OXFORD WORLD'S CLASSICS

AN AUSTRALIAN GIRL

CATHERINE MARTIN was born on the Isle of Skye and migrated to South Australia as a colony, in 1855. While earning her living as a clerk, she wrote a wide range of poems and essays, publishing her work sometimes under pseudonyms or anonymously. She married Frederick Martin, an accountant, in 1882. Her first and best-known novel, *An Australian Girl*, reflects the passionate commitment Catherine Martin felt to her adopted country as it moved from the status of Britain's interlinked colonies towards nationhood. In later years Catherine Martin revisited her native Scotland and spent long periods in Europe, but always returned to South Australia, where she died in 1937.

GRAHAM TULLOCH is Professor of English at the Flinders University of South Australia. He has edited Scott's *Ivanhoe* and, for Oxford World's Classics, Clarke's *His Natural Life*, and he writes on the Scots language and Scottish literature.

AMANDA NETTELBECK is a lecturer in English at the University of Adelaide in South Australia. She is the author of *Reading David Malouf*, editor or co-editor of three books of essays on Australian writing, and has a particular interest in South Australian literary history.

OXFORD WORLD'S CLASSICS

*For almost 100 years Oxford World's Classics have brought
readers closer to the world's great literature. Now with over 700
titles—from the 4,000-year-old myths of Mesopotamia to the
twentieth century's greatest novels—the series makes available
lesser-known as well as celebrated writing.*

*The pocket-sized hardbacks of the early years contained
introductions by Virginia Woolf, T. S. Eliot, Graham Greene,
and other literary figures which enriched the experience of reading.
Today the series is recognized for its fine scholarship and
reliability in texts that span world literature, drama and poetry,
religion, philosophy and politics. Each edition includes perceptive
commentary and essential background information to meet the
changing needs of readers.*

OXFORD WORLD'S CLASSICS

CATHERINE MARTIN

An Australian Girl

Edited by
GRAHAM TULLOCH
with an Introduction by
AMANDA NETTELBECK

OXFORD
UNIVERSITY PRESS

Oxford University Press, Great Clarendon Street, Oxford OX2 6DP

Oxford New York

Athens Auckland Bangkok Bogotá Buenos Aires Calcutta
Cape Town Chennai Dar es Salaam Delhi Florence Hong Kong Istanbul
Karachi Kuala Lumpur Madrid Melbourne Mexico City Mumbai
Nairobi Paris São Paulo Singapore Taipei Tokyo Toronto Warsaw

and associated companies in Berlin Ibadan

Oxford is a registered trade mark of Oxford University Press

Published in the United States
by Oxford University Press Inc., New York

Introduction, Select Bibliography, Chronology © Amanda Nettelbeck
Note on the Text, Explanatory Notes © Graham Tulloch

First published as an Oxford World's Classics paperback 1999

British Library Cataloguing in Publication Data
Data available

Library of Congress Cataloging in Publication Data
Martin, Catherine, 1848-1937.
An Australian girl / Catherine Martin ; edited with an
introduction and notes by Graham Tulloch and Amanda Nettelbeck.
(Oxford world's classics)
I. Tulloch, Graham, 1947- . II. Nettelbeck, Amanda.
III. Title. IV. Series: Oxford world's classics (Oxford University Press)
PR9619.2.M385A97 1999 823—dc21 98-41802
ISBN 0-19-283922-5

1 3 5 7 9 10 8 6 4 2

Typeset by Best-set Typesetter Ltd., Hong Kong
Printed in Great Britain by
Cox & Wyman Ltd., Reading, Berkshire

CONTENTS

ACKNOWLEDGEMENTS

We would like to thank Anne Chittleborough, Dawn Partington, and particularly Judy King for research assistance of various kinds including help with chasing some of Martin's more obscure allusions, and Peter Monteath and Sue Tulloch for their interest and support. We have been greatly helped by the staff of the Flinders University Library, the Barr Smith Library of the University of Adelaide, and the Mortlock Library of South Australiana and we are grateful to the Barr Smith Library for providing a photocopy of the 1891 edition of *An Australian Girl*. We would also like to thank the staff of Oxford University Press: Joanna Rabiger and Elizabeth Stratford and, especially, Judith Luna for her patience and encouragement in the longer than expected gestation of this project.

A.N.
G.T.

INTRODUCTION

Readers who do not wish to learn details of the plot will prefer to treat the Introduction as an Epilogue.

When *An Australian Girl* first appeared anonymously in 1890, it was widely received by its reviewers as an example of domestic romance. Yet to regard the novel simply as a romance is to overlook Catherine Martin's detailed scrutiny of colonial Australian society, particularly its views on gender, class, and nationalism. The story itself follows, in part, the narrative structure of a *Bildungsroman*. Stella Courtland, the beautiful and somewhat immature youngest daughter of a genteel pastoralist family, considers a problem of love and marriage (two states which, she shrewdly understands, are not necessarily mutually inclusive). Her choice is between Ted Ritchie, a wealthy, good-natured but unintellectual local pastoralist whom she has known from childhood, and Anselm Langdale, a cultured young doctor from England who is her intellectual equal. Cheated of her natural choice, Stella considers the options available to her within the framework of late nineteenth-century morality.

The plot might contain many of the ingredients of domestic romance fiction, but it deviates from that genre in two important ways. First, we are not allowed the satisfying closure we might expect of the romance novel, either in the contentment of a good match or in the unambiguous tragedy of a lost love. Second, Stella is not quite the heroine we would expect. She is passionate about the writings of the German authors Goethe, Heine, and Kant; her attention is drawn by themes no smaller than future nationhood, the social role of the church, and women's independence from husbands; her challenges to the institutions of Victorian value position her on the edge of the womanly ideal, and her dislike of British social codes reflects her insistence upon Australia's cultural independence.

In these senses, the title of *An Australian Girl* immediately signals its two most pressing themes: the question of what 'Australianness' might be and the values which the generation of the turning century, particularly its women, might represent. These themes are certainly not discrete in *An Australian Girl* but are intimately bound together in the fate of Stella; to a significant degree, Stella *is* the face of a new Australia. Her pride as an Australian girl (as opposed to a 'colonial' one) anticipates the declaration in 1901 of Australian Federation, which legally and politically transformed Australia from a collection of colonies into a single nation. Catherine Martin's expression through Stella of Australian identity as unique and homegrown, rather than as derivative of English social models, corresponds with the nationalist sentiment which emerged in the literature of the 1880s and 1890s. The 1890s in particular were, as literary historians have shown, the most prolific literary years of the century, and romance fiction predominated as the favoured genre. In these years before the turn of the century Australia was creating its own literary tradition, one which imagined the country as the site of stoic survival and freedom. The *Bulletin*, the Sydney-based periodical which began life in the 1880s, is widely regarded as the vehicle of this tradition, and is often cited for its promotion of a national sensibility which privileged the values of masculinity and the Bush frontier over those of domesticity and urban social life.

Yet although such values held powerful mythic force, this was a literary movement to which women writers did contribute, and which did address themes other than those of masculine adventure.[1] *An Australian Girl* celebrates the Australian bush but it does so through a feminine consciousness. The bush frontier which stretches from the gate of the Courtland family property is not, as the conventionally regarded *Bulletin* tradition would suggest, the province of men's exploration and adventure; it is personalized, even feminized, by Stella's identification with it. What is more, in *An Australian Girl* the land is not isolated from the urban expansionism of nineteenth-century Australia; although Stella is the mouthpiece for much of Martin's satire on metropolitan society, she is a young woman who moves readily between rural and urban life. She is, indeed, the image of the New Woman who emerged in the public

[1] Recently, literary historians such as Joy Hooton have suggested that the long neglect of women writers of the period is due not so much to the overwhelming masculinity of the late nineteenth-century literary movement as to the fact that women writers were forgotten by the literary historians who catalogued an Australian 'canon' in the mid-twentieth century. ('Australian Literary History and Some Colonial Women Novelists', *Southerly*, 50/3 (1990): 310–23.) That this argument carries weight is reflected in the dates between published editions of *An Australian Girl*: after its Australian edition of 1894, it was out of print until 1988.

consciousness alongside a burgeoning national awareness during the late nineteenth century. Ethel Castilla's popular 1888 poem 'The Australian Girl' offers a similar picture of the coming generation in feminized terms as self-possessed, independent-spirited, and both physically and intellectually fit for the future:

> She has a beauty of her own—
> A beauty of a paler tone
>   Than English belles;
> Yet Southern sun and Southern air
> Have kissed her cheeks, until they wear
> The dainty tints that oft appear
>   On rosy shells.
>
> Her frank, clear eyes bespeak a mind
> Old-world traditions fail to bind
>   She is not shy
> Or bold, but simply self-possessed.
> Her independence adds a zest
> Unto her speech, her piquant jest,
>   Her quaint reply.
>
> O'er classic volumes she will pore
> With joy, and true scholastic lore
>   Will often gain.
> In sports she bears away the bell,
> Nor under music's siren spell,
> To dance divinely, flirt as well,
>   Does she disdain.[2]

In 'The Australian Woman', written in 1899 on the eve of Australian Federation and the new century, Castilla indicates that the future of the Australian Girl lies in her power as the mother of the next generation to mould the coming nation:

> The dawn of a new nationhood
>   She waits with hopeful eyes to see;
> The bursting of the bonds she hears
>   That sets her country's strong soul free,
> And feels her power, in future years,
> To mould its mighty course for good,
> To write, in characters of gold,

---

[2] Ethel Castilla, *The Australian Girl and Other Verses* (Melbourne, 1900).

> Brighter than seer has yet foretold,
> Her children's destiny.

Catherine Martin's own life history was more humble but in
some senses more liberated than the one she paints for her heroine.
Whereas Stella enjoys the given privileges of the Australian-born
middle class, Catherine Mackay (as she was born) was the seventh
child of Highland crofters who migrated to Australia in 1855.[3] While
Stella's life is that of the leisured gentlewoman, whose commitment
to social aid is part of her genteel femininity, Catherine Mackay
worked in paid employment after her father's death. From 1867 she
helped her sister Mary run a small school for girls in the south-east
of the colony, where the family had settled. Her Australian education was informal, but this did not prevent her from developing a
knowledge of German language, literature, and philosophy, presumably gained from her association with the German community
there; neither did it deter her from publishing her own and translated German poetry in various colonial presses. From the mid-
1870s, having moved to Adelaide, she attempted to support herself
from freelance journalism. This proved to be a difficult endeavour.
Writing was a precarious profession in the best of circumstances, and
was especially so for a woman. In her autobiography, Martin's friend
and the doyenne of South Australian women writers, Catherine
Helen Spence, gave this account of her life during the 1870s:

when I found she was litterateur trying to make a living by her pen, bringing out a serial tale, 'Bohemian Born,' and writing occasional articles, I
drew to her at once. So long as the serial tale lasted she could hold her
own; but no one can make a living at occasional articles in Australia, and
she became a clerk in the Education Office, but still cultivated literature
in her leisure hours.[4]

---

[3] Biographical information on Catherine Martin, here and in the Chronology, is owed
to Margaret Allen, 'Three South Australian Women Writers, 1854–1923' (unpub. Ph.D.
diss., Flinders University of South Australia, 1991). For a briefer account of her life,
see Patricia Clarke's *Pen Portraits: Women Writers and Journalists in Nineteenth Century
Australia* (Sydney, 1988, 153–4).

[4] Catherine Helen Spence, *Catherine Helen Spence: An Autobiography* (Adelaide,
1910), 55. Margaret Allen notes that the serial tale Spence was referring to was more
likely to be 'The Moated Grange', which was published in the *South Australian Chronicle and Weekly Mail* between 3 Feb. and 27 Oct. 1877 (Allen, 'Three South Australian
Women Writers').

Unusually, Catherine Martin retained her position in the Education Department after her marriage in 1882 to Frederick Martin. Yet neither her working life nor her marriage replaced her literary commitment. Throughout the 1870s and 1880s she continued to publish poetry, stories, serials, and occasional articles; her four novels—*An Australian Girl*, *The Silent Sea*, *The Old Roof Tree* and *The Incredible Journey*—were published between 1890 and 1923. Spence praised her writing as reflecting 'the highest level ever reached in Australian fiction', positioning herself 'a very humble second place beside her'.

In 1890 *An Australian Girl* certainly drew attention to the new novelist, evoking a wide and largely positive response. Yet although in many ways it fitted comfortably within the literary conventions and concerns of the period, the novel still produced a mixed reaction from its Australian and English reviewers. On the whole, they approved of what they regarded as a 'truly' Australian novel. Stella's freshness and beauty provided an inspiring image of Australia's future. Her middle-class gentility, set against the physically impressive background of pastoral South Australia, offered a glimpse of what Australia's newest generation might be. But although her dilemma in love fulfilled the expectations of domestic romance, her less conventional interests did not, and this seemed to produce what reviewers regarded as a problem of form in the novel.

The reviewer for London's *Spectator* (31 January 1891) was one of several who were disgruntled by what was regarded as the novelist's 'misapplication' of material. He declared that the novel suffered from an absence of 'form', arguing that 'it requires more mental concentration than most people care to devote to a novel'. He concluded that the author (rightly divined as a woman) would do better to try her hand at 'essays or sketches': the kinds of writing, presumably, which would demand less mental energy of both writer and reader. The reviewer for the Australian journal the *Australasian Critic* (1 November 1890) was more impressed by *An Australian Girl* in so far as it reflected an 'Australian feeling', a feeling he compared favourably with the 'timidly imitative' literature of the past which had 'been weakened by conventional following of British patterns'. He praised the novel for its unapologetic 'local veracity', its quality of being 'spontaneously and unreservedly Australian', and hailed Stella as 'the ideal woman of the future', a future belonging to the

new world of 'Australasia' rather than the old world of European tradition. Yet even this warm appraisal of a desired literary 'nativism'
was moderated by the reviewer's disapproval of Martin's 'excursuses
(they are nothing else) on Kant's "Kritik", on Socialism, on the
access and decadence of religious fervour, on charity organisation,
and a number of other subjects'. The novelist, it seems, had mistaken
the extent to which she (and her protagonist) could overstep the
romance genre. A similar opinion was expressed by the reviewer for
London's *Athenaeum* (19 July 1890), who, having been impressed by
the novel's 'decisive literary vigour' and its 'finely drawn' portrait of
Stella, was disappointed by its attentions to philosophical and religious subjects, 'dragged in without much regard to the plot of the
story'. Amongst Martin's contemporaries, then, there was tacit
agreement on the desirable possibilities and boundaries of 'plot'. The
most pressing insistence upon adherence to these implicit boundaries
came from the *Sydney Mail*'s reviewer (15 November 1890), who
claimed never to have encountered an Australian Girl 'who had
Kant's "Kritik of Pure Reason" at her fingers' ends, and spoke and
wrote interminable pages of reflections on life, death, and theological doctrines'. The reviewer was not without hope, however: with 'a
good deal less philosophy', he concluded, 'we see no reason why
this writer, who is apparently a "new hand", should not at the next
attempt produce a really readable novel'.

Although most of Martin's first reviewers were impressed by the
novel's 'local veracity' and 'vigour', they were also irritated by what
they regarded as its two competing aspects. One is an (approved)
expression of a fresh, localized Australian voice; a voice, in other
words, of the dawning age of Australian nationalism. The other is
a (disapproved) portrayal of an incredible heroine; one whose pro-
gression through a romance plot is hopelessly weighed down by her
distracting entanglement with philosophical and theological debate.
It is telling, that when the London publisher George Bentley released
a single-volume edition of *An Australian Girl* a year after its three-
volume appearance, the new edition contained much less philosophical content. When Bentley released an Australian edition in 1894,
that edition was based upon the reduced version of 1891.

Stella is by no means, of course, the only socially critical and
independent-minded heroine of nineteenth-century literature,
either in Australia or elsewhere. Readers have compared her to

her English predecessors Emma Woodhouse and Maggie Tulliver, who queried the institutions of social conduct, religion, and marriage. Yet while the stories of other nineteenth-century heroines tended to resolve themselves in happy marriage (as for Emma) or death (as for Maggie), Stella's relationship to her world remains open and even ambivalently treated to the novel's end. She is married, it is true, but to the 'wrong' suitor. Her relief from grief, in a sublimation of the self to a newfound devotion to higher social purpose, both ties her to and frees her from the Victorian ideal of middle-class married womanhood.

However, the theme of femininity and its role in the coming age is only one aspect of *An Australian Girl*. Central to the novel, as to most of Martin's work, is a strong attachment to South Australia as a regional site of national progress. At the time of the Mackay family's arrival, South Australia was barely two decades old as a formally declared colony of Britain. Proclaimed a province with political status in 1836, South Australia was carefully planned upon principles of economic and political progressivism. It was to be a model free society, and the utopian idealism which accompanied its foundation was reflected in the names initially suggested for it by the social philosopher Jeremy Bentham, 'Liberia' or 'Felicitania'.[5] An absence of the convict labour which had built Australia's other colonies, open trade, religious tolerance, democratic ideals: these were the grounds on which South Australia was promoted to its targeted emigrants in Britain and Europe. The population of the colony with Europeans would not be random but rather based upon a programme of deliberate government assistance. A principle of regulated capitalism would encourage the growth of a prosperous society in which enterprise could be followed by social mobility. Adelaide, South Australia's metropolitan heart, would become 'the commercial emporium, the London of Australia'.[6] This mood of liberalism was intended to extend to South Australia's Aboriginal population. The proclamation of South Australia as a province included the stipulation that colonization should not affect the rights

---

[5] See Douglas Pike, *Paradise of Dissent: South Australia 1829–1857* (London, 1957) and Eric Richards (ed.), *The Flinders History of South Australia: Social History* (Netley, 1986).
[6] Cited by Eric Richards, 'The Peopling of South Australia, 1836–1986' in Richards (ed.), *Flinders History of South Australia*, 117.

of 'any Aboriginal Natives of the said Province to the actual occupation or enjoyment in their own persons or in the persons of their descendants of any lands therein now actually occupied or enjoyed by such Natives'.[7]

Not surprisingly, the spirit with which South Australia was founded was countered by various disappointments. Economic depression in the early years, in addition to such social problems as the seepage of convicts from the eastern colonies and conflicts of class interest, gave a different face to the colony's much-publicized image. The ideal of harmonious race relations, too, meant little in the face of colonial expansion. Although the principle of continuing Aboriginal land rights was upheld by London's colonial office, it did not weigh much against settler greed for land, and enjoyed neither popularity nor respect. Indeed, the kind of stable race relations hoped for in 1836 had already been compromised by earlier grievances suffered by Aboriginal peoples in encounters with whalers, sealers, and sheep or cattle drivers on overland expeditions from other colonies. During the 1840s, as settlers moved further out from Adelaide and Aboriginal communities became more marginalized from their traditional lands, Aboriginal–settler relations deteriorated into recurring instances of frontier violence.

By the time the Mackay family arrived in South Australia in the mid-1850s these patterns of settlement, the tensions underlying the utopian ideals, were well established. But the colony's economy was prospering and rural centres were developing, attracting a greater share of the settler population than the metropolitan centre of Adelaide, a demographic pattern that would not change until the 1920s. For a family like the Mackays, who did not represent middle-class capital, South Australia presumably offered liberating opportunities and the real possibility of economic and social mobility. Catherine's father died not long after the family's arrival in the colony, but his sons went on to become successful pastoralists. When Catherine Helen Spence first met Catherine Mackay as a young woman in Adelaide, she took her to be 'the daughter of a wealthy squatter'. The Mackays' emigration to South Australia, then, no doubt enabled more advantaged lives for the younger generation than they would have enjoyed as a crofter's children in Skye.

Catherine Martin, it seems, strongly considered herself to be

[7] Feb. 1836; cited by John Summers, 'Colonial Race Relations' in Richards (ed.), *Flinders History of South Australia*, 285.

South Australian, and everywhere in her writing her attachment to
the local is affirmed. This is particularly evident in *An Australian
Girl* in the close depiction of the regional landscape, which becomes
a recurring motif for the veracity of Australia's 'essence'. Here
Martin reveals her debt to a romantic literary tradition. The South
Australian landscape embodies the essential truths of the country,
which present themselves not in the terms of pastoral beauty but in
all the features of the sublime. This, for instance, is Martin's description of the South Australian mallee scrub:[8]

These vast parched domains, lying in all their nakedness under a sunless
sky, have nothing to befool the soul. They have a terrible sincerity in whose
cold light not the picture which we so fondly weave of life, but life itself
in all its pale disenchantment, makes a sudden seizure on the questioning
spirit. In such an hour the multitudinous trifles that choke the soul like
the white ashes of a burnt-out wood-fire are blown away as with the breath
of a strong west wind winnowing the chaff from the grain. In face of so
stern a solitude we cease to deceive ourselves. (p. 102)

Here there is an edge of bleakness: the landscape is exalted,
untempered, and above all indifferent to human habitation. These
qualities, though, make it all the more appropriate as the scene of
Stella's self-development. It may be infinitely more powerful than
her small form, but its 'vast solitude' makes it the perfect background
onto which she can pitch her energetic sense of self. It is to this landscape that Stella devotes her private time, and it is in this landscape
that her love affair with Anselm Langdale unfolds. The Wicked
Wood, where she and Anselm first declare their attachment, is dense
with all the heightened power of a Gothic setting and so serves as
foil to the European order and 'cultured beauty' of the family's more
manicured property. Stella writes of the place to her sister:

the Mallee sinks into tameness compared to the Wicked Wood. It seems
to stretch out unseen arms and compel you to stand and look from tree to
tree, and try to draw in the secret of its strange fascination. It is too terrible, one says; and then, because of this, one visits the place again and
again. It nourishes the imagination. (p. 233)

The depiction of landscape in Gothic terms was a common feature
of colonial literature. Marcus Clarke's well-known account of
Australian scenery, published in 1894 as a preface to Adam Lindsay

---

[8] mallee: a variety of eucalyptus which flourishes in arid areas.

Gordon's *Poems*, evokes the sense of uncanniness it inspired in the Europe-trained consciousness: 'What is the dominant note of Australian scenery? That which is the dominant note of Poe's poetry—Weird Melancholy . . . The Australian mountain forests are funereal, secret, stern. Their solitude is desolation . . . In Australia alone is to be found the Grotesque, the Weird, the strange scribblings of nature learning how to write.'[9] Yet whereas Clarke's account of Australian scenery highlights a sense of oppressiveness, Martin's landscape is compelling and nourishing to the imagination. It is indeed the constant background to Stella's story of development; it provides her with her sense of Australianness, which is equally her sense of self. This scene, for instance, supplies the backdrop to Stella's and Anselm's evolving companionship:

They flew over the great smooth plain, while the spring wind, vivifying as a sea-breeze, blew in their faces. At times they came to a stretch of kangaroo grass, tall and rustling, swayed by the wind that came now and then running up in little fitful gusts . . . The earth and sky equally had an unfamiliar boundlessness that at first lay like a weight on the spirit, and yet gradually soothed it as the imagination gathered impulse and repose from the sad magnificent horizons, unbroken by wood or hill, or the gleam of water. (p. 257)

In contrast to this 'boundless' landscape is the calm and cultivated garden of the Ritchie family's estate, the scene of Stella's sense of containment. The garden's imported flowers, 'bending above the earth with angelic benedictions' (p. 302), may be pleasing to the eye but they produce in Stella nothing but the reminder of her entrapment by Ted's affections.

In honouring the South Australian landscape, Martin makes a point of evoking the presence of Aboriginal people as part of its essential, pre-European character. At one level this very acknowledgement of Aboriginal life displays a relative sensitivity; Aboriginal people are either notably absent from or demonized in a good deal of colonial writing. Stella is portrayed as being unusual amongst her peers in maintaining an interest in local Aboriginal custom; presumably this is intended by Martin as a sign of Stella's attachment to her country, a sign of her own 'nativeness'. Not surprisingly,

[9] Marcus Clarke, 'Weird Melancholy', Preface to Adam Lindsay Gordon, *Poems* (Melbourne, 1894), pp. ix–xi.

though, Martin's depiction of Aboriginal cultural life is closely framed by the Social Darwinism which dominated late nineteenth-century colonial thought, and according to which European-Australian advancement was perceived to be as natural as indigenous decline was perceived to be inevitable. Indeed, Stella's nativeness can only be affirmed in the novel if Aboriginal cultural life is taken to be a thing of the past. When Stella praises 'the bare, untrammelled aspects of her native land' which 'hold no claim from the past' (p. 420), she promotes Australia's departure from the traditions of Britain. Yet her celebration of Australia's vigorous youth simultaneously forgets the currency of Aboriginal cultures; the very creation of Australianness entails the omission of already existent Aboriginal sovereignty. In this sense, Stella's approach to Aboriginal custom as its self-appointed collector and custodian does not so much protect the local culture as render it something of the nostalgically recalled past. When Ted Ritchie brings her an Aboriginal 'Kooditcha' shoe, he does so because he knows she collects culturally 'quaint' myths and artefacts. The shoe represents for the Australian-born Stella, as Aboriginal culture did for most European settlers earlier in the century, the notion of mystery: it is, she thinks, a 'cunning, gruesome-looking sort of thing' and 'strangely wicked' (pp. 20–1), and she assures Ted that 'of all the myths I have gathered about the blacks, none are so dramatic as this relic' (p. 22). The shoe, viewed as a dramatic relic, is thereby made to seem symptomatic of the mysterious history of a doomed race. Later the narrator discusses the apparent divergence between sophisticated Aboriginal social law and what is referred to as a 'very primitive stage of savagedom' and suggests that such a 'curious contradiction' can only accrue to Mother Nature's 'strange pranks' (p. 166); and so again, Aboriginal life becomes aligned with the mysteries of Nature and dissociated from the progressive rationalism of a new Australian culture.

The principles of Social Darwinism are most evident in the tale of Caloona, a 'half-caste woman' who returns to her own people after her white common-law husband Thomson beats their small son (pp. 94–9). The remorse-stricken Thomson's efforts to rediscover mother and son come to nothing, and he hears of their fate from an exmissionary only on his deathbed: 'She had lived for years with white people, and then gone back to her tribe. But the savage life was too much for her, and when her strength began to fail she found her way to the mission, anxious to have her boy properly cared for after her death' (p. 98). The sorry tale closes with the news that now both mother and son 'are buried in one grave in the mission churchyard at Mandurang . . . their dust repos[ing] there in the sure and certain hope of the resurrection of the just' (p. 98). There may well be a satirical intention in this last passage, since Martin reveals elsewhere in the novel her lack of faith in the missionary project to Christianize 'the natives': she gives to Stella, for instance, a strong note of irony in recounting the efforts of the well-meaning but misdirected missionary Mr Ferrier (p. 99). The broader theme of the story does, however, support the conventional nineteenth-century view that church-run missions, regardless of their spiritual success, rescued Aboriginal people from an impossible position between 'the savage life' and existence on the margins of 'civilization'. Indeed, in the early twentieth century the mission would become central to government policy in maintaining state control over and surveillance of Aboriginal life under the guise of protection. But the focus of Martin's story of Caloona is not so much upon the success (or otherwise) of Aboriginal missions as upon their perceived function to 'smooth the dying pillow': there is little space, she suggests, for those caught between a 'declining' Aboriginal culture and a pervasive white culture. Caloona's story serves to articulate a standard perception of the day: the (regrettable but) inevitable departure of the Aboriginal race.[10]

Underwritten by these traces of evolutionary discourse, *An Australian Girl* suggests that a new page is needed for the scripting of a new Australia. But in contrast to the Australianness most predominantly imagined in the 1890s literary tradition—an Australianness based upon masculine self-sufficiency and anti-traditionalism—the new Australian generation realized in Stella Courtland is characterized by a wider commitment to intellectualism and social enquiry. Stella may identify with the local environment, but she is equally stimulated by what the world has to offer; the philosophical traditions and social conditions of Europe, and in particular of Germany,

---

[10] The theme of White Australia's neglect of Aboriginal life, which figures as a background to Australia's emergence as a nation in *An Australian Girl*, received much fuller development in Martin's last novel, *An Incredible Journey*, published more than thirty years later in 1923. Aboriginal responses in politics, art, and literature have challenged the assumptions which, even if intended as sympathetic, emerged as forms of popular and governmental paternalism from the time of settlement to the present.

are subject to her passionate interest. Australianness for Stella, then, is imagined not as defensively regional but as framed by broader cultural traditions. Her patriotism springs not just as a reaction against anti-colonial sentiment but also from an absence of doubt about Australia's deserved place with 'older' countries on the world stage.

In the late nineteenth century, though, the cultural confidence expressed so fervently by Stella was still underpinned by the continuing importance of empire to Australia's future directions. As Ken Stewart recently put it, the power of Britain might have been redefined by the years leading to Australian Federation, but it was not removed. The nationalistic tone of the period's literature lent an optimistic note to what was still, in many ways, an age of political conservatism and economic instability.[11] And if the issue of cultural validity was infused by the continuing influence of empire so, inevitably, was that of class. Australia's early national movement, and the principles of democracy and economic freedom on which the South Australian colony in particular was founded, nurtured an ideal of egalitarianism. It goes without saying that such an ideal was more a fiction than a reflection of social realities. It is also true, however, that colonial society was fluid rather than fixed. If insecure social boundaries were a feature of post-industrial expansion in nineteenth-century Europe, they were even more pronounced in colonial Australia, where the terms of economic and political power were still being formed. The status of given gentility, enjoyed by the Courtland family in *An Australian Girl*, became in the colonial context more difficult to define. Despite his lowly birth, for instance, Sir Edward Ritchie's success as a pastoralist ensures him significantly more economic weight than the well-bred Courtlands can carry, as well as his family's place within the most fashionable and distinguished of Melbourne's social circle. Yet in the face of social mobility, the principle of 'real' respectability did not die. As a response to the flux of colonial society, those with given (rather than cultivated) respectability could still call upon indirect means by which their gentility could be recognized. Such a task rested particularly with women, who, more than men, were the keepers of society's codes of conduct.[12]

---

[11] Ken Stewart, 'Introduction' to *The 1890s: Australian Literature and Literary Culture* (St Lucia, Queensland, 1996), 5–6.

[12] See Penny Russell, *A Wish of Distinction: Colonial Gentility and Femininity* (Melbourne, 1994).

Some of this social ambivalence is apparent in Martin's treatment of class relations. In Stella she portrays an Australian generation which rejects an outmoded attachment to colonial social hierarchies based upon connections to old-world nobility. This dislike of classed affectations is played out in the politely veiled irony with which Stella treats Mrs Anstey-Hobbs. Yet while these scenes of social satire might affirm the egalitarian ideal which predominated in the litera-ture of the late nineteenth century, they might also be read as Martin's clue to the separation of 'real' gentility from 'false'. Cer-tainly *An Australian Girl* offers plenty of shrewd parody, particularly on the frenzied, excessive world of metropolitan Melbourne inhab-ited by Laurette, in contrast to which the quiet pace of Stella's pas-toral life appears natural and uncontrived. Martin's social satire is not, however, all-inclusive. Although she finds comedy (via Mrs Anstey-Hobbs, for instance) in colonial society's attachment to old-world respectability, that respectability is also naturalized (most clearly in the Courtlands) as something implicit and beyond commodification. Here, the portrait of Mrs Anstey-Hobbs is intended to caricature the self-proclaimed cultural élite of colonial society:

'It is sordid wealth without culture or the traditions of refinement that stifles our artists and poets,' she would murmur ... the fact being that Mrs Anstey-Hobbs had a talent for assimilating ideas from the books and magazines she read in such numbers monthly, but had not an equal felic-ity in their application. The thought that wealth was detrimental to mental expansion was one which had from various sources become dear to her—so much so, that about this time Mrs Anstey-Hobbs had made a deter-mined effort to put down, as far as possible, the overwhelming power of money in Melbourne society. She had struggled to establish a salon—a weekly gathering to be open only to people of culture and esprit. (p. 129)

Yet such satire is countered elsewhere in the novel by an affirmation of tradition's real value. This is particularly apparent in comparisons of the Ritchie and the Courtland family histories. Godolphin House, the Ritchie family home inherited by Ted, is a symbol of vulgar display. Like Laurette, it is ostentatious and absent of real distinction:

Everything was on a large scale—the house, the grounds, the conser-vatories, the trees, and even the views ... [T]he emissary of a great 'decorative' firm had prevailed on Sir Edward to have the 'mansion' 'done up' from top to toe. This took the form of a carnival of unlimited expenditure, and that unhappy outburst of British Philistinism known as the aesthetic craze . . . But the culmination of all was the library . . . a room full of lame and impotent compilations in 'books' clothing.' Thinglets fit only to wrap candles in, or make winding-sheets in Lent for pilchards, or keep butter in the market-place from melting. (pp. 42–4)

Unlike the Ritchies, Stella and her family are given natural distinction, which comes not from wealth or the display of connections but from their menfolk's professions as Anglican clergy and Mrs Courtland's 'high-bred refinement' (p. 29) as the descendant of an old Highland family. So in contrast to Godolphin House, this is Fairacre, the Courtland family home:

Fairacre both within and without bore the traces of easy affluence. The house was a large one-story building, substantially built of stone, with a deep veranda, furnished with Venetian shutters, running all round it. The principal rooms were large and lofty, and opened by wide doors, half glass, upon the garden, which from one season to another was never seen without the radiance of many flowers. The sparkling old silver, and the delicately fine table-linen, were family heirlooms, as were also several rare works of art, and a large proportion of the rosewood furniture. (p. 29)

Interestingly, the 'natural' distinction we see reflected in the Courtland family home is tied to a sense of the 'genuinely' Australian (the deep veranda, the wide doors and cool, lofty rooms), while the cultivated ostentation of the Ritchie home is associated with the slavishly followed fashions of Britain's latest 'craze'. 'Real' Australianness and 'real' gentility become merged in an image of true cultural value.

The reader's cue to recognize this value is also prompted by Martin's appeal to physiognomic principles. As a branch of the nineteenth century's new sciences, physiognomy judged moral character from the cast of physical features. In the colonial context, in particular, physiognomic principles corresponded with evolutionary ones, and were enlisted to determine such things as the presence of an undesirable convict ancestry or the intellectual and cultural 'inferiority' of Aboriginal people. In *An Australian Girl* they emerge to define the differences of character and distinction between Stella and Anselm on the one hand, and Ted and Laurette on the other.

[Stella's] brow was singularly noble, and gave promise of unusual mental power. The complexion was very fair and clear, and when she talked it was often tinged with swift delicate rose-pink, that died away very slowly, leaving a soft warm glow in the cheeks like that often seen in a moist sea-shell. It was a face whose every line and feature indicated that Stella was endowed with rare qualities of intellect and imagination, quick to feel, to see, to think. (pp. 11–12)

Anselm, too, possesses a 'brow strikingly noble—an air well maintained by the rest of the face, more especially the finely-moulded chin and mouth, whose short upper lip was defined rather than hidden by a silky black moustache' (p. 179). Anselm's rival, Ted, is 'good-looking in a not uncommon and distinctly unintellectual way', but his brow and mouth give away his real weaknesses: 'The forehead was low and square . . . The jaws were too heavy, and the lips, partly concealed under a heavy drooping moustache, were over-full. Altogether, it was the face of a man who could be firm and determined in action, yet morally lacking in force of will' (p. 12). The meanest of features are reserved for Laurette, including the utter invisibility of the all-important brow: she is given 'fair fluffy hair, lightened by gold dust, descending in a fringe of infantile curliness to within a short distance of her eyes, which were . . . like those of a parrot that is bent on finding out a great deal. An expression that was further carried out by the nose, which took the liberty of turning up a little, and a mouth which, though it smiled very often, had something rather hard and beakish in its formation' (pp. 30–1).

This alignment of appearance and character as a signpost for reading differences of class is also extended to the 'lower orders', who are rustic, given to gossip and simple tastes, and inclined to base behaviour when beyond the redeeming influence of gentlewomen. The woman who emerges from the Bush near the Courtlands' property had never, until her encounter with Stella, 'acquired any of those amenities that, even among the lower orders of women, help as a rule to keep social intercourse on a higher plane than the primeval scramble' (p. 212); the Courtlands' household servants show more dignity, having become 'accustomed to the refined courtesy of gentlewomen' (p. 212). The responsibility of social care, which was an important part of Victorian middle-class femininity, is carried by Stella with genuine sincerity but none the less with all the presuppositions that confirm her sense of the social hierarchy. One of the success stories of her Anglican charity work, for instance, is that of the hopelessly Catholic Mick Doolan, 'a dreadful little old ragged, drunken Irishman' who, under her charitable care, becomes 'one of the best little men she ever knew' (p. 194).

In these ways the landscape that is dear to Stella as the open space of Australia's potential is, after all, already encoded by many of the social and intellectual conventions of the late nineteenth century. In other ways, though, Martin's treatment of contemporary social issues cannot be easily framed within the dominant mores of her day. In particular, the character of Stella raises many questions about the role of middle-class femininity in colonial society. Certainly Stella's access to some affluence and much leisure allows her a degree of freedom in indulging her interests, but her position as gentlewoman also sets the terms of behavioural constraint. She can privately read as many tracts of German philosophy as she likes, but she has no way of applying her intelligence to the public world. This is largely due to limits within nineteenth-century practices of femininity, but it is also due to the colonial community's own limits; and until she can marry, she has no opportunity for changing her environment. With the exception of her brother Cuthbert, and until the arrival of Dr Langdale, who keeps a copy of Molière's work in his coat pocket, pastoral South Australia provides no one with whom she can discuss her interests. Still, as the woman of Australia's future, Stella's intelligence is balanced by her physical health, and to a degree the absence of intellectual activity in her life is compensated by physical freedom to explore the country beyond her family's fences. In this her natural companion is Ted, the image of sun-browned and youthful strength, who, like Stella, is a 'native' Australian. The compensation is inadequate, however; Ted's athleticism is not rounded by an enquiring mind, and he is no match for Stella.

Stella's frustration within a world which allows little room for bright and able women is vented in her cynicism about marriage, a state of 'terrible disillusion' (p. 24) which, she suspects, maintains men's privilege at the cost of women's independence. Her preference that she and Ted remain 'fast friends', against his insistence that they become 'man and wife', causes her to suppose with her characteristic wit that 'we could hardly be both' (p. 8). The more disturbing aspect of women's lot in marriage is signalled early on in the novel by the tale of Stella's friend Cicely Mowbray, the abused wife of a violent alcoholic who is scorned by society when she leaves her marriage. Cicely's story serves both as a precursor to Stella's own future, in which Ted will be revealed as an alcoholic, and as an indication of Stella's commitment to natural justice rather than to social convention. Unlike her other acquaintances, Stella supports Cicely's decision to leave her husband as an option 'less immoral than staying with the man she married' (p. 14). The radical nature of Cicely's decision is modified, however, by some residual access to decorum: she is rescued from an unhappy fate by a better man; one who, though an overseer by profession, is 'a gentleman by birth' (p. 27).

Yet curiously enough, some of Martin's most telling criticisms of women's unfortunate position within marriage centre upon the novel's villain, Laurette. Married to a philanderer and a gambler for whom she feels no love but on whom she is dependent, Laurette understands too well the difficulties of serving out a contract which offers few benefits in return. After the revelation of Ted's intemperance—a revelation which staggers the naïve and protected Stella—the more pragmatic Laurette advises:

Take my word for it, forgiveness is the quality that best suits us women—even when we are most sinned against. It does not become us to be too logical, or look too far ahead . . . Where would I be to-day, and my two little ones, if I had not swallowed a great deal more than ever you will have to overlook? (p. 348)

Martin does not invite much sympathy for Laurette; she is the novel's Iago, the cunning manipulator 'who knows how and when to strike the desired key-note, [who goes] on her way conquering and to conquer' (pp. 353–4). However it is Laurette, far more than Stella, who suffers the inequalities of marriage, and the commitment of her energy to deceit reveals the narrowness of her options. If she ruins Stella's hopes by contriving the marriage with Ted, it is because she sees no other available way of protecting her own financial welfare. We despise her willingness to sacrifice Stella's happiness to her own gain, but as a man a character like Laurette—pragmatic, ambitious, and shrewd—would have had available more approved outlets for such unfeminine talents. The novel's antithesis of Laurette is not Stella but Dora, Cuthbert's bride. The Victorian ideal of feminine goodness, Dora is sweet, mild-mannered, and pretty; in short, she is the perfect model for a clergyman's wife. (It is perhaps significant that Dora bears the same name as David Copperfield's 'child-wife',

Dora.) Yet against the image of Stella, who encapsulates the new generation of Australia, Dora seems unbearably insipid. Lacking in character, passion, and opinion, Dora is no more Martin's model of Australian femininity than Laurette.

Cast then in a mould which falls somewhere between the unacceptable Laurette and the too acceptable Dora, Stella is the true Australian Girl. Her independence of spirit, physical vitality, and sharpness of mind are balanced by her sense of social responsibility and moral integrity. Catherine Martin may have created in Stella an image of femininity capable of surviving the coming century, but it is also an image buoyed by the principles of the closing age. In 1884 Martin had published a review on the Victorian social critic John Ruskin which reveals a strong admiration for his views on women's roles. 'In "Sesame and Lilies"', she affirms, 'we find every page fraught with utterances which are worthy of undying remembrance. A woman who has not read the second of these lectures "Of Queen's Gardens" has missed the truest and the wisest words spoken to or of her sex in this generation—indeed in any generation.'[13] It is interesting to note the passages of Ruskin's work which Martin chooses to highlight as his 'wisest words' on women's vocation. She is clearly inspired by Ruskin's views on women's education, a great debate of the 1860s which Ruskin addresses in *Sesame and Lilies*: 'not only in the material and in the course, but yet more earnestly in the spirit of it, let a girl's education be as serious as a boy's . . . [A]ppeal to the same grand instincts of virtue in them, teach *them* also that courage and virtue are the pillars of their being.' Yet Ruskin's vision of girls' education was, of course, established on a principle of sexual difference, according to which women's distinct feminine virtues would be upheld and realized. In admiring Ruskin's vision of women's equal 'seriousness' to men's, a seriousness which indicates, she says, 'the capacity of human nature for nobleness and "infinite height"', Martin also supports his conservative vision of women's distinctive social place as the custodians of home and moral responsibility. Here are the well-known words of Ruskin she finds most worthy of quotation: 'Wherever a true wife comes, this home is always round her. The stars only may be over her head, the glowworm in the night-cold grass may be the only fire at her feet; but home is yet wherever

---

[13] C. E. M. Martin, 'The Works of John Ruskin', *Victorian Review*, 10 (July 1884), 281–303; 298.

she is.' And: 'the lives of many deserving women are passed in a succession of petty anxieties about themselves, and gleaning of minute interests and mean pleasures in their immediate circle, because they are never taught to make any effort to look beyond it'.

Martin's response to Ruskin in 1884 as the inspiration for women of her generation is again visible when, six years later, she creates for Stella a choice between love (for Anselm) and commitment to higher duty (in marriage to Ted). Yet despite the unambiguous direction of Ruskin's moral vision for women, Stella's choice is not readily made. Her discovery of the plot which precipitates her marriage to Ted results in a nervous breakdown. And here, Martin's depiction of Stella's 'brain exhaustion' opens a window on the Victorian perception and treatment of women's 'hysteria' or the related nervous disorder neurasthenia. The perceived links between women's mental 'illness' and their efforts to expand the social and intellectual limits of their lives were noted not only by the medical practitioners of the period[14] but by other women novelists. Charlotte Perkins Gilman's 1892 novella *The Yellow Wallpaper* famously highlights the mental collapse which follows one woman's domestic confinement. Complete with all the symptoms of the Victorian medical institution's paradigm of women's nervous disorder, Stella's unhappiness, which begins with her removal to Godolphin House as Ted's wife, gradually emerges as fullblown 'hysteria': 'She tried to smile, but broke instead into wild, hysterical laughter. The blood had surged to her head. Her lips and cheeks were crimson—glowing like coals; and there was a glittering light in her eyes' (p. 383). According to the American neurologist Silas Weir Mitchell, creator of the 'rest cure' which saw women bedridden and deprived of 'dangerous' stimulation, recovery depended upon domestic isolation and passivity.[15] But for Stella, recovery lies with the development of emotional maturity, which she gains from the social experience of Europe, where she and Ted have travelled for their honeymoon. From this point, the story

---

[14] According to Elaine Showalter, the neurologist George Miller Beard ascribed nervous illness in the 1860s to five features of social change: 'the periodical press, steam power, the telegraph, the sciences, and especially the increased mental activity of women'. Elaine Showalter, *The Female Malady: Women, Madness and English Culture 1830–1980* (New York, 1985), 135. For a fuller study of Stella's nervous breakdown and its effects, see Christopher Lee, 'Strategies of Power and Catherine Martin's *An Australian Girl*', *Southerly*, 52/2 (1991), 189–206.

[15] Showalter, *Female Malady*, 138–9.

continues in Europe, specifically Berlin, which changes the terms of Stella's perception of the world. A sense of her own place in the scheme of things comes to her through the recognition, in the old world, of the forces which create both cultural greatness and social injustice. This recognition enables her to confirm Australia's unique-ness in relation to Europe, as well as to find the path back towards balance in her own life.

Initially she imagines that recovery of balance is achievable in a plan to travel with Anselm and his family; her decision is forged on a sense of natural justice, which will end her marriage to Ted and restore Anselm to her. The real lesson of the education awaiting her, however, is that women's best role is the unselfish aid of others rather than the gratification of self-will. This lesson is given the authority of divine will when, after years of the absence of faith, she enters a church and experiences a moment of epiphany. Her realization is that the effacement of her own desire represents not a loss to herself but a reconciliation 'of matter and spirit':

A scorching sense of shame at her infidelity to the higher loyalties of justice, self-sacrifice, and generosity overcame her . . . She was consumed with shame and sorrow, and yet she was quickened by the thought that here her downward course had been arrested by the presence of that priest of the Most High whose words had so early fastened on her heart. Once more she had been drawn as with irresistible cords to the foot of the Cross. (pp. 425, 426)

For a contemporary readership, Stella's renunciation of her own desire is no doubt vexatious. Indeed, the nineteenth-century female *Bildungsroman* has always presented problems for late twentieth-century readers because of the fact that, unlike the male protagonist, the female protagonist has a limited number of destinations in her journey of self-education. Stella has already been compared with George Eliot's Maggie Tulliver, whose restoration to the world she longs for is achievable only by her death in the flood. The figure of Maggie may well have been influential for Catherine Martin; that she was an admirer of George Eliot's work is clear from her 1885 study of Eliot's life in *Victorian Review*. In it she admires 'that passion for knowledge' which informed Eliot's life (and which also of course informed the lives of Eliot's fictional women like Maggie Tulliver and Dorothea Brooke), but equally she admires a quality she discerns in Eliot's work of an 'unshrinking acceptance of the solemn facts of life, its limitations, its bitter inheritance'.[16] The negotiation between passion for knowledge and acceptance of limitation is Maggie's particular struggle in *The Mill on the Floss*, and the novel's climax has created a puzzle for its feminist readers: does the flood mark the fact that a character like Maggie can have no future, or does it in fact offer a symbol of her own power, which liberates her from narrow social duty? Whichever way it is read, Maggie's story is one with no ending other than the flood and her death: it can be enacted only upon its own social stage, within the terms established by mid-Victorian morality.

A similar awareness of historical conditions needs to be brought to the ending of *An Australian Girl*, which modern readers have regarded as both Stella's restoration to and escape from social convention. On the one hand, Stella's rediscovery of Christian faith and resignation to a future as Ted's wife seem to affirm the value of those most powerful of Victorian civil institutions: the church and marriage. On the other hand, such an outcome seems to free Stella from the narrow limits of the romance plot, lifting her decision beyond a personal acceptance of duty to the broader, public level of social commitment. Like Maggie Tulliver's, however, Stella's story is more complex than either one of such polarized readings can suggest. Her choice needs to be read not only in terms of its implications for Victorian femininity but also in relation to other social debates.

One of the most forceful debates in late Victorian social politics centred on the dangers of intemperance, and it was one in which women held an active and influential role. In the last decades of the nineteenth century intemperance became the object of considerable social anxiety in Australia, as it did in Britain, Europe, and America. In South Australia the temperance movement gathered pace from the early 1880s, leading to the formation of the Temperance Union of South Australia in 1884. In 1893 Francis Bertie Boyce published a lengthy study called *The Drink Problem in Australia*, which connected 'the manifest evils' of drink to poverty, crime, lunacy, and the degeneration of both family life and state order. Indeed, in these years before Federation, alcohol acquired the status of one of the social evils which most threatened to poison the future nation. But

---

[16] E. C. Martin, 'George Eliot's Life', *Victorian Review*, 12 (June 1885), 162–89; 163.

if it represented one of the worst perceived social ills, women represented the 'army' which could defeat it. Australian women's power in the temperance movement lay, as Boyce asserts more than once, in their given role as 'the mothers of the coming generation'. In their capacity as wives and mothers, women were given a political voice and the responsibility of social reform: 'Let women arise in their might and work', Boyce urges. 'May God inspire the fair daughters of Australia in . . . their sacred duty to be energetic and aggressive . . . May they put forth all their strength to for ever remove the relentless adversary of the home, and almost the only terrible enemy this fair country has to fear.'[17] In *An Australian Girl* Ted signals the danger of this national enemy; various clues (beginning with that description of his overly full mouth, indicating an absence of moral will) alert us to what will later emerge as his 'fatal weakness': alcoholism. Stella's decision to remain with Ted rescues him from a life of intemperance, and in this she plays out two important social roles. First she becomes, in Ruskin's terms, the saviour of fallen man, the symbol of womanhood's capacity for moral influence. This is a role which is realized in Stella's experience of renewed faith in God:

Yes, out of the abysses of exceeding darkness which first fell on her . . . there gradually emerged a faint dawn of hope. After all her weary wanderings—after her blindness and hardness of heart—after her long conviction that God could only be darkly groped after, never securely hoped in—she knew once more that the chastisement of our peace was upon Him . . . (pp. 424–5)

Her second, closely related role is that of womanhood as the voice and vehicle of social conscience, on which the future of national good rests. This is a social conscience which is not only forgiving but also healing. Against a resigned view of men as inherently sinful is this more hopeful one of redeemability, which comes to Stella with her renewal of faith:

on the first evidence of the power of evil habit over her husband she had stood coldly aloof, as if wrong-doing on his part absolved her from all lot or concern in his fate. She recalled how, in speaking of him she had even inferred that he could not help himself—assuming that the spirit of man,

---

[17] Francis Bertie Boyce, *The Drink Problem in Australia, or the Plagues of Alcohol and the Remedies* (London, 1893), 277.

no more than his body, can have any source of impulse or action apart from the inexorable links of material causes. Could the spirit of evil itself help to wreck men with a darker atheism than this? . . . The belief that evil may be overcome—this spring of moral hopefulness—how basely she had denied it by word and action! What . . . if the half-understood dicta of pseudo-science regarding heredity, and the insignificance of man's will, had prevailed rather than the Divine rule, 'Believe, and thou shalt be saved'? (pp. 425–6)

The promise of Ted's redeemability makes the reader more inclined to accept him as Stella's future, despite his position in the novel as the 'wrong' lover. Not only is Stella's moral and social conscience affirmed here, but so is Ted's potential as a suitable husband for her. The devotion and 'unfailing thoughtfulness' which he brings to his marriage, unlike Cicely Mowbray's violent alcoholic husband, strengthens his potential as a morally upright citizen. Yet most of all, the positive potential of their union is suggested by the fact of their mutual Australianness: a quality Stella does not, after all, share with the Englishman Anselm Langdale. Writing to Stella from England, Ted displays a commitment to Australian nationhood which is as strong as Stella's:

We must have a country of our own, governed by ourselves, and not have the name of being ruled by fellows sent out of the heart of London, to do no good but set people by the ears with their twopenny-ha'penny Government House cliques. . . . 'Our colonies,' they say, as if we were bad figs they bought at fourpence a box. I hope that shell-parrot gave me the straight-tip about living to be seventy-six, if only to live to see Australia a properly independent country. (p. 371)

The closure of Stella's story may well be an ambivalent one, but it is none the less filled with a sense of potential. The principle of reform which she brings to her union with Ted is extended in her plan to use their lucrative pastoral land for social good. Two hundred acres of Strathaye, Stella announces to Ted, will become farming lots for poor (though 'self-respecting') European emigrants. In her vision, the unhealthy social decline facing post-industrial Europe will be countered by the fresh spaces of Australia. What is more, her new commitment to social improvement is accompanied by colonial entrepreneurialism. When Ted expresses doubt about the financial sagacity of her plan, Stella replies, 'It will be an investment'. ' "At first you'd better make up your mind to *lose* four per cent.," put in

Ted. "No, I won't lose," she answered confidently' (p. 441). Stella, as much as her husband, holds in her hands the economic development of her country as well as its social reform.

Finally, then, the conventional moral lesson of Stella's return to the church and acceptance of the 'wrong' marriage is underpinned by a profound optimism about her capacity to wield enough influence to make it the 'right' marriage, as well as about the investment she shares with Ted in the unfolding age of a new nation. It is clear, in retrospect, that the new century would bear witness to the same kinds of cultural violences as had the nineteenth century, from the marginalization of women in the process of creating national myths to the systematic elision of Aboriginal cultures in the process of reinventing the country. Yet it would be impertinent to burden Catherine Martin with the responsibility of resolving such deepseated cultural fissures. If, in *An Australian Girl*, there is an implicit acceptance of the conservative forces of history, there is also a challenge to their limits and a powerful faith in a future of independence and equality.

NOTE ON THE TEXT

An Australian Girl first appeared anonymously in London in 1890 in a three-volume edition published by Richard Bentley. In 1891 Bentley published a new one-volume edition which corrected some mistakes but also omitted sections of the original edition. Although the preface to the second edition describes the excisions somewhat disingenuously as 'some slight omissions in one or two passages in the course of the book, which simplify the construction without impairing the interest of the story' they are in fact substantial. While Martin no doubt accepted the correction of obvious mistakes, the excisions were not her work and were in opposition to her desire not to cut the novel.[1] In 1894 the second edition was reissued by Bentley as an 'Australian Edition', this time with ascription to 'Mrs Alick Macleod' as author. (Bentley had in the meantime published Martin's *The Silent Sea* under this pseudonym.) The layout and pagination of this third edition is almost exactly identical with that of 1891 but there are a few minor corrections (and at least one new error).

The present edition reprints the text of 1891 with the correction of some obvious errors. It must always be controversial to publish a text which has been abridged by someone other than the author, but the 1891 excisions certainly produce a text which is more tightly focused on the story of Stella's relations with Ritchie and Langdale and shorten a very long text to a length which might be more acceptable to a modern reader. Nevertheless some interesting material was lost in the passages omitted from the 1891 edition. The omissions are mostly of two to three pages at a time but there are longer passages in all three volumes, notably from Volume I a two-chapter conversation in which Stella describes to Cuthbert her attraction to Roman Catholicism and her subsequent disenchantment (47 pages), from Volume II a whole chapter about a meeting and conversation between Stella and Langdale (25 pages), and from Volume III Stella's encounters with the poor and with various Socialists (10 pages and 32 pages). The excisions in the first two volumes are arguably less

---

[1] The correspondence between Bentleys and Martin can be found in *The Archives of Richard Bentley and Son 1829–1898*, British Publishers' Archives on Microfilm, Part 2 (Cambridge, 1976–7).

significant than those in the last, which lead to the disappearance of a minor character, Signorina von Gerstenberg, who makes a passing reference to Marx. The shorter cuts also contain some significant material, particularly the cuts to Stella's letters to Cuthbert which include, amongst other things, Stella's endorsement of euthanasia. In general the cuts have been made with some skill in the particular sense that they leave a narrative which still makes sense. However, a few minor puzzling allusions remain in the abridged text: Stella's mention of her 'Satan letter' and of a 'merlodeon' (with that particular spelling) can only be fully understood by reference to the longer text (see notes to pp. 123 and 229). Its planned publication in the Academy Editions of Australian Literature will bring the longer version back into print for comparison with the edition printed here.

The 1891 text was clearly prepared and printed with care, although there is a certain amount of inconsistency in the spelling; the spelling has not been standardized for this edition as in every case each of the alternative forms is an accepted spelling in other nineteenth-century British texts. This edition is not the result of a full collation of the three editions but rather reproduces the 1891 text (from the copy in the Barr Smith Library of the University of Adelaide) except for the correction of obvious errors (missing or inverted letters, wrong accents in foreign words, omission of full stops or of quotation marks at the end of dialogue, question marks where there is no question) and the following more substantial changes:

Page.line	*1891 reading*	*Emended reading*	*Source of emendation*
35.24	in only	is only	1890 edition
45.2	biblia-a-biblia	biblia a-biblia	editorial; follows source (see note)
64.4	*raillement*	*ralliement*	editorial
73.28	Montague	Montaigne	1894 edition
88.32	doleur	douleur	editorial
96.1	nia–mia	mia–mia	editorial
102.10	topical	tropical	1890, 1894 editions
114.10	Laracor	Fairacre	editorial
131.21	northern territory	Northern Territory	editorial; capitalized at 105.3–4
199.15	lute	flute	editorial; follows source (see note)

Page.line	*1891 reading*	*Emended reading*	*Source of emendation*
216.10	too	to	1890, 1894 editions
224.25	filette	fillette	editorial
224.26	J'aime	T'aime	editorial
238.38/239.1	Noyou	Noyon	editorial
265.20	hearts	heart	1890 edition
351.26	Viene ...	Vieni ...	editorial; follows
	fra questi	tra queste	source (see note)
355.30	come	comes	editorial
376.35	same	came	1890 edition
399.10	vol	nol	editorial; follows
			source (see note)

SELECT BIBLIOGRAPHY

Novels

The Silent Sea (Mrs Alick Mcleod, London: Bentley, 1892).

The Old Roof Tree: Letters of Ishbel to her Half-Brother Mark Latimer (anon., London: Longmans, 1906).

The Incredible Journey (London: Jonathan Cape, 1923).

Poetry

The Explorers and Other Poems (Melbourne: Robertson, 1874).

Serials

'The Moated Grange: An Original Tale' (serialized in *SA Chronicle and Weekly Mail*, 3 Feb.–27 Oct. 1877).

'At a Crisis' (serialized in *Adelaide Observer*, 14 April–23 June 1900).

'Born an Orphan' (serialized in Melbourne's *The Leader*, 31 Aug.–5 Oct. 1912).

Catherine Martin also published a wide range of travel vignettes, articles, and reviews.

Select Criticism

Margaret Allen, 'Catherine Martin, Writer: Her Life and Ideas', *Australian Literary Studies* 13/2 (1987), 184–97.

—— 'Three South Australian Women Writers, 1854–1923' (unpub. Ph.D. diss., Flinders University of South Australia, 1991).

John Byrnes, 'Catherine Martin and the Critics', *Australian Letters* 3/4 (1961), 15–24.

Miles Franklin, *Laughter, Not for a Cage* (Sydney: Angus and Robertson, 1956).

Christopher Lee, 'Strategies of Power and Catherine Martin's *An Australian Girl*', *Southerly*, 52/2 (1991), 189–206.

—— 'Women, Romance, and the Nation: The Reception of Catherine Martin's *An Australian Girl*', *Australian Feminist Studies*, 17 (Autumn 1993), 67–80.

Elizabeth Webby, 'Introduction' to Catherine Martin, *An Australian Girl* (London: Pandora, 1988).

The following are reviews of the re-released Pandora edition of 1988:

Bronwen Levy, 'Marriage and Mateship in the Colonies', *Australian Society* (Oct. 1988), 48–9.

Margaret McCluskey, 'The Archaeology of Women's Writing', *Australian Book Review*, 104 (Sept. 1988), 30–2.

Michelle Slung, 'Australian Women Writers: The Literary Heritage', *Belles Lettres*, 4/3 (1989), 7.

General Background

Debra Adelaide (ed.), *A Bright and Fiery Troop* (Ringwood: Penguin, 1988).

Joy Hooton, 'Australian Literary History and Some Colonial Women Novelists', *Southerly* 50/3 (1990), 310–23.

Patricia Clarke, *Pen Portraits: Women Writers and Journalists in Nineteenth Century Australia* (Sydney: Allen & Unwin, 1988).

Eric Richards (ed.), *The Flinders History of South Australia: Social History* (Netley: Wakefield Press, 1986).

Penny Russell, *A Wish of Distinction: Colonial Gentility and Femininity* (Melbourne: Melbourne University Press, 1994).

Catherine Helen Spence, *Catherine Helen Spence: An Autobiography* (Adelaide, 1910).

Ken Stewart (ed.), *The 1890s: Australian Literature and Literary Culture* (St Lucia: University of Queensland Press, 1996).

A CHRONOLOGY OF CATHERINE MARTIN

1848   (est.) Born Catherine Edith Macauley Mackay, seventh child of Samuel and Janet Mackay, on the Isle of Skye, Scotland.

1855   Emigration of the Mackay family to South Australia.

1856   (est.) Death of Samuel Mackay.

1867   (est.) Catherine and her sister Mary establish a school for girls at Mount Gambier in the south-east of the colony.

1874   Publication of a collection of poetry, *The Explorers and Other Poems*, under the pseudonym M.C.

1875   (est.) Catherine moves from Mount Gambier to Adelaide to make her living as a journalist.

1876   Catherine's first meeting with the influential South Australian writer Catherine Helen Spence, and the beginning of their long friendship.

1877–85 Catherine works as a clerk in the Education Department.

1882   Catherine marries Frederick Martin, an accountant, whose family had migrated to South Australia from England in 1851.

1890   Anonymous publication in London of her first novel, *An Australian Girl*, in three volumes. The novel was reissued in a single-volume edition the following year, and in an Australian (single-volume) edition in 1894.

1891–4   The Martins travel to Europe, living in a variety of cities.

1892   Publication of a second novel, *The Silent Sea* (also in three volumes), under the pseudonym Mrs Alick Macleod (perhaps a variation of her brother Alec's name. Alec had died in a shipwreck off the Queensland coast in 1875).

1904–7   The Martins travel again to Europe, staying in Germany, Italy, and Spain.

1906   Anonymous publication of *The Old Roof Tree: Letters of Ishbel to her Half-Brother Mark Latimer*.

1909   Death of Frederick Martin from tuberculosis.

1910–11 Catherine travels again to Europe, visiting Skye, her place of birth. In her later years she would make various trips abroad.

1923   Publication, under her own name, of *The Incredible Journey*.

1937   Dies in Adelaide on 17 March.

AN AUSTRALIAN GIRL

PREFACE TO THE SECOND EDITION

THE appearance of the present edition has been somewhat retarded by the absence of the author in Italy.

Advantage, however, has been taken of the interval to correct a few clerical errors which escaped notice in the revision of the first edition, and to make some slight omissions in one or two passages in the course of the book, which simplify the construction, without impairing the interest of the story.

In view of the favourable reception which has been on the whole accorded to this work by the leading critical organs, one is reluctant to take exception to adverse criticism. But in one instance an able and otherwise appreciative critic implied that the plot of the story was in some degree derived from that of another Australian tale which appeared earlier in the same season. It is right to state, therefore, that though the book was not published until July 1890, the MS was in the publisher's hands from November, 1889, that is to say for several months before the other book came out.

July, 1891

CHAPTER I

I⊤ was one Sunday afternoon in the middle of December and in the province of South Australia. The grass was withered almost to the roots, fast turning gray and brown. Indeed, along the barer ridges of the beautiful hills that rise in serried ranks to the east of Adelaide, the herbage was already as dry and bleached as carded flax. In the gullies, thickly timbered and lying in perpetual shade, the ground still retained the faint graying green distinctive of Australian herbage in a state of transition from spring verdure to summer drought.

But soon even the shadiest recesses would bear witness to the scorching dryness of the season. For even before the middle of this first month of summer, two or three of those phenomenal days had come which furnish anecdotes for many successive months alike to the weather statist and the numerous class who cultivate community of soul by comparing experiences of those dreadful days on which 'the hall thermometer stood at 104° before noon.' This Sunday had not quite been one of the days that make the oldest residents turn over heat averages extending to the early dawn of the country's history. But, nevertheless, it was a very hot, still day, without a breath of wind stirring, and in the distance that faint shimmering bluish haze which, to the experienced eye, tells its own tale of days to come.

The masses of white, silver and messmate gum-trees that clothe these same Adelaide hills so thickly, formed a grateful resting-place for the eye, wearied with the steadfast glare of sunshine. So did the vineyards that dot their declining slopes, and the gardens and orchards that are scattered broadcast to the east of the town. But even Adelaide itself is interwoven with the foliage of trees, which do so much to mitigate, both for eye and body, the severities of a semi-tropical climate. This fascinating embroidery of trees is more especially observable in glancing over North Adelaide. This extensive and important suburb, which is divided from Adelaide proper by the Torrens Lake and Park Lands,* lies considerably above the city and adjacent suburbs. So large a proportion of the houses are surrounded by gardens, that from some points of view North Adelaide looks like a well-trimmed wood, thickly studded with houses.

And these gardens are, as a rule, neither suburban slips,* with precocious trees selected for their speedy power of growth, nor the painfully pretentious enclosures which auctioneers delight to term 'grounds.' No, they are genuine gardens—roomy, shadowy, well planted, well watered; rich in flowers and many fruit-trees, bending in due season under their fertile loads; haunted with the hum of rifling bees, fragrant with the perfume of old-world blossoms. In such a garden on this Sunday afternoon a young man and woman were slowly pacing up and down a broad central walk, thickly trellised with vines. The gadding tendrils,* the wealth of wide emerald leaves, the countless oval clusters of ripening grapes—Crystal, Black Prince, and delicate Ladies' Fingers—which clothed the trellis on the sides and overhead, made a delightful picture. So did the great rose-trees hard by, garlanded after their kind with pale pink, yellow, white and blood-red roses. Parallel with this vine arcade there were loquat trees loaded with thick clusters of clear-skinned creamy fruit, and orange-trees, with dark-green globes nestling among glossy boughs, sheeted in waxen blossoms, whose penetrating odour loaded the atmosphere. But as so often happens when a young man and woman are engaged in a *tête-à-tête*, neither the objects round them nor any topic of wide social importance engrossed their attention.

'Do you know why I asked you to come out into the garden, Stella?' said the young man, breaking a pause that had followed some previous talk.

'Oh, to admire the roses, and flick the poor vine-leaves with your riding-whip now and then.'

'I wouldn't mind betting a thousand to one you know as well as I do; but that's the way with you. You'll never help a fellow out of a hole. Why didn't you come to Melbourne last month?'

'Ted, that reminds me. Shouldn't I congratulate you on your horse winning the Melbourne Cup?* Or is it an old stupid story by this time?'

'It's the things that don't come off which make the stupid stories.'

'Well, I congratulate you, then. How long have you been on the turf?'

'I haven't been on the turf at all, in one way. I've bred racehorses, and bought and sold them, ever since my uncle died, leaving me Strathhaye; that's now six years ago, come Easter.'

'Well, for six years you have been more deeply interested in young horses than in anything else in the world——'

'You know a jolly sight better than that.'

'You have talked of them, dreamt of them, been with them; several times you have nearly died for them; always you have lived for them, and now at last you have won the blue ribbon of the Australian racing world. How did you feel when you saw your horse pass the winning-post?'

'I didn't see him at all. He was a dark horse,* and sold the book-makers right and left. There was a packed mob of them yelling like devils, calling out this horse and the other. When the number was put up, and people kept shouting "Konrad!" I saw blue stars for a bit.'

'It must be delightful for something to happen that makes you see blue stars. I almost wish I had been there.'

'I wish you had. I would have had a new drag* in your honour, and a team that would have made most of those there look silly: Why didn't you come when Laurette wrote to ask you?'

'Oh, let me see! I know there were very good reasons, but I forget them.'

'Now, Stella, don't sham. You wouldn't forget them if they were very good reasons.'

'What nonsense! the better they are the more completely they go under sometimes. Think what good reasons there are for being good, and things of that sort.'

'Now, I'm not going to be put off. You've often served me that trick. I ask you a question and you start a new quarry, and the night after I wake up thinking, "Stella never told me whether she still writes to Billy Stein," or whatever it may be. Why didn't you come?'

'Must you know?'

'Yes, certainly.'

'Well, as I was walking by the Torrens, I found a little palm-basket sewn up in the most cunning manner with a red worsted thread.* I unpicked it, and out flew a little milk-white dove, crying: "Don't go to the Melbourne Cup, don't go to the Melbourne Cup!"'

'Well; I'll be hanged if ever I saw a girl that can make up a fib patter than you can when you like!'

'Now I know why you wanted to come into the garden—so that my mother shouldn't overhear you talking like a jockey.'

'Oh, that's all you know about the way jockeys talk! You never heard them. Besides, you know, you shouldn't tell a crammer.'*

'It's not a crammer—it's a parable.'

'That's blasphemy, isn't it, calling yarns you make up as you go along after things in the Bible?'

'Do you think there are no parables except those in the New Testament?'

'I know a parable is when a fellow asks for a long drink in ever-lasting fire, and the other chap in Isaac's bosom won't even wet his lips.* By Jove, I've often thought there wasn't much to choose between them for goodness! One had his good time here and turned his back on the beggar; but the beggar was more spiteful—he had all eternity to behave better, but didn't.'

'Oh, Ted! you are too delightfully literal.'

'I wish to the Lord you really believed I was too delightfully any-thing. Surely you might have dropped a fellow a line when Konrad won, seeing you had the naming of him.'

'Did I? When?'

'Why, a month after he was foaled. Don't you remember that frightfully stupid ball at Government House, where a fellow couldn't put a hoof down without treading on some old tabby's* train? There was Mrs Bartholomew Gay with one from here to the Polar regions—white satin embroidered with Chinese dragons, or something. I had to stand with one foot in the air, like a circus-tumbler, so often, for fear of stamping on her tail; at last I firmly planted my foot on it, and tore it out of the gathers. By Jove, didn't she look daggers at me! But she trundled it off the floor after that.'

'What a memory you have!' said the girl, laughing. 'I remember now—we sat out a dance, and you told me about some signally tal-ented yearlings, and this foal, who had such a brilliant pedigree—I am proud of him; I shall kiss the star on his forehead when I see him.'

'You remember he has a star? You had much better let me take it to him—not that I would give it to him, though.'

'Now, Ted, if you are too bold I shall return to my book.'

'No, no, you wouldn't have the heart to do that. You can always go to your books while I am mostly three hundred and fifty miles away. How many months is it since I saw you last?'

'Oh, two or three, I suppose.'

'It was in July, nearly six months ago; and you then said you would most likely come to Laurette's in November. But you didn't. You wouldn't come to the Cup, and you wouldn't drop me a line to say you were glad about Konrad—all to avoid giving me a chance. Now, don't make your eyes big, as if you didn't take in what I say. Why don't you ask me what chance?'

'Well, then, what chance?' returned the young lady, laughing, but with a heightened colour.

'To once more ask you to marry me.'

'Only once more? Then after that we may be fast friends.'

'Not at all—we shall be man and wife.'

'Oh, Ted! Well, I suppose we could hardly be both.'

They smiled in each other's faces, but the young man soon became grave.

'Stella, how often have I asked you to marry me?'

'Do you mean counting from the very beginning, or since we have grown up?'

'I don't think it's fair for you always to poke borax at me.* Why don't you be serious?'

'I don't like being serious. I have been to church once already. The proper way to spend a hot Sunday is to be like chaff that the storm carrieth away———'*

'What do you mean by that? Is it another parable?'

'I mean to lie in a hammock in the west veranda, and think whatever idle thoughts choose to come into your head, or read your favourite poets, or listen to a bird on a branch hard by. Do you hear that white-breasted swallow in the top of the Moreton Bay fig-tree?'

They were silent for a few minutes, and the liquid, melodious carols of the little minstrel filled the air.

'But I would much sooner listen to you than to that little rubbish,' said the young man in an emphatic tone.

'Oh, what bad taste! Wouldn't you like to know what it really feels like to float in the air like a sunbeam?' asked the girl mischievously.

'He only flies and sings for his tucker*—I can get mine without that. Besides, I would sooner be on the earth near you than anywhere you could mention. Stella, it was close to this very spot I first asked you to be my wife, when we were both of an age to marry. Do you remember it?'

The girl looked at her companion with undisguised amusement.

'I should think I did! You were barely nineteen.'

'And you were nearly eighteen—a very good age for both, considering I had been left my own master twelve months before, with twelve thousand a year. What more did we want?'

'A little wisdom, a little love, a little sympathy, and power of companionship—everything that we ought to have mutually.'

'Do you mean that I didn't love you enough, or didn't know my own mind?'

'But surely marriage is the sort of bargain which needs two to make it?'

'Well, at any rate you refused me out and out then, and were as solemn as if you were going into a convent. Larry always declares you were thinking of doing it then. I know you had a picture of the Virgin, and said she was our advocate, and talked about the soul and all sorts of Papist things—enough to make a Protestant's hair creep.'

'Did your hair creep? And how did you know you were a Protestant? Because you never go to church, I suppose?'

'That's neither here nor there. But now, do you remember the second time I asked you?'

A quick wave of colour swept over the girl's face.

'Ted, what is the use of going over all this?'

'Well, I'll go over it—and you check me if I make a mistake. It was eighteen months later. We hadn't seen each other for nearly a year. You were in the garden when I came. Is that right?'

'Yes.'

'I saw your mother and told her I was going to try my luck again, and she said I had her consent and good wishes. The moment you saw me you asked if any gifted year-old colt had hit his leg, I looked so serious; and then you said: "Oh, you are going to be foolish again"——'

'And you were, and I was still more foolish—for you knew your own mind, and I didn't know mine.'

'Foolish! By George! when I think about you, and feel rather savage I remember that once in your life, anyhow, you were good and sensible; and that's the day you promised to be my wife, and sat beside me in the arbour of Spanish reeds, with the scarlet japonica hanging on it in bundles.'

'You certainly have rather a dreadful memory.'

'Yes—you wore a cream-coloured dress like the one you have on now. I could tell you every word you said—and, by heaven! I could tell you, too, how I felt a week afterwards when I got your letter at

Strathhaye breaking it all off, and saying it was a frightful mistake on your part.'

'Well, Ted, do you want me to say again how sorry I am? Do you want me to grovel in the dust all my life because of that blunder? After all, you brought it on yourself by being so persistent when I was in rather a weak-minded mood.'

'Weak-minded? You never were half so good before or since. And you had quite got rid of all that stuff about convents and Papists.'

'You must not speak so disrespectfully of these things.'

'Well, you know very well you may have any notions you like—as long as you have me.'

'That is rather a strong bribe.'

'I'll make it much stronger if you'll tell me how. You don't suppose it does a fellow any good to come a cropper like that, do you?'

'Why, three months afterwards I heard you were going to be married to Miss Julia Morton. Why weren't you?'

'I did try to like Julia—if it were only to vex you; but, by Jove! when she began to be in earnest, I found the shoe was on the wrong foot. You might be vexed for a day, but I should be vexed for all the rest of my life.'

'What makes you think I would be vexed for a day?'

'Oh, just because I've come to belong to you—in a sort of way— like that goggle-eyed owl and the little gold pistol hanging at your watch-chain.'

'I use the little gold pistol to wind up my watch with, and the owl has sparkling ruby eyes into which I look in church when I am very tired. The one is useful and the other beautiful, you see, Ted.'

'And I am both,' said the young man imperturbably. 'Besides, I can give you whatever money will buy—take you anywhere.'

'But then, you see, you would be always there.'

'Yes; and when I wouldn't be about you would nearly cry your eyes out. You may laugh, but women always get fonder of their husbands. Look here, Stella, you said "yes" once before; you'll have to say it again and stick to it. The last time I spoke to you you said you would think over it. You've had plenty of time. You're close on twenty-three. A girl should be married by that time.'

'Or not at all. You seem to forget that many women never marry.'

'But you're not one of them. Now, Stella, look me in the face and tell me, do you intend to be an old maid?'

'Oh, one doesn't intend it; but sometimes circumstances are more merciful than one's intentions.'

'Has any fellow come along that you care for more than me?'

'N—no.'

'Thank the Lord for that! All you know have been in love with you already—Willy Stein, Wigram, Lindsay, Andrew——'

'Ted, you really are too absurd! Don't you think it is wrong to trifle away the precious moments that never come back again?'

'Ah, yes, they do. When I've been with you the time comes back over and over again. Besides, Stella, how can you call it trifling when I ask you to marry me? Will you?'

'No, thank you.'

'You speak just as if I offered you a mouldy bit of bread.'

'No; as if you offered me some rich cake for which I have no appetite.'

'What if you did not get another chance of refusal?'

'Do you suppose I expect you to turn up periodically all my life, asking me if I am "game" to come out with you into the garden?'

'Well, it's what I'll do, unless you get married to someone else.'

'Or unless you get married yourself.'

'I shall never marry any woman but Stella Courtland, and that's as sure as my name is Edward Ritchie.'

The two had paused in their pacings to and fro, and stood facing each other at the end of the vine arcade furthest from the house, close to a great white Fortuniana rose-tree, thickly covered over with roses and buds in all stages of unclosing.

The girl was tall and very finely formed. Her face in repose was apt to be rather cold and pale. The eyes were extremely beautiful—starry, large, deep and liquid. When we try to describe eyes or flowers, we find that language is extremely destitute in precise colour terms. They were dark gray-blue—sea-blue is, perhaps, the term that most nearly approximates to the hue of this girl's eyes, and as that tint in the waves is subject to rapid changes, to deepening intensity and gleaming flashes of paler light, so did those bewitching orbs reflect each passing emotion. They were as sensitive to her moods as the surface of water is to the sky's influence. Thus it will be seen that their range of expression was infinite. The same might be said of the whole countenance. When moved or animated, it glowed and sparkled as if a light shone through it. The brow was singularly noble, and gave promise of unusual mental power. The complexion was very fair and clear, and when she talked it was often tinged with swift delicate rose-pink, that died away very slowly, leaving a soft warm glow in the cheeks like that often seen in a moist sea-shell. It was a face whose every line and feature indicated that Stella was endowed with rare qualities of intellect and imagination, quick to feel, to see, to think. And yet a very woman, far from indifferent to admiration and the sense of power that the homage of men gives a girl. Yet, withal, liable to that quick disdain of the more frivolous aspects of life, which to those who understood but one side of her complex nature appeared in the light of wilful caprice. She made a captivating picture as she stood under the thick woof of clustering grapes and vine-leaves that threw flickering shadows over her well-poised head, with its abundant coils of silky hair, which had a slight wave and was of that deep golden-brown colour that is seldom retained after childhood.

The young man was good-looking in a not uncommon and distinctly unintellectual way. He was close on six feet in height, with a well-knit, athletic figure, a sun-bronzed face, inclining to be florid. The forehead was low and square; the eyes dark-brown; the hair lighter in tone, cut close, but crisply curling to the roots. The nose was thick, but straight and well defined. The jaws were too heavy, and the lips, partly concealed under a heavy drooping moustache, were over-full. Altogether, it was the face of a man who could be firm and determined in action, yet morally lacking in force of will.

The contrast between the two faces in form, development, and expression was so striking that a casual onlooker might conclude there was that essential difference of nature and temperament which might somehow form a basis for marriage. This impression would be strengthened by a lurking air of indecision in the young woman's face as her companion delivered his resolve in a voice that well carried out the robust air of knowing what he wanted, and a determination to compass it, which was conveyed by his general demeanour.

'I don't know whether I should say that I am sorry or glad you are going to be a bachelor,' she said reflectively. 'Will you grow very thin and cross, or stout and good-natured? The worst of it is, if you get stout you will hobble and have a bad toe. It will be really gout, you know, but you'll call it a sprain or something. And then, when you come to see me, you will tread on dear Dustiefoot's paws. I suppose

I may be a little deaf by that time. Ah, I can never bear to think of growing old or dying!' and Stella stopped abruptly with a little shrug of the shoulders.

'Why didn't you finish your fancy sketch? If you were a little deaf I would bawl at you: "Do you remember that Sunday in December when the garden was full of roses, and that little beggar of a bird was singing?" And then you'd say: "Ah, Ted, why didn't we get married when we were young?" . . . You know, Stella, you'll have to give way in the end. Twice you've named a horse for me, and twice it's turned out most lucky. Now, tell me—suppose we had been married this morning at church, what would you think the very worst part of the concern?'

'That you wouldn't drive to the railway-station and set off for Strathhaye—alone.'

'Well, that's flat. I often wonder what makes me so ridiculously soft about you, Stella. You say such horrid things to me, while every other girl I come across——'

'Now, Ted, if you boast, your very last fragment of a chance is gone.'

'Oh, I have got a fragment of a chance, then? Come, that's the best thing you've said yet. Look here, Stella, have you ever been in love? Now, honour bright?'

'Well, hardly—except with people in books.'

'But how the deuce could you be in love with people in books?'

'Oh, I assure you they are far the nicest people to fall in love with.'

'Because you can put them on a shelf and leave them there.'

'Yes, that is one great charm. It is partly what ruins life, the way people see so much of each other, till they know each other by heart, up and down—all their stories that once were funny, their pet theories, their stupid idiosyncrasies——'

'What are idiosyncrasies?'

'Let me see. It is your idiosyncrasy to wish to marry; it is mine to think it too dangerous an experiment.'

'Fancy calling it an idiosyncrasy when a fellow is spoony.* But I expect that is not the dictionary meaning. Well, you are all but twenty-three, and you have not been in love. You may depend, if you are not heels over head before you are twenty, you never will be. So you may as well save waiting any longer.'

The girl laughed out loud.

'Well, Ted, you are the first I have heard use inability to love as an argument for getting married. You are really very humble.'

'Oh! a fellow is always very humble when he's up to the hilt in love.'

'It is afterwards, when the fair is over, that he isn't quite so meek and beseeching.'

'Well, you wouldn't have him be a humble jackass at a distance all through? It's too much like making your dinner off peaches. Besides, a girl like you always has her own way, hand over fist, single or married; and when to that you add ever so many thousands a year——'

'Always when you have been to Melbourne you harp more and more on your money.'

'Maybe. You see, the more you see of the world the more you find how much people think of money, and how much it gets for you.'

'And yet to be poor in the midst of riches is the worst kind of poverty.'

'But you see,' said the young man eagerly, misinterpreting the drift of this remark, 'Strathhaye is none of your big leasehold affairs. It's nearly all freehold—a good deal of it fit to carry three or four sheep to the acre—where never a cockatoo nor a free selector* dare show his nose.'

'Oh, I feel as if I knew every inch of Strathhaye!'

'Well, a good tale is none the worse for being twice told. Besides, I am coming to the point. You might marry for love to-morrow, and in a few months find you were quite insolvent in the article—have to pay a bob in the pound, or even less.'

'True—become an utter bankrupt; such things happen.'

'Yes; there was your friend Cicely Mowbray——'

'Oh, please don't!' said Stella, in a tone of quick pain.

'Well, not speaking of things doesn't make them different. You know how completely gone she was on the man she married; and in less than three years she ran off with another fellow!'

'And that was less immoral than staying with the man she married,' said Stella, a hard expression coming into her face.

'Still, it isn't what people mean to do when they marry for love. You see, the point is that you may fall as completely out of love as you may fall into it. But you can't wake up one morning to find eighty thousand acres first-class arable land, freehold, all gone to kingdom come like a rainbow. May I smoke a cigarette?'

'Yes. What a pretty case, and what elegant little cigarettes!'

'They ought to be. Do you know what they cost each?'

'Oh heavens! You are going to be just like Croesus* Henway, always telling the price of things.'

'Or you might say like my father. He likes to mention the figure that things cost. Still, I might easily take after a worse old boy than the governor. Though, mind you, I don't mean to go into Parliament ever, and give ninety Affghanistan camels for an exploring expedition,* and get a handle tacked to my name because they came on a desert a hundred miles by ninety.'

'You're like a good many more Australians. You'll never do as much for your native land as your fathers did for their adopted one.'

'Oh, I don't know! I've half a dozen gold medals for my wool; and my horses are far-away the best in the district. But there—I'll put my foot in it again if I say much more. Would you like me to be Sir Edward Ritchie, Stella, like the old man?'

'Surely that is a very foolish question to ask me, of all people.'

'I am not so sure about that—Sir Edward and Lady Ritchie. If you really have any fancy for the title, I might give another big dose of camels to the Government. There's plenty more desert to be opened up for selectors to perish in.'

'Your speaking of the desert reminds me that I am getting parched with thirst. There must be some afternoon tea going on by this time. Haven't we been here a good while?'

'About five minutes. I don't care for tea. But I'll go and get a split soda* for myself and bring you a cup. Oh, if we go inside you won't come out again—and we haven't settled anything yet. But here comes Kirsty with a tray.'

Kirsty was a tall spare woman, who was getting to be more than middle-aged, but whose active, vigorous ways forbade the imputation of old age. She was invariably attired in black, a snowy cap, apron, collars and cuffs, and a face in which all the cardinal virtues ran riot. But it was withal tempered by a certain severity of expression that would seem to be seldom absent from the bearing of trusted Scotch servants who have lived nearly all their lives in one family.

'I hae brought your pet Chiny teapot, Miss Stella,' said Kirsty,

putting the tray down on a little wicker table that was fixed beside a
rustic bench in the arcade. 'And Mr Tom bade me ask ye, sir, whether
ye wadna rather hae a glass o' soda water?'

'Yes, if you please, Kirsty; but tell Mr Tom to draw it mild.'

'Where is Maisie, or Sarah, Kirsty?' asked Stella, as she poured
herself out a cup of tea. 'You shouldn't be attending on us here, when
we really ought to go inside.'

'Weel, Miss Stella, ye see there's whiles when people disna
want ither folk aboot,' answered Kirsty, with a demure smile; 'Sarah's
gone to Mile End* to see her aunt; as for Maisie, I've set her to learn
a page o' the Shorter Catechism.* She used to ken every question in
it; but ye suld hear her when I pit a few till her to-day. It's just
awfu' hoo this climate seems to be against proper grounding in the
fundamentals.'

'Poor Maisie!' said Stella with a smile; 'fancy learning a page of
the Shorter Catechism on a day like this!' She fanned herself softly
with a wide pink satin fan, tipped with marabout feathers, and slowly
sipped her tea.

'What is the Shorter Catechism when it is at home?' asked the
young man, who was sitting near the girl and watching her every
movement.

'Oh, it's just a little Scotch book, full of questions and answers
about things people are supposed to believe—but don't.'

'What sort of questions?'

'The first is, What is the chief end of man? Now what answer
would you give to that?'

'Being in a garden with the girl who won't have you—but will
some day——'

'No; but in a general way, what do you think is the chief end of
man? what he should most live for?'

Ritchie knitted his brows for a moment. 'Well, I should say it is to
sell on the rise and have a good time.'

'Sell on the rise?'

'Yes, if you sell on the rise you make a pot of money. If you
don't, the other fellow collars the tin.* Now, what is the answer in
the Catechism?'

'The answer is that the chief end of man is to glorify God, and to
enjoy Him for ever.'

'But, of course, that means when people get to heaven.'

'But why should they get to heaven if they do nothing to deserve it?'

'Well, there you ask me a question! Ah! here comes Kirsty with my seltzer.* Here's to you, Stella—and many of them,' said Ritchie, clinking Stella's cup with his tall tumbler, and tossing off half its contents at a draught.

'What a pretty pale amber colour! Is that ordinary soda water?' asked Stella.

'Yes, ordinary soda water—but not ordinary old Irish whisky. I'd back your brother Tom's judgment in that article against any man's. Have a little nip. It's ever so much better than tea. I say, Stella, why does the old woman—Kirsty, I mean—set her daughter to learn such stuff?'

'Ted, I am afraid you are almost a heathen. Do you ever read the Bible?'

'Well, I sometimes begin to read it on Sunday evening after a game or two at billiards. But I generally drop off to sleep. I seem as if I always knew what was coming.'

'I wonder how much you really know of it?'

'Oh, lots! You try. Ask me about Noah or any of those old buffers.'

'Then what can you tell me about Noah?'

'Ah, Noah! Well, he was the one that put all the insects into an ark and drank too much wine,* and was going to put a knife into his son Esau, till the ram called out, "Here am I."* If he had been a proper prize animal he'd never have given himself away like that. Well, what are you laughing at?'

'Oh, Ted, Ted! Then what about Abraham?'

'Abraham was one of those fellows that was always getting into a fix because he didn't leave his wife at home.* It shows how wrong it is for a man to take his wife everywhere.'

'And Isaac, what about him?'

'Well, he was about as sly as a Jew pawnbroker. He put on a kangaroo skin, or something, so as to get a mess of porridge.* But he didn't make much out of it, for he got put into a fiery furnace afterwards—but no, it was a pit.'*

'And how many sons had he?'

'Well, there was Jacob and a thundering lot more; but ten of them got lost, you know—the ten tribes—so you can't expect me to know *their* names. One of them—Joseph—had an awful swell coat. He went down into Egypt.* But I never could swallow all the yarn about him. Do you think you ought to laugh so much at things out of the Bible?'

'Ted, do you really think all that is in the Scriptures?'

'I bet you it is; and a lot far more unlikely. Yes; I'd lay you all I hope to make when next I sell on the rise you couldn't ask me much in the Old Testament I wouldn't give you an answer to,' said Ritchie, with the elation of a man who has passed a creditable examination.

'But what things do you sell? I thought you sent your wool to London and sold your surplus stock to station-brokers, as my brothers do at Lullaboolagana.'*

'Oh, I don't mean station stuff. I mean shares of all kinds. Gold in Victoria; silver in New South Wales; rubies, copper, and tin in South Australia; opals in Queensland; pearls in Western Australia. I have had a share in a pearling boat at Shark's Bay* for two seasons. I mean to show you a specimen of the pearls before long. But, after all, no speculation comes up to betting on thoroughbreds that go flashing by with a feather-weight on them. But, you know, it strikes me that no one with a lot of money gets such a curly half-hour out of betting or plunging* as those that put their last copper* on something they know nothing about, and then hold their breath till they see whether they go to gaol or make a haul.'

'Well, this is very edifying. It seems the great thing in selling on the rise is to rob your neighbour and have some excitement. I had no idea you were such a financier.'

'Oh, a fellow must do something. As for wool and sheep, you shear your flocks and ship the wool off. The sheep are turned into the paddocks and begin to grow their next clip, and the London market goes up or down a few farthings in the pound. It's all as slow as a christening.'

'Were you ever at a christening?'

'Yes, I was, worse luck! and stood godfather, too!'

'You a godfather? Oh, Ted, this is too ridiculous!'

'Well, I thought it meant just to give the little beggar a silver pot and a five-pound-note now and then. But it appears you tell the most barefaced crammers about renouncing the devil and all his work.* It seems to me the moment you have anything to do with the Church you have to tell lies till you're black in the face.'

'And who is the happy babe that may be left to your spiritual guidance?'

'Why, Henrietta's last baby. She's John Morton's wife, you know. Aren't we somehow related through the Mortons? You see, my sister is married to John Morton, and your brother Claude is married to Helen Morton, John's sister. Now, what relation am I to you?'

'Oh, the relation that should sit a little further away. We always come back to talking of ourselves.'

'Well, there's nothing else half so interesting. By the way, I was coming part of the way from Melbourne with Dick Emberly, and he said your brother Cuthbert was going to take charge of a congregation in one of the Melbourne suburbs. I didn't know he was a full-fledged parson.'

'Yes, he was ordained three months ago. He is going to take a congregation at Hawthorne* for some months for a clergyman who has fallen ill.'

'Oh, now you'll come to Melbourne. Larry said she would make you come for part of the season. Have you seen her yet since she came to my father's?'

'No; she called the other day, but I was out. She left word that she wanted to see me particularly, and I meant to call one day this week. How does her husband go on now?'

'Oh, much as usual. It's always head you lose, tail I win, with a man like the Hon. Talbot Tareling. No member of the "British nobility," as Larry was so fond of calling it, that I've known in the Colonies has much idea about money, but to grab as much as possible without doing a stroke of work.'

'Well, I cannot help liking Mr Tareling. He has such very good manners, and he is very amusing.'

'You see, it's all he's got to show for himself and for being descended from goodness knows how many lords, and for having an uncle a K.G.* and his elder brother married to the daughter of a duke. Lord, how Larry used to cram them all down our throats, till we found out to our cost what an expensive trick it is to have a sister marry into the "British nobility." Look here, Stella, shall you be in to-morrow afternoon? Because, if so, Larry will drive across and settle when you'll come, then. You see, you can't get out of it now that Cuthbert is to be in Melbourne.'

'Oh, let me see. I'll have to consult my mother and decide about all sorts of things. You see, I've promised to go to Lullaboolagana in May or June.'

'Very well; take Melbourne on the way. I am going to see the old people this evening, and I shall tell Larry.'

'Didn't you come from Godolphin House?'

'No; you see, when I got in by the inter-colonial* last night, I went with one or two other fellows straight to the club. Then I didn't get up very early, and so I came direct here to see you.'

'When did you see your parents last?'

'Oh! about six months ago—the same time as I saw you before.'

'Well! and the way your poor mother dotes on you—her only boy! Why do people think it is a blessing to have children? Very often it seems one of the bitter pleasures of life.'

'Well, you see, if people didn't think things were a little better than they are, the world wouldn't gee up at all. And doesn't it say even in the Bible that a man shall leave his father and mother and cleave to his wife?* Then how much more will he do it for the girl who doesn't want to be his wife!'

'Ted, your logic is irresistible.'

'You may call it logic if you like—but it's true.'

'Which logic seldom is; but then it's correct, and you can so seldom combine the two,' said Stella in the light, mocking tone which came to her so readily; 'I declare I've nearly emptied my teapot! It is fatal to begin to drink on a day like this.'

'Yes; the more you drink, the more you want to—that's the mischief of it,' said the young man, with a gloomier expression than the occasion seemed to call for.

'By Jove! I nearly forgot I had this for you, Stella,' he said presently, taking a small parcel out of his breast coat-pocket, sealed and addressed as it had come by post. 'You're always interested about the niggers. Myers, my book-keeper, is a great dab at finding things out about them. By the way, he corresponds with your old friend, Dr Stein. Well, some time ago Myers fossicked* out about a very rum sort of shoe that the blacks use on particular occasions. I told him to get me one if he could, and when I got to the club last night I found this waiting for me. Oh, it's over three weeks since I left Strathhaye; I've been in Melbourne and other places.'

'Let me open it!' cried Stella. 'I love unfastening an unknown parcel; it is one of the simple pleasures of life that never palls. Oh, Ted, what a cunning, gruesome-looking sort of thing!' she said, as the shoe was revealed to view.

It was light, and compressible into a very small compass. The sole was composed of emu feathers, matted together with a dull red coagulated substance. The upper part was a sort of network of small plaited strands crossed and re-crossed. This curious shoe was extremely crude in shape, being exactly alike at both ends.

'Why, Ted, this is hair!' cried Stella, after examining the net closely, and touching the plaited strands, which had still a dull gloss.

'Yes—a woman's hair.'

'Ah! only a woman's hair. How strangely wicked this shoe begins to look! Not a scrap of difference between the heel and the toes— and yet one could tell it is meant for a shoe; and it looks as if it would keep well on the foot. Let me see how it would look.'

Stella quickly slipped off her own shoe and put on the aboriginal one.

'Put it off! put it off! I can't bear to see it on you,' cried the young man vehemently.

But the girl merely laughed, and walked a few steps, and found that this curious covering for the foot, though much too large, yet clung to it with strange tenacity.

'Do you know that it is the most unlucky thing you could do?' said the young man quite gravely.

'Really!' said Stella, smiling at the sombre tone of conviction in which he spoke. 'Well, give me my own shoe, Ted. No—I can put it on.'

Ritchie half reluctantly returned the pretty little bronze shoe with its silver buckle and dainty bow, and then took up the aboriginal one.

'Now, do you know what this is called, and what it is used for?' he said, holding it at full length on his outspread palm.

'No; but I am dying to know, for I never before heard that any of our blacks made any attempt at shoeing themselves. Could they walk far in a thing of that kind?'

'Far enough for their purposes, I dare say,' returned Ritchie grimly. 'That is a Kooditcha shoe,* and a black fellow never puts a pair of them on except when he steals at night upon an enemy to kill him.'

'Oh, Ted, are you making that up to give me what you call a "curly half-hour"?'

'Oh, but you've not heard all yet. Do you see that reddish stuff holding the feathers together? Well, that is human blood.'

'How horrible! I wish I had not put it on,' said the girl, with a little shiver. 'It really has an assassin-like look, and such strange sombre tints.'

'You see, it would make no more track than a butterfly, and nothing to show it was on a foot. The blacks say they can track anything that walks or crawls, from a horse to a young snake; but not a ghost or an enemy in Kooditcha shoes.'

'Well, of all the myths I have gathered about the blacks, none are so dramatic as this relic. Thank you so much for getting it for me.'

'Well, I'm glad you like it. I wouldn't touch the thing with a pair of tongs, for my own part.'

'Human blood and a woman's hair! I wonder if anyone ever wore this to creep up to a tribal foe at midnight? But why did you say it was unlucky to put it on?'

'Well, the blacks say if you put one on and don't kill anybody, you'll live to wish someone had killed you.'

'Clearly the only thing for me to do is to kill someone. Who shall it be?' asked Stella, with mock gravity.

'Well, I'd offer myself, but you did for me long ago.'

'Why, Ted, you are getting quite epigrammatic.'

'Oh, I can't make a stew of my heart and put it into a letter, like some fellows. But look here, Stella. Ah, here comes Cuthbert. By Jove! he looks almost like a Bishop already.'

The newcomer, Cuthbert Lionel Courtland, was three years older than his sister. He was a young clergyman, with perhaps something of the ultra-gravity of demeanour that may sometimes be observable in those that have recently entered on the sacred calling. He had the finely-developed brow that was a characteristic of the Courtland family, dark gray eyes, something like Stella's in expression, and a beautifully-chiselled mouth, that helped largely to convey the calm, sunny expression which marked his face.

The two young men greeted each other as old acquaintances.

'You're a full-blown parson, Courtland, since I last saw you; I suppose I ought to congratulate you, but——'

'But you're not quite sure, Ritchie? Well, I'll take the half-will for the deed.'

'The fact is, I never know what to say before a parson; and though we've been kiddies together, I don't believe I can forget after this you belong to the cloth. The white choker and that makes you look, somehow, as if you had belonged to the clergy all your life.'

'Well, shall I put a spotted necktie on, Ted—for old acquaintance' sake?' laughed the young clergyman.

'Oh, I'm just going, thank you. Stella has been blowing me up* for not being with my parents. There's a little filly I've had sent to my father's for you to ride, Stella. May I come and take you out on Tuesday morning?'

Stella hesitated, and then consented to the arrangement. The brother and sister accompanied their guest to the house, where he made his adieus to the rest of the family. He then mounted his horse and rode away.

CHAPTER II

THE brother and sister returned to the arcade. Cuthbert was the first to speak.

'Stella, there is a question I want to ask, and I'm almost afraid to put it.'

The girl looked up quickly, and then a smile slowly crept over her face.

'Dear darling boy, don't be afraid to ask me questions—as if they were lighted matches that might fall into gunpowder.'

'Has anything special passed between you and Ritchie?'

'Yes.'

'Have you accepted him?'

'No.'

'Then why do you go out riding with him on Tuesday?'

'Because I haven't accepted him.'

'Stella dear, don't trifle about this. Is it fair to him?'

'I think it's not only fair, but generous. He asks me to marry him. I cannot make up my mind to do so at present. In the meantime, I bind up his wounded spirit with the balm of friendship.'

'Yes, that's it. You refuse him time after time——'

'Not invariably. Do not blame me too severely. You see, I have tried all the recognised modes of treating a lover. I have refused him and accepted him, and sometimes done neither. When he has asked me for a stone I give him bread*—the nourishment of occasional social intercourse instead of the terrible disillusion of marriage.'

'All this may be very well from a comedy point of view. But remember, it is not for the amusement of a passing hour that a man persists in asking a woman to be his wife year after year.'

'No. But still, dear, remember how much more amusing it is than if she had married him the first time of asking.'

'But now let me ask you seriously, what is to be the end of it all? I cannot understand you in the least, Stella, in this matter. To begin with, it is a mystery to me that you should find pleasure in Ted's society, and yet I believe you do.'

'Ah, Cuth, you haven't heard Ted give an account of the Bible Patriarchs'—and the girl burst into a peal of laughter so infectiously merry that her brother was forced to smile. 'As for asking what is to be the end of it all, why, that is a question we keep on asking as long as people live, and, most of all, when they die.'

'Yet people must decide something in a rough and ready fashion. You have allowed yourself to drift into a very undesirable position. You refuse to marry Ritchie—and there I, at least, feel you are right. But I think you are wrong to go out riding with him, for it gives him hope that in the end you may change your mind.'

'And so I may. If I could only be sure that he would be always as amusing as he was to-day——'

'Well, I suppose sex must count for something when a certain friendship has subsisted since childhood between a young man and woman. I must say that to me the chief quality of Ritchie's conversation is a careless—well, perhaps graphic—commonness of speech.'

'There is more than that. There is a direct appeal to life as it presents itself to him; and when we have all tacitly agreed to blink so much, the trait has a certain fascination—at least to me.'

'I could understand that so much better if Ted's point of view were not essentially that of the average sensual man. Pardon me, dear, if I say anything that vexes you.'

'You must not forget that I have never been in love with Ted.'

'Well, that troubles me sometimes more than if you were.'

'Isn't that just slightly contradictory?'

'Perhaps it may be; but what I mean is, that if you could really be in love with him, and married him, you might transform him. But if you marry him without being in love—well, I fear that one or both may fall over a precipice.'

'Why, Cuthbert, you must have been reading tragedy lately.'

'What makes you think so?'

'Because it is only tragedy which is so merciful in finishing us up in a speedy, impressive manner when things go wrong, till at last the ghosts have to come on the stage to explain how people fell over a precipice.'

'Every word you say there makes me feel afresh how disastrous it would be for you to risk a *mariage de convenance*,* or marriage with anyone to whom you could not look up in some measure, with whom you would not have that deeper mental bond without which marriage, in some cases, is not justifiable.'

'Well, it seems to me that marriage of all subjects is the one that most eludes dogmatizing about to any successful issue.'

'I admit that; but the more difficult a position is, the more one must avoid an obvious danger.'

'"To save the soul," says one of the old Spanish saints, "it is necessary to have as little intercourse with people as possible."'*

'Please don't say that in order to be happy in marriage the same axiom applies; for you are quite capable of proving it,' said the young man laughingly.

'Did you ever notice a funny old book in tarnished gold that was given to Grandmother Loudon on her wedding-day, called "Letters to a Granddaughter"?'

'Yes; I never read it, but I always understood it was published for private circulation only by an ancestress of our own.'

'Oh, very likely. It is full of the acute platitudes I find crowding to my pen when I try to write, so I suppose it is an hereditary strain. Well, the thinglet is divided into "School Life," "Coming Out," "Betrothal," "Marriage," "Maternity." Each section except marriage has about a hundred pages devoted to it. But under marriage there are only five or six pages, beginning: "It must be evident to my dear intelligent young female friends that this is a subject on which every woman who enters the holy estate must be left to make her own special reflections. They cannot be anticipated."'

'Really, Stella,' said her brother, laughing, 'you never seem to look into an old, unknown book without finding a joke in it.'

'Do you call that a joke? You wouldn't if you had turned the grandmother's letters over as I did, when I was seriously trying to make up my mind about entering the holy estate. But the old woman was right to a certain extent; for there you have to do with all the uncertainty of untried depths in two natures, brought into a previously unknown relationship. Who can tell how the venture is to turn out?'

'Therefore, I say, let there be the sympathy of two responsive natures or the differences that arise from two minds consciously alive.'

'Yes; and after building on all these hopeful auguries, you find the result a failure more elaborate than the ordinary type.'

'I cannot quite make out why you are so radically sceptical on the subject of marriage. I am sure a great many of those we know most intimately have made harmonious unions. Ah! I can see by your face you are thinking of poor dear Esther. Certainly, that marriage turned out a failure, though at first it promised to be an exceptionally happy one. But, at any rate, the more mistrustful you are the more careful you should be not to run risks. Even when people start with a good stock of affection, what terrible ruin often overtakes them! There was your poor friend Cicely——'

'It is curious to have the poor woman quoted from two such opposite points of view in one afternoon. Well, at this moment she is living in a four-roomed weather-board cottage in a township in New South Wales, where her husband plays the harmonium in a little Baptist Chapel on Sundays. I do not say that there is not an element of terrible ruin in this, but not in the sense you mean.'

'Her husband?'

'Yes; as soon as she was divorced they were married. I found out where they are living, and sent some help at a time when she badly needed it. We have corresponded from time to time since then.'

'Does mother know this, Stella?'

'Well, no. There are some things one's mother should be spared. The first letter I had was too pitiful.'

'Of course, I know you used to be very fond of each other, but——'

'The friendships of women should always have a limit. I admit it is very dangerous to find out how things have really happened. You then find there are cases in which, if you knew all, you would connive at "terrible ruin" rather than avert it.'

'But, Stella, we must not let our sympathy with people blind us. There are some actions that cut away the roots of friendship. I would rather you had found a way of helping the poor woman without corresponding.'

'I wrote to her regularly after I knew she was living with a horrible man, who used to lock himself up and drink till he was in delirium tremens—one who was a dipsomaniac before she married him, and yet managed to conceal it from her till after they were married. I know she is living a purer life now than she could then. The only child that was born to her was paralytic and imbecile. Fortunately it died. What sort of a crime would it have been against herself, and still more against society, if she had gone on adding to the probable criminals of the world—to its certain weaklings?'

'I know how frightfully hard life may become; but at the worst, no matter how we may be sinned against, we may at least refrain from joining the ranks of those who have wronged us.'

'Meaning the criminals?'

'Yes.'

'Do you consider suicide a crime?'

'Need you ask, dear?'

'Because there were two courses open to Cicely—to kill herself, or go away with the man who had for over two years protected her at intervals from the maniacal conduct of her husband.'

'Who was this man?'

'An overseer on their station—a gentleman by birth. I suppose every country evolves its own special tragedies. You see, Mowbray's run is four hundred miles north. When he came to town now and then before he was married, he managed to keep sober. At any rate, Cicely, during the five months' engagement, never heard a breath or had the least suspicion; and if her aunt did, she took good care not to mention it.'

'Surely she would never be guilty of such atrocity!'

'Oh, but she would. After the death of the child Cicely told her all, and implored her to let her stay in town. No; a woman's proper place was with her husband. That's the sort of venomous old lynx she is—always comfortable and decorous, and going about with a bottomless pouch of gossip. If ever she comes to a steep place she throws herself upon tradition and conventional morality to save herself from the least collision with virtue.'

'Stella, dear, that is very severe,' said Cuthbert, fondly stroking his sister's glowing cheek. There was summer lightning in her eyes. Her voice, when she was moved, had a resistant silvery tone, whereas when she was indifferent or merely amused, she drawled a little.

'You wouldn't say so, Cuth, if you knew the old dame. But she was the only relative Cicely has in Australia; so there was nothing for her but to go back. Two months after she did so I heard she ran away with Stoneleigh.'

'I remember how dreadfully cut up you were.'

'Yes, we are often sorriest for people when the worst is over. Now, Cuth, don't sermonise; I see it is in your eyes. Just look how the hills are catching the sunset glow.'

'Is it so late? Let me help you up on your beloved gum-tree stump to see the sun set.'

The ivy-covered gum-tree stump, thirty-five feet in circumference, relic of an old monarch of the primeval woods, was close to the northern boundary wall of the garden. This point of vantage commanded varied and lovely views. Beyond North Adelaide and its sub-adjacent villaships, looking to the east and south-east, one saw St Peter's, College Town,* Norwood, and Kensington lying in graduated perspective, and beyond these pretty prosperous suburbs full of charming houses and rose-filled gardens, stretched the Adelaide hills. Their bases and quiet darkling gullies were now in clear blue and pale purple shadows, their summits beautifully flushed with the gold and crimson splendour of a brilliant sunset. Northward the wide fertile Gawler Plain stretched beyond sight, thickly sprinkled with tree-encompassed homesteads, and great corn-fields, now ripely yellowing for the harvest. Westward lay Hindmarsh and Bowden, the manufacturing suburbs of the city, Torrenside in the foreground, with some delightfully old-fashioned, many-windowed houses, their cream-coloured walls gleaming through fig-trees and vine-trellised verandas. Beyond these might be discerned Port Adelaide, with its forests of ship-masts lying along the wharves, and beyond all, the ocean flushed to the verge of the wide horizon with the setting sun. For a moment it rested like a quivering ball of flame on the level waters, and then dropped out of sight, leaving a fiery glow wide and high in the sky, passing towards the zenith into the most delicate tones of pink. The same tints were reflected on the hilltops for some time, as vividly as though they were mirrors throwing back a not distant picture.

The two gazed on these lovely scenes with crowding associations that stretched back to the first twilight of childish memories, and lingered in the garden till the sound of the dinner-bell summoned them into the house.

Fairacre both within and without bore the traces of easy affluence. The house was a large one-story building, substantially built of stone, with a deep veranda, furnished with Venetian shutters, running all round it. The principal rooms were large and lofty, and opened by wide doors, half glass, upon the garden, which from one season to another was never seen without the radiance of many flowers. The sparkling old silver, and the delicately fine table-linen, were family heirlooms, as were also several rare works of art, and a large proportion of the rosewood furniture. Mrs Courtland was now close on sixty-five years of age, invariably attired in widow's weeds since her husband's death years previously. She was descended from an old Highland family, and in face and bearing she bore the unmistakable stamp of high-bred refinement. Her features had never been strictly beautiful, but her countenance must always have been marked by the calm gentleness, the sweet, kindly serenity which imparted to it so much charm and distinction. It must even in youth have been distinguished by that guileless sincerity which formed an index to a mind curiously free from any taint of worldliness or self-seeking.

The Courtland family numbered eight in all, though there were at this period but four of them under the paternal roof. The eldest daughter, Barbara, was married to the Rev. Joseph Wallerton, an Episcopalian clergyman settled in Sydney; the second daughter, Esther, Mrs Raymond, was a widow of over two years' standing. Her husband had been a wealthy squatter in the south-eastern district of the colony, where Mrs Raymond and her four children chiefly resided. There were two unmarried daughters still at home—Stella and Alice, eighteen months her senior, but looking incredibly young for her age, being *petite* and rosy-cheeked, with overflowing spirits— circumstances which were, perhaps, providential, as she had recently entered on an engagement that threatened to be rather indefinite. Tom, the other son who was at home, was a lawyer in good practice, and three years older than the young clergyman. The other two brothers, Hector and Claude, the eldest and second eldest

respectively, had been for over twenty-one years engaged in squatting pursuits with almost unbroken success in the adjacent colony of
Victoria. Ten years previously a wealthy cousin of Mrs Courtland's
in the Indian Civil Service had left her a legacy of thirteen thousand
pounds. This had been invested in Lullaboolagana, the Victorian
station, which not only ensured the increasing prosperity of the two
squatters, but added handsomely to the general income of the old
home.

The visitors at Fairacre on this Sunday afternoon were Mrs
Harrison, a daughter and two sons. It was to Felix, the younger of
these, and an architect by calling, that Alice was engaged. The
elder brother, Andrew, was a journalist. The support of the rest of
the family depended largely on the two young men, as the father, a
clergyman and an old college friend of the late Mr Courtland's, had
died a few years previously, leaving his widow with but a small
annuity and younger children to be educated. The elder daughter,
Fanny, was now eighteen, and there were growing symptoms of an
attachment between herself and Tom—a circumstance which drew
the remark from Stella that it seemed as though some families had
hereditary tendency to catch infantile maladies from each other. It
was when she made observations of this kind that Tom used to
wonder why the youngest of an otherwise well-conducted family
should be hopelessly spoiled.

CHAPTER III

ON the following Monday afternoon Laurette Tareling, or, to give
her the designation which was dear to her as a title, the Hon. Mrs
Talbot Tareling, paid the call of which her brother had spoken on
Sunday.

She was of the medium height, though something in her face and
figure gave the impression that she was small, being slight and fair
with a faint colour deepened with a little rouge so skilfully that it was
unsuspected by all save the most practised eyes. She had fair fluffy
hair, lightened by gold dust, descending in a fringe of infantile curliness to within a short distance of her eyes, which were dark brown,
rather small, but very bright and keen, and altogether somewhat
like those of a parrot that is bent on finding out a great deal. An

expression that was further carried out by the nose, which took the liberty of turning up a little, and a mouth which, though it smiled very often, had something rather hard and beakish in its formation. Yet, on the whole, Mrs Tareling was considered pretty. She dressed extremely well, and was never seen beyond the domestic circle without an air of determined vivacity. She had the reputation of being one of the 'smartest' talkers in Melbourne society, and had a knack of telling a story against those to whom she owed any grudge, which at once made her popular, and created many enemies.

Mrs Courtland and her two daughters were in the drawing-room when the visitor was shown in. Mrs Tareling bestowed sharp little explosive kisses on each, ending with Stella, at whom she looked inquiringly, her head a little to one side.

'Why, Stella, you have grown thinner,' she said, half pensively. 'My dear Mrs Courtland, has Stella been ill?'

'Oh no; Stella is never ill!' answered the mother with a fond smile.

'Well, just look at the two—who, to see them, would think Allie was older?'

'Ah, Laurette, you are letting me down gently,' said Stella, trying to keep back the mischievous smile that lurked round her lips. 'What you mean is that I am "going off"—that my first youth is over.'

'Oh, well! in a climate like ours we must make up our mind that we shed our first youth when we leave our teens—except fortunate people like Allie, who discover some elixir——'

'Which they don't give even their sisters,' laughed Stella. 'Well, Larry, I promise you if ever I get the chance I shall have a sip—if only to save you pain.'

'Oh, as for that, who is such a wreck as I am myself for my age? I assure you the day before I left Melbourne I nearly wept at finding that I was suddenly an old hag. Oh, positively! In the morning I found two gray hairs in my comb. I always heard people speak of the first gray hair, but there were two, showing that somewhere my head was getting powdered with the frost of age. And that wasn't all. In the afternoon I stood in a cross light, opposite a mirror. I turned round with a start; who is that creature, thought I, with her cheeks so hollow and a faded colour, and lines deepening round her mouth? And then, to crown it all, Talbot came in that moment leading Gwendolen by the hand, looking atrociously tall for her four years——'

'Is that your little daughter, Laurette?' asked Mrs Courtland, who was getting a little hard of hearing, and did not quite catch the drift of these remarks, which were delivered in a rapid, semi-staccato tone levelled especially at Stella.

'Yes, dear Mrs Courtland; and growing such a big girl, and so precocious. She wanted to know, the other day, whether her little brother Howard would not be Lord Lillimore when he grew up. And then she was sure, she said, that Uncle Ted would be Sir Edward Ritchie.'

'My dear, you must not let her be too much with the servants. You should get a nice young lady as nursery-governess for her,' said Mrs Courtland, in a motherly way, never dreaming that this precocious tattle had been invented by Laurette on the spur of the moment.

'Well, life is full of accidents; who knows but both these events may come off one day,' said Alice solemnly, though there was a merry gleam in her eyes.

And then Mrs Tareling went off on another tack.

'You are always so beautifully quiet and sedate in Adelaide, it is really like coming to another world from Melbourne. And the season was so late with us this year. What with the Russian and German men-of-war* and the visit of the Sultan of Morocco, it was a perfect whirlpool. I felt at last I would like to retire to the Grande Chartreuse.'*

'But I suppose you find the dear little farinaceous village almost as quiet. Hardly anything happens with us,' said Alice. 'People die occasionally, but only once, and very seldom. Yes, and holes come occasionally in the carpets—of the poorer classes, you know;' and Alice glanced half ruefully at the Brussels pile* which had been in the drawing-room for twenty years and began to show signs of wear in places.

'Yes; and even your Governors last longer than they do elsewhere,' answered Mrs Tareling. 'Now, with us in seven years we have had two; and next month Sir Marmaduke leaves; and who do you think is his successor? Why, Lord Weavelow, whose wife is Talbot's first cousin, and Lord Weavelow a connection of his sister-in-law, Lady Gertrude. It is rather trying to be so closely related to the new Governor in our circumstances.'

'Oh, my dear, it is very likely they will be quite nice people. I dare say you will like them very well,' said Mrs Courtland soothingly, which amused her daughters not a little.

'Mother never did, and never will, comprehend the little subtleties of a snob,' as Alice said afterwards half despairingly.

'Oh, I dare say we shall like them very much. But then we are so poverty-stricken; and the people who entertain most in Melbourne get more ostentatious every year—private theatres, and enormous ball-rooms, and French cooks who keep a tandem* and a Cremona violin.'*

'Fancy all these complexities off the back of the idyllic sheep!' said Stella, laughing. 'Well, Laurette, if I were you, I would go in for a sweet and severe simplicity. It would really be more *distingué*.'*

'That is true. But nothing is so costly as the only form of simplicity open to you if you have the right of tambour at Government House,' returned Mrs Tareling, with the air of one who is laying down axioms for the guidance of society from Olympian social heights.

At this moment a little diversion was caused by the entrance of two elderly Quaker ladies, maiden sisters, in soft dove-coloured dresses and bonnets, and white fichus of Indian muslin. They were followed by afternoon tea, over which the older ladies fell into a group to themselves, talking softly over sick and afflicted people, and new candidates for admission to the Asylum for Incurables.

'Still, I suppose you will hardly retire to the wilds of Kannawi-jera* when your relatives begin to reign at Government House?' said Alice, taking up the thread of conversation as she presided at the tea-tray.

'No; not this coming season, at any rate. We had to give up our house at Yarra Yarra; they raised the rent so atrociously. But we have secured a smaller one at Toorak, with the principal rooms *en suite*;* almost all the partitions in folding-doors, that can be pushed back in the most wonderful way. Just like one of those knives—at least, they look like knives, but when you open the handle it turns into corkscrews, and toothpicks, and glove-buttoners, besides several blades. Everyone says Melbourne will be awfully full by May; so we caught time by the forelock, and took this house from November. But we don't pay a penny more than if we waited later. It is to be a most brilliant season, everyone says. And now, Stella, I want to arrange about your long-promised visit.'

'Oh, you are very kind,' said Stella.

'Don't say that: it's a bad omen. Always before when I asked you to come, you said, "You are very kind," and didn't turn up. It's no use coming for a couple of weeks, like the girls who come from the wilds of the Bush for a birthday ball, and don't know a soul but a few lanky men in split gloves, who don't waltz, and huddle up together behind the doors.'

'Ah, Laurette, you had better think twice before you are burdened through part of a brilliant season with a country cousin like me,' said Stella, laughing merrily at the picture called up by Laurette.

'I suppose it would be no use asking you to come as well, Allie, just for a couple of weeks?' said Mrs Tareling graciously.

Allie raised her hands in mock despair.

'How can you ask? I am in training to keep a house on nine or ten pounds a week, and save out of that for a rainy day.'

'Oh, how very romantic! But surely no rainier day can come than nine or ten pounds a week?' said Mrs Tareling, with well-simulated wonder.

'You see, Larry, you who are poverty-stricken on over three thousand a year can hardly plumb the depths of real destitution,' said Alice. 'There is the poverty of hot joints and "frugal days of interlinear hash——" '*

'Allie, whatever you do when you and Felix marry, do not have large joints,' said Stella gravely. 'I am confident that the happiness of the Australian household is more frequently wrecked by hash than any ethical point.'

'Well, I am studying the question. Perhaps I may one day publish a shilling cookery-book for young couples who ought not to have married.'

'Surely Felix's income must be considerable now. They say he is the best architect in the place,' said Laurette somewhat abruptly.

This laughing raillery about poverty did not commend itself to her in the least. It is mortifying, when one wants to make a girl feel how comparatively humble her prospects are, to find her treating the subject in a serio-comic vein.

'But then there are the younger children to provide for—quite dependent on Felix and Andrew,' returned Alice.

'Well, it's a pity you girls couldn't go in for a little division of poverty,' replied Laurette. 'Here is Stella's *fiancé* rolling in money.'

'As it happens, that young woman hasn't got a *fiancé*,' returned Stella quickly.

'No? You and Ted keep on such good terms, I always forget the affair was broken off,' said Laurette rather maliciously. 'But now for your visit, Stella.'

'I must talk it over with mother before making ultimate arrangements.'

'But we all know beforehand what that means. Your mother says, "Yes, darling," to all you propose. Pray, my dear, don't forget that I've known you from childhood. It was never a secret you were rather spoiled.'

Thus pressed, Stella said half hesitatingly:

'Well, if you let me come to you on my way to Lullaboolagana, without pledging myself to the length of the visit. But do you know that Dustiefoot insists on coming wherever I go?'

'Oh yes; and you always take Maisie when you pay a long visit— at least, someone said so the other day——'

'Yes,' put in Alice; 'we spare Maisie to Stella because she could never bear to brush her dresses or sew on bits of braid. It is a case of atavism. She has reverted to the only duchess that was in our family—more than three centuries ago.'

'That is curious,' said Stella, maintaining the mock gravity with which her sister spoke; 'for after twelve generations the proportion of blood of any one ancestor is only 1 in 2,048.'

'At any rate, it is settled you are to come—Dustiefoot, Maisie, and all,' said Laurette. 'By the way, how did you enjoy the Emberly ball?'

'Oh, immensely,' answered Stella; and then a quick wave of colour suffused her face, mounting even to her forehead.

'We enjoyed it "not wisely, but too well."* We fancy there has been no nice weather since that ball was over,' said Alice, who sympathetically noted this uncompromising blush, and tried to attract Laurette's gleaming eyes from her sister's face.

But Laurette had in an eminent degree what Talleyrand considered the whole art of politics—that is, the art of seeing—at any rate, what was on the surface.*

'Oh, very much, did you? And you used to be so disdainful of dancing. But, to be sure, that was when you were much younger. And those alcoves one heard so much about—were they a great success? I declare, Stella, there must be something behind this. Do you know you are blushing most furiously?'

'Oh, I always blush when I ask Alice for a second cup of tea,' replied Stella, recovering her self-possession. 'As for the alcoves— the half was not told you. There are eight windows in the ball-room, and round each window an alcove much larger than an ordinary bay-window, all lined with salmon-coloured satin with a seat running round each; up the front, on both sides, brackets with great vases full of ferns and roses, and lotos blooms and aspho-del; overhead an electric light in an opal globe, exactly like a great piece of the full moon put into a crystal prison, only more lambent.'

'And don't forget the cream lace curtains in front lined with salmon satin, Stella,' said Alice, looking at her sister with a dancing light in her eyes. And then turning to Laurette: 'The thing was to meet Prince Charming at the ball—dance and chat with him, and then sit out the rest of the evening in an alcove, behind the curtains and two chaperons, just fashioned by Providence so as to completely screen you from the other men to whom you might have promised dances.'

'Indeed, and who—who was your chaperon?' said Laurette, looking from one to the other of the sisters.

Stella had grown suddenly grave, though the remnants of her 'furious' blushing still lingered in her cheeks.

'Oh, Mrs Marwood and Tom and Felix and Andrew,' answered Alice lightly.

'And which of you retired into the alcove with the imprisoned moonlight and asphodel—and Prince Charming?'

'How literal you are, my dear!' said Alice, laughing. 'But you see, after one's ideals of life have been exalted by such alcoves you must not expect Stella to fall quite prostrate before the grandeurs of Melbourne society.'

Laurette seemed only half satisfied with this explanation, but feeling that further investigation would be useless just then, she allowed the subject to drop.

'I wonder what has given Laurette this ardent attack of friendship just now,' said Stella, when the sisters were alone.

'About insisting on your visit? Oh, she means to show you the king-doms of the world and the glory thereof.* And I expect it's not so much Laurette as Ted. It's a change of venue so as to get a different verdict. You have got into the habit of saying "no" at Fairacre, but in that "smaller house" at Toorak, surrounded by magnates who have private theatres and French cooks—after all, Laurette is very amusing.'

'Oh yes; for a day or two. But get a little below the surface, and she always has the hard, crude touch of the social amateur. And Allie—how could you be such a little jackdaw as to say that to her—about Prince Charming?'

'Well, it was partly my instincts as an artist. I could not bear to hear you give the light, graphic touches of the setting and leave out the very core. Besides, even Laurette cannot unravel that little mystery. Do you know, Stella, it's the nearest thing to a romance that has happened for—twice one year. A great brilliant ball—a wonderful Austrian band—electric lights, flowers—an introduction without surnames—one dance—intellectual kinship—mysterious sympathy between two souls—a long talk behind ferns and chaperons in an alcove—duty thrown to the winds—till the fugitives are discovered by an irate ci-devant lover who is down for two waltzes—separation without even a lingering farewell—disappearance of the Prince before midnight—no name—no trace. Even the people who got him the invitation depart next day by the P. and O. steamer. Ah me! he was on his way to the Princess of China*—or to awaken the sleeping beauty with a kiss. Would I were the sleeping beauty! He really *had* a distinguished air.'

'I wish Felix would overhear you,' said Stella, who listened to this little rhapsody with a half-tender smile.

'Ah, my dear, when people are so desperately fond of each other as Felix and I, the shadow of romance never eclipses their gaiety. But the more I have thought over the episode, the more does it appear to me in the light of an allegory. You were from childhood the victim of the ideal. You always forsook your dolls when you perceived they were stuffed with sawdust. When you found the kitten of commerce mewed by means of a spring, you would have no more of it. And so in the central fact of a woman's life, as someone has called marriage.* You ask for better bread than is made from wheat. Well, just for one evening you saw one cast in that higher mould, and then you were for ever secured from disillusion.'

'Allie, you have got into one of your random fits. Remember, it is you who have been spending yourself on theories and imaginings concerning the unknown.'

'Ah, my dear, it is what you do not say that I try to interpret. But take it, I say, as an allegory—not a real event; and then turn your mind to the sober realities of life. Now confess, if at the end of October you had not gone to a certain assembly, in November you would have fulfilled your engagement and gone to Laurette—seen the Melbourne Cup and made certain promises—renewed them, rather. Remember our conversation two days before the ball, when our dresses came home.'

'I like your way of measuring life, Allie.'

'By the dressmaker's thread? Well, it's much more cheerful than that of the Parcae.* But you *do* remember that conversation?

'Yes, I think we came to the conclusion that some people married because they were in love; others because they thought they were; but the majority because they couldn't be.'

'And that you belonged to the last named; but would very likely find the unholy estate of matrimony as brilliant an affair as most others.'

'Well, for goodness' sake don't let us go on quoting ourselves as if we were classics in Russia backs.* I still hold to that. I begin to see that Ted is my fate. I shall have to succumb. On the whole, it will be less tiresome. And then I want to go to Rome and places.'

'You might have gone with Claude and Helen.'

'Well, it was heroic of them to offer to take me; but I think it would have been still more heroic of me to have gone. Oh, every reason— Can there be anything in life more unendurable than the confident air of prosperity which envelops your newly-married couple? The melting stolen glances, the becoming humility, the timid anxiety to please that in pre-nuptial days marked their demeanour, disappear as if some witch had exorcised them with black magic.'

'Oh, let it be white magic, Stella, if only for my sake!'

'Till at last we have that placid semi-unconsciousness of each other's presence which decks your full-blown married pair as a cankerworm adorns the rose.'

'Oh, Stella, Stella! I believe you really were born with a mistrust of marriage,' laughed the elder sister.

'Yes; ever since I have been able to think or observe I have been convinced that marriage is the most foolish, faulty old institution going.'

Alice at this laughed louder than before; and then, still smiling, with the joyous, confident smile of a woman triumphantly in love, she said:

'I wish, dear, you would throw out a few hints for the improvement of this heaven-forsaken arrangement.'

'Well, you see, really to improve it would be to destroy it. To begin with, people see too much of each other, which seems to be destructive alike to passion and good manners. Oh yes; you are ready to *mourir à rire** at all this. Nevertheless, fate and the comedians are lying in wait for you.'

'As for the comedians, I care nothing for them. Most of them were men who married dreadful creatures—as even Molière did.* And fate—well, the most terrible sting it can have is that after living all our lives together, Felix and I may not die together.'

'Like the babes in the wood,* or Philemon and Baucis.'*

'Yes; or those dear old people one so often sees in common life, who survive each other only a few quiet uncomplaining weeks or months. But as for you, Stella—well, I suppose you would have your husband come with his hat in his hand, asking in an agitated voice when he might pay you a morning call?'

'Yes; and then I would look at my ivory memory—the pretty one you gave me a year ago, with a tablet for each day in the week—and I would say, "To-morrow is Goethe's birthday,* and I see only people who write sonnets in honour of that occasion. Ah, but yours, my friend, do not scan! No; nothing in prose, however felicitous, will pass muster."'

'Well, the next day—wouldn't you let him come on the next day?' pleaded Alice, a wicked light gleaming in her eyes.

'No; the next day, "I have an appointment with a white fairy rose-bush. It has four hundred and fifty buds, and some of them have promised to open on that day. Well, yes; perhaps Wednesday. But, mind, you must be very amusing, and whatever you do, don't tell me old stories."'

And so, grave and gay by turns, they talked of love and marriage, as girls are wont to do in the sheltered sanctuary of the parental home, while life is a sort of isthmus between early youth and the deeper responsibilities of womanhood. Behind them lies childhood, full of sunshine and laughter, of bird calls and opening roses and passionate little griefs that passed into oblivion in the sleep that came with the glimmering twilight. Yes; looking backward there lie the fairest meadows, sunny nooks made cosier with the blue haze of smoke rising from familiar hearths; and always in the air the refrain of cradle songs, the sound of bells calling to prayer, the faces and voices that they first loved, that they must love to the end. They are still merely onlookers, seeing but selected replicas of the play of life, jealously guarded from the vulgar collisions of the crowd. But what is there on the farther side of the isthmus? It is far off, and the land is veiled in mist.

But there are arenas there in which terrible things happen. There is reckless trampling as of wild beasts, and there are dark stains of bloodshed quickly sanded over. Often there come rumours of those overtaken with worse than the throes of dissolution. The shadow of the valley of life is much more intolerable oftentimes than that of death.* There are whirlpools that suck in more than life.

And those who have been so delicately guarded: will their path trend towards sinister pitfalls? will they be overtaken by those catastrophes that mutilate human lives, smitten with those fiery darts that with a touch work moral paralysis? How will it be with them in the unborn years, far from the old sacred shelter of their early home? Will they moan for help in the darkness, with no ear to listen to their cry?

Ah, dear God! how strange and pitiful it all is—this incredible saga of human life, whose beginning we have lost, whose end we cannot tell; in which we lose one by one those who are our companions, and in the end lose ourselves; in which we are first robbed of all we love, and then of all we know.

The sisters had wandered from lighter topics, and were talking in hushed tones of their father's death, when Mr Edward Ritchie was announced, and the young man entered with that air so characteristic of him, of being in and belonging wholly to a world without visions or anxious forecasts. His mere presence threw discredit on the sophistry of speculation. He was, to use an old figure of speech, for ever planting cabbages,* and when one foot was on the ground the other was not far off. Nothing in books, or the destiny of the race, or the life of the soul, had ever moved him. But, then, he was never without a horse or two that had achieved something wonderful, or were just going to do so, or might do it if they chose. Without being exactly excited over this, he was so deeply interested, and so sure people wanted to know all about it, that he often, even in the breasts of those who cared little for equine performances, created a glow of enthusiasm, which banished every subject of a less abstract nature than an animal of good lineage, with four legs and a mane.

There was Spindrift, now, who could do anything he liked at home, and yet, put him on a race-course, you would swear he was dickey* on every leg he had got, and had sprung a hock into the bargain. It was enough to make a fellow eat his hat, and the horse, too. And such a beautiful creature—almost perfect in all his points— perhaps the shoulders were not quite oblique enough. But the only thing by which you could guess there was a bad 'nick'* in him was his eye. Never trust a horse unless his eye is bold and full, etc., etc.

Ted's ostensible mission, on this occasion, was to invite the Court-lands to a dinner-party at his father's house before Cuthbert left for Melbourne.

'My mother and I put our heads together, and planned it after Larry came to see you to-day,' he explained. 'When Larry comes on a visit to the old house now, she wants to drive everyone tandem, full swing. But we just gave her the slip, and settled how many and all, and I wouldn't even wait till to-morrow morning—I shall be here at ten sharp to take you out riding, you know, Stella. I thought perhaps Cuth might have some parsonic concern on, if he didn't get early notice.'

'But a dinner-party on the 26th December!' said Stella, in a voice of consternation. 'Everyone will be so frightfully used up with the tradespeople's Christmas cards, and the heat, and the Athanasian Creed* the day before!'

But Ted overruled every objection. He had to return to Strathhaye soon after Christmas, and the 26th was the only day, and come they must.

Then the three went out into the garden to see the sun set across the sea, which was one of the traditions at Fairacre. All over the west the heavens seemed on fire, and underneath lay the sea, wide and silvery, and calm as a great inland lake. A white-sailed craft going southward stood out with startling distinctness.

'Where lies the land to which yon ship must go?'* said Stella, watching its course with a far look in her eyes.

'To Normanton, I expect, for potatoes,' said Ted promptly.

And then when his companions laughed involuntarily at this explanation, he asked very placidly where the joke came in.

'Well, Ted, you must know that a man called Wordsworth wrote sonnets, and that is a line out of one of them,' said Alice.

'I'm blessed if ever I could make out why these old buffers of poets want to jaw so much about things. If he didn't know where the boat was going, why didn't he ask at a shipping office, instead of writing a sonnet?'

This reflection, delivered in a wondering, half-aggrieved tone, made Stella laugh more than before. Though Ted could not always very well divine the cause of her clear rippling laughter, no sound was pleasanter to his ears. The elder sister watched the two with an amused interest that was always renewed. It was apparent that the blunt, shrewd way in which the young man so forcibly used his limited outlook on life, formed a kind of attraction to the girl, who had that wide sympathetic range of view which a many-sided culture imparts; who was infected, too, by that dreamy, sceptical attitude of mind born of a nature innately introspective, and early inured to flights in mental dialectics.

'I suppose I ought to go now,' said Ted lingeringly.

'No; stay to dinner and spend the evening with us,' said Alice. 'Oh, it doesn't matter about your clothes. Tom and Cuth seldom dress when we dine *en famille** in the summer-time.'

'Will you play two-handed *euchre** with me for sixpenny points if I stay, Stella?'

'Oh, I must play for love.'

Ted coloured with pleasure to the roots of his hair, and Stella hastened to explain.

'You see, it is near the end of the quarter, and I have nothing in my purse but a doubtful threepenny-bit and a damaged stamp.'

CHAPTER IV

GODOLPHIN HOUSE, the town residence of Sir Edward Ritchie, was a large pile of buildings near the foot of the hills, a few miles to the south-west of Adelaide.* Everything was on a large scale—the house, the grounds, the conservatories, the trees, and even the views. The place had been well planned and built, from the neat little semi-Swiss lodge at the chief entrance, to the handsome gable-ended stables, with their luxurious appointments, at some distance to the rear of the house; and the house itself lacked no comfort or convenience of modern days, and, to a certain extent, had been even pleasant to the eye, till, in an evil hour, the emissary of a great 'decorative' firm had prevailed on Sir Edward to have the 'mansion' 'done up' from top to toe. This took the form of a carnival of unlimited expenditure, and that unhappy outburst of British Philistinism known as the aesthetic craze. There was one apartment, known as the peacock-room, which upset an old Bush comrade of Sir Edward's in a surprising way. The man was one to whom money had no value apart from the excitement of earning and losing it. His life was impartially spent in tents in the wilderness and costly hotels. He and Sir Edward had worked together as wood sawyers in a great gum-forest for over seven years. This long period of hard lucrative work had laid the foundation of the worthy knight's large fortune, while for the other man it started the habit of alternately drinking bad champagne, etc., at a guinea a bottle, out of a quart jug, and humping his swag to the last new rush. For it was always gold that attracted him, and that, with astonishing frequency, retrieved his fallen fortunes. But through all the reverses of the one, and the climbing grandeurs of the other, the friendship between the two men was unbroken.

It was when Godolphin House was at its most appalling stage of unmodified aestheticism—from sage-green portières* to nymphs with exaggerated chins holding bronze lamps aloft—that the Bushman paid one of his periodical visits. Sir Edward took him all over the house, and finally the two sat down in the peacock-room. Here they dug their sawpits and felled mighty giants of the forest over again. But the more adventurous spirit had recently 'knocked down' a large nugget,* and his nerves were not what they ought to be.

'Ned, my boy, I can't stand these blazing eyes any longer. They get upon my liver somehow. I'll take a turn in the fresh air.' With that he stepped on the terrace, but the next moment he rushed back white and breathless.

'Look here, old man, I must hook it out of this.* Why, you've hung the very birds with these damned staring eyes!' He had come upon a row of peacocks sunning their gorgeous tails on the terrace on which he had taken refuge.

Even Ted used to grumble that it was all very well to lick the place into a cocked hat* with screens, and fans, and dados,* and soup-plates, but it was a jolly shame not to leave a den or two in which a fellow could live. Laurette adored all the transformations as long as they were 'quite the thing'; but when the tide turned she wrought various changes from time to time during her visits to her parents, and in several rooms had quite wiped away the disgrace of conventional aestheticism. But the air of 'no expenses spared,' and of being *en rapport* with* a rampant art–decorator, who has forsworn the old honest British hideousness for a sickly unreality, was apt to weigh heavy on the spirits. It was a house in which above all others to taste the wormwood of ennui to its last dregs; in which to be overcome by that lassitude of body, and bitter languor of mind, in which these symptoms may be successively noted.

You have a growing conviction that you can draw your breath but an hour longer without a change of environment.

You find yourself yawning irretrievably when you essay to add your mite to feeble anecdotes of the weather.

You find your face turning to stone when you strive with all the anguish of despair to call up a smile in response to a faded joke.

You reply with withering platitudes to every observation, and you find the kindliest attempt at pleasantry an unpardonable offence.

You sit on and on with the uncommunicating muteness of a fish, till you are overpowered by the thought that if you do not creep into the solitude of your own room you will be driven to commit some desperate deed, so that you may be imprisoned or sent to an asylum for the insane, or some equally genial retreat that will mercifully shield you from the joys of social intercourse.

But the culmination of all was the library. It was a marvel in its way. Horace Walpole somewhere speaks of one that contained only a broken chair, a chart, and a lame telescope.* But this was an enchanting bower for the muses compared to a room full of lame and impotent compilations in 'books' clothing.' Thinglets fit only to wrap candles in, or make winding-sheets in Lent for pilchards, or keep butter in the market-place from melting. There were rows upon rows of such stuff as the Rev. Ebenezer Slipslop on Corinthians; awful Encyclopedias and Treasuries of Knowledge, and biographies of self-made men who, to the prime sin of having existed at all, added the no less unpardonable one of swelling the dreariest form of fiction. So many and so many and such woe.* In proportion to the keen pleasure we associate with real books is the gloom which the bare sight of such biblia a-biblia* can induce. The tradition ran that Sir Edward had ordered 'a ton of books' from a third-rate bookseller in distress, and that this enterprising tradesman had bought up and bound for the Godolphin House library an astounding collection of the young men's mutual improvement type of rubbish. There was probably not a fact in the known world of the callow sort one hears only to forget which did not repose on these shelves.

Even in venturing out in the grounds at Godolphin House, everything still breathed of money recklessly lavished by hirelings. One was constantly taken to gaze at some double or triple monstrosity, perpetrated by gardeners who were so highly paid that it would compromise them to let Nature have much of her own way.

When Ted returned to his father's house that night, he found Mrs Tareling—Larry as he usually called her—in a bitterly discontented frame of mind.

'Who do you think has come to stay for two weeks, Ted?' she cried, the moment she caught sight of him.

'Tareling?' questioned Ted carelessly, taking possession of one armchair and resting his feet on another.

'Oh, you know very well he wouldn't come to stay so long, especially at Christmas-time. It is Uncle John!'

'Well, I'm glad the old chap came while I'm here. It's ages since I saw him. Did he bring aunt along with him?'

'Upon my word, Ted, you are horribly provoking sometimes. You take it as coolly as if he were the most agreeable company in the world.'

'Well, one's relations aren't often that; but still, there they are, you know, and there they were, before we showed our noses in the world. Has the old man gone to bed?'

'Yes, long ago. That's his way. He'll go to bed when the hens do, that he may rise at daybreak, to go creaking all over the house and burst into guffaws of laughter at the decorations and things, and tell abominable stories before the servants.'

'Now draw it mild, Larry. The old fellow can tell a shady* yarn as well as most men of his age, especially if he's a bit sprung,* but he doesn't before the servants, and I'm sure he wouldn't before you.'

'Oh, I don't mean what you call "shady yarns." It's much

worse when he tells how he left London as a stowaway, with two and threepence in his pockets, and not a second shirt to his back.'

'Yes he had. Don't you remember the little bundle done up in a red cotton handkerchief—a pair of go-ashore breeches and a Crimea shirt?'*

'Goodness knows, I ought to remember it all; I've heard it often enough.'

'Well, it's natural when a man comes to be sixty-eight he should like to tell how he kicked up his heels at seventeen. If a horse has got much gumption, he doesn't care to race after he's two years old. But a man goes it as long as he can, and afterwards he likes to speak of the old days. And, by Jove! it's only what you might expect,' added Ted reflectively. 'I'd sooner be a stowaway, without even a bundle, to-morrow, than be close on seventy with a million of money.'

'Ah, yes; but if you became a stowaway to-morrow, it would be a very different tale. You've been brought up with the command of money and servants, and never took your hat off to anyone save on equal terms. But when Uncle John tells his stories, you know, he used to stand in his smock frock, staring at the "gentry" as they drove by. And the way he eats his soup, and chuckles when the servants say "your ladyship" to mother!'

'You see, Larry, he didn't have four daughters to sit upon his manners, and train him up the way he should go, like the governor,' said Ted, smiling broadly, as certain reminiscences rose in his mind.

'The worst of it is that Colonel and Mrs Aldersley are coming here from Friday till Monday. Yes, they came over here from Melbourne three weeks ago. They've been at Government House for two weeks. Look here, Ted, couldn't you take the old man away somewhere during that time?'

'Well I'm blowed!* You have got a cheek, Larry,' said Ted, sitting straight up at this proposition. 'Smuggle the old bird away as if he were a convict, and all for what? An elderly frump of a woman, who says "Yes, to be sure," eighty times a day, and a man who would rook a young cub that had hardly shed his milk teeth. Oh, I happen to know a good deal about Aldersley. I tell you what, in the matter of straightforward, fair play, the man isn't fit to brush Uncle John's shoes!'

'He never wears shoes—it's always great creaking Wellington

boots. And can't you see, Ted, that to have embezzled money years and years ago would be pardonable compared to taking an orange in your fist, and sucking it at dessert, as Uncle John does? But nothing is so bad as his stories; and it's no use interrupting him: he only gets red in the face and talks louder.'

'Yes; as he did when he was telling once how he and father borrowed an old donkey to go and see the young squire's first meet; and there were you and Henrietta, pitching away about the Queen's drawing-room, at which our Lotty was presented. By Jove, it was as good as a play,' and Ted laughed.

'As good as a play!' echoed Laurette, her face reddening with vexation. 'Yes, I dare say it will be as good as a play for the Aldersleys. You may call Mrs A. a frump and think she's slow, but let me tell you she is as sharp as a needle. She agrees with everything, so that people may give themselves away more completely. She keeps a diary, and writes pages upon pages in it every night. Two people that know her well have told me she means to publish a book on "Life at the Antipodes" when she gets back to England, and, of course, Uncle John would be regular nuts for her.'*

'But who the deuce cares what these tourist people say? They either put down stuff that everybody knows from the beginning of creation, or they tell crammers that suck in nobody but their own friends,' said Ted, lighting a cigar, and resuming his semi-recumbent attitude.

'And it isn't even as if one could make him out to be eccentric or an oddity,' went on Laurette in a bitter tone. 'He won't change his boots in the house, but he'll put on a dress-suit and a white tie that goes slipping round his neck like a third-rate hotel waiter's. And it's ten to one if he doesn't blurt out how long his wife was in service with him before he married her.'

'Well, you may put your money on it that all the world over people have got to be in service, or have enough money of their own to live on, or live on someone else,' returned Ted, with philosophic calm. 'You're always kotooing* at Government House here and in Melbourne—and aren't they all in service? Living on money they get out of the country for looking on while other people manage affairs. It's a perfect chouse.* When Aunt Sally was in service at Kataloonga she worked for all the money *she* earned, I bet.'

'You talk as if you hadn't a scrap of proper pride about you. You take good care only to ask a lady to be your own wife,' retorted Laurette rather vindictively.

'It's not because she's a lady; it's just because she's Stella, and I've known her all my life, and every other girl seems common and flat beside her,' answered Ted, holding his cigar in his hand as he spoke.

A half-resentful expression came into Laurette's keen dark eyes at this speech. But before she could make any rejoinder Ted laughed softly in that gratified way which is significant of pleasant recollections.

'By Jove! I had a jolly evening! I never knew any girl that can make as much out of a little thing as Stella does sometimes. We played euchre together,' he went on, in answer to Laurette's interrogative 'Oh?' 'Stella at first wouldn't play for money, because she hasn't a sou, being near the end of the quarter. Think of that, you know; and me with over a hundred and fifty thousand pounds in spanking investments, not to mention the yearly income of Strathhaye. I'd like to fill all her pockets with gold and diamonds, and I can't offer her even a shabby tenner.* She had a great run of luck with the cards at the beginning—right bower* and joker and a couple of high trump cards—time after time. At last she consented to play for money, and then—confound it!—the luck changed. I tried to pack the cards so that she might win. But she's got eyes like an eagle-hawk, and bowled me out at once. You should hear all the penances she set me. She lost five shillings and gave me an I.O.U.' Ted took a note out of his pocket-book and gazed at it fondly. 'I'll keep this till all I've got belongs to her.'

'Well, I sometimes fancy that will never be the case, after all,' returned Laurette, who, for various reasons, was in that 'put out' frame of mind in which one finds a gloomy satisfaction in dashing the hopes of another.

'What do you mean by that?' asked the young man quickly. 'Hasn't she promised to come to see you in Melbourne?'

'Yes; in a sort of a way. Instead of being grateful and pleased at the idea of seeing some good society, she said, "Well, if you let me come on my way to Lullaboolagana, without pledging myself before-hand as to the length of the visit,"' and Laurette mimicked Stella's tone as well as she could, grossly exaggerating her little drawl.

'Excuse me for saying so, Larry, but if the Lord meant you to talk like Stella He'd have given you a prettier mouth,' said Ted, with slow deliberation. 'And as for good society—what have you better than she has been in all her life?'

'Oh, yes; a narrow, Churchy little clique, mixed up with all sorts of outsiders. People here always rave about Mrs Courtland being so sweet and unworldly. It's my belief she's full of old Highland pride at heart. They're on a sort of little suburban pinnacle, without the least idea of anything like real style or *chic*. And that Alice speaking of themselves as "the poorer classes." If that's not the pride that apes humility* I should like to know what is. . . . I don't know why you've set your heart so on wooing that girl. Why, with your fortune you might easily marry a lord's daughter.'

'But what the devil do I want with a lord's daughter?' cried Ted, in an amazed voice. 'The only one I ever knew had a scrag of a neck, and was as yellow as a buttercup.'

'Oh, it's just like a man only to think of looks. I'd like to know who all Stella's partners were at the Emberly ball. I fancy there was something in the background. The moment I spoke of the affair she blushed up to the whites of her eyes——'

'But Stella always does that. I never see her but she colours, off and on, twenty times an hour.'

'Yes; she's one of those girls that always look more charming when an admirer is by, whether they care for him or not. She has that slow kind of half-smile and a droop in her eyes, as if to show her long lashes, and she sometimes says the most biting things with that gentle sort of drawl, and then she laughs right out when you least expect it. I never did like girls that find things so amusing which are serious to other people. They're always coquettes, more or less. Oh, you don't half understand Stella Courtland!'

'Well, perhaps a fellow sees rather more than is good for him of the sort of women who are too easily understood. . . . At any rate, I understand this much about Stella. I'd sooner hear her laugh without quite understanding why she's amused than have any other woman in the world at my feet. And, by George! if she throws me over at the last—well, it's all U P with me.* I know that. . . . They're coming to dinner on the 26th,' he added, relighting his cigar, 'and we're going out riding together most mornings till then.'

'Well, Ted, you've always been very good to me when we've been in a financial fix,' said Laurette, 'and I'll do what I can for you. As I said before, I think part of a season in Melbourne among people who are really in the swim may open Stella's eyes a little. She'll find what it is to have a fashionable connection and good horses, and dresses from Worth,* and the last touch in a Parisian bonnet. She'll see the crowds of girls nearly as well born as she is, and more fashionably dressed, and handsomer, whose mouths would water at the chance of an offer from you.'

'Now, Larry, there you're out of it completely. The girls you call handsomer would have their numbers taken down* the instant they stood in the same room with Stella. As for being more fashionably dressed—why, whatever she puts on is the best and most fashionable. And it's just the same with what she says. She may mock at me, or say things I don't quite catch, or laugh when I don't know the reason why; but whatever she does is just right—except refusing me—and, by the Lord, I sometimes think that just a proof she's really long-headed. And yet I believe I could make her as happy as any other fellow would.'

Ted had ceased smoking, and now stared before him with a look of care on his face which was very unusual.

'Now, Ted, whatever you do, don't let your spirits go down,' said Laurette. 'Of course the life of a man is as different from that of a girl as chalk is from cheese. After all, the more high-falutin' a girl is, the more she has to knuckle under to the inevitable. ... I remember when I used to stay at Fairacre in the old days Stella was always reading some rubbishy old fathers, or tragedies, or wild German stories. Her father used to call her his little "improvisatrice," and she would sometimes start off and tell stories that would make your backbone quiver. She always had too much imagination; and that's the one thing a woman can best do without. It makes her draw pictures of life each one more unlike reality than the other. But in the end she'll have to put up with things as they are, just like the rest of us. Women have dreams, only to give them up when they marry.'

When Laurette took to moralizing it was in the robust strain of one to whom delicacy of mind was not a lost, but an unknown attribute.

'Well, Larry, if nothing comes of this visit to Melbourne—if before this time next year Stella is not my wife—why, I think I must give the affair up for good and all.'

'Quite right, Ted. The end of everything ought to come before it's too late. Whatever lies in my power shall be done. I think Melbourne will open her eyes a little.'

'And if you're in a fix for some tin, Larry, before the end of the season—why, just let me know,' said Ted, who knew by experience that a season in Melbourne seldom passed in which a hundred pounds or two was not a welcome, if not an indispensable gift to Laurette, notwithstanding the station in the Mallee country, worth over three thousand a year, which her father settled on her when she married the Hon. Talbot Tareling five years previously.

A look of vivid interest suddenly came into Laurette's face. It was the being 'in a fix' for some time which had mainly inspired her present visit to her father.

'Well, Ted——' Laurette began, and suddenly paused. Various thoughts swept through her mind, and then what she had intended to say ended in the bald statement: 'It is really very late.' But at that moment certain seed had dropped into fertile ground—seed that was destined to bear fruit in the not distant future, which, to their bitter ruing, must be eaten by others rather than by herself.

CHAPTER V

CUTHBERT COURTLAND left for Melbourne on the 28th of December. On the afternoon of the same day Edward Ritchie called at Fairacre to say good-bye.

He looked dejected and very much out of sorts; weary, with an unusual pallor on his face.

'You really were ill, then, on the 26th?' said Stella, noticing the change in his appearance.

'Yes, of course. Did you think I would stay away for a trifle when you went to my father's? It was a horrid sell altogether. Two of the best horses behaved like shoe-trunks.'

'Why, I thought you were at Mr Edwin Emberly's place near Reynella?'

'Yes, and we had a private steeplechase—gentlemen riders—and the day was most abominable. Everything went wrong. If I had only stayed at home——'

'You see, Ted, you cannot have your cake and eat it.'

'Cake? it *was* a cake. You seem to have an idea I stayed away on pleasure.'

'Well, you know, it was an atrocious day, with a fierce east gully wind. It's always a little cooler at Reynella.'

'Not on the 26th, with an amateur steeplechase and only a mob of young bachelors together.'

'But then, in the evening, instead of dressing for dinner, no doubt you lounged in pyjamas and smoked, and had "long drinks" out on the verandas. Whereas we fanned ourselves languidly through thirteen courses, and listened to the good old Bishop speaking on surpliced choirs and the ultimate cost of the cathedral.* I certainly thought you had the best of it. But now I see you really were ill. Did you have a sunstroke, or did your horse roll over you—or what?'

'Oh, it was just what!' answered Ritchie grimly. 'The fact is, I'—he was staring hard at the girl as he spoke, but something in her gay smiling unconsciousness arrested the words on his lips—'I believe my heart has gone back on me rather badly. It keeps thumping about in the most confounded manner.'

'Your heart, Ted? Now do you know what side it is on?' she asked laughingly.

'Oh yes, Stella, it's all very well for you. You're on the right side of the hedge. You never had a day's illness in your life since you were a baby. I've had many an attack. And to have old Mac and his wife bringing you in beef-tea you can't drink, and lie awake half the night, and no one to talk to, or ride out with in the morning and have some fun—— You can't wonder I run off to Melbourne pretty often. What is there to keep me at home? Now, if you were there—but I'm not going to say any more just now. I am going on to Strathhaye, to see to a few things there; and then I'm going to have a complete change for some months. I've been feeling rather dicky off and on for some time. Oh yes, I look well enough generally; but you can't always go by that. I think I shall give up horse-racing—it keeps a fellow racketing about so.'

'What! sell Konrad and Circe, and all the rest, and have no more "sweet little fillies" and year-old colts, that are so knowing and thoroughbred they take to racing almost without being told? What in the world would you talk about, Ted?'

'Oh, I wouldn't sell them all. I'll always keep good horses. I can't stand any other kind; but not to go flying about from one race-meeting to the other. It begins to tell on a fellow after a few years. I think I'll try and read a little more. You remember the list of books I got you to give me once? Well, there's a big boxful at Strathhaye never opened. I'll take it with me. But I don't think I can ever make much out of sonnets, Stella.'

'Why, have you actually been reading sonnets? Ah, poor Ted! you must have been feeling bad.'

'Yes, I felt very low last night, after I got home; and I thought I would try to improve my mind, as Edwin Emberly calls it. I thought I would try to understand more about the things you care for. I have a Wordsworth that was given me for a prize at St Peter's.* Oh, it was for regular attendance. When a fellow was there for a couple of years, and they couldn't give him a prize for anything else, they gave him one for not playing the tally. As I was a boarder, I couldn't do that very well.'

'And did you really get out your prize Wordsworth and read it?'

'Yes, I read some of the sonnets; but it was for all the world like a bullock trying to jump in hobbles. He makes a great clanking with the chains, and he heaves up his horns, but he doesn't get any further. And there's no story in the thing. At least, if there is, it's so thin I can never catch it. Now, when I was about ten, I remember, you read me "The Lady of the Lake"* once, and, by Jove! it made my heart beat. It was one Saturday. I came from St Peter's to stay till Monday. Cuth was always very kind to me, though he was at the head of his class and I was always at the bottom, and one below my age. You sat up in the branches of the Moreton Bay fig-tree, and I sat beside you and turned the leaves. Good Lord! I wish I was ten to-day, and you nine!'

'Why?—that we might go and sit in the branches of the fig-tree? Perhaps it isn't too late even now——'

'I hate those words "too late!"' said Ritchie, with unusual irritability.

He rose and strode about the room, and stared out through one of the windows overlooking the garden.

'Really, Ted shows himself in quite a new aspect to-day. It is as though he had the first faint beginnings of a soul,' thought Stella, looking at him with a new interest. 'Why do you hate the words "too late," Ted? Have you any association with them?' she said, going up to him where he stood at the window.

'Yes; we had a knock-about hand* at Strathhaye once, and I can't forget the way he said the words over and over at the last. Well, he was hardly middle-aged, really; but the life he led made him seem so. He belonged to one of the old swell families in England, and got engaged, but had no money to marry on. So he sold out of a crack regiment and came to try his luck at the diggings. He was among the lucky ones—he and his mate, who had been a gamekeeper on his uncle's estate. They got one nugget worth four thousand pounds, and there was more to follow; and there, in the very middle of his luck, came a letter telling him his sweetheart was married to an old baboon with ever so many thousands a year. It put him off his chump entirely. He went completely to the bad. He was two years at Strathhaye. He would go off every now and then with a cheque, and come back blue with the horrors*—even his coat and his blanket sold for a last nobbler* or two. At last he stayed away for over a month, and came back one night more dead than alive. Why he didn't do away with himself, I can't make out. Sometimes, I believe, people get too miserable even to hang themselves. We had the doctor for him; but there was nothing he could do except give him some stuff that made it easier to die.'

'Was there no one to look after him?' asked Stella, her eyes large and dim with pity.

'Oh yes; he was in the men's hut, and Mrs Mackenzie used to go to him for a couple of hours every day. I used to go in, too, most days; but, by Jingo! I can't think of anything more awkward than to sit by a fellow like that when you know he's dying, and he knows that you know. You can't even say you hope he'll soon be better. You know nothing of where he's going; and it would hardly be decent to talk of horses and classifying wool to a man with the death-rattle in his throat, so to speak. I offered to read the Bible to him, but I was always coming across some queer yarn that made one feel anyhow. At last he gave me a little purple Book of Common Prayer to read; but there, what was the good of reading "The Publick Baptism of Infants," or "The Churching of Women," or "The Solemnization of Matrimony"——'

'Oh, Ted! why didn't you read "The Psalms," or "The Visitation of the Sick," or a collect?' said Stella, unable to refrain from a smile, though the picture called up by the young man's unstudied narrative touched her deeply.

'Well, you see, you know the run of the Prayer-Book, but I don't; and I just used to start off where I opened it. Once I began with "The Burial of the Dead;" but I wasn't sorry, for it made poor old

Travers laugh so. "Not yet, my boy—not yet!" he said. That was a few evenings before he died. And just two days before, a lawyer's letter came, telling him he was heir to his uncle's estate. The old man was dead, the eldest son had come to grief hunting buffaloes somewhere in North America, and the second had got killed in the Zulu War* years before. So there was this estate, with thirteen or fourteen thousand a year, for Travers to step into, just as he got his last marching-orders—barely two days before he turned up his toes. I was sorry the letter came before he died. He was rather gone in his mind, what with sleeping-draughts and one thing and another. And after he read the letter everything about him passed out of his mind, and he thought he was a young fellow with the ball at his feet, and he and his Nellie were to be married. I sat by his bedside in the dusk, and he kept on saying, "I am so glad this has come before it was too late, Nell! It is sometimes awful. I knew of a fellow that went to the dogs away in Australia; but then the girl he loved threw him over. You would never do that, Nellie darling! Thank God, it's not too late—it's not too late!" By Jove! you know, it gave me a lump in the throat as big as a potato. Somehow it was worse than if he said it *was* too late; and he kept on hammering at the same thing, and thanking God she was so true to him, and marking down on a map where they were going for their wedding-trip. And then he would say, "Now, Nell, don't keep me waiting long at the church. I have been waiting such a long time; and sometimes I had the most awful dreams. But it's not too late!" he would begin again. I was glad when it was all over.'

'Ah, what pitiful broken episodes many lives are!' said Stella softly. 'All that might have saved them is defeated—every touch leads to the catastrophe, and then silence and darkness—and the great play goes on just the same. And yet how good it is to be alive and see the sky and look at the roses!'

'Will you give me a rose before I go, Stella?'

'Yes—what kind would you like?'

'One of those you're fondest of.'

'Well, those I love the very best are the white fairy roses, and the cruel east wind on the 26th scorched the last of them, buds and all. But I can give you a Gloire de Dijon.'

'And, Stella, would you mind giving me that book with the "Lady of the Lake" in, and——'

'Oh, with great pleasure!'

'And just write my name in it, Stella—and the date—and here's a little parcel. Don't open it till I'm gone. You know you said you liked opening parcels.'

'But, Ted, I should see what it is before I take it.'

'No, you can settle about that when I see you in Melbourne.'

Stella took the little square parcel, and looked at it doubtfully. 'It's not another Kooditcha shoe?'

They passed into the library, where Stella got the book, and wrote 'E. Ritchie, 28th Dec.,' on the fly-leaf. Then they stepped out into the garden, and got an unopened rose, fragrant and smiling red at the lips.

'I am sorry your mother and Alice are out—say good-bye to them for me, Stella——next time I meet them I hope—well, we shall see. . . . Now, Stella, give me your two hands, and say, "God bless you, Ted!"'

She gave him her hands, and he looked into her face so long and steadfastly that she suddenly crimsoned under his gaze, and said with a little pout:

'Ted, you mustn't be so solemn. One would think you were going to Central Australia, or whale-fishing to Greenland in very bad company.'

'Say it, Stella.'

'God bless you, Ted!'

He bent and kissed her hands, and then hurried away without once looking behind.

Stella stood where he left her, till she heard the sound of his horse's hoofs ringing on the roadway as he passed up Barton Terrace. And then traces of contending emotions swept over her face.

'Poor old Ted! I believe he is in some trouble. What if his health is really affected? But I can't believe it. That is a way men have if the least thing is wrong—they take themselves as seriously as if they were stuffed llamas. Well, I'm almost sorry I wasn't more sympathetic . . . only it is so dangerous.' And the thought of Ted trying to read sonnets for her sake overcame her with amusement. Yet this was soon followed by a feeling akin to self-reproach. In the old days she had read to him—talked to him of what interested her most—but for the last two or three years, when they met, her chief feeling was a wondering amusement that one who had learned to read at all should so completely escape all tincture of books. She had got into the habit of listening to him—of apprehending his point of view— almost avoiding any direct personal talk that might influence him or modify his mental habits. But was he so entirely beyond any intellectual sympathy—so far removed from kinship with matters that lay beyond the common grooves of common life? Why had she relinquished those ardent dreams of being a power for good in the lives of those to whom she was dear?

Her face grew hot as she recalled the frivolous way in which she had met his half-expressed resolution of giving up horse-racing. And yet was there any other pursuit that seemed so completely to arrest the better development of a man's nature—to paralyze the worthier interests of life? The perpetual contact with the ignoble rabble, whose keenest interest was the excitement of betting, and winning money for which they had not worked—must not this render the mind more and more callous to all that was worth living for? And yet she had almost mocked his recoil from his past devotion to the racecourse.

Her action suddenly appeared to her in so odious a light that she longed to see Ted again for a few moments, to ask his pardon for her mocking indifference—to encourage him in his new-born resolve— to tell him that their native country was full of work which needed honest men and honest money. How many fields were white for the harvest—how many labourers were needed to dedicate their whole powers to the world's service!

'Oh, I shall have to come back to being as much in earnest as ever,' she thought, half smiling at her rising zeal; and then the thought of Ted blundering through 'The Publick Baptism of Infants' beside the poor dying man made her feel inclined to laugh and cry at the same moment.

The strange, bitter pathos of that human wreckage which drifts into so many currents of our Australian life fastened on her mind— men delicately nurtured in the old homes of the Old World, as well as the luxurious ones of the New, and in the end going completely under, in the rough, wild manner of the veriest waifs. This is misery of the kind which weaves the most tragic thread in the web of existence. The slow but inexorable deterioration of character makes oftentimes a strong seizure on the startled spirit.

'Oh, it is all too cruel!' said the girl to herself. And then a curious sense of undefined peril came over her—one of those quick unreasoning apprehensions, often strong enough to give a sense of physical pain, to which minds of over-reflective fibre are sometimes subject. It is as though chains of consciousness, apart from the centre of thought, were at work storing up half-understood impressions, piecing together disconnected events, casual words and signs that have floated through the brain without leaving traces strong enough for waking memory, till the total is summed up in an expression of imminent or latent danger which is suddenly flashed on the mind with bewildering vividness. And yet the process by which this is conveyed is sealed from knowledge. There is no orthodox channel of intercourse between these swift intuitions and the workaday brain immersed in the details of daily life.

'Do you think it does a fellow any good to come a cropper in that way?' was one of the reminiscences Stella found rising in her mind after the vague little shock of dread had left her.

She went back into the drawing-room, and there was the little square parcel still unopened. It was a brown morocco case which opened on pressing a spring and disclosed a magnificent pearl brooch in the form of a horse-shoe—row upon row of graduated pearls, with a very large one in the centre, and large ones round it; the next a little smaller, and so on to the last row, which were small exquisite pear-shaped pearls. There was a little note in Ted's round, schoolboyish hand:

'DEAR STELLA,

'This is for your birthday in April. They are Shark Bay pearls, got by the boat I have an interest in. You used to take little presents from me before on your birthday. Once I brought you a little beggar of a sparrow, with only a few feathers, and tried to get a kiss for it, but you didn't see it. By Jove! you owe me an awful lot, you know. I hope you will like the pearls. I got the jeweller—should there be two *l*'s or three in that word?—to make them up in a horse-shoe for good luck. Mind you, I know very well I'm not half good enough for you; but then neither would any other fellow be. I wish to-morrow was the day I was to see you in Melbourne. You must be a bit of a flirt, Stella. The governor is always quite gone on you afresh after he sees you. He likes a girl with plenty of go in her; and you always tell him some funny story over which he keeps on chuckling. If you're not in when I call to-morrow, I may tell you that I was awfully cut up I couldn't leave Heronshaw on the 26th, so as to dine at home. I'm getting full-up of races. I shan't go to one till I see you again. I am going quite into the Bush for a thorough change.

'Good-bye, Stella,

'Always yours,

'ED. RITCHIE.'

Stella looked long at the pearls. They were so soft and lustrous, with that glowing moist look as if damp with the sea under whose myriad waves they took shape and grew within a creature that had the breath of life. Is it this that gives them the wistful tenderness which marks them from all other jewels? That, and perhaps the melancholy moanings of the sea in which they were cradled.

'It is much too costly a gift—unless, indeed, this endless wooing is to have an unfortunate close,' thought Stella with a smile. 'Well, it should rob matrimony of some of its terror to marry the youth who at nine or ten tried to bribe one to kiss him with a half-fledged sparrowlet.'

From that day till she met him again she consciously from time to time faced the possibility of this 'unfortunate close.'

CHAPTER VI

SOME of the letters which Stella wrote to her brother will best convey the tenor of her life during the months that intervened before she left for Melbourne and Lullaboolagana. They were the last she wrote from the home of her infancy and girlhood—that serene and happy resting-place in the chequered journey of life. They show her on one side gay, playful, open to every impression, in love with life and beauty as ardently as a Greek, finding food for mirth at the core of much which outwardly wears a mask of solemn gravity. On the other side she exhibits a cold logical faculty for drawing pitiless inferences from the laws of nature, from those lives which had touched her own and had become bankrupt in all life's promises of joy. Prone also to that severe disenchanted estimate of human affairs, springing from the austere strand inevitably woven into minds that have at one time been nourished on the sustained enthusiasm of supernatural ideals—on the writings of saints and fathers whose keynote is the lofty renunciation of those who look on the world and its most coveted distinctions as the empty pageant of a passing show:

'Fairacre, N. Adelaide, 15th January

'You ask me to be sure and write when the thought arises: "How I should like to tell Cuthbert about this!" "If I could only have a good long talk with him now!" But consider, my friend, what a cold little viper a pen is when you want really to talk face to face! When a word, a look, suggests thoughts that had else hardly struggled into existence! And then, apart from the chill which the frosty tip of a pen engenders in one's most communicative moods, has not ink an immemorial right to be dull? Still, I perceive a certain advantage in saying whatever I like, feeling sure that in a day and a half you will gravely read it all. Whereas in a *tête-à-tête* one is open to contradiction—to interruption—to be skipped like an elderly newspaper, yawned at like a tedious play. One is afraid to skip a letter too cavalierly. There might be something in it. For after all life has many surprises.

'As women generally sit by the hearth all their lives, like a cat that has given up hunting, they should early learn how to purr and write letters. Do you know the tradition among some of our aboriginal tribes, that their Creator taught men how to spear kangaroos and women how to dig roots? Now that you are on the pacific war-path of a spearer of souls—what a vile simile! I am sorry, but that is the worst of primitive races—they seldom afford good metaphors. I imagine that I meant to say I must learn to dig with my pen—grow intimate with it, make it loyal to me, so as to keep at bay that estrangement which often creeps between people when they are apart. What a fierce jealousy stirs me at the thought that time and absence might dare to nip with lean fingers at our lifelong friendship!

'Shall I divide my letters between daily events and the natural sprouts of my own understanding? Someone has said that matter of fact is the comfortable resource of dull people.* But when you come to fold it up in pages, stamp it and send it five hundred miles or so, matter of fact should have its whiskers trimmed, and its obesity buttoned up in a slim jacket, like an organ-grinder's monkey.* But if you do this when you are so good and calm that you have no history, what remains?

'All this day the north-east wind has abused the privilege it has of being intolerable. How I envy people who, unless they go out on foot, hardly perceive that this *bise** of Australia is running riot! You know the habits of our climate at such times. The air dry and parching, with ever-recurring puffs and gusts, warm as if they had escaped from caldrons of red-hot sand, and that unceasing undertone, whether the wind blows high or low, as of things being swirled along the earth. It is the motion of countless little twigs, of skeleton leaves, of bits of bark, of old frayed nonentities, of desert grit borne along in a whirl of dead resurrection by a wind that surely has not its compeer on earth for dragging things from near and far that have been long spent and buried into the unmerciful light of day. You were spared another page or two regarding the hot wind by Kirsty, who came half an hour ago to the library-door, saying that poor old Honora wanted to see me.

' "She's the warse o' drink, and as hoarse as a corbie.* There's nae use in helping her at a'. It's mony a day sinsyne* that she began thae* evil ways," said Kirsty, with those severe lines round her mouth growing still severer. "Sall I say you're too busy, Miss Stella?" Needless to say I was not. Poor Honora! She was more sunburnt and draggled than ever, her clothes more weather-beaten, her hat more desperately broken. Altogether she looked one of the most forlorn targets of the darts of misfortune that could well be seen on the world's turbulent stage. Still, with it all she maintained that inflexible air of being only one more victim of the stratagems of fate.

'Oh, she was well, all things considered! Many a poor thing with a bad husband and undutiful children would even now like to change places with her. But things had gone against her again. Work was not easy to get, and since she had set up housekeeping she had more worries. "Yis, Miss Stella, wid the foive shillins' ye gave me whin I met ye three weeks ago, and I had neither bed nor sup, nor anny other av the luxuries av loife for two or three days. May the Blissid Virgin reward ye, and pray for ye, now and at the hour av your death. Ye see, it was loike this, me darlint."—Honora always grows more affectionate when she is going to tell you a bit of her life.

' "I luked at the two half-crowns, and thought to meself, 'There's a dale may be done wid so much capital. If 'twere one mane shillin' it wouldn't help anybody to turn over a new leaf, so to speak.' So I spint two an' a penny on a supply of groceries, and I bought a taypot and cup, and an old tayspoon in a second-hand shop, kep' by an honest, hardworking, straightforward, onfortinate woman as ever the sun shone on, Widdy* Ryan, in Brown Street.* I tould her how I was resolved, wid the help of God and a little capital, to be no longer a sthray vagabond, loike a cat left in an impty house. And she, poor crather, knowing what the hardships and mocks av this world are, let me have the few crockeries as chape as dirt. Thin I hired one room from an old comrade, Johanna O'Connor, a cook, who has come down from the north to take a spell* for a few months. Indade, Miss Stella, I was as proud as an Impiror when I heard the chip crackling under the saucepan I got the loan av from Johanna, for 'twould have made too big a hole in me funds to buy a taykittle. And nixt day I just tuk it aisy, and wint for a walk in Loight Square,* and who should I meet but two av the Sisthers av Saint Joseph,* that used to give me a bed now and thin, but av late have been moighty cool. 'Well, Honora,' sez Sisther Lucy, 'we haven't seen ye at chapel at all av late. Where do ye go?' 'Indade, sisthers,' sez I, 'I must go to thim as will help me. I've been thinking of giving up religion altogether and turning Proteshtant.'" Do you not find this interview worth all the "capital"?

'Kirsty is quite scandalized at my liking for the poor old soul. I suppose it is a sad vulgar taste, but I love to listen to these details. I want to go and see them all: Widdy Ryan, with her secondhand shop, who knows what the mocks of this world are; Johanna, who is taking her ease in her own rinted cottage; and Honora boiling water for tea in a saucepan.

'Dustiefoot is well, but, can you believe it? not quite so young as he was. It seems that as soon as he is a year old a collie dog begins to fall into sombre reveries on the flight of Time, on free will, and the yoke of necessity. Or are there infinitely more important themes that occupy the thoughts of a creature who has the felicity to be born with four legs and an oblique tan spot above each eye? I whispered your name to him this moment, and he wagged his tail thirteen times. Have angels a more eloquent mode of expressing goodwill? Certainly man has not. Still, I am not sorry that in our arduous ascent in the scale of nature we lost our tails. Do you not know by instinct the people who would jocularly catch us by them, as a token of good fellowship? Notably those who pride themselves on being too sincere to take kindly to the conventionalities of life, and on being the artificers of their own manners. Now think over it, and see if Blank, and Dash, and Snap do not appear to you in a more lurid light than ever. Do you not find a fresh glow of dislike welling up as you reflect: "Yes, that is the stamp of man who would infallibly pull one's tail"?'

CHAPTER VII

'Fairacre, 13th January

'WHEN a benevolent fairy bestows on me a cast-off island, or some old-fashioned kingdom upon the mainland, I shall have a carriage as capacious as a state barge, drawn by two iron-gray horses, tall and high stepping, likewise a slim footman, and a fat elderly coachman. This is the state with which I was encircled yesterday, when I drove out with Mrs Marwood in her brand-new equipage. And let me tell you, my dear, that I found the change from our lowly pony carriage, and Leo's diminutive trot, to these exalted prosperities very sooth-ing. How deferential shop-people and all that ilk are, when one goes about with such a halo of wealth! But never suppose that I am going to revile human nature on these grounds. No; when I reflected on the matter, I was unmoved and dispassionate to an edifying degree. "After all," I said, "money is a great power." Pray, are you dazzled with the brilliant originality of this? But don't interrupt reflections, for though doing so may add much to your joy, it is death to the homilist. "Money is at the root of all civilization and art."

'At this point an aboriginal family bore in sight, who pointed the moral in a striking way—father, mother, and two picaninnies were all barefooted. In a word, a tattered Government blanket, a couple of waddies,* and the rakings of a dust-bin, by way of clothing, com-prised all their worldly possessions. Thrilled with the justice of my remarks, I went on: "Society is held together by mutual wants. The unfortunate devils who have not wherewithal to satisfy these must go to the wall. How unavoidable, then, that money should confer distinction! It is true that wealth draws out the flunkyism of the average week-day mortal in a pitiful way. But may not flunkyism itself be termed the exaggerated respect of poor natures for an absolute power?" etc. I do not know any place in which one may make reflections so fairly and comfortably as in a deep-seated, plush-lined carriage.

'Do you know how profoundly benevolent and incoherent Mrs Marwood is in her charities? She really is a perfect *point de ralliement**of incongruities. You find her telling you how atrociously Worth charges for a simple gray silk, and before she has finished marshalling her figures she ejaculates, "But why should we worms of the earth* take so much thought wherewithal shall we be clothed?* The sheep and caterpillar wore that very clothing long before." My imagination is not nimble enough to take in so varied an assortment of metaphors without bruising its shins. First as to the phrase "a worm of the earth." I no sooner hear it than I picture myself as a creeping thing, without hands or feet or face, living in a carcase underground, without light or sun or air. Before this gruesome picture is complete, enter a sheep with a waist, in a fine homespun, and a caterpillar trailing a trained silk. You see, they wore "that very clothing long before." 'Tis to no purpose for a sober man to knock at the door of poesy, says Plato.* So it is with me. The flights that people take to read a lesson to man's pride confuse rather than edify me.

'One of the visits Mrs Marwood paid as we were on our way to her house was to a family whose head she described as a "brand plucked from the burning."* Judge whether one who lounges about his house in the afternoon with unlaced boots, a stubbly beard of a week's growth, and smoking a short black pipe, seems a fit subject for such a description. But then perhaps the appositeness of a "plucked brand" rests with the eye that sees it. Certainly he might have been engaged in drowning his youngest child in the tank, or dancing on the prostrate form of his wife.

'You hope that I am going on with my collection of aboriginal myths and customs? I hope the same. So it is evident that life is partly given us that we may keep on hoping, and nothing come of it. "Why do I not set to more seriously?" In the first place, I hate to "set to"; in the second, I abhor "more." And if I could hang myself for aught, it would be because there is such a word as "seriously," not only in the dictionary, where one may endure anything, but also in people's mouths. Have I expressed myself too strongly? Then I repent—but without any thought of amendment. This, I believe, is the only thing that makes repentance tolerable.'

CHAPTER VIII

'Fairacre, 3rd February

'THANK you for your kind inquiries after my chickens. They thrive apace. Ten out of twelve of them seem to have gained a firm footing in the world. One especially, a buffy white, nimble creature, is so trenchant a warrior in the battle of life that we have named it Hector, not after the family, but the classical hero.* He picks crumbs out of his brothers' mouths as if he were a Christian merchant; he hops on his mother's back, and, stretching his neck, spoils twenty muscatel grapes in half a minute. He snatches happy insects out of the sunshine, and, with one slight arch of his neck, hurls them into an unshrived* eternity. The place where his tail ought to be is fast developing; a tiny yellow comb is faintly visible. Alas! I see plainly that Time, who scatters his poppy-seeds with a ruthless hand, is bent on his destruction. For the day on which he becomes what Kirsty terms "a cockerel,"* his fate is sealed. But, then, our own special doom awaits each of us; and Hector has this advantage in being shelled a fowl: he never sinks into sallow meditations as to his coming fate. The present hour, with its worms and sunshine and sweet opportunities of theft, is enough for him. He listens to all the speculations that can be addressed to him with unmoved composure. Only this morning one held him in her hand, and said: "Ah, little feathered atom, so lately shelled from one eternity into another; fleeting pilgrim in a passing show; confined to a few roods of earth, yet linked by subtle chains to the remotest star—nay, perchance, to spirit itself! To know thee wholly, how largely must the boundaries of human knowledge be widened. Time and space, and the solar system—all are necessary to thy existence——"

'Hector listened with round rolling eyes, but at this point he made a sudden dart at the speaker's mouth, as if it suddenly struck him that it was alive, and possibly as good to eat as a beetle.

'Yesterday I made several visits to sick people. Two of them—Mrs Rupert and Mrs Morland—have been slowly dying for nearly two years. Do you remember hearing mother speak of them? One of consumption, the other of some internal malady. Can one witness such long unavailing struggles without pondering why human beings should endure so much, all to no purpose? . . . People speak about waiting for the end. But has not the end of the body come when it is smitten with an incurable agonizing malady?

'It would seem that when I enter on moralities, my dear, you and I are undone, like salt in water. At any rate, you will not feel disposed to grumble that, just at the moment I was dipping the inquisitive beak of my pen in ink, to come without further phrase or disguise on the yolk at the heart of euthanasia, who should call but Mr Willie Stein. You know how he makes these sudden appearances from the far north. The thermometer is very high; the wind is from the east, and threatens to veer to the north; there are crowds of undelightful things that ought to be done the day before to-morrow; Duty, like an old hag that ought to be burnt at the stake for sedition, peers in at you from time to time, and then, to fill up the measure, in comes Mr Willie! Here is an aboriginal myth he told me: Once upon a time the pelicans went to fish and found a great deal of barracoota, which they left in a gully while they went for more. Up came some greedy thieving magpies and stole the booty. The pelicans, in revenge, rolled them in the ashes, and that is the reason why they are partly black.* This belongs to the same class of legend as that of the venomous snake who made the moon angry by killing so many blacks, till at last she burnt its head as it slept in the grass at night. So that is the reason why its head is black and its bite harmless.* You see, Australian myths have this in common with those of classic Greece, that they also endeavour to give an account of the origin of things.

'You ask about my translation of "Faust."* I have not done so many lines per day since you left. You see the second part is to our speech, with its many one-syllable words, a perfect trap for the translator. I am glad, however, you encouraged me to undertake this task, for in no other way can one draw so near to the heart of a work in a foreign tongue. But as for any literary value, of course the thing is naught. I could make you die of laughing at subtilties, screwed words, and rhymes hacked and raked all to no purpose. The performance is like nothing so much as a bar-horse that hath his eyes blinded trying to race a soar eagle. But then I feel that I have climbed a little nearer to Goethe—and is there anything in life more delightful than the tranquil friendship that grows out of long and frequent intercourse with a great writer? One who is not only among the most majestic sons of light, but a frontier savant of life—who penetrated to the outposts of human nature, and unflinchingly noted the vantage-ground of good and evil.

'Early next week I am going on one of my periodical visits to Dr and Mrs Stein. They have staying with them, just now, an old friend, who arrived from Germany a few days ago—a man who is as steeped in research as a seaweed is in ozone. But is it? Well, if not, it ought to be.

'It is cruel of you to vaunt the praises of the Melbourne climate over ours, when we are having such atrocious hot winds. Yesterday, some of us did nothing but lie on the floor in Apostolic raiment, swallow ice, and feebly murmur the old aboriginal incantation: "Sun, sun, burn your wood—burn your internal substance and go down!"'

'Fairacre, 15th February

'If I were a South Sea Islander, this is the day on which I would beat my idol black and blue. I have completely fallen out with myself. Dearest dear, do not put up your eyebrows in that unbelieving way. You should have heard me speaking to myself a little while ago. "What sort of a creature do you call yourself?" I said. "If the wind is from the north-east, if a dress is a misfit, if people say the same things to you, if they say nothing at all, you are like a bundle of stinging-nettles—cross and disagreeable all over. What have you done to your soul that it does not raise you above the petty malice of the passing hour? Go away—go to someone who does not know you so well as I do—no, I won't have you at any price."

'And, lo! my friend, here I am, with a pen and a scrubby little ink-bottle, and a sheet of paper, and a shivering, homeless ego, thrust from its accustomed throne. May I come to you? Do not ask me inside if you are busy writing sermons. No, it wouldn't be safe. Just give me a mat at the door and one of the old poets till you have finished. It would be no use making a confidant of me. You could not feel for me. If I said my pretty pink *crêpe de chine* has been spoilt in the sleeves, you might try to look sympathetic, but you would really be smiling inside. And yet greater failures have much greater consolations. If you construct a wrong system of ethics you make your claim surer to be ranked a philosopher; if you make it clear that the majority of mankind must be damned, you may possibly be reckoned severe, but are sure to be considered a sound Christian. But what comfort can be drawn from having the wrong sort of sleeve? I defy you to find any; or if you do, 'tis because you are not a woman.

'*You*. Is that the only reason why you have become "a house divided against itself"?* Well, some of your sex have ere now pretended to be racked with toothache, when they were really suffering from heartache.

'But I deny the imputation; besides, what so reasonable as to be quite out of humour with one's self from time to time? And yet an invincible self-approbation is one of the boons I envy your full-blown Philistine, man or woman. Take Mrs Towers, for instance, who chants eternal paeans to everything she possesses, from her eleven children to her apricots; from her husband to her Ligurian bees.* You know how one seldom meets her, without hearing of some visitor who has travelled far and wide, and yet regards his visit to Hawthorn Vale as the happiest event in a life not barren in joy. How it must save the tissues of the brain to be in such a state of mind as that perennially! . . .

'This afternoon Esther and the three children arrived. Poor dear! it is so sad to see her in mourning still. Unless husbands have been very angelic, it seems rather a mistake to wear mourning so long. But I think this is one of the subjects I should skip. I have some thoughts in future of trying to imitate Providence in letting events fall heavily or lightly as they may, but without remark or expostulation. This will be all the easier, because the children have taken entire possession of me. To-morrow we are going for an endless ramble by the Torrens away towards the hills, beyond Windsor,* and all the other pretty little townships, crowded with gardens and orchards and orangeries and fields of vegetables. Perhaps we shall see some mountain ducks on the river, and hear the loud ringing calls of ash-coloured cuckoos away in the gum-tree tops. Here is a *bon mot* from your nephew Clement:

'*I*: "Why, Clem, you are growing frightfully tall! And yet it is not so very long since you were in petticoats!"

'*Clem*: "No; but you, Aunt Stella, are in them still; will you never grow out of them?"

'I felt too crushed to attempt a reply. I think I shall send this to Mr *Punch*,* as a specimen of an Australian boy's idea of repartee at nine.'

CHAPTER IX

'Fairacre, 1st March

'I HAVE just returned from Mrs Stein's, laden with roses and early white China asters and double balsams of the most celestial pink. You know of old what a delightful event a visit to Rosenthal* is. But you do not know what it is to listen for hours to Professor Kellwitz, the Primitive Dwelling man, talking for hours on the pre-Deuteronomic Pentateuch* and "Die assyrisch-babylonisch Keilinschriften,"* and the early twilight of man's history on the earth. Nay, he one day went back still further, even to the time when our world was without form and void—when what is above was not called heaven, and that which is the earth beneath had not a name*—ere a sprout had yet sprung forth and "the generative processes at work were all hidden in chaotic vapour." The two old friends spoke, of eourse, to each other in German, and sometimes I lost the thread of what they were saying, and I would not ask a question for the world. I love too well to listen to men talking when they are oblivious of a woman's presence. The second day I was there is especially memorable to me. Mrs Stein was busy preserving Duke cherries in brandy. The sparrows are so bad this year that the cherries have been gathered off some trees before ripening. Don't you think the sparrow in Australia is an awful example of a bird with a conscience seared as with a hot iron?* In his native countries he is, it seems, undainty to a discreditable degree, seldom tasting fruit and never red nectar. But with us he not only becomes an epicure beyond the wildest dreams of the pagan world, but a reckless destroyer—a small Attila* with a pair of brown wings. Not merely does he disdain to eat the skin of a freestone peach and the transparent rind of sweet-water grapes, but for each one he eats he spoils twenty by pecking at them. Here at Rosenthal, where he lives meal-free and at ease, the ungrateful little varlet nibbles two score of cherries to each one he eats.

'Ah, true! I have not told you about the second day of my visit. There was rather a horrid gully wind blowing. So early in the after-noon the Doctor and the Professor established themselves in the western veranda with the curtains drawn, with their pipes lit, and between them a table that groaned under its array of Lager-bier bottles. I was sitting, with a book and a small Rupert garment half made, by the French window of the drawing-room, when the two took up their quarters close beside me, with only the window-curtains between us. There were peals of Homeric laughter as they recalled incidents of their student days; and there was talk of a Lischen, who seems to have been celebrated for the length of her golden hair, "long since turned to dust." Then they talked of their work. The Doctor told tales of the early days of the colony, and how, twenty-four years ago, he and Courtland became intimate friends. When he spoke of father's learning and rare goodness of nature, it was all I could do to keep myself from stepping out and kissing him on the mouth. Then the Professor spoke of his early struggles. For many years he held a subordinate post in a small university, where he had three-quarters of the day to himself. He seems from the first to have been devoted to that kind of literature which no reference library should be without. One of the incidents he told was of a far journey he made during one vacation to a little town, to which some Grand-Duke had bequeathed a singular collection of books. It was a long journey, and cost more than he anticipated; so that before he returned he was forced to leave his watch in pawn, though he trudged the greater part of the way. And the object of all this was to authenticate *one date*. On hearing this, I shifted my chair, so that I could see the Professor's face better. A spare keen face it is, with many lines and furrows, and yet distinctly human, as though in all his researches and wanderings he had never lost sight of the fact that man himself is a more insoluble interesting problem than any facts to be gleaned regarding him.

'There was a sound of cork-drawing, and discovering that I was thirsty, I went into the dining-room for a glass of seltzer. When I returned the talk had veered to Australia—its inhabitants and resources, and future prospects. The Professor found a grave drawback in the thought that as most colonists orginally came to the country for material reasons, true patriotism must be of tardy growth; "Your young people do not love it as their native land in the same way that ours do."

'"Yes, Herr Professor, they do!" I cried, obeying an irresistible impulse to bear witness to the love I have for my own country. And then a long animated talk followed, during which I was obliged to turn to my own tongue—for the Professor talks English much better than I talk German. I drew up the veranda curtain, and bade the good Pundit mark the loveliness of my birthplace—the city with its white buildings and scores of spires encircled by shady parks, the sea beyond stretching to the western horizon, the fertile plain to the north sprinkled with wide fields that yield bountiful harvests from year to year; the hills close at hand, with their tree-crowned heights, and graceful curves, and shadowy gullies—all thickly studded with prosperous homes, with orchards, and vineyards, and flowery gardens, and olivets*—and over all the overflowing sunshine, which encompasses the land year in, year out. Who could be born in such a place and not love it for its beauty and fertility? If our fathers were crowded out of the old world—or left it because they feared their children might sink into poverty—was not that an added reason to love the new one, which had offered them comfort and prosperity, and a fair field for the energies of their sons? We have great wastes and atrocious hot winds—but shall we receive good and not evil also?

' "Yes, after all, each one must remain in his own skin," said Dr Stein, taking up the parable. "If I were in bitter poverty in the Fatherland, as many men are who are more gifted than I am, I might be a dangerous Socialist hatching plots against the safety of the State. There is a point beyond which history and the traditions of the past touch the heart but little. The great kings and nobles who figure so largely in our history were mostly men who commanded the lives and wages of others, while they themselves were hedged round with privileges and wanton luxury. I want my own share of the pleasant things of life, and the country which gives me this, and in which my children were born, has as strong a claim on their love and gratitude as the oldest country of them all. Practically you owe your life to the country in which you were born. Stella, here, who is the granddaughter of a man that fell fighting for Old England, do you think she would not make as much sacrifice for her native land as any German maiden of old times?" "Hear, hear," said I, clapping my hands in honour of myself in true democratic fashion.

'Enter Mrs Stein, followed by Hetty with a trayful of slender pink glasses, and a flagon of Rosenthal cup. The pure juice of the Australian grape mellowed by ten years' repose in the Doctor's cellar. It was a lovely amber colour, with an excellent bouquet, and

though I always like wine best when I do not drink it, I felt bound
to honour the Professor's toast, which was "The Old Fatherland and
the New." We became great friends, and, in fact, I have promised
that when you and I go on our travels we shall pay him a visit in
Berlin.'

CHAPTER X

'Fairacre, 14th March

'MY DEAR CUTHBERT,

'A very disconcerting thought hopped into my head after reading
over your last letter. You seem to go to see the Rev. S. Carter very
often. Tell me true—is it the quality of the good man's theology, or
his daughters, that attract you? Perhaps you have not yet arrived at
the conscious stage. Oh yes, I am quite an authority on the tender
passion. I have read and re-read Mr Harrison's play, and made
endless suggestions. There are two young people who are madly in
love with each other, but do not know it till a certain crisis. I object
to this rather, but A. says that it is for the stage, and not for poster-
ity. You would have laughed if you had heard us deciding such knotty
points as to whether a certain young man would have the presence
of mind to improvise a story when he was interrupted in making a
declaration of love; whether the heroine was not disloyal in believing her lover guilty of a crime because appearances were strongly
against him, etc., etc. There is an unusual and interesting plot, and
the dialogue is crisp. A. calls it "Macaroni" for the present, because
he says I have been sticking feathers* in it. I found him out using up
some things I said, and he declares it is because Evelina resembles
me, and would naturally speak a little like me.

'I have now a very nice riding-horse, from Zembra's, named Ivan.
Our favourite ride is to the seaside, which we reach in half an hour
when we make for the Grange or Henley Beach.* The latter is
my favourite ride. We pass such old-looking gardens, and hedges
still full of Macartney roses—altogether a flat, shadowy tract in
which there are always sea-birds wheeling slowly above the trees—
sea-gulls, white terns, and occasionally those lovely little gulls, snow-
white and pale gray, with blood-red feet and bills. When disturbed
by the trampling of our horses they utter mournful cries, and fly

before us seaward. They remind me of something in an old author somewhere on the shelves: "About thee gathered the daughters of old ocean, uttering cries of grief. They spread over thee vestments perfumed with ambrosia."*

'But I have been strangely neglectful in not introducing you before this to Major Foster and Mr Paul Ferrier. Though we have known them only since you left, they are now habitual visitors—in fact, they may be called our *amis de la maison** in the antique line.

'The cause of the Major's visit to Adelaide is a great joke. He came to administer consolation to an old friend who had lost his wife, and was inconsolable—for nine months. Do you not find this very funny? But when I tell you that this friend is Mr Inglis Taylor! During the first six months of his widowhood Mr I. T. wrote repeatedly to his old friend, urging him to come on a long-promised visit; he was so broken-hearted, but could not leave his clients to go for a change. But the Major being long a widower, with his only daughter settled, and having retired from the army, why should he not come? So, moved by the sacred ties of old friendship, and the duty of administering consolation, the Major came, and found his friend enjoying the sober ecstasies of his third honeymoon. You know already something of Mrs I. Taylor and her many matrimonial adventures. I have not the slightest doubt that on the voyage the Major read standard works of philosophy and religion, so that he might be better able to bind up a prostrate and bleeding spirit. I have tried to glean information on this point, but the Major is reticent. In fact, I think he mistrusts my motives. He does not know that my curiosity arises from my wish to be a beautiful soul. Don't you remember that Montaigne says the beautiful souls are they that are universal, open, and ready for all things; if not instructed, at least capable of being so?* Now, I do want to be instructed how a man feels when he has come fifteen thousand miles to weep on the neck of a widower, and finds him married for the third time to a woman who has been thrice married before. Well, perhaps this is only her third husband, but I cannot make any other reduction in the number. I never see her without recalling the woman of Samaria. But I suppose it makes a difference if there is only one of them living at a time—I mean of the husbands.*

'Mr Ferrier is an ex-missionary. He lived among the blacks for twenty years; but he has been so much concerned for their souls that he does not know any myths, and their customs, I suppose, are not to be spoken of. He called shortly after you left, to ask if mother would subscribe to the mission in which he was so long engaged till severe and repeated ophthalmia threatened him with blindness. Indeed, he had almost lost his sight when he came to be treated in the hospital here six months ago. Even now, when he is outside, he always wears a green shade over his eyes. He has about sixty pounds a year to live on, and out of this he subscribes ten pounds a year to the Mandura Mission. He is nearly seventy, but looks older, being very weather-beaten and brown, and his eyes so dim. There is something heroic and ardent about the old man; and imagine being so enthusiastic about the conversion of the aborigines! You know mother's angelic kindness to poor and lonely people. He is quite alone in the world, and no doubt his leisure engrosses most of his time. It is an understood thing that he comes to Fairacre twice or thrice a week, and we all subscribe to his beloved mission. I think he has more of Don Quixote* in him than any other I have ever known.

'You say that you never think of me now as doing anything but making snares for the stubble-loving grasshoppers or watching birds on the wing. Well, we do pass a great deal of our time outside. The worst ardours of the summer are over; the woods are so shady, and the children and the dogs tempt me out constantly, when I have serious thoughts of confusedly tumbling over divers authors. After breakfast we go out to feed the pigeons and the chickens. There are so many pigeons now, they darken the air, flying down to be fed. They alight on our shoulders and make such pretty cooing sounds. It is not to be credited though, how long-legged and everyday Hector grows in common with his family. Time, who is the most impertinent busy-body in the world, so soon spoils chickens—and alas! I suppose I ought to say, young women. Ivan begins to distinguish my voice, and makes me very happy sometimes by whinnying when I speak to him. . . . Often we follow a string of ants to their home, and watch them descend with the booty they have gathered. We drop crystals of sugar and grains of wheat and rice so as to watch them carrying off their loads in triumph. This afternoon we discovered a hive of bees in Hercules. Is it necessary to explain that this is the gigantic gum-tree opposite us in the Park Lands? Their hum is never absent there; but near that great old tree it is as though one were inside a hive. We watched numbers passing in and out of the hollow stump of a broken limb, high up, and, looking closely, we saw the ends of their waxen cells. How many jars of honey are hived away there is now an all-absorbing thought—second in interest only to the chrysanthemums, which are swelling visibly and promise to open early this season. After discovering the wild hive, we wandered homeward; and when we got back, we ate grapes in the vine arcade. It is quite a show, literally bending beneath its loads of grapes; so are all the fruit-trees, each after its kind. The jargonelle pears are as yellow and soft as cream, and the large purple Turkish figs melt on the trees. The peaches and apricots blush at each other, like lovers in a play. (Mem.: Offer this comparison to Mr Harrison for "Macaroni.") There are some pomegranate-trees, whose fruit looks like fiery blossoms. They are not quite ripe yet, but we got one each, and sat down picking seeds from the crimson rinds, like sparrows.

'"Now, Dustiefoot, it is extremely wrong of you to thrust your cold black nose in my face——" My dear, don't you think it is time I stopped? That is the way with us in our dear, quiet Adelaide! We have so little to distract us, that when we begin to do anything the difficulty is to leave off.'

CHAPTER XI

'Blumenthal,* Easter Sunday

'I MUST write to you while I am at Pastor Fiedler's. I came on Saturday, so as to be at the Dankfest* to-day.

'You know what an old-world charming little German-looking township Blumenthal is, with the Coolie Hills in the distance, to the south-east, and the quiet, shadowy woods all round, broken up by farms and vineyards and numberless homesteads, nestling among fruit-trees. St Stephan's, the new little Lutheran church, is nearly a mile from the pastor's house, with a delicious untilled valley full of tan wattles lying between. There is a good-sized garden and a glebe attached to the pastorage—a glebe with two milch-cows, like-wise two calves, that come up and let you kiss them on the forehead, and rub their charming little chestnut noses against your hand. There is also a fat gray cob, lazier even than Leo. You may doubt this; but that is because you do not know Hans as intimately as I do.

But I want you to come to the little church. The pastor went at ten; Mrs Fiedler and I half an hour later, and we brought immense posies of chrysanthemums. They are out in wide bushes; at this moment there is a great bowl of them close beside me. They are in the little hall, in the sitting-room, on the tiny lawn, in the garden— everywhere. We also brought some of our best roses and crocuses. How I love the yellow crocuses that come up in wide golden bubbles, so close to the ground! Sunday was an entirely perfect day. I believe it was really the first day of autumn. The sun was at times half veiled with fleecy gray clouds. The sky was not so staringly blue; a tender tint of gray had stolen into it. And there were such gentle pastoral sounds: the distant tinkling of bullock-bells; the bleating of sheep not far away; the lowing of a cow whose calf had been weaned; the high, sweet carol of a white-shafted fantail. Autumn leaves fluttered in the wind down from the willows and fruit-trees; but they did not speak of decay, only of rest. Everything rested— from the great foliage masses that bounded the horizon on every side, to the bees whose buzzing was faint, as if they were half drugged with the ambrosia of deep flower-bells. No rumble of dray or waggon, laden with wool or wheat or grapes or hay, invaded the Sabbath quiet.

'My old friends the Schulzes, Grossvater and Grossmutter, greeted me with all their old cordiality. Their seat was crammed with sturdy young Schulzes of the third generation. I should be afraid to say how many of the sept there were in all. It was good I was in the church before the service began, for I could not have kept my eyes from wandering. Such lavish heaps of flowers, fruit, and vegetables! No wonder the good Germans of Blumenthal hold a harvest festival. There are ten windows in St Stephan's, with wide, deep sills to them. On each side of these an overflowing horn of plenty had been emptied.

'It was a triumphant exhibition of what Nature can do in our land when her lap is shaken out. The apples alone were a feast to the eyes—so large and smooth and beautifully tinted. As for the pears, they were so ripely yellow one dared not look at them too fixedly lest they should melt at a glance. There were mounds of great purple figs gaping with mellowness. Citrons large as pumpkins, quinces not much smaller, plums of all kinds, from the little piquant damson to the generous Orleans; blood-red mulberries, fragrant peaches with their crimsoned cheeks, nectarines, and oranges of a lordly size, though still, of course, unripe. On the altar—a plain table with a white cloth and crucifix—were grapes, heaped up in splendid profusion. The robust Black Prince, the small berries of the Cabernet Sauvignon—no, I must not put you out of patience by naming all; besides, if I did, half would still be forgotten, if you will pardon the bull.* I noticed one bunch of Doradillas which must have weighed five pounds. You are in deadly terror of hearing about the spies and Eshcol*—but I spare you. I also let you off in the matter of vegetables. They were all there, from the asparagus to the virtuous potato. The ends of the seats were wreathed with hop and vine leaves, and round the chandeliers were hung sheaves of fine wheat, of oats, of barley, and maize. The pastor preached a divine little sermon— sincere, simple, and to the point. It was the discourse of a man who knows that there are two sorts of ignorance, and two sorts of lying, in the world. The ignorance that knows and cares for little beyond the daily round; the ignorance that cares for so much, yet apprehends that so little can be really known. The lying—that of statements known to be untrue; the other, which takes the form of treating as certainties matters that can never be subjectively proved true. And yet, because he knew all this, it seemed to me that he was all the better fitted to speak with authority on what we do know to be true. We know that if we put aside the baser temptations of life we can bear our share of fruit to nourish man's spiritual nature, even as the fields around us, year in, year out, bear harvests that sustain material life.

'As we came home the wattlewood valley rang with the peculiar mournful pipe of some birds. "They are quite new here," said the pastor and pastorin* as we stood to listen, I felt I ought to know whose notes they were, yet could not tell without seeing the birds that uttered them. I left Dustiefoot in the pastor's charge and stole away as noiselessly as an aboriginal in Kooditcha shoes. Dear, how you will begin to hate this comparison—to me it still has something of the freshness of primeval woods. They were white-winged choughs. I saw three of them perched in the very top of a tree. One knows them from afar by their scarlet irides and the glossy green reflections of their plumage.

'In the afternoon we drove to the Schulzes'. Grossmutter, as usual, kissed me repeatedly, as if I were a little child—and very good. But it is true, if ever I am good at all, it is among these kindly, sincere German people. Not even the sort of impertinent pen you wot of would tempt me to cast reflections now on a world that produces such fine grapes and wholesome-natured people.

'Grossvater was in one of his blithest and serenest hours. Their golden wedding-day is next month—on his eighty-first birthday. After that he will give up all active part in the management of his vineyards. His son Karl is a good and skilful vigneron. "I counsel him to be true to his Australian Fatherland—to make nothing but good wine from good grapes," said the old man, with the genial smile that makes his face so young. "Wine fit to drink at the table of the Lord's Supper, at the marriage feast, at the christening of the eldest son, on the death-bed, when the dear God calls us to another world."

'One sees how much better it is for the pastor to be in the country with a congregation that grows grapes and tills the soil. Life passes with such leisurely tranquillity, and the baser denominations of our kind seem more unreal. I feel sure, too, that no one here tempts him to read the "Kritik of Pure Reason."'*

'Fairacre

'I left Blumenthal yesterday, vowing to make a longer visit in the spring. I carried away with me from the pastor an old ballad in early German, called "Two King's Children,"* which I am translating into English for your special benefit. This is the anniversary of Esther's wedding-day. No one had the courage to say a word about it. After what you said so admirably as to the necessity of sometimes showing a little of the sympathy that one feels, I made an effort. But, heavens, how I blundered! It was after sunset. I sat in the drawing-room bow-window sewing, when Esther came and sat in a far corner already dusky with the gathering twilight. She sat with folded hands, her face pale and set. At last I crept up to her and touched her cheek with my hand; and presently we were both crying. To make one weep bitterly who had before been calm, is that shedding any of the balm of consolation? Don't you think you had better dissuade rather than encourage me in such painful bungling? It is better to recognise one's limitations. If people are badly hurt, I can make them cry worse, but can never tell them it is all for the best. I could tell them that no one understands the refinements of hangmanship like Nature, and that life is a finished artist in defeating the heart's insatiable yearning for happiness; but on the whole I think I had better hold my tongue—likewise my pen. But not till I tell you a little *conte à rire** related to me by the pastor when he drove me into Gawler for the two o'clock train. Two Sundays ago he visited the little Lutheran Sunday-school at Detmold, and found the teacher—a very stout, placid-natured man, who likes to arrange things in a tranquil, unexciting way—with a class around him repeating the Creed. The plan was that each child should say a clause, thus: "I believe in . . . the Holy Catholic Church;" next child, "the communion of saints;" next, "the forgiveness of sins." Then there was a long pause, till a small boy at the tail-end of the class piped out: "Please, teacher, the girl who believes in the resurrection of the body has got the mumps!"'

CHAPTER XII

'Fairacre, 10th April

'ALAS! the young gentle autumn was a treacherous make-believe. For the last week we have had an inordinate fit of hot weather—frequently the sky overcast and lowering: it promises to rain, but the clouds turn to vapour; the wind changes, but it is not cool. To-night, again, the barometer has fallen; the moon and the stars are all hidden, the air is intolerably sultry, and there is that further sign of change—unending swarms of insect life. I write by my open window, and they come floating in, hovering round the lamp, creeping on the table, getting in the way of my pen—creatures on foot and on wing—thinglets that fly one moment and fall down helplessly the next—morsels that crawl with half-spread wings, and things that fly as if with legs. They terrify me—these purposeless hordes that struggle into existence one moment and the next are crushed by a foot-fall, the accidental turning of a leaf, the scratch of an idle pen. Do they not throw some light on the cataclysms of human history? Are they not linked closely to our race and lot—part of an incomprehensible world in which, stronger than righteousness or justice, or any figment of morality, reigns the impulse of every single organic being to increase in numbers? Is it true that some form of thought underlies the lowliest manifestations of life? What instinct or purpose is subserved by those pretty little pearl-gray moths, with silver dust on their wings, who dash into the flame of lamp or candle, as if it were the source of life? Here is one of them which I have twice saved from consuming itself. One wing is scorched and it is very limp, as if rescuing it from burning were defeating its only purpose, snatching it from the one possible joy of existence. The thought possesses me that some higher intelligences than we know may thus regard our lives. But have we more power to fashion and to mould them than this helpless thinglet that was called into being by forces over which it wields no control, and seeks nothingness by an impulse equally beyond its influence?

'Last night the rain came down in torrents; towards morning there was a thunderstorm, of which I heard nothing. But to-day the air and the sky are clear and fresh, the Torrens is babbling, and the birds are singing the blithest legends imaginable all over the Park Lands. The Major and Mr Ferrier are spending the day with us. Poor Mr Ferrier is forever telling us about the conversion of some aborigine. I often wish we could keep an old black fellow on hand at Fairacre for him to convert from time to time, and then perhaps he would spare us these endless recitals. But my heart smites me for speaking like this of the zealous ex-missionary, and I am sure mother likes to listen to him. Then he is so entirely in earnest. Perhaps you would like to know his story of to-day? It was about a half-caste boy who, after being at the Mandurang Mission Station for a year, began to show signs of repentance and grace. One day he stole some sugar. "Was that after he showed these signs?" asked the Major. From some people the inquiry would sound ironical, but not from the dear guileless Major, who is evidently quite unused to theological phrases, and was merely trying hard to comprehend all he heard.

'"Yes, sir," answered Mr Ferrier; "it was some weeks after we had great hopes of him. The old Adam* is strong in all of us, but perhaps especially so in our poor half-caste natives. Do you know, my dear sir, that there was a canon law of the Church in the early ages which rendered converts from heathenism ineligible for the priesthood to the second and third generation? Well, I knew Thomas—we always gave our people Christian names at their baptism—had taken the sugar; but I said nothing to him. I felt the time had come when he must be allowed to stand or fall. The boy was dear to my wife, and she wished me to take him aside and remonstrate with him. But I

said, 'He knows good from evil now; we must see whether the root
of the matter is in him.'* We read the Word of God, and had prayers
in the evening as usual. My dear wife offered the prayer; she wres-
tled with God mightily for the soul of the half-caste boy. Ah, my dear
friends, I wish you had known her—not a thought for self. Her only
thought was to win souls for the Saviour, and many of these poor
people were verily brought through her means to the foot of the
Cross. It was only nine months after this it pleased God to take her
from me."

'There was such pathos in the old man's voice, it gave one a lump
in the throat. The Major hastily drew out his handkerchief and pretended to cough. But Dorothy at four and a half can make-believe
much better than the Major at fifty-seven.

'Mr Ferrier went on to tell how, after the natives retired for the
night, he sat in the sitting-room writing out his monthly report,
leaving a blank where he was to write of Thomas, till he found
whether he would repent him of his theft. His wife sat with a book
in her hand, but he knew that she was crying, not reading. At last a
tap came at the open window, and a timid voice saying: "Missie,
missie, me want to gabber!" It was Thomas. The wife at once went
out, and the boy talked to her for some time. Presently she came in
with "a light on her face," as Mr Ferrier expressed it, and she said:
"Paul, you need not leave a blank for Thomas now. The Lord has
given him to us as a prey snatched from the snarer."* "And though
he had a passionate temper, and sometimes gave way to it, yet from
that day till the hour of his death I never had reason to doubt that
he was a chosen vessel* of grace," said Mr Ferrier solemnly.

'No one could doubt the good man's sincerity. But I confess I never
hear him talk in this fashion without a great longing to know what
conception an Australian aborigine could really form of the profoundly metaphysical dogmas of Christianity. They are so kneaded
into our literature, so imbedded in the marrow of our minds by
inheritance and instruction, we could not if we would really cast
them from us at least as phases of thought. But a savage who cannot
count beyond three, and goes out to murder some tribal foe because
a kinsman has been killed by the fall of a tree—what idea looms up
in the twilight of his mind when he is kept at a mission and taught
the Creed and the Ten Commandments? Here is an anecdote I fished
from Mr Ferrier, when I was trying to glean aboriginal myths from

him. An old man, badly wounded, came to the mission one day. They nursed him and fed him, and he seemed so docile and to accept all he was taught so readily, that they thought he was in a short time ready for baptism. One thing puzzled them, however. Though he bathed often, and had clean clothing on, a peculiar odour always hung about him. A few days before he was to be baptized, it suddenly struck Mr Ferrier that this was caused by something with which he smeared his hair. But this was not the case. It was the kidney-fat of an enemy rolled up, and secured among his locks. He would allow no one to touch or remove it, for it was a point of honour with him to keep this ghastly memento until he had also murdered the brother of his victim. In the meantime he was very anxious to be baptized.

'The rain has rather battered some of our chrysanthemum bushes. But then there are such angelic multitudes—in all shades—white and pale-cream, pink and rose; red are our special favourites among the Japanese. This last shade has for me as irresistible a charm as the pink ear of the maiden which in Tom's Turkish song robbed her lover of his reason.'

CHAPTER XIII

'Fairacre, 20th April
'AFTER listening to innumerable tales of conversion, after hearing of aborigines who talked on their deathbeds like leaflet tracts, ever since we first knew Mr Ferrier, he has at last told me a charming little myth. It bears no traces at all of being the production of natives that, to use Dr Stein's expression, had been "tampered with by the missionaries." You might put everyone of them that ever laboured in Australia in rows, and bribe them with the promise of a whole continent of blacks, all ready to talk broken English and wear second-hand store clothes on Sunday—and yet between them the worthy missionaries would never produce anything with the peculiar *cachet* of an aboriginal myth. But if I say much more you will vow that I am enamoured of the subject—it is as a master passion on which people must notoriously be mistrusted. It is such a short myth, dear, after all, that I am obliged to add to it with a preface. Do you notice how Tom is training me to dabble in bulls?

'The sun is a woman who courses over the sky all day, keeping up enormous fires. But at last she uses up all the wood she has for that day, and she goes down at night among the dead. They stand up in double lines to let her pass, and do her reverence. She has a lover among them, who gave her a great red kangaroo skin. Each morning, when she rises, she throws this over her shoulders.*

'Another thing I learned yesterday is that the good little man's special blacks noticed the stars, and had names for some. The evening star they called Kyirrie; the Milky Way Kockadooroo; and there is a cluster of stars visible in the western sky, during the winter months, that they knew by the name of Amathooroocooroo, which signifies "claw of eagle-hawk."* Please to reckon it henceforth among the classic constellations.

'Then, floating in the Milky Way, is still to be seen the bottom of the ark of Neppelle, who transported himself in it to heaven to escape the waters with which another god flooded the earth to drown his unfaithful wives.* And did you ever hear that three of the stars in the Southern Cross are two aboriginal Helens and their lover, who escaped with them to that far retreat from the fury of the deserted husband?* The astronomical lore of our natives may not have been very scientific—but at any rate they knew which sex was always causing mischief. But there, dear—it is a sore subject—and I know many of you are now sincerely repentant.'

'Fairacre, 30th April

'You would be very much shocked to hear of Mr Stanhope's sudden death. It took us all dreadfully by surprise. It is only seven days ago that Allie and I met him and his mother at Sir Edward Ritchie's; and then, as always, he looked the picture of health and strength, and overflowing with merriment. We had great fun about Leo, who really is getting quite past any whipping I can give him. In his wildest days he would sit at the kitchen-table and eat sugar, but now he almost gets into the pony-carriage instead of drawing it. Mr Stanhope was particularly diverted at the trick I told him Leo has acquired of stopping short when he sees any very poor or disreputable-looking persons, making sure mother is in the trap and wants to speak to them.

'"When you drive those glossy thoroughbreds that are being trained for you, you will wonder how you could ever bear to sit behind Leo," he said, and laughed when I pretended not to understand. Then he took out a little pocket-calendar and said: "My mother and I are going to Cape Town in November. Mind, the event must come off before then, for it is a pact between Ritchie and myself that we should see each other go off the hooks." The next day he was attacked with violent congestion of the lungs. He was ill barely five days. He was buried this morning. I write the words, but they seem to convey no meaning. I see him strong and young, his eyes full of laughter, turning over the calendar filled with engagements and appointments; but not a word of this one inevitable assignation. Nothing left of all that eager, vivid personality save a poor clod of earth hurriedly hidden out of sight! Good God! is not this the bitterest insult that could be devised for the last scene of the last act?

'There is a wonderful fund of unbelief in the heart regarding death. Yes, we must all die; but individually it is as though immortality were a birthright we are to inherit without tasting the bitterness of dissolution. Is it very bitter? and in the hereafter, does it indeed matter very much if we pass away with empty lamps? In that supreme moment when the soul is sundered from the body, do we perceive that the life which was all in all to us was but a dream grafted upon a dream—a passing vision crowded with phantoms? . . . And now the curtain is drawn. We see no more. All beyond is so shadowy and faltering.

'How is it the thought of death does not haunt us more? The event is so tremendous. I have often had the feeling after the death of one I knew, that never again could I be lulled into such entire forgetfulness of this one absolute certainty. But gradually the impression vanishes. We are planted so deeply in the life that now is—we may be shaken and horrified and apprehensive—but the world is like one of those hydra-animals which may be turned inside out, and the exterior surface will then digest and the stomach respire.'*

'Fairacre, 7th May

'Fanny Harrison has returned from her Melbourne visit, and has been telling us tales about your overworking yourself—visiting sick people day and night—reading to incurables and blind people by the hour—making superhuman efforts to save larrikins from themselves. Don't, dear darling; at any rate not so much. It gave me a shiver all

down the vertebrae when I thought, "What if Cuthbert should turn
out one of those clergymen who take life so seriously that they die
of it like a dose of arsenic?" Do not forget that it was a neglected
cold when he was so much engrossed with the sick and poor one hard
winter that brought on the lung complaint of which father died.

'I cannot get over a certain awkwardness of not knowing exactly
what to say when I first visit people who are very poor, and hopelessly ill. So I mostly listen to them, and read a little only if they wish
it. Poor Thomson seems to like this, for the last time I visited him
he aired his grievances. People are very kind, he said, and lots of
ladies always visit him; but they do read so much to him. "No doubt
'tis very good of them, but when a chap lies in bed month after
month, never expectin' to get up again in health, and often cuss-
ing himself for having been a fool and partly to blame for his
misfortune—why, then, a lump out o' the Bible don't seem to hearten
him up much. Now, there's Mrs Cannister and Mrs Meadows, and
her dorters—'tis my belief as they uses Bibles not properly divided
into chapters. In course there's a good deal of it taken up with Jew
names, and stories not meant for gineral use. But I don't see why
them ladies should pick out the melanchorliest psalmses for me. Well,
I mean them as is all about the horrors of death bein' on me, and the
waters goin' over me, and my eyes bein' consumed from weeping,
and bein' a worm and no man, and the arrers sticking fast in me, and
bein' in a pit, and in a dry thirsty land, and arskin' the Lord why He
cast me off for iver, and that I forgit to eat my bread, bein' like a howl
in the desert and a perlican in the wilderness, and a sparrer atop o'
the house without a mate, which is what niver happens, as far as I
know the varmin; and coals of juniper, and scattered at the grave's
mouth and lying in wait for my soul.* Yes, Miss Stella, ye may laugh,
but it's true—the creepingest things. Yes, I remember what's read to
me pretty well, but then I've heerd it all over and over agin—some
days twicet over.

'"And then Mrs Cannister—she sits there as you may be now, only
more frontin' me, so that she can fix her eyes onto me—and she
reg'lar ivery week says to me: 'Now, my good man'—if there's anything I hates it's them words; if she said 'my wastin' away toad,' I'd
like it better—'now, my good man, do you not begin to feel that it's
all well, and all for the best in the hands of the Lord?' And if I'm
tired I just mostly gives a nod, so as she may stop jawing. But other

times I says: 'I donno as to things being so very well. If my family was pervided for, an' I didn't lie awake half the night coughin' and spittin', I might be more sartin on the point. As to things bein' in the hands of the Lord, I know well, if I'd have been stiddier and different-like in many ways, I wouldn't be in the fix I'm in now.'

'"When I says anythin' like that, the old dame looks for a more dismaller psalm the next time. It licks me, though, how people can go on saying it's all in the hands of the Almighty, and He does everything for the best. Now, Miss Stella, if you take it that me—and a good many of the chaps I've knowed—was the handiwork of the Lord, I'd like to know who has spiled more horns nor He before making a good spoon!"*

'You may not think very highly of this man's theology, but I like him for his honesty in admitting that he is to blame for what he calls the "fix" he is in, and a straighter way of looking at things than people generally allow themselves.'

'Fairacre, 1oth May

'The Fortuniana and tea-roses, and the heliotrope and various other sweet-smelling flowers, still flourish in our garden in golden abundance. I brought a great posy to Frau Kettig this afternoon, with various other things of a more material kind, but the flowers delighted her most.

'Yes; I have just returned from seeing her. How angelically good and uncomplaining she is all through her illness! She is more grateful for being destitute than I am for all I possess. I assure you, dear, I threw stones at myself nearly all the way home. I talked with the dear old woman for a long time, and read her favourite hymn to her, "Ein feste Burg ist unser Gott."* Then she chanted the two first verses—her thin, old, toil-marked hands devoutly clasped, her eyes half closed. . . . Through the little window at the foot of her bed I could see the sky, clear blue and serene like a great heavenly web woven throughout of hope and love.

'"Surely it must be so," I thought, looking at the frail old woman with her load of eighty winters—with all her cruel bereavements and losses, and now in her diseased old age, after moiling like a slave for sixty-eight years, dependent on charity for her bread, yet lifting up her trembling aged voice and hands in tearful love and gratitude to God—the great Father in whose hands are a thousand worlds full of treasures—who yet has bereft this sincere loving soul of all. If there were not some tremendous force of love behind the "mocks of this world," could spirit achieve so signal a triumph over matter?

'"It is a fair summer day of the Lord, full of His sunshine, and yet cool; and the flowers thou hast brought me, beloved child, take me back to the sweet Thuringian woods," she said, with the simple directness which makes the grand old German sound like one's mother-tongue. I could not trust myself to speak. After a little she said, as if suspecting that I was too sorry for her: "When one no longer hopes to rise again, how good and dear it is to think on the day when all waiting and weariness are forgotten in beholding the face of the beloved Redeemer!"

'Here is Fatima at my elbow, rubbing herself against me and purring benevolently, looking a little askance at Dustiefoot, who has indeed too often tried to make a play-thing of her tail. But he is fast asleep just now, with his nose against my shoe. Fatima likes those lucid intervals in which Dustiefoot slumbers and she can purr of "auld langsyne"* without interruption. Dear old tabby! tell me quick and tell me true, is your ardent liking for fish a proof that in another world you will sail a boat and cast a net into the sea? Certainly, though you love fish even to felony, you cannot go a-fishing in the life that now is—which things are a parable. I begin to see that this infatuated pen of mine will get me into trouble if I do not stop.'

CHAPTER XIV

'Fairacre, 17th May
'WE do not think mother is as strong as usual. But as neither the seaside nor the hills suit her as well as Fairacre, we do not like to venture on a change to either. She will, however, most probably accompany Esther to Coonjooree for some months. Allie has gone for a couple of weeks to the Emberlys; and I do most of mother's sick-visiting for her. She consents to this more readily because I think she believes it is good for me. But personally I cannot help feeling how much better it would be to send Kirsty instead of me. She thoroughly believes that under all circumstances people are better off than they deserve. If a man has broken his leg, she is ready to say,

"What a blessing it is not his neck!" If a poor woman is confined of her tenth baby, Kirsty reflects, "How much better than to have typhoid fever!" And when people have typhoid fever, she says, "What a mercy it is from the Lord to have medical attendance!" I confided to mother the other day how, in average sick-visiting, I am haunted by the feeling that I can do no good, and sit with a long face thinking how horrid it is to be in bed, and wondering awkwardly what I am to say next. Then the flies put me out of countenance. With the poorer people among us they are a veritable plague—in their bedchambers, and upon their beds, and in their ovens, and in their kneading-troughs. Mother answered very gently: "Charity, my dear, is a kind of Bezer in the wilderness,* a city of refuge, which we must always keep open, because of the many accidents and misfortunes of life. Our visitings and readings and half-hours spent by lonely sick-beds, they may perhaps be compared to the 'Refuge, refuge,' written in every double way on the parting of the ways, to aid those who, without help or sympathy, might be in danger of perishing in the great desert. Think, my dear, what it is to lie, for month after month, in a poor little room, without ever hoping to be well again. Even to make hours a little pleasanter, that would otherwise be dark and lonely, is something. In such matters we must be content to live from hand to mouth, without looking for great results."

'You know how mother's words, "delicate as honey born in air,"* at once soothe and convince the heart.

'Yesterday the Major told us about one of his funny episodes with Adolphe. That is his man—an Austrian by birth, but with a cosmopolitan command of tongues. The Major and he bid each other an eternal farewell every three months, if not oftener. Adolphe went yesterday morning to send a telegram for his master, and did not return till late in the afternoon, very much the worse for liquor, which he often takes beyond the bounds of moderation, as he candidly explains, "pour la guérison de douleur."* He always knows when he has taken too much, and his custom is to come to the Major with a virtuously determined air and say, "Sir, it is wrong that I should longer anguish the heart of a true and loving woman. I must return to my Julie—and yet to leave you——" then he breaks down. Often as this little farce has been acted, with variations, it always seems to rouse the Major's ire, and then make him relent all in one scene.

'"If only his conscience could be touched!" murmured Mr Ferrier. Would the Major allow him to give Adolphe some little books on the evils of alcohol? Certainly; but the Major thought it was only fair to tell Mr Ferrier that Adolphe was always ready to sign a pledge against intoxicants. But when he is tipsy, next day he explains with great fluency how the necessity for nervine aliment* is insurmountable in a climate like this.

'No; I am not going to Laurette at as early a date as was fixed, because it is now quite evident that mother is out of health. I cannot go until she is better. Dr Stein is in attendance, and I am head nurse, Allie bottle-washer, Kirsty major-domo. Dr Stein tells me that our friend Professor Kellwitz contemplates matrimony—at sixty-three, and for the first time!—and to a lady who has been his intimate friend for over twenty years. Is it not dreadful to spoil so tried a friendship in this ruthless way?'

CHAPTER XV

'Fairacre, 1st June

'POOR, dear Mr Ferrier has had a severe disappointment with Adolphe, who, under the ex-missionary's unwearied efforts, became not only a total abstainer, but to some extent a lecturer. He devoutly read Mr Ferrier's good little temperance booklets—nay, learnt much of them by heart; so that when it occurred to some zealous tee-totalers to put him on the platform, Adolphe became at once very popular, and was always greeted with cheers. No doubt, like M. Jourdain's dancing-master, who hungered after *un peu de gloire*, Adolphe found that *applaudissements me touchent.** Last Tuesday he went with Mr Ferrier to address an evening temperance assemblage at a little township four miles away. It seems that on these occasions it is customary sometimes to make certain experiments with alcohol to show its evil effects. When it came to Adolphe's turn to address the meeting, he gave what Mr Ferrier called "an able and earnest address." At a certain point he broke an egg into a glass and then poured some brandy on it to show what a deleterious effect it had on the albumen. The audience cheered lustily, and were much impressed. But when the next speaker rose, Adolphe was seen to slip behind him and swallow the experiment in a few gulps. Loud expressions of disapproval arose, and Adolphe instantly came forward to defend himself from the "calumny." It was then apparent that he must have been previously imbibing, and, in fact, he had taken a quarter of a bottle of the Major's best brandy to make experiments which should revolt the popular mind against "nervine aliment." When he returned home that night he went weeping into the Major's room, imploring him not to take any more stimulant of any kind, and holding himself up as an example of its evil effects—and all through swallowing a small experiment by an unaccountable error!

'Two days ago I was on a visit at Mrs Marwood's, and went from there to what the profane called a "disorganized charity meeting," along with Mabel Towers. We, too, went as Mrs Marwood's deputies. But what singular instructions we received: "Here, you see, girls, is my list," said Mrs Marwood, producing two octavo sheets with various names and figures, etc.; "you see, there's a large committee of us, and we have to be very business-like. Here are the numbers of things to be given opposite each applicant's name. We decided that at a meeting some days ago. Sometimes we run short, and are obliged to give a pair of trousers instead of a dress; but if any complaints are made, give them a form to fill up and send in, for we have to be very strict and accurate. And if you happen to give too many things to one person, mind you give nothing to the next. Mrs Benjamin Ezra is to be there to-day; and you must keep an eye on her that she does not give away my share. Her plan is to give heaps away till everything is gone. She either loses her list, or else never looks at it. This is very awkward in a society on such strict business principles as the organized relief."

'Yes; so determined are we to imitate all the charities of the mother-country, that before this "great fertile young Hercules"* is yet fifty years old, we not only provide relief works and soup-kitchens and free breakfasts, as we did last winter, but this season we have also an organized relief society, which, among other nefarious tricks, distributes cast-off clothing. But, my dear, I warn you, do not send any money to the philanthropic novelties of our Metropolis. They are frightfully mischievous, and the really deserving poor do not go near them. There is quite enough discriminating benevolence everywhere in the country to cope with all honest poverty. It is when we begin to tease charity-mongers with salaries that impostors and

the cunningly vicious have their innings, and that the unabashed professional pauper appears in the land. We have now not only the weaklings, that have been industriously sent us by emigration agents, but
the greasy loafers of other provinces who are attracted to ours by our
notoriously indiscriminate distribution of alms. Let me tell you of
the two first cases on our list, which may, I believe, be taken as
average specimens of what the rest were.

'No. 1 applicant: Mrs O'Mulligan, with two girls.—Causes of destitution: Husband, an ex-publican, long out of employment, large
family, furniture seized for rent. Mrs O'Mulligan soon set us to
work, I can assure you. We were the first to arrive, and were ushered
into a room lined with wide shelves, full of clothing of all kinds, a
great deal of it as good as new. It was like a clothes pawn-shop
without the pathos, fortunately also without the dirt. Mrs O'M. was
down for one woman's dress, two ditto for girls; one man's coat, one
ditto trousers, one ditto boots. She and the girls followed us into the
clothes-room. We soon found dresses for them. Then came the
mother's turn; but as she weighed over fourteen stone, it was no light
task to fit her. "Shure, now, and you see for yourselves, young ladies,
that wouldn't kape on me little finger. Yes, that's a foine thick stuff;
but where 'ud I be in it?—outside the most av it." At last she selected
a pale blue cashmere, not nearly as large as some useful dresses she
had rejected. Mrs Marwood said this choice must have been made
with a view to selling or pawning, and no doubt that was the explanation. Then came the husband's turn. He must have been phenomenal in his proportions, judging by the yards of tape with which
Mrs O'M. measured the upper parts of trousers we turned over for
her. At last came a pair that looked as though it must be the gift of
a benevolent elephant; so this she put aside. Then she pulled an
endless sort of string from her pocket, which turned out to be the
measure for a pair of boots. Of course there were none of such an
impossible length.

'"It's not, thin, that Mr O'Mulligan has such a large fut at all at
all, but he gets the swelled rheumatzises so bad. Indade, he had an
ilegant fut in his young days. But what with the throubles and the
sorrow, they seems to git larger ivery year." As the string was twenty
inches long, it was evident some mistake was made. It was, in fact,
"the lingth av little Paddy's throusers." After all the articles for which
this woman was put down had been produced, we politely asked her

to take them away. "Is it that this is all I'm to git?" she asked, with a tragic air. We asked her what else she wanted, and she said: "I have six helpless childer, and I want a complate shuit for each. Ye see thim two girrls wid me? Wan av thim has a good ulster* on, an' that's a lind; the other, she has a good pair av boots, an' thim is a lind; so is the hat wid a feather on top av my head, an' the gloves on me hands, an' the mantle on me back wid a bead collar." She raised her voice and she flourished her arms as she spoke. Finally she took up three pairs of boys' trousers that were near her and went away, saying she would put us in the papers for cruelty to an "onfortinate rispictable woman wid a husband that had seen better days, and a large family and no support." She turned back at the door and said: "Ye have a great roomful av things sint by the charitable, an' ye sind me away wid a few miserable rags for reasons best beknowns to yerselves!"

'Our next case was a small thin woman with an extraordinary facility for tears. She wept copiously the moment we spoke to her. She never had accepted charity before in all her life, and it was very hard to begin now. With this she made a dart at a heap of boys' shirts that were near her quite new, Mr Marwood and other wholesale drapers having sent various parcels of clothing from their warehouses. She wiped her eyes, and folded up three shirts. She was down on the list as a widow with one boy; name, Eliza Trimton; and the written oracle restricted her to two articles for herself and three for the boy. I explained this to her, and added that we were bound to keep to our list. Yes, of course—she knew that; and she began to shed tears afresh, and pounced on an elaborate tea-gown that had been sent by someone who had more money than wit. Next she fixed her gaze on a very good ulster, and she instantly began to cry afresh. No one, she said, but those that had seen better days knew how bitter it was to accept alms. With that she folded up the ulster, and put it with the other spoils. "It comes very hard to accept charity for the first time," she murmured, seizing on a blue cloud,* a boy's vest, and a pair of merino stockings all at one swoop. For the second time I read over to her the articles to which she was entitled, and thought she had taken the hint, for she began to tie up her bundle. But presently her tears flowed, and she picked up a woman's hat, a boy's greatcoat, and a pair of boots in rapid succession. "But really, you know, this is a great deal more than your share," said Mabel. "More than my share!" retorted Mrs Trimton, wiping her eyes vigorously. "Who took it on theirselves to know all I want? I never breathed it to anyone I needed so much. Never having accepted charity before, my feelings was too delicate-like." With that she dried her eyes and went away.

'By this time most of the committee-ladies had arrived, and one of them said, as so many applicants were coming to-day, they had better not be admitted into the room where the clothing was. "Of course that is the proper plan," said another lady; "but there will be a heap of letters in the papers saying the public gave so generously to the clothing fund, and that the poor people were not allowed to fit themselves." However, the applicants were finally made to wait outside, and served in their turn alphabetically, an arrangement that gave great umbrage to some. I heard one woman say it was a real shame she should have to wait so long because her name began with Ho. Another woman was in tears because a baby's hood given to her had no pink lining. A neighbour of hers, she said, had one from the Relief Society last week lined with beautiful pink silk, fit for a little princess! "Look at this," said another recipient of aid, holding up a child's handsome scarlet mantle. "There's where the tassel should be, and I won't go away till it's found." Still another woman spoke in broken accents of despair of a pair of shoes that were given to her with one buckle missing. It would be unfair, however, not to mention one old woman who seemed to be quite grateful. We came upon her in the lobby rearranging a man's greatcoat and some other articles of male attire. Someone near her asked if any mistake had been made. "Yes, my dear," she said, in a semi-confidential whisper. Her face was very red, and she carried with her a strong odour of some liquor. "There's been some blessed mistake, and I'm just hurrying away before it's found out. I can get far more for these than for any flimsy perticoats they'd give an old woman like me."

'I am this instant going into the Park Lands with Dorothy to see if a magpie does not give us an act out of a bird comedy. By the way, talking of birds, the last time Mr Lindsay was here he told me a very Haroun al Raschid anecdote* of a man who lost a very peculiar sleeve-link on the Murray Flats, and found it a year afterwards in the playhouse of a silky bower-bird,* dangling beside the capsule of a brandy-bottle and the scarlet flowers of the pretty native wistaria. Mem. for my note-book—Would this make a peg on which to hang an alibi? I asked Mr Lindsay the question, and he promptly said: "Oh, if it was to save a fellow from swinging,* of course it would never be found." Now, you know how little speculative or "morbid" he is. Is it possible that life itself is often more morbid than any reflections regarding it?'

CHAPTER XVI

'Fairacre, 9th June

'I CANNOT report that mother is better; but she insists on thinking of other people as much as if she were quite well. Poor Thomson is failing rapidly. Yesterday at her wish I spent part of the day in taking care of him. I must tell you what happened. After I had chatted with him for a little he said: "There is a chapter, Miss Stella, as I liked when I was a boy—somewhere in the Old Bible part—'tis about being took up by the hair, and looking in at places, and seeing the women-folk weep for Thomas. I'd like you to read it to me."

'Would you be able to find a chapter in the Bible by this? I doubt whether I would, only that lately I have been rather fascinated by Ezekiel. It was the eighth chapter he meant—where the likeness as the appearance of fire put forth the form of a hand, and lifted the prophet up by a lock of his hair. "Then he brought me to the door of the gate of the Lord's house which was toward the north; and, behold, there sat women weeping for Tammuz."* "I like them parts o' the Bible, so strange, and yet they seems quite real like." You may be sure that I did not attempt to foist any interpretation upon the text. There is a point at which those who have read much of the best, and those who have read very little, seem to meet—enjoyment of vague mystery and wonder, leading to a subtle sense of the marvels that lurk under the masking raiment of commonplace. Just as I rose to go, the storm, which had been gathering all the morning, began to come down in torrents. The rain beat sharply against the window-panes, and the room suddenly darkened. I noticed the sick man gazing at the window with a very sombre look, an expression that had in it something—how shall I say it?—more tragic than poverty or disease. "Miss Stella," he said in a low voice, "do you believe as them that is gone could ever come back from the other world?" "I don't know. I have often wondered whether they do or can," I answered, awed by a sudden conviction that the man, to use our nurses' phrase, had at some time "seen something." He moved restlessly, as though his head were uneasy. I smoothed and shifted his pillow, and then to my dismay I saw that great tears were rolling down his cheeks. No doubt he had moved so that I should not see them, and I had done the very thing I ought not to have done. Some strong wave of emotion swept over him, his bosom heaved convulsively, and he sobbed half aloud.

'I felt horribly distressed, and not knowing what else to do, I tidied up the fireplace and put some wood on the fire. "I saw his face as plain as daylight at that very window, a week ago," he said, when he recovered himself. And then he told me this little story. He came to South Australia twenty years ago, a lad of eighteen. He was for some weeks a knock-about hand on a sheep-station near Jarranda Bay. One of the shepherds suddenly left, and he was sent to take his place. A few days after he went to the Stone Hut, as it was called, he found an old black woman, who was dying, and had with her only her daughter, a half-caste, a slip of a girl of fourteen. They were beside a little creek, and had had nothing to eat for three days except a big snake the girl had killed near the water. They were on their way with other blacks to a great corroborree that was to be held eighty miles further on, when the mother was taken ill and left behind with her only daughter Caloona. Thomson fed them, and gave them all the comforts he could. In a week the old black woman died, and then the girl lived with him. He engaged himself as shepherd for two years, and stayed altogether for eight. Caloona, he said, turned out mighty handy, and she was always so wonderfully thankful. "When you told me about that little dog of yourn, Miss Stella—Fly you call him—I thought he was for all the world like my poor Caloona. She would follow me about, and wanted to wait on me hand and foot, and thought so much on me. I tuk to reading the New Testament, and minding all the good things my grandmother used to tell me. Caloona soon learnt to cook and do things much handier nor many a white woman, and she kept the hut as neat and clean as a new pin. I bought clothes and things for her from a hawker, and, if you believe me, Miss Stella, she looked much prettier in them than many an altogether white girl. She would be up and working before it was light, so as to have breakfast and dinner cooked and come out with me after the sheep. Even when the little boy was born she stopped in the hut but a few days. She was that proud of the little chap—he was fairer than you could believe—and he grew very fast. He was out all day long in the woods

with his mother and me, and when it rained we just made a mia-mia*
of boughs for him and put a 'possum* skin over it. He was sharper
nor a needle; and many's the time he made us lie down on the grass
roaring with laughing at his old-fashioned ways.

'"But onfortinately as he grew older he showed signs of a very bad
temper, and he would turn and strike his mother for the least thing.
I could not stand that, but Caloona only laughed, and that encouraged him. That was what come between us. I allays heard as mixed
bloods was worse nor full blacks or full whites, and I was afraid how
the youngster might turn out. When we was out shepherdin', and in
the evenings, Caloona used to tell me tales o' her mother's tribe, how
they quarrelled and fought, and in the end murdered each other,
sometimes, perhaps, for the sake of an emu-skin. As the boy got
older I couldn't bear to hear her laugh over them things. Then I
thought, 'It's no use beginning to teach the boy if the mother knows
no better.' So I began to learn her to read and write. She was not
long in learning to read out of a big Testament my mother give to
me when I was leaving the old country. But she didn't seem able to
take in as Jesus Christ was man and God, and she gave Him a native
name as vexed me—meaning, 'him as makes believe.' And I suppose
I couldn't explain proper, for when I tried most hard she would
go off in a fit of laughing, and the youngster would wake up and
laugh too, fit to crack his sides, and somehow, when the two laughed
in that way, it used to rile me oncommon. The boy was very sharp—
everyone as saw him said that—but somehow he was sharpest in
doing things he oughter not to do; and when I was trying to teach
him like he allays seemed duller, and given to cryin', and his mother
used to watch me, her hands all of a tremble at whatever she was
doing.

'"Well, Miss Stella, to make a long story short, when the boy was
a few weeks over seven I found him setting a puppy on to some sheep
with young lambs. I took him by the hand to the hut, and before pun-
ishing him I asked why he did such a thing. His mother stood there
shiverin', looking at us, and the boy burst out cryin' and denied it
hard an' fast. He said he was callin' the dog off. This riled me so
much that on the instant I give him a bad thrashin'—worse, I know,
nor I should have—so that the mother turned on me very fierce like.
I got into a bad Scot,* an' told her if she didn't let me bring up the
boy proper she had better clear. In course, I never meaned a word of

it, and never thought as Caloona would take it to heart. But the boy sulked and would eat no food, an' made believe he was very badly hurt. God knows, perhaps he was, though I didn't believe a word of it, an' I felt very hard agin him for telling such barefaced lies. Next day his mother stayed in the hut with him, and wouldn't even look at me when I was going out. When I came home that night they were both gone, an' from that day to this I never set eyes on them. 'What became of them, an' where are they now?' that's what I says to myself over an' over agin. An', then, a week ago, before the lamp was lighted, I saw the boy out there at the window in the rain as plain as I see you now, Miss Stella.

'"This morning the Canon said as I ought to take the Sacryment, and I was thinking over things. The moment I heered your voice I says to myself, 'I'll tell Miss Stella; she'll understand as 'twasn't through my being such a bad lot.' I haven't got very much longer to live, and I've many times heard that at the last people felt quieter like if they told all that was on their minds. I couldn't tell the Canon, Miss Stella; for in course he'd tell his wife, an' then Lord only knows how many melancholry psalmses she'd read to me next day! An' yet 'twas through trying to do my best that it all come out wrong, as it were. I never told a word of this to my wife; what'd be the good? 'Twould only fret her."

'The more simply anything is told, the more is lost in re-telling it with the cold little snout of a pen. The very *mise-en-scène**—the homely little room—the door leading into the kitchen behind, where the worn-out wife rested—everything so quiet and common-place— the rain dashing against the small window, through which the sick man fancied he saw his half-savage boy out in the gloom—all helped to make a quiet but forceful seizure on the heart. Thomson had hardly ceased speaking when Mr Ferrier entered. The moment I saw him it flashed across my mind that the half-caste boy he told us of some time before might be Thomson's child. The poor man was so exhausted that in a few minutes he fell fast asleep. I motioned Mr Ferrier to the window, and asked him if he knew anything of that lad's mother. Yes; she had been at the Mandurang Mission six months before she died. Her native name was Caloona. I told him Thomson's story as briefly as possible. "Oh, how wonderful are the ways of the Lord!" he ejaculated at the close—not very relevantly, I thought.

'The sick man was soon wakened by a fit of coughing. When this was over, Mr Ferrier took his hand and said: "My friend, instead of reading to-day, will you let me tell you a little incident that happened at the Mandurang Mission Station?" Thomson nodded a weary assent, as if he knew beforehand that this could have no interest for him. I was about to slip away, but Thomson asked me to stay a little longer. The ex-missionary's little incident was soon told: How, late at night, a young half-caste woman, with a boy of nine, came to the mission spent with illness and weary wandering. She had lived for years with white people, and then gone back to her tribe. But the savage life was too much for her, and when her strength began to fail she found her way to the mission, anxious to have her boy properly cared for after her death.

'When he learned the names of the mother and son, Thomson's strength seemed to return to him in a strange way. He half sat up, his face all alight, asking a torrent of questions.

'With the tenderness of a gentle-hearted woman Mr Ferrier gave full details. He divined that this strong, rugged nature, wearied with mortal illness, stricken with remorse for the past, craved hungrily for all that could be told him of the poor fugitive mother and her boy.

'"A few days before her death she seemed to wander," said Mr Ferrier, "and she kept on saying: 'We got back to the Stone Hut one evening—big one tired and hungry; but strange man there and we went away. Me want to tell masser boy very good now; but masser gone.'" There was the sound of deep sobs in the room, and Mr Ferrier's voice failed him. I went to the little window and looked out. The sky was overcast, and on the horizon sheet-lightning played in wide flames. There was thunder in the air, and the atmosphere was heavy, and made me feel that the world is full of desolate women and fugitive children. The murmur of voices went on after a pause— question and answer—and then the one grave voice, with its fervent accents:

'"They are buried in one grave in the mission churchyard at Mandurang. Not far from them my own wife and only daughter lie buried. Ah, my dear friend, their dust reposes there in the sure and certain hope of the resurrection of the just.* In the words of a holy man of old, 'Every body, whether it is dried up into dust or dissolved into moisture, or is compressed into ashes, or is attenuated into smoke, is withdrawn from us, but is reserved for God in the custody of the elements.'"* I do not know that poor Thomson took in much of this. "She went back again—she went back again," he said several times, in a low voice.

'"I knew well the youngster was dead ever since I seen him at the window," he whispered to me as I went away. I spare you my reflections, as I walked home in the gathering dusk, on the strangely pathetic threads mingled in the yarn of all lives when we know something of their inward history. What passionate affections to end in a little mound of earth! What fears and agitation and anguish that avail nothing! What vivid hopes held close in the heart, only to vanish fruitlessly as morning mist! What glowing plans, stretching out into the coming years, to end in bitter disillusion and disenchantment with life!'

CHAPTER XVII

IT was the first week in July before Stella left home for her visit to Melbourne and Lullaboolagana. This delay was occasioned by her mother's illness, which at first seemed trifling, but eventually developed into slow fever. At its worst—and the worst lasted four or five days—the gravest fears were entertained as to the issue. During this time Stella could not be prevailed upon to leave her mother day or night, except at very short intervals. She could sleep only by snatches, and affirmed that she was more rested in the sick-room than she could be elsewhere. Periodical sleeplessness was the only ailment from which she had suffered since her childhood, and at this anxious period her incapacity for sleep took a very pronounced form.

As soon as the invalid was fit to travel, it was arranged that she should accompany Mrs Raymond, the widowed daughter, to her Coonjooree property—a small sheep-station in the Tatiara district,* distant from Adelaide by rail half a day's journey and a quarter of a day's drive.

'You look as much in want of rest as I do, my child,' the mother said fondly, when the preliminary arrangements were made, and Stella sat, pencil in hand, jotting down memoranda of the things Maisie, who was to accompany her in the capacity of maid, should pack up for two or three months' absence from home.

'Do I look like an invalid, mother, really?' she said with a bright smile. 'Esther, why don't you ask me to your sanatorium for the sake of my health? It will sound so dignified.'

'My dear, you know I would be only too happy; but Mrs Tareling is in despair at your already missing the most brilliant part of the season.'

'Yes; and to make up for missing more, I shall come to Coonjooree for a week. You were afraid to tempt me? Have you not yet learned that to be tempted and fall is our one form of wisdom in some things?'

'Well, that is a delightful item added to our programme,' said Mrs Raymond. 'The old place will be almost forsaken for two months.'

'Yes, July and August. The memoirs of the Courtland family during this time, in the year of grace 188—,* were strewn with events. Fairacre, the paternal home, inhabited only by Tom and Alice, in the guardianship of the Misses Kendall. Esther, I should like to be an invisible onlooker during this régime. Oh, can't you imagine how the two dear Quaker doves will spend their time in chivying after Allie with wraps when she goes out into the garden with Felix? And then there will be Tom and Fanny—of course they will be engaged before we come back.'

'And you, my dear—what will have happened in your case?' said the elder sister wistfully.

'Oh, I shall be two or three months older!' laughed Stella.

There was a difference between her and Mrs Raymond of thirteen years, but there was a bond of sympathy between the two which was independent of all differences of age and experience.

Stella's week at Coonjooree lengthened into ten days.

'Laurette will understand the fascination that the Mallee Scrub has for one,' said Stella, laughing, as she recalled Mrs Tareling's undisguised horror of Cannawijera,* the station settled on her by her father, and distant from Coonjooree about fifteen miles.

And yet to many the Mallee Scrub,* like all deserts, comes to have an inexplicable charm. To realize the change that may gradually be wrought on the mind in this respect, one should, perhaps, enter the Mallee country when the mask of night is falling on the land, and travel for hours under a moon struggling ineffectually for supremacy with driving clouds. In the uncertain light all that can then be seen is an endless succession of densely-scrubbed, low, undulating rises, or plains that stretch indefinitely on every side with clumps of scrub cypress rising here and there above the Mallee bushes. The traveller should further be a guest at one of those home-stations in which a stranger asks himself incredulously what he has ever done to deserve the unbounded hospitality and kindness showered on him. It should be winter-time—or what stands for winter in this dry waterless region. He should waken at sunrise, and gaze for the first time at the Mallee Scrub in the light of day through an eastern window. And there the scene that meets his eye, far and wide as he may have wandered, will be stored in the cells of memory for all time to come. The sight has in it something which compels him to dwell on it long and fixedly, and turn to it again and again, while a strange weight falls on the heart, and the mind for some time vainly seeks a clue to the mingled and contradictory feelings that are awakened.

There, as far as the eye can reach, lies tier beyond tier in endless succession, low chains of ranges, with dense gray-green bushes, tall brown clumps of grass-trees, with patches of white and yellow sand showing between. During winter in the early mornings the sky is often one unbroken mass of gray clouds. As the sullen red in the east that proclaims sunrise dies away, there is no tint or suggestion of colour anywhere visible in heaven or earth. All around, without break or alloy, are the uniform monotonous tones of sand and gray-green bushes; above is the more sombre gray of clouds, in which the eye vainly loses itself, seeking for a lighter tinge. They are so austere and thickly piled—those clouds that promise rain, but pass away oftentimes week after week without a shower. They hide the blue of heaven, and the sunshine, and rigidly shroud the horizons, as if to make the picture more ineffaceable—an arid, formless mass above a sombre, colourless desolation. It is as though one came upon the rigid skeleton of a spent world, or upon a living presentment of primeval chaos, when the earth was without form and void.

A bitter loneliness falls upon the spirit. All the well-loved sunny nooks of the earth seem so far away. Life seems so fleeting—happiness so unreal. The mind is thrown in on itself, and an immense ennui takes possession of the heart—clutches it, oppresses it, as though it were suddenly touched by a heavy hand. It is as though all that men most cling to in life passed away like mist before the sun, till nothing remained but this arid wilderness, without the song of bird, or sound of water, or gleam of flower, or even the over-arching foliage of a tree. In these regions, severe and desolate as the Dead

Sea wilderness, in which the Son of Man was assailed by the great enemy of souls,* the petty distinctions for which men and women scramble and cheat and lie in everyday life shrink into trivial toys. These vast parched domains, lying in all their nakedness under a sunless sky, have nothing to befool the soul. They have a terrible sincerity in whose cold light not the picture which we so fondly weave of life, but life itself in all its pale disenchantment, makes a sudden seizure on the questioning spirit. In such an hour the multitudinous trifles that choke the soul like the white ashes of a burnt-out wood-fire are blown away as with the breath of a strong west wind winnowing the chaff from the grain. In face of so stern a solitude we cease to deceive ourselves.

The country is not wild. It is in appearance sterile to a degree; it is tame; it is dull; it is oftentimes solitary as a tomb. Few see it for the first time without experiencing a causeless melancholy—nay, often dark forebodings, as of some dread disaster slowly drawing nearer; and yet this wears away, and the country (how is one to account for it?) comes to have a fascination of its own. It is so silent, so severe, so implacable in its veracity. It has no arts with which to allure, no winning surprises, no breaks in its uniformity through the greater part of the year. And though at first this scenery agitates and weighs on those who lie open to the charms that usually draw us to nature, yet after the first shock is over this strange landscape bends the mind to itself, and gains a subtle hold on it—a hold based not so much on tenderness as confidence. It fulfils far more than it promises. Notwithstanding its parched and barren appearance, a little irrigation makes it blossom into wonderful fertility: and though no water is ever seen on its surface, it is believed by those who know the region best that great reservoirs extend far below these infinite leagues of sandy ground. The theory is so far borne out by the fact that, where artesian wells have been sunk in this district, water has been struck in overflowing abundance. Fruit-trees planted where water is available are in four and five years loaded with luscious fruit. Here, as in so many other directions, Nature waits to be governed by obedience to her conditions. Dig, and ye shall find; water, and ye shall reap.* If the principle that anyone who makes wasteland productive became its owner were enforced, the Mallee Scrub, instead of being a barren waste, even in appearance, might soon become a great granary of fruit and corn. But even in its present state it has a brief hour of beauty. In the zenith of the Australian spring this scrub is in places sheeted in blossoms: brilliant little orchids; scarlet and yellow pea-like flowers; the pale lemon blossom of the native clematis; the small purple geraniums, with their poignant fragrance when crushed under foot—these, and many other wild blossoms as yet, alas! nameless to the laity, invest the country with a charm all the more deeply felt because of the contrast between these fleeting weeks and the sombre monotony which prevails during the rest of the year.

In July the country was at its dreariest, for the rains which fall, oftentimes with tropical fury, are instantly absorbed by the sand, whose thirst is never satiated; and though there is then more herbage than through the drought of the summer, the uniformity of tints is seldom varied. The sombre olive of the Mallee shrubs; the sterner green of the dwarf honeysuckle, whose pointed leaves when ruffled by the wind show their silver under-lining, like pale buds that never blossom; the solemn deep-sea hue of the scrub cypress; the pallid sage-green of the salt-bush—all are minor tones in the same sad, monotonous, lacklustre hues; yet day by day, as Stella became more intimate with the Mallee Serub, its nameless attractions grew on her. And one day, as she rambled miles away with the two elder children, she discovered a whole range-side of early epacris. The brief blossoming season of the region was yet two months off, yet here were acres of this radiant native heath, white, and scarlet, and tender pink. The feast this made for the eyes in the midst of the harsh setting all round made Stella feel as if for the first time she knew what the joy of colour meant. And then they were constantly coming upon stores of white immortelles*—those snowy blossoms of the desert, so lightly rooted in the sand, it seems as though a passing breath would bear them afar. But no; though the sand-laden wind blows shrill and high, the everlasting-flowers of the wilderness remain in myriads of loosely-rooted clumps. The snowy coronals of silky petals round their deep-gold hearts, on brownish dry stalks, with a few slender leaflets sadly gray-green as the salt-bush itself, all give a tender charm to the flowers. They are scentless, and have none of the dewy bloom of ordinary blossoms; but, seeing that their faces are seldom wet with rain, and that the tips of their roots never touch water, the marvel is that their pensive radiance ever illuminates this parched-up land. Of all the flowers that grow, they are those that one may pluck with least compunction. Weave them into photograph-wreaths or thimble-baskets, and at the end of two years they are as white and silken as on the day they left their native scrub.

CHAPTER XVIII

IT was to these placid pursuits that Stella devoted herself on the afternoon preceding her departure for Melbourne. During the past few days she had experienced a curious shrinking from the visit. To read and sew and meditate, to listen to her mother's gentle voice, to wage mimic warfares with her sister over their best beloved authors, to ramble with the children, looking for new flowers and strange birds, seemed just then the plan of life best worth having.

These tranquil days succeeding hours of acute anxiety soothed her into a mood in which the prospect of change and the clamour of strange voices repelled her. She knew so well how she would weary of herself in the society of women whose highest ideal of life was to stifle it with futile details. And then the inevitable meeting with Ted disturbed her in anticipation. In the solitude of the Mallee Scrub those vagrant glimpses of a future wholly pledged to him came to wear the air of a grotesque dream. But she told herself that the strong temptation which assailed her to break faith with Laurette was only another example of her instability. And now Maisie was engaged in labelling the luggage for their early departure in the morning, and Stella sat with her sister in the western veranda busily weaving the immortelles she had gathered with the children that morning.

'I solemnly entrust these four photograph-wreaths to your charge, Esther,' she said, as she gave the finishing touches to one. 'All my life I have seen these little wreaths round pictures, but never have I had any for myself till now.'

'And whose will your pretty wreaths honour?' asked the elder sister.

'One for father and mother—that last one taken of them together—one for you, one for Cuthbert, and one left over.'

'Ah! perhaps for a "nearer one still, and a dearer"?'*

'Yes; if he has to sail the salt dividing seas, and go to strange countries, and kill lions like enclosed birds, etc.'

'But why these hard conditions?'

'Oh, just the power of association. Don't you know the way girls have of hanging a man in a cosy nook in their own rooms—a bearded, sun-burnt being, who is away exploring, or in the Northern Territory, or pearling, or gold-digging, or taking stock across an unknown tract of the Continent? There the pictures are so safe and snug, with white everlasting flowers round them, while the men themselves—goodness only knows what they are doing, or what is happening to them in the wilds.'

Stella wreathed a few more immortelles into places less thickly covered, and then held the wreath at a little distance to judge it more critically.

'Yes, that will do; it is worthy to surround the picture even of the unknown one,' she said, with a dawning smile.

'Stella, will you think me inquisitive? Tell me all there is to tell about your unknown partner at the Emberly ball. I have heard broken hints and laughing allusions from Alice,' said Esther, regarding her sister narrowly.

'It is only Alice's idea of a joke,' said Stella, but she coloured slowly. 'There is not much to tell, but I will tell you. Shortly after the ball began Mrs Leslie came up to me just after a dance, saying, "There is a friend of my husband's, a stranger here, who wishes to be introduced." Some woman seized upon her at the moment to ask a score of questions about the Leslies' departure for Europe. They were going, you know, the very next day. Then Mrs Leslie tore herself away and led the stranger to me, and all I heard was, "Miss Stella," and I think, perhaps, "Doctor——"; but I am not sure, and I rather hoped I did not hear aright.'

'But why?'

'Well, it is very stupid; but this stranger had what you might call a distinguished air, with a noble brow, and a look as of one dissoci-ated from the vulgar tide of life.'

'But surely a doctor may be and look every inch a gentleman?'

'He may; but then, as a rule, he is not—with us, at any rate. He is the highly-respectable bourgeois, who has taken to expensive habits of living before he can quite afford it. And so he must have a great deal of "tact," and cultivate a trick of looking wise, and of listening reverently to the twaddle of a rich hypochondriac; and, in short, of all the professions, the medical is the one that most easily degener-ates into a trade.'

'I think, my dear, you are prejudiced. What about your beloved Dr Stein?'

'But then, you see, he is a German. Oh, you may laugh; but culture lies at the root of all the professions in Germany far more than in England. As I know neither country, except from an Australian standpoint, I feel qualified to pronounce judgment. But seriously, now—isn't your average doctor exactly like your average pianiste, profoundly out of touch with most of the wider issues of thought or research?'

'But, you see, the profession is a very arduous one. To be a successful doctor a man must be a specialist to a great extent.'

'To be a successful doctor a man, as a rule, gets into the narrowest of grooves; and the more money he makes the more furniture and gew-gaws he heaps about him, instead of limiting his practice and dusting his mind a little more. I don't know whether it is matrimony that destroys the profession, as it ruins the influence of the Protestant clergy.'

'Stella—Stella! you are incorrigible about marriage,' said Esther, laughing. 'The worst of it is you partly mean all you say. But we are not getting on very fast. Let us conclude that the stranger was not a doctor, though, after all, if he resembled his friend Dr Leslie——'

'Yes; he also is one of the exceptions. But, then, the stranger had the look of one so much—how shall I say it?—devoted to ideas, and not jostled up with the meannesses of ordinary life. And then his mind had an alert literary kind of side to it. You might very well retort on me by asking how I should judge of all this; but, you know, one gets so awfully and wonderfully weary of the commercial stamp of mind and face, one quickly recognises the difference.'

'You must have had a good deal of talk with him.'

'Yes; we wasted no time, not even in dancing. He danced only square dances, and after going through a quadrille we sat out a waltz, which stretched into nearly two more dances. Yes; it sounds rather serious, but so much depends on the way things happen—and you must know we were not on a staircase, nor the recesses of a conservatory, nor on a veranda lit only by moonlight—we were in one of those alcoves that Allie and I have raved about ever since; and in front there was dear, amiable Mrs Marwood and a large elderly lady from the country, who seemed to have daughters married in every known quarter of the globe. There the two good old dames sat chatting away like two fountains, and there were we two others getting more and more charmed with each other in the irresponsible way of people who meet once—at least, I hope he was charmed with me; I can answer for myself.'

'Oh no! I dare say he was dreadfully bored,' said Esther, smiling. 'And, then, was there not a wonderful Tasmanian fern that partly screened you from the partners you cheated?'

'Yes; a tall, graceful creature, with hundreds of yellowish-green and dusky-brown fronds drooping one over the other, and baby ones curled up tight, fold within fold, looking as though they had taken a vow never to emerge from their infant dreams of the woodland dell where they first saw the light.'

'I should very much like to know what you two others talked of, but perhaps it was too much *à cœur ouvert et à langue déliée** to be confided to a mere elder sister?'

'Oh, nonsense! But what remains of the talk that has delighted us most? One may as well try to recall a walk on the seashore on a summer night. There was the moonlight and the "sparkle of the glancing stars,"* and there were the waves breaking on the beach, and others coming after them endlessly; but how much can we convey of the scene to another?'

'A good deal,' smiled Esther. 'Do I not remember how your first exercises in composition were writing conversations down verbatim? The pieces of moonlight globed in crystal, as I have heard Allie call the electric light in the alcoves, the flowers, and the crush of people, and the wonderful Austrian band—all that would make talk after a first dance, but not for so very long.'

'Well, after our quadrille my partner said he was only in Adelaide two days. He had just landed, and was on his way to some of the other colonies, though he had fallen into such a piece of luck. I thought it was a very fleeting form of fortune, and said:

> 'Das Glück ist eine leichte Dirne
> Und bleibt nicht lang am selber Ort.'*

A pleased look came into his face. His mother was a German, though brought up in England, and the language was his second mother-tongue. I read Heine, then? Oh yes; and nearly all the German writers; and I had translated Goethe. His face fell comically. I know he was astounded at such conceit, and—you know what a delightful sensation it is to see a little downright fun looming on the horizon— so I said with unmoved seriousness, "I know Kant, too, very well; and it is a great consolation, for when the hairdresser comes to dress my hair for a ball I pass the time by remembering bits out of the 'Kritik of Pure Reason.'"'

'Oh, Stella! what put such a comical thought into your head? Of course, he found you out then?'

'Yes; and we both laughed heartily; and that, you know, is like eating salt together—it is a sort of mental latchkey. When Tom came to claim his dance after my partner and I had sat out a waltz we were both in Rome. I told Tom I would let him off his duty dance, and so we still talked on. An unfortunate man slipped and fell with his partner in front of our alcove. "Surely that is one of the thirty-six tragic situations of life," said my partner. I said there must be a great many more than thirty-six, and we began to count; but we fell out at once. He declared existence would be honeycombed with tragedy if my contentions as to tragic situations were allowed. We grew serious and laughed the next moment, and flouted each other's arguments. "But I will tell you one of the thirty-six," he said: "to dance and talk, and then to part." I was just on the point of saying, "Especially if you do not know your partner's name," when, to my horror, there was Mr Andrew Harrison, and the polka-mazurka, for which he was down on my programme, almost over.'

'I suppose you did not say you would let him off his duty dance? And did you and your unknown partner meet no more?'

'No; we smiled and bowed and parted, and I saw him no more. And the Leslies sailed next morning; and, of course, the Emberlys could tell nothing of any special stranger, there were so many whose names and faces were equally unknown to them. Now are you satisfied?'

'It is like the beginning of a story—an overture that should be followed by a concert. I wonder——'

Esther paused abruptly, scanning her sister's face with an inquiring look.

'You must not get on the wrong track, Esther,' said Stella, who was now weaving a little thimble-basket out of some everlastings that were left. 'Tom and Allie could not get over my sitting out nearly three dances with anyone. I never did such a thing before; but the attraction was unexpectedly meeting someone who seemed to have all the makings of a friend in him.'

'A friend, my dear? Like Willie Stein and Mr Harrison, I suppose?'

'How horrid you can be, Esther! It is the very fact that most men have so few strings to their nature that makes one so soon under-stand the sort of people that are different. I have for a long time thought that one of the greatest pleasures of life would be a real, great, lasting friendship. It takes so much to form a true one. There is, as a wise man says, in human nature generally more of the fool than of the wise.* Yet the part of us which is not a fool responds so gladly to the sane, enlightened strain of another mind. But it must be different from one's own. That is why the best friendships require the difference of sex.'

'How very sage and calm that sounds,' said Esther, with an amused expression. 'But, after all, what shoals there are! Most men and women are either married or expect to be.'

'And yet my pair of friends must be single or widowed. They must have an interest—and a deep one—in books, but still deeper in life itself, so that they are like the spectators of a play in which nothing can happen that has not some significance. Only life being so much greater, so much wider, and more complex than any picture of it can possibly be, it always strikes people—men and women especially—from opposite points of view.'

'You are quite convinced that your ideal friendship must be based not only on difference of sex, but dissimilarity of view? Well, you may be right, but how long would it last between two disengaged people? How many weeks would pass before that strong interest in books, and in the general play of human affairs, would be centralized?'

'Oh, Esther, you are too tiresome. Of course, that is the rock on which the ordinary friendship of an ordinary man and woman strikes—and it is odious—it is worse than disillusionment.'

'My dear, you have gone through the process more than once,' said Esther, a smile hovering round her lips.

'Yes; and the soft, silly look that comes into a man's eyes—the way in which he is perpetually on the look-out for some point of personal vantage—for the opportunity of paying some inane compliment—of course all that is the very antipodes of true unbiassed intercourse. Flattery is the lethal spot of friendship. It is the cryptogram for betrayal.'

'And yet I suppose friendship, like love, must be nourished by admiration to some extent.'

'Yes; but then love, or at all events, the thinglet that usually goes by that name, is always seeking its own ends, whereas friendship— well, it is a root of that divine severe force which constantly calls upon us to be true to our best capabilities. "No receit openeth the heart, but a true friend to whom you may impart griefs, joys, fears, hopes, suspicions, counsels, and whatsoever lieth upon the heart to oppress it, in a kind of civil shrift or confession." And again, "The best preservative to keep the mind in health is the faithful admonition of a friend."* You know who says this?'

'Yes; but how rare such intercourse is between man and woman.'

'So it is, and that makes it all the more precious.'

'Well, if ever you form such a friendship, Stella, you must tell me, and do not conceal the end,' said Esther with a smile.

By this time the sun had set, and a light mist hung over the sombre ranges that stretched westward, giving them a mysteriously limitless aspect, as though they extended beyond the confines of the world. This impression was deepened by low masses of clouds driven before a rising wind. The outlines were so uncertain and broken, and the prospect so wide and lonesome and silent, that the whole formed a picture which for weird austerity could hardly be surpassed.

'I'll tell you what, you must live at Coonjooree, and ask me to stay with you, Esther,' said Stella. 'I am only just beginning to find out all the allurements of the place. Last night I watched the moon setting, and the look of the desert in the pale lessening light was indescribably solemn. The place seems to have been created to make up striking pictures that somehow make one in love with desolation.'

'And to carry a sheep to three acres—don't forget the sheep, Stella. Would you really come and stay here with me? But I confess I would be afraid of so much solitude. One must be either older or younger than I am for that. I think we had better set off on our travels, you and I and the children, and their governess——'

'Do you not find it chilly out there, my dears? There is such a charming fire of Mallee roots here,' said Mrs Courtland, opening the window under which her daughters were sitting in the veranda.

The twilight was deepening, and the clouds were gathering more impenetrably. But within the quiet, warm little drawing-room, fragrant with the breath of violets, it was that charmed hour when the hearth 'smiles to itself and gilds the roof with mirth,' and it would be 'a sin to light the lamps as yet.'* Some old writers speak of a substance called Babylonian naphtha, which is so inflammable that it kindles into flame if it is placed near fire without touching it.* Old dry Mallee roots when split up have something of that quality. They are strangely twisted and gnarled, as if the waterless wastes in which they grew had thwarted and stunted them till they are fit emblems of a defeated existence. But when they break into flame, it is as though they pass into a brief life of ecstatic joy. No other wood makes so vivid and pure a fire. The flames are a delicate clear jonquil. The roots on the least touch flash into ardent, lustrous arrows of light, whose glow seems to warm the mind as well as the body.

The mother and her daughters sat round this glancing, softly brilliant fire, and talked of the past and future, of things that had been and that were to be, in the calm unapprehensive way which gradually returns even to those who have sustained many of the storms and shocks of life.

CHAPTER XIX

HER brother was absent in Tasmania when Stella arrived in Melbourne. For the first two days nothing more noteworthy than drives and calls and invitations to coming festivities marked the hours. The 'smaller house' which the Tarelings had taken was in Toorak, 'one of our most fashionable suburbs, as I dare say even you may see,' Laurette said, as they drove by spacious mansions and large, well-kept grounds. Monico Lodge was not distinguished by these advantages. It had that irritating pretentiousness about it which takes the form of several large reception-rooms and diminutive sleeping apartments. When Stella entered her room she looked round it with a feeling of comical dismay. It seemed as though the walls were not far enough apart to enable her to breathe freely. As for the dressing-room, in which Maisie slept, the wardrobe filled it up so completely that the poor maid seemed to have been smuggled into the closet for some nefarious purpose. There was a conservatory devoted entirely to exotics and gardeners' plants, but there was no garden; and the 'grounds,' a most conventionally formed snippit of land, were chiefly adorned with trees which refused to grow, rooted in tubs that refused to be concealed.

But even more uncongenial than these surroundings was Laurette's constant society, with her unconcealed triumph at being in the thick of all that was most distinguished and fashionable in Melbourne, as she herself expressed it. When this triumph seemed on the point of being a little dimmed, she fell into transports of delight at the prospect of an indefinite stay in town.

'If Talbot had not made this lucky hit in mining shares, I could only have been here for a couple of weeks,' she said, 'what with the low price of wool and papa's fearful losses with the rabbits. He has given us a great deal of money from time to time, but he has turned very rusty of late. As for Ted, you might as well ask a doornail for money. I hope he will marry some nice girl soon who will teach him to despise filthy lucre a little.' This with a side-long look at Stella, who laughed at this pious aspiration, but made no comment.

Everything jarred upon her so much that at first she could not even write a letter. The day after her arrival she sent a telegram to Coonjooree, proposing to write the next day. On the morrow she wrote a post-card. On the third day she scolded herself seriously, and sat down at her desk. She had only written the words, 'My darling Mother,' when she leant her head on her hand and went into a long reverie, during which a curiously wistful, softened expression came into her eyes. She was roused by a tap at the door.

'Are you here, Stella?' It was Laurette, and she wore an impromptu air of surprise. 'Guess who has come?' she said, with an arch smile.

'Oh, Cuthbert!' exclaimed Stella, her face radiant, as she hastened to join him.

'No; your brother cannot be here till the evening. It is Ted.'

Stella's face flushed, but it did not escape Laurette's keen gaze that with this deepening colour the sudden radiance of gladness died away.

'He is so delighted to find that you are here. I hadn't time to say three words when he sent me off for you. I must interview the cook about luncheon. You will find Ted in the breakfast-room.'

There was something in Laurette's tone and manner which Stella greatly resented; but it was, on the whole, easier to ignore this than call it in question.

Edward Ritchie met her in the hall, and took both her hands in his with so eager and impassioned an air that Stella instinctively stepped back and drew her hands quickly away, saying lightly, to hide her confusion:

'At last I shall know whether you have been in Egypt or Central Australia.'

'You look thinner than you used to, Stella,' said the young man, so absorbed in gazing at her that it seemed as though he heard nothing.

'And you—you have grown stouter. Yes, really, Ted, you remind one of the beauties in the Arabian tales.'

'Like the beauties! Oh, come now, Stella, draw it mild. What kind of beauties were they?'

'Oh, they used to have adventures. Sometimes they were put in a box, the box in a chest with seven locks on it, and placed at the bottom of the sea, beneath the roaring waves.* Sometimes they were put in baskets sewn up with red thread.* But whatever happened to them, they always turned up all right again, with faces like the moon in the fourteenth night.'*

'So that's why you compared me to those beauties, Stella. Well, I couldn't believe you were paying me a compliment. But tell me now, are you glad to see me?'

'Oh yes, of course. But why do you always alight like a bomb? Is the wind from the east?'

'Oh, bother the wind! Tell me all about yourself. Have you been well all the time? I don't believe you have. You used not to have circles under your eyes; and they look bigger.'

'The better to see you with,' answered Stella, smiling.

The most obvious quotation, however, was always thrown away on Ted.*

'But why are you not looking well?' he persisted.

'Well, you know, mother had a fever. But dancing is good for me; so I have come to stay with Laurette, that I may dance for weeks before going into the Bush.'

'How often will you dance with me, Stella?'

'Well, that depends; you used to waltz out of time. Have you had any practice during your travels?'

'What travels? You seem to think I have been gallivanting about amusing myself, whereas—oh, Stella, I barely know how to hold myself with joy for seeing you again. And, do you know, you hardly shook hands with me!'

'But if someone held your ten fingers in a vice, could you shake hands?'

'Well, give me your hand again; I will not hold it hard. Or, I'll tell you what, you just hold my hand about as tight as you wish me to hold yours. You see, I'm perfectly reasonable.'

'Thank you, Ted. The way I want you to hold my hand is not to touch it at present. We have a little Irishman who comes to work at Fairacre, and I have learned to talk Irish, you see.'

Stella was sitting on a low chair near the fire. Ritchie stood over her, leaning against the mantelpiece. Carried away by a sudden impulse, he knelt down and held her hands to his lips. They were so hot that they seemed to scorch her fingers.

'Oh, but really, Ted, it appears to me that you are too absurd!' she said, the feeling of amusement with which this faithful squire usually inspired her struggling with a sense of growing discomfort.

'Do you remember the last time I saw you?' he asked, drawing a chair close beside her.

'I cannot speak to you, Ted, without twisting my neck. Do, please, go a little further off.'

'Oh, hang it all! Haven't I been far away long enough?'

He tried to hold her hands in his. She slipped away and took a chair opposite to him.

'Now we can talk comfortably,' she said. 'Tell me, have the rabbits eaten all your father's sheep, as Laurette says?'

'Do you remember how long it is since we parted?'

'We are just like two people in a burlesque,' said Stella, smiling. 'We fire off question after question without once answering each other.'

'Well, why don't you answer me, and sit down nearer to me, and be a little jollier?'

'But that is the point. I would not be at all jolly if I twisted my neck. Oh, I assure you it is much worse than spraining one's ankle.'

'Do you remember the day we parted so many months ago?' persisted Ritchie.

He was a man to whom rapid thought was impossible. But it was equally impossible to divert his mind from the point of view which was uppermost with him.

'Oh, heavens! yes. I remember everything,' cried Stella, with her low merry laugh—a laugh that always had a magical charm for her companion.

'You remember everything,' he repeated slowly. 'I am glad of that, for you know very well——'

He stopped abruptly. His eyes had been fixed on Stella's face intently, and he noticed that it grew cold and a trifle hard. The change made his heart heavy with apprehension.

'Yes; what do I know very well?' she answered, taking up the ravelled thread with an impatient weariness.

She felt that this long serio-comic wooing must end once for all. Then, as she noticed the agitated, breathless way in which Ritchie looked at her, an acute apprehension of all that this long courtship meant to him suddenly smote her, and therewith a pang of remorse as she realized how far she had somehow travelled from the old tolerant half-responsive standpoint, when she had decided that if she married anyone without being in love it must be Ted.

He looked at her for some minutes without speaking, and Stella knew it was because he feared to put the old question into words. She was always ready to see how faulty she was—ready to blame herself where blame was due. She was all the more conscious of any blame that might attach to her in this long intermittent wooing, because by some process which she herself could not have explained, the moment they met it became clearer to her that those fugitive resolves that she harboured from time to time after they last parted, of accepting Ritchie as her lover—her future husband—were, in truth, impossible—or, at least, possible only at some indefinite period—not now.

'Ted, I am very sorry,' she said humbly, after a pause.

'Sorry!' he echoed. 'Why are you sorry? I don't expect you to love me as I love you. It's not the way of girls—like you.' Ted would sometimes make running comments on herself and things in general that amused Stella. Speculations, theories and musings on things in general were quite foreign to his nature, while they were part of her daily atmosphere. And yet she was vaguely conscious that, one-sided as his point of view might be, it rested on contact with more sides of life than were open to her ken. 'If you'll—you'll only just put up with me at first, Stella, I'm willing to run the risk.'

'Oh, it isn't your risk I think of so much,' she answered, looking up into his face smilingly.

He was standing nearer to her again, leaning on the mantelpiece, pulling a large red rose asunder and letting the petals fall on her one by one.

'By the way, I heard Konrad jarred his knee—how is he?' she said, with rather a barefaced attempt at getting away from the subject.

'All right again. But I haven't been thinking much of horses lately. I've had other fish to fry.'

'What fish, Ted?'

'You—mostly.'

'Oh, Ted! To call me a fish, and speak of frying me, and pull that beautiful burning-red rose to pieces at the same time! Why, it had hardly opened, and roses just now are scarce.'

'What would you like me to do?'

'Why, let me see. I think, in this crisis of Australian history, every squatter should study how to exterminate rabbits and conserve water.'

'Confound the rabbits and conserving water! Look here, Stella, you always twist me round your fingers in this way.'

Stella held up her hands deprecatingly.

'What makes you say such dreadful things about my poor fingers?'

'Oh, you know very well what I mean. Time after time I've asked you to marry me, and said to myself, "Now I'll decide it one way or the other." But you turn it into a sort of joke. "What has put this funny notion of marrying into your head, Ted?" you say; or you hold up your fingers before I've said a word, and laugh, saying: "Now, Ted, when you knit your brow in that way it always means something spoony."'

'Oh, Ted! I never used that word—never!' cried Stella, laughing despite her efforts to keep serious.

'Well, it doesn't matter about one word. You know what I mean, don't you?'

'Yes, I know what you mean—and I feel I have been very much to blame.'

'No, you haven't,' retorted Ritchie almost roughly. 'You haven't been to blame; it's me who used to feel that I'd sooner be made a fool of by you than have any other girl throw herself at my head. I've drawn back as frightened as a wombat when you began to be serious.

I wanted things to be the same, for fear I mightn't even come to see you from time to time. But everything must have an end. I'd like you to marry me on any terms—unless—you're not fond of anyone else?'

She did not reply at once, and the young man recalled the hints that his sister had thrown out at Godolphin House.

'Why don't you tell me?' he cried in a husky voice.

'No! But then I can imagine that I could love; and I think, before a woman risks marrying, she should. We have been friends so long, I will be quite frank with you. I have sometimes thought I could marry you since we last parted——'

'Oh, Stella, Stella! God in heaven bless you for saying that,' cried Ted breathlessly.

'But then, Ted, I have oftener thought I could not. I think that we should be a little more alike. It is such a frightful long time——'

'Not always. Some people die off before they're anytime married.'

'But it would be unwise to count on that form of happiness,' answered Stella; and then she gave way to an uncontrollable burst of laughter.

'And as for not being alike,' said Ted, who always enjoyed the girl's merriment even when not a muscle of his own face moved, 'why, there's not many fellows that would care to have their wives like themselves. And I would, perhaps, get a little bit like you after we married, Stella. We would have so much time together at Strath-haye—or we could travel, or whatever you liked.'

The door-handle was turned in an ostentatiously preliminary way, and then Laurette came in.

'Would you mind keeping away for a little longer, Larry?' said her brother; on which Laurette laughed in a knowing way, bowed, and disappeared.

'Oh! how could you, Ted? Laurette will imagine all sorts of absur-dities.'

'She will imagine that we are getting engaged; and that's what's going to happen, Stella. You never could throw me off after all these years. You know that I love you with my whole heart and soul, don't you?'

'I believe that you love me a great deal more than I deserve. But try and put yourself in my place; think how different the thought of marrying me would be if you did not love me.'

'It's no use my trying to think that; I've loved you ever since I was that high,' said Ted, holding his hand four feet from the ground.

'Well, it goes to my heart to think of grieving you; but——'

'Don't, Stella—don't say it. You can't know what a God-forsaken good-for-nothing I'd be if you took away all hope from me. Let's stay as we are and think over it—get used to the thought that you are to be my wife.'

'Don't plead with me so much—it worries me. I feel as if I must give way; and that would be fatal. Do not interrupt me. You don't understand what a hatefully cold-hearted creature I feel when I get indifferent to people.'

'But you are not indifferent to me—not quite?'

'No, not now; but then I see so little of you!'

'Well, I wouldn't be always at home; don't think it. I'm away from Strathhaye sometimes for weeks; and when I'm there, I'm out most of the day. Well, you can laugh as much as you like, though I'll be shot if I can make out often what amuses you so much!'

'Well, you really are too original in some ways. You tell me that sometimes people die off early in married life, and that we would not see much of each other—all by way of encouragement.'

'Yes, because I'm trying hard to follow your lead; though, by Jove! it would go very much against the grain with me either to die or be away from you after we are married.'

'Heavens, you make my flesh creep when you talk as if it were an accomplished fact! There is one thing I want to say to you, Ted.'

'One thing?—say a thousand! Say so many that you will never be done till we are both old and gray-headed.'

'I must go away and write my letters if you are to be so foolish.'

'No, no—no, Stella; I'll be dumb as a sonnet. Tell me the one thing.'

'Those pearls that you left the day before you went away——'

'What about them? Don't you care for them?'

'They are very lovely; but wait a moment.'

Stella went to her room, and presently returned with the morocco case in her hand. On seeing this, Ritchie's face became very sombre.

'It was very kind of you to think of my birthday; only mind you must forget so tiresome an anniversary after I'm twenty-five. But you know I cannot take such a costly gift from you.'

'All I have is yours. Why shouldn't you take this? It's a horseshoe, isn't it? You know that is for luck.'

He pressed the spring, and looked at the pearls.

'No; they are too superb to be given or accepted in a careless way. You must take them back, please: I did not even show them to anyone.'

'Take them back!' repeated Ritchie, his face flushing with vexation. 'What should I do with the damned thing?'

'Is it right for you to say that before me?'

'No; and I beg your pardon. But you should not vex me so much. You *must* keep them. Now, I've got to see my trainer at one o'clock, and after that to take a spin down to St Kilda. But I want you to promise to come out for a ride with me to-morrow morning. I have the neatest, best-bred little colt for you that ever you saw. Now I can see you are trying to think of an excuse.'

'Indeed I am not. I shall be delighted to ride. The air here stifles one. I am only thinking how I shall be dragged to give an account of all these friendly rides and talks the next time the spirit moves you to have a "square understanding."'

'Well, you needn't think anything of the kind. You *have* sometimes thought you could marry me. Why, Stella, I could live on that for a year. The last thing I do at night is to look at your picture. When I look at it to-night, I shall hardly be able to believe you said that. Now put both your hands in mine—I won't hurt them—and say, "God bless you, Ted," the same as you did in the Fairacre garden.'

She gave him her hands, and repeated the words with a little tremor in her voice, which thrilled him through and through with happiness. He held her hands very gently, and lifted them one after the other to his lips, and then he hurried away.

Stella threw herself into an arm-chair. For some moments she was buried in one of those profound meditations in which every faculty of her mind became absorbed in a tyrannous, compulsory looking-on at her own special span of the past as part of an unfathomable enigma. She was presently roused by Laurette's shrill voice.

So Ted had not even stayed to lunch? Oh, she made no complaint. She knew too well that at certain times in a man's life sisters, in common with all the rest of the world, must take a back seat—look on like people in the pit of a theatre, who see as through a glass darkly,* and see little.

Laurette's eyes fell on the pearls, and she uttered a little cry of delight.

'What a splendid jewel! Why, this looks like business, Stella! It's better to be born lucky than rich,* after all.'

Laurette surveyed herself in the mirror of the over-mantel, and held the brooch under her chin admiringly. Then she fastened it in the lisse ruffling of Stella's dress. But Stella quickly unfastened it, put it into the case, and closed it with what Laurette mentally called 'a vicious snap.'

'It does not belong to me,' she said coldly, in answer to Laurette's look of amazed inquiry. 'It is meant for the young woman who has been born more lucky than rich,' she added, with a mischievous smile.

CHAPTER XX

THE Hon. Talbot Tareling was at this time absent at Banjoleena, a new gold-mine which had recently excited much attention. No form of work had ever attracted Mr Tareling unless it was of a light, irregular nature, with a strong element of gambling. Hence, dabbling in mining shares was the one Australian industry he found tolerable. He made erratic excursions to mines from time to time, ostensibly for the purpose of getting the straight tip. This, as a rule, proved very disastrous; but lately Fortune had smiled on him. He long held shares in a mine which neither development nor sensational rumours could galvanize into popularity. By-and-by, however, there was an assay which yielded an enchanting result. Instantly a boom set in in favour of the Celestial Hill Mine. Its dingy branch office in a dingy back street in Melbourne was besieged by eager applicants for shares. Middle-aged women in rusty black; unsuccessful business men, who had long eschewed mining ventures, but had got tired of seeing idle, brainless clerks turning ten-pound notes into fifties; spinsters who had saved one or two hundred pounds by toilsome years of penurious saving; clergymen with families far in excess of their incomes; artisans who were weary of the faded simplicity of investments at seven and six per cent—in a word, that numerous class with whom the longing to widen or enrich life takes the form of narrowing it—who are always preparing to live, but never begin—were especially to the fore in buying Celestial Hills.

It was so safe. It was no bogus concern. It had been worked for a long time, and now they had 'struck oil.' And here was the average: four and a half ounces to the ton; and everyone knew that half an ounce paid. Then scraps of paper would be produced, and rapid memoranda made, and eager faces flushed with excitement at the splendid percentage. It was while the results were at their best on paper that Mr Tareling sold out nearly all the shares he held. A week afterwards they were not worth a withered fig.

Then ugly rumours began to circulate. When people are aching with the loss of money, slander seems to be a balm to the wounded spirit. The mine had been salted;* a false balance-sheet had been drawn up; a clandestine lump of gold had been dropped into the smelting-pot. How was it, too, that the *intimes** of the directors had sold out rump and stump?* Mr Tareling was one of these; but, like Pilate, he washed his hands in public.* He still had all the shares that he originally held; the fact being that the bulk had been bought with his wife's money and in her name. He was supported in his inno-cence by Ozias, the son of Lazarus, popularly surnamed Judas. This man wrote to the press bearing testimony to the childlike faith which the Hon. Talbot Tareling still put in the Celestial Hill gold-mine. On which some people arched their eyebrows, and prophesied that if this scion of an ancient family had recourse to many more testimonials of this kind, his business career in Melbourne would soon be blocked. Naturally all this duplicity rendered Mr Tareling still more wary. He upheld the practice of finding out whether a mine really existed before investing in it. Such a plan, as some of the brokers remarked, would upset any system of mining that had yet been in vogue.

Laurette, in the meantime, found the present in many respects the most beatific season she had ever passed in Melbourne. Her growing intimacy with the viceregal family more than realized her most ardent expectations. She was fast rising to that social eminence in which her dresses, opinions, and parties would form topics of eager interest among women who a short time previously had barely acknowledged her as an equal. If it were not for increasing money difficulties, her enjoyment would have been almost without alloy. But Ted's presence gave her a feeling of security. She vaguely felt that in some way she would turn it to account.

She went with him to the theatre on the evening that followed his arrival, and Stella anticipated the pleasure of a long *tête-à-tête* with Cuthbert, who arrived that afternoon from Tasmania. Alas! it was not an unmixed happiness. What her soul feared had come to pass.

After the first greetings and inquiries were over, Stella fixed her eyes on her brother's face in an inquiring way.

'Cuthbert, you look very radiant. Has anything happened? But no—you came to me the first evening. I am still—— Oh, heavens! you are colouring up to the roots of your hair!'

'But, Stella dear, you misrepresent yourself. You know that you would be the first to congratulate me—to be glad with my gladness.'

'Now you are breaking it to me gently—Nebuchadnezzar, King of the Jews!* Yes, I can bear it all. Is it the Rev. S. Carter's daughter?'

'You are a little witch! You pretended to tremble about these daughters before I ever thought anything about Dora, except what a charming girl she is.'

'As if that were not the Alpha and Omega of the infatuation that precedes marriage.'

'You little heretic! Oh, there is not much of a story, except that we are both perfectly happy. Dora went with her mother to Launceston a week before I did. We met frequently. The day before we left we went mountaineering with a few others. It was all settled before we returned. Mrs Carter charged me with her kind love, and wishes you to come and spend a day, or as long as Mrs Tareling will spare you. Can you come to-morrow? Well, the day after. Dora and I will call before twelve, so that you may see a little of her before you meet the whole family.'

Stella fell in with this arrangement with rather a disconsolate little look.

'And so you are "perfectly happy"? But don't smile too often, Cuth, or you will spoil the serious lines in your face I like so much. Let me look at you sideways. So that's the way one looks when one is first engaged. Ted is stouter than you are; I am afraid the joy of being accepted would quite ruin his profile.'

'You will love Dora, Stella. You cannot imagine what a darling she is—already quite fond of you. I have often shown her your letters, and she is quite charmed with them, except——'

'Ah, I was waiting for the cloven hoof "except."'

'Well, dear, she is very devout, and has the beautiful untroubled faith of childhood. She is vexed to think that you should be so uncertain, so——'

'So infidel—that's the ecclesiastical word.'

A look of pain came into the brother's face, and then, of course, Stella repented.

'I am horribly jealous, I know that,' she said. 'Lay a charm over me, Cuthbert; sprinkle me with holy water; beat a brass pan to drive the evil spirits away—but don't be cross with me.'

'Cross with you, Stella? Have I ever been that? Have I not loved you fondly ever since you were a dear, funny little baby, who would not let people lead you when you were a year old, but preferred all the bumps you got to being held by the hand?'

'Yes, my ownest boy, you have always been to me like a guardian angel. Oh, far better. Yes, let me be unorthodox while Dora isn't here. After all, a guardian angel keeps at a discreet distance, but you——'

To the girl's own astonishment she burst into tears. Her brother, it must be confessed, was rather pleased. He always a little dreaded the vein of hardness—of *diablerie**—of which the 'Satan letter'* was so signal an example, that would at times become apparent in Stella. It clung to his mind at times like a superstition that, in a mood of angry defiance, or disgust, or impatience of the sweet inevitable humdrum of life, she might take some course which would lead to bitter misery, or, at the least, cloud and hamper the better possibilities of her nature. She was human through and through, but a mocking, ironical tone came to her over-readily. She wept very rarely, and when tears did come they became her wonderfully, and made her for a time adorably gentle. But it seemed this was not one of these occasions.

'Can you believe, my dear Stella, that my love for you will ever be less because of other ties? It seems to me rather that this new sweet love makes all other affection deeper and fuller.'

'Yes, dear, I know,' said Stella, smiling through her tears. 'It makes you feel like our Torrens after the winter rains.'

'No, I won't accept that comparison. You must think of a prettier one. Do I not know how the Torrens gets in the drought of summer? Do you believe that the leanness of dry December will ever overtake my love for you?'

'I know you will never be anything but what is dear and good. Still, it is quite evident to me that I must either get converted or married; and I fear of the two the latter is the more practicable. You see, dear,' she said in answer to a half-reproving smile, 'it is not to be endured that I should write or say anything which would vex Dora. So you and I can no longer be intimate friends. Oh, I know the atmosphere in which an *average* clergyman's daughter is brought up. There is a standard for everything—there are so many clauses of a creed, so many articles to be believed. Then all the evil and misery and astounding chaos of life is made out to be a jumble between God and the devil and man's free-will. Sometimes it is one, sometimes the other—but the reputed Creator of all must never be blamed. And in the face of everything there must be an amazing kind of optimism— a thing that leads a precarious kind of existence by brigandage on the understanding, by injecting minute doses of morphia into the pores of reason. Judge how many letters of mine could be anything but a snare and a grief to one who has been saturated with that way of thinking.'

'My dear, you must not talk like that,' he said, taking her slim, fair hands between his brown, vigorous ones. 'If I did not know you so well I should be afraid you and Dora would not get on. But you rail against most people theoretically, and end by charming all—as you certainly will charm this dear new sister who is to be.'

'You speak as though a sister were a kind of rare exotic to me, Cuthbert. Don't forget that I already have six. Yes, certainly I must always count myself, and this, with Hector and Claude's wives, makes up the unromantic half-dozen—then Dora seven. Did you know that the sacredness of the number seven was fast rooted in the pre-Semitic civilization of Babylon?'*

'I know that you are sometimes the most whimsical monkey under the sun, and that to this day I don't always know when you are in fun or in earnest.'

'I am in earnest now, Cuth. I wish you every joy and blessing. Yes; now I have got over the first shock. To-morrow I shall be glad that you are happier; the day after that I shall begin to love Dora. God bless you, Cuthbert!'

She kissed her brother on the forehead, on each cheek, and on the lips—an old form of embrace which she had instituted in token of reconciliation after their rare quarrels in the old childish days.

'I wonder,' said her brother, after a pause, 'when I shall have to congratulate you under the same happy circumstances?'

'Now, if you like, dear, leaving out the happy,' she said solemnly. 'Is Ritchie in town?'

'Yes; he came to-day, and to-morrow morning I go a-riding with him on the trimmest little colt in the world.'

This ride took the form of going to Brighton and a delightful gallop by the seaside, during which the colour leapt into Stella's cheeks with charming vividness, while her eyes seemed to imprison rays from the glancing sparkles of light on the softly-moving waves. Ted could scarcely take his eyes off her face. He longed to say a hundred things, but seeing that she was disinclined to talk, he also kept silent.

It was almost pathetic to notice how implicitly he responded to her moods as far as lay in his power. He did not understand her veiled irony, her bookish allusions, her sudden sparkling merriment at those 'trifles light as air'* which touch the keen edges of a mind fully alive to the incongruities of life. But he understood when she wished to be silent or talk, when she wanted to hear about his horses, and when the wonderful bay colt, who promised to surpass all previous records, became intolerable to her.

Before turning homeward they paused at a little headland. The waves, crested with foam, broke against this in rollicking tumbled masses. There was a breeze fresh enough to ruffle the sea surface, so that the waves stretching out to the vast horizon curled here and there into foam, and broke on the shore with a long-drawn shuddering cadence, which was momentarily lost, and yet rose again, making itself distinct from the deeper symphony of the multitudinous waters far off. There were voices in the sea that morning which made Stella's heart beat as if she were listening to passionate music. Singly and near at hand the waves lisped and prattled; but altogether and far off, what solemn and terrible strength, what possibilities of sudden irretrievable shipwreck! Did they symbolize the Mount Tabors and Gehennas* that darkly lurk within the human soul—its inappeasable longing for happiness—its certainty of storms and sorrows?

'A few moments here are worth a month of stupid Melbourne drawing-rooms, incessantly mimicking other mimicries,' said Stella, taking off her hat, so that the ozone-laden breeze might sweep away the tags and knots of tiresome thoughts that would thrust themselves between her and the sunshine.

'How long are you going to stay with Laurette?'

'Oh, I hardly know. You see, I must be several weeks at Lulla-boolagana, and I want to get back to Adelaide before the spring is over.'

'I hope to be in Adelaide, too, before the spring is over. Shall I come first to Fairacre?'

'Oh yes! I am sure mother and all will be very glad to see you.'

'Won't you?'

'Yes—certainly; but as a friend, mind.'

'Do you know I was quite cut up when I heard there was some talk last year of your leaving the old place.'

'Were you really, Ted? Why?'

'Well, you know, I spent many a happy holiday there. Cuth and I don't chum much now, somehow, but we were very good friends at St Peter's, though he was always miles ahead of me. . . . Do you remember the day we walked up to the weir, and you crouched for half an hour behind a rock watching two mountain ducks or some other comical little brutes that paddled about in the water? . . . Do you remember showing me the head of a bull-dog ant through a microscope? By Jove! I can't imagine how they make a few glasses tell such thundering lies! . . . I believe I remember the first time I saw you—when you were four. Then you came with your mother to stay for a week when you were eight years old. You climbed up to the top of a she-oak tree with me, and told me you liked me ever so much better than Laurette.'

'Now then, Ted!'

'Honour bright you did! You were the jolliest little trump of a girl I ever saw. You played leapfrog with me, and tore the lace of your pinafore. You didn't want anyone to see it, so I got a needle and thread and helped you to sew it. I ran the needle into my finger to the bone. I remember it well, because I went to St Peter's the next Monday, and my thumb was swollen. I wrote so badly they put me into pothooks and hangers.* We used to have Latin every day, and spelling once a week. I never took to Latin, and I hated spelling, and even if I liked it, five lines of dictation once in seven days wouldn't make a literary character of a chap. I'm rather weak in spelling to this day, as I dare say you notice when I propose to you from time to time. I always get my book-keeper to write my business letters.'

'Yes. I suppose that's easier than to learn to spell?'

'Oh, much! You see, it's in this with me like everything else. Once I make up my mind to a thing I can't alter it. And it seems I generally make up my mind wrong in the spelling line. But I say, Stella, do you remember that birthday I got a little sparrow without many feathers on it in your Moreton fig-tree?* Oh, I can see you do. I asked you to give me a kiss for it, but you wouldn't. When will you?'

'Have you bribed many girls since then to kiss you, Ted?'

A dull red mounted into Ritchie's face.

'That isn't the question—stick to the point in hand, Stella, and tell me.'

'Well, perhaps never. Indeed, most likely never.'

'I don't believe that. Count it on your left hand as we used to do with the cherry-stones. Begin with the thumb, saying, "Shall I ever give Ted a kiss?—yes—no": go on.'

'Shall—I—ever—give—Ted—a—kiss? Yes—no—yes—no!'

'No, no, no; that's not fair, Stella. You must stop with the little finger, and the dear little finger says yes. I shall get a diamond hoop for that little finger. Now, then, ask it when this is to come off: say spring—summer—autumn—winter. Spring, hurrah! exactly when I thought.'

'This is a charming horse of yours, Ted.'

'Yes, I've had him trained on purpose for you. I thought he was about the style of horse you would like.'

'Now I think of it, you always get into this sort of carnival when we come out riding. I don't think I shall come with you again.'

'Don't say that, Stella. You must come for rides in the morning as long as you are in town; and when I go back to Strathhaye I shall almost believe you are coming. When shall I see you there, Stella?'

'Ted, you are far from amusing when you keep on harping on the same string in this way. It is about time we turned back. We are going to lunch with some of Laurette's prize hens to-day. It would be rather nice to play the truant.'

'Lord! Stella, don't tempt me in that way, or I shall really carry you off. Yes—no—yes. Don't you hear it in the horses' hoofs? Spring—summer—autumn—winter. Spring: it's as plain as a pike staff. You never look half so jolly anywhere else as you do on horseback. We shall spend our honeymoon on horseback—part of it, at least. Oh, I can't help it, Stella! You get into my head when we come out riding. Say a sonnet to me, and it will take my spirits down. "Where is the ship to which yon land must go?" '*

Of course Stella laughed at this unconscious travesty, and the absurd memories it revived; and Ritchie, seeing her laugh, was wise enough to say nothing more that would recall the dreadful threat that she would not ride out with him again. Before they parted she had promised him three dances at a ball to which they were going that night.

CHAPTER XXI

'YOU and Ted must have had a very pleasant ride,' said Laurette, a little maliciously, as they drove to the Anstey-Hobbs mansion.

'Yes, the sea and the air were delightful,' answered Stella calmly.

'If you keep that charming colour, Mrs A.-H. will fall in love with you on the spot. Since reading some book or other she is quite enthusiastic about healthy, well-developed girls—especially if they combine what she calls a rare organization with dabbling in the fine arts. You don't model in clay, or paint, or sing, do you?'

'No; I'm like the cat with one trick*; my one accomplishment is reading.'

'Still, I fancy you'll take with my Melbourne friends. Why do you laugh?'

'You made me think I must be cow-lymph* or a new shade of ribbon. What do people have to do when they take?'

'Oh, sit in a corner and try to be as good as little Jack Horner.* Do you know, Stella, it strikes me that you are more spoilt than ever. I suppose it comes from your being the youngest, as Tom says.'

'It is awfully good of you to make excuses for me,' said Stella, with a heightened colour.

Mr Anstey-Hobbs was popularly credited with being a million-aire. Certainly the surroundings and appointments of his town house gave colour to the belief, not to mention the number of idle servants who hung about the place. 'Just like an English nobleman's house,' as a governor from one of the adjacent colonies had said—a say-ing which some of Mrs Anstey-Hobbs' friends treasured up and repeated to select circles of their friends' friends, basking in the reflected glory of a viceregal compliment respecting an abode in which they were so much at home. As for Mrs Anstey-Hobbs herself, she never repeated anything that savoured of vainglory. Indeed, one would imagine at times that wealth was quite a mortification to her. She would take precautions to have scores upon scores of callers on her reception-days, and then take a bosom friend aside, who entirely believed in her and had an incontinent tongue, and say, 'Ah, my dear, how are we to cultivate our minds as we should, when we are swallowed up in social maelstroms like this?' And so, when she donned a specially magnificent visiting dress—one of Worth's highest flights—indicating yet chastening the possession of wealth, she would sit in a remote corner of her carriage, with a melancholy air, as if she were bowed down with the thought that all is vanity and vexation of spirit.* And then, in talking to her friends at such times, the words 'our terrible climate' and the 'severe limitations of colonial life' were often on her lips.

'It is sordid wealth without culture or the traditions of refinement that stifles our artists and poets,' she would murmur, as if shoals of such gifted beings were annually offered up on the altar of Mammon*—the fact being that Mrs Anstey-Hobbs had a talent for assimilating ideas from the books and magazines she read in such numbers monthly, but had not an equal felicity in their application. The thought that wealth was detrimental to mental expansion was one which had from various sources become dear to her—so much so, that about this time Mrs Anstey-Hobbs had made a determined effort to put down, as far as possible, the overwhelming power of money in Melbourne society. She had struggled to establish a salon—a weekly gathering to be open only to people of culture and esprit.* Those who had neither, asserted that the line must certainly be drawn at Mr Anstey-Hobbs, but habitués of the salon said it was drawn at those who were neither amusing nor had made any contribution to art or literature. But then a liberal interpretation had been put upon the latter term, for among the gifted beings at the first reunion was a wealthy young squatter, a neighbour of Ritchie's, who was by no means amusing, and had never been suspected of wandering on the slopes of Parnassus.* On inquiry, however, it turned out that a year previously he had written a letter to the Melbourne *Argus** on 'Fluke in the Liver of Sheep.'

The luncheon-party at which Stella made her début in Melbourne society, as Laurette grandiloquently phrased it, was made up of ten women in all, supplemented by two young men, who stole furtive glances at each other, and at first spoke chiefly in monosyllables. According to the hostess, one was a poet, the other a painter. Stella sat at Mrs Anstey-Hobbs' right hand, the painter at her left. Some funny talk went on about allegory.

'Well, Mr Vincent, I still think that your first idea of representing Australia as a wood-nymph, with an opossum-skin thrown carelessly over her shoulders, was exquisite,' said Mrs Anstey-Hobbs.

'That may be, dear madame'—Stella found that this was the title by which young souls, touched with the sacred fire of genius, and therefore admitted to the salon, addressed the hostess—'that may be; but are our public educated up to the point of reading this allegory? I lay it down as one of the canons of art that a picture must tell its own tale. Now, the tale that would be conveyed by the figure in its first inception would be that it was not Australia, but a young black woman.'

'But suppose you introduce a kangaroo on one side and an emu on the other?'

'There would be two objections. The introduction of these typical animals would strengthen the aboriginal theory with one class, and afford an element of mockery to another.'

'Of mockery? surely not! Abandoned as our so-called newspaper critics may be—and, alas! we have no higher standard for leading the masses to sweetness and light*—they would never dare to sully with their profligate satire so pure and original a conception!'

'You have hit the very point. That is exactly what they would do, madame. The figure of a young female inadequately clad, with a bewildered-looking kangaroo on one side and a nerveless emu on the other, suggests nothing so much as an exhibition trophy of colonial wine and olives. You know the *banal* and *borné** tone of newspaper judgment.'

'Ah, you have so much penetration, such marvellous insight into the envious writhings of inferior natures!' murmured Mrs Anstey-Hobbs, gazing at her 'painter' with pensive admiration. 'Indeed, I doubt whether the very strength of your analytical judgment does not stand in your way as a great creative artist.'

Mr Vincent blushed with pleasure, but still maintained a gloomy frown, as became an artist who had to bear the burden of genius in a world beset with inappreciative masses and unilluminated critics.

'And what form, then, have you decided on finally?' said Mrs Anstey-Hobbs after a pause. She had always a lady on the premises who took the more prosaic duties of a hostess, and so left her full scope in her efforts for developing the less material forces of colonial society.

'Well, a figure more after the classical school, with silken drapery, gauzy and flowing. You wished to say something?'

'Does it not strike you that it would be better—always, of course, with an eye to the untrained masses; and as I wish to make a gift of this allegorical figure to our picture-gallery, we must think of them— would it not be better to array the—the young woman in a product of colonial growth, or, rather, manufacture?'

'There you display the subtlety of the born critic as distinguished from those who exist merely because they get so much per column for squirting muddy water. But unfortunately our manufactures are still too crude—too entirely limited to the more fustian uses of life. Tweed and flannel could hardly be used to drape a lithe young female whose contour must show through.'

'But we grow cotton in Queensland and the Northern Territory.'

'Yes, and we can also grow silk; at least, silkworms and mulberries thrive with us.'

'I am vanquished, Mr Vincent. I have not another word to say. The silken drapery is perfectly legitimate.'

'But still, as silk is not yet one of our established industries, we must enhance its effect by something characteristically colonial,' said Mr Vincent, with the dispassionate fairness of a mind too broad to be puffed up with a sense of its own critical acumen.

'Quite true—quite true. The salt-bush is very typical. How would it do to have salt-bush for the background, with a couple of sheep nibbling at it? They might be rather lean, to typify that this bush has often kept our flocks from starving.'

'If I were painting for such as you are, madame, my task would be an easy one—my labour of love, I should say; for on the day on which I cannot feel it is such, I never touch a brush. But to the ignorant on the one hand, and the malicious on the other—and in the colonies these are the two great classes for whom artists work—I say to these the sheep would be a stumbling-block. The one would think, and the

other would say, without thinking, that the young woman was a shep-
herdess—"a reminiscence of the worst rococo period of unreal land-
scapes!" That's what the critic with a little wit and no conscience
would say. No—my own idea, after long, and I may say painful
thought, is to paint the figure with a garland of colonial flowers,
holding a basket of colonial fruit, with a colonial bird on her shoulder pecking at it.'

'Oh, charming—charming! Really too exquisite, Mr Vincent! *Do*
tell me what flowers and what bird. The fruit—would you have
grapes and oranges and peaches, and so on, or one kind?'

'I do not know about grapes. The colonial wine is really so very
—— Well, I fear I am fastidious with wine.' It may be mentioned,
en parenthèse,* that Mr Vincent usually smoked a strong cigar over
his wine, and smacked his lips ecstatically when he gulped British
champagne made of unripe gooseberries.

'Yes, and then one likes to encourage teetotal principles among
the masses,' answered Mrs Anstey-Hobbs. 'Perhaps we had better
discard the grapes? And the flowers?'

'Well, I don't know the names of any colonial flowers; but I must
ruralize* a little in the Botanical Gardens. I suppose they have native
ones there?'

'No doubt—no doubt! Oh, how very charming and natural it will
all be—quite a bush idyll! Now about the bird—you see I am all
impatience!'

'Well, I thought, a native companion*——'

Here, to save herself from absolute disgrace, Stella dropped her
napkin, so as to have an excuse for stooping and hiding her face for
a moment. The movement drew Mrs Anstey-Hobbs' attention to her
right-hand neighbour. It may be imagined that Stella had listened
with both ears to all that had passed. Her eyes were literally dancing
with suppressed merriment, her cheeks glowing like a well-sunned
peach. She was flanked on her left by an elderly woman, who was
rather deaf, and who ate her way stolidly through every dish on the
menu, so that the girl's attention had been undistracted.

Mrs Anstey-Hobbs put up her pince-nez and looked at her admiringly. The lady had very good eyesight, without any defect of over
long or short sight; but an English countess, who had visited Melbourne and stayed some days at Toorak House, had always put up
her pince-nez when she wished to look attentively at anything, being

so short-sighted that objects at a little distance were all blurred and indistinct to her unaided eyes. So, with the curious humility of a parvenu, Mrs Anstey-Hobbs had ever since zealously imitated one afflicted with impaired vision.

'My dear young lady, I fear you are not eating,' she said.

On which Stella answered with wreathed smiles that she had been so very much interested in the conversation on painting, etc. Indeed, her face was so radiant with what her hostess mentally called naïve delight, that she instantly took a liking to the girl.

'You are, perhaps, colonial-born?'

'I am an Australian,' answered Stella, who had to keep on smiling in what she felt was an imbecile way. The image of the allegorical figure of Australia, with a native companion perched on her shoulder, was really too killing.

'You make a distinction, then, between colonial and Australian?'

Mrs Anstey-Hobbs was the daughter of an English country attorney, and having in her provincial youth been familiarized with the term 'colonial' as somehow expressive of a state of things far below the status of the great British under-middle classes, she still clung to the term in her days of grandeur, fondly deeming that it somehow marked her as one whose bringing-up was more aristocratic than could fall to the lot of those who were born and bred in Australia.

'Surely,' answered Stella, 'when there is so much difference.'

'Now do tell me how. You see, I came to the colonies only when I married. I believe I was the first of our family to leave England.' There was a vague flourishing emphasis on 'our family,' as though it represented great territorial magnates.

'Well, a colony—does it not suggest a handful of men ploughing scraps of land in an insignificant little state or island, or, at any rate, the first scattered handful of pioneers who have an uncertain footing in an alien land? Australia is not a colony; it is a continent, a great country where generations have already lived and died—the birthplace of thousands upon thousands who love it more dearly than any other spot in the whole world.' The light of patriotic love and pride shone in the girl's eyes, and her voice was musical with deep feeling.

'Really, you know, I am very glad to have this explained to me,' said Mrs Anstey-Hobbs, with the indefinite awkwardness of one who has unawares awakened a chord in an unknown instrument.

'I grant you, though,' Stella went on in a lighter tone, half piqued at herself for betraying any emotion, 'that we cannot dispense with the word "colonial."' She was deeply tempted to add, 'as long as we have people who hang idly about Australian cities, painting foolish pictures for money that should be better spent.'

'Well, you heard what my friend Mr Vincent said. Tell me, do you think a native companion——'

There was no help for it. Stella had to laugh.

'Dear Mrs Anstey-Hobbs, a native companion is much larger than the domestic goose, and is mounted on legs over two feet high, with a neck almost as long as its legs.'

'Ah, I fear it would not do, then, to perch on the shoulder of an allegorical figure of Australia,' said Mrs Anstey-Hobbs, dropping her pince-nez, and turning to the artist, who was staring at Stella sombrely, as if he suspected her of inventing the dimensions of the unfortunate fowl.

'Now tell me, Miss Courtland, are there any pretty bush-flowers that would do for a garland—any that may be considered nationally Australian, like the lily for France and the rose for England?' continued this enthusiastic art-patron.

'Oh yes; it is an embarrassment of choice. To go no further than the exquisite blossom of our tan wattles, the white scrub immortelles, the epacris, and the lovely myrtle-blossoms of the eucalyptus, cream and pink. Have you ever seen the curve of a low hillside in the depths of our woods all one mass of epacris—white, and pale-pink, and scarlet?'

Mrs Anstey-Hobbs murmured an apologetic negative, with an involuntary glance at the gorgeous orchids that adorned her table. It struck her, perhaps, as being a little out of place to speak with so much enthusiasm of things that grew in masses in the bush to one who could command such rare exotics.

'The tan wattle is of rather a crude and violent tint,' said Mr Vincent in a tone of authority.

'I can imagine that it would very easily become so on canvas,' answered Stella with a sweet smile, which quite confirmed Mrs Anstey-Hobbs in her first estimate of the young lady as being 'delightfully naïve, you know.' It is to be feared she would have changed her opinion if she had overheard Stella that night describe to Ted the accessories of an allegorical Australia, that had been evolved in her hearing by a 'colonial' painter and his patroness.

CHAPTER XXII

STELLA was still sitting over a late breakfast with Laurette when her brother called with his *fiancée*, having driven Dora from her father's house in the family pony-chaise. He watched the first greetings between the girls with keen pleasure. Dora was very pretty; fair and *mignonne*,* with pale-gold hair in crisp wavelets, a pure English complexion, and large blue eyes that had something of the expression of a child's who has suddenly been told a pleasant piece of news.

'Oh! you are a sweet little darling. No wonder Cuthbert has thrown me over for you,' said Stella, looking at her critically.

'But Cuthbert has not thrown you over, dear Stella; he has given you one more sister to love.'

'Do they teach each other what to say already?' thought Stella. They babbled away pleasantly for some little time, going over those reminiscences and simple personalities in which old ladies and newly-engaged lovers so readily indulge. Presently Laurette joined them, and the talk became more general. The plan was that Stella should spend the day and stay the night at the Carters'. Cuthbert was preparing to go, having parochial work, when Ted rode up to Monico Lodge, followed by a groom leading Shah, for Stella to ride.

The discovery seemed to have something of the nature of a sensation to Dora when, after she and Ted were introduced, he said: 'Why, Stella, I thought I would find you ready. Shah is in fine form for you to-day.'

'You have appointed to go out riding?' Cuthbert said a little coldly to his sister.

'You see I had no idea that you children would be so good and kind as to come so early. I am sorry, Ted, but I am afraid I cannot ride this morning.'

Ted's brow darkened visibly. 'But that's nonsense, Stella,' he said impatiently. 'If you haven't finished your jabber, I can wait.'

Cuthbert's face became more and more impassive. Dora looked from Cuthbert to Stella in a mystified way, and then Laurette came to the rescue, proposing that she should drive back with Dora. She wanted to see dear Mrs Carter so much. They could take Stella's dress-basket and maid, and then Ted would take Stella direct to the parsonage.

'That's the very ticket,' said Ted. 'Go on, Stella; see if you can't get ready in five minutes,' and he pulled his watch out, and Stella, without further ado, hastened to obey.

Incredible as it was to Cuthbert, this rather illiterate and over-bearing young man seemed destined to triumph in his suit. His heart sank strangely at the thought. He left for town before Stella reappeared, and when they met again at the parsonage in the evening, he knew by the wistful droop of his sister's mouth that she had somehow felt bored to death. Bored in this exquisitely refined Christian home, and yet tolerant of Ritchie as a lover!

Poor Stella! She had indeed passed through some evil hours that day. In the first place, the seaside and Shah, the blue serenity of the day, the great, measureless crescendo of the waves, and Ted's touching goodness in entirely keeping off forbidden ground, had beguiled her into prolonging her ride beyond what she intended. The moment she entered the house, she became aware that lunch had been kept back on her account. There are some households in which unpunctuality is made into one of the seven deadly sins, and it seemed this was one of them. There were three daughters older than Dora, and it transpired that the day was pigeon-holed for all, with set duties for each hour, so that when thirty minutes were lost in waiting for a guest who was inexcusably late, the rest of the day threatened to resolve itself into a scramble to make up for lost time and wasted opportunities. The Rev. S. Carter and the two eldest daughters had to excuse themselves and hurry away before the meal was over, in order to catch a certain train to one of the suburbs, where a sale of gifts in aid of a church school had to be opened. Directly after their departure, a friend called by appointment to accompany the third daughter on a periodical visit to an orphanage. And thus silence prevailed for a little, which Stella endeavoured to break by saying: 'I feel most awfully guilty, you know; but the sea was too divine. And the sky—have you noticed, Dora, how widely vaulted it is to-day?'

'Oh yes; very pretty!' answered Dora, with a faint smile, and Stella resolved, for the hundredth time since she left home, that she would not try to drag the things that captivated her so insanely into conversation. It was like offering people coin for which they had no change.

'Cuthbert did not mention you were engaged,' said Mrs Carter, when they had settled themselves in the drawing-room, each with some form of needlework.

'Oh, but I am not!' answered Stella. And then mother and daughter exchanged a quick look, and Dora, colouring very prettily, said:

'I thought, dear, by—by Mr Ritchie calling you Stella, and your going out riding——'

It certainly behoved Stella to explain the long-dated friendship, or at any rate acquaintanceship, which had established both customs. But she was little in the habit of apologizing for herself, and, partly through indifference, partly out of perversity, she allowed the subject to drop. Not so Mrs Carter, however, who found a roundabout way of approaching the subject again. Mrs Tareling was Mr Ritchie's sister then. What a very brilliant marriage she had made. Stella opened her eyes wide in surprise. Of course, the younger son of a British peer was considered so in the colonies, Mrs Carter presumed. 'No doubt you knew her before she married?' Ah, yes; they knew each other since they were children. And Mr Ritchie, the young man, was one of those who had so many sheep and cattle and things. Stella believed he had over fifteen thousand a year. On hearing this, Mrs Carter sat more upright, and regarded Stella with new and respectful interest. And then the lady slid into a long and tedious account of her own family. It was rather involved, or else Stella's attention wandered, for at the close she was not certain whether it was Mrs Carter herself or her mother or her grandmother who had been governess to an English princess of the Royal family. It was clear, however, that they belonged to a good family; that they had been much reduced; that those who had married had espoused rising clergymen. One sister was married to a bishop. 'Poor woman!' thought Stella. Mrs Carter seemed to pause as if for some expression of awe or admiration. When she found this was not forthcoming, she went on to explain how wide was the gulf fixed between a colonial and an English bishop. The Carters were only temporarily in Melbourne, and proposed to return to England at no distant date. There was money in Mr Carter's family: one of his nieces was married to the first cousin of a great duke. Stella lost herself in calculating what share of lustre this connection with the British aristocracy shed on her brother. When she emerged from this depth, Mrs Carter was dilating on the pang it would cost them to part with dear Dora. But Cuthbert was all they could have wished: they had every confidence in him, etc. It seemed to Stella that the good lady was applying the phrases of a governess's testimonial to her brother. Yes, decidedly it must have been Mrs Carter herself who had held brevet rank as a governess. She placed so tiresome and so didactic an emphasis on the less alluring aspects of life, coupled with an implication of having been, since early childhood, engaged in laying the moral groundwork of society. Then, in the midst of this gentle, consequential, self-complacent purring, she suddenly asked Stella whether young ladies in the colonies— those who had been born in them, and had never lived elsewhere— took more after the American stamp than the English?

The question somewhat revived Stella's drooping spirits. It opened the door for a frankly mischievous sketch of her own existence at Fairacre. The sick-visiting, the calls, the church-going, the walks with the children, the rides with her brother, etc., but not the remotest allusion to what she knew had been chiefly in Mrs Carter's mind: not a whisper of Platonic friendship or suitors. One might imagine, from Stella's easy rapid sketch, that a 'colonial'-born girl was like the angels in heaven, and never even remotely glanced at the question of marrying.

By-and-by there were visitors and afternoon tea-parties, but both of a very mild, not to say tepid, character. Dull people do not understand the grateful fillip that the beverage, when quite fresh and fragrant, gives to the spirits and imagination. Nor did matters improve much when the rest of the family returned. When they were all together, the atmosphere was pervaded with snatches of ruined lives—parlour extracts from the careers of reprobates of both sexes. Something had always happened which was too 'shocking' to be gone into. Either a mangle or a daughter seemed to have disappeared clandestinely from most of the poor houses they had recently visited.

Stella listened in vain for some touch of fun or genuine pathos— something that these poor people had said which would throw an illuminating ray on what they really thought or endured. But no; if anything was repeated that had been said by the fatherless, or the widow, or the backslider, it had a chilling echo to her of conventional make-believe—of the kind of pulpit-slang the needy catch up so readily, with alms given on condition that they repent. Or it was still more like what one of the middle classes might have said after being led astray and made decorously repentant by the pangs of hunger.

There are multitudes who all their lives visit the poor without ever catching a true lineament of their minds. Such people are often suffused with an hysterical kind of earnestness which makes them utterly impervious to any true apprehension of what is going on in the minds of others. Or they are swaddled in a complacent egoism which makes them quite invulnerable to any true appreciation of the bearings of life. They are capable only of one standpoint, and this one is all distorted and awry.

'You do not look very much entertained, Stella,' said her brother when he found an opportunity, shortly before he left, of speaking to her alone.

'No? It must be the ravages of a troubled conscience you notice. Shah was too dear this morning. I kept the whole household waiting for me, and then—you must notice that the eldest Miss Carter sings methodically out of tune? Or don't people mind such trifles when they are in love?'

Cuthbert flushed hotly. He was indeed very much 'in love,' and this, coupled with the conviction that his sister had decided to accept Ritchie's devotion, made him impatient—for a moment angry even. Like other angry people, he took up the first weapon that came to hand.

'Perhaps the charms of Ritchie's society make you impatient of ordinary intercourse,' he said almost sternly.

Stella looked at him with startled, dilating eyes. It was almost the first time in her life that Cuthbert had spoken and looked at her unkindly. She felt it like a stab, but she strove to conceal all appearance of being hurt.

'I dare say,' she answered, smiling. 'You see, we Australians understand one another. We have a wicked love of enjoyment, of horses, and sunshine, and the seashore. Did you hear that Ted has a new bay colt, which has twice covered a mile in an incredibly short time?'

'No; I have never been much interested in the performances of horses, as you know.'

'Well, it has an amusing side. Ted is always pursued by a trainer, or a jockey, or a man in a funny necktie, who is dying to buy the little brown filly out of Lady Glendora, by Victor, you know.'

'I never believed till now that you would end by accepting him. Stella, it seems to me little short of an infatuation.'

'But do you know, my dear, that there are women who marry even bishops?'

Was it perversity, or the outcome of some nascent feeling of a deeper nature than even she herself was aware of, which led the young woman to answer her brother's remonstrances with so much reserve that a sudden change in her real attitude towards Ted would not have seemed inconsistent? Perhaps there was something of both motives. Nevertheless, the chief one which made these long morning rides so precious to her was a passionate love of being in the open air, of riding, of getting away from people who were, more or less, tiresome—she herself, at times, most of all. On horseback, more completely than anywhere else, she threw every haunting shape of troubled thought to the winds. Life then became a glorious ecstasy— a glad, bounding motion in which simply to be was enough, without any foolish looking before and after.

That night, before she fell asleep, Stella recalled her brother's face and words in the brief conversation that had passed, and she felt her heart failing her in a curious way. 'It is true,' she thought; 'the chief attachment of my life is crumbling away. As long as I was first with Cuthbert, he did not see what a faulty, foolish, inconsistent creature I am. Dora's placid little perfections show me up in a lurid light. After this he cannot see me without criticising me—without wondering how, at one time, I seemed to him so dear and lovable. And I—I shall always be conscious of it, and always say horrid things. Oh, it is no use my drawing out a little set of rules, resolving to be more gentle, and sweet, and patient. The things I say, for which I afterwards hate myself, come to me with handles. "Is this a dagger that I see before me?"* No, it is a stupid little bodkin, that generally contrives to scratch me. I seem to have got to that stage of life in which I must take myself for better or worse, as people do in marriage—meaning mostly for worse. Perhaps, when the glow of courtship and the honeymoon are over, Cuthbert may cease to criticise me—but that is too far away to be consoling. I have the unfortunate Australian temperament. I want the share that falleth to my lot now.* And then there will be not only Dora, whose eyes get rounder at everything I say, but there will be an elder sister eternally singing out of tune—practising a little song with a moral in its tail, to sing at a servantmaids' friendly association. Poor things! it is no wonder they disappear like the mangles that are bought with subscriptions. After all, Shah and Ted are less objectionable than many things in life.'

She mocked herself, as she habitually did when she was bent on keeping sterner, more serious thoughts at a distance. Yet before she fell asleep her pillow was wet with tears. In the days that followed the brother and sister gradually drifted apart. He was constantly with the Carters and their friends during his hours of relaxation from parochial work. Stella, swayed by a variety of motives, conceived almost a horror of the Carter household. She even repented of having called Dora 'a little darling' at their first interview. She described her to Ted as opening her eyes wide like an automatic doll.

'You don't like having your nose put out of joint, I can see that,' answered Ted, with an amused chuckle.

Stella made a slight grimace at him, and gave Shah his head. As they were trotting up the Toorak road, Ted spoke again:

'You see, Stella, that's one strong point about me. I'll never throw you over for anybody.'

'Oh, for the matter of that, Cuth hasn't; only he's got engaged to the wrong sort of family. When you get engaged, Ted, please see that the lady you love has not three unmarried sisters—the eldest desperately unmusical, but bent on singing.'

'Well, you see, the lady I love has only one unmarried sister. But, of course, you had that in your mind when you spoke,' said Ted, smiling to himself under his moustache.

Stella laughed merrily at the imputation.

'Now confess,' said Ted, as they slackened their horses' pace and dropped into a walk, 'you would be horribly cross if I came tomorrow morning and said I had got engaged, and instead of begging you to ride Shah, took out the other young woman.'

CHAPTER XXIII

NEXT morning the rain came down in torrents. It was out of the question to go out riding. Nor could Ted make an appointment for the afternoon, in case it cleared. Mrs Anstey-Hobbs had formed one of those sudden attachments for Miss Courtland which characterized the Melbourne lady's social career. Already, in writing to Stella, she addressed her as an 'ever dear,' and this was the day on which the new 'ever dear' was to be at Toorak House at twelve o'clock, and spend a quiet evening with a few special friends.

'That means the people who have souls and pens, Stella,' said Laurette. 'Mrs Anstey-Hobbs always reads people's characters at a glance. She quite took you in the first day. You are so sweet and fresh and naïve—so open to new ideas. Fancy my listening to all this without betraying you!'

'By Jove! you women are a rum lot,' broke in Ted, who stood staring out through the window, beating a tattoo on his boot with a riding-whip.

'Thank you, dear,' said Laurette, with a pert little bow.

'Yes; here's that Hobbs woman flying at Stella with both arms when they meet, and Stella going for all the day and most of the night with her; and then I'll swear she'll have some comic story when she comes back, like that one about the lean sheep and the Mallee and the native companion.'

Laurette looked thoroughly mystified. Though Stella dearly loved to tell a funny story, she was very careful not to make a confidante of one with so slippery a tongue as Laurette's. Ted perceived the situation, and his heart beat with joy. Stella was sitting on a low arm-chair near the fire, cutting the leaves of a magazine. Ted sat down on the fender-stool at her feet, and said in an undertone: 'After all, what you told me in the top of the she-oak so many years ago is quite true.'

'Oh, as for Mrs Anstey-Hobbs, she gives herself away to everyone,' said Laurette viciously. There had been an ardent friendship at one time between the two, which had long since been offered up as alms to oblivion,* and Laurette suspected that Mrs Anstey-Hobbs had confided some story to Stella under the bond of secrecy. 'There was that absurd story about herself and the Russian commander last season. Oh, I mean when the Russian man-of-war was here. Of course, Mrs Anstey-Hobbs gave a grand ball, and Joseph—that's her husband—rather forgot himself. She was so mortified, she began to speak to the commander in a bow-window, and a broken voice, of the withering bonds of the conjugal life, just merely to show off how sensitive and refined she was. She didn't mean a word of it, you know. The commander thought she was proposing to elope with him, and explained in fragmentary English that his official position would not permit any irregularity, but that he hoped to return before long.'

'Really, Laurette, I don't think you should tell a story like that before me,' said Ted, who was engaged in trying to purloin a bow of ribbon off Stella's shoe.

'And then the way she dresses,' said Laurette, who, like many others, found it difficult to curb her enthusiasm as soon as she had begun discussing an absent friend. 'You noticed her the other evening at Government House, arrayed in an extraordinary pea-green, with yellow marabout feathers on the train? She reads the "Court Circular,"* you know, and makes a point of dressing like a young princess—quite forgetting she is getting on in life, and never had a complexion.'

'If you say much more, I shall stay to see you hugging and kissing her when she comes in,' said Ted, slipping a knot of crimson satin ribbon into his vest pocket.

'That reminds me; I must write a note or two before I go,' said Stella.

One of these was to Louise, her brother Hector's wife, at Lullaboolagana.

'You say you are not very well, and are longing to see me,' she wrote. 'Well, if you write in your answer "I want you at once," you will see me twenty-four hours after I get it. I feel an ungrateful wretch—for Laurette is all kindness in her way—but the Mallee Scrub spoils one for the kind of society in which money is the one great distinction, and where women have no time for anything but to be insignificant victims of those sinister successes of life which end in choking it with superfluities. As for Cuth—ah me!—one little dimple of Dora's pretty face is worth all I am or can be. Yes, this is partly jealousy—a mean sort of reptile which I used to think I was quite above. I suppose we are above most failings as long as there is no temptation.'

'Well, Ted,' said his sister, when the two were alone, 'it seems to me that you and Stella are getting on.'

Laurette did not really think so; but money affairs were day by day assuming a sterner aspect, and she was anxious to make belief in the success of Ted's suit a ground for making 'sacrifices' on his behalf. Laurette's ideal of a sacrifice was making someone pay very heavily for an action that had cost her nothing.

'Oh, do you think so?' answered Ritchie. Then he walked up and down the room for a little. 'Look here, Larry,' he said suddenly, 'do you think Stella has heard anything?'

Laurette was just then like a *chiffonnier*,* who discards nothing that comes to hand till it is examined at leisure.

'I do not know,' she answered slowly; 'what makes you ask?'

'Well, at times she is so merry and full of fun; then she gets a silent fit; and though we are friendly, we never seem to get any further. The more I see of her the less I know what is going to happen.'

'She doesn't know herself. Stella Courtland is one of those girls who seem to be wise and even strong-minded—but all the time she is torn in twenty directions. It runs all through her. At seventeen she wouldn't be confirmed, because she wanted to be a Catholic. She has never been confirmed to this day, and never turned Catholic. She stays away from Church far more than I do, and yet she'll read her Bible by the hour, as if it were a French novel. She scoffs at people thinking they can do any good to the poor, and still she has a trick of going to see them and listening to everything they choose to say far more patiently than she would to you or me. She has been absurdly fond of her brother Cuthbert all her life; and instead of being glad he has got engaged to a pretty well-connected girl, she mopes over it. I have no doubt she thinks in her heart that I am a very poor shallow creature; but at any rate I know what I want, and I generally succeed in getting it; and for once I change my mind, she changes hers fifty times. Let her go on a little longer, and if the whim should take her in the end that she doesn't care to marry you, I think I can bring her to her bearings. It used to be a great weakness with her, even as a girl, to believe she could do good. It's a sort of family superstition. She may not have it very strong now; but still enough to get at her through her conscience.'

'Through her conscience!' repeated Ritchie; as though in the case of a woman this were a theological abstraction, not to be lightly brought up in secular conversation.

'Yes, precisely,' returned Laurette, with a firm voice. Conscience was, on the whole, the mental faculty of which she knew least, and she felt therefore all the better qualified to reckon on its mystic influence with a character so unstable. 'But after giving you so much encouragement, she'll never finally reject you.'

'Well, as to the encouragement, Larry, it's more that I won't give in, you see—and take "no" for an answer.'

'Then don't be impatient. The longer you are thrown together in this sort of way the better for you.'

When Stella came back from Mrs Anstey-Hobbs' that evening, she found Laurette looking very much discomposed over a telegram that awaited her return from a musical evening at Sir Thomas and Lady Danby's, who were next-door neighbours at Monico Lodge. She said nothing, however, as to the cause of her evident vexation, but chatted about the events of the day until Ted came in. He launched into details of a dinner that had been given at the Melbourne Club to Colonel Aldersley, prior to his departure for England.

'There was little Jingo of Wyoming,' he said, 'laying it on as usual with a trowel: "The presence of men like Colonel Aldersley amongst us," says he, "has more than social significance. It is the influence of such high-toned people that rivets the bonds that bind us to the mother-country," and a lot more I can't remember. And there was the colonel trying to look as if he believed it, and the other fellows jogging each other, and little Eardley Everson—a brat of a boy of eighteen, who has lost over £20,000 to the colonel—pinching himself to see if he was awake.'

Stella was much diverted by this, but Laurette re-read her telegram with a care-laden face. Then she left the room, saying she would be back in a few minutes.

On this, Ted entered into more personal talk.

'I say, Stella, what do you call that dress you have on—I mean, what stuff is it?'

'Crêpe de Chine—pale pink, as you see!'

'And that stuff peeping out round your shoulders?'

'Cream-coloured crêpe lisse.'

'Would you mind being married just in a dress like that?'

'Why, Ted, that's like fishing for an invitation!'

'Nothing of the sort. Who ever heard of a bridegroom asking to be invited to—— Now, Stella, don't move; sit just as you are. And what are these roses in your hair and bosom?'

'Scarlet fairy roses. Aren't they too dear and sweet? Mrs Anstey-Hobbs still has heaps of them, though they were nearly over with us when I left home.'

'Tell me about Mrs Anstey-Hobbs before Larry comes back. I won't let the cat out of the bag on you this time!'

Stella was sitting on her favourite chair, near the fire. The flames leaped rosily, and cast rosy reflections on her face—stealing to it on each side of the Japanese screen, with its flock of wide-winged storks hovering above their slender bamboos. Ritchie had planted himself straight in front of her, sitting horseback fashion on a chair, his hands, which were crossed on the back of it, supporting his chin.

At this request Stella began to laugh, and her eyes sparkled with amusement. It was the expression that her companion best loved to see her wear. When she looked like that he always understood what she said.

'Oh, the *salon*, Ted; it was really too funny. You must know that after dinner we assembled in what Mrs Anstey-Hobbs calls her boudoir, but it is as large as any ordinary drawing-room. It is hung with panels of peach-coloured satin, very beautifully embroidered—some with Graces and Cupids tumbling over wreaths of roses. But the design I liked best was a great spray of double white cherry-blossoms, with a pair of sweet little gray love-birds billing in the midst——'

'Yes, they're jolly little animals. I wish some people would take a little more after them.'

'Now, if you interrupt I must remember how late it is. Perhaps I ought to tell you that this work was done by a Russian countess that Mrs Anstey-Hobbs met abroad. She got into trouble with her husband, or the Government, or something. So one night, instead of returning home from a ball, she ran away to the Riviera, where she designed and worked lovely things for people who have two hundred thousand sheep in the woods of Australia. When you come to think of it, there is something that fascinates the mind in the idea of eloping with a crewel-needle from the reach of the police, or an objectionable husband.'

'Nonsense, Stella; no woman worth her salt runs away from her husband like that,' answered Ted promptly. He may have had reasons of his own for entertaining strict views on this point. 'Besides, if you knew all, you may depend it was not with a crewel-needle she eloped.'

'Well, at any rate it was with a crewel-needle she lived. And she was known as the Countess Olga. But where was I? Oh, the *salon*—well, you must figure to yourself that Mrs Anstey-Hobbs was draped *artistement** in a wonderful Indian fabric, and that she lived in an enormous armchair covered with citron-coloured velvet. Beside her was a little octagon table carved out of Angola ivory; on it the daintiest little notebook in the world with jewelled clasps—a notebook in which to enter the *bons mots** of the evening.'

'What are *bons mots*? Have I ever heard any?'

'Oh, Ted, Ted—to think that I climbed trees with you in my infancy, and have seen you at intervals ever since, and that you should ask such a question! How shall I explain—it must be in the concrete. You remember the last time you were out riding you told me of an Oxford man who was a knock-about hand at Strathhaye for some time, and how, speaking of the old Greeks once, he said their only idea of trade was piracy, and I answered it remained for modern times to combine the two? Well, that was something in the nature of a *bon mot*.'

'Oh, you are always saying things of that kind. But why the dickens should the old frump want to put them in a notebook?'

'Why, indeed,' answered Stella, laughing heartily. 'Well you see, Ted, the prosperity of a *salon* depends on its *bons mots*—but I am obliged to confess I did not hear any. There were twenty of us, and the first part of the evening was monopolized by a Yankee newspaper-man, who sends columns of lies every week to a daily paper in New York. He stood with his back to the fire, and held forth through his nose for nearly an hour on the merits of cremation. He proved conclusively that a casket ten inches by eight would contain the calcined ashes of an adult. And then he asked the host in an audible aside for a "nip of dog's nose." What in the world is that?'

It was now Ted's turn to laugh. 'Why, it's a horrid mess made of gin and beer mixed.'

'Then that accounts for Mrs Anstey-Hobbs' confusion. She told me beforehand that in striving to establish a *salon d'esprit** she was determined to keep the grosser pleasures of the palate in the background—to have nothing more material than macaroons and lemonade. I think Mr Hobbs himself went to brew the unholy mixture. I am sure he would not dare to ask it from the butler, who is a magnificent creature, whose former life has been passed in the bosom of the British nobility. What can be keeping Laurette so long?'

'Oh, I dare say the kiddies have got measles or something,' answered Ted. 'Go on, Stella, tell me some more. Were there many to dinner?'

'Yes, about a dozen. These endless costly dinners are my horror. I like my food plain and unmixed, like a bird or a peasant. On one side of me there was a parched-up-looking woman, who seemed to be in a state of nervous tension about her spoons and forks. On the other a man hardly middle-aged, who gobbled away till the veins on his forehead stood out. Pastor Fiedler's nine little pigs used to dine much more peacefully, and then their grunts were so much more eloquent than anything he said.'

'I've been to Toorak House a few times,' said Ted, laughing. 'It always seemed crammed up with things from everywhere.'

'Oh yes; I should think that temples in the far East must have been rifled for screens, and rugs, and mantel-drapes. There are some things I have quite fallen in love with. One is a very old Egyptian drinking-cup—greenish-gray, in the shape of a lotus-leaf. Another is a slender Etrurian vase in jade. . . . But how late it is!' she cried suddenly. 'Laurette must be seeing the children through all the phases of a lingering malady. Good-night, Ted.'

'Good-night.' But he did not release her hand. 'Oh, Stella, if you would let me take one kiss—just one. You did once before, you know, when we were engaged—that afternoon in the garden at Fairacre.'

She drew back, but he had taken both her hands, and held them firmly in his.

'Let me go at once, Ted,' she cried in quick anger and something of dismay.

'Stella, when is this to come to an end? How long am I to wait and beg, and play the fool? Have pity on me. You do like me a little. That's all I want to begin with. You *have* thought that you might marry me; you must have thought that you would let me kiss you. There, don't look as if I frightened you. Try and make up your mind——'

'I have made up my mind,' she cried, sweeping past him, an indignant flush on her face.

It was nearly one o'clock in the morning, and she found Maisie fast asleep in the dressing-room, where she had been waiting her mistress's return. Stella made her go to bed at once, but she herself sat in a dressing-gown by her bedroom fire. She was angry; first at Ted and then herself. It was ridiculous of her to sit and talk with him so long. Laurette was a sneak, who had no doubt purposely stayed away. Even chaperons had not been invented without a cause. Probably the most jaded institutions of society were founded upon some battered relic of reason. But was it necessary to run full tilt against them before acknowledging this?

How absurd it was getting, this determined, endless wooing! What would be the end of it? Her anger died away as she tried to answer the question. She could not pretend to dislike Ted. She reflected on the endless variation of dulness that entered so largely into the lives of the bulk of women. After all, money was one of the greatest safeguards against that mildew of unexpectant monotony with which the years were so largely infected when once one began to find things out. She was really beginning to feel as if Ted had a right to her. Finally, she resolved that she would hasten her departure for Lullaboolagana, and there make a final, an irrevocable decision. Then she pictured herself writing to Ted; no, she would see him, it would be kinder; she would ask him to meet her in Melbourne on her way back. 'Ted, this must come to an end. You must take my final answer; I cannot marry you.' Would he call it 'coming a cropper,' and rend her with reproaches? And then a little panic seized her, that no reason she could urge would stand the tide of Ted's remonstrances. She did not acknowledge it to herself, and yet a vague consciousness underlay her musings, that the masterful way in which he had held her hands, and looked at her with ardent eyes, made some hitherto unknown chord of her nature vibrate in unison with his will. Perhaps it was a faint reminiscence in her blood of the remote ancestresses of pre-civilization, who were knocked on the head if they did not fall in with the marital arrangements made for them.

CHAPTER XXIV

STELLA had not been unfair in conjecturing that Laurette's absence from the drawing-room, after her brother came in, was not accidental. It had not, however, been her design to stay away so long, a circumstance which was in point of fact due to her having a bitter fit of crying. This was with her an extremely unusual circumstance, and was caused by no sentimental weakness. The laconic telegram she had received would not of itself have thrown much light on her emotion. It was dated from Sydney, and merely contained the words:

'Cannot be back for some days to come.

'TALBOT TARELING.'

That was all; but its bitterness, like that of many other events, lay in the context. There was no legitimate excuse for his sojourn in Sydney. Even business, elastic as it is in the hands of a wary and

unfaithful husband, could not in any possible guise be held account-
able for this move. In order to go to Sydney from Banjoleena, Tareling must have passed through Melbourne. Laurette had no need to
waste time in asking herself why he had done so, like a fugitive. It
was owing to the recent departure for Sydney of a wretched little
opera singer who was Tareling's last infatuation. Laurette reviewed
the situation in the light of past events.

Cheered by his success in Celestial Hills, she had, without a
murmur, allowed him to retain possession of the nine hundred
pounds that had been netted by the timely sale of her shares in that
mine. Tareling had gone to Banjoleena with this money to his credit,
confident of doubling or trebling the amount in a few days. Perhaps
he had. But she knew that he would return from Sydney penniless,
yet imperturbably unrepentant. It was one of Tareling's aristocratic
characteristics, that he never attempted the *rôle* of the Prodigal Son.*
He was obliged to come home when the fun was over; but there
any simulacrum* of repentance began and ended. So it had been
before, so it would be no doubt to the end. But just now, owing to
a conjunction of untoward events, this spell of riotous living meant
for Laurette—unless she could by some means or other raise the
wind—the almost immediate giving up of the costly furnished house
at Toorak, and retirement to the intolerable solitude of Cannawijera.
And this to Laurette presented all the concentrated bitterness of a
hopeless defeat in the hour of greatest triumph. She had married
Talbot Tareling not for love, for even if she had been capable of it,
he was the last one qualified to evoke any such passion when the two
met; not for his good looks, for he had none; not for his morals, for
if he ever possessed any, the world, the flesh, and the devil had wholly
despoiled him long before he left his native shores. She had married
him simply because he was the younger son of an English peer;
relying on this circumstance, and her own tact and heiress-ship, to
become one of the elect of Melbourne society. Yet, with all these
advantages, the struggle had been very uphill. Her income, when the
marriage took place, was over three thousand a year. The Hon. Talbot
was supposed to have five hundred a year, but it was invariably in
the hands of disreputable Hebrews twelve months in advance. The
sinews of war* were wholly inadequate to the sort of campaign that
Laurette undertook. And then, even in a frankly democratic country,
the cadet of a noble house, bankrupt in money and reputation, does

not meet with unqualified social success. But Laurette was indefatigable, and year by year she made a little headway. Only year by year there was an accumulation of debt, and tradespeople made their terms harder, and her father and brother were more reluctant to supplement her income from Cannawijera by random cheques for a couple of hundred pounds.

But then came the brilliant windfall of the new Governor and his wife—high in rank, and nearly connected with her husband's family. This gave her at one stroke that right of tambour at Government House which had been her cherished dream from early girlhood. She planted her feet on the neck of recalcitrant tradesmen and spiteful foes of her own sex, in the inner cliques of that curiously disintegrated mass which calls itself 'good society' in the capitals of Australian colonies. Her hour of victory had come. The Governor's wife was not only closely related to Tareling's family, but an intimate friend of his mother's. Before leaving London she had pledged herself to do all she could for Talbot, vaguely imagining that, in a wealthy young country like Victoria, it would be easy to smuggle a relative into some cosy sinecure worth, well, say seven or eight hundred a year.

But a very brief sojourn in Australia reveals the fact that to appoint a man to a post worth even one hundred a year, apart from fitness for the work or claims on the country, would at once arouse a ferment of Parliamentary inquiry. Now the Hon. Talbot Tareling's fitness for any appointment was limited to a well-cultivated and hereditary incapacity for any form of steady employment. His claims on the country consisted in having spent all his own and a great deal of his wife's money in very equivocal ways. The profound etiquette and the glamour of monarchical institutions are needed to elevate such traits into an irresistible claim on the public finances.

But at least it was in Lady Weavelow's power to shower those delicate attentions on her cousin and his wife which, from a vice-regal personage, are objects of keener ambition in Melbourne than money or appointments. In Laurette, Lady Weavelow was agreeably surprised to find a lady whose demeanour, dress, and general *savoir faire* would bring no discredit on her husband, even among the order to which he belonged. Stella had once spoken of the hard, crude touch of the social amateur in Laurette. But like all who do not possess the ultimate distinction of manners moulded by hereditary culture, or the spontaneous courtesy of an essentially kind heart, Laurette's behaviour was largely dependent on circumstances. With people like the Courtlands, whose unostentatious family pride made them indifferent to those forms of social distinctions which had the keenest fascination for Laurette, she was probably at her worst. Their simple mode of living, their ardour for books and ideas, their absence of *chic* measured by local standards; the humble nondescript sort of people, marked only by unselfish aims of life, that one constantly met at Fairacre—all gave her a certain sense of superiority to them, and yet a baffling sense that they would regard such an assumption as very amusing, and not to be taken seriously. She was at her best with those whose rank and position towered above her own. She was then on her guard against the robust vulgarity that formed the real substratum of her nature. She was quick and clever in her own way, and prided herself on knowledge of the world. In her case, as in that of all intrinsically shallow natures, such knowledge is largely, though unconsciously, founded on the dictum of the Scotchman: 'There is no an honest man in the world; I ken it by mysel'.'

But probably the very narrowness of Laurette's aims made her feel all the more acutely the prospect of speedy social extinction. After she reached her own room, she re-read the telegram with a sickening heart. She recalled her father's obstinate refusal at Christmastime to advance a few hundred pounds till after shearing-time. Of course he knew that to 'advance' was merely a euphemism for giving. He told her that till the rabbits were exterminated on his runs he would neither give nor advance a single copper, and advised herself and her husband to live quietly on their Cannawijera property, instead of running head over ears into debt in Melbourne. To go to these desolate wilds from the very apex of her triumph—from the haunts and assemblies whose open-sesame had cost her so many toilsome years of guerilla warfare with millionaire women, whose dull resentment she had aroused with the unguarded malice of a sharp and vindictive tongue! In a week after her departure her place in society would know her no more. The world abounds with those who are terrified at nothing so much as being forgotten. If people are buried in the Mallee Scrub, society has no alternative but to forget them. The thought suffocated Laurette in advance. And then Talbot—she knew—he would not stay at Cannawijera more than a week at the outside.

To make life endurable to him in such a *cul-de-sac*, it would be necessary to erase twelve hours out of the twenty-four. Even in Melbourne he was often dull. Against dulness he had not one honest resource. Still less would this be the case when his wife was permanently at Cannawijera, and he was permanently a man about town. He had an incredible knack of obtaining credit. It must have been inherited with his blue blood. A man habituated to the brutal habit of paying for what he got could never attain such perfect mastery of the art. He was skilful too, or lucky rather, at games of chance. Yes, he would keep afloat for a few months. But after that? He would join some theatrical company, and leave the colonies. Laurette was sure of it. He was a good amateur actor: he had been trained by experts. There were *rôles* in many popular plays in which he could give well-salaried actors points, and yet come off winner, from the fact that in such *rôles* he had only to present his own character in the less habitual parts that were fitted for stage representation—that of a well-bred, cool, unscrupulous man of the world. It was his one chance of getting a livelihood. He had more than once spoken of taking it up, when the dark desolation of Cannawijera loomed in the foreground as the only refuge open to him apart from gaining an independent livelihood. 'He will attach himself to Mademoiselle de Melier's company, and go to San Francisco,' thought Laurette; and she turned cold and faint with the conviction the thought carried—all that she had lived for seemed to be crumbling around her.

She covered her face with her hands, and felt better after she was able to cry. She heard Stella leave the drawing-room, and she debated with herself whether she would go to her brother and throw herself at his feet and implore him to save her from the ignominious series of defeats, of social annihilation, which she saw in store for her. But the next moment she rejected the thought. If a couple of hundred pounds would do her any good Ted would give a cheque at once. But he was far more obdurate about larger sums than ever her father had been. He knew too well what Tareling's mode of life was. He himself had worked hard from the age of sixteen till his uncle's death left him sole master of Strathhaye, and he had an invincible objection to placing an unlimited supply of cash at the disposal of 'an image of a man who never did a stroke of work in his life, for himself or anyone else.'

Laurette buried her face in her hands, and one design after another flashed hastily across her mind. To write and tell her father that some dire catastrophe impended, unless he could send her, say, a thousand pounds? No, she had done that more than once before. It was the story of the shepherd-boy and the wolf* over again. Then slowly something like a feasible plan suggested itself. But she determined to ponder over it for a day or two. At the end of that time, however, events ranged themselves precisely in the direction she wished. Stella announced to her that Louise was not well, and asked her to hasten her visit as much as possible. 'If you will let me leave by the early train to-morrow, Laurette, I shall write and let Mrs Coram, and the others whose invitations I accepted, know that I have been called away, and then I can see you again on my way home if you wish.'

Stella spoke in an apologetic tone, feeling half guilty for beating so hasty a retreat. But the enforced companionship with Laurette began to be intolerable. Her sustained enthusiasm about trifles, the glow of inextinguishable interest with which she retailed Lady Weavelow's opinions and sayings and doings, the solemn reverence with which she went over the connections of Lord Harry, the aide-de-camp, and entered into endless details regarding those she held to be the great people of Melbourne, bored Stella to the last point of *ennui*. It was like being in the society of servants, but without the interest of the servants' point of view at first hand. Then the whole atmosphere of Monico Lodge oppressed her so that she could not even read any book she cared for. The very walls and chairs seemed to whisper endless anecdotes full of foolish self-importance, and count over the provincial notabilities who paid them visits. 'We never know,' says Goethe somewhere, 'how anthropomorphic we are.'* Probably those who do have a glimmering of it conceal the fact, because the habit of endowing lifeless objects with a personality of their own has, in the eyes of most practical people, something in it dangerously silly.

'Well,' said Laurette, a sudden light coming into her face, 'I will let you off on condition you promise to stay two weeks with me when you return. There is an English man-of-war to be here early in September, and a French royalty *incog.*; so we shall have the place *en fête** again.' But as Laurette spoke her heart sank as she thought: 'I may then, perhaps, be entombed in the Mallee Scrub.'

Stella had spent the previous day with her brother by the seaside. Had she made any irrevocable decision? Perhaps she meant to write to Ted. Laurette had noticed the pearl horseshoe wrapped up on Stella's toilet-table, in an isolated fashion, as if she did not mean to include it in her belongings. Ted had gone to St Kilda, and would not be back till the next afternoon. Stella's departure in his absence was so far fortunate—if no communication passed between them. Laurette was just then in a curiously strained and watchful mood. She was all eyes and ears.

She determined on a little conversation that might help to fetter Stella's action till they met again—a conversation that might also aid in the development of her little *coup*. It was not that facts were at all necessary to her when she found a little impromptu history helpful. But facts, even when twisted entirely from their true drift and context, are valuable as imparting a certain *vraisemblance* to supposed events. There are people who will report an entirely imaginary conversation, and find a kind of moral support in adding: 'Yes; he sat in an armchair all the time, with his slippered feet on the fender.' The 'he' in question may not have uttered a word of the many ascribed to him—but then he did sit in an armchair, and his feet were really on the fender. After all, human veracity has severe limitations. We cannot have everything limning the severe countenance of truth. Let us remember this when, in contemporary history, we have the conversation all askew, but the armchair, the slippered feet, and the fender true to the life.

'Stella, may I speak to you a little about Ted?' said Laurette, with an engaging air of timidity.

She was really very quick at times in diagnosing the frame of mind in which people happened to be, and she had a prevision that her subject just then must be cautiously broached. Stella had not gone out riding with Ted since the evening he had offended her, and he had admitted to Laurette before he went to Flemington that he had been a deuced jackass, but when she questioned him he had relapsed into dogged silence.

'Why, Laurette, you speak as though Ted were at the other end of the world. What do you wish to say?'

'Well, no doubt I am rather foolish to be so much concerned. You see, Stella, you have so many brothers, you do not know how a woman feels when she has only one. Poor dear Ted is so unhappy just now. He offended you. Well, I undertook to make his peace with you. He did not go into particulars; perhaps he begged for one of the many kisses you owe him. Dear me, what a freezing air! I wonder how many kisses your brother Tom snatched from me; and yet he never proposed to me even once. Certainly I never set up for a monument of icy hauteur. Still, I never forgot that I was Sir Edward Ritchie's daughter, any more than I am likely to forget that I am the wife of the Hon. Talbot Tareling.'

Laurette drew herself up to her full height, and Stella was too much amused to retain an air of offended majesty.

'At the same time,' said Laurette, astutely taking advantage of this to show a sudden change of front, 'I don't think you need be afraid of Ted pestering you again. Now, my dear, let us have a proper talk over this. Sit down here; we may as well be comfortable, and not stand staring at each other like two strange cats on the roof. I believe there were tears in Ted's eyes when he took me into his confidence. "What do you think I'd better do, Larry?" said he. "Do?" said I. "Why, nothing." "But I am afraid she's very angry," said he. "She hasn't even ridden out with me since, and now she's away for the whole day. It feels as long as a month of Sundays. I shouldn't wonder if she sent me back that dashed horseshoe"—indeed, I am afraid he used a stronger word. Poor old Ted! you know he is a little rough sometimes. But how good and generous he is!—though I sometimes call him stingy in fun. There he was yesterday, trying to make me take a cheque for I don't know how much. But, of course, when a woman is married, there *is* a limit to what she can accept, even from a brother. Besides, I had a sort of feeling that it was more for your sake than my own—a sort of testimonial because I am nice enough for you to visit me.'

Laurette, when it suited her purpose, was a finished mistress of that adroit flattery which seems inseparable from radical insincerity of nature.

'I must say that was very humble of you,' said Stella, laughing outright.

It is foolish to flatter people with a strong sense of humour; even if they like it, they must see through it.

'Well, but to return to this storm in a teacup. I couldn't help laughing about the horseshoe; and I said, "If Stella wants to get rid of that in a huff, why, I'll take charge of it."'

'I wish you would, Laurette. I'll leave it in your hands,' said Stella.

'Oh, certainly,' returned Laurette, with an indulgent smile; and she mentally ticked this off as one point gained. But she had not finished yet. 'Then Ted said to me, "Now, Larry, tell me—do you think I'm any nearer the end of this long courtship, one way or the other? Is it more likely or unlikely that Stella will have me?" "Ted," said I, "don't ask me what Stella will do or will not do. I've long ago felt about this affair as if I were looking at a play—one of the sort that nearly makes you fall in pieces with yawning, don't you know. It's so long, and people come on and off, and you sit through one act after another, thinking that surely something will happen soon; but it doesn't, and there you gape till the curtain is rung down, and you feel like a perfect fool." At that Ted got rather angry, as if I were prophesying evil. Of course, I didn't mean to do that; so I simply said, "When a girl lets a man dangle after her for years——"'

'You had no right to say——' said Stella, colouring hotly.

'Well, please remember this was a confidential chat with my only brother. "When a girl lets a man dangle after her for years, and prevents him from thinking of anyone else, and in the end doesn't know whether she'll have him or leave him—why, then I think it is time for him to take his fortune into his own hands."'

'Well, that, at least, was good advice,' said Stella, 'and I hope Ted will act on it.'

'Will you believe it?' said Laurette, laughing—'he has solemnly made up his mind that unless you write to him about something, or give him some direct encouragement, he will from this time forth try to think of you only as a friend. I believe that is partly why he has gone to Flemington.'

'I am glad that he is reasonable at last,' answered Stella; but, notwithstanding the words, Laurette felt sure there was some pique in the flush that settled in the girl's cheeks.

CHAPTER XXV

WHEN Ritchie returned, and found that during his absence Stella had taken her departure for Lullaboolagana, his chagrin was extreme.

'She asked me to say good-bye to you for herself and Dustiefoot, and gave her kind regards to Shah,' said Laurette, as she sat skimming a budget of letters and notes that had just been delivered.

Ted felt like one who has suddenly been dragged out of the

sunlight, and has had the key turned on him in a cheerless dungeon.

'She is to finish her visit in September,' said Laurette, when she found that Ted made no response.

He stared at the *Age** for some time in gloomy silence, glancing from one column to another as if he were reading, but not seeing a line.

'Well, I don't suppose it's to make much difference to me whether she comes here or anywhere else,' he answered.

Laurette made no reply.

'Was that all Stella said?' asked Ritchie after a pause; 'just to say good-bye? Was she at all put out that Louise wanted her at once, or was the thing a plant, do you think—just an excuse to be off?'

'Ted, don't ask so many questions, or I shall betray confidence,' said Laurette.

'Betray confidence? Bosh!' retorted Ritchie in a disdainful tone. 'You can't run with the hare and hunt with the hounds. At Christmas-time you thought you were going to do great shakes by getting Stella here, and showing her what a dash you cut; and now she's gone off in less than two weeks without even saying good-bye to me. And then there's something that you know in confidence. I should think I am the proper person to be taken into confidence, if there's anything to confide.'

'You asked if Stella only said good-bye,' said Laurette, in an impressive tone. 'Well, we had a long, private talk.'

Ted leant forward, no longer pretending to read the newspaper.

'Yes; and what was the talk about?'

'Before telling you that, I must get your promise that you will not let Stella know I told you.'

'I'm not such a confounded blab as to carry yarns between people.'

'Then tell me, has Stella, since she came here, said anything that led you to think she had been debating in her own mind whether or not she would accept you?'

'Yes; she told me that since I last saw her she had sometimes thought she would come to the scratch.'

'Ah! Well, after all, you understood her better than I do. They say that women have so much penetration; but I think some men have. You asked me one day if I thought Stella had heard anything.'

'Well?'

'She has.'

'Ah, I suppose Cuth, the parson, has fossicked?'

'I don't think so. I believe it is a slight rumour, but enough to disquiet her—to make her uncertain.'

'I shall write and make a clean breast of it; tell her all.'

'Not for your life. At least, not if you don't mean to lose her.'

'Lose her? I haven't got her, and not likely to now!'

'Ah, there you are mistaken. Stella *loves* you, Ted,' and Laurette, without a quiver of her eyelid, gazed into the young man's face. He flushed deeply, and walked about the room with signs of evident emotion.

'If I could believe that——' he said, and stopped.

'You may believe it,' she said, in a tone of quiet confidence which thrilled him with joy.

'And in spite of—what she has heard?'

'Yes; and when she returns here in September—well, I can only judge by what she said, and by what she did not say, which is often quite as important, and by what I observed—I believe you will get a speedy answer. But, whatever you do, don't write to her till you do see her, for she would instantly think I told you all that passed between us, and I have not done that, and don't mean to.'

'Well, Larry, this is very good news you have given me,' said Ted, and he was so much moved that his voice trembled.

Some visitors were announced, and Ted took himself off, and went for a long spin on Shah, trying to realize that his tedious years of waiting were after all to be crowned with the one great joy that had so long seemed a vision beyond his reach.

The next little scene in Laurette's *coup* took place three days later, in the evening. Ted was to return to Strathhaye on the following day. A servant brought in some letters on a salver. Among them was one which Laurette had posted to herself, containing a long letter that Tareling had written to her a year or two previously. Latterly he never wrote long letters, even on business. Laurette crushed the envelope into her pocket, and began to read this letter with an air of absorbed attention. Presently she gave a little sharp cry.

'What's the row?' said Ted, looking up. 'A letter from Tareling?' he said, glancing at the sheet, which Laurette re-perused with a most dejected countenance. But she said nothing. She read one or two more notes; one of them a delightfully intimate one from the Hon.

Miss Brendover, Lady Weavelow's sister, asking Laurette and Miss Courtland to spend an afternoon at Government House in an informal way two days hence.

'Tell me, Ted,' said Laurette suddenly, 'how much is father really affected by the rabbits?'

'How much? Well, there, you ask a question that neither he nor I can answer at present. Within the last twelve months he has spent £9,000 on sending the bunnies to kingdom-come; and how much he'll spend during the current twelve months, the Lord only knows!'

'But I thought this rabbit extermination was partly at the expense of Government?'

'Exactly; and that's why the vermin have been increasing head over heels. Why, the governor himself has had forty-three rabbits trapped, with the scalp taken off, and let run again that they may go on breeding. You see, these scoundrels in Government pay mean to make a permanent job of it. They get so much for every scalp, so, instead of killing the little brutes, they sometimes carefully take the skin off the top of the head, and in the course of a few months there are thousands more bred by the animals they have been paid for killing. When the governor saw what was going on he jacked up at once—gave the Government notice he would see to doing away with the rabbits on his own account. So there he is paying at the rate of £30 a day, and putting up a rabbit-proof fence between his land and the land in Government possession.'

'But, then, of course, father has been saving a lot of money all these years. It doesn't take more than eight or nine thousand a year to keep Godolphin House going.'

'Yes, he has unfortunately put four or five hundred thousand pounds into good investments in South Australia,' said Ted grimly. 'He had £150,000 in Commercial Bank Shares, which at the present moment may be had wall-high for an old song; he has £100,000 in the Town and Country Bank, which is more shaky than a poplar leaf; he has a pot of money in tram lines that will yet be sold for old iron; and he has heaps of tin in houses that cost him a handsome sum every quarter for broken windows, and advertisements for tenants that don't turn up. Perhaps you thought the governor cut up rather rough when he had to shell-out a thousand pounds over that shady concern of Tareling's six months ago; but, by Jove! if you knew how much money the old man has dropped lately in one way or another——'

'Well, I suppose we'll have to take up our abode permanently at Cannawijera,' said Laurette in a resigned tone.

'Yes. It licks me why you don't make more of a home of that place,' said the unsuspecting Ted—'make a garden—you've only got to irrigate, you know: it's ridiculous to pay a manager on a little station like that—and make the place trim and comfortable. In fact, Stella told me she liked Coonjooree so much the last time she was there, she means to go again before long. Jove, I hope I may be there if she does!'

'Well, you see, I am not one of the gifted souls that love a worm-eaten old poet so much better than my fellow-creatures,' said Laurette a little viciously, and the next moment regretted giving any indication of the loathing that the place excited in her mind: but she had the faculty of saying sharp things, and found it hard to resist the temptation. 'But now that nothing else is left to us,' she said with a pensive resignation—'well, I dare say we shall make the best of it. Perhaps, if you come to see us next month, Ted, you will find Talbot planting a grass-tree against the wash-house wall.'

'You must bet him it won't grow, Larry, or he'll never finish the job,' said Ted, laughing. 'You mean next year, though; not next month?'

By way of answer Laurette unfolded her husband's letter, and read aloud:

'"It is only fair to let you know at as early a date as possible that I have lost every stiver of the money I brought with me, and am probably liable for as much more. This comes of trying to earn money by downright honest work——"'

'Baccarat!' interjected Ted; but Laurette did not heed this.

'"If I had been content, as so many are, to take the words of thieving brokers, instead of coming here to see for myself, we would probably have trebled our little haul from the Celestial Hills. But it's no use crying over spilt milk. And I am determined that neither you nor I will ask a loan or an advance from your father or——"'

Laurette stopped short.

'That close-fisted hunks of a brother of yours, that's about it, isn't it?' said Ted, without a *soupçon* of malice. 'Don't mind me, Larry; Tareling and I understand each other. Well, what then?'

'"But we must at once leave Melbourne. So please put the house immediately in Sibworth's hands, and make all your preparations for leaving on or before the 24th of this month."'

Ted gave a low whistle, and Laurette folded up the letter with an inimitable air of resignation.

'But if you go, then, what of Stella's visit?' said Ted, with folds in his brow.

'Stella's visit?' repeated Laurette absently. 'Oh, to be sure! To tell you the truth, my dear Ted, I am too much taken aback by the position to think much of anything beyond the domestic horizon. It is so sudden—yes, and unexpected—for if Talbot had had a little luck we should have paid off nearly all our little arrears; and then, of course, there would be the shearing in October.'

Laurette avoided allusion to the fact that this had been long ago discounted and the advance used up, and creditors appeased only with fictitious promises of payment after the shearing already disposed of.

'Of course you will see Stella at her own home, though I think there is something in the wind about her going abroad with Mrs Raymond. It is to her I trace the rumour that has set Stella—— But there, I must not mix up things and other people's secrets!'

'Larry, you mustn't leave—you mustn't give up Monico Lodge till after September.'

'Ah, my dear boy, I would be only too happy, but it's beyond my power. It did flash across my mind that I would write and ask father; but now that you've explained about the rabbits and things——'

'But there are no rabbits at Strathhaye!'

Laurette looked wonderingly at her brother, and then a sudden light seemed to dawn on her.

'Oh, Ted, don't tempt me. I'll be honest. It isn't what would keep Monico Lodge going; but being so nearly connected with the Weavelows, we are in the swim of everything. I wouldn't undertake to stay for the rest of the season—not unless Talbot's aunt was kind enough to die, and he got the few thousand pounds for which he is down in her will. But she was always a cantankerous old cat. I dare say she'll live for fifteen years to come. And lately she has taken quite a passion for the Burmese. She helped to send two missionaries among the Chins* there, but they were eaten or something. I don't know whether they do eat them in Burmah; but at any rate she's going to send more. How old ladies of the aristocracy of England should send missionaries anywhere while the young men of their own class are what they are—and the old ones, too, for the matter of that!—but I dare say they know how hopeless it would be; whereas people that you never see, you can believe all sorts of romantic things about them, their conversions and things; and then, I suppose, wild creatures, who haven't got a stick of furniture or a shirt to their backs, can afford to be really Christianized.'

Laurette had taken up a seam from a work-basket near, and was sewing away most industriously, while she rambled on in this artless fashion. Ted rose abruptly, and, without saying a word, went to his own room. He returned presently, and Laurette noticed, with a beating heart, that he had a cheque-book in his hand.

He sat down at a davenport in the corner of the room, and wrote for a few minutes rapidly, blotted the cheque, and stood near his sister.

'Don't talk in that cold-blooded way about the old woman, Larry. I think you may always reckon that the Australian side of your clan will do more for you than the "English-nobility" side. Keep this as much as you can in your own hands; and, if you want it, you can have as much again at the end of September.'

With that, Ted put down the cheque before Laurette, and hastened to leave the room. It was for fifteen hundred pounds. It seemed to Ted that Larry didn't look at the amount at all, when she rose with a little exclamation of joy, intercepted him, and threw her arms round him.

'There, Larry, don't slobber! I think you ought to say your prayers for that old woman. It sticks in my gizzard entirely to hear people talk in that way of old people—grudging them their bit of tucker and their own fireside. Why, even the niggers never knocked the old ones on the head unless there was a big famine.'

With this little homily, Ted went out; and Laurette, hardly able to believe her senses, stared at the cheque with beaming eyes. She had hardly dared to hope for such complete success.

'As much again at the end of September!' But of course that was spoken in the elation of believing his suit was to prosper. Like a wary general, Laurette began to sum up the situation. She was secure against detection as to those excursions of the imagination she had dealt in till her brother and Stella met; and as far as Ted was concerned, probably altogether secure; for if that idiotic girl finally rejected him, that was the ultimate misfortune to him, and everything else would sink into insignificance. Stella would be the first to let the cat out of the bag; for if she were still obdurate, the first thing she would say, no doubt, would be: 'Now, Ted, I thought you had made up your mind that we were just to be friends. That is not the sort of thing friends say.' She mimicked her half aloud, and for the first time felt her smouldering dislike to the girl warm up to something like hatred. She was almost sure Stella would cheat her out of the other fifteen hundred pounds. Well, but it was good of Ted—at least good, considering he had never given her more than three or four hundred pounds at a time before. But, after all, a young man with about fifteen thousand a year: 'If we only had a run like Strathhaye instead of that desolate hole! Oh, thank God, we can stay in Melbourne after all!'

It may seem curious that one should thank God for the result of so much devious by-play and deception. But when we consider how a strong nation will attack a weaker one for no better motive than greed or ambition or the lust of tyranny, and then go to church *en masse* to chant the praises of the Almighty because tens of thousands of human beings have been slaughtered and tens of thousands of homes have been desolated and impoverished, the wonder of the solitary case diminishes. It is not safe to assume that the individual conscience is invariably less frayed than that of the collective nation.

CHAPTER XXVI

THE home-station* of Lullaboolagana was one of those delightful places which at once convey an assurance of welcome, comfort and repose. It was partly of wood, partly stone, with additions that formed an irregular chronology of the past. The snug-looking detached cottage, with a billiard-room and two or three bedrooms, marked the season in which the number of sheep shorn touched fifty thousand. The addition with the gable end dated the year in which the little Courtlands first had a governess, etc., etc. The house had deep verandas round three sides. The roof, washed snow-white, so as to lessen the force of the summer sun, gleamed with a seductive cheerfulness and air of salutation among the encircling foliage. Several outbuildings at varying distances made the home-station look at a little distance like a miniature village. The wool-shed and shearers' house, with two or three huts, formed a second group of houses

westward, beyond the confines of what was known as the Home
Field. This consisted of over forty acres of land, which had been
subjected to an artless form of landscape gardening by a relative of
the Courtlands, who had left England under sentence of death from
consumption, and had lived at Lullaboolagana for eighteen years,
though it had been authoritatively predicted he could not survive the
long sea-voyage. Here, then, he had employed his lease of semi-
invalid life in testing the capabilities of Australian soil in growing
trees and plants from widely-separated countries. Here, like Shenstone, though on a smaller scale, he planted groves and avenues and
alleys, diversified his woods, pointed his walks, and entangled his
shrubberies.* The result was a charming semi-English *milieu* of the
kind that the British race are so skilful in creating in the far regions
of the earth, giving their dwelling places under alien skies a touching resemblance to the old quiet homes in which their forefathers
may have lived for many generations.

There were avenues on every side of the Home Field, composed
chiefly of Italian pines, which in twenty years had attained a size
almost incredible for that period. The Home Field was not closely
planted. All over it there were wide open spaces between the groves
and woodlets and groups of trees that embraced endless species,
from the firs and pines of the north to the palms of the torrid zone,
with a liberal proportion of Australian trees. Simplicity was certainly
the governing taste, but combined with a blending of effects which,
when perceived, added a new attraction. All round the house there
were blossoming shrubs, rose-trees, and a great variety of flowers
that kept up a procession of blooms year in, year out. The secret of
perpetual spring in flowers is well-nigh solved by gardeners in the
more favoured portions of Australia. There were several gentle
hillocks in the Home Field, which lent themselves to landscape
effects in a very agreeable manner. But the most charming
natural feature of all was the creek known by its native name, the
Oolloolloo. It meandered through the whole length of the Home
Field. The orchard, which was half hidden in a deep little valley, lay
in two unequal portions, one on each side of the creek. Its course
was still marked by the tall eucalyptus-trees, seldom absent from
the banks of creeks. Indeed, these trees never attain their finest
development except by running water; and yet they have to live
through centuries in waterless wastes. Is there not here something of

the same curious contradiction that we find between the complex social etiquette of the aborigines and their very primitive stage of savagedom? It is often forced upon the observer of nature in Australia that in the past she has been playing strange pranks; among other trifles, brewing pepper for her children instead of nourishing them with milk.

But the eucalypti were far from being the only trees that grew by the Oolloolloo. Side by side with these natives of the primeval woods were copses of alders, overgrown bushes of sweetbriar, bamboos springing up tall and slender, and falling wide apart, making pictures against denser foliage like Japanese screens; here and there a hazel with its 'artless bower';* wide clumps of pampas grass, with their silky, flax-like blooms softly stirred by every breath of wind. Then one would come on a dense little grove of elms and native cherry-trees, mingled with scrub cypress—a combination which, of all others, makes the most alluring secular cloisters; a place in which to dream with open eyes; to catch phantasies by the wing; to read Shakespeare to one's self aloud; to muse, to brood, to meditate. Over all there was an enchanting air of leisure, of tranquil repose, which was heightened by the woods that lay on every side except to the south, where Minjah Millowie, a township of seven or eight hundred inhabitants, extended in an irregular fashion within two miles of the Lullaboolagana home-station.

This was the direction the house fronted, and opposite to it there was a bridge across the Oolloolloo of solid masonry. It was the third that spanned the creek in the Home Field, but the only one that could be depended on when the winter rains were heavy, and the sluggish little creek, with its silent pools connected by a slender trickling thread of running water, was transformed into a rushing, turbid fury of a rivulet that filled the adjacent groves with its enchanting sound. The second bridge was an enormous gum-tree, which from time immemorial had lain across the creek as it fell, its great old withered branches extending over a hundred feet beyond the creek on the Home Field side of it. There were marks all along the upper side of this tree made by the stone axe of the aborigine, who had climbed it in quest of opossums, or to place his bark-enclosed dead among the boughs,* or perhaps to scan the surrounding country for the little column of pale blue smoke that might proclaim the presence of a tribal foe not far off.

The third bridge, so called, was beneath a tall, slim white gum-tree, close to the orchard, and was a little rustic erection perched high up, completely covered on both sides with trailing creepers, conspicuous among them the wide-leaved passion-flower plant, now loaded with blossoms, scarlet and pale purple and white.

'What a graceful creature it is, garlanded with leaves and flowers!' said Stella, as she approached it with her sister-in-law the morning after her arrival. 'It looks like the beginning of a poem, or some place that should come into a story. Has nothing ever happened there?'

'Let me see. Hector and I often walk to and fro on it in the moonlight, when the nights are very warm.'

'Ah, if you were only lovers—that had to part, you know, Louise——'

'Thank goodness we are not!' laughed Louise.

'Not lovers? Oh, of course not—you are married people.'

'Well, Baby, you are as wicked as ever. I do like to hear Hector call you Baby. You see, though you may be very grown-up, and serious at times, Hector best remembers you as the baby of the household, when he left home twenty-one years ago. What ancient folk we are getting, to be sure!'

They had by this time reached the passion-flower bridge, which was provided with seats on each side, and was, indeed, much resorted to as a sort of outside sitting-room. It was a point of vantage, and commanded a good view of the country round. Eastward there were low ranges. Between those and Lullaboolagana lay one of the tracts of dead trees that in Australian scenery make up so weird a picture of desolation. It was known as the Wicked Wood, from some unknown aboriginal tradition. Looking steadily northward, one became sensible of a break in the distant woods that betokened the beginning of a great plain, which stretched many scores of miles in that direction.

'The Messmate Ranges, where I first saw a lyre-bird; the Wicked Wood, where only grass-trees and scorpions live; the Weeloo Plain, where a buggy seems to glide along like a boat—everything is just as it was over three years ago,' said Stella, looking around with glad recognition.

Here the sisters-in-law indulged in one of those long wandering and delightful chats possible only to people who have had interests in common for many years. This lasted till a servant came to announce that Mrs and Miss Morton had called.

'My dear, how you have grown since I saw you!' were Mrs Morton's first words as she kissed Stella. 'This is Julia; you did not see her when you were here—how many years since?'

'Oh, a dreadful long time ago,' said Stella; 'but not long enough for me to have grown, Mrs Morton.'

'Oh, but positively you have, love,' said Mrs Morton, surveying the new arrival with fond eyes.

She was a fair, stout woman, long past middle life, but endowed with one of those exuberantly kind natures which seem to defy the worst inroads of age. She certainly never wore a face of joy merely because she had been glad of yore.* The annals of daily life almost invariably supplied her with food for wreathed smiles. Not that she was callous to the accidents that marred other people's pleasures, though mishaps of all sorts had hitherto been unfamiliar to her personally. Only, though she knew well how to mourn with the unfortunate, she made an offering to oblivion of all that bordered on sorrow in an incredibly short time. Still, no one unconnected with a local catastrophe took it to heart so thoroughly for a day and a half as Mrs Morton did. And on this very occasion she gave proof of this.

'Oh, my dear, have you heard of the dreadful accident?' she said to Louise after a few casual remarks had been interchanged.

'No—what accident?' said Louise, a little startled by the concern depicted on Mrs Morton's face as she spoke. It is curious how the people who feel the most acutely connect any show of deep concern with personal misadventure.

'Well, it was at Dr Morrison's yesterday evening. We called at one of the Minjah shops on our way, and heard all about it. A man came in from the Bush with a fearful gumboil. Dr Morrison found the tooth would have to come out. He put the man under chloroform, and extracted the tooth most successfully—but the man never got over it. The chloroform killed him. Oh, my dear, wasn't it dreadful?' and Mrs Morton took out her handkerchief—not unnecessarily, for the tears were trickling down her cheeks.

'Oh, I am sorry—and poor dear Mrs Morrison so easily upset, it would give her a dreadful shock,' said Louise.

'That is the best of using ether,' returned Mrs Morton tearfully.

'If it hurts the patient it does not show till afterwards. But for a man to die under your hands—without getting away from you! Oh, it is so very shocking!'

'But, after all, mamma,' said her daughter, 'he was quite a common man, and very fond of drink.'

'Well, Julia, my dear, if you were his wife, or his mother, or his sister, that isn't the way you would speak,' said Mrs Morton, wiping her eyes. 'It's of them I think.'

'But he didn't have any, mamma. He was just a knock-about hand on the Tarra-tarra Station.'

'Oh, my dear, not have a mother? how thoughtless you are. If Dr Langdale had been there, I cannot help thinking he would have seen the man couldn't stand chloroform.'

'But isn't Dr Langdale there? He was here the day before yester-day, and didn't say a word of leaving for any length of time.'

'He is at Nareen, staying with the Kenleighs. You know, they worship the ground he walks on since he performed that wonder-fully successful operation on Mark.'

'Do you think he'll really stay in Australia, Mrs Courtland?' said Miss Morton.

'I do not know,' answered that lady; 'I am afraid not. You see, it was not to stay he came, but for a year's change and rest.'

'But then he's always writing—he must be writing a book,' said the young lady. 'I asked Mrs Morrison the other week whether he wasn't, but she only shook her head and smiled. I don't know why some people are so fond of making secrets of things. Either he is or he is not. Why shouldn't she say "Yes" or "No"?'

'Perhaps she doesn't really know,' answered Louise, smiling. She knew that anything in the nature of a secret was abhorrent to Miss Morton, who loved nothing so well as talking of other people's affairs, except talking of her own. She was a tall, good-looking young woman of twenty-five, with large brown eyes, a brilliant complexion, and that stamp of figure which milliners call 'stylish.'

The visitors stayed for many hours in the friendly leisurely fashion of neighbours in the Bush, who are separated by fifteen miles of unpeopled woods. Miss Morton had three weeks previously returned from a visit to her brother, Mr John Morton, coming back by way of Melbourne, where she had stayed a couple of days with Mrs Tareling.

'I would have seen you there,' she said to Stella, 'only you were so long in coming. Laurette thought you were going to give her up altogether. What a dear Laurette is, to be sure!'

To this Stella assented, in the facile way in which we all help to swell social fictions.

'I do not feel as if I remembered much of my new sister-in-law. Is Helen like Julia at all?' Stella asked a little hesitatingly, after the Mortons had gone.

'Not much. Helen takes more after her father. Not but what Mrs Morton is the dearest and kindest of women. You will like Helen, dear,' said Louise, who was essentially one of the peacemakers of life, who not only prophesy smooth things, but help materially to bring them to pass.

'And who is this Dr Langdale you all conspire to——'

'Now, Stella, I warn you to say nothing disparaging,' said Louise, laughing. 'Dr Langdale is an immense favourite with us here. You are sure to see him as soon as he returns from Nareen. He strolls across from Dr Morrison's house in Minjah Millowie most days in the afternoon, when his writing for the day is over. He does write, for Hector told me. You know how slowly Hector makes friends.'

'Does he? You see, I really know very little of Hector and Claude.'

'I always forget that. Of course, you see them only at long intervals, and for a short time. Well, it's about five or six months since Dr Langdale came. He had been in the other colonies some little time. He and Hector became great cronies almost at once. He is related to the Morrisons. We heard a good deal about him before he arrived. He has inherited a pretty good income, and does not need to work for his living. But he always had a great liking for the medical profession. He is much interested, too, in all sorts of social questions. He had an appointment in a large London hospital; in fact, he has never practised anywhere else. He previously held a merely honorary post there for two or three years. Then an uncle—a great physician in the West End—died, and his son wished Dr Langdale to enter on a partnership with him. Before deciding on this, he came away for a year's rest and change.'

'How old is he?'

'About thirty-one, only, like most Englishmen, he looks younger, at least as compared with Australians. But he isn't all English; he is German on the mother's side.'

'Indeed! What is he like?'

'Now, Stella, you are interested. You do so love the Germans. I know you will like Dr Langdale, if only for that reason.'

'Yes; and because you are giving me such a vivid description of him,' said Stella, laughing. The soft flush in her cheeks would have shown one who knew her that she was more interested than she chose to appear.

'Well, I'll do my best, only the moment you see him you'll say——'

'Oh, here you are, both gossiping away nineteen to the dozen! Well, Baby, are you tired from your journey yesterday? After all, you are really quite grown up.'

It was Hector Courtland who made this little speech, standing in the doorway of the drawing-room, where his wife and sister were seated, with Lionel, the eldest boy, just then an invalid, on a couch, buried in the enchanted pages of the 'Arabian Nights.'* Courtland was a tall spare man, with that slight stoop which tall men, who are in the saddle often ten hours out of the twenty-four, are apt to acquire. He was bronzed with the sun and constant exposure to all sorts of weather. He was barely forty, but his dark-brown hair, beard, and moustache were plentifully sprinkled with gray. His face, when in repose, was grave almost to sadness, and he would often pass hours without uttering a word. These are some of the characteristics of a life passed in the Bush from early manhood. Courtland had been at Eton three years, when sudden and disastrous reverses, coupled with failing health, led his father to decide on leaving England for Australia. No one who knew Hector Courtland when he left Eton—a lad of seventeen—would have prognosticated that he would become grave, silent, and unmirthful long before he reached the uplands of middle age. But there are probably few natures which are not profoundly modified by a semi-Carthusian* existence during the most susceptible years of life.

'You look tired, Hector. Wouldn't you like a cup of tea?' said his wife.

'Yes, a quart potful. Some sheep got boxed up at the seven-mile hut, and we had a high old time of it drafting them. Well, Liny, what are you doing, young man?'

'Reading about Sindbad the Sailor, father. Do you know that Aunt Stella can tell stories just like a book?'

'No; I never heard her. What sort of stories?'

'The one she told me this morning was about strange people who live always in the woods.'

'What kind of people, my boy?'

'Well, when they are in the sunshine they are all light. When they are in the moonshine, it goes through them, so you must step very gently, and follow them till they get into the shadow; and when they are in shadow, you cannot tell them from the darkness.'

'Then it seems you do not see them at all?'

'No, father, never; and all the time they are there doing the strangest things. They catch falling stones and toss them back into the sky, and there they give more light than ever, and don't fall down any more. They take old bits of dead bark and make them into butterfly wings, with gold and purple spots on them. When an old log is burnt up they make the little geraniums, that smell so sweet, out of the ashes. They never go to sleep, and they never stop working, and they are never tired and never seen, and they never let the tiniest scrap of anything go to waste.'

The father listened with smiling seriousness to these wonders of the wood. Later on he pleaded to be among the audience when Stella told twilight stories to the children, and he would listen with profound interest to the mystical events and subtle fancies that rose to 'Baby's' lips with tireless vivacity. She certainly had something of the improvisatrice in her, for never, except when she threw the reins on fancy's neck in speaking, did such winged words, luminous reaches of imagination, and quick touches of pathos come to her. Sometimes, when the grave elder brother listened, he would almost question whether this could be the merry little child with wide open eyes who had been the baby among them all when he left home. She had in a manner remained 'Baby' to him ever since.

There is something pathetic in the way that those who are most closely related may come to be entire strangers. When we are in daily communion we inevitably weave fancies one concerning the other, which stand to us in place of knowledge. But all the time—between not only dumb natures, but those most subtly gifted with utterance—there is that baffling, inexorable wall of division, that unfathomed abyss in which each human soul is shrouded from the cradle to the grave.

CHAPTER XXVII

IT might seem at first sight that station life in Australia must be a very slow and dull kind of existence. As a rule, the centres of civilization are far off, the nearest neighbours many miles away; and the ordinary modes of amusement, balls, parties, opera, and theatre-going, etc., are unknown. To many, no doubt, a life so cut off from external excitement would seem a very maimed and incomplete affair. But, on the other hand, it must be remembered that all the most healthful forms of recreation, as opposed to pleasure-seeking, are opened to squatting life. There are books and magazines to read, buggies to drive in, horses to ride, visits to be received and paid, and all the engrossing interests of family life for the women-folk. For the men there is the ceaseless round of duties, which are on the whole not more monotonous than the calling of average professional men, and less arduous, after the early struggles are over, than most other forms of work. And, then, who has lived for years encircled by great woods without finding that these unpeopled spaces exercise a fascination, all their own, over the mind? The tranquil gullies, in which the slender, stringy bark-trees grow so thick that every sun-ray is intercepted; the scrubby ranges, which the radiant epacris sometimes turn into a mass of colour; the swamps, with their wide, gray-green fringe of reeds and rushes and flocks of water-fowl, that come to them in straggling lines from far districts that have become water-less; the treeless plains, that stretch like a mimic ocean to the verge of the far horizon; the swelling hills, that break the monotony of well-timbered, undulating country; the sombre vegetation, the gleam of brilliant desert flowers, the calls and songs of birds, all have a charm of their own, and rise up in the memory of the Australian exile with an allurement which he never finds in the crowded cities—nay, not even in the scenery of the Old World.

Stella took very kindly to station life. She found it delightful to be so closely neighboured by the great unmeasured woods of her native land. She even regretted that the township of Minjah Millowie was so near. The views she liked best were those that swept the woods to the north and west, where one might travel on and on for days without striking any signs of human habitation. Next day she was on the passion-flower bridge, alternately absorbed in Keats and in looking across the Home Field and the stirless masses of foliage beyond, when she heard approaching footsteps. She turned, to find herself face to face with her unknown partner at the Emberly ball.

'Miss Stella! Is it possible?' he said in a delighted tone.

They shook hands cordially.

'I believe I know your name now,' said Stella laughingly.

'Oh! it is Langdale. Did you not know that night?'

'No; but since I came here things I have heard of you made me believe that Dr Langdale and you were one and the same.'

He laughed with beaming eyes at this division of his individuality.

'Well, I knew you were Miss Stella; and now, I suppose, I may add to that, Courtland? This is another stroke of good luck—not so fleeting, I hope, as the first. By the way, should I not ask whether you have got over the fatigues of the ball?'

'Oh yes! This is the day after.'

'Only, I suppose, you would say it was one of the thirty-six tragic situations of life that one can never really make believe?'

'You still remember our little debate?'

'Surely. Tell me, do you still think of the "Kritik of Pure Reason" when the hair-dresser comes before you are going to a ball?'

She laughed merrily, and then said seriously:

'Do you know, I haven't been to any ball half so nice since.'

'And I haven't been to any at all. But they are not much in my line. I wonder if that exquisite Tasmanian tree-fern is still flourishing?'

'No; it died next morning of pure chagrin.'

'I am sorry to hear that. But why?'

'Because someone near it began an anecdote about Heine, and then went away without telling it. If there is anything in the world a Tasmanian tree-fern cannot brook it is an interrupted anecdote.'

'Well, I felt it a great misfortune that your partners discovered you; but I didn't know the tree-fern sympathized with me. Shall I tell you that little story?'

'Please. I have often since tried to imagine what it was.'

'It was told to my mother by an old lady who knew Heine. She visited him one dull day in November, a little over two years before his death. She found him spent with pain, that had defied his sleeping potion all through the night. But he was propped up on his mattress-grave,* writing on a tablet. He said it was a poem, which, like life, had turned into a bad joke on his hands—too long for wit, and too pathetic for the publishers. It was the story of a peasant-boy from the Thuringian woods, who had climbed mountain-peaks for edelweiss, gathered violets before sunrise, who, with tears in their eyes, told him why their petals were the same in number as the eggs of the swallows, and other weighty secrets; a boy who made love to the stars at night, and watched a maiden spinning till he believed that he was a poet. He came to Paris—the beautiful heathen Circe, who slays her lovers by thousands with the simples she culls with a brazen sickle by moonlight.* But her simples had no power over the peasant-boy. He played woodland melodies on his oaten pipe early and late, but no one heeded him. Then he fell ill, and longed even to death for a sight of his native woods, but most of all for one of the white violets that Gretchen used to wear at her throat. Then the evil spirit came to him one midnight, and offered him a white violet for one of two trifles—a song or his soul. The boy had no longer the power to make a song in the cruel city that had broken his heart, so he gave his soul. He held the flower against his lips, but when the dawn crept into his garret he saw that the violet was a purple one, bleached with brimstone. Then without a word he turned his face to the wall and died. They say he looked so young and beautiful that Beelzebub* himself shed tears. "I do not believe this part of the story, however," said Heine, "for in that case he would give up pinching my nerves with red-hot pincers in the night when Mathilde* is asleep, and there is no one to drive him away." Of course, much is always lost when a thing of that kind is repeated from one to the other; but that is the little anecdote as my mother told it me, as nearly as I can recollect.'

'Well, I think it has Heine's *cachet** on it. Poor Heine, it seems like a peep into his room where he lay so cruelly long!'

'Yes, it was a bitter period—those lingering years—when, as he said in one of his letters, he was no life-enjoying, somewhat comely Greek any more, who would laugh merrily at morose Nazarenes; but only a poor Jew, sick to death; a wasted picture of sorrow; an unhappy man.'*

'What a crown of thorns life has for the most part offered to the goldenest-mouthed singers.'

'That is true; but we must not forget that they themselves plaited the thorns too often, just as we other ordinary mortals do.'

'Ah, but they suffer more; they have less "certainty of waking

bliss."* Genius has never been truly acclimatized in the world. The
Philistines always long to put out the eyes of poets, and make them
grind corn at Gaza.'*

There was a touch of scorn in Stella's voice and a light in her eyes
which were not lost on her companion, who, indeed, found an
evident pleasure in looking at her, as well as hearing her speak.

'But you must not forget that poets are by nature very vocal, and
able to record their joys and woes with cunning effect. Now take
the dumb, patient way in which the poor—women among them,
especially—suffer. It is nothing uncommon to find a woman has
been enduring acute pain at intervals for years, and all the time
going about her work as if nothing were the matter, and saying
very little about it. That, to my mind, is true heroism. If a poet
could ever suffer in the same way, for a month, say—ye gods! what
despairing odes—what declamatory appeals to an unrighteous
Heaven!'

'You talk almost like a heretic.'

'Perhaps I say what appears to me true; that is often the worst sort
of heresy.'

'But surely not if your truth is really true,' said Stella, with an
arch smile.

'Ah, that is a burning question,' returned Langdale, with an
answering smile. 'But without going into the more serious aspect of
affairs—though we should not *choose* to be in error—yet are there
not many things in which illusions help people more than the truth?
Isn't that perhaps one reason why things, as they are, remain for the
most part so carefully masked?'

'I must think over that before I commit myself. But about the
poets; isn't it their vocation to see the "passionate expression"* not
only in the face of all science, but to put into words what others
dumbly endure? When Shelley says:

> '"I could lie down like a tired child
> And weep away this life of care,
> Which I have borne and still must bear,"*

he was speaking not only for himself, but for multitudes who have
had the same feeling, but lacked all gift of expression.'

'That just points what I wanted to say. A feeling of that kind is,
after all, fleeting; it takes up but a small part of a working day, and

a working day is, on the whole, a hopeful one. Only the things that make it so would not produce a lyrical cry.'

'That sounds so reasonable; it is more provoking than a downright attack.'

'No; but really it is so. Think what it takes of endeavour, of effort, to make up one day of this world's life. Most of this may be called downright drudgery. Things that have to be done over and over again, in almost exactly the same way, simply because people need three meals a day. And yet the work done has its own interest to each healthy individual.'

'What, to the women who make buttonholes all their lives, and make dolls' arms for a shilling the hundred dozen; to the men who break stones for the road, and work in gangs in factories and mines underground?'

'Do not forget,' said Langdale with a smile, 'that you are thinking of these monotonous employments with a highly sensitized imagination. And even when the work is in far more imaginative grooves—when it brings the mind into touch with things that do not pass away with the using—how much more effective for poetry is the reaction, the mistrust, the vague disappointment, than the moderate satisfaction at moderate success—the feeling of expectation and looking on, and waiting for what is to follow, which, after all, give their zest to the average days of existence?'

'Well, are we to come back to the old idea of banishing poesy because it is misleading?'

'By no means. Only I think we do not enough realize its tendency to heighten what is sad in life—often, I think, to exaggerate it. It isn't the people who have most to do with life that write criticisms on it. And in all criticisms there is a heightening and a deepening. It is the craft of the ready writer.'

'You make me think of an expression people often use when anything dreadful happens—"It is like a dream." And yet the worst things always happen when we are wide awake. Still, I feel the force of what you say about the poor. I have often been struck with the uncomplaining, almost stoical, way in which they take misfortune.'

'Yes, one cannot help being struck with it. "It does feel rather bad," they will say, when "intolerable agony" would be our only adequate expression for what they are enduring. And how simply often they face death. "I wouldn't mind going, if it weren't for the children," I have heard poor, long-suffering women say over and over again. What a sinewy, insinuating expression for passing away from all that we know. There is no art of the rhetorician here—of the shoemaker who can make a great shoe for a little foot.'

The two had left the passion-flower bridge by this time, and were slowly sauntering through the Home Field towards the house. It was the afternoon of one of those perfect Australian days in which the sky is widely vaulted in a dome of crystalline clearness; the horizons so indefinitely enlarged that the limiting-lines are beyond sight; the world overflowing with sunshine, as though day had been added to day; while a cool westerly breeze was blowing, that stirred the boughs into jocund sprightliness, and revealed in the searching light how large the buds were growing on the limes and birches, and all the old-world trees that lose their foliage in winter.

'You almost tempt me to think that it is more poetical to be "to dumb forgetfulness a prey"* than to interpret nature and our own hearts to us,' said Stella. 'But still, I suppose you do love the poets a little?'

'Fortunately I have got a voucher with me,' he returned laughingly, and pulled a small brown volume of Molière out of his pocket.

'Ah! that is one of the beloved among the classics. One reads him each time as if afresh—for the first time.'

'Yes. As I walked from Minjah Millowie I laughed over Harpagon's instructions to his servants to conceal the defects of their liveries as if I had never read them before. Is there anyone else who has the secret of touching the springs of laughter so irresistibly? And it isn't so much with broad effects, or even the finer point of wit, but the perpetual play of the human comedy—the ironical surprises life has in store for us.'

'You make me long to steal the volume from you. I don't think I have read "L'Avare"* for years.'

'Suppose we exchange? I know Keats very imperfectly. This is just the atmosphere in which to read him. Now, that is a sort of pledge of friendship,' he said, as they exchanged books.

'Yes, so it is', answered Stella heartily.

'Do you know, I often wondered if we should meet again,' he went on. 'I quite made up my mind that we might be friends if we did, if you will forgive such boldness.'

'So did I,' returned Stella frankly; and she recalled her conversation with her sister at Coonjooree.

'Thank you very much,' he returned, with a simple cordiality which was a marked trait in his manner. 'I foresee that we shall quarrel occasionally,' he continued gaily, a little afterwards.

'Yes; there is an exasperating reasonableness about you,' she said, with a soberness only belied by the dancing light in her eyes, 'and that must breed mischief sometimes. I suppose it comes of your belonging to two old civilizations firmly rooted in the past.'

He maintained his gravity till her eyes betrayed her, and then they laughed together.

'You have a way of taking temporary rises out of me which you must expect to hear of again,' he said; and this threat made food for more laughter.

And then at that moment Louise, accompanied by two or three little ones, came in sight among the trees.

'What will my sister-in-law think?' said Stella, with an amused smile. 'She does not know we are old friends.'

What Louise thought as she approached the two was that they looked extremely companionable. Stella was attired in a close-fitting cream-coloured cashmere, with a cluster of passion-flowers at her throat, and a broad straw hat looped up at one side with the same flowers. A smile hovered about her lips, and as she talked her long thick lashes and dark slender eyebrows heightened the radiance of her eyes and cheeks.

Her companion was little over a head taller, with a muscular, well-formed figure. His eyes were dark gray, his head and brow strikingly noble—an air well maintained by the rest of the face, more especially the finely-moulded chin and mouth, whose short upper lip was defined rather than hidden by a silky black moustache. His hair was of the same colour; his skin a clear olive tint.

'I do not think I need offer to introduce you to one another,' said Louise, smiling.

'Well, no. We have just been finishing a talk we began the day after I landed in Australia,' said Langdale. And then Louise was speedily told all there was to tell.

'You were sitting on the passion-flower bridge, then, when you met Dr Langdale?' said Louise afterwards, when the two were alone. 'Well, something has happened there at last. For don't you think, under the circumstances, it was almost an event?'

'Oh yes, it *was* an event; for we are going to be friends.'

Louise might smile covertly, and feel as sceptical as people usually are regarding friendship pure and simple between an attractive young woman and a man barely eight years her senior. But Stella, who was weary of being made love to, found this prospect of friendship very alluring; and from the first moment she met him something which she could feel, though not define, made her feel sure that Langdale was a man capable of being an intimate friend without degenerating into a lover.

CHAPTER XXVIII

THERE come epochs in some lives to which the thoughts in all after-years return with infinite tenderness, and a vague wonder that, in an existence so beset with common pleasures and turmoils and disillusions, there should be this tranquil sanctuary by which always there seem to glide the sweet waters of Siloe that go with silence.* Such a period for Stella were the weeks that followed. The spring was an unusually lovely one—calm, overflowing with sunshine, and yet cool. Our Australian woods do not greatly brighten or darken at the approach of any season. And the monotony of form and colour must often deepen the tendency of all well-known objects to fail in making us apprehend our surroundings with eyes quickened by imaginative insight. But here at Lullaboolagana there were groves and little woods of European trees, whose bare branches were starred with leaf-buds that swelled from day to day in the liberal sunlight and the kindly air, making the heart beat with involuntary gladness at their revelation of the dawn of returning youth. This miracle, perpetually renewed, of vegetable life so largely drawn from unseen material, has a subtle power to draw the mind into wondering conjecture as to presences, unknown as well as unseen,* which may be all around and near us.

It seemed to Stella as if she fully felt for the first time the mystical significance of this ceaseless throb of returning vigour. And then the growing intimacy with a mind equipped by training and natural endowments, with a keen apprehension of the more novel forces that are moulding thought and life in the present day—equipped, too, with a calmer, more assured outlook on life than had yet dawned on her introspective, more apprehensive nature, seemed in a delightful

way to realize that ideal of friendship she found so attractive. They
had so much in common, and yet they were so wide apart. And this
led them often far afield in talk which, though at first chiefly impersonal, yet led to a growing sympathy. This may be better realized by
recording, though imperfectly, some of the talk that passed between
them on successive occasions.

The second time they met at Lullaboolagana was on the wide
western veranda closed with a thick screen of creepers, where Stella
sat sewing beside her little invalid nephew.

'I wish you had come in time to hear Aunt Stella's story of the
little lost angel,' said the boy.

'Well, hadn't you better tell it to me, Liny?' said Langdale
coaxingly.

Lionel, nothing loath—he was one of the children who like to tell
a story almost as much as to hear one—told in his own way the
strange adventures of a little angel who, viewing the earth a long way
off, fell in love with it and came to see it closer. He could fly down
easily, but his wings were not strong enough to bear him back. There
was a little cottage in the woods, in which a girl and her mother lived.
The girl found the little angel, wet with the dew and blue with the
cold, and brought him home. When his wings had dried, the mother
plucked most of the feathers out to stuff a pillow with them. This
grieved the angel so much that he wandered off to the woods, and
sat in a very lonely place waiting for his wings to grow again. But the
dragon-flies deafened him with their buzzing, the crows tried to peck
his eyes out, and at last an emu put sand over him, so that he might
be hatched like one of her own chicks.

'That is all,' said the boy. 'Aunt Stella won't say whether the angel
grew its wings or was choked. I think myself the sand would smother
it—or make it blind. Poor dear little angel!'

'I wonder why your aunt told you such a doleful story as that?'
said Langdale, speaking to the boy, but looking at the culprit, who
showed no signs of repentance.

'Are you of the same persuasion as my sister Louise?' said Stella.
'When she tells the children stories they are lightened of all disasters—even "The Babes in the Wood" have a happy time in the end.'*

'Well, don't you think the chief justification of stories is that they
are pleasanter than the worst that may happen?'

'Do you really think so?' said Stella, looking very sceptical.

'Yes, I do. I have a grievance on this point. I am fond of novels—English and French—and always have been. Now, if you begin to read stories at eight, by the time you get to be thirty-one you are at the mercy of contemporaries for fiction. Oh, I assure you, some of my contemporaries who write novels would fare very badly if they fell into my hands. What doleful evenings they have given me, when the day's work was over, and I have sat down in solitude, proposing to forget problems and maladies and the imbecile people who so constantly beset us in life! But, no! the modern novelist, instead of taking the good the gods provide us in wholesome cheerful lives, shows invention in nothing but incredible disasters. If they give us anything new, it is in the way of fools and diseases and villains, and every conceivable shade of human meanness.'

'While all the time you want a glorified Arcadia,* where all the good people are happy and the wicked ones either overthrown or turned from the evil of their ways?'

'Or why don't you say ignored? Think how intolerable human society would be if people were not agreed to ignore a great deal, and rightly so.'

'I do wish you would give me some idea of what your favourite novels should be. At present—what between hiding away the misery of life and ignoring the evil of it—I can only think of fairy tales with the fairies left out.'

'Well, you amuse me. Here are you, quite evidently blessed with a physique without flaw—with all your time to spend in the way that seems best to you—with money, position and friends, and a healthy capacity of enjoyment—and yet you affect to believe that books cannot be real unless they are waking nightmares of misadventure.'

'But how could a tale be made that anyone would read out of good health and immunity from destitution? Not that I am one of those happy beings; for I am awfully poor,' said Stella.

'Are you really?' said Langdale, looking curiously at the pale pink crêpe de chine which was one of Stella's favourite materials of wear.

'Yes; I have only thirteen pounds a quarter for everything.'

'What, for rent and food and the incidence of taxation? You must manage very well.'

'Oh, you are laughing at me! Of course I mean for my clothing.'

'And do you mean to say you are poor upon that?'

'Yes; the worst of all poverty, debt. My notebook is full of entries, in my brother Tom's handwriting: "Lent this day to Stella, five pounds; to be paid again to me when she can. I say five pounds!"'

'That has a very business-like sound,' said Langdale, smiling.

'Oh yes; and after these notes I also write: "I owe unto Tom five pounds, lawful money of Australia, which I did borrow of him. Heaven grant he may get it back." But this is a digression.'

'Not at all, as far as I am concerned,' answered Langdale, speaking quite gravely, but with a lurking smile in his eyes. 'A young lady who has fifty-two pounds a year and sundry pound-notes for mere dresses and ribbons, and yet is desperately poor, is just fit to be a member of that growing fraternity of malcontents who are so ready to rail at Nature and Providence.'

'Now you are quite mistaken,' said Stella, with equal gravity. 'It was only yesterday afternoon I saw a laughing-jackass* swoop down and swallow a great blind-worm that Dunstan, our gardener, turned over, and yet I asked neither Providence nor Nature a single question. It was an ugly creature, and I was quite content it should be gobbled up out of sight.'

This delicate insinuation that, when we find little to complain of in life, it is because we ourselves are protected from the worst barbs of misfortune, was not lost on Langdale.

'But then an angel is higher up in the scale—nearer to our own sacred caste of humanity,' he said with a quiet smile; 'and so you protest against accident to one of these by making a poignant little tale out of its disasters. How characteristic that is of so much of our modern literature, which piles up often the outward accidents of existence and all the time leaves out its very kernel.'

'Tell me what you think is left out.'

'Life itself. The strong warm instinct of clinging to the earth even when its harvests do not whiten fully to allay our hunger—the instinct that makes the man who has writhed in pain through the night carry food in trembling spoonfuls to his lips in the morning, while a glow of thankfulness rises in his heart because he yet lives to see the light of day—ah! it is a subtle ensnaring game, this life of ours. And to most—I am sure of it—the very fact of being alive is a good that outweighs the bitterest evils.'

'And yet you have been so often in the presence of the terrors of life. In London there must be swarms of people about whom everyone must feel it would be better if they never saw the light. It seems to me that in hospitals and poor-houses a doctor must often feel that death rather than life would be the great boon.'

'I am afraid you will think I am very callous,' said Langdale with a smile; 'but such a thought has very seldom forced itself on me; and when it has, I have rejected it as treasonable. I dare say you are right. Habit may engender a bias on the side of life apart from its conditions. Fortunately for us, we have only to take one part at a time in the stage of life.'

'Yes, you are concerned with pulling a man through, not with the question whether it is worth while. Now, I am one of the lookers-on at the play. I do not hold a retaining fee on one side or the other, and so I perceive how unmoral this ardour for prolonging this existence really is.'

Stella spoke with extreme gravity; but seeing that Langdale really thought she was in earnest, she could not refrain from laughter.

'It is very charitable of you to assume that this ardour for keeping people in life counts for so much,' he said, smiling. 'But, joking aside,' he added after a pause, 'there is an absorbing interest often in watching how incredibly near a human being may draw to the unknown bourne,* and yet struggle back to health once more. What is the subtlety of man compared to the subtlety of Nature? someone has said.* And Nature is in nothing so subtle as the extraordinary rallies she makes on the side of life. And thus, in a great crisis, when one pang of remorse or a dark foreboding as to the future might turn the scales against recovery, the senses are wrapped in unconsciousness as impenetrable as that of early childhood.'

'You make me feel that a struggle against death might be more entertaining to watch than the life that followed.'

'But when you are a little older you will find that the great thing is the game itself,' returned Langdale, with the frank, catching smile characteristic of him; 'the endless interaction of motive and expectation, of work and play, of the wider outlook on human affairs, which is so distinctive of modern days, lend the world an interest that outbalances its dreariness.'

'Yes; as long as we do not try to peer below the surface,' returned Stella half smilingly.

'And then,' went on Langdale, 'there is a strong element of *opéra bouffe** in the world, apart from moral or deeply serious considerations; so much interplay that lightens work.'

'Even in the wards of a hospital?'

'Yes. I had to laugh as I rode out yesterday, recalling a case that was admitted into our casual ward a week or two before I left hospital. It was a man who had been run over, and whose head was badly hurt. It appears he had been drinking for some time. He explained to me, as he was getting better, that he was a poet, whose ideas would flow only under alcoholic stimulant. This unfortunate accident made him lose the thread of a great epic, which would have made his fame. "Oh! what was it—what was it?" he would say, and then he would implore me to help him to recover his epic. It was a theme colossal in its grandeur, and yet full of pathos and interest. I suggested heaven and hell. "Ah! don't you see, that when people have ceased to hope for one or fear the other, such a theme is impossible. Besides," he said, "the critics would at once say I was imitating Dante and Milton." Then I said, "A great monarch—one dethroned," etc. "A monarch!" he said, in a tone of disdain, "a creature that nowadays has either to ape the manners of the common herd, or keep himself locked up like a criminal!" "Woman?" then I said in despair. "Oh, woman—woman, who broke my head, and has stoned the prophets in every age——" he replied, beginning to sob.'

They both laughed at this reminiscence. Then Mrs Courtland and the governess joined them, and the conversation became general.

CHAPTER XXIX

THREE weeks of Stella's visit at Lullaboolagana had passed, when her brother Claude and his young wife returned from their travels. It had been arranged that they were to live at the head station a year or two before starting an establishment on their own account. Mrs Claude was a good-looking, vivacious young woman, who, as is the wont of travellers, had brought back many tales of the countries she had seen. They had spent February and March in England among relations on both sides, and this, on the whole, was the part of their foreign experience which oftenest afforded themes of reminiscence.

'Some days would begin bright,' she would say, 'and then all at once a fog would come on. After peering into the sky for some time you would find the sun in the most awkward position, looking for all the world like an old worn-out rose-coloured platter. But even when there was no fog you would think the sky was coming down on top of you. It was so awfully low and dark, and all the trees shivering—I used to long to put a petticoat on the poor things. And at Uncle Courtland's rectory in Devonshire I found a little blue gum trying to live. Oh dear, I nearly cried over it.'

'Why? well, you must have been homesick!' said Louise.

'Well, I don't know—but at any rate I was very dull. They went to church so often, and I felt I ought to go too. One of the girls had been to Girton,* and she is a little like Stella in some things—but the rest seem to look on her as a pagan. . . . I couldn't believe you had more sunshine here than you liked. You begin to understand why English people laugh so little.'

'But do they?' questioned Stella, who was listening and sewing by a French window that opened on the veranda. 'I think all the English people I have known laughed as much as we do; and what other nation has produced such humorists?'

'Oh yes, long ago. Now they laugh most when they are here—like Dr Langdale. I should think there must be millions of women in England who never laughed out in all their lives. I suppose that's why they take everything so seriously. If you're five minutes late for breakfast they look at you as if you had stabbed the cook—or worse; for they would say a cook can be replaced, but if you waste the time you can never get it back.'

'You see, dear, we get rather lax ideas of punctuality in the long hot summers,' said Louise apologetically.

'Oh, my goodness! how I should like to see some of our relations there—panting on their bedroom floors instead of seeing that every-one is at the table to the minute! Such a fuss over wasting the time! Claude says it's part of *"le cant Anglais*."* What better can you do when the sun never shows himself?'

'You speak as though you had been rather in a wet blanket there,' said Stella, smiling, 'and found the people rather *agaçant*.* Now, I think nice English people are the nicest of all.'

'Yes, in Australia, away from the rest,' said Nell, with a sparkle in her eyes; 'but a houseful gets upon the nerves—and as for a whole country full of them, nothing but the thought of leaving it for Australia, say, keeps you up. I can see you don't take that in quite; but wait till you go there, Stella. I don't believe you would stay two days at your uncle's. They are for ever talking of church and the anti-Unionists.'*

No doubt Mrs Claude could have enlarged eloquently on the subject had it not been cut short by the entrance of her mother and sister Julia, who were speedily followed by Dr Langdale. He stayed only a few minutes, however, being on his way to Nareen, and having merely called with a book for Stella. Mrs Morton could never see Dr Langdale without entering on conjectures as to whether he might not settle in Victoria, instead of returning to London when his year was up.

'We do so need good doctors in this country,' she said; 'and really the young men who take their degrees in Melbourne and Sydney seem anxious to cut people up just out of curiosity to see what's inside them.'

There was a general laugh at this, but Mrs Morton did not speak in a joking spirit.

'Indeed, girls, it is true. There was that young Dr Jones at Warracootie. Not a fowl could they keep. He was trying to invent a liver pill, and used to try its effects on hens and ducks. They all died in convulsions. He said it was in the sacred cause of science and humanity—but surely it's better to have your own eggs fresh laid. And then, if he knew as much about the liver as he should, would his pills act in that way?'

'But, for all we know, Dr Langdale may be engaged to be married, and obliged to return,' said Miss Morton, and she managed to watch Stella's face as she spoke. But she did not glean anything from the survey. Then Mrs Claude, who knew the rather callous way in which her sister was prone to investigate and thresh out any subject that interested her, changed the conversation. But the subject was one on which Miss Morton was conscious of an aching void for information, and next Sunday, when Claude and his wife were spending the day at Broadmead, the Morton station, Miss Julia returned to the subject again.

She was a young woman who took her prospect of settling in life, as she would have called it, very seriously. It was now nearly three years and a half since she and Mr Ritchie had been, as she thought, on the verge of becoming engaged. She had had frequent opportunities of meeting him during her visits to her brother and his wife, Ted's elder sister. She believed that Ted still admired her a good deal—that she formed, in fact, a sort of second string to his bow, which he would soon fall back on, if only he were finally convinced that Stella was not to be won, or, better still, if Stella married. This was a calculating, not to say mercenary, way of looking upon marriage for a good-looking young woman of twenty-five. But we sometimes forget that the freedom of choice in marriage, which is permitted to women of the Anglo-Saxon race, has the effect of making some of them regard the institution on cool business principles. It is an 'arrangement' made by themselves, instead of by the mothers, as in France. Indeed, no French mother could go to work in a more disenchanted way in this respect than a certain type of Australian girl. 'I am getting on in life,' she will say, examining the corners of her eyes and the parting of her hair critically. And then she counts over the number of eligible men in her circle, and makes a mental tick against the name of the one who combines most money with good looks. If he dies, or marries the wrong woman, the process of ticking has to be gone over again.

But to do Miss Morton justice, affection, though not of an absorbing nature, had something to do with her designs on Ted Ritchie. She could readily have loved him, and would much sooner have married him than, say, the dissipated younger son of an English peer, as her friend Laurette had done. She had, indeed, during the period when Ted seemed seriously bent on coming to the point, discarded a local suitor, who was quite as wealthy as the recreant knight, but twenty years older, and with a fringe of crimson hair scantily surrounding a singularly flat crown. His eyes, too, were of the protruding order, and his chin fell away a good deal. Altogether, he had very much the look of a frog that has lived through many winters. Still, he had fifteen thousand a year, and such an income always placed a marriage above the odious category of scratch matches. But he was a shy sort of creature, and seemed to have taken a woman's 'No' as being final. He would doubtless require unmistakable tokens of goodwill to bring him to the point once more. Now, though Miss Morton was not romantic in her disposition, though she had started in life with few ideals, while those that she had were of a tough, serviceable kind, yet she hesitated, and delayed showing those tokens while Ted was still in the land of the living—in other words, unmarried. If she could only write to tell Laurette that Stella was engaged! Before she left Melbourne the two had canvassed the whole affair in that exhaustive, unreserved fashion habitual to many women in talking over their own and other people's affairs.

'I consider Stella as good as engaged to Ted after all that has passed,' Laurette had said. And when Julia came home, it was with a fixed resolve to regard Ted as no longer among the quick; and she had even planned those overtures which would convince Mr Timothy Haydon that, though a girl might decline to leave the parental roof over three years ago, it did not follow that she would always be in that negative mood. He would come home with them from church one Sunday, as he sometimes did, and a little accidental stroll in the garden together and a judicious leading would surely be enough. But, then, before this visit or stroll came off, she found that Stella Courtland and Dr Langdale were 'as thick as two thieves,' as she expressed it in writing to Laurette. On getting this letter, Laurette had instantly written back asking Julia to be sure to let her know if anything happened. It was rather early days for anything to have 'happened' in Laurette's sense of the term; but, then, speedy wooings are not rare in Australia, especially when there is a separation in near prospect. Stella's visit was not to extend beyond the middle of September, while Dr Langdale's original intention was to return to England in October. And then they saw so much of each other: they had so much to say, and looked grave, and laughed, and interested, and animated all in turn. What could such proceedings mean, but that they were fascinated by each other and falling in love?

And then, in the midst of her dubitations on the point, Mr Timothy Haydon suddenly announced his intention of visiting England after shearing. It was well known to his friends that he had a tribe of unmarried elderly female relations in England— cousins of all degrees of nearness and remoteness. He would never return 'alive,' Julia was certain of that. If she was not prepared to resign him, to let him become the victim of a foreign brave of the female 'sect,'* she must take speedy action. But what if, after the day on which that stroll should come off in the garden with a successful issue, she heard that the knell of Ted's hopes as far as Stella was concerned had been rung! It was a cruel position for a young woman whose fate lay in her own hands, as far, at any rate, as the second best match possible to her was concerned. It was like the story of the old woman who was driving her pigs to market. In her perplexity Julia resolved to play the part of the rope in that legend of the nursery.* According to the light that was in her, she resolved on a little experiment of her own to bring matters to a crisis.

Two days before Mrs Claude returned there had been a lawn-tennis party at Dr Morrison's. Dr Langdale was one of the players, and during an interval in which Miss Morton and he were looking on, the lady took the opportunity of speaking of Stella's play as a prelude to playing the part of the rope.

'Miss Courtland never strikes the ball except on the run. Now, which do you think is the better way to play a stroke, Dr Langdale?'

'The way in which you are most successful, I should say,' answered Langdale, smiling.

'I would like awfully to learn how to put on twist when I give a service as Miss Courtland does. I wish she were to settle here when she marries; but her future home will be a long way off.'

'Yes?' said Dr Langdale. But Julia could not detect any show of surprise. There was, perhaps, a slight, slow alteration of colour, and in a little while he added: 'I did not know that Miss Stella was to be married.'

'Oh, it is a very old story! She was engaged for a short time years ago to the gentleman and broke it off, and now it is on, or as good as on, again—at least, so her sister-in-law that is to be told me. Perhaps I should not have spoken. But'—with an arch smile—'I thought, as you are such good friends, that you knew.'

'Well, I hope the happy man deserves his good luck,' returned Langdale; and there the matter dropped.

In thinking over it afterwards, a panic seized Julia that she might have put a rachet in the wheels instead of giving them a spin. But no; she felt certain people could not be so intimate without 'talking over' things that concerned them. If Langdale was at all affected, he would not rest till he found out whether this was true. Such rumours often advanced affairs in a marvellous way; but since then eight days had come and gone, and there was no sign. Miss Morton used to lie awake at night thinking that after all she might fall between two stools. And now shearing would soon begin, and she was as undecided as ever about that stroll in the garden with Mr Timothy Haydon.

So on this Sunday she resolved to glean all that she could, hoping for some light that would help her to come to a decision. After dinner she and Mrs Claude went into the banksia-covered arbour at the far end of the garden, the very spot in which Julia had pictured herself gently leading her Adonis of fifty* into the primrose path of dalliance. She recalled him as she had seen him that morning (his pew was not far from theirs in church), and her heart fell. His fiery fringe of hair was getting scantier, his eyes paler and more blinking, his wrinkles more obtrusive. And then she thought of Ted. The contrast between the two gave her a sense of faltering dismay. Then she thought of Stella as an interloper, whose unpardonable wilfulness overshadowed her own (Julia's) plans like a nightshade.

'Well, Nell, and how do you get on with Stella Courtland, on the whole?' she said, suddenly rousing herself out of the reverie in which the probable and possible husband formed a disconcerting foreground.

'Oh, charmingly! Who could help liking her?—so full of fun, and all kinds of unexpected fancies.'

'You seem to have rather a trick of standing round her at Lull, when she talks; but, for my own part, I like a girl with a more open disposition. Now, who would see her with Dr Langdale without thinking they were lovers, or going to be?' said Julia, with much animation.

'Well, and supposing they were?' said Mrs Claude, a little surprised at her sister's tone.

'Supposing they were! And she as good as engaged to Ted Ritchie!' retorted Julia.

She was determined to put her case bluntly, so as to extort her sister's opinion all the more quickly.

But instead of evoking any sharp denial, as she hoped to do, a sudden light seemed to fall on Mrs Claude.

'Well, now, that explains what has begun to puzzle me,' she said slowly; and at these words poor Julia's heart fell.

'What has been puzzling you, Nell?'

'The sort of fast friendship there is between Stella and Dr Langdale, without any approach to love-making.'

'Without any approach to love-making!' echoed Julia bitterly. 'Well, Nell, you must be a greenhorn to be taken in by such stuff. Why, you cannot see the two together without knowing at once they are playing at being friends; but it's about the shabbiest disguise *I* ever saw.'

'Oh, I know how you look at it, Julia,' said Mrs Claude, with a quiet smile. 'You only see part of the play, and the other part you put together all endways.'

'Well, I see only part, but enough is as good as a feast,* they say. Why, last Thursday when I was over there I saw them meeting at the passion-flower bridge, and it took them a solid hour to get from there to the house! And yet till Stella appeared you know the sort of deadly calm the Doctor always maintained to young ladies. Indeed, Mrs Waring felt certain there was something behind it all—that he was privately married, or a woman-hater, or something.'

'Oh, we all know Mrs Waring's talent for working out patterns for other people's lives,' said Mrs Claude, with a superior little smile which Julia found very trying. 'You see,' she went on, with the combined experience of one recently married and travelled, 'people in the Bush think, as a rule, that if two people like Stella and Dr Langdale have long interesting talks, it must somehow mean love-making. So it does in ninety-eight cases, but they are the ninety-ninth, and with them it doesn't. And when you see a little more of the world you'll find there are plenty more like them. Why, when we were at Geneva we met an American lady and her mother. I suppose I ought to name the mother first, but she was really as much in the background as an extra dress-basket. Well, the daughter was not young, and there was a countryman of hers, the Consul there, who had been her intimate friend for fourteen years. During all that time when they are apart they write long letters to each other every other week.'

'Good gracious! what a waste of time! Why in the world don't they marry?' cried Julia energetically.

'Well, you see, they only want just to be friends,' answered Mrs Claude, with unconscious irony; 'and they had all sorts of things to talk about, only they were always very serious. But Stella and the Doctor have great fun very often.'

'Why, do they chaff each other much? Because, you know, that's a great sign sometimes. That's the way Dan Wylie and Milly Waring used to go on.'

'Mercy on us! do you suppose that Stella and Dr Langdale go in for that sort of horse-play?' said Mrs Claude, with a comic look of horror.

'Well, I wish to goodness you would give me some idea of what they *do* go in for. I might then get an opinion of my own. You mustn't think it's just idle curiosity,' said Julia, with a solemn expression. 'Any time I overhear them they laugh and smile at things that don't seem to me in the least funny. And Hector, too, who is the slowest coach I ever saw in my life, he seems quite lively and talkative with these two.'

'Well, you know, Hector and Dr Langdale were great friends before ever Stella came.'

'What was that talk going on about novel-writing on Thursday evening?'

'Oh, there is a theory that each is writing a novel. Stella declares the Doctor is bent on making his book so agreeable that there are crowds of obliging fairies in attendance on his characters, picking crumpled rose-leaves out of their way, and so on. And he imagines that her people in the end resolve to sit still all their lives, as the only way in which they can avoid doing evil; and then when things go wrong they call Nature, and Life, and Providence to the bar of judgment, and decree that they ought to be hanged, so as to give the world a fresh start. The Doctor declares that reaping as we sow* makes up two-thirds of the misfortunes of life. Then Stella asserts that life is so arranged that you sow tares when you mean to sow wheat, and that when you do sow honest grain an enemy comes in the night, who spoils the harvest.'*

'Well, it's rather silly, don't you think, to go on so about far-off things?* And then they seem to turn even people's misfortunes into a joke. They were actually smiling over Mr Dene's compound fracture.'

'Oh, Julia, how can you take up things in such a crooked way!' said Mrs Claude warmly. 'They did nothing of the sort. Hector had been to see Mr Dene, and said he was getting low-spirited through being confined to the house so long. And then Stella said, quite gravely at first—she often makes one believe she is in earnest when she is not—"I suppose in writing a novel fit to be read when one smoked a pipe after the labours of the day are over, an accident of this kind should be termed one of the agreeable amusements of old age—or would you ignore a compound fracture altogether?"'

'Well, I am sure that is chaffing, if not more so,' said Julia sturdily. 'And then, what did Dr Langdale say?'

'"Not if it pointed one's pet moral so completely," he said. "You must perceive that if an old gentleman at seventy-three persists in riding a fiery horse imperfectly broken in, he lays himself open to accident; in fact, he was so likely to get his neck broken, that a compound fracture may be, in comparison, called a gentle warning."'

'And then Hector and Dr Langdale have taken to calling Stella "St Charity." What is that for?'

'Oh, because she has the most extraordinary way of finding out creatures that are hurt. Before we came, she found a little calf with a broken leg when she was out riding. One of the boundary riders set the leg for her, and she has nursed it in a fashion. It is now nearly well. Then early last week she came upon an old crow badly wounded, and she brought that right home, and tied up its broken wing and treated it with vaseline. Hector and Dr Langdale call it Satan; but Stella won't have that name. She says the only time Satan was hurt it only made him cleverer than ever. But it's a dreadfully cross old crow, and we all think it is the queerest pet. But it really begins to hop after Stella.'

'Oh, she's a spoilt thing; she always does just whatever comes into her head, however queer it may be,' said Julia impatiently. She really seemed as far as ever from any guiding light as to that walk with Timothy.

'Well, what comes into her head in that way is very kind and sweet,' returned Mrs Claude. 'There is poor old Mick——'

'Mick? Is that a crow, or a calf, or what?' said Julia pettishly.

'Not nearly so interesting—to most people, at any rate,' laughed Mrs Claude. 'He is a dreadful little old ragged, drunken Irishman, who has eight young children. He used to come to Lull sometimes asking for a job; but Dunstan and some of the other men thought so badly of him, Louise dared not give him any work. But one day when he came, Stella met him by the creek, and had a long chat with him, and coaxed Dunstan to give him work; and now he is in constant employment in the Home Field, and hardly a day passes but he says something ridiculously droll to Stella. She declares that naturally he is one of the best little men she ever knew.'

'What, that awful little Mick Doolan, that has been so often in gaol for drunkenness?'

'Yes; but Stella has found out it is his wife who drives him to the public-house. She is a perfect virago, and every now and then Mick comes with a black eye and a funny shade over it. He says he was breaking wood, and a stick flew up and hit him. Stella goes to see her regularly now when she goes into Minjah, and we fancy things are a little better. But Stella does not like to talk of her charities. She says they nearly always turn out addled eggs.'

'I don't wonder at it if she takes up people like Mick. Mrs Wylie met her near the cemetery the other day, and she watched her go into it with a basket of flowers. What does she do that for?'

'She weeded Rupert Courtland's grave, and puts flowers on it once or twice a week. The cousin, you know, who planted the Home Field, and lived there with the Courtland brothers so many years. He was so fond of trees and flowers, and planted so many rose-trees that are now in full bloom.'

'Well, you may say what you like, but I think she is rather queer,' said Julia. 'Then, do you really think, Nell, that neither Stella nor Dr Langdale care for each other, except as friends? Mind, as I said before, I have good reason for wishing to know.'

'But what good reason can anyone else have to know what chiefly concerns themselves? I should be very sorry to answer decidedly for either, especially for—well, I don't think I should say it.'

'For whom? What a close sort of thing you are getting, Nell!'

'Well, for Dr Langdale, if you must know. When he walks across in the afternoon, if Stella is not in the room, or in the veranda where we sit so often, and he catches sight of her coming, or hears her voice, his whole face lights up. You see, his is a face that must show what he feels more than most men's. There is no part of it hidden. The eyes and mouth sometimes look as tender as a woman's, and yet there is something a little hard about him. And suddenly, when he is talking, something makes him look almost stern.'

'Well, Nell, you always were one to notice a great deal and find things out long before other people did!' said Julia with sisterly admiration. She herself seldom noticed things unless they had a distinctly personal bearing; and then she invariably interpreted them according to her own wishes.

'It seems to me you have been taking Dr Langdale out of winding pretty completely,' she said after a pause.

'Well, you see, one must do something when one has to keep indoors so much, and do a lot of sewing,' said Mrs Claude with a pensive little sigh, unconsciously hitting upon one of the keys to that passion for psychological observations which, with some women, develops into a sort of sixth sense; 'but for all that, you know, I shouldn't be a bit surprised if they parted friends and nothing more. Certainly Dr Langdale doesn't talk of returning to England much, lately; and Stella too, sometimes, when she speaks of returning to Fairacre, suddenly turns very silent. But that may be because she thinks of Ted. She is to stay at Laurette's on her way back.'

'But what do Louise and Claude say? As for Hector, he's such a stick-in-the-mud, he wouldn't see anything unless several people told him plump.'*

'Claude and Louise? We none of us exchanged a syllable on the matter. Oh, you mustn't imagine we sit and talk things over, and try to ferret things out, as—as we girls used to.'

'Well, I call that a very cold, reserved sort of way for a family,' said Julia, with a touch of scorn. 'And that's one of the things that the tourist people who come here for a few weeks, and write books, praise us for. They say we have such an open, unreserved, easy way.'

'But then you see those tourists mostly see the people who have made money in business in the towns, and they are nearly always garrulous everywhere. It's their life,' said Mrs Claude, with a touch of her husband's manner that was not lost upon Julia.

'Yes, and no doubt the Courtlands are extra reserved because of their ancestry,' she said, tossing her head. 'It's good of you to keep so friendly with us, Nell, after marrying into such a set.'

'Don't be so absurd, Julia; and whatever you do, don't mention a word of what I've said to anyone.'

'What have you said, then?' cried Julia, in high dudgeon. 'I could imagine ten times as much in half a minute. I believe you know more than you say. I think Stella Courtland is a perfect flirt, and you don't like to—to tell on her. But, after all, I don't believe she'll ever give up a man with fifteen thousand a year for one that has to look at people's tongues for a living.'

Mrs Claude could not refrain from laughter at this incisive summing-up.

'Dr Langdale needn't if he does not like. You know he has seven hundred a year private income.'

'Yes; his father was in business, at any rate—a London fruit-broker. I don't think that was so very aristocratic,' said Julia, who really was in the mood in which certain women love to fling their tongue abroad like a javelin.

'Yes, his father was a London fruit-broker and the grandson of a baronet,' answered Mrs Claude calmly. 'Oh, Mrs Morrison only mentioned it in the course of conversation, just when I told her that my pretty moss-green bonnet was bought in London, in a shop kept by a lord's daughter.'

'Well, if Stella didn't feel it was wrong to make such fast friends with one man when she's engaged to another, surely she would have said something to you or Louise about Ted,' said Julia, making a last despairing effort to 'fossick' out some more highly coloured hint than she had yet obtained.

'Oh, as to that, Stella got so much blamed on all sides for getting engaged to Ted for a week and then breaking it off: we none of us expect to hear of her being engaged till she's on the eve of marrying. You know it was after that affair she came to see Louise, over three years ago; and she said then she never would be engaged for more than a few days. The temptation of throwing it all up again might be too great.'

'Oh, she's a conceited thing! I always think there's something almost impertinent in the cool way she treats everything,' said Julia viciously.

'Look here, Julia, if you don't like Stella, we'll stop talking about her,' said Mrs Claude; and with that she returned to the house. Julia lingered for a few moments in the arbour, trying to decide whether it would not be safer to have Mr Haydon to dinner next Sunday, and renounce all chance of Ted for good and all—'that Stella is too risky a creature to let anything hang on her ways,' she thought, and she slowly followed Mrs Claude into the house.

'Oh, my dears,' her mother was saying, 'did you hear that Sally Richardson died on Saturday night at twenty minutes past twelve? She ate a little sago, with a tablespoonful of port wine in it, only half an hour before; and she said the whole of "Gentle Jesus, meek and mild,"* a little afterwards. Her poor dear mother——' and Mrs Morton wiped her eyes.

'Well, mamma, you know what a fearfully tiresome creature Sally always was,' said Julia tartly.

Sally had been a housemaid in the Morton family for some time, but indeed it needed not this tie in the past to make Mrs Morton dwell with effusion on every small particular she could glean of a death, or on the blank that it caused. It is sometimes curious to observe the modifications which parental traits undergo in a second generation. Julia had inherited all her mother's ardour for the details of other people's lives, but utterly divested of her mother's quick sympathy. There was really no personal gratification which Mrs Morton would have purchased during any period of her life, had it been in her power, at the cost of a finger-ache to a Mandarin in China. Whereas there was no kind of ache Julia would have saved any young woman she knew, if such pain could advance her own scheme of life. Perhaps when the laws of heredity are better understood, the danger of saddling a daughter with callous indifference to the claims of others will serve to curb the too expansive altruism of mothers like Mrs Morton.

'The idea of mamma going to sit up with that Richardson woman all Friday night!' said Julia in a discontented voice.

'Well, my dear, you ought to be used to your mother being a real Christian by this time,' said her father, not without intentional sarcasm.

He was a hale old man of seventy-five, who enjoyed the distinction of being the only squatter in the Warracootie District who had lived fifty years of his life in Australia. He was one of three brothers—descendants of an old English squire who had lost his land—who had come to Victoria with a little capital, which had all been lost in unprofitable speculations, so that they were for some time knock-about hands, till a fortunate gold claim formed the foundation of the wealth which they now enjoyed.

CHAPTER XXX

THERE are many days of an Australian spring on which to remain within doors is an impossible heresy. This Sunday was one of them. The two who afforded Miss Julia Morton so irritating a theme for conjecture and comment were wandering in the Home Field in common with the rest of the Lullaboolagana household. Dr Langdale had a little old-fashioned-looking book in his hand, and was engaged in the congenial task of supporting a theory Stella had started some days previously. She had found Virgil's 'Eclogues'* full of notes in her deceased kinsman's handwriting, and it suddenly occurred to her that the Home Field was full of hints from those stately pastoral poems.

'Suppose we trace the resemblances one day?' said Langdale.

'May I say it?' asked Stella, smiling.

'You will say it, whether you may or not, when you look so mischievous, St Charity.'

'Well, don't you think it is the German in you who suggests that heartless form of crushing my poor little fancy?'

'Now, as a penalty for that speech, I shall pelt you with proofs,' said Langdale, laughing.

And now he was going to make good the threat, armed with the little book in tarnished gold that bore traces of having been a treasured companion.

'I am waiting to be pelted,' said Stella.

'Well, there is Amaryllis,* to begin with; swift as a fawn, lithe as a young pine, flitting by, pretending she does not hear the lay that Tityrus pipes on his flute——'*

'But where is she?'

'Oh, a commentator is always allowed to see a little more than his readers or hearers. I see her. And then there is the spreading beech under which the swain reclines. Look, there are three beeches hard by—all spreading as far as their age permits. Could the beech-tree under which Tityrus reclines* do more?'

'Oh, I see that in the matter of proving a theory you were born to destroy Afreets,'* said Stella, her face sparkling with fun at the extreme gravity which her companion had assumed.

'But there is much more to follow. A little further on Meliboeus says—— May one read a little Latin to you without scandal?'

'Surely that is an anachronism! What else would he read?' said Stella, pretending to misunderstand.

They both laughed at this; and then Stella said: 'Yes, one may.'

'Then, "Hic inter densas corylos."* The Oolloolloo is haunted with dense hazel-bushes. Tityrus, in his reply, says that Rome lifts up her head among other cities as high as cypress among bending osiers.* I am not sure about more than one patch of osiers, but cypresses you have in abundance.'

'Yes, and of all the trees that grow, none look lovelier in the rose twilight of sunset. See those clumps of them between the house and the orchard, mingled with tamarisk-trees. At mid-day the cypress looks dark and stern compared with the silky tamarisk locks. But when the sunlight is dying, the cypress seems to disentangle its feathery foliage, till it looks like an airy vision of a tree rather than one that has roots underground.'

When Stella spoke of trees, or animals, or flowers, one could see that they were like living humanized creatures to her.

'Now, I have often wondered why I like cypress-trees better at sunset. Tell me some more about trees.'

'Oh, you haven't finished your proofs yet.'

'Well, Meliboeus speaks further of pine-trees, fountains, and vine-yards.* Pines you have in hundreds; you have two fountains, and over an acre of vines.'

'Really, the resemblance becomes quite startling!' laughed Stella.

'Yes; and then there is mention of willow-bloom on which the bees feast.* Then you have flocks of pigeons, and elms and turtle-doves without number. In view of this, you must perceive that the lines concerning the hoarse note of the wood-pigeon, the turtle-dove's complaint, and the towering elm* serve—first, either as a prophecy regarding Lull, or second, that the place has been moulded upon these lines. I incline to the *latter* view. The emphasis is my own.'

'But seriously, it is an interesting coincidence that all the natural objects named in the "Eclogues" seem to abound in the Home Field.'

'As you are convinced, even beforehand, my labours are at an end,' said Langdale, closing the book. 'Now tell me, have you any funny little stories of Mick or Dunstan?'

'Oh, Mick was better than a comedy yesterday. He hardly opened his mouth without making a bull.* He told me about one of his girls who is at service and very much overworked. The mistress, it seems, gives music-lessons. "But she's no great hand at the music," said Mick, lowering his voice mysteriously; "indade, Miss Stella, they say she niver saw a pianny till she came to Minjah four years ago, and thin 'twas an harmonium."'

'Well done, Mick!' said Langdale, laughing.

'Then I asked after the eldest boy, who has got a situation lately in a little store. He doesn't get on with the mother—no one can long—so last week he went to board at an aunt's. Poor Mick was much scandalized. "'Why, Patrick,' says I to him, 'what do people's children do who have no parents but lodge wid their father's sister? And thin the house is near the swampy end of the town, and people die there that niver died anywhere else.'" Well, you may laugh, but there is sound sense under it all. I shall miss Mick's little anecdotes sadly when I go away.'

'When you go!' repeated Langdale, and his face fell visibly. On meeting his eyes a deeper tinge stole into the girl's cheeks. Then he added in a lighter tone: 'There are days in August when people who speak of going away should be fined, or at any rate set to counting the vine-buds and gadding tendrils.'*

'And yet how very human it is to go away, even as human as it is to come. You see, I am catching a little of your reasonableness,' said Stella.

'That may be; but on a day like this, when the veriest little locust chirps in the sun as "though he never should be old,"* I maintain it is little short of felony to speak of the accidents that mar life. . . . You see, I am catching a little of your unreason,' he added.

They had crossed the stone bridge, and stood on a hillock clothed with elms, she-oaks, and scrub cypresses, where the breath of hidden violets came and went on the air like tremulous music. From this slight eminence they had a far-reaching view of the country round—the Messmate Ranges, with their dim gullies; the Wicked Wood, spectral in its bareness; the break in the far distance, where one became sensible of the Peeloo Plain; the flat, well-wooded country, and the contour of ridgy hills that stretched beyond Minjah Millowie. On every side lay the still wide woods, motionless as a great picture framed between heaven and earth, all clothed with the overflowing sunshine as with a garment.*

And yet these two, as they stood there and looked afar and listened to the songs of birds and all the woodland sounds which filled the air—what influence was it that stirred both so deeply in the midst of this peaceful idyllic scene? Who can tell what vague outward gropings of the spirit make the heart turn on itself in some rare soft-footed hour as with a quickened sense of the sweet calm of the present, a shrinking fear of the uncertain days to come which may be clouded with futile agony, drenched with the storm-spray of life's keenest sorrows? For some moments neither spoke.

'You will never know how good it is of me not to talk like your friend Ivan Michalowicz just now,' said Stella, breaking the silence. 'I could believe the air is full of unseen presences——'

'That is a plagiarism from Mick. Go on—and unheard wails,' Langdale said, laughing.

'Well, good dressmaking, for my own sex. Do you remember what Frenchman said that women take the outward polish of civilization more quickly than men, but that inwardly they remain more truly savage?'*

'Ah, that is the sort of paradox which even a luminous-minded Frenchman cannot resist. It is so glaringly untrue—there must be something in it—so it is wrapped up in a neat little epigram. But about the dressmaking?'

'Well, I think a woman who makes dresses that fit perfectly, adds more to the practical Christianity of the world than most people are aware of. If you could peep into the mind of a woman when a costly dress comes home that makes her waist what it shouldn't be, you would believe the Frenchman a little more. She may have sat at the feet of sages and be in touch with much of the wisest and the best, but in that moment she has taken a great leap back to the anthropoidal era.'*

'But when her waist is what—no, I am afraid—but when the dress-maker has done her work nobly?'

'Why, then a sort of flow of philanthropy suffuses one's whole being. Yes, to make a dress well—without a pinch or a wrinkle in it—that is one of the least mischievous things a woman can do. As for your sex—— Well, what do you say to a shoemaker—one who does not cripple the foot, and makes good shoes with honest workmanship? With such shoes, one feels impelled to walk more; and to walk more is to be in the open air; and to be in the open air is to be—dare I say happy?'

'Oh, why not! "On the whole, stick close to words."'

'Where is that?'

'"On the whole, stick close to words, then shall you go through the sure portal into the temple of certainty."* That is Mephistophe-les speaking to the student. Don't you think it is time you spoke German to me?'

'Yes, I have two anecdotes to tell you in German. But for the summit of well-being in the open air, don't you think we are more indebted to the horse than the shoemaker? You see where the Mess-mate Ranges fall off into flat country? That is the beginning of one of our unoccupied spaces; and the scenery—but perhaps you know it?'

'No, I don't think I do.'

'Claude and I rode there the other morning early. I had Duke, a delightful horse who skims the ground like a bird.'

'How far did you go then?'

'Thirteen miles. We reached No Man's Land, which stretches away close up to the New South Wales boundary. Nothing but sand and slender stringy bark trees, that grow so thick the sun can hardly pass between them. It was a most glorious ride, in the keen morning air loaded with the fragrance of gum-leaves.'

'I wonder if you would let me come with you some morning?'

'Oh, we shall be delighted; but then it is in the mornings you write your novel. Tell me how are your people going on? Do the wrong ones still make love to each other?'

Stella went on to sketch imaginary plots, ending in the most fabulous forms of happiness and good-luck, and introducing such extraordinary dialogues that, by the time the sound of a gong summoned them to afternoon tea on the western veranda, the two were laughing continuously, like a pair of school-children.

CHAPTER XXXI

Two days later, Stella had again ridden in the direction of No Man's Land; but this time she was alone, except for Dustiefoot and her horse, and she had an 'adventure.' Shearing was soon to begin, and all hands were busily occupied on the station. Under these circumstances, Stella insisted on her birthright, as an Australian born, to ride through her native woods without any companionship beyond a swift well-bred horse and her beloved dog. There was some talk of getting Maisie to practise riding on a not very young pony, whose wildest pace had long been a gentle canter, so that during the time there was a premium on all male workers she might accompany her mistress. But Stella rejected the proposal with comic horror. Maisie by herself, or Andy by himself, might be borne; but the united caution of the two would mar the most delectable ride that could be offered by spring and Duke. If they really objected to her riding alone—'Look at the hypocritical Baby pretending to give in!' cried Claude, 'as if she ever failed to get her own way in anything!' 'I wish I could go,' said Mrs Claude, making a rueful little face; but her husband did not echo the wish. 'I shall ask Dr Langdale to come with me,' thought Stella; but somehow she did not, which could hardly be deemed the action of unbiased friendship.

It was her second ride alone, one breezy sunshiny forenoon, when four miles from the head-station on the road that led to No Man's Land, Stella came upon the strangest spectacle she had ever seen. It was a very old-looking waggon, with a tilt-cover, drawn by two horses, followed by another, tied to the vehicle behind, and all three lean to the last degree of emaciation, while the pace at which they went was that of animals worn out with famine and fatigue; and everything else was in keeping with the worn, famished look of the horses. At each slow revolution of the wheels, the waggon creaked and groaned as though it would fall to pieces. The woodwork was warped and splintered, with here and there dim greenish streaks—faint reminiscences of having, at some remote period, been painted. The canvas cover was draggled and patched, saturated with reddish sand and long-accumulated dust, frayed into tatters at one side and flapping dismally in the wind. The harness was entirely composed of untanned lengths of kangaroo skin; the horses had no bits in their mouths, but there was a ragged remnant of a bridle on each, to which knotted ropes were attached, that hung loosely on the poor lean necks. Every rib might be counted at a distance. They crawled on with drooping heads, the sound of their worn unshod hoofs completely drowned by the perpetual rumbling and groaning of the disjointed waggon. No hand guided them; no voice urged them on.

It was all so unspeakably forlorn and dreary, that the sight filled Stella with dismay. Dustiefoot, who was trotting on gaily in front, paused as he drew near this battered vehicle, drawn by horses that looked only fit to be the food of carrion crows, and he, too, was plainly smitten with something akin to fear. Whether this was occasioned by the strange rumbling and groaning or the weird appearance of the whole, it would be hard to say. But he suddenly stopped short, and, with the hair round his neck bristling angrily, began to bark in a loud defiant way. 'Quiet, good dog; quiet,' said Stella coaxingly. She had reined in her horse, and it suddenly flashed across her mind that this extreme misery must be rooted in some catastrophe. At the sound of the dog's barking the horses came to a stand-still. It seemed as though they were glad of an excuse to give up even the snail's pace at which they crawled. Still no sign of life in the waggon.

Women of well-descended natures, who have been protected from every form of harm all their lives, are usually not lacking in courage. Stella was certainly no coward. But she had a powerful imagination of an essentially picture-forming kind.

Was there anyone in this spectral-looking conveyance alive?—or was its occupant worn with fatigue and asleep? She had heard strange stories of people who had been overtaken by drought or illness, and had been imprisoned sometimes for months, sometimes for a year, in a far-away corner beside a permanent water-hole, unvisited by any human being. She advanced slowly to the side of the waggon, and using the well-known Bush salutation, she said 'Good-day,' in a loud, clear voice. But there was no reply. Her own words came back to her with mocking emphasis. She shrank from dismounting to look into the waggon, shrank still more from the sight that might meet her there. Should she return home and get Hector or Claude or one of the station-hands to come to the rescue? Whether there was a human being in distress or beyond it, the famished horses needed help sorely. To Stella, an animal in want or pain was very little, if at all, less important than a human being. The sight of these three poor creatures, with their bones almost projecting through the skin, with drooping heads and dim eyes, standing in their patient dumbness, went straight to her heart. No; she could not bear the thought of leaving them. She would start them on and take them home, where they would be fed and rested; and if there was anyone in there—— 'Oh, I must not be such a coward,' she said to herself impatiently; and then, with a fast-beating heart, she rode close to the side of the waggon, on which the cover was tattered and fluttering in the soft spring wind that blew from the west. She reined in Duke, the proud, graceful young horse she rode, who had come off victor in many well-contested local races, and who was gentle and tractable as only a well-bred horse can be when ridden by an affectionate well-trained rider.

She bent down and looked in. The first thing she saw was a woman's long, fair hair—unkempt and matted. The next was a dingy white cockatoo that had been fast asleep, and now woke up and began to mumble, 'Confound your eyes, confound your eyes,'* in a faint, rapid way that was infinitely eerie. The woman's face was partly hidden by one hand, which covered her eyes and the upper part of her face—a brown, sunburnt, grimy hand, very lean and unwashed, and unwomanly-looking. No, she was not dead, as Stella at first feared. She moved and moaned, and as the bird went on mumbling, descending to a still lower depth of imprecation, the sound, and then Stella's sympathetic voice saying, 'I am afraid you are very ill,' seemed partly to rouse her. She half sat up, but her eyes remained glazed and unresponsive. 'Gee up, Jerry; Jill, Jill!' Her tones were shrill, though quavering, and at the words the horses pulled and strained, and once more resumed their weary, incredibly slow walk. They kept in the middle of the road, and Stella could but try to make Duke fall into the same pace. But this was impossible. He could stand stock still, or he could walk his slowest. But being neither lame on four legs, nor starved, nor born to drudgery, he could not absolutely crawl. It took this strange little procession the best part of two hours to get within sight of Lullaboolagana home-station. No words can express the air of mingled pride and responsibility with which Dustiefoot marshalled them all. He made circles round them, he trotted on in front, he walked behind, he panted; his scarlet young tongue hung out with joy and anxiety, his handsome bushy tail was arched upwards more airily than ever. He had the same insuperable difficulty that beset Duke of being unable to regulate his pace by that of animals so famished, so overborne and jaded, that even their hides would have been worthless. As Stella examined them more closely she saw that they had sores all over them—under the jagged collars that were held together with half-untwisted strands of rope, on their shoulders, sides, and thighs. So utterly maimed and defeated did they look as they dragged one quivering, shrunken leg after another, the only wonder was that they had not long since lain down to die.

When Dustiefoot found himself getting too far ahead—and if a young dog walked at all, that was inevitable—he turned round and waited, gazing at his mistress, and then at the horses and their load, till he was forced to give expression to his feelings in one or two barks, which might be classified as of the glad-excitement order. Those who have the privilege of being intimate with dogs are aware that no living creature is so pleased all over at an unusual event as a collie in the second year of his age.

Before the strange little cavalcade had reached the house, it was seen and met first by some of the children, then the maids, and finally by Mrs Courtland and Mrs Claude. Dunstan was at once despatched for Dr Morrison. But before he came the poor woman was refreshed with wine, washed, arrayed in fine linen, and comfortably in bed. It was a case of collapse through long privation and exposure. There was nothing to eat or drink in the waggon beyond the stony remains of a damper, and a little muddy water in a brown earthen jar. She partly recovered consciousness after she had been in bed for a couple of hours. Dr Morrison, on seeing her, came to the conclusion that careful nursing and dieting would bring her round in a few days. There was some dispute as to who should be chief nurse, but finally Stella convinced her sisters-in-law that, as she had discovered the patient, she must be primarily held responsible.

'You have a name for finding many ailing sorts of creatures, Miss Stella; but I think this is the biggest cargo of any,' said the doctor, with an amused twinkle in his eyes. And then he gave his instructions with due emphasis. 'I shall be away to-morrow, and perhaps the next day, but Dr Langdale will look after her. By-the-way, how is your last patient, the crow? Langdale had grave fears as to his recovery at one time.'

Soon after the doctor left the patient fell into a deep sleep, and leaving Maisie in charge of the sick-room, Stella went to see after the horses. She found Dunstan giving them small measures of bran and oats, and looking at them with a mingled pity, amazement, and scorn that was irresistibly funny.

'You have unharnessed them, Dunstan? That is right. Oh, you poor, poor, dear things!'—and Stella stroked each in turn.

'Unharnessed them, Miss Stelly? Well, yes, if you calls them bits o' broken rope and rawr hide harness. I'm jiggered, but it's the very rummiest turn-out ever I seed. And what can have come to her husband?'

'Oh, she may not have one, Dunstan.'

But Dunstan shook his head. 'Ah, Miss Stelly, you don't never find a female get into such a hole without she's a married 'oman. That's the way along o' some women. If they want to enjy themselves at all, and are proper-like, they gets married, and then mostly they has a very bad time. They're like these yaller little birds; you sticks 'em in a cage, and they buzz agin the wires; and yet, if you let them go out into the wilds, they get knocked about, and can't get proper tucker.'

Dunstan spoke in a leisurely, high-pitched voice, which had a very odd effect. He was given to moralizing, and had those quaint reaches of fancy that are often found with men whose lives are passed out-of-doors in gardening, or shepherding, or other undrudging avocations.

Stella with difficulty refrained from laughter at this summing-up of the disabilities of her sex.

'I don't think you would like to be a woman, Dunstan?'

'Well, no, Miss Stelly. If so be that such a thing could happen, and God A'mighty give me the pick to be a female or a worm, I'd say a worm, if you please; meaning no disrespect to the A'mighty or to you, Miss Stelly. A worm, to be sure, has a lowly life, and unless it's cut in two or swallered alive, not much happens in the span of its days. But what's that to having things allays happening, and each one worse than t'other? I ought to know. I'm married to my third wife, and not one of the three ever had six months proper health on end.'

Dunstan was portioning out further doles of oats and giving them to the horses as he spoke, so that Stella could enjoy these reflections without checking the flow of his thoughts. Dunstan himself seldom laughed, and when others did so at his serio-comic sayings, it disconcerted and, in the end, silenced him.

'I b'lieve they have had enough; but the poor old karkisses look so starved,' he said, as the horses set to once more.

'And they are so galled. Dunstan, don't you think if I bathed their sores with a little warm water—oh yes, I am sure of it.' Stella hastened away, and soon returned with a china bowl of tepid water and a soft sponge, with which she deftly bathed one sore after another.

'They seem to enjoy it just as if they was Christians,' said Dunstan, and then he went to the kitchen and brought out a pailful of warm water, as that in the basin soon got discoloured with the dust and sand. Then he stood by as Stella went from one poor skinny creature to another, caressing and speaking to them in a low, fond voice.

Both were so much absorbed that they did not notice the approach of Hector Courtland and Dr Langdale, who stood at a little distance looking on at the scene with faces full of an amused interest, and some deeper feeling withal, as they watched the girl's tender ministration on the poor galled scarecrow horses.

'Why, here's Dr Langdale with the master,' said Dunstan, suddenly perceiving them. 'It must be serious for the poor female if she must have two doctors.' Though Langdale was so frequent a visitor, Dunstan somehow connected his appearance at that juncture with the event of the day.

'Well, Stella, this little performance of yours caps all your previous finds,' said Hector, looking at the three horses with beaming eyes.

'St Charity, I would give much to have your picture painted as you stood here bathing the sores of these horses,' said Langdale, and as she returned his greeting there was an expression in his face which made her look quickly away.

'And this is only part of the caravan, sir,' said Dunstan, addressing his master. 'Besides these horses that the crows would hardly get a mouthful on, there's the waggon, fit only for firewood, a cockatoo that would set your hair on end with blasphemy, and a onfortinate female as can't say a word, good or bad.'

'We cannot permit you to keep the cockatoo, St Charity,' said Langdale. 'I understand he is worse than any of the orthodoxies, consigning people to eternal and entire perdition irrespective of their opinions.'

'Well, he does swear very badly,' said Stella, smiling. 'We fed him and put him in exile. He is on a perch in the stable.'

'But who ever heard of a backslider being reformed in a stable? Look here, Courtland, cannot you suggest a better asylum for a foundling whose moral nature has been perverted?'

'His native woods, I should think; unless you take him in hand yourself, Langdale, as well as the "onfortinate female" as Dunstan calls her.'

'Are you going to look after my patient, Dr Langdale?' asked Stella, who stood sponging the roan horse's neck for the second time.

'Yes—free, gratis, for nothing, unless you are a refractory nurse; in which case I shall charge you a guinea a visit. Now, if you let me put a little vaseline on these sore places, your new pets will recover all the sooner.'

Stella went immediately to beg a pot of vaseline from Louise.

'There must be a semi-tragic story behind this curious little adventure,' said Langdale, examining the waggon. And then Courtland recalled some curious stories that had come to his knowledge in past years of people who had attempted to make long journeys with horses or teams of bullocks through unknown country and came to signal grief. 'But this is the first time I ever heard of a woman and a blaspheming cockatoo journeying through the Bush, evidently for months.'

CHAPTER XXXII

THERE are probably few who have passed their first youth without indulging now and then in conjectures as to how many would really befriend them if they were completely stranded in life—say, without money or position, and under the shadow of some imputed crime. We begin the world as a rule with pathetic confidence in ourselves and others. Heaven is full of beneficence, earth crowded with friends. There is so much that we can do; there are so many whose eyes will brighten at the prizes we are to pluck by the way. And then our contests are to be won without stooping to the stratagems of canvassing; we are to head our polls without the indignity of hedging. Later on, there is still much to be done; but little quite so well worth dying for as our own hearts and the poets whispered in the early days. We begin to suspect, too, that Providence sends biscuits chiefly to those who have no teeth.* Our dearest aims have a trick of eluding us, and leaving the tedious hours full of the memories of spent bubbles. The rude breath of experience—that *figmentum malum** in the life of man—has shrivelled so many tender illusions. Life is not so amusing. Some of its most comical jokes are elaborated at our own expense. This kind of payment impairs one's sense of humour. And those myriad orbs that were to sparkle at our feats? Alas! most of the eyes we now know are keen only to detect that the plumage of our prize-bird is gray rather than white. And so in our more egotistical moments—and these come to all—the question may arise, 'If I were entirely defeated in this tiresome drama, which begins in youth, like the rising of a curtain on a fairy scene, and goes on like a scene in which there is nothing fairy-like, save gold, how many would really stand by me?' If one were thus defeated, in fact as well as imagination, probably the very best thing that could befall one would be to find one's self in the Australian Bush not very far from a head-station.

So at least it proved in the case of the poor woman Stella Courtland had come upon. She was dangerously ill for several days.

During this time, Stella and Langdale saw each other daily, and drew very near to each other. The woman's first coherent inquiry was for 'Jack,' which turned out to be the cockatoo. Stella brought

'Yes; and souls that can find no home. But I forbear.'

'Well, I must admit that on a perfect day like this—and the only fault it has is that it keeps time to a clock—a kind of sadness creeps over me. It is the penalty for looking before and after.'

'Yes; neither a cat nor a marigold uses the sunlight as an invocation to call ghosts into a circle.'

'Ghosts? You know nothing of them!'

'At this very moment the air is drenched with ghosts. Ghosts of days to come—lean and gray, when youth is left far behind—when those that look out at the window are darkened, and the daughters of music are laid low.'*

'It is good of you not to speak like Ivan,' said Langdale gravely. 'He said once that the great melancholy steppes of his native land had got into his disposition. I think the vast solitudes of your Australia have got into yours.'

'But do you never think how dreadful it is to grow old? And it goes on all the time. Why, since we have been here, if your eyes were keen enough, you would see wrinkles deepening on my face.'

'Thank Heaven my eyes are not so precocious!'

'Ah, now you have betrayed yourself. You are not so hopelessly reasonable after all. I may yet hear you rail at life in good set terms.'*

'But don't you think it is time enough to speak of wrinkles when they come?'

'Ah, but they have come. I discovered a little sly wretch of a crow's-foot at the corner of my eye the other day. Look there when I stand sideways in the light,' and Stella stood so that her crow's-foot might be more clearly seen.

Langdale could not resist laughing. 'My eyesight is not sharp enough, or else your crow's-foot does not exist,' he said.

'Spoken like a courtier. But it would be more friendly to see it, and then to say something out of Seneca* to comfort me. When will your profession make some real advance?'

'And invent an elixir for renewing youth—or perhaps you are thinking more of the happy despatch of superfluous beings?'

'But as it is, you are chiefly concerned with screening fools from their folly——'

'And thwarting the beneficent severity of Nature? Yes, it is painfully humdrum. Have you ever thought what calling in life might put one in the way of doing least mischief?'

him into the bedroom the woman occupied. He erected his crest, and fluttered about, muttering imprecations of various kinds.

'He knows me, sure enough,' said his mistress in a gratified tone. 'You can't think, ma'am, what a comfort it was to hear him when I was alone. He do swear badly, but it was like having a Christian body near one to hear him. . . . He never come back. I didn't expect he would, after hearing the shots; but, if I live long enough, Bill Taylor will swing for it. . . . The saddle—oh, the saddle, Miss Stella!—was it took care of?' (She started up in bed in great excitement. Stella assured her it was all right in the harness-room.) 'Oh, but I must get it—I must see it. I'll put somethin' round me, and go out to look at it.'

Stella thought this was but a freak of the fever that still lingered in her brain; and to keep the woman quiet, she sent Maisie for the saddle, which was old and worn and externally destitute of any points that would justify one in setting such high value on it. But appearances are proverbially deceitful.

The woman clutched it eagerly. She had never acquired any of those amenities that, even among the lower orders of women, help as a rule to keep social intercourse on a higher plane than the primeval scramble in which egotism was the sole standard of conduct. And yet she had many distinctly human qualities.

Maisie went out of the room, and resumed her sewing in the nursery, where the upper nurse sat with the six-months-old baby in her arms.

'Is your young lady going out riding this morning?' she asked.

'Indeed, Jane, I cannot tell ye,' answered Maisie with a toss of her head. 'What Miss Stella's ma would say to her nursing an ill-mannered person like yon I don't know. Miss Stella should leave her till us, and then she'd be cured a little of whims and whams. There, she has that awfu' swearin' cockie in the room, and now a dirty old saddle, and there comes the doctor. I wish he would cure her soon, and let her be packing with her duds and screws of horses.'

Servants who are accustomed to the refined courtesy of gentle-women resent nothing more strongly than being spoken to roughly. This, indeed, is one of the causes which often creates a disastrous barrier between them and men in their own rank.

The sight which met Dr Langdale on entering the sickroom that morning was a curious one. The large, dingy cockatoo stood on the toilet-table, close to the bed, muttering, 'Hang him—hang him!' in a rough, deep voice. The patient was sitting up in bed, an old saddle turned upside down before her, the lining ripped open, disclosing underneath one side a deep layer of extremely soiled bank-notes, on the other nuggets of gold, ranging from the size of peas to pigeon-eggs, some embedded in quartz, others with the earth still clinging to them. Stella stood at the foot of the bed, looking on in silent wonder. Neither had heard the doctor's tap, and even when he opened the door, saying, 'May I come in?' the patient went on with a calculation which absorbed all her faculties.

'Ten—twenty—forty—fifty—fifty-five; yes, that's the one-pounders—that is right. Then, two, three, four, five, six, seven, eight, nine, ten—tenners; and five twenties, and two fifties. And the gold——'

'I fear you do not approve of this proceeding, Dr Langdale?' said Stella as they shook hands.

'If anyone is to be blamed it's me, sir,' said the woman, who seemed to be thoroughly roused by the process of reckoning up the hoard before her.

The doctor tested her temperature, and found it rather high. 'If you throw yourself back, you know——' he began, in a grave voice.

'Well, sir, I know it makes my head beat; but it would have been worse to keep on thinking p'r'aps it was lost. I don't rightly remember things for days before I got here. That's my marriage lines, ma'am,' she said, holding out a very soiled slip of paper to Stella. 'I don't know what makes you so good to me, such an object as I must have been when you saw me. You couldn't tell what sort I might be. And I'd like you to know I'm an honest woman. And if things go wrong——'

'Oh, things will go all right, if you keep quiet,' said Langdale. 'You have an iron constitution.'

'Thank you, sir; but I'd sooner tell the young lady and you how it was, in case; and then I know I'll feel more restful like. I've laid here many an hour turning things over when I wasn't able to wag my tongue. I don't know whether you've heard of Poor Man's Diggings ever. They don't make no flare, but from seventy to eighty men have been working there quietly for two years. Jack and me was there eigh-teen months—that's my husband. The men called the cockie after him, because he was a great swearer, and the bird was the dead spit of him in that way. Jack was a digger, and we had a little general store and a sly-grog shanty. But he was fined so often, at last I said to him it would be cheaper to take out a license, and so he did. But he took to hard drinking and gambling, and six months ago we left, for we had enough money to go back to our friends in Sydney. We was both born there. There was no one to take the license off our hands, so Jack carried away all the grog that was left, and that was the ruin of him. When we came across any teamsters, he used to gamble for a couple of days at a time. I've seen him play at poker and lose two bottles of rum and a five-pound note and one of the horses all within an hour. And then he'd have to buy his horse back.

'At last I took and planted the money and the gold you see here. It was once when he was drinking very bad, and gambling with a little man called One-leg Bill. He had followed us from the diggings—'t any rate, so I believe, though he pretended to come upon us quite by accident. But none is so surprised as them that gives their mind to it, and that was the way with One-leg, I'm pretty sure. Jack was that given to the gamble, when there was no one else he'd play with me. But then there wasn't enough "go" in it, for if he lost to me, he could take it from me. Well, One-leg had his horse and swag and kep us company for near a month, winning a good deal more money nor he lost. At last, when Jack wasn't by, I told him to clear, and I'd give him twenty pounds without no playing nor cheating. He was a unhonest vermin, if ever there lived any!

'Well, he tuk the twenty pounds, but still he hung round, till one day we camped at a water-hole, and he said he was going to take a cut off for the nearest railway line to Melbourne in the morning. I dunno why, but I didn't b'lieve him. Certainly, he never told the truth, unless he had an accident in speaking like. But it wasn't that only. In the middle of the night I heard a noise, and I put my head out quiet-like, and there was One-leg sitting by the camp fire, polishing up his revolver. That gave me a turn, and I didn't sleep another wink. Of course, people has to keep their firearms in order travelling in the Bush, but still——

'Well, in the morning Jack was very drowsy-like, and when he woke up he didn't seem inclined to make an early start. No more did One-leg. I gathered up the things and put-to the horses in the afternoon, and One-leg saddled hisen. Then, just as I thought we was going to start, they both set off for a little stroll. I knowed well that what Jack wanted was to gamble. He had took a Bible oath to me two days afore not to touch a card with One-leg again, and he was 'shamed to do it before me. Many's the time since I wished I'd let him alone; but I meaned it for good, though it come out very crooked. I made signs to Jack to come to me and ast him to take his rifle. But when a man has been drinking off and on so long, he don't have his wits about him much to speak of.

'I watched 'em go out of sight in the woods, and all to once I began to cooey after Jack as loud as I could. But he never turned his head. One-leg turned round and waved his hand with a grin, and then hobbled on. He had a wooden leg and used a stick, and there was his lather bag with the revolver on his back. I waited and waited, but they didn't come back; and then about sunset I heard two shots— one after the other. I went cold all over, and, if you b'lieve me, I felt as if the blood was running out of my side, and a horrid, burning pain. I sot* where I was in the waggon, not able to move; and then it went through me like sparks of fire: "One-leg ull come and put a bullet through me next, and then he'll have everything, and never a soul to peach on him."

'With that I tuk the reins and made a start, and then I thought, "If I leave his horse Sambo, he'll overtake me in no time." So I put a piece of rope round his neck, and tied him to the waggon. He had got used to following like that when Jack and One-leg sot playing cards, and I druv. They was all pretty fresh, for there was good grass round the water-hole, and we had spelled* for nearly two days. Everything was swimming before me, and somehow I tuk the wrong turn—came back istid of going towards New South Wales boundary. I thought of turning round, but there was One-leg coming out of the wood—alone, and yelling after me like mad. I just whipped up the horses as fast as they would go, and Sambo come on after the waggon fine. But the way that One-leg run and roared no one would b'lieve. It made me go cold all over to think Sambo might break the rope and fall into his hands. But he didn't, and he was soon out of sight. I travelled all night, and kep the horses up to it as fast as they would go, and took cross roads. Next day they was so knocked up I had to spell them.

'But my sleep went off altogether. I was waiting always for One-leg to come and shoot me. I dunno how long it was—I dunno what country. I met people now and then—teamsters and hawkers mostly, and I passed the time of day, but I never ast one a question. I'd got to be suspicious of men—they seemed, all of 'em I knew, such a poor mean lot. Sometimes when I passed people I kept up a talk as if poor Jack was sitting inside. But at night that made me feel creepy. Jill began to be very raw and knocked up, so one day I put Sambo in, but 'twas as if the very mischief was in him. He broke the bridle all to pieces, and ran away with all of us till he couldn't move. Everything got worn out. When I put the other bridle on him that was broke too; till I had never a bit—leastways, I had the bits, but nothing rightly to fasten them to. Not that it mattered much, for they was now that tame—what with no grass, and very little water, and going on and on, not knowing where, but hoping always to come to a little township, but never one. I used to take a track this way and that—and I think many a time I turned my back straight on what would have took me to a township with womenfolk and children and police.

'At last, when I was getting to know I'd got some sort of fever on me, I met a hawker, and I asked him the nearest way to a township, and he said to keep on and I'd come to Narryhoouta, or some such name. And I kep on, but I lost count of days, and I hadn't strength to take the horses out of the waggon, and I could see they wouldn't go much farther. I dozed away like, seeing all sorts of things, just like poor Jack when he had the horrors. Then it came like a dream that a young lady looked in at me, and spoke to me so gentle I couldn't hear what she said. And then I saw more ladies, but everyone was so kind it seemed all dreams. And then I woke up at nights, and I thought maybe 'tis true about heaven—but 'twas a deal more cheerfuller than I've ever heard tell about heaven; what with one soft light burning, and no crowd, and one kind woman to attend on me, and nothing to do, not even to sing, but just lie still in white soft things, and no awful creaking going on and on. And then in the daytime you come to me—often in white, ma'am. I just used to shut my eyes and keep still for fear it would all go different. And then there was you, sir, as kind as anyone, though a man.'

'Yes; but I'll not be kind if you say any more to-day,' said Dr Langdale very gently.

'Very well, sir—I'm quite content to lie still now. The money is all safe, and the young lady and you knows all. Yes, the saddle of course must go, but if the young lady would put the notes and gold

away till I get about; and if I don't there's the address of my father
and mother on the back of my marriage-lines.'

'That was a curious little story—so characteristically Australian,'
said Langdale, after they had left the sick-room, leaving Mrs Claude
with the patient, and were strolling toward the orchard, close to
which Stella had discovered a hymenosperum in bloom a few days
previously.

'Yes,' she answered slowly, 'it seems as if there were more heart-
beats in situations that belong essentially to new countries. That
reminds me of a little story I heard from a sick man before I left
home.'

'May I hear it, St Charity?'

'Yes—that is, if you are good, as the children say.'

'How can I be otherwise when I am with you?'

'A fine for saying that. Friends do not pay each other
compliments.'

'No; nor yet fine each other for telling the truth.'

'Another fine. But seriously, you do not know how bad it is for me
to be made vain.'

'If you wish to malign yourself, St Charity, you must get a more
sympathetic audience.'

'What has put you into this mood to-day?' she said, laughing in
his face.

'To-day?' he echoed, his eyes kindling. 'Do you think a man can
be privileged to be near you so often, to watch your gracious kindliness, your perfect courtesy, your varying moods, each one more
charming than the last, without——'

He stopped abruptly—and then Stella, who had grown suddenly
pale, replied in a voice that was a little tremulous:

'Werthester Freund,* I remit all those fines; for when you speak
like that I feel as lowly as Dunstan's worm.' At this they both
laughed, for Stella had in due course related the worthy gardener's
reflections and reminiscences on the day she had first dressed the
wounds of the 'caravan' horses, as they were called. Their sores were
now quite healed, and the poor animals were rapidly putting on flesh
in the adjacent stock-paddock. Indeed, Sambo had been observed to
kick up his heels on more than one occasion.

'Hush,' said Stella suddenly; 'there are strange bird-notes,' and
sure enough there were plaintive long-drawn calls heard on the banks

of the swallow-pool, in the Oolloolloo, near which the two were then standing. Stella stole on tiptoe nearer the bank, and Langdale followed her as noiselessly as he could. 'Oo-da-warra, oo-da-warra,' the groves resounded with these cries. They came from two bronze-winged pigeons on the brink of the pool. It would be difficult to name any other birds whose plumage forms a more perfect model of harmonious tints. The wings gleamed more lustrously than precious stones—dark, and pale-brown feathers, with iridescent gleams as of mother-of-pearl on the coverts; a deep, gleaming purplish tint on the breast, and the legs a perfect carmine. They drank repeatedly of the water, rested for a little, and flew on their way westward.

'Charming woodland visitors—they drank of our swallow-pool, rested in the shade of our trees, and then flew away!' said Stella wistfully. 'Did you notice,' she added, 'what soft appealing eyes they had?'

The truth was that Langdale had watched her face rather than the bronze-winged pigeons.

'Yes, they were lovely!' he answered, jesuitical fashion—speaking of those he had seen, while his words conveyed another meaning.

'So are all pigeons' eyes!' Stella went on, encouraged by her friend's evident enthusiasm; 'very different from parrots, who have hard beady eyes—even the sweet little shell parrots, perfect sonnets as they are in emerald and pale jonquil.'

'And parrots scream rather badly, too; don't they?'

'Yes; but there are times when they warble most musically; not only the smaller kinds, like the shells, the porphyry-headed, and the little ones with deep-red faces, but also larger ones, like the rock-pebblers. We watched some of them in the orchard the other day, wandering on the ground, picking up seeds and things and making the gentlest cooing sounds imaginable. The male bird was a magnificent creature, in scarlet and dark green and yellow and lazuline blue.'

And while chatting after this fashion, they reached the hymenosperum, a beautiful tree of Eastern Australia, with glossy eucalyptus-like leaves and drooping clusters of long slender bell-blossoms, from eight to twelve in a bunch, ranging in colour from delicate cream to saffron, and fragrant as orange-flowers. Stella uttered an exclamation of surprise when she saw the tree arrayed in opening blooms.

'There were so few out two or three days ago,' she cried, 'and now they are out in hundreds! But that is always the way in our spring. It is like what Pliny says of the oak-galls, that they break out altogether in one night about the beginning of June.'*

'But don't forget,' said Langdale, smiling, 'that Pliny the Elder gave good reason for being styled *mendaciorum patrem*.* But this tree of yours is perfectly lovely. When your Australian trees do blossom, they do it in a wonderfully generous fashion—and how exquisitely scented!'

Then Stella drew his attention to a bee that was struggling hard to penetrate into the depths of one of the deep flower-bells. It was too slender for the industrious creature's body, or its thighs were too heavily laden with wax; for after writhing for some time, with a muffled half-angry hum, the bee drew out its head and shoulders. Instead, however, of going to any of the myriad flowers around, it still clung to the coveted blossom, and began to bite a hole at the base of the delicate waxen tube, so as to get at its honeyed treasures from the outside.

'I must put that into my country journal,' said Stella.

'Do you put everything into your journal?' asked Langdale.

He noticed a soft flush mantling in her cheeks as she answered:

'Yes; spiders and bees, when I catch them "writing deep morals upon Nature's pages."* As a special favour you may come and see our pet spider web; it is in a hawthorn-bush, whose first spray budded yesterday, that is, on the third of September.'

On their way to this treasure, Stella pointed out wide groups of her favourite spring-flowers, now in full beauty—here a clump of the Santa Maria narcissus, blue Apennine windflowers, and other wide white ones of the Japanese variety; everywhere golden daffodils and settlements of the velvet-soft many-coloured polyanthus.

'How little notice you take of these brilliant bushes of flowers, St Charity!'

'Oh, the petunias and rhodanthes! Well, most of them are so hard and scentless. With a cunning pair of scissors, wire, and a few sheets of French-coloured paper, one might turn out basketfuls of these you would hardly know from the originals.'

'Now, how can you urge that as an objection when you love the native "immortelle" so dearly?'

'But don't you see the difference between flowers so much cared for and cultivated, and those that spring up in sandy deserts? Flowers in gardens are the Hebrews, with prophets and leaders and angelic visitations. But when Marcus Aurelius says, "If there are no gods it is ill to live; if there are gods, it is well to die"*—that is an everlasting in the desert.'

'I humbly crave pardon for my foolish objection. Yet I am glad I made it, for the sake of your answer.'

'This is our spider-web!' said Stella, pausing by the hawthorn-bush. 'See what a delicate tracery of silk and light it is, with a cloud-like little woof in the centre. Now, is that to turn into the spiders of the future?'

'Yes, I imagine so, when the time is fulfilled,' said Langdale, looking at the web with grave attention. 'Who bent this spray, and fastened it so as to protect the web?'

'I did. You see, this tiny hammock—the most exquisite baby-cradle of nature—looked so forlornly exposed to all the caprices of fate: the wind, and insects, and fowls of the air.'

'Yes; we all live at each other's cost, whether we dwell in palaces or the crevices of a tree's bark; but the spider has a sterner struggle than most: he hangs perpetually in suspense, unless St Charity devises schemes to protect him. But why does she watch this little cocoon with so much interest?'

'I have an incredible curiosity to see one or more infant spiders of unblemished life, "ere sin could blight or sorrow fade"*—even before they have tasted the blood of a fly. It is a sorrowful thought that though I have seen so many thousand spiders, I have never seen an innocent one!'

He laughed, but all the time one who observed him closely might see that he was becoming more constrained and preoccupied, as if there were some struggle going on in his mind.

'You have not told me that other little story yet. Suppose you tell it to me by the hymenosperum tree; and, by the way, you must say something distinctive about that graceful creature—something that will go with the image of it when it rises in my memory: tall and slender, arrayed in pale saffron, like an Eastern bride.'

'I am sure I cannot think of anything more distinctive than that,' laughed Stella. 'I shall borrow a metaphor and give it to you. "As a saint is to ordinary good people, so is a hymenosperum to other flowering trees."'

'Here is our tree,' said Langdale, 'with a little rural seat near. Now, please tell me your story.'

She told him Thomson's little narrative, not forgetting to give a rapid, brilliant little sketch of her old friend Mr Ferrier—'the best little man in the world; but he is like cheese o'er renneted: so much in earnest that he can enjoy hardly any of the play of life.'

'I think we may put that down as a thirty-seventh tragic situation,' said Langdale; 'the poor man trying in his simple fashion to Christianize the savage mother of his child; and the two breaking into loud laughter at him in the night.'

He took out a little pocket diary as he spoke, and with it an unopened letter.

'Oh, I had forgotten this,' he said. 'The English mail was delivered as I left the house this morning.'

'Do you put aside letters without reading them?' said Stella in surprise.

'Well, not as a rule,' he answered, smiling; 'but there were family letters that kept me occupied till I got here; and then, you know, at Lull there are things so much more interesting than letters from one's lawyer.'

'You may read it now—I will excuse you,' said Stella, and she went to gather clusters of the fragrant hymenosperum blossoms, picking out those that had just opened, which were pale cream, and mixing with them a few of those that had been opened a few days, which had assumed a delicate saffron tint. Then the clear musical song of a superb warbler rose near, and she saw one on a laurustinus bush not far off—a little male bird, gorgeous in its spring attire of shining pale azure and dark blue, its little tail erect as that of a fantail pigeon.

Stella was away long enough to permit the perusal of many pages. But when she returned Langdale still stood engrossed with his letter. He looked hard at the girl as she drew near to him, and his face, usually so calm, betrayed curious signs of agitation.

'You have had no ill news, I hope?' said Stella softly.

'Ill news?—no. St Charity, is it true—— But I have no right to force your confidence. Only there are affairs that hasten my departure for England—and there is something I want to know. Will you think my curiosity an abuse of our friendship?'

'Oh, no. I am sure I shall not,' she answered promptly.

'Then—are you engaged to be married?'

'Certainly not. I was once, for a short time,' she added, colouring deeply; 'but it was a mistake.'

She saw his eyes suddenly grow radiant.

'Then, sweet St Charity, I am going to ask a great favour. May I write to you after I get to England?'

His face was very pale, and his voice shaken. No one who heard and saw him could deem that the permission he asked was concerned with the interchange of merely friendly sentiments. Least of all Stella, whose quick insight played round even indifferent matters with the fellowship of wide sympathy.

She struggled with some rising emotion. But her voice was clear and firm as she answered:

'Yes—you may; and here is a little bouquet I have gathered for you.'

He took it and held it to his lips. And then for a little time, as they turned homeward, neither spoke. There are moments in life when speech is an impertinence—when words the most winged and penetrating are too leaden-soled for the thoughts that rise in endless succession—swift and golden as sun-rays glancing upon waves.

'I shall write to your mother and Hector, you know, at the same time,' he said, as they drew near the house.

'But the longest letter must be to me,' she answered, trying to speak lightly; 'and it must be very wise, and partly in German.'

'When do you leave, St Charity?'

'On the fifteenth—eleven days from this. And you?'

'I should like to leave the same day you do, only I must stay till Morrison gets his assistant. He is overdone and overworked. But he is advertising in the Melbourne and Adelaide papers. I shall be back in four months, I suppose, from the time I sail. Will you——'

He stopped abruptly. He was evidently struggling with conflicting currents of thought. Stella, who, in the tumult of her own emotion, was keenly conscious of the agitation that betrayed itself in Langdale's voice and manner, tried in vain to speak of some indifferent subject. But seeing Louise near at hand among the shrubs, her courage returned.

CHAPTER XXXIII

STELLA sat that night writing till late, and then for hours, by her open window, looking into the starry skies, an expression of peaceful happiness on her face, which for a time was unclouded by even a passing shadow. She had been sure for many days past that her ideal friendship was in peril. She knew that, time after time, words and questions had risen to Langdale's lips which he had kept back. She had seen that he strove with contending emotions, and once or twice she had lightly parried one of those leading questions which, if not turned aside, would have been as the letting in of waters. She found it so entirely exquisite, the bliss of loving and being loved, without the gadgrind of outside opinion, without the desperate seriousness of having to think of the future as a fixed, imponderable, menacing responsibility; nay, without any avowal spoken by the lips. And now the precious secret would be hers for four long months to come. There would be no interchange of vows, no assurances. They had met as friends, and as friends they would part. She laughed a low, glad laugh to herself, as she pictured Esther's face when she would tell her this. It would be quite true—till he returned.

Till he returned? How her heart beat at the thought. If he left in October, he might be back in March at the latest. The late roses would be still in bloom, and the chrysanthemums would be coming in. He loved her to wear great clusters of roses at the throat. What time of day would it be when he came to the dear old Fairacre home? She hoped it would be twilight—just before the lamps were lit. There would be great china bowlfuls of roses in the hall, and delicate pink and pale cream-coloured Japanese chrysanthemums. 'I love the Japanese for making a festival in honour of this flower,'* she thought. And then she mused over far-away, strange countries. Would they see them all together? Oh! what leaps to make! and they had not yet been betrothed. Yes, in the twilight. There would be a golden glow lingering in the west, and far above that the inimitable rose-lilac colour which steals so often into the evening sky, when the wearying languor of the long summer is over. Rose-lilac? no, that was a burlesque of the real tint. There was in it the pink of wet sea-shells, and a faint tinge of a very pale lilac pansy, and over all a divine haze,

as if a great white star had been melted in the air. What name was
there for such a colour as that? None. What name was there for the
flood of happiness that thrilled her through when their eyes and
hands met at parting? Love! But all the dreadful, commonplace,
earthly creatures who ever got engaged took that word in vain. Come
back, ye wandering little imps of thoughts, and finish this twilight
scene. Would she be in the garden when he came? Of course she
would know about what time the vessel would reach Glenelg.* It
would be telegraphed first from King George's Sound,* and in less
than four days afterwards it would be sighted off Cape Borda.* When
Tom went to his office that morning, she would take him aside, and
say: 'Can you keep a secret? I don't suppose you can. You mustn't
laugh, you mustn't cry; you must do the best you can.'*

'What is it, Baby? Have you given away your last half-crown to
Honora, or some other old vagabond, and haven't got a pair of gloves
to put on?'

'No, Tom, it isn't that. But the———'. What would be the name of
the ship? The *Nepaul* or the *Lusitania*? Some such name very likely.
But she would give it one of her own—the *Pâquerette*. Where did
that come from? Oh, from some lines her old French master had
taught her, telling of a custom the village maidens had in France for
testing how much they were beloved:

> ' "La blanche et simple Pâquerette,
> Que ton cœur consult surtout
> Dit: ton amant, tendre fillette
> T'aime, un peu, beaucoup, point du tout." '*

Yes. 'But the *Pâquerette* is coming in to-day, and I want to know the
exact time she reaches Glenelg. Send me a telegram. Oh! put it in
your official note-book, and, whatever you do, don't forget. Ah, you
are very good; I know you never forget. But this is more important
than the creation of the world, or the Christian era, or anything.'
She wouldn't go anywhere that day, and if any visitors came, she
would retreat into the study—the dear old little library with the pale,
sea-green cretonne curtains, with brown sedges and water-lilies all
over them. She had bought them herself when the green damask
ones had grown so very faded, and she had climbed up on the ladder
to fasten them, and caught sight of a little row of books behind the
old Divinity ones that were never disturbed, and the first one she

took up was *Candide*.* She read twenty pages of it standing on the ladder. Was there any domain of life so pungently vulgar as those twenty pages? Or were books like *Candide* hidden away behind tomes of Divinity because these last were so fanciful—women and children might read them—while the others were too true to be left within reach? Would she ever tell Anselm? Well, perhaps; if he persisted in calling her St Charity. What beautiful intonations there were in his voice when he was talking very gravely, and how deep and steadfast his eyes were! Would he ever look angrily at her? Sometimes she had tried to provoke him, but the more she tried the more he was amused. But then, after years of married life, would not some taint of marital coldness creep into his manner? Heavens! what a bound to make— and they had not yet met!

She would retreat into the library if visitors came that day. But she would be unable to read. Nothing that ever was written could interest a girl who was waiting for the beloved of her heart—the only man she ever loved or ever could love. Oh, what a dreadful creature she had been to think of marrying when her heart had been as unmoved as the nether millstone.* What could have possessed her on that steel gray day in June, when Ted pressed his suit so ardently, and laid his thirteen thousands a year at her feet, and told her he could never care for anyone but herself; and at last she gave a shud- dering half-reluctant consent, and he trembled with happiness, and she allowed him to kiss her? Great heavens! how could she? She rose up, and laved her face in cold water as she thought of it.

She wished that no one had ever loved her; and yet how could she tell that she could not have loved anyone but Anselm if no one else had wooed her? But then she should not have found it so amusing. Yes, she knew well she had a thread of the coquette in her. She liked to know that people thought her charming and admired her. How unworldly she had been at one time! How incredible it seemed that her keenest ideal of joy had been to give herself wholly to God— to the lowliest services of life. What voices were these that came wandering back, austere with renunciations and sleepless vigils? Poor earthworm, yearning for security in the contentments of this fleeting show—a perpetual day-drudge to the delusion of perfect earthly happiness—consider how slight a breeze may scatter thy bliss—even as a gust of wind levels a small dust-heap! Hast thou forgotten what a thankless runaway slave is joy? She had read so many of the Saints and Fathers, she could have run on in homilies for hours. But, after all, there was something unreal in their depreciation of life—they spoke in the hieratic style, as Anselm had said. . . . Would she get into the trick of quoting him eternally, as so many wives did? Wives! Do people ever know how bold girls can be in their imagination?

No, she could not read while she waited. She would sit in the chair in which her father always sat when he taught the three of them—Cuthbert, Alice, and herself. How kind and gentle he always was—how he taught them to love the best books, and make fast friends of them, and as far as in them lay to do good to all men. How brave and pure and just his life had been—how full of kindly deeds and thoughts; and yet to the last his mind retained that lambent play of humorous irony—that quick perception of what was droll or incongruous. She could see the quiet half-smile that played so habitually round his lips. Only two days before his death, she had read to him some scenes out of *Cymbeline*. . . . That was a strange awakening before dawn, when, at the last, the end came so unexpectedly. The cocks were crowing when Kirsty called herself and Alice, and there was a strange grayness on his face when they entered the room.

How often since, when she woke at cock-crow, she had gone over the story of her father's life—thinking even of the day on which he first saw light—and then his brilliant student days, when he had won scholarly distinctions; and the long vacation, one summer, when he met his future bride in the old Surrey deanery where she was spending the summer. She was nearly twenty-one and he was twenty-four, and a year later they were married. And now it was all over; but surely—surely somewhere that spirit, so keen to feel and love up to the last, was enshrined in a fuller, larger life than that can ever be where the soul is clogged by a material companion. . . . Could Anselm be now content to believe that we became a thread in the living garment of the Infinite only by being transmuted into lowlier forms? . . . How quickly they had crept into each other's modes of thought and opinions and most cherished fancies! They never spoke to others of the things they discussed together. Would they ever listen to each other with a yawn, and even forget in time the anniversary of their wedding-day? What, married again—and they were not yet plighted lovers. . . .

Well, when the visitors were gone, she would go back into the drawing-room and watch the clock. The sun was setting, and the

Pâquerette had come in at five. Would she stay in the garden till some one came and told her he had come? Yes, of course, Alice would know, and her mother; for Anselm was going to write to her from England. What would she wear? Pink crêpe de chine and cream-coloured chrysanthemums—no; cream-coloured cashmere and scarlet fairy roses. She would pluck them at sunset, so that they would be fresh and fragrant; and at that moment Alice would skim down the vine-arcade: 'He is here, Stella; your *friend* has come!' Her heart beat so loud and hard, that she placed her hand over it. She went up through the vine-arcade, that bent under its great clusters of grapes—a white-breasted fantail carolling overhead, mad with mirth, as though it had sipped some frantic liquor; and now she was in the hall, her hand was on the door. Stella!—Anselm!—and then she shrank from his encircling arms with the thought, 'I am glad it will be yet four months before we meet as lovers!' And then a quick, sudden fear awoke in her heart. 'Oh, my love—my love, you have come back. All the way across the salt-dividing sea!'* and with that she burst into low sobs: 'Oh, the way is so far—so far; and some-times there are dreadful storms!' she moaned. The adder that lies ever at the heart of passion had awakened, and stung her.

What light was this stealing into the room? She looked at the stars and found them pale and shrunken; there was no need to turn to the east for tidings of the dawn. Already the birds had learned the secret. A Boobook owl gave a loud sad koor-koo, as if the light had suddenly smitten it blind. A curlew called in the distance by the Oolloolloo, and near at hand some magpies began their finished trills and flutings, but stopped short as they seemed on the point of breaking into the mellow ripeness of summer song.

There are some dawns that enfold the earth as with the unspeak-able beauty of Holiness. This was one of them. There was none of the fiery splendour that so often heralds day in Australia—especially in the summer, when the whole east is often kindled into a throbbing ocean of almost intolerable beauty. But this divine hue was the self-same '*dolce color d'oriental zaffiro*'* that blessed Dante's sight when he escaped from the murky atmosphere of hell. Morn, treading proudly on golden sandals, spread from horizon to horizon, till it seemed as if day were added to day, and the whole world overflowed with light. It was so keenly luminous that the trees on the Mess-mate ranges stood sharply outlined instead of being merged in a

continuous mass of foliage. Then, gradually, a deep rose-tint stole
into the east, as if halls were disclosed heaped up and running over
with rose-leaves. Never does heaven draw so near earth, and the earth
lie so open to heaven, as in those moments when we can first say it
is morning.

Stella could not remain within doors. She threw a soft woollen
shawl over her shoulders and went out among the shrubs and trees.
There was a great bush of Rosamond's glory near the front of the
house, and the heavy clusters of burning red roses that open their
hearts so lavishly to the wind, keeping back no folded petal, drew her
to them as with silken cords. The roses quivered fitfully in the breeze,
scattering their petals on the ground, where they glowed like delicate leaflets of vivid flame. 'Oh, what passionate prodigals you are to
shed yourselves on the relentless earth in this fashion! Why do you
not tarry a little longer, you generous spendthrifts?' said Stella softly,
looking at them with dimmed eyes. Why did the tears rise so quickly,
when beforetime they came to her so tardily? Had the weak destiny
of a woman at last overtaken her? The dawn had always before
been so full of joy and promise—like a great exulting *Te Deum*,* the
triumph of light over darkness, the glad beginning of a new day. But
now it was strangely solemn, charged with thoughts of those who
had been and were no more, of quiet chambers in which women had
watched their dying children, their husbands, their lovers. Oh, the
sadness and the strange mystery of those never-ending changes that
strike a chill to the heart in its gladdest hours of fruition! How many
there were to whom the pale splendour of this dawn brought only
the awakening consciousness of a life emptied of joy! How many
idylls of youth and love would come to a tragic close before night fell
once more upon land and sea! There were husbandmen sowing grain
which they would never reap, young mothers making garments for
babes that would never see the light of day, men working and waiting
for brides that would never be theirs, gallant ships sailing the main
which would never reach their haven. Oh, why did these dismal
thoughts rise in that hour full of the budding promise of the crowning happiness of life? And all the time every bird that had a note was
pouring out melody ceaselessly, vehemently, as if it would sing
its little heart into shreds. The sparrows were deafening each other
with their breathless chatter—but high above this rose the clear
sweet treble of the fantails. One might suppose that the swallows saw

glancing water for the first time, so buoyantly did they skim its surface, singing snatches of madrigals the while that were composed long before the first cave-man scratched rude figures on stones. Among the bamboos the reed-warblers poured out with pauseless haste those melodious but capricious lays in which many stolen goods are brought to light. Now a stave from a warbling grass-parrot, then a careless parody of the swallow's tittering; anon the cadence of a shell-parrot's love-song—and in between liquid blithe little legends all their own.

'They are perfect little rogues, these brown water songsters,' thought Stella, with a smile. 'They have as wide a range of musical sounds as Sir Thomas More's wife, who took lessons on the lute, the cithara, the viol, the monochord, and the flute, which she daily practised to her husband*—poor man: and I cannot play a single instrument, though I love music so insanely. If Anselm is fond of musical evenings we must get a "merlodeon." '*

At this thought she laughed outright. And then she went inside lest she might be seen in evening attire like a strayed reveller*—for it was now close on sunrise, and smoke was ascending from the kitchen chimney, from the men's hut near the wool-shed, and Dunstan's cottage. She knew that sleep was impossible; but after bathing and putting on a crisp morning dress she felt quite refreshed.

But how endless the day seemed! At ten o'clock it was difficult to realize that so much of the day still lay before her. At that hour a note came from Langdale to Mrs Courtland explaining that he would be unable to visit Mrs Parr, the caravan woman, as the servants called her, on that day, as he was going to see some sick people at a distance for Dr Morrison. There was a message to St Charity, directing her to take the patient's temperature, and permit her to sit up for some hours if it was not over one hundred and one. Stella carried out these instructions, and wrote a note for the patient to a brother in Melbourne. Then Mrs Morton and Julia came to ask all the Lull household to spend the day after the next at Broadmead, it being the fortieth anniversary of Mr and Mrs Morton's wedding-day. 'I don't suppose Hector and Claude will come till the evening, but you three, and the older children, can come early in the day. It does seem like a tale that John and I should be married for forty years, and never a cross word in all that time, my dear,' she said, turning to Stella.

'Not *one* cross word, mamma? And Claude and I have not been married a year, and we have had lots of little rows. But then I think it's more interesting, for we are always better friends afterwards,' said Mrs Claude reflectively.

'Well, my dear, people must have their own way, but I prefer always to give in,' said Mrs Morton. 'And when I don't really give in, your papa has so got into the habit, he thinks I do. And now, my dear, tell me about your woman.'

On being thus appealed to, Stella told the curious little story she had heard the previous day.

'Oh, my dear, if Miss Kibwell only heard that story, she would make something quite beautiful out of it,' said Mrs Morton enthusiastically. And then she went on to tell who Miss Kibwell was—a young English lady who wrote such beautiful stories for pious English magazines. 'We met her at Basle, dear, where papa and I stayed for a month; and there was a French curé staying at the same hotel. He spoke English nicely, and when I pointed out to him the evils of idolatry, he listened to me most attentively. I gave him two tracts on Mariolatry,* and he thanked me quite nicely and put them into his pocket. I prayed for him at sunset regularly, as I noticed that about that time he always read his poor Popish Breviary.* And do you know, my dear, this young English lady made such a pretty story of this for *Sunday in the Parlour*. She showed how, when the curé was at his Popish prayers, some influence—occult, I think she called it—was at work with him, till at last the "Hail Mary!" stuck in his throat, and he could not get it out. She showed how my few words and the tracts worked on him so that at last he had to renounce his errors. And then, at the end, she made what she called a word-picture of him—married, and with three or four children—the whole family saying the Lord's Prayer at sunset on the very spot where the lady from Australia—that was me, my dear!— first met him. But the editor of *Sunday in the Parlour* changed this into the family going to church on Sunday morning, for he feared some of his readers might find a Popish taint in prayers at sunset. Oh, they are wonderfully careful in these pious magazines. Not a word of the worse things that really happen will they allow into their stories.'

Stella, to whom this little tale was chiefly related, listened with both ears. Nor did her interest relax when the good lady took up her parable about Dr Langdale, whose speedy departure was a subject of thrilling interest. And to return again so soon. It must be some very important piece of business.

'Had anyone died, or what had happened?' said Julia, in the sharp way in which she invariably hankered after the concrete facts that underlay events.

'He said it was some private family matter,' returned Mrs Courtland, 'and that he expected to be back in Australia again in four months.'

'Well, that was just what we heard from Mrs Morrison as we came through Minjah Millowie,' said Julia. 'It seems funny, doesn't it, for one to go for such a short time?'

Very recently Miss Morton had written to Mrs Tareling a letter, in which the words occurred: 'You may depend the next news you hear will be that of the engagement of Stella and Dr Langdale. Stella picked up a dying woman—at least, she turned out not to be dying—and Dr L. is attending her; so they see more of each other than ever.'

Indeed, so great an impression had this made on Miss Morton's mind that, though Mr Haydon had been the previous Sunday at Broadmead, she had not stirred beyond the veranda. Still, it was comforting to know that he had made one or two artless plans to lure her away beyond the family circle.

The afternoon turned out very cloudy and sultry. Tantaro, the native boy, had had an accident with Duke a few days previously in riding to one of the out-stations. In jumping a fence the horse had struck his near fore-leg and cut it so badly that he could not be ridden for some days. Louise had not ridden for many years, so there was not a great choice of ladies' horses. There was Andy, voted an impossible little animal by Stella; and there was Norman, just then in a distant part of the run; and Orlando, who was in the stock-paddock close to the house, but had an evil name.

'He has splendid paces, and a head like an Arab,' pleaded Stella.

'Yes; but he has a concealed vice which is now an open secret,' returned her brother Hector. 'He shies at the most unexpected moments. Yes, you'll be on your guard if you see a lumbering bullock-dray, or a white log lying close to the road, or anything else that a nervous horse objects to. But how if he gives a sudden swerve when you are cantering along a tract as smooth and level as a bowling-green?'

'In that case I should either stick in my saddle or have a fall; and that reminds me, I've never had as many falls as people say go to the making of a good rider. Hadn't I better improve the shining hour?'*

'You had—in keeping out of mischief. No, Baby, you must have no experimental bursters* when you ride alone. You can have Andy to go anywhere with, and you can ride Orlando in the stock-paddock, then on Thursday you may have Norman.'

Stella rode Orlando once or twice round the stock-paddock, and highly approved of him. It is true he shied once or twice, but nothing to signify to anyone who knew how to sit in a saddle. On this dark, sultry afternoon she felt an uncontrollable longing to ride for miles in the open air. She was weary, but she could not sleep; restless and unable to work. She would ride to the Wicked Wood. It was only between seven and eight miles away, with a well-made road leading through it, little frequented by any save riders or the light vehicles of surrounding squatters, or people journeying between Minjah Millowie and Nareen. This wood had made a strange impression on Stella. It was only a few days previously that she had written of it to her sister Esther:

'Are there such tracts of utter desolation in any other country? Acres upon acres, nay, in one direction, mile after mile, with each tree bleached and bare as the planks of a wrecked ship that has lain for centuries on the coast of an uninhabited island. They are tall, and gaunt, and white, standing close to each other, so that their limbs—their poor skeleton-intertwisted branches—touch each other overhead. They look as though they had been convulsed with throes of mortal agony, and were then suddenly petrified. They are like the numberless trunks and bones of dead things reared in air instead of being kindly hidden in the bosom of the great mother. Are the limbs of living trees twisted and twirled and twined and twinged in this way? Is it possible that bark and leaves and the breath of life have such magic that they do not let us catch one glimpse of the real anatomy of a tree until their masking raiment is entirely gone? Some of the great old trees in the Wicked Wood have, through all these years, kept their tiniest twigs in extraordinary completeness. Standing under them and looking upward, they look more like delicate carving in ivory, like marvellous etching in silky-gray and pure white against a deep blue background, rather than the corpse of what was once dense foliage. It seems as if no great storm could

ever have swept through the wood since it became a burial-ground
of trees, whose hold of life was so strong that even in death they
stand upright. Else how is it that those delicate cobwebs of interlac-
ing twigs, those fine slender branches, dry and brittle-looking as an
old grass-tree, have not been strewn in crumbling fragments—in
dust, I had almost said? Underfoot there is a little vegetation—a sad
gray-green, with wide patches of yellow sand showing between. I
thought the Mallee country round Coonjooree might be taken as a
type of the most weird aspect of our scenery, but the Mallee sinks
into tameness compared to the Wicked Wood. It seems to stretch out
unseen arms and compel you to stand and look from tree to tree, and
try to draw in the secret of its strange fascination. It is too terrible,
one says; and then, because of this, one visits the place again and
again. It nourishes the imagination. There are some spots in it of
which I dream by night. In the daytime I try to think of stories into
which they could come. But then their barrenness—their lean
detachment from all the glad life of the world around, freezes the
impish fancies that seek to give them a local habitation and a name.*
The Wicked Wood is a sort of belt half a mile wide as one passes
through it from here to Nareen, but miles away on each side, to the
right hand and to the left. A mile further on, within sight of Nareen,
there is a wide stringy bark valley, in which a bush fire raged not very
long ago. It must have leapt from tree to tree and up the trunks to
the very tips of the branches, for all are blackened and charred, and
many are dead. But most of them have put forth young twigs and
leaves. Some among them are, indeed, a perfect idyll of spring—all
a mass of tender young leaves, clad in pale green, the youngest and
smallest of them tinged with a pure bronzy shade, fluttering above
the charred branches and along the coal-black trunks as if planted
by some fantastic gardener in hidden vases.'

Now that the thought, 'The way is so long and the sea so treacherous,' kept rising in her mind like the refrain of a ballad heard long
ago, and chiming perpetually beyond her power to still it, these gaunt
writhing trees seemed to draw her to them as by a spell. It lay in her
nature to seek serenity in a scene that had not one of the charms
which ordinarily woo the heart. The cultured beauty of the Home
Field, with its wealth of leafing trees and budding roses and spring
flowers, disquieted her.

CHAPTER XXXIV

STELLA resolved that she would merely reach the Wicked Wood and then return—keeping unsleeping guard on Orlando all the time. Not even the sight of two yellow-rumped geobasileus birds, twittering on a dwarf honeysuckle near the road, made her forget to be cautious, though their notes were symptomatic of housekeeping, and one of their curious double nests was a thing she much longed to see. Orlando seemed to enjoy the spin as much as his rider—and that was saying much. Those who love riding find a fascination in the exercise it would be difficult to define. Care, or the shadow of trouble, has in it something unreal, while the free-bounding motion of a horse seems to add a new strength and buoyancy to one's flagging vitality. The air is lighter, the horizon widens, heaven is nearer, and the songs of birds come in ecstatic rain while mile after mile of forest, or wood, or plain is rapidly passed.

Within a mile of the Wicked Wood Dustiefoot lagged behind and barked in a way that told his mistress he was out of breath. She slackened speed, and then for the first time noticed the strange change that had come over the sky. Up from the north a long wide column of clouds, low and black, was rushing with incredible velocity. The wind, too, had shifted, and suddenly lost its warmth, and seemed to be gathering strange voices from the wilderness. It was evident that a storm was brewing. It was in this moment of surprised inattention that her brother's mistrust of Orlando's open vice was justified. Without any ostensible reason he suddenly bounded from one side of the road to the other, and Stella, who sat at ease, her eyes fixed on the quickly gathering clouds, found herself in the twinkling of an eye low in the dust, with one shoulder feeling very numbed, and a general sense of dislocation weighing heavily upon her. 'I have had an experimental burster after all,' was the first thought; and then she attempted to rise, but she could only limp very slowly and painfully. Orlando cantered out of sight, the loose reins and flying stirrup, and all that marks the demoralizing contrast between a horse ridden and guided and one who is a lawless runaway, prompting him to flee from the scene of his escapade. Dustiefoot looked after the defaulter lost in amazement, which presently gave place to an indignant bark. Then he came and fawned on his mistress, and held her riding-whip in his mouth till she took it from him.

There are few occasions in which the pangs of conscience make themselves felt more acutely than after being rolled in the dust by a horse that one has been warned not to take beyond the stock-paddock. As far as she could ascertain, Stella had no limbs broken, but both the right shoulder and arm felt extremely stiff and sore, and there was some twist in her right foot which made it impossible for her to walk even a mile, much less seven or eight. The only alternative was to sit by the roadside till some one passed who could take her home. And then arose the very unwelcome and disturbing thought that tramps and vagabond sundowners* were just as likely to pass as friendly squatters in buggies, or a resident from Nareen or Warracootie eager to show a kindness to anyone belonging to Lull. There was a large fallen gum tree on one side of the road at about thirty or forty yards away from it. With considerable pain Stella dragged herself to this, and sat so as to be as much as possible protected from the storm, which would evidently soon break in its wrath.

Even as she reached this place of refuge, there was that curious lull which foretold a fierce outbreak. All heaven was now clothed with a shroud of storm-black clouds. The wind, which had quickly risen and broken into keen shrill voices, seemed for a moment suspended. The birds had betaken themselves to the covert of the trees, and were as silent as though night had fallen. Then, with a sudden obscurity of darkness, there was a great sound as of many rushing waters—a far-off gathering murmur, that had at first something plaintive, almost musical, as of many harpers harping on their harps. But this was soon drowned in a hoarse, ever-rising roar. Gust after gust of terrific violence, each one higher than the other, swept over the woods, till all the air was darkened and thick with dust, with branches torn from the trees, with fragments of blackened grass trees, with withered boughs that had been long dead of old. The spirits of the tempest were all abroad—a thousand jarring voices seemed let loose at once, rising in wails, and shrieks, and fiery confused sounds, as of battle and lamentation. Then a great flame of lightning swept the horizon, and peal after peal of thunder broke and resounded as though the earth were undermined with Cyclopean* chambers, through which the deafening crashes hurtled and reverberated end-lessly. Quivering, wide-drawn flames swept constantly across the face of the sky, as if the darkened heavens were being searched with flaring torches.

Dustiefoot cowered close to his mistress, and both were fortunately sheltered from the brunt of the storm by the closely interwoven branches under which they had taken shelter. Every now and then sticks and broken limbs, and all the débris that floats at large when the wind is blowing with hurricane violence over great tracts of thickly wooded country, fell around them. Now and then a branch was broken off overhead, and lifted high up as though it were a feather-weight. At each peal of thunder the dog gave a low growl, the hair round his neck bristling on end. Stella called him by name from time to time, but a trumpet-blast would have been lost in that terrific din as completely as a whisper. The touch of her hand on his head, however, seemed to reassure him. It was certain that the almost human intelligence of the dog's eyes, as he alternately fixed them wistfully on her face and looked abroad wrathfully when he gave a low growl, as if warning the elements not to go too far, gave Stella a sense of companionship, even of amusement. But the air seemed loaded with sulphureous vapours that gradually made her head feel at once giddy and very heavy. Once or twice she caught herself opening her eyes with the sudden start of one who has dozed. At such times Dustiefoot seemed more than ever on the alert with a brisk, protecting air. It was when the fury of the storm was spent that the thick end of a bough, which had been denuded in its flittings* of all the lighter branches, crashed through the thinned-out boughs overhead, grazing Stella on the temple and falling heavily end-ways on poor Dustiefoot's left paw. He gave one low, yelping bark, but did not whine or moan once, though the jagged end of the storm's missile had cut and bruised him badly. The sight of the blood dripping from the wounded paw made Stella turn faint and cold. She could not spare her handkerchief in all that blinding dust, but she had a fine white silk one round her throat, and tearing this in two, she bound one half of it round the maimed limb. Dustiefoot lay close by her, his head in her lap, and more than ever, as the storm subsided, Stella felt that she could not keep her eyes open. She felt sure, however, that Dustiefoot would not let any vehicle or horseman pass by without giving timely notice. Already he had started up barking clamorously, but the passer-by each time was a stray bullock, which hurried into a thicker part of the woods as if fearful that the worst was yet to come.

Once or twice Stella aroused herself with thinking of the consternation her absence, through such a storm and on a horse of Orlando's character, would cause at Lullaboolagana. Well, at the worst they would send out in search of her when the evening drew near. And Dunstan had seen her take the road that led to Nareen. The atmosphere and the shock of the fall, and perhaps, too, the little blow on her temple and the previous night's vigils, all combined to bring on a queer feeling of stupor. She was not asleep nor insensible, and yet she felt as if even to move were a trouble. She felt a slow trickling on her temple, and thought it must be rain. A few large heat-drops had fallen as the storm abated, but nothing more. It was a little rivulet of blood which trickled from the left temple, where it was grazed by the tree-branch. She rested her head against a large, smooth bough behind her, and sat with closed eyes, deathly pale.

It seemed to her that hours passed as she sat in this way—never wholly unconscious, yet overcome with an irresistible languor. In reality only half an hour had passed, till one drove up rapidly in a buggy, with Orlando led captive behind it. It was Dr Langdale on his way from Nareen. He had been caught in the storm, but was fortunately in the stringy bark wood where the trees were covered with vigorous young foliage. In the Wicked Wood the ground was simply littered with dead wood, which the violence of the storm had strewn broadcast like chaff. Half-way he saw Orlando, which he failed to recognise as one of the Lullaboolagana horses, but he knew the side-saddle daintily embroidered with scarlet. A horrible fear shot through his heart, but he strove to believe that it was misplaced. He could never quite recall how he got through the Wicked Wood. He kept glancing from side to side at the great withered trunks and limbs that the storm had felled, his mind filled with a sickening apprehension of what the next turning might have in store.

He breathed more freely when the Wicked Wood was left behind. A few minutes afterwards he recognised Dustiefoot's barking. Then, in one awful moment, he saw his worst forebodings beggared by the ghastly reality—Stella white and death-like, her face stained with blood. 'My God! my God!' he cried, with the intolerable agony of a strong man suddenly smitten beyond endurance. Stella heard the words distinctly, and recognised the voice. She had a struggling consciousness that if she willed it she could open her eyes and speak, but a kind of hunger fastened on her to hear what further he would say on perceiving her thus apparently insensible. She did not know

how cruelly like death she looked—her face ghastly white, stained
with dust and blood. In a moment he was by her side, kneeling
by her, his breath coming in quick gasps. 'Oh! my darling, my
darling—my darling!' he cried, his voice failing him with mortal fear.
And then quick compunction seized on Stella, and she sighed softly.
So extreme was his agitation, that for a moment he could hardly
believe she was not mortally hurt. But he found that her heart beat
with energy, he saw her eyelids quivering, and a faint tinge of colour
stealing into her cheeks. She recovered consciousness slowly, so that
he might not know she had heard those impassioned words which
held the sweetest music that had ever fallen on her ears, also that he
might not know the perfidy of which she had been guilty.

'You are badly hurt, I fear,' he said, as she at last looked up. His
voice still thrilled with the sharp emotions which had rent him, but
he had regained his self-possession.

'Dustiefoot is worse than I am,' she answered. She felt so absurdly
happy that it was a surprise to her to find her voice so thin and faint.

Langdale went to his trap and produced one of those cases which
are sometimes called the 'Bushman's Christian Companion.'

When it is remembered that such a case should contain a flask of
the best brandy, with a neat silver top that can be used as a cup, also
a flask of water and a pound or so of biscuits, the term will not seem
out of place, especially if it is further remembered that those who
make journeys in the Bush may often go scores of miles without
seeing a human habitation of any kind. But perhaps the term is never
so beautifully appropriate as when, as in the present instance, it is
incumbent on the possessor of such a case, in the interests alike of
science and humanity, to play the Good Samaritan.*

'Now, one, two, three—and you are to drink this, every sup.'*

'Do you really carry medicine about with you?' said Stella, with a
little pout, as she sniffed the mixture.

'No questions, if you please. Remember, people who are picked
up wounded and insensible are "cases."'

'Ah, that isn't so very inhuman!' she said, after gulping down the
dose. 'It takes the breath away, but then it seems to bring back one's
soul.'

'I am sorry to say that the noble art of healing does not invent such
remedies. We cannot say, like the Bishop of Noyon, that this recipe
came out of our own heads.'

'And who was the Bishop of Noyon?'

'A worthy ecclesiastic who used to say at the close of his sermons, "My brethren, I took none of these truths which I have just uttered from the Scriptures or from the Fathers—all came out of the head of your bishop."* That was not a pharmacopoeian drug you swallowed; it was brandy and water.'

'Dr Johnson's beverage for heroes!* Well, I felt heroic impulses the moment I drank it—no less than a resolve to mount Orlando. Oh, you unfaithful creature!' she said, looking reproachfully at the horse.

'Nonsense, you must submit to be driven home in my buggy, and I really must wash that wound on your temple.'

'A wound!' cried Stella, with incredulous amazement.

'Yes; was it the blow of a stray branch that threw you off the horse, or was it the fall that made you insensible?'

'Oh, I was not——' she stopped abruptly.

'Oh no, you were not insensible, I suppose, and you have not been hurt, and Orlando did not run away. In the meantime, this looks very much like blood.' He had wetted a handkerchief, and with the delicate touch of a trained hand washed away the clotted blood. Then he perceived that the wound was very slight, being, in fact, a mere scratch.

He assisted her to rise, and as she was determined to ride home, she repressed all sighs of pain. But he noticed her sudden paleness and the contraction of her lips.

'You *are* hurt. Pray let me drive you home.'

'Oh no, please. Claude will never let me forget it if I am ignominiously wheeled home.' And then it all came out—how she had persisted in leaving the stock-paddock on a horse notoriously unsafe, except, perhaps, for a buck-jumper.

'Well, do you know, Miss Stella Courtland, I begin to think you are rather a handful.'

'Yes, and I begin to see that you are rather tyrannical. Will you send Dr Morrison to see how many of my bones are broken?'

'Yes, I shall send him; but I think it is a duty to warn him of the sort of patient he is likely to have. Poor old boy! your paw is really rather badly hurt. Would you like a biscuit, old fellow?'

Dustiefoot ate several. Then the 'Christian Companion' was put back in the buggy, Orlando's reins were mended with a piece of twine, and Stella rode him back, while Dustiefoot sat by Langdale's side in the buggy looking quite like an invalid. How incredibly happy they were as they went back through the woods, exchanging a few words now and then, laughing at the veriest trifles, watching Orlando's ears to see if he meant to shy once more, counting the notes of the birds that had found their voices once more now that the storm was over!

They parted at the avenue gate of the Home Field. 'I shall send Dr Morrison at once. I know he is at home, because I took his distant patients for him to-day. To-morrow I shall probably call in to see how Mrs Parr and—Dustiefoot are going on.'

'Happy dog!' said Stella, with a mischievous laugh.

'Is it only a day since we sat by the hymenosperum tree?' she thought as she rode up the avenue. All her incipient fears and forebodings had vanished. The four months would speed away almost too swiftly—before she could fully realize this vast happiness which had come to her. There was some duty he had to fulfil before he asked her to be his wife. She accepted the fact without even speculating over it, so complete and whole-hearted was her confidence.

> 'I could not love thee, dear, so much,
> Loved I not honour more,'*

were the words that rose to her lips as she thought of the firm self-repression which had so speedily succeeded his agitation. Not for worlds would she have missed hearing those passionate words of endearment, and yet she resolved to be very guarded during the days that lay between their separation—to help him in every way to keep to a purpose which would not have been formed without good reason.

It was near sunset next day when he called. Mrs Parr was making rapid strides towards recovery. Dustiefoot was as well as could be expected. Stella was with her sister-in-law, Louise, in the drawing-room, her injured arm in a sling, the youngest Courtland on a big white bearskin at her feet, the 'Arabian Nights' on a little table near her.

'Behold how tragedies are made when common chances happen to wilful girls!' said Langdale, laughing, as he sat near her. 'What have you been doing in Arabia?'

'Oh, I drank coffee with the three ladies of Bagdad,* and then I met Aladdin, the son of Shamseddin,* on his way to that city. You know he left Cairo with fifty mules laden with merchandise?'

'Was he overtaken with a storm, and——'

'"Did he have an experimental burster?" Pray do not spare me, or let me for a moment forget that I was thrown in the dust like a foolish sack of potatoes.'

'Indeed, Baby dear, it might have been very serious,' said Louise, laughing.

'I assure you it looked serious enough when I saw her,' said Langdale gravely. 'And as it is, your arm is a good deal hurt,' he added in a lighter tone, turning to Stella.

'Yes; and I swallowed some dust.'

'And a tree hit you on the head and wounded your dog.'

'And before I entered the house yesterday the whole family met me in a procession—like one of those sculptures they dig up in Nineveh,* you know—all asking what could possibly have induced me to ride Orlando.'

'Yes; and to-day I have come with my pockets full of mulberry-twigs to whip you till you repent or die.'*

CHAPTER XXXV

IT was easy to keep on neutral ground when someone else was by, but next day, when Langdale called, all the rest of the family were at Broadmead, and Stella was alone on the western veranda with a large basket of flowers she was arranging in glasses and opal dishes containing clear fresh water from the creek.

'Are you allowed to sit up in this defiant attitude and do things?' Langdale asked, as he sat facing her.

'Oh yes. Dr Morrison says I am going on famously; and that if no one scolds me I may ride Norman—say next Monday.'

She held up a great cluster of half-opened white fairy-roses as she spoke, looking at them sideways in the clear emerald light that came in through the thick woof of greenery that enclosed the veranda.

'I wonder if anyone ever really scolded you?' he said, drawing nearer, so as to hand her the flowers she was arranging in the glasses with such cunning effect.

'Yes, everybody in turn—except Dustiefoot. Do you know, he runs about as if nothing had happened to him, with merely the prettiest limp in the world.'

'Are these white roses off the bush close to the myall acacia by the Oolloolloo?' he asked, bending over to count the number clustered on one slender spray.

'Yes; it is only rose-trees close to flowing water that bear such roses. How I should like to paint them or embalm them in fitting verse!'

'But they come back again next spring in all their old witchery. It is only human lives that can never be repeated—never be acted over but once.'

'Unless they are like the tags of old rhymes and the rain-clouds that fall and are evaporated and come back in a dragon-fly's wings, or a plant struggling for life on the edge of a desert.'

'Wicked child! you are laughing at me to my face. But whether or not we come back like the roses, or the creatures you so much object to that have more legs than four, every day is as fresh and keenly interesting now as if it were created for us individually.'

She felt that they were getting on dangerous ground, and sought safety by retreating to a more impersonal region in the persiflage that came to her so readily.

'And yet to superior beings on a better ordered planet, I suppose our lives would seem little better than blobs in a world heaped up with tumbled cobwebs.'

'What is a blob?'

'Do you go out into the woods in the early mornings?'

'Often, since I have learned from you what an exquisite hour the dawn is in Australia.'

'Then, have you not noticed transparent little webs pearled with dew hanging on bushes and tree-trunks?'

'I have occasionally. Why don't you look at me to-day, St Charity, when you speak to me?'

She attempted to do so in a laughing, careless way; but her glance fell under his, and her fingers trembled as she wreathed a long spray of native clematis with pale-green tendrils and delicate citron-coloured blossoms round the slender stem of a cloisonné vase.

'Well, have you not noticed,' she went on, making her work an excuse for not looking at him, 'how, when something has brushed against these webs, the side touched has curled up in a little blister? That is a blob.'

'Thank you. And do you really feel like one when you are arranging flowers like these?'

'Oh, let us speak in a broad general sense,' she said, laughing.

But, curious to say, he disregarded the suggestion.

'What do you call these white single roses?'

'They are the Macartney. Are they not lovely, with their golden centres and wide cups with "leves well foure paire"?'*

'I shall always think of it as the Stella rose. It is so starry,* and seems to look abroad with such fearless inquiry,' he said slowly.

At the words a deep damask flush mounted into her cheeks and remained there. Her deep lustrous eyes were, in truth, shining like twin stars. The pale-blue tea-gown she wore, with a cluster of white fairy-roses at the throat, threw the pure tints of her face and the soft brilliancy of her eyes into clear relief.

'You think they have an inquiring look? Yes, perhaps, something like the wide-opened eyes of calves, or the beaks of hungry sparrows.'

How angry she was at herself to find her face flushing more hotly, her fingers getting more tremulous, her heart beating more wildly!

'Give me one of them, Stella.'

She held out one to him, and their hands met. He took the rose, but did not release her hand.

'Were you quite unconscious when I reached you yesterday?' he said in a low voice.

But she could not speak; her reply was a long, shuddering sigh.

'You know my secret; and you are not angry, Stella?'

His voice was very agitated; and, as for her, she seemed to be enveloped in a throbbing haze through which she could not clearly see nor hear.

'Tell me, my own, that you are not offended,' he said, drawing nearer to her.

'No, I am not offended,' she said at last, her voice lower than a whisper.

'And do you know—oh, you cannot know—how I love you, with my whole heart and soul, as a man can love but once in his life!'

A fantail began suddenly to sing near them as if its heart would break with joy—the selfsame bird that trilled its golden carol above the vine-arcade when he came back in the *Pâquerette* four months later on! What strange confusion of time!

'You must not say more till you return,' she said, looking up at him, vainly trying to smile. The full knowledge that he loved her filled her with joy so keen that it bordered on pain.

'But, Stella, I must say more. I must hear you tell me that you love me just a little; say it, Stella—say "Anselm, I love you a little!"'

'But—Anselm—that would not be true.'

'Stella—my own sweet love—do not trifle with me.'

'Yes, it would be untrue, for I love you'—there was a pause in which he could not breathe, till the words came with a great thrill of gladness—'more than I can say.'

He knelt down by her side and folded her in his arms. Their lips met in a long, long kiss.

What a strange, memorable hour followed! It was almost unreal in its tumultuous happiness. It was to both the great sacrament of life—consecrating it; giving it fulness and meaning; seeming to lift it for evermore above the meanness of chance, and accident, and disaster; giving them a heavenly anchorage from all peril and storm.

'And now you must say no more,' said Stella at last, smiling through her happy tears; 'and there is to be no solemn revelation to anyone. It is our secret till you write from England, as you purposed at first.'

'Ah, but that was when I thought I was Stoic enough to keep to my purpose—now——!'

'Now it must be the same, Anselm,' she said quickly. 'Oh, do you not understand how frightfully tiresome it would be to have anyone else talking over this precious secret before we have realized it ourselves? In four little months I shall have got used to the thought. The same reason exists now that existed yesterday—does it not?'

'Yes, my own,' he replied, a shadow falling on his face. 'But now I think you ought to know all.'

'No, Anselm, let it be as though you had said no more. We need make no promises. Let what was your wish in this be my law till you return. Let us be friends a little longer. Oh, it has been so dear and good a bond! Can any other be better?'

'You little sceptic! You have sat too long in the scorner's chair. People have often told you their little stories, Stella. I also have one to tell you. But as you wish it, let it be when I return.'

'Yes, sir—some evening when we begin to yawn at each other.'

'Very well, madam—when we have worn every subject threadbare.'

'And we have learned to say "Not at all, my dear," with tightening lips.'

'When the honeymoon is quite over.'

'And the first quarrel an old, well-known story.'

'And poor little Cupid has been sent to weed poppies.'

'And you wonder why you used to call me St Charity.'

'And life has turned into a blob.'

'Now we must lay down rules. You must not take my words without leave. You did not know that was in the English language till I used it. Say, "Dear Stella."'

'Dearest beloved Stella!'

'"Please may I say 'blob'?"'

'Oh, you artful, captivating rogue! Tell me, Stella, how do you manage to be such a wonderful darling?'

'Just because I want you to be in love with me—oh! so much that you don't know whether you are on your heels or your head.'

'And then?'

'Oh, then you must keep an eye on Cupid at his weeding.'

'Stella, my belovedest, don't encourage yourself to be cruel. It is a taste that grows on people, like eating opium and stealing umbrellas.'

'That reminds me. Shouldn't I ask you how many of the commandments you have kept, if any?'

'Certainly not. It is the most dangerous habit a woman can contract, that of asking questions, more especially when she is going to be married.'

'Oh, how boldly and brazenly you pronounce the word! How glad I am that it cannot be for some time!'

'Not so very long, thank God! Let me count on your fingers.'

'Oh no—no, please,' she said, suddenly drawing her hand away.

'But why?'

'Superstition!'

'Ah! Have those beloved fingers of mine—yes, you are mine; you know you are!—have they been counted before!'

'It is the most dangerous habit a man can contract, that of asking questions, more especially when he is going to be married.'

'You have said it. Oh, you bold child, how brazenly you repeated the word! But, Stella——'

'Well, once upon a time, as you know already, I did think of marrying; but I never loved before.'

'And I, Stella, my darling——'

'Ah, that is part of your story!—ah, of course I know! I have read so many plays, and then there is Tom and people. How many sonnets did you write to eyebrows before you were eighteen, let us say?'

'Would you like me to count?'

'No. After all, you couldn't tell what a darling I am if you had not found how foolish it was to love anyone else.'

'Stella, will you be a good, loving child? Kiss me once of your own free will.'

'Oh, Anselm—next time, perhaps——'

'Will you really?—and after that?'

'And after that—and on and on till—— Can it ever be a tale too often told?'

'Never, never! But what has become of my rose? Give me another one. Let it be a "Stella" rose. What stupid people have the naming of flowers!'

'Oh, yes! and of most things. If only lovers were among the convocations that decide saintship, how easily the ultimate distinction of the Church would be obtained!'

'But the truest saints never get canonized, St Stella—"ora pro nobis."* Why that stifled sigh, my little heretic?'

'May I not sigh any more when I wish?'

'Yes, while I am away. Oh, I think I must set off to-morrow!'

'So that I may sigh?'

'So that I may return quickly. Ah, Stella darling, I have been waiting for you so long; and now I have found you—I have found you, in spite of everything!'

They fell into the sweet, endless repetitions of lovers' talk—grave and gay by turns. The sun was setting before Langdale could tear himself away. And then, before he rode off, Stella walked with him to the passion-flower bridge; and there they lingered till a great white star glowed in the rose twilight of the west, which spread far up, almost to the zenith of the sky. This great roseate wave of colour was a beautiful phenomenon of the season, and increased in brilliancy as the summer drew near.

'Perhaps it is star-mist, out of which new worlds are to be fashioned,' said Stella.

'Are you sorry for them, Liebe?'*

'No; perhaps after long ages there will be people in them who love each other as we do—and that will make up for all.'

A proud smile stole over his face as he listened.

'Are you mocking or in earnest, Herzblättchen?'*

'In deadly earnest. I foresee I shall be fearfully serious, Anselm.'

'No, no; you must not be a whit different—that would be a schism I could not bear. Stella, may I give you an old keepsake?'

'Do you love it very much?'

'Yes; and I have worn it for twelve years.'

'Then you may.'

He detached a small, old-fashioned gold ring from his watch-chain.

'It is a motto ring that was left by an old relative to my favourite sister Margaret, who gave it to me before her death.'

'Ah! she died?'

'Yes, at eighteen. "A pard-like spirit, beautiful and swift."* Do you know, Liebe, you reminded me of her the first night we met—and oftentimes since.'

Stella took the ring and kissed it gently.

'I shall wear it next my heart,' she said. 'There is a motto on the inside—"Amore."'

'Yes. "Amore e 'l cor gentil sono una cosa"—"Love and a noble heart are one and the same." It is out of the "Vita Nuova."'*

'Ah, the great master. From first to last he speaks more nobly of love than any other of the sons of light.'

'Shall we read him together next spring, Liebe? You know we shall be old married people by that time. Are you cold, Stella? You seem to shiver.'

'No; not cold. When you spoke of next spring, someone must have walked over the earth in which my grave is to be.'

'Oh, Blättchen,* what a weird idea! You should not speak of such a thing.'

'Yes; we shall read Dante together. But won't that be reversing the usual order of married people—to be first in the Inferno, and then go on to Paradise?'

They laughed softly. They were so far removed from the sagging prose, the dulness, the satiety of the 'usual order of things.' The hour was one of the charmed soft-footed fairies which come once or twice in the years of man's earthly pilgrimage—bearing in both hands a cup filled to the brim with life's costliest wine. The soft rose-glow in the western heaven thrilled through the transparent atmosphere; the Oolloolloo babbled merrily on its way, its course as yet unstayed by the fiery ardours of the approaching summer. A solitary curlew called in the distance, but near at hand the liquid songs of the little reed-warblers fell thick and fast, like swift melodious raindrops. They turned at last towards the house with lingering footsteps.

'How can we meet after this like mere friends, Liebe?' said Langdale, as they paused at the end of the little passion-flower bridge. 'It is very good and generous of you only to think of what I could have wished, but——'

'I would like to see the sort of being that represents me in your imagination, Anselm. Oh, please don't make a Dalai-lama of me, for you will be most dreadfully disappointed by-and-bye. Remember that we propose to face the ordeal of matrimony——'

'I wish to heaven the ordeal were to begin——'

'You must not interrupt—I am going to make a confession.'

'Well, your father confessor is waiting to hear it, and, if possible, to grant absolution.'

'"Father confessor!" Oh, Anselm, if you could see your own eyes just now you wouldn't call yourself such names. But don't try to look different. You are one of the few people who can be happy without looking foolish. I am quite in earnest. When people have the wrong sort of profile, they pay a very heavy penalty for being glad. You know when you cried out on first seeing me—I heard you. I was not insensible. I could have moved and opened my eyes—at least, I am sure I could—but I didn't even try.'

'You cruel child! why didn't you?'

'Because—because—I wanted to hear you say "My darling." I was at once bold and hypocritical.'

'This is too sweet a crime to be lightly forgiven,' said Langdale gravely.

'Oh, what infatuation! Well, don't you see it was like waylaying you—surprising you out of your declaration? I ought to be sorry, but I cannot, for we would have lost this day, and no other could be quite so perfect. Only let your reason hold good. After all, it concerns only us two really. And do you not know how I love to fold this secret in my heart from everyone in the world but you for a little time? I could not bear to have it profaned all at once. So many women chatter about such things in a common, callous way. There is Helen's elder sister—a perfect image of earth—who gossips away perpetually. Her favourite subject is engagements. You may smile, but I am quite serious. She asks questions until you feel that you are lying about in fragments; then she puts you together and begins afresh.'

'Very well, sweet St Charity, let it be your penance to have your own way in this.'

'And now, while we walk back to the house, you can practise talking and looking like a mere friend.'

'In that case, when I speak to you, you must look away.'

'Look away! that is what people in love do in a comedy. Why, the very magpies would point us out as lovers.'

'But what am I to do when you look at me with those eyes?'

'That is not the way to practise. Devise anecdotes about the weather, and try to be reasonable once more, for you have suddenly forsworn the art.'

'There is not the same call for it. You seem to have left off railing against nature and Providence, and the treacheries of life; remember what you said about the new world!'

Stella watched him ride away, turning at intervals to look at her till he was out of sight, and her eyes became suddenly dim with the thought—'Only eight more days before we must part!'

CHAPTER XXXVI

YES, these eight lengthening golden spring days swept on with cruel swiftness. And yet they held so much. The hours in which the heart is most deeply touched have something of the quality of eternity. They stretch backward and forward, allying themselves with all that is deepest and most enduring in human experience. Stella's was one of those complex, yet essentially feminine, natures which can only be gradually kindled with love. But when it comes to full being it is a passion which transforms all life. In place of discord there is harmony that before lay mute and unsuspected, like Hassan's gold covered over by common wood.* The friendship which had ripened into the perfect blossom of love had been a very real one. Social intercourse is for the most part a pitifully shabby concern, in which the ashes of mere existence smother aspiration, the quick play of fancy, and the sympathetic flow of thoughts that range beyond merely egotistical aims; an affair in which men and women largely bear themselves as though they were automata moved only by the wheels of custom, taking thought mainly for the things that perish with the using. But fellowship with the kind of vitality which wakens deeper chords of thought and feeling is as the salt of life. There were moments at first in which Stella could have found it in her heart to be sorry that her friend had 'degenerated into a lover.'* But if he had not, how unhappy she would have been! And how much she would have lost! Even the old faith she had given up seemed in some way gradually flowing back. When she prayed she no longer lost herself in weary conjectures as to its futility, doubting that her weak pitiful words could reach the great Omniscience, whose thought of order was the fixed law of all the starry hosts, doubting and wondering, till she seemed to be obliterated in a chaotic universe where nothing seemed certain but uncertainty.

And these long beautiful days passed without any of the jar and fuss and congratulation that would have robbed them of their serenity if the sweet fiction of mere friendship had been abandoned. 'Please tell us about one of your hospital people,' Stella would say, as she often said before in the presence of her brothers, or their wives. And she would sit sewing and listening, hardly raising her eyes. There were so many people she had learned to know in this way— the old Scotch charwoman who never read fiction because, she said, it was mostly taken up by things that did not signify for this life or that which is to come; the little lame boy who told the sister of charity he did not believe God heard people about legs; the costermonger who had been run over, and whose wife candidly explained that the Lord had made him 'naterally so silly,' one could not tell oftentimes whether he was drunk or sober. And when they were alone after one of these episodes had been talked over, Stella would say with unaltered demureness, 'Dr Langdale, do not go into partnership with your cousin in the West-End.'

'Why not, Miss Stella?' he would say with responding gravity.

'Because you like the poor so much, and'—dropping her voice with a quick change of manner—'we shall have enough money. And medicine has the trick of turning into a trade when it makes a big income.'

The 'we' had a magical sound to Langdale. Then sometimes they would talk of the work on which he had been engaged. At first he persisted he would tell her nothing about it till his return.

'You have woven so many brilliant fancies about it, St Charity, and the reality is such homespun stuff.'

Then she found he had been engaged on a dual task—one a treatise on some aspects of hypnotism, the other on the conditions of factory labour. On this she expounded a brilliant plan by which they might be unified, and so produce a novel with a solid realistic background, relieved by incidents of ideal romance, in which 'suggestion' should play the part of the genii.

'Never were so many plots thrown away on a material, semi-Teutonic mind before,' laughed Langdale.

Before these charmed days were over he could not forbear confiding to Hector Courtland that his purpose in returning so speedily to Australia was to visit Fairacre, on which Courtland heartily wished him good luck, and prophesied that he had a good show, but said not a word to Stella.

He told his wife, however, and she was delighted, but a little provoked at what she thought was some sort of caprice on Stella's part. She assumed that Langdale had put his fortune to the touch, and that the girl was too wayward or too proud—too much in love with her dearly cherished liberty—to be at once entirely guided by her heart.

'She will be sorry when he is gone, and it serves her right,' she said, a little vindictively.

'Oh, Stella may as well have a good long think over it; she is just the sort of girl that might be happier single all her life,' returned her brother meditatively. He fully adopted his wife's opinion, without, however, ascribing his sister's supposed action to caprice.

'Oh, you think Stella means all those wicked little speeches she makes about marriage?' said the wife.

'Well, she means some of them, or they would not occur to her,' returned Hector, with a touch of that fine discrimination which often characterizes reticent natures.

Mrs Courtland's resentment was not of a serious nature, and, indeed, chiefly took the form of contriving to give the friends that solitude *à deux* which so often leads to a change of programme, and even of life. Thus, on the afternoon of the day preceding Stella's departure, the two, after strolling for some little time with Mrs Courtland and Mrs Claude among the rose-trees by the Oolloolloo, found themselves left alone, heartlessly deserted by their companions. It was the fourteenth of September. The season was dry and warm, and already the time of roses had begun at Lullaboolagana. Some were out very early, some were half open, some just in bud, but all of them were very lovely. The white and pale cream Banksias were out in clustering festoons against walls and espaliers; there were tall standard rose-trees of Fortune's yellow, cloth of gold, white and pink moss, the Safrano and the generous old cabbage—all were loaded with opening roses. The Ophiric, with its shining, unserrated leaves and roses of pale flame, the delicate yellow of the Narcisse, the camellia-like pure pink of the Princesse de Hazel, were among those that were opening earlier. The Solfataro, too, with its large, greenish-white buds, pale, wax-yellow when they first unclose, but later white as the breast of a sea-gull; La Brillante, with its fiery, coal-like buds; the Gloire de Dijon, dark-red in early infancy—all were slipping their sheaths and coyly uncurling their outer petals. Dry as the season might be, the roses never lacked for water in the Lullaboolagana Home Field. They were its great glory—the joy of its mistress and the pride of Dunstan's heart. There were stations not twenty miles away in which roses paled and dwindled like rare exotics under an inclement sky. But here on the banks of the little Oolloolloo, and all within the spacious field, they bloomed early and late.

'How do you manage it, Dunstan?' visitors used to say in wondering admiration; and the old man, who was careful always to conceal his pride, would reply:

'Oh, it's the sile as does it—the sile and the creek and the underground tank and the tubing. You see, if I say to the mistress, "I wants this or that—or the t'other must be done," why, there 'tis, you know. 'Course, I don't say that I'm a born jackass, and don't know that one rose wants to be treated one way and another quite contrairy.'

Gardening was a topic on which Dunstan was never unwilling to enlarge when Stella spoke to him as he worked in the Home Field. He did so on this afternoon, when she stood lost in admiration of a young Murray wattle, whose great golden racemes, drooping one over the other, all the folds of the wide woolly tufts fully open, formed a sight of exceeding joy.

'Yes, 'tis purty fair,' he said, giving it a sidelong look; 'and yet, if I hadn't a-pruned it a bit last season and given it more water, 'twould have give up the ghost. A man may put as much work inter ground as would make trees and flowers spring up like shiverin' grass, and he may get naught but barrenness, if so be his work isn't what it should be. 'Tis for all the world like a man going out shootin', Miss Stelly. He may fire away till he's black in the face, and yet not bring home a crow's feather—like Bill Wilton, who's so fond of carryin' a gun—why, the Lord only knows, if it's not to show how much powder and shot may be wasted, and no harm to any creature with a wing, though I've known him to graze the tail-end of a bullock pretty bad. 'Twas after that I was out with him once at Swamp Desolation, and he kep' on blazing away in such a permiscous way, I said to him at larst, sez I, "Look here, Bill, if you're to go on firing like that, I must go into the swamp and sit down among the wild ducks; 'tis the only spot where I'll be sure of a whole skin."'

Stella, who had stayed behind her companions to talk to Dunstan, was laughing merrily over this incisive illustration, when Langdale came back alone; and then the two wandered by the Oolloolloo, whose silvery whispering was growing fainter day by day.

'Teach me before we part, ever belovedest, how I am to live so long without seeing you or hearing you laugh!' said Langdale, as they stood to watch the ripple of the wind among the tender leaflets of a beech-tree. 'Don't sigh, Stella. See what a perfect love-day has been sent us to-day by——'

'Heaven—say Heaven, not Nature, Anselm. A little while ago I kept wondering what they could grow in heaven lovelier than a Murray wattle and rose-buds. And now look up there, where tiny flakes of cloud leaflets seem to be floating. They are really young angels, who are waiting for an excuse to come down.'

'Do they despair of seeing people as happy up there as here? But tell them, Liebe—for they will hear your slightest whisper—if they want to see perfect happiness, to come all the way down next spring. Do you remember what brave old Homer puts in the mouth of Ulysses when he wishes that Nausicaa may be happily married?—

"Nothing is better or more beautiful than when a man and a woman inhabit a house being one in heart." "*

'We must not have too many possessions, Anselm. People get so fearfully stupid—so swallowed up in furniture. It would be adorable to start life like Hassan the camel-driver, with a cruse of water and a plume of curled feathers.'*

'You often gibe, Liebstes Herz,* at the commonplace, as though it were a penal settlement; but I confess I have often seen a day-labourer return to his home at night with feelings akin to envy.'

'Dear darling, you have often been lonely, and I wasn't there to comfort you. But after this——'

'Tell me, Stella, when I return home will you hasten to meet me, walking buoyantly on the fore-part of your feet like a figure in antique sculpture, as you walked among the rose-trees just now? Come and sit in this charming little summer-house—all one mass of jasmine and passion-flowers! Why, Stella, my darling—good God, you are crying!'

'Anselm, how foolish of you to be alarmed because I shed a few tears! Did you think I never, never cried? I believe Cuthbert is quite pleased when he sees me reduced to tears. Not that he has witnessed me often in that plight. You see, we were so much together, and, as boys do not cry, I got quite out of the habit.'

'But, my child, all this does not explain why you weep now. Herzblättchen, I cannot bear to see you anything but gay—or smilingly serious.'

'It is because we are too happy, Anselm. All day it comes over me afresh every now and then like a great wave of incredible gladness. Sometimes I cannot sleep, thinking it is all too like a fairy-tale. The first thing in the morning, before I open my eyes, my heart begins to beat wildly for joy—every bird that sings has a lilt in its song to which I could dance; and then in the middle of it all comes a sudden shiver of fear. Ah, there are such frightful accidents—such catastrophes in life! I think of my old friend Stanhope cut off in a few days! It all came up so vividly last night.'

'And the tears are in your eyes still, you fearless, fun-loving little Australian, with strong roots of the Keltic melancholy and superstition lying deep under all. Get a "pâquerette," and pluck the leaves to see how I worship you. Daisy petals are truer than dreams.'

He drew her close within his arms. Here she was safe. Here the billows of life's bitter waters could not reach or affright her. The jasmine summer-house was over-arched by a tall white poplar, whose young leaves with fair silver lining quivered on the slender stalks with as swift a motion as on the day that the old Greek poet compared the maidens to them who spun late and early in the household of King Alcinous.* Through the roof of leaves and blossoms overhead, and the poplar limbs with their mist of tender leaves, the blue crystalline dome of the sky could be seen, stretching above all like a great benign smile. How peaceful it all was! How much more reasonable to believe the waking assurances of earth and sky than the vague presentiments of a sleeping girl!

> 'O gentle wind, that bloweth south,
> From where my love repaireth,
> Convey a kiss from his dear mouth,
> And tell me how he fareth.'*

She chanted the words with the old glad light in her eyes, and laid solemn charges on him to turn towards Australia night and morning and waft her greetings.

They did not say farewell that evening. Hector Courtland was to accompany his sister part of the way to Melbourne, and was to take her by way of the Peeloo Plain, on the borders of which his friend Mr Dene lived, and Langdale proposed to pay a long-promised visit at the same time. But many farewells had to be spoken, nevertheless, and do what she would, the feeling lay heavy at Stella's heart that in leaving Lullaboolagana, the dearest, tenderest chapter in the book of her history was over. Here life's dearest mount of vision had been scaled, its sweetest idyll had been told.

Poor old Mick wept effusively when she bade him good-bye; Dunstan made it very clear that it was her duty to come back to Lullaboolagana early next spring, if not sooner.

'Why, Miss Stelly, the place was made for you, I may say; and what will become of the vagabonds that get their legs broke, I dunno. The crow has took to no one but yourself, and that poor female as went away with her brother last week whole and well, and the three horses a kickin' up their legs as if they never knew what it was to be skelingtons; and even that blasphemin' cockie had forgotten some of his worst curseses——'

Dunstan lost himself in enumerating the caravan procession that had so deeply impressed him.

The next afternoon Stella and her brother reached Peeloo Station, where they were to stay the night. Langdale came near sundown, after paying some professional visits for Dr Morrison by the way. There was but a meagre garden at this station, though it was a wealthy one, like most in the district. The house, too, had a curiously makeshift appearance. The fact was that the family from year to year proposed residing in the vicinity of Melbourne. Near sunset the host proposed an evening ride to all who cared to go over the great Peeloo Plain, which stretched for over sixty miles westward. There was an artesian well ten miles off, on the plain of weeping myalls, he wished to show Courtland.

'Whom the gods love ride across a great Australian plain in the evening,'* said Stella; and Langdale, of course, was instantly converted to the same opinion. So the four set off westward, when the sun was low on the horizon. There were heat clouds piled up in an unmoving bank, through which the sun burned, as it sank, like a smouldering fire that the wind has fanned till the coals kindle into red heat and the flames break out, eating their way through the fuel. For a moment before setting the sun stood all undimmed on the level horizon like a great fiery ball, and then dropped suddenly out of sight, leaving a deep soft glow which reached high up in the heavens, and so remained for hours. This beautiful, unusual appearance was more vivid that evening than it had ever been before.

The riders followed no road, but took their way across the plain, still clothed with the luxuriant winter grass, which here and there was beginning to be touched with the heat languor that a few weeks later would turn the verdure into sapless flax. But as yet the herbage was so close and rich that the hoof-beats of the horses scarcely awoke an echo. The few sounds that were borne with startling distinctness through the sonorous air died away. The shrill scream of a black cockatoo in the depths of a weeping myall, the twitter of a little emu wren bounding through the grass, the loud calls of the white-fronted honey-birds in a flowering acacia, the hysterical chorus of laughing jack-asses in the wooded bend of a watercourse densely lined with ti-tree, the sudden caw of a solitary crow in a box-gum, all became silent, one by one. Now and then a red kangaroo, with his beautiful ruddy tints and faint flush of dawn-rose on the under-neck, or a doe, clad in delicate steely blue, bounded near them as they passed.

They flew over the great smooth plain, while the spring wind, vivifying as a sea-breeze, blew in their faces. At times they came to a stretch of kangaroo grass, tall and rustling, swayed by the wind that came now and then running up in little fitful gusts, till the faint billows formed an exact image of the half-formed waves seen in mid-ocean in placid summer weather. The earth and sky equally had an unfamiliar boundlessness that at first lay like a weight on the spirit, and yet gradually soothed it as the imagination gathered impulse and repose from the sad magnificent horizons, unbroken by wood or hill, or the gleam of water. At rare intervals the marvellous uniformity was heightened rather than interrupted by the course of a creek whose abrupt banks were marked by a wavering line of box-wood or weeping myall, and sometimes dense undergrowth. The light of day and the brilliant blue of the sky were replaced by the dreamy paleness which falls on the world when the heavens are cloudless, yet hold the stars for some time out of sight, and the earth lies stretched below without limit and without shadow.

There was no cold look in the sky, no bleakness on the earth. It was noble in its vast breadth, its virgin promise of fertility—fit to be the dwelling-place of a race strong, free and generous; careful not only for the things that advance man's material prosperity, but caring infinitely as well for all that touches the human spirit with quick recognition of its immortal kinships.

'It is like no other scene I have ever looked at,' said Langdale, at length breaking the silence.

'Don't you feel you will remember it all to your dying day?' asked Stella softly.

'Yes; perhaps when we die we shall remember it better than ever. It is like a picture of the old classic underworld, with its pale light and its wide, homeless pastures.'

'Oh, if it would only last for ever—the world flooded in mysterious light, the horses never tired, the horizon never visible! Why are you smiling?'

'I would not wish it to go on for ever. I have an earth-creeping imagination that would soon pine for a local habitation—and Blättchen waiting for me inside. But how often we shall recall this ride till we meet again!'

There were cadenced cries far overhead, as if among the stars, which began to swim into sight all over the firmament, and looking upward, a long line of great birds, with dusky wings wide spread, became visible.

'They are swans going to their nesting-places by some swamp,' said Stella. 'How plaintive and musical their notes are! Don't they make you understand what someone meant when he said that virtuous melodies teach virtue?'*

'And what virtue could they teach Herzblättchen that she does not possess?'

'Handfuls! Try to believe this in time: gentleness, resignation, hope. Did you not tell me yourself, some time ago, that I was curiously lacking in hope? I always knew that a friend was more faithful than a lover!'

'But, Liebe, I am both; only the more I know you, the less I could bear to have you different.'

'That is what I am always promising when my happiness makes me afraid to be different. I take refuge in the thought that I am going to be so useful and helpful—to make some lives happier that without us might be intolerably hard; to make our future home a little radiant centre. Anselm, I had rather be a cat and mew at the moon than be self-complacent and wrapped up in my own prosperity like a cocoon.'

Langdale laughed softly at this quick vehemence of speech.

'But, Stella, how little danger there is of that! Do you want to make me believe that you have not always been helpful and loving—full of sympathy and tenderness and quick insight, ready always?'

'Ah, but you don't know how indifferent in between—how ready at any moment to believe that after all it does not much matter. You do not know this vagrancy of temperament. You are protected by your nationalities and your love of work. That gives you an ideal of duty apart from whim and sudden changes of mood.'

'I always knew that a friend was more faithful than a "Little-heart-leaflet." '*

'Don't laugh at me, Anselm. We shall recall this ride so often, as you have said: when the days are too long—when people are wearisome: and that is one of the great qualities of our race everywhere.'

Langdale laughed again, and took off his hat in acknowledgment of this wide compliment.

'Forgive me, Liebe,' he said, recovering his gravity; 'but this air seems to get into one's head like champagne. But I promise not to interrupt again.'

'Well, always while you are away—when I am bored, when I am overcome with the feeling,

> '"Only my love's away,
> I'd as lief the blue were gray"—*

I shall think of this ride, and remember that I made resolutions to be better—above all, to be more patient. I can so well understand how it was with the Foolish Virgins. It is never amusing to wait long. I should have gone to sleep, I am sure. I should have been caught with my lamp extinguished.* Do you know that seeing you so un-wearied—so lost to every thought but the welfare of that poor woman during the days when she was so near death—has given me, I think, a more abiding sense of duty.'

'Sweet St Charity! how divinely serious your face is just now—heroic in its earnestness!'

'My heroic moods are exotics; the wings of my soul are not full-grown, and it takes but very short flights; it comes nestling back to earth so quickly; it will follow in the wake of your vessel all the way; you may not see it, but it will be there—especially at dawn. Leave your cabin window open; for it is only the spirit of a dead soul that can go through cracks and bars of iron and glass.'

'And will your beloved little soul come and lay a kiss on my face?'

'No. It is not the vocation of a soul to kiss.'

'Nor even to whisper those delicious little *niaiseries** that make me so happy? Cruel little soul! Why, then, will it come all that long way?'

'To get into your waistcoat pocket with your watch, and count how fast time flies.'

It was past nine o'clock when they returned to the Peeloo station. The host and Courtland lingered at the stable after they dismounted.

Langdale and Stella bade each other farewell on the wide veranda covered in with passion-flowers and a luxuriant Queensland bignonia.

Langdale had to leave by daybreak, as he was anxious about one of the patients he visited that day—a splitter* living among the great tiers of peppermint eucalyptus that lay behind the Messmate Ranges—a man who had been injured by a falling tree. Stella was very brave, and kept a smiling face to the last. Then she went in and chatted for awhile with the lady of the house, while the men smoked on the veranda. She had gone to her own room before they came in.

CHAPTER XXXVII

LAURETTE had never been more airily cheerful and full of gossip than she was on the day after Stella's arrival.

'We have all the morning to gossip in. I asked Mrs Carter and Dora to afternoon tea, so there is no chance of their dropping in at some unearthly hour. To-morrow evening we are going to rehearsals of private theatricals at the Jorans'. By the way, they have returned from England since you were here. They are among our *crème de la crème* in Melbourne. What confers the distinction? Well, at present, the very inner circle is rather High-Church, and of course has the right of tambour at Government House, and one must be very wealthy or'—Laurette made a slight pause, so as to make the point with emphasis—'one must be connected with the British aristocracy, or with the viceregal family.'

'When the two are combined, one must hold every blessing that this life affords in the hollow of one's hand,' said Stella with a becoming gravity.

'Yes, my dear, unless one has to retreat to the depths of the Mallee Scrub, as I must shortly do. But I shall devote myself to the education of the children. But about the Jorans. Thomas Joran has had what you might call a romantic career. The very earliest glimpse of him in colonial history: he hawked elderly cabbages in the streets of Melbourne—at least, they would have been streets if they had been made. Well, I don't mean that any decaying vegetable is romantic; but then compare the status of a man employed in that way and one who entertains a Duke and goes to Court. But it was rather a sell about the Duke. You see, the Jorans entertained him sumptuously. Some people say that, in all, they spent four thousand pounds on him in less than a week. What it must have cost them in special trains alone! I myself have sometimes seen Joran haggard with anxiety, hunting up railway officials, while Mrs Joran stood sentinel lest a common populace should even peep in at the blue satin lining, or the butler, who was in a separate compartment, in charge of the ice and champagne. Naturally a man could not have all this gold and incense lavished on him without making some return. So when the Duke left our shores, he cordially invited the Jorans to visit Rookcourt when they were next in England, thinking he was safe because they had only just returned.

'But "the dear Duke" had scarcely sailed, when weighty reasons compelled the Jorans to do likewise. In fact, Mrs Joran, in a burst of confidence, confided to me that it would be unpardonable not to respond to the Duke's pressing invitation. But sad to say, the only recognition his Grace accorded them was that a younger son asked Mr Joran to lunch with him at a Radical Club. You may talk of the aboriginal myths, but I think they are very paltry compared to spending five or six thousand pounds, and getting in return a five-shilling lunch! It could not have cost more, for out of compliment to his guest, Lord Augustus had colonial claret, the kind we can buy in Melbourne at fifteen shillings a gallon. Oh, I assure you, it was quite five or six thousand pounds the Jorans spent, between the voyages and a mansion in Park Lane for three months, and servants that made them believe the nobility never ate beefsteak that cost less than two-and-sixpence a pound. Still this last visit to England was not altogether without consolation. The British Government was about that time bent on what is called "knitting the bands of the empire closer." So people from the remotest isles and colonies were patronized and invited in troops, like tenants on rent-day, to various very funny entertainments. The Jorans went with a crowd of others, to lunch or breakfast or something at Windsor Castle. The greatest mar-joy in the arrangement was that an over-worried Court official was heard to exclaim in despair, "Good Lord! I thought this was the day for the negroes!" Mrs Joran never mentions the Windsor visit to me now; she did so once or twice to begin with, but I invariably said, "Well, it must have been comical to see all those darkies from Benares and Ceylon and the Malay Peninsula. And, by the way, were there any of the Chins from Burmah who hang missionaries to make the rice grow? I take an interest in them, because the Dowager Countess of Essington—Talbot's aunt, you know—spends a small fortune on the dreadful creatures—— But no, I am mixing things up like the poor gold-rod-in-waiting, or whoever it was. . . . Haven't you heard the story, dear Mrs Joran?" Naturally she doesn't give one the chance to trot this out too often.'

'Well, I suppose Mrs Joran does not sheathe her claws when she gets a chance to tell you amusing anecdotes,' said Stella, who sat listening to this sprightly malice with a good deal of amusement. 'I have always heard that kindness and a wish to please are at the root of true breeding—so you seem to have the article here to perfection.'

'Oh, that's all very well, when one is in the country,' returned Laurette. 'Why, when I am at Cannawijera, and the squatters' wives around ask me my opinion of their bonnets, I assure them they are perfectly *chic*—awful things, you know, with black cotton lace, and the wings of those *demi-monde* African parrots, that tear your eyes out with their staring yellow and green. Oh, Talbot is well, thanks. He has gone into some sort of partnership with a man who buys land at a shilling a yard, and sells it at £10 a foot. Mining is so frightfully risky—perhaps land is, too; but you can cut up land, it seems, into minute globules, and yet build houses on it. I don't understand exactly how it is done, and yet I have seen it in a way, just as I have seen conjurers' tricks. You give one of these men your handkerchief and he gets eggs out of it—though you know there were none when you gave it to him.

'Driving about in the suburbs, I have often seen vacant pieces of land for awhile. By-and-by there are great placards as big as a house put up on lofty poles: "This valuable piece of land, situated in the very best suburb of the metropolis of the Southern Hemisphere, is to be sold at a ridiculously low price," and so on. That is what they write on these enormous placards. And though there is nothing to be seen near them, except, perhaps, a few dirty children and rusty kerosene tins, when you see such an announcement in big letters for a few weeks you somehow begin to believe it.

'Then there are columns in the newspapers about the rising suburb—the suburb which is coveted by the *élite* of Australia; the suburb where the irritating hum of the sanguinary mosquito is never heard. Then you get a fat letter containing an elegant circular, with daisies and butterflies round the border, and a map of the place—all showing that in some way every blessing this earth affords is grouped round the rising suburb. If you read the advertisement and the circular, and have a five-pound note to spare, and never go near the land, you're sure in the end to buy an allotment. You see, you need pay only a few pounds to begin with. But then you pay a few shillings a week as well, for the rest of your life, or till you throw it up—I mean the land, not your life, though some unfortunate people have done both. But if you do that you lose all you have paid. So altogether it comes to a lot of money—only I am afraid the "boom," as they call it, is going off, for at a sale last week, only the auctioneer, and the boy that rang the bell, and Talbot, turned up. But now tell me about Lull and Minjah-Millowie, and all your people there; and the Mortons, don't they live not far off? And who is this Dr Langdale all the good people rave about?'

Only once before had Laurette seen the colour flash into Stella's face in such endless wavelets. To hide her confusion she broke into a laughing account of some of Mrs Morton's funny little stories. But without this Laurette had concluded that all Julia's surmises were well founded. The girl looked so radiantly, so insultingly happy. She fell into such dreamy little reveries—her lips softly parted, her eyes shining with a gentler irradiation than of old. And then she studiously avoided Langdale's name. Heartless coquette that she was, after encouraging Ted's addresses for years, she was now prepared to throw him over at a moment's notice to satisfy an absurd whim of being in love. As if there were no such thing as duty in the world! Nothing was more characteristic of Laurette than the way in which she always fell back on the moral foundations of life as the true mainspring of her actions when she found herself in what she called a 'fix.' She ignored everything that it suited her to forget, and when meditating some paltry little scheme that had every element of meanness and treachery on a small scale, a virtuous glow stole over her as if she were reinforced by the law and the prophets, and obedience to the Ten Commandments was what she lived for. But here she seemed to have entered a *cul-de-sac* in which there was no move in her power that could further her purposes.

'There is nothing so easy to make as a tradition,' one of our best-loved novelists once wrote;* and many lesser people find it also very easy upon occasion. There was no tradition, oral or written, that Laurette was not prepared to invent. But to what avail? Ted would come, and the first few words between him and Stella might serve to explode all Laurette's painstaking efforts to keep the girl in the strait and narrow path* of duty. A point had come in which invention without deeds was valueless—but what could she do? Nothing except wait the course of events with a heart prepared for any little justifiable artifice that would keep her brother's life from being wrecked by the selfish perversity of a heedless girl—one bent only on her own scheme of happiness, regardless of the sacred claims of the past! She was undoubtedly in love with this man—was she engaged to him? A hundred times the question rose to Laurette's lips. A feverish sort of hopelessness grew on her as she marked those little signs that in themselves are so slight, and which yet, linked together, furnish so strong a chain of evidence.

Many things had conspired to tax Laurette's nerves lately, and she found this additional suspense intolerable. But the instinct of secrecy, of concealment, which comes to be a second nature with those in whom a life of small intrigue has grown and waxed strong, restrained her. Nothing could, after all, be gained by asking this question. She would wait and watch.

Stella escaped early into her own room that night, and wrote for a long time, a happy light on her face, and warm blushes often mantling in her cheeks, which would have told their own tale to an onlooker. This was what she wrote:

'DEAREST FRIEND,

'I was half glad and half sorry that we did not meet in the morning. Our homeward ride was so altogether precious—so far removed from the ordinary grooves of life—it was better to part in the starlight and see each other no more. I almost wish we should not meet again till you return from England. And yet, of course, it is only my pen that says this. Yes, I soon went to my room; I sat without a lamp looking out into the beautiful night, with its soft, deep glow and ethereal starlight, and I made a picture of it all in my mind, which I will keep forever and forever. Oh, I am so very sure that nothing we can see in any other world in any other life can be dearer or more alluring than that ride together over the great plain, stretching indefinitely on every side as if it passed beyond the confines of the world. The shadowy clumps of trees, the dark lines that marked the watercourses, the talk kangaroo grass undulating gently like stormless billows, the cries of water-fowl far overhead, the muffled hoof-beats of our horses, the boundless expanse, the solitude, above all, the pale, wistful light, making visible the faint lilac of the sky, the uncertain gray-green of the earth—I held them all, making a picture of them that should not pass away. I looked at them long and steadfastly till the secret of their changeless uniformity, their unbroken peace, their sweet serenity, penetrated my heart. Do you remember the fragrance of the wild geraniums that our horses crushed under their hoofs in one place? It comes floating in with the moonbeams at this moment. But to be the elixir of life it must be accompanied with the sound of a voice—*the* voice which in all God's wide universe—— But is this what one writes to a "friend"? And what is the use of trying to make a pen say all that rises in the heart?

'Oh, you little cold, good creature! I say to it; you are sometimes wonderfully cunning. You have a tongue of your own that often dives down after thoughts, and brings them out triumphantly, after a fashion that sets stammering speech at defiance. But where are your eyes, that brighten with happy smiles, and grow dim with excess of joy? And where are your cheeks to glow and turn cold in a breath? And, above all, where are your hands that with a touch, a little timid good-night clasp, make the tongue feel like a clown who has nothing to say but the worn-out tags of songs long known by heart? All these gifts come to you only in the hands of a master from whom you learn the strange magic of playing on the hearts of men from generation to generation, like a clarion heard at dawn. . . .

'But I have no power to teach you how to tell the thoughts that rise in my heart in these days—the wonderful long, swift days in which so many thousand strange, sweet, shuddering thoughts storm and foam, and then flow in strong deep tranquillity, like an impetuous mountain brook that grows ever wider, till it becomes a river and loses itself in the sea. But help me, little pen, to tell a few of these myriad fleeting thoughts that will not let sleep come beyond the threshold. Is it true, then, that this dear friend and I belong to each other for time and eternity? That neither life nor death, nor principalities nor powers, can ever mar the perfectness of our love?* Is this true? Yes—yes—yes. Yesterday is irrevocably ours, and to-day belongs to us, and to-morrow dawns that we may still know how perfect life may be. Henceforth our lives are double—one within the other, in heart and spirit—never to live apart, even though seas may roll between and continents divide us.

'And can it be that from year to year the heavens will be so high and golden, the earth so wide and loving, that the heart will thrill with a power of loving which lifts the soul as on eagle pinions, till life and death are but twin brothers, equally welcome so that we are undivided?

'Ah! what a strange thought, almost to wish for death now! Yes, would it not be good to escape a possibility of the cruel ironies that Nature keeps so often in store for the children of men? Can any mortal measure the power which time has to bring in its train change and weariness? What if the day should come when this love, so strong and ardent now, should become one more of the beautiful illusions of life, a deserted pavilion flecked through and through with the mildew of indifference? Has my heart been too readily given? Is it not written in song and story that men prize most what is won with difficulty? But as for me, the first time we spoke to each other, did not my heart stir tumultuously? Could I not have opened my eyes if I had willed that day when the storm had raged so fiercely—was it not because I hungered to hear him speak his love? . . . Well, be it so. I am glad that I know the truth—that it will be with me through these long months of separation, like a nest of singing birds whose wings grow strong for flight, and who yet, like doves that fly afar in the day-time, always return to their dove-cotes before night falls. . . . Tell me of the gentle, tender thoughts which cast out every lurking shadow of fear; of the new ties that may arise to knit us ever closer, heart to heart, in the higher duties of life, till we

' "Learn by a mortal yearning to ascend,
  Seeking a higher object,"*

till in imagination I draw near to the dim bourne without any heart-quaking. Yes, even Death must doff his terrors when we know that the infinitely beloved of our soul must pass through the shadow of the dark valley. Ah! gentle, kindly Death, grant us that last favour of life—not to be long apart after the last farewells are spoken. After all, it is the might of love that takes the victory from Death and robs the grave of its terror.* We learn to know too well that not a clod can ever touch the outer bark of the spirit's life. Abide with me, thoughts of pensive gentleness, that fill the mind with calm till all forecasting doubts and fears are swallowed in the azure of peace, like clouds that wander on the wide horizon till they are spun into the flawless dome of heaven. . . .

'After all, little pen, there is a touch of the laity about you, so that the heart cannot take you into its full confidence. But do not stand in the outer court of the Gentiles*—the dear friend for whom you are writing loves our babbling. What other small broods of fancies do you hear chirping out their slender roundelays? No, let us not speak of our happiness. It is foolish to cut snippets out of so endless a theme. What was that little whisper of fear or regret?—no, nothing so resolute as these feelings, but a vagrant little misgiving, that trips so swiftly before one looks it in the face. One cannot say whether it is a scout, or a forerunner, or an idle little gad-about, who has nothing to do but snatch an ear of corn, melting melodious airs to the most wayward woodland fancies. Are you not afraid to marry when you are so desperately in love? Ah, wicked little rover! I have caught you merrily whistling your treasons. Now I have put the tip of my pen through your errant fancy, and transfixed it for my friend. I should not wonder if he would beat you as blue as a violet when he catches you. But what treacherous little arrow have you let fly? Let me get at the core of this half-jocund lay which leaves a sting behind. Youth, love and marriage, are these the three fearful felicities of a woman's life, and is the most fearful of these marriage? And love, the most exquisite vision which life holds, is it in imminent peril when it is imprisoned in the service of every-day life? . . .

'Lovely as one of the muses, and crowned with the first violets of spring, this vision loved to wander solitary on mountain peaks, when they were first lightly touched with the vermilion of brightening day. It came and went at will—this radiant dream, casting a glamour over the world, like the reflection of a damask rose falling athwart the half-opened chalice of a white magnolia. Dreams shun the glare of day; but one morning the voice of him to whom this vision of right belonged called to it to come from its lonely haunts, and abide by the altar which he had dedicated to it in a secure dwelling-place—alas! is it too secure, too untroubled? Who could believe that a little air of revelry, whistled on an oaten pipe by the most *insouciant* of wandering minstrels, should awaken such qualms? Go on, little pen—an altar fitted to guard the fairest dreams. Even Love's purple wings and golden arrows are touched to finer issues when they are consecrated with life-long vows. Yes, like other monarchs, he comes to his kingdom by making covenants; and yet, and yet, we cannot give up the dream for the reality without heart-quaking and doubt, and something of poignant regret. Flashes of thought come like cloven tongues of fire, in whose light the soul waxes faint and timorous and cries in anguish. Is it, then, true that love's inmost life is rooted in the senses, are its keenest aspirations to be tamed like caged birds, to be merged in the commonness of every day content? Yet, for all possible fears and doubts and questions there is an answer: Perfect love casteth out fear.* Love, the crowning felicity of life, that light of the world which shines more unquenchably than the stars of heaven. It is strong, not only to bear sorrow and anguish, but also to meet the common needs and common joys of daily life, buoyant enough to sustain the secure happiness of wedded as well as the despair of parted lovers.

'Dear friend, does this appear to you as the cloven foot of those heretical images of marriage which haunt me so often? But who can go through life with open eyes and not perceive that the average run of married people seem to have but entered on business contracts, in which anything like the ardour of love is absent as conspicuously as in any huckster's bargain? Do you remember my telling you one day that I could not be so very sorry for Romeo and Juliet? You asked me why, and a coach-whip bird flew snapping by, and I followed it to make sure whether it had a white spot above each eye. And then, though you may not think it, ever belovedest friend, I often hesitated to say things because of your calm, clear reasonableness. But now there is no coach-whip bird, and you are three hundred miles away. Therefore do I thank the gods that here and there we have the immortal story of lovers who died before their hearts and lives were touched with the corrosion of life's invading commonness. Why should we regret those who knew how to die so well for dear love's sake? So many and so many live to bear false witness to it—to sit under a ragged banner and eat garlic, nor ask to be stayed with flagons and comforted with wine.* But then, again, there are the fortunate few. I must stop. I should have written to my mother this evening, but I wrote to you instead, though I parted from you only the day before yesterday. Oh, Anselm Langdale, do you not call this the utmost peak to which ingratitude can climb? A mother's love; whose is like it?—giving so much, asking so little! Do not pretend that you ask little. History, poetry, the drama, your eyes, all betray you. But this first tender love that enfolded us from the dawn of life, that bore with all our waywardness, that watched over us in illness, that was with us like the benediction of God when we first folded our hands in prayer. And then, like long-legged, every-day chickens, we leave the loving mother to scratch up the dust for ourselves, without the shadow of an excuse that she pecks us away in favour of a younger brood. Don't I know? Have I not watched my old hen, Augusta, rearing brood after brood? And now I watch myself looking forward to the return of the *Pâquerette* with hardly a pang. Hardly a pang? You hypocrite—with a heart that keeps time to dance-music all day long; yes, and beats wide awake at night to keep up the revel. Think of it—coldly to leave the sweet mother when the night is drawing on apace, when all the vivid personal gladness of being alive is over, to wander to the far ends of the earth, perhaps to meet never again. Oh, infinite pathos and mystery of our being! Life, hast thou never a draught of joy to offer that is sparkling throughout? I am ashamed I did not write to my mother instead of writing to you; and yet, no, because to-morrow is Friday, and I would not write my first letter to you on that day for the world, it would be a bad omen. Why do you smile so? I could prove to you that from the first dawn of history until now, omens have played a strange part in the life of man. Think how ominous of their future career it was that all the Ten Commandments were broken even before they were given to mankind! I spare you the rest. This in itself is an army set in array.

'Tell me if that poor splitter, who was so badly hurt, is better? Has he anyone to look after him? Did you stay long? Did you see a lyre bird standing on a little hillock showing off its tail-feathers like a peacock? Did you see someone peeping from behind a window-blind after you at daybreak yesterday morning when you rode away? And now not another word. I am going to get you that keepsake I promised you on the veranda of Peeloo station. Always your friend—likewise your sweet St. Charity, and,

> 'THE INNERMOST-LITTLE-LEAFLET-OF-
> YOUR-HEART.'

When Stella finished, she rose and unfastened the coils of her hair, which fell below her waist like a mantle of dead-leaf gold. She cut a thick full-length lock, soft and silky, with a ripple in it as if it had fallen out of curl. She folded it up in silver tissue-paper, which had been wrapped round a small vial of attar of roses. Then she enclosed it in the closely-written sheets, sealed and addressed the letter, and put it on the hall-table in the receptacle for letters to be posted at ten.

CHAPTER XXXVIII

A LITTLE afterwards, Laurette came out into the hall with some notes, saw this letter, and regarded it as the answer to all her conjectures. She took it up and looked at it with a strange expression on her face. It was bulky, with double postage on it, and that Eastern fragrance clung to it of a thousand rose-leaves crushed into a pinpoint of liquid, which had been dear to Stella from childhood. Laurette remembered as a girl seeing some of the hermetically-sealed little vials full of this essence, which some connection of the Courtlands sent to the girls from Persia, where he was in the diplomatic service of his country. Laurette could hardly have explained why the reminiscence heightened that half-vindictive spite never very distant from the feeling with which she regarded Stella. It was merely one of the insignificant little events that is part of the life of a family whose cadets have for generations pushed their way into every quarter of the globe in the civil and military service of Britain. But such circumstances had, to Laurette's sharp envious mind, marked the gulf which, in the old country, had separated her own people from those to whom the Courtlands belonged, though in Australia the position was in some degree reversed. She held the letter a moment in her hand, then put it back with the rest.

If any object could be gained by destroying or opening it, she would not have hesitated to take either course. There would have been no balancing of sentiments—no struggle between good and evil—but simply a swift calculation as to the chances of detection, and if that could be evaded, prompt action, as it would serve her interests. When men or women have passed many years in an atmosphere of small habitual duplicities, shifty meannesses, and unscrupulous self-seeking, all the time tempered by a cunning caution, the nature becomes ingrained with a moral imbecility that seems absolutely proof against any stirring of conscience.

Laurette returned to the drawing-room, and shortly afterwards her husband came home. His appearance at that early hour was a little shock to her. Nor was it misplaced. He at once broached the subject which led to his phenomenal movements.

'That Riverina fellow has seen me to-night again. He is willing to give an advance of two hundred pounds for this place, on the rent we pay. I have told him he may most likely have it at the end of this month.'

'Well, that was kind of you,' said Laurette, trying to laugh; but it was an unsuccessful attempt, and her face had blanched. To this Tareling made no reply.

'I am going to sleep at the club to-night, and make an early start to Beechfield to-morrow about some land there. I thought I'd better tell you as early as possible about giving up this place.'

'And going to Cannawijera with the children and the maids?'

'Precisely; unless your father wishes to have you at Godolphin House. What the devil made them give the place such a name as that? It seems like a bad joke.'

'Most things do in the Colonies, don't they?'

'Ah! I don't know that we need go into these details. You understand about the house? I have not given an absolute promise.'

'No; and you must not!' said Laurette, suddenly rising with quivering lips. 'If you suppose that I am going to bury myself in the heart of the Mallee Scrub——'

Tareling shrugged his shoulders with such an imperturbable air that Laurette at once checked herself.

'You have a good deal of temperament at times,' he said smoothly, after a little pause; 'but if you think over it you will see that here it is really worse than useless. I must have six or seven hundred pounds early in October, and two hundred pounds clear is more than I can afford to lose. Besides, you are only getting into debt every week.'

'And you? what will you do?'

'Oh, I shall manage, thanks,' answered Tareling, examining his watch-chain critically.

'Yes; you will manage to get into debt.'

'Probably; but there will be compensations.'

'And then my father will have to pay another thou——'

'You are developing a remarkable turn for figures, and I notice you do not mix up amounts like some women. I wish you had been as accurate when we first met, and you dropped those artless hints about being heiress to the tune of five or six thousand a year.'

'Oh, good heavens! if I had only known; if I could have foreseen!'

'Ah, exactly. If we could both have foreseen; but as that was a gift

denied to us, we married. But if you will excuse me——' Tareling
stood up, taking his watch out.

'Well, Talbot, I'll excuse you if you excuse me,' said Laurette, with
a sudden change of tone and manner. 'I should have told you before
that Ted is going to give me another fifteen hundred pounds at the
end of this month—only I must not leave Melbourne at the latest
till the season is quite over.'

'Why didn't you tell me this before—when I first spoke of
re-letting the house?'

'Well, you see, I thought I would keep all this second cheque for
current expenses and the most pressing bills—as you had nearly half
of the first lot; but you can have what you need early in October.'

'Oh, well, I suppose I had better tell this fellow circumstances have
turned up that prevent our letting the Lodge.'

And with a nod the Honourable Talbot Tareling left the domestic hearth.

For some time after he was gone Laurette sat sunk in reflections.
Early in October. Yes, that was about the time that the company to
which Mademoiselle de Melier belonged was to leave for San Francisco. Laurette had known for some time that her husband contem-
plated a change of scene. People who had known him intimately
before his marriage were amazed that he had remained in the
Colonies so long. Countries in which work is the paramount social
factor are always more or less crude in their resources of amusement.
And then the Ritchie family was cutting up so confoundedly rough
about money matters. Laurette had long recognised that there was
nothing in her husband's nature to which any appeal could successfully be made that clashed with his own ideas of enjoyment. His
intrigue with this wretched little singing actress affected Mrs Tareling little, if at all, from an ethical point of view. As she had once said
in a burst of confidence to an old school friend: 'When a girl marries
into the British nobility she must give up bourgeoise notions of
morality.' Neither could she be deeply wounded through the affections. But there is always a vulnerable spot—and that with Laurette
was her social success. If Talbot worked out his present plans,
Laurette's prospects centred not only in social extinction in the
Mallee Scrub, but something also of social disgrace. Laurette rose
up almost gasping at the prospect.

She did not in the least expect the second munificent cheque from

Ted, knowing too well the tissue of deceit by which she had secured the first. But then, this Riverina family was choked off, and every week made it less likely that anyone else would make as good an offer for Monico Lodge—and she gained time. To leave Melbourne at this juncture would be to give up all. She regretted not having opened Stella's letter. Was it not possible she was dallying with a new admirer—yet unable to commit the extravagant folly of resigning a man with fifteen thousand a year for love of one who had not half as many hundreds? She had written to Julia urging her to find out by all means in her power what this sudden departure of Langdale's portended. She must somehow find out the truth of affairs before telegraphing for Ted, as she had promised to do on Stella's arrival. In fact, it might be necessary to prevent their meeting at all under her roof. She reflected that if one is called to account for conflicting statements it is always easier to explain by letter. 'My anxiety for your success, dear Ted, may have led me to exaggerate in your favour,' etc. As for Stella, she would be too happy and self-absorbed to care about such trifles. 'But "there's many a slip 'twixt the cup and the lip,"'* thought Laurette vindictively.

Next morning's first post brought letters to Stella from Lulla-boolagana, and one in a hand strange to Laurette, bearing the Minjah-Millowie post-mark. But there was not much room left to her for speculation as to the writer. The moment Stella saw this letter her face was suffused with happy blushes, and she presently made some excuse to escape with it to her own room—actually leaving the rest behind. Laurette herself had a note from Julia. 'I have fished it out of Nell,' she wrote, 'that Louise *knows* Dr L. has not yet been accepted, but hopes to be on his return. He is to be back in three or four months. What can be taking him away? Perhaps you will see him in a day or two. Mrs Morrison told me yesterday that a Dr Grey, a friend of her husband's, has come out by the last P. and O. steamer, and is most likely coming to practise here in partnership with Morrison.'

On Monday Stella went to stay for a day and a half with the Carters. An hour after she had driven away with her brother a servant brought a card to Laurette. It was Dr Langdale's, and he was waiting to see her. Was he going by the French steamer which sailed in the afternoon? Could she prevent him from seeing Stella, or would this do any good? He would have had her letter on Friday night, while his must have been written on Thursday. A hundred thoughts flew through Laurette's mind, but she felt the impossibility of seeing her way far ahead before she knew what Langdale's plans were. Only she decided if he were really leaving by the *Salagie* she would say Stella had gone—where? Some place not to be reached in a few hours. But lovers were such awful fools—they would attempt the most imbecile feats. Well, to avoid all rash venturing she would state Stella was on her way to Mount Macedon by an uncertain route.

Who that saw this pretty, fair woman in her fresh blue morning dress greeting her visitor with an amiable smile could have dreamt what her resolves had been a moment before? Langdale apologized for his early call. He had arrived by the morning train, and was to sail by the *Salagie* that afternoon, and being anxious to see Miss Courtland before leaving——

'Oh, had she any idea you were coming?' broke in Laurette.

'No,' Dr Langdale answered, smiling; 'he himself had not known till six hours before he left Minjah–Millowie.'

'Oh, a thousand pities,' said Laurette, in a sympathetic voice. 'Miss Courtland is now on her way to Mount Macedon. I cannot even say by what route, or whether she will reach her destination this evening. She may stay with friends on the way. Your woods seem to have spoiled Stella for town life.'

This was said with an arch smile, and Laurette was quick to note the awakened look, the swift flash, with which Langdale heard this.

'Miss Courtland is well, I hope,' he said a little anxiously.

'Oh yes, radiantly well; but more addicted to silence than formerly,' returned Laurette meaningly. She thought if she were sufficiently cordial and encouraging, if she comported herself as if she were quite behind the scenes, she might glean a little more intelligence. At any rate, such a manner would be likely to inspire confidence. And nothing was more valuable than confidence when you were bent on thwarting the confidee's little plans. 'But, after all, perhaps you need not go to–day?' added Laurette.

'I must,' he answered—and he went on to say that his passage had been booked in the *Salagie* by telegram, that she sailed at seven in the evening. And then he asked leave to call later with a letter for Miss Courtland.

'Well,' thought Laurette, as the door closed behind him, 'this looks like the finger of Providence.' She seemed to hold possibilities in her grasp that would be valuable, and yet Stella was so unmalleable in some respects, and Laurette divined, even from her brief interview with Langdale, that one who knew him, much less one who loved him, would not be easily duped into doubting the man. But Laurette was content to take short views. He was going to the other end of the world, and to entrust a letter to her care. Yes, people often wrote on the way, but on a French boat one could not write earlier than from Mauritius—five or six weeks ahead at the least; while what Laurette was scheming for was to get that other fifteen hundred pounds at the end of September on the plea of serving Ted's cause so well.

She did not stir out of the house till Langdale came and left the letter. She took it at once to her own room and locked the door. She opened the letter carefully, and it yielded under her supple fingers without a tear. Of course, if nothing could be gained by destroying it, she would close it up again and deliver it. But a glance served to show her that it placed undreamt-of opportunities in her hand, if only she could devise means of putting them to use. There was a long letter with a separate enclosure. It was this that first caught her eye, and brought the blood into her face, while her heart beat tumultuously. Then she read the letter:

'SWEET ST CHARITY,

'Your first letter reached me an hour ago. Will you ever know the extreme joy it gave me? And the great lovely lock of hair it contained! I drew it to its full length, and laid it against my cheek. But Blättchen knows the fatuity of pens in speaking of things so far beyond their reach. How shabby my letter was compared to yours! But, if I do not take care, I shall not remember to answer one of your questions.

'As I rode away, in the dawn, from Peeloo, I looked back and thought I saw a face I knew at one of the windows. It came with me all the way, and showed me the profound loveliness of the early morning light falling upon the still woods. The splitter is better. I stayed with him two hours, and he told me a little story that would have delighted St Charity's heart. I may, perhaps, tell it to her when I see her in Melbourne; and there is something else I must tell her also—the full reason for my visit to England. Yes, darling, it may pain you, but your letter makes me feel that it is unworthy of us both to hold it back. But this is my first reply to a letter of Liebe's, and therefore there must be nothing in it to pain her. And I may be with her for a little in a day or two. How I long to set out, so that I may hasten back! My first reply to you, dearest. What have I to say? Oh, I have a great and solemn secret to whisper in your ear. Don't let Dustiefoot hear it; and be sure you do not tell it to the pert Fairacre birds, who do nothing but chatter from morning to night. The secret is this. Oh, little-leaf-of-my-heart, I love you—I love you—I love you! Did I ever tell you before what a darling you are, and how entirely I worship you? But that I could not tell you adequately—no one could! Oh, my own, do you know what your love means to me— how it has gladdened my life as I never expected it to be gladdened? I told you once that I had suffered; but some sorrows have power to make strong and build up, while others seem to eat up what should go to the woof of calm daily happiness. That was the sort of sorrow I have had; yet I felt and acknowledged that I myself was to blame, as most of us are in the misfortunes that fall on us apart from bereavement. But the darkness is over. Already I see the gold of dawn which is to broaden into the perfect day of our happiness.

'Darling, does it not seem in some ways as if we could not be really separated any more? Now and henceforth you are part of my inmost life. Each sight and sound of Nature is more vivid—more beautiful since I knew you. Here are some lines that I keep crooning very often when I am alone:

> ' "She gave me eyes, she gave me ears,
> And humble cares and delicate fears,
> A heart the fountain of sweet tears,
> And love and thought and joy."*

'Yes, love and thought and joy. How grateful I am that the unspeakable gift of your love was given to me before time and bitter memories robbed me of the capacity of joy! It does happen in life that people are sometimes so crushed and made desolate that, when the possibility of happiness is restored to them, it comes too late. It is not only that Joy is so prone to put his hand to his lips bidding adieu, but that often, when he approaches, his sovereignty is over. If necessary, we can endure our lives and do our work in the world without the possession of vivid personal joy. But, ah! when it comes, and our hearts are still fresh and young enough to bound at its approach, what is there that we would barter for its possession?

'Belovedest, did I not see tears glisten in your sweet eyes when we parted? Do not allow too many sad thoughts to nestle in your heart when I am not near to chase them afar. There is but a step between being dejected for individual reasons and harbouring melancholy forebodings relative to wider issues. It is good to remember that the problems of life do not crowd pell-mell into our daily path in the way that they do into our minds, and that in the end we have not to solve inextricable riddles in order to do our best in the world. There is one maxim you quoted out of "Wilhelm Meister" I would have you, Liebe, keep in mind all the time I am away—"Remember to live."* Do not let spectres come between you and the sunshine you love so well. By this I do not mean try to drive solemn thoughts from you. Ever-belovedest, I love to think of you too well as you are—to recall how in the most mirth-provoking mood a sudden seriousness would often fall upon your face. No, I would not have Liebe different from her dear self by the twentieth part of the petal of a milk-white fairy rose. Her quick moods and rippling fancies are all too precious to me. All I plead for is that she should drive sombre dreams to the far ends of the earth; that she should let no reflection of the shadow that has burdened part of my life throw any darkness on hers. Keep all your buoyant fancies, darling, and your tender sparkling gaiety, for my sake.

'I have often felt that the exacting routine of labour to which men must school themselves, brings in its train something wooden and inflexible, even when their work makes constant demands on their sympathies. I suppose it is because of this that a woman's more inward and leisured habit of thought exercises so deep a fascination. She has time to keep all these things and ponder them in her heart,* so that she comes to have a kind of second sight, a sensitive delicacy of perception, which, with most men, is either undeveloped or swallowed in the grind of daily life. A woman sees a thousand things that from their duller, or, let us say, more preoccupied eyes, are almost wholly obscured. To achieve anything in the world, a man has to learn to be hard on himself, and that often produces a certain hardness in other respects. It would seem that to work long and constantly, even though the work is what interests us most, begets a certain strain of insensibility. Thus I often smile when I think that though I could draw separately, and in skeleton form, all the bones of a swallow's wing, I learned the full poetry of its flight through your bright eyes. But what is the use of my talking, or rather writing, in this way, when Liebe persists in making the most adorably comic little faces at me, and making up a wicked little story about what happened to someone who had an evil habit of writing in a didactic, reasonable strain? After all, your chrysanthemums will not be out before I return. But there will be roses, and mind you wear great clusters of them on the day the *Pâquerette* steams into Glenelg. Dear day, filled with soft-footed hours! Is that one of Liebe's phrases, and will she inflict penalties on me for using it without leave? So she may; only I must draw up a list of the penalties.'

Here followed a page or two of the ardent nothings that come so readily to a lover's pen. Then there was a break, and the rest was dated that day, 'Scott's Hotel, Melbourne,' deeply regretting Stella's absence from town, explaining how the prompt acceptance by a friend of Morrison's of a medical partnership at Minjah-Millowie had occurred in time to permit Langdale taking his passage by the outgoing French boat, which enabled him to set out at once, and he was incredibly anxious to get away, so that he might be back in February.

'And now,' he wrote, 'I am going to tell you, Stella, what that business is, because ever since I got your precious letter I felt it was impossible I should conceal it from you; my only reason for doing so was that your keenly sensitive, apprehensive nature might dwell on the bare possibility that there may still be a barrier to our marriage; but with the exquisite trust and love you have shown, no consideration has force enough to make me keep this back from you, only it must not be included in this, my reply to Liebe's first letter. Are you satisfied that I am not so calmly reasonable after all, and that I may even be infected with a little superstition? No, not superstition, but "delicate fears." I shall not say farewell, but merely what we said that night after our most memorable ride—"Auf baldige Wiedersehen."'*

After reading this, with beating temples, Laurette turned once more to the enclosure. There were four thin sheets of foreign paper, the last being but half written. As Langdale wrote a firm, rather heavy hand, he had written on one side only. It was a trifling circumstance, and yet it was of material service to Laurette in carrying out the plan that eventually took shape in her unscrupulous little brain.

'At the age of twenty-two, while still a medical student in London, just a year after my father's death, I met a lady a good many years older than myself, who fascinated me greatly. She was an Italian, and very beautiful. Still, infatuated as I was, I shrank from the idea of marrying her. But, under circumstances which I need not now detail, I married her four months after we first met. The marriage turned out a disastrous failure. After three years we agreed to live apart. A year later I knew that she had proved unfaithful to me. I had sufficient evidence to secure a divorce, but partly because I shrank from the exposure—only a few of my most intimate friends knew of the union—partly because she had fallen into very bad health, and besought me to spare her, as she had not long to live, I desisted. She gave my lawyer a written acknowledgment of her guilt, duly attested, resigned my name, and left England for Brussels, where some of her friends lived. On these conditions I settled an income on her, which she named as being adequate, and was to be paid by my lawyer half-yearly.

'The letter I opened in the Home Field that day was from my lawyer. He wrote to say that the last receipt he had received for this half-yearly payment was evidently a forgery, that he had caused inquiries to be made through a trusted agent, and found that the lady to whom the money was payable had died, but that the fact was concealed by a relative who endeavoured to make capital out of the imposition. He found that the lady who died was buried under the name of the one with whom she lived, and an application was for a second time made for the annuity, with a statement that the difference of writing was caused by illness. But a request that an interview should be granted to one who knew both ladies was denied. No doubt could exist in my lawyer's mind, nor in my own, as to the facts of the matter. But you will understand, Stella, that it is one of the points on which one is satisfied with nothing less than legal indisputable proof. It was my intention to possess this before doing more than asking leave to write to you. I cannot but be glad that the course of events led to my departing from this resolution. The assurance of your love is too precious. But you have been so loyally trustful, you have shown such entire confidence in me, it seems to me now I should have frankly told you the position. But I shrank horribly from marring the first glow of our happiness with this sordid story. And then there are some misfortunes in life that men are more sensitive about than many forms of evil-doing. And yet, my own, now that I have won the treasure of your love, I feel more than ever thankful that in this early, ill-judged, ill-fated bond I was the betrayed, and not the betrayer. It hurts me horribly that the bloom of your gladness must be touched with the thought of a life which closed so darkly stained. And yet, Stella, it is best you should know all now— that our happy reunion on my return should not be spoilt by going back to this. It will then be the past for both of us. From the moment I resolved to tell you I felt a relief, for the conviction haunted me that I should not have yielded to your generous wish in the matter, saying that I had been surprised out of my secret. Do not be too sorry, Herzblättchen. Think chiefly of what carries so much joy for both. Think of the day on which the *Pâquerette* will gaily sail into port.'

After this came some lines that had been blotted out, but so quickly dried that the words were readable:

'Will you forgive me if I say that one of the memories which gives me the most unalloyed happiness is your timorous confession that you felt you could have moved or spoken after your accident when I reached you, only you wished to known how it would really "affect me"?

'Yours, Stella, with the profoundest respect and love,

'ANSELM LANGDALE.'

Laurette's head throbbed with swiftly succeeding and conflicting thoughts as she reached the close. It was apparent at once that the first letter must be kept back, if only on account of its allusion to Stella's imagined absence from Melbourne. And the other, the enclosure, which, taken by itself, would begin with such strange abruptness?

'Chance—chance,' says Ste Beuve in one of his critical essays, 'if we wish to be truthful, we shall never allow enough room for you, nor shall we ever make deep enough incisions in any philosophy of history.'* Probably Laurette herself could hardly say how far the form of this statement, the way in which it was written on one side only of the paper, and the suggestive air of the effaced lines, helped her to work the scheme which she put into execution with unshrinking completeness.

She sat for an hour or two reading and re-reading the words, regarding the statement from all sides with concentrated intentness. Her eyes glittered strangely, and a brilliant flush reinforced the *soupçon* of rouge which lent point to her complexion. It was characteristic that though, on first reading Langdale's little narrative, no doubt entered her mind as to the death of the unfortunate woman whose life had made his run with so dark a current for some years, yet the moment she decided on her plan of campaign, she convinced herself that the news was illusory.

'People never die when it adds to their friends' happiness,' she said to herself, with the decision of one who argues from the knowledge of experience. 'Well, Stella won't run such a fearful risk if I can help it.'

She destroyed the letter there and then, setting fire to it in the grate, and watching it till the last scrap was reduced to a thin black cinder. Her next step was to ring for Sarah, the parlour-maid who had admitted Dr Langdale and brought her his card.

'Sarah, I want you to get ready to go to Wandalong, Mrs Morton's place, you know, by the early train to-morrow. She needs a little extra help, and I must spare you for a few weeks at any cost. Your wages will be fifteen shillings a week as long as you are there.' Then she sent a telegram to her sister:

'Feel sure you need more help. Sarah goes to you to-morrow for a month.'

'I must run no risk of servants' tattle,' she thought, with forced calm. Then she sat down and wrote two notes—both brief. The first was addressed to a Mrs Anson, and ran:

'DEAR ROSE,

'What an age it is since we met! Can you imagine that your grief and undeserved misfortune have changed your friends? As it seems useless to expect you to come to me, unless some pressure is brought to bear, I shall send the carriage for you at ten to-morrow morning, and you must spend the day with me. I shall take care we have no visitors and no interruptions. You see I am determined to take no excuse.'

The next note ran:

'DEAR STELLA,

'As I know the Carters are dying to have you a little longer, I write to say that I shall not grudge your remaining till we call for you to-morrow evening on our way to the theatre. Just demi-toilette and a few flowers. They say the comedy company is in splendid form.'

After that Laurette set about her task of manipulating the enclosure.

Sarah left by the early train, and at half-past ten Mrs Anson came. She was the wife of a man who had been high up in the Civil Service, but who had, six months previously, been convicted of defalcating the public funds, and sentenced to six years' imprisonment. Mrs Anson was a gentle, sensitive woman, who since her misfortune shrank into retirement as much as possible, yet felt a melancholy pleasure in being so warmly remembered by an old friend. Laurette, on her part, was all chastened sympathy and delicate attention, kissing her sweet Rose on each cheek, and holding her hands in a gentle, detaining clasp.

'You have hurt your hand, dear?' said Mrs Anson in a tone of concern, noticing that the forefinger of Laurette's right hand was tied up.

'Oh, a mere bagatelle—a little cut with the bread-knife. I gave my nursery governess a holiday yesterday, and saw to the little one's dinner myself.'

'You are always doing someone a kindness,' murmured Mrs Anson, suddenly struck with the thought that hitherto she had hardly given Laurette credit for all her good qualities.

'Well, my dear, it would be a poor world if we did not help each other with little deeds of kindness,' replied Laurette, not only without a blush, but with a little glow of virtuous self-complacency. Then she sat and chatted about all the people her friend had known intimately in days not long gone by. Some who had married, and some who expected to marry, but did not, and all equally repentant. No little tale of social disaster lost its piquancy on Laurette's lips. Indeed, at her best, she had a gift for heightening effects, and shading, which many an artist in journalism might envy. The hours passed very agreeably. There were callers, but Laurette was denied to them. She had promised herself a treat for the day, and she was not going to be cheated out of it. There was so much insincerity and hollowness in the world. 'As I grow older, I sometimes long to turn my back on it all,' she said, with a gentle little sigh. Poor Mrs Anson, though far from being a bitter or envious woman, yet could not wholly escape a slight tinge of the gratification sometimes experienced by the unfortunate when the reflection is forced on them that the disparities of life are, after all, not so great as they appear on the surface.

As they sat over afternoon tea, several letters were brought in to Laurette. One of them seemed to distress her.

'Oh, how very thoughtless of me not to have written that note as I promised!' she cried, with a little gesture of despair. 'Rose, dear, will you excuse me while I pen a note that I should have sent away last night? Thanks, so much.'

She opened a little morocco writing-case that was on a small table near her. Presently she uttered a sharp ejaculation of pain.

'Who would have thought that such a slight cut would be so painful?' she cried.

'But the cut appears to be on the front of the finger,' said Mrs Anson. 'You see the moment you attempt to write the pen presses against the wound.'

'Oh, how very provoking!' cried Laurette, knitting her brows prettily.

'Is it anything I can do for you, Laurette? Pray let me, if it is!'

'Oh, thank you, dear,' said Laurette, her face brightening. 'It is only an old friend like you I could have as an amanuensis in the matter. It is something to be enclosed in a friend's letter in corroboration. A matrimonial quarrel—only more serious than the average run. A wretched affair—jealousy, estrangement, broken hearts. I must not burden you with a knowledge of names; secrets are so often a nuisance. One is so afraid of betraying them, and of course, if it comes to being questioned downright, one tries to tell a fib and fails. I shall be able to put the beginning and sign my name.'

Mrs Anson was more and more convinced that Laurette was one of those people who must be well known before they get credit for all the minor deeds of charity, and little merciful acts of an unstrained quality, they scatter on their way through life. She sat down and wrote, to Laurette's dictation, in her elegant, careful handwriting, with a sincere wish that what she wrote would effect its kindly purpose.

After her visitor was gone, Laurette looked over the shipping news in the *Age*, and found that the *Salagie* had not left Williamstown till eleven o'clock on the previous night. Dr Langdale's name was safe in the passenger list; but what if the delay had led to a chance encounter between himself and Stella? If she and Dora had gone shopping in Collins Street, as not infrequently happens with young ladies, late in the afternoon! Laurette put the conjecture from her. She was somehow upheld by the thought that her efforts at putting crooked things straight would not be so ruthlessly crushed by an overruling Providence. Laurette thoroughly believed that this power was always on the side of the strongest battalions,* and as matched against Stella, Laurette felt that at this juncture she was as one armed and lying in ambush to trap an unsuspecting foe. As some of the lowest organisms in which nerves cannot exist are yet somehow sensitive to light, so even the least noble natures, when contriving a great baseness against a fellow-creature, are often dimly conscious of remorse. But few have ever practised treacherous artifices with less compunction than visited Laurette at this crisis.

She had never known anything of those delicate instincts of morality which are motive powers in many minds that have received far less moral culture. She had many impulses of generosity and kindness, but they were rudimentary florets that never blossomed into habit. Of principles she knew nothing beyond a determination to make the best of her opportunities—to get all she could out of life. She would never transgress the rules of outward decorum, nor know anything of the better aspirations of human nature. She was now threatened with social extinction, and her insatiable thirst for pleasure and ease, and the footing she had gained in society, urged her to make a desperate struggle, using such means as lay within her grasp, as little checked by any feeble glimmering of conscience as a street urchin when he sucks an orange and throws the rind away.

And yet, with all this, she had an inimitable trick of assigning, even to herself, virtuous motives to the shadiest of her shady little intrigues. 'It is not only Stella who must be protected from an entanglement with a married man,' she reflected, 'but then there is Ted, and there is Talbot, whose movements I must watch. A husband and father must not be left to the wiles of a wretched little actress at a crisis. I shall have that fifteen hundred pounds after all, for, if I know anything of Stella Courtland, the letter she is to get to-morrow morning will set fire to her pride in a way that will put things in a new light. And her jealousy—I had no idea she had so much of it till her brother got engaged—to find he hurried away without even seeing her—and to a living wife! It must succeed!' she said half aloud, as she went over the main features of the affair.

CHAPTER XXXIX

'THEN you did not care very much for the play last night, Miss Stella?' said Mr Tareling at breakfast on the following morning. 'Tell me what you objected to most.'

'I had no choice of dislike,' answered Stella. 'I thought the whole of it was overgrown with the scurf of commonness—the sort of thing that gets acted because of the permanent stupidity of our kind.'

'Goodness! I feel quite annoyed that I enjoyed it so much,' said Laurette, with mock humility.

'I wouldn't if I were you,' answered her husband with a laugh. 'In a democratic country you are always right if you are on the side of the majority. But come now, Miss Stella, weren't you a little touched by the despair of the lovers? There was a big woman in a purple satin dress near me who mopped her eyes till her handkerchief dripped. You *must* have found their despair pathetic.'

'Despair!' echoed Stella. 'Why, a marionette wouldn't be imposed upon by such a paltry device! They were engaged in the first act. It would never do to let them be married in the second—in fact, the play would not come into being—and what would then become of the worthy fathers of families who are supported by the drama? So of course there must be a misunderstanding through six or seven scenes. Oh yes, it might melt a heart of stone, to see a middle-aged female, rouged up to the eyes, weeping bitterly without shedding any tears! Did you see how she held her handkerchief so as not to brush the powder off her nose?'

'I am sorry I didn't show you my big woman in the purple satin. She wept for herself and both the lovers,' said Tareling, looking very much amused.

'But I suppose you will admit that misunderstandings do come between people—and—why, even your Shakespeare makes a man smother his wife because of groundless jealousy,' said Laurette, who had taken up a morning paper and glanced over it.

'Yes, and with such a fiend incarnate as Iago to poison his mind he could not have been Othello without being driven into madness.'

Laurette was glancing over the paper, but there was something restless and nervous in her manner.

'Then what would you consider a sufficient reason for an estrangement in a modern play?'

'Oh, I cannot say! I imagine if people really love each other, nothing that another could say or do would estrange them, unless there is an Iago in the case, and such a man is much rarer than——'

'Than a grand passion?' put in Tareling. 'Ah, Miss Stella, it seems to me you have a very charming colour this morning.'

She turned on him, and parried the insinuation, with a laughing, radiant face.

'I don't think I can quite forgive you for not showing me the woman who wept so copiously when the despairing lovers could not even move a muscle. How the sight would have consoled me!'

Letters were brought in; several for Stella. Among them she discerned one addressed in a handwriting the sight of which made her heart throb stormily.

Laurette was trembling with excitement. She had opened a letter, but instead of reading it she looked over it furtively at Stella, whose face at that moment was irradiated as if a rosy flame shone through it—her lips slightly parted in a happy smile, her eyes lustrous as stars. The Honourable Talbot Tareling's home correspondence was chiefly of the kind that takes the disgustingly prosaic form of requesting payment—applications which, as a rule, rouse neither enthusiasm nor curiosity in the recipient's breast. Tareling turned over his with an air of profound indifference; then he glanced from his wife's face to Stella's with an expression of curious inquiry. Laurette caught the look, and coloured violently, instantly taking refuge in her open letter.

'It is evident that I shall have to spend part of the morning at my desk,' said Stella, rising and gathering up her letters.

'Please remember we are due at Mrs Joran's in the afternoon,' said Laurette.

'Who is he?' asked her husband, as the door closed after Stella.

Laurette pretended not to understand.

'Oh, aren't you behind the scenes, then? A young lady does not colour like Aurora* because a handful of letters come from the family circle. And such a dewy smile! Ye gods, what it must be to be a girl and in love! The girl has a lovely face!'

'Oh, probably there was a letter from Ted,' returned Laurette, trying to speak carelessly.

Tareling looked at her narrowly, and then gave a short laugh.

'Fancy a girl like Stella colouring up to the whites of her eyes, and smiling timidly, because she got one of Ritchie's croppy, jockey-like epistles! You are sometimes too funny, Laurette. What is your little game now?'

A sickening fear shot across Laurette's mind. She knew that, in the decorums of life in which she herself was founded as on a rock, her husband scarcely knew the draping of virtue's garment. But it was also equally clear to her that, if he knew a third part of her 'little game,' in this instance, he would overwhelm her with anger and scorn and unsparing exposure. It seemed to her as if Stella might appear at any moment, denouncing the palpable treachery that had been practised on her. But there was no tremor of fear in her voice as she answered:

'Ted is a dreadful cub, isn't he, except when he signs cheques that may be treated as blank ones?'

'It appears to me you are acquiring a habit of repeating yourself. Of course a man doesn't expect to be amused in a *tête-à-tête* with his wife. But—ah—don't you think you might hit on a variation?'

Laurette did not permit herself to attempt a reply. Indeed, to do her justice, it was only at periods of unusual strain or irritation that she so far tested how bitter and unalloyed are the dregs of a contract entered upon for life, without love or mutual respect, when the advantages which were the governing motive seem to be gradually becoming less.

When Stella entered her own room, she stood for a moment by the open window, that soft rapture still kindling her face with which a woman receives the first love-letters that are precious to her. She opened it, and after the first strange, unreal moments, sank in a chair, covering her eyes as if to shut out a sight too terrible to be looked upon. Again and again she forced herself to read over the words mechanically:

'At the age of twenty-two, while still a medical student in London, just a year after my father's death, I met a lady, a good many years older than myself, who fascinated me greatly. She was an Italian, and very beautiful. Still, infatuated as I was, shrank from the idea of marrying her. But, under circumstances which I need not now detail, I married her four months after we first met. The marriage turned out a disastrous failure.' Here there were several lines completely effaced, and then: 'On these conditions I settled an income on her, which she named as being adequate, and was to be paid through my lawyer half-yearly. The letter I opened in the Home Field that day was from my lawyer. He wrote to say that'—here three more lines were effaced—'the lady to whom the money was payable had died.' After this, two half-sheets had been bodily left out by Laurette; and the half-sheet which concluded bore only the signature, all the writing that preceded it having been obliterated, and yet not wholly. Looking closely, three lines at the close could be made out: 'Your timorous confession that you felt you could have moved or spoken after your accident when I reached you, only you wished to know how it would really "affect me"?' Then the concluding terms were obliterated also, but the name 'ANSELM LANGDALE' was clear and distinct.

Then there was a sheet of paper, which was evidently part of a letter.

'You are entirely in error in every particular regarding your wife. Return as quickly as possible, and all these miserable misunderstandings will be explained and set right. You need not hesitate nor imagine that you will be asked to believe this merely on bare assertion. *Proofs* are forthcoming. As to the rumour of death, it is as ill-founded as the first mistakes. But your long-continued absence has reduced my poor friend to such a state of despair that she is too indifferent to take even the slightest trouble. Pray—pray do not lose any time after getting this. Return to her, and all will yet be well.'

When a great blow suddenly falls on one, it can hardly be said that at first coherent thought is possible. The throbbing temples, the parched throat and flickering vision, the slow, dull, cold beating of the heart, make the physical anguish as pressing as the mental suffering. Then the creeping stupor that succeeds the swift exhaustion of all the faculties paralyzes coherent thought. It is as though all the powers of the mind and body were concentrated in sullenly keeping hold on life—dreary and hopeless as it has been made in a few wild incredible moments. Cold and trembling in every limb, Stella cowered by the window over these fragmentary sentences. Every feature that under other circumstances would have thrown discredit on these strange communications was even, at the first glance, a

strong link in a chain of crushing evidence. Here there was no
hearsay—no perhaps. It was a bald, commonplace little story. An
unhappy early marriage—a separation years ago. Then the news of
his wife's death. That was the letter he read out in the Home Field
that happy spring day—O God! how long, how long ago! She seemed
to see herself through the lapse of gray years out in the sunshine
with the birds singing all round, and her heart leaping with a sudden
passion of joy as Anselm asked leave in a broken voice to write to her
from the other side of the world. She went over all that followed—
moaning faintly now and again as her breath failed her. Already all
the rapture and bounding hope and insane gladness were part of an
unreal fable. She turned to his letter written the day after they parted.
She knew it by heart. She had read it the last thing at night, and had
wakened up with the first faint approach of day to read it again. Then
this letter had come to him. No wonder he wrote in a disjointed,
halting fashion, blotting out almost as much as remained legible—
beginning and closing abruptly. Where was he now? Oh, she must
see him. She opened a letter from Louise, and near the beginning of
the letter she read: 'You will, of course, have seen Dr Langdale before
he sailed on the 22nd'—that was two days back. Why had not the
letter reached her before? Ah, he had taken precautions. Would it not
have been kinder to see her when this torturing revelation was to be
made—or did he understand her too well? Did he know that she
would have thrown herself at his feet and implored him not to leave
her—not to believe this woman who urged his return? Merciful
Heaven! what frantic thoughts were these? Would she indeed have
been so lost to pride and maidenly reticence? She went and con-
fronted herself in the looking-glass. But the face she met there—the
eyes like those of a creature trapped and wounded to death—made
her turn away shuddering. He was gone. He had found it possible to
leave without one more look or word, though they were never to meet
again. There was something in this that wounded her beyond
endurance. And he had not made one allusion to her long letter.
Perhaps it was wiser. Wiser? Yes, wiser—she repeated the word as if
trying to understand it. She felt dimly that to her wisdom, prudence
or caution were but empty word-echoes in face of this overwhelming calamity. How could she have looked at him and borne the
thought—'It is for the last time'? Yes, he had been wise and reasonable. As for her, she could not have left him thus if ten thousand

obstacles had stood between them. Ah, yes, he understood the wild passion of which her nature was capable. Sometimes she walked up and down the room; at other times she stood staring out of the window, trying to recall what she had been thinking of. And so the hours wore on to noon. . . . Then there was a tap at her door, and Maisie came in asking something about a dress.

'Oh, Miss Stella!' she suddenly cried out in dismay, as she looked full in her mistress's face, waiting for an answer which did not come. 'There's ill news—there's ill news! Is it from Fairacre, dear Miss Stella?' cried the maid, overcome with terror at the white impassive face.

'No—no—it is only—a little faintness,' murmured Stella. It was all over, and the world swept on as usual, and she had somehow to face the lie that life still went on with her. Maisie bathed her face and hands, and stood fanning her by the open window. She was still half fearful that the news of some catastrophe had wrought this sudden change—but when she saw that her mistress shed no tears she was reassured. Maisie, fortunately, had no knowledge of those stabs which are so deadly that they bleed but little outwardly.

'You were to go out in the afternoon, Miss Stella—but I doubt you suldna,' said Maisie, who in moments of agitation returned on her mother's accent and phrases with curious fidelity.

'Oh yes—yes; don't speak so loud, Maisie,' and then Stella forced herself to open the Fairacre letters, and read bits of them to Maisie, who at once became certain as she listened that all was well. There were honeybirds in swarms in the Park-lands, especially the Botanic Park, all during the spring. The Torrens was determined, so Alice wrote, not to give up running and singing as it went till Stella returned. The roses were extraordinarily fine this season, especially Stella's favourite white fairy and Macartney roses——

The girl dropped the letter with a little miserable moan. Then she compelled herself to read on. Weighty changes were imminent in the old home. Felix Harrison had won so many distinctions of late, and his income showed so liberal a margin over former years, that he and Allie were to be married at Christmas. Then Tom was also an accepted lover, and there was not a single reason forthcoming why their wedding should be delayed. 'Can you fancy only you and mother in the old home?' wrote Allie. 'You would have to see all the visitors that came, instead of retreating to the library, you spoilt child! But no; Esther and the children will share the old home with you. It is time Clem went to college—and, after all, no one expects you to linger long in the paternal nest. Oh, you monkey, what secrets have you not kept from me!' She crushed the letter into the envelope—and there was the maid still waiting an answer.

'Thank you, Maisie. I must write some letters. The dress—the navy-blue velvet? Oh, any way you like.'

She was left alone—but she tried to read no more of her letters just then. She was stunned, insensible, though not unconscious. There is a kind of moral syncope which falls on the heart and brain after the first shock of a great calamity. A sort of lethargy crept over Stella, in which no thought, no feeling, was acutely present. She read the words over repeatedly, till she could have said them by heart. She could so well understand those erasures—that stern avoidance of all empty words of regret. And then the lines at the close, which had been so hurriedly blotted that the forms of the letters were still traceable, caught her attention: 'Your timorous confession that you felt you could have moved or spoken after your accident when I reached you, only you wished to know how it would "affect me"?' Her heart gave a strange leap, and the blood came back to her face in an overflowing wave.

As if the anguish and despair that held her did not fill the cup of her supreme agony to the brim, she saw in the words, coupled with the cold, bald statement that preceded them, a record of Langdale's consciousness that her love for him had caused the avowal of his when he had meant to keep silent. It had been his intention to sail for England without making a sign—merely asking leave to write to her from there. She had been quite happy in her confidence that he loved her, even before his avowal. Oh, what madness, when the mere thought that he cared at all for her, and kept silence, should have at once suggested some insuperable obstacle! She, who had ever been so ready to question, to doubt things that were beyond the scope of human knowledge, while here, in a simple every-day matter, in which silence was in itself suspicion ready forged, she had found no cause for inquiry, for a moment's uneasiness! He loved her; he did not wish to say so for a time—that had been quite enough. Oh, fool and blind that she had been!—ready to give her love before it was asked—ready to see no peril in anything so long as she knew that he held her dear.

He had loved this woman once, then, that he had made his wife?

His wife!—she shuddered and cowered down on her bed as if seeking to hide herself; and then she rose up and read over again and again the words written in a woman's hand—in fair, even, well-formed characters, on the face of them the writing of a lady: 'All will yet be well!' Was this possible? Would he, perhaps, learn that he had been in error—that the wretchedness of the marriage had been caused by misunderstandings on which light would be now thrown? Would he be thankful that the rumour of her death was untrue? Would he, perhaps, learn to love her? Oh, God in heaven forbid!

The next moment she was thrilled with horror at the prayer—the imprecation, rather. But no quick involuntary horror, no reasoning, could hide the truth which forced itself on her—that the thought that he should love this woman was even more torturing than the knowledge that she was his wife. Should not this in itself serve to loosen the dominion of this love—this passion that had insidiously rooted itself in every fibre of her nature?

She satisfied herself that he had really sailed. Every hour that passed widened the distance between them—brought him nearer to her who might win his love. The thought worked like poison in her veins. She threw her unread letters aside, she put away out of sight these miserable fragmentary ones that had brought her the tidings which seemed more to wreck her soul than her life—even the envelope, with its firm, clear writing, her name written in full, as if he had lingered over it in the old lover-like way, hurt her intolerably. And his ring which she wore next her heart like a charm, with its noble motto, now the bitterest irony. All that was best and highest to her seemed touched with this mildew of mockery. Yet she would keep this to the day of her death. When the world was mercifully shrouded in oblivion, this golden amulet would lie against her heart, while all its stormy throbbings were overpast. But oh, merciful Heaven, what a long and weary eternity lay between! She had come to one of those epochs that arise in the lives of women who have souls, when nothing is left but death and the love of God—both seemed equally remote.

Dustiefoot, who had patiently waited for his mistress, finding that she did not come as usual to caress and talk to him, jumped lightly through the open window. When she spoke to him he instantly noticed the change in her voice, and looked at her with that keen, almost human intelligence in his eyes which Langdale had once compared to those of a dog painted by Piero di Cosimo in his picture of the death of Procris.* Ah! those endless memories! Each thought, and emotion, and association, all were steeped in the dye of those days which seemed to hem her in on every side.

Laurette waited in almost trembling impatience for Stella's appearance. She did not leave her room at luncheon-time; she had letters to write, and could not eat. Maisie brought her some tea, and biscuits for Dustiefoot, who lay at his mistress's feet, looking up in her face from time to time with watchful solicitude.

Laurette longed to go into her room—to know in what way the letter that had been so subtly changed had wrought. 'If she takes it fighting,' thought Laurette, 'I shall send for Ted this very afternoon.'

Four o'clock was the hour at which they were to leave for Mrs Joran's. A few minutes before that time Stella joined her hostess in the drawing-room, faultlessly dressed, a damask flush on her cheeks. Her eyes glistened like those of a creature that has been dangerously wounded, and there was a livid aureole round them; but beyond this, and a curiously toneless timbre of voice, there was no outward sign of the fierce storm which had swept over her.

If she could have been thankful for anything at that time, it would have been that no one knew, as she believed, of the disaster which had overtaken her. A weight seemed to press on her head, and voices that were near sounded at times as if they came from a great distance. Her lips were hot and parched; occasionally a shuddering sigh, that threatened to become a low moan, roused her to greater vigilance. She had not shed a tear, but at times a film came over her eyes as if a mist fell on all around. The strain of bearing such torture, without the relief of solitude or rest, or any touch of gentle resignation as to an inevitable grief, was cruel in the extreme. But it seemed to induce an apathy and a deadly fatigue, so that sleep came to her almost at once when, late that night, she went to bed. She slept for two or three hours, and then she woke up sobbing uncontrollably, with tearless eyes. She rose up and lit her lamp, trembling in every limb. There was an unbearable burning weight on her head. She opened her desk, hardly knowing why. She searched for those fragmentary letters, and sat down, going over every word afresh. The thought had suddenly lodged in her mind that she was the victim of some strange delusion. But as she read, all the thoughts and events of the past day came crowding back. The contrast between the overflowing happiness of the woman who had opened this miserable letter, and the stony misery which had fallen on her, fortunately touched the source of tears. 'Oh, my lost love! my lost love!' she moaned, and the tears rained down and blistered the paper through and through. The light of day surprised her still crouching over that strangely-pathetic record of the days that had been illuminated with a light now quenched in the darkness of despair. She knew that the new-born loveliness of the day flooded the sky with its accustomed tenderness and splendour, but she shrank from the sight as though it had the poison of asps in it for eyes outworn with weeping.

Turn where she would, she saw no gleam of consolation. And in these first hours of intolerable suffering, pain and anguish were more hateful to her than they had ever been before. She was scorched under the agony that had fallen on her, as a flower exposed in its opening freshness is shrivelled by a furious hot wind. All those tendrils of hope, of dawning love to God—those moments of exalted consciousness in which she seemed to draw closer to the vivid faith that had once kindled her heart—were put to flight, withered, and entirely slain. It was as though the air around her, which had before been fanned by the dove-wings of ethereal hours, was suddenly darkened by the sweep of vulture wings. Even that last resource of an unhappy love—the remembrance of happier days—was impossible to her. She knew that for her these days had been the flowering point of her life; but as for him, was it more than a brief episode—one soon to be forgotten, perhaps, in a happy and unlooked-for reconciliation with *his wife*? The words had in them something that crushed all the finer tissues of thought and sensation. She lay hiding her face from the light, quivering at times from head to foot. She was thankful to feel that apathy creeping over her that comes to the overstrained mind like the insensibility of muscles which have been severely bruised or scalded.

She rose at the usual hour, and Maisie was again startled at the sight of her mistress's face. It was one in which expression played so large a part that the absence of vivacity and light, of a quickly mantling colour, as well as the dark rings round the heavily-lashed eyes, made a startling change.

'Indeed, Miss Stella, I doubt but we should get away home sooner than you spoke of. This place doesna agree with you. The room is too small, and ye miss the woods, and the birds, and your rides. Wouldn't you be glad, ma'am, to leave for Fairacre soon?'

Stella, at the words, swiftly realized what a terror the thought of returning to her peaceful home had for her. Those calm existences—her mother and sister, who had lived their lives, who had passed their keenest joys and sorrows; the children whose lives were to come, whose life was made up of sunshine, and flowers, and gentle schooling, and all the healthful, untroubled influences that for the more fortunate bridge the isthmus from infancy to maturity—how could she take up the ravelled threads amongst them? Nature and books, and the sweet serenity of home, all had become equally impossible. All the force of her strong, complex organization rose in revolt against the perspective of a faded, insipid existence which the prospect called up. How could she endure that faint replica of life with those agonizing memories in the background? Birds, and flowers, and trees, and running water, the dawn of day, and the music of childish voices—they had not only lost their enchantment: their very memories were barbed with fiery darts—part of a past which had worn a faint simulacrum of happiness before the keen flame of love had breathed on her and transformed her being. What were they all now to her—the persons and scenes and events that had made up existence? Links in an inexorable chain that bound her, like a galley-slave, to her ineffectual, inept post in the world, when life itself had really passed from her grasp! Oh no; she had not lost all affection for those dear, but they could do without her, and she could do without them for a time. She must throw the past from her like a stained chalice emptied of all the wine of life. She must be somewhere in the stir and tumult of the world, where things would hold her and draw her away from herself—where she could live without happiness, and those foolish dreams that had been the dearest possession of her soul.

'But maybe ye would like to stay for the ball?'

'Oh, of course, Maisie. Use the hard brushes for my hair this morning.' She spoke in an impatient, imperative tone, which surprised the maid so much that she offered no further suggestions.

At sight of her pallid face in the glass, Stella sponged her cheeks with pungent aromatic vinegar. The delicate skin responded at once to the touch, and her determination to keep at bay the rising sorrow that at times threatened like a great flood to sweep all embankments into its whirling eddies, kept the colour in her cheeks and the fire in her eyes.

'Only four more days till our ball,' said Laurette, who in her heart had ejaculated a fervent little thanksgiving to Providence at sight of Stella entering the breakfast-room. She had looked so deadly weary and done on the previous night, fear, like a chilly snake, had lodged in Laurette's bosom that the girl would certainly fall ill.

'I think, Miss Stella, you had better come with me for a riding expedition till the evening of the ball,' said the master of the house, who, with the wisdom of the serpent,* generally cleared out on the days immediately preceding such festivities.

'But I thought you were to be the villain in Mrs Joran's comedietta to-morrow night,' answered Stella, with a faint smile.

'Ah, true—the man who drugs people and steals letters.'

'Surely that is not the *rôle* of a real villain—to drug and steal letters merely. You are going to be a philanthropist in disguise.'

'Thank Heaven! she believes it all,' thought Laurette.

'Do you know, Miss Stella, that sounds a little misanthropical for one who gets letters in handfuls.'

'But how should I know it would be a boon from the gods to have them stolen if I did not get a few?'

'Still, you would not like them all stolen?' He could not help watching her a little curiously. There was some inexplicable change in her whole face and bearing since she had sat in the same place twenty-four hours ago. He saw that, notwithstanding her effort to keep an indifferent, smiling look, her face hardened, and he hastened to change the conversation. 'Are you going to fall into Mrs Anstey-Hobbs' plan of getting you for the heroine of her little adaptation from the French?'

'No, I think not. One's own little part in life gives me so many *jours insipides*,* without dabbling in other people's.'

'Thank God! she is in a fighting mood,' thought Laurette.

'I am sorry. Mrs Anstey-Hobbs consulted me, and I told her I thought her idea was an inspiration, as you constantly remind me of a cousin of my own, of whom a French diplomat once said that she had a Parisian edge to her mind. She had, too, as he said, that vivacity *dans ses moindres mouvements** which Englishwomen so rarely possessed. She had, in fact, an infusion of Irish blood, as you have of Highland.'

'Wasn't Mrs Anstey-Hobbs shocked at the mention of anything Parisian in connection with Stella? You never told *me* the funny story

Ted was laughing about once. I shouldn't wonder if he turned up to-morrow.'

This remark seemed to be addressed to the teapot more than to anyone in particular.

'But shearing is in full swing at Strathhaye,' said Tareling, who instantly connected this announcement with Stella's presence, and began vaguely to speculate whether, after all, there was anything in it. Women were such queer conundrums—one could never tell. How many impossible marriages he, Tareling, had seen in his day! But Australian girls were not as a rule so keenly alive to the fascinations of wealth as those inoculated with the aims and standard of London society, where to lack money was to be out of the swim of everything that held life together. That same Lady Mary, his cousin, who in Tareling's memory held the shadowy place of what might have been; who had at times scolded him, and somehow got him out of his first serious scrape at Eton, and written him letters, and promised to marry him if a Chinese mandarin left him a mine in Golconda;* whose radiant gray eyes and brilliant sallies had often been recalled by Stella Courtland—what a strange hash she had made of her life, first marrying the wrong man, then running away with the wrong one, and finally taking the wrong dose of chloral!*

Would she have fared so very much worse if she had married him, though they were both as poor as church mice, with something less than nine hundred a year between them, and no one likely to leave them a mine in Golconda? She in her dishonoured grave—and he in his dishonoured life, gambling, and drinking deep at times, and playing the *roué* generally in third-rate society at the far ends of the earth, 'sponging on his wife's relations,' as old Ritchie had once said in a fury, after he had been called on to shell out a thousand pounds or so to keep a very shady story from the light of day? Probably they would have quarrelled; and to quarrel in one of those tiny establishments in which people lived on nine hundred a year was the very deuce—one had to get down so completely to hard pan*—or be a plumb idiot* the next moment, and kiss and be friends. He rather thought they would have done the latter. But at any rate would they quite have come to this; she in a nameless grave at Monte Carlo— he married to a colonial heiress, intriguing to keep a firm hold among the mixed lot that formed the *crème demi-double** in a pushing, vulgar

colonial city? Yet even Lady Mary's marriage lacked some of the
utter incongruity that would attend one between Ritchie and this
young woman. A mammoth scratched on a bone by a prehistoric
man, and a statuette by one of the old Grecian sculptors, that was
what would represent the comparative quality of their minds.

Tareling was not a man who had retained much of the faculty of
being even touched by the higher possibilities of human life. He
would have had to purge and live cleanly before he could be the moral
equal of many among those he contemptuously classed as a 'mixed
lot.' Whatever semblance of the hero had once lived in his heart had
long since atrophied. His aims and ideals were to the full as ignoble
as those of that lower division of the common herd who value money
chiefly for the physical excesses and mental excitements that it com-
mands. Yet it may be taken for granted that one has not generations
of well-born and cultured people behind him, without retaining
some keenness of perception that belongs to a well-descended creature, whether he be man, horse, or dog. Stella interested him not only
because of the resemblance he fancied in her to the unhappy girl who,
in her brilliant youth, had been so much his friend, but also because
of that element of personal fascination which is inseparable from
some women. Why had the glow and the sparkle of her face been
suddenly quenched? Why those livid circles round the eyes that did
not in the least respond to the smile she called up?

'You will be glad to have some riding, Stella. No doubt Ted will
bring a hack or two a lady can ride,' said Laurette, emboldened by
the inferences she drew from observing the girl to handle her subject
'like a lad of mettle.'* She began to think that Stella, after all, was
not such a very bad sort of nettle to manage.

'Would you like to ride to-day?' said Tareling suddenly. But it
seemed there were too many engagements of one sort or another.
Indeed, if there had not been such, Laurette would have invented
them. No one allowed himself to be more easily hoodwinked than
Talbot when it suited him; but, on the other hand, no one had a more
unerring vision in piecing broken hints into a whole, once his suspicion or interest was thoroughly roused. He had, too, curious tact with
people whom Laurette herself might deceive or mislead, but whose
confidence she could never win. She could see by the way he glanced
under his heavy, deeply-lined eyelids from herself to Stella, that
something had presented itself to him as a problem.

'Oh, it will be delightful to ride!' Stella said, looking up, with a faint flush rising on her face.

The word 'delightful' had a sardonic ring in her ears. But language cannot serve its purpose, as legal tender between beings whose first care often is that nothing of what surges most vividly in the mind should pass into speech, without at times sounding in the ears like a mocking echo.

CHAPTER XL

RITCHIE arrived at Monico Lodge on the forenoon of the next day. Laurette met him in the hall, and drew him into the breakfast-room.

'Yes, Stella is in; she is in the drawing-room,' she said in answer to her brother's eager inquiries. 'But, Ted, I am in despair. I absolutely do not know what to think. Heaven knows if ever a woman tried to serve a brother as I have.'

'Well, what's in the wind now—anything fresh?'

'Oh, goodness only knows! When she came, she was in almost wild spirits; one would say she counted the moments till you came. Now——'

'Now she ain't so jolly! Well, that is Stella all over. What is there to wonder at in that? Hurry up, Larry, if you've got anything to say; I am famishing to see her.'

'Only this, Ted. Feel your way cautiously; and whatever you do, don't breathe a word of anything I said to you before you went to Strathhaye.'

'Of course not—I told you before I wouldn't,' answered Ted impatiently; 'but look here, Larry, you're a trump to take so much trouble on my account.'

'Oh, if one could only be sure of her; but one day to be full of hope and all smooth sailing, and the next——' Laurette gave a deep sigh, as if she were in the depths of perplexity. Then Ted made his escape into the drawing-room.

'Well, Stella, are you still cross with me?' he said gently, holding her hand.

'No, I think not,' she said with a wan smile, endeavouring to re-collect the reason why she should cherish offence. Everything was so incredibly misty at times, so far away and indifferent. The days seemed to stretch on and on, like eternity. Three had not yet passed since the morning on which she opened that letter with its pitiless tidings. Yet the most remote epoch of her life seemed to be the days in which supreme happiness was neither a threat nor a vague possibility, but a secure possession. And now it was all over—all over, with nothing left but those recurring periods in which she was alive in every nerve to the horrible misery that had overtaken her—periods in which she seemed to see nothing but a ship that sailed on, night and day, bearing the only man she had ever loved, or could love, to his *wife*. The thought stung her so intolerably that she often rose up, seeking for relief in motion, as if a heavy physical load crushed her which she must endeavour to throw off.

Ritchie looked into her face with startled inquiry. What ailed her? Was it possible that the knowledge which Laurette said had partly come to the girl should give her so much pain? The thought touched him strongly. But he remembered Laurette's warning. He might interrupt her counsels and little incipient homilies roughly; but yet no one else could help him so much, nor tell so well what motives swayed Stella.

'I don't believe Melbourne agrees with you one bit,' he said, still holding her hand, which she left passively in his.

'No, perhaps not; and yet I don't want to go back to Fairacre.' They stood side by side in the bay-window, she looking out with heavy, tired eyes at the scrubby little trees and scantily-flowering rose-bushes that decorated the 'grounds' of Monico Lodge, but seeing nought of all that was around her.

'Where would you like to go, Stella?' said Ritchie slowly. His breath came fast, but some instinct warned him to keep down his rising joy.

'Oh, I don't know! where I would not see these woods and skies eternally—away to the far ends of the world.'

'Stella, let me take you wherever you would like to go. It's all I've got to live or care for.' He was looking eagerly into her face, and suddenly saw a gray paleness creeping over it. All became dim around her. She put her hands out like one groping in the dark. He passed his arm round her, and for a moment her head fell on his shoulder. Her face was like that of one dead, and its pallor terrified him. But she did not entirely lose consciousness.

'How dark it has grown!' she said in a faint whisper.

'It will soon be light again, Stella,' answered Ted, hardly knowing what he said. The profound sadness of her face, and her sudden, unaccountable weakness, smote him to the heart. 'Stella, has anything happened that hurts you? Is there anything in the world I can do for you?'

His voice trembled, and he tried to draw her nearer to him. This roused her, and sighing heavily once or twice, she disengaged herself, and sat on the seat that ran round the window. Ritchie's presence had recalled, with a paroxysm of acute agony, all that lay between now and their last parting. Such moments of overpowering pain were succeeded by hours that were passed rather than felt. The intolerable edge of suffering was gradually dulled—became for the time blunted. Apathy put a foil on grief, and robbed memory of its piercing barbs. In the reaction, Ted's familiar voice and unswerving devotion soothed, nay, even reassured her. Her stern, proud self-control had not broken down before anyone till now. And with her self-possession came the thought that he had claims on her. She had once consented to be his wife. But her heart had rebelled against a marriage without the quickening pulse of love and tender mutual sympathy. Now she knew that these were forever sealed against her. The glow and romance of youth were over. She had loved and lost. But the years could not be thrown aside like a stupid story. She had dreamed a dream of life, and it was over, but existence still remained to be got through.

'Stella, we have been friends since we were little children. You do care a little for me. Be my wife!'

She heard the voice so long familiar pleading with her brokenly, and it touched her in that strange hour as it had never touched her before. The thought welled up strongly in her heart: 'This love is to him what mine was to me—the one great affection of his life. In this was centred the keenest possibilities of his happiness.' The very depth of her own suffering and infinite loneliness moved her to compassionate sympathy. She had almost forgotten him in the brief triumphant days of her joy. But no one had ever usurped her place with him. Could she now confer on him the boon that was so priceless in his estimation—for which he had so long pleaded? And for herself? . . . Would this not, after all, be the best solution of the cruel enigma into which existence had resolved itself? The old home life, full of leisure and calm and well-loved books—how could she take that up when her one fierce longing was to forget? It would be an endless stifling life in death; in which the weary days would stretch before her, to be filled only with bleeding recollections, with famished imaginings of what might have been. Her pursuits and meditations there would touch those treacherous springs which woke all the cells of memory, and flooded her being with unbearable agony, with the wild, baleful pangs of jealousy. Yes, jealousy unreasonable, uncontrollable.

It was the bitter humiliation of this that stung her beyond endurance. Sorrow in any other form she might have borne—but this scorched her, degraded her, bit into her like some virulent, immaterial poison which nourishes the blood in order that it may consume the soul. Jealous of a man's wife! These were the words that came to her perpetually, more venomous than the hiss of a serpent. A marriage in which some kind of friendship was possible—in which travel, movement, variety, were open to her—this was the least objectionable scheme that remained to her. Ted's allegiance was so unshaken—he exacted so little. He watched her face with keen emotion.

'Stella, you are going to consent,' he said, drawing near to her. But she drew back.

'Don't, Ted. You must not be affectionate if you want me to marry you.'

Ted smiled under his moustache. Then a servant came to announce the arrival of his groom with the horses.

The day was perfect in its warm, serene loveliness. The sky was like a vast bed of blue hyacinths, bending above the earth with angelic benedictions. Already the sun-rays had something of the ardour of summer heat, but there was a cool southerly breeze, and a recent fall of rain had laid the dust.

The sight of the sea lying as calm as a great lake, its bosom glancing in silvery sheaves rather than waves, brought back to Stella, with irresistible vividness, the memorable ride over the wide Peeloo plain. A great wave of anguish swept over her afresh, in which it seemed as if she must call aloud to find some relief from the fierce torment. So great was the agony, that for a little time she could neither hear nor see. 'Oh, my love, my love, have I indeed lost you?' were the words that rose to her lips. For a moment a wild revolt rose within her against all the obstacles that could part them. On the wide horizon she seemed to see the faint film of smoke which a great steamer leaves as it speeds on its way to the old world. 'All will yet be well.' Did this hope animate his heart? Did he, perchance, count the hours till he saw her again—till those proofs were given him of faults imputed that were groundless—of years made dark with unde-served blame? Would a fresher, stronger bond rise up in place of the old unhappiness? Would he learn to love her—his *wife*? Ah, what a pitiful, humiliated creature had she become to harbour such thoughts! Hell seemed to yawn at her feet when she found her heart torn with savage jealousy as these thoughts rose in quick succession.

The riders had ridden fast, and Dustiefoot, who could not bear to lag far behind his mistress, panted and showed such signs of being overdone that they rode back slowly.

'Will you take him with you on your travels, Stella?' asked Ted, who watched with a feeling akin to envy the tenderness with which Stella regarded her dog.

'On my travels? Oh yes, wherever I go. One should always have a dog to keep one in countenance.'

'In countenance?'

'Yes. Most human creatures remind one of the characters in an old morality.* As—enter God's Visitation; enter Time, who maketh people weary and melancholy with a similitude of rust and dust.'

'And what is an "old morality," Stella?'

'Well, Ted, you really must go to school.' She laughed, and the sound was music in his ears, though it was a strange, mirthless little laugh.

'Yes, I should like that very much—if you keep school, and take just one scholar. Where would you begin with me, Stella? How many books have you read?'

'Heaven only knows! Quite enough to convince me that I do not know anything.'

'O Jupiter! is it worth while learning so much to know that? What is the good of reading so many dry old fogies of books?'

'Well, sometimes it makes people better companions for them-selves; but other times it makes them the worst of all company, I believe.'

'I read very slowly. If it is a dull book like the Bible and poetry, I forget what one page is about before I get to the next. It would take me a thundering long time to read books, and if they don't teach me much in the end, and make me worse company for myself, why, we'll give books the go-by. What's the next on your list, Stella?'

'I haven't got a list—and there isn't a next. Ted, you mustn't ask me questions. I do that to myself endlessly, and I hate them; there are no answers to most, and those that have answers are scorpions.'

'What questions do you ask yourself? There, I've put my foot in it again! Well, look here, Stella, your school will be the jolliest affair going. You only teach reading, and that game isn't worth the candle. So there I'll be, bright and early, and nothing to learn but to stay with you. But I'll pick up a lot in that way. Why, some time ago I put the stuns on a fellow with just only remembering that the line, "Where is the land to which yon ship must go?" is in one of Wordsworth's sonnets.* Oh, he's just a racing fellow! he comes from one of the old swell families in England, but nothing like such a bad lot as Tareling. He's as straight as a die, and never borrows money, and he's quite gone on books, though he took his degree at Oxford. He and another fellow were talking about poetry in the smoking-room after dinner at the club the last time I was in town, and the other fellow asked Dacre, that's his name, where that line came from. I was reading the sporting part of the *Australasian*,* but the words came on me like seeing you unexpectedly, and I looked up and said: "Why, that's from one of Wordsworth's sonnets." By George! they were more astonished than if I had stood on my head. Yes, upon my soul, they both stared as if they had paid a bob to see me! "Why, Ritchie, do you actually read sonnets?" said Dacre. He has written a bookful himself. He is one of those fellows who think that all men write poetry when they are spoony. I could tell him better than that. Do you remember, Stella, one Sunday evening when I was staying from Saturday till Monday at Fairacre? Billy Stein and Herby Lindsay were there, too. Billy knew a fearful lot of German stuff that you were always fond of, and as for poetry, he could spout it by the hour. It was shortly before I left for Strathhaye—I suppose you were fifteen at the time—you used sometimes to get perfectly wild with making fun of one thing or another, and your eyes, and cheeks, and lips all used to make flashes. Oh, you may laugh! but I know what I mean. Your eyes are awfully heavy just now, Stella. Well, you put the four of us in a row—Cuthbert, and me, and the other two—and you wouldn't let us move till we each made some sort of verses. 'Pon my soul, I nearly squirmed my eyes out trying to think of words that sounded alike. When I did get any, the spelling was out, and there was that little beggar Billy making up something as long as my arm

about a rose, and a maiden, and a nightingale. But I put the kybosh
on him there, for I said there were no nightingales in Australia, and
how did we know whether they sang as he said? And you took my
side, but I think it was out of pure wickedness. Everyone got finished
long before I did, and at the end I could only make up four lines. Oh,
I remember them well enough:

> '"A lamb's tail
> Caught on a rail;
> The mother humming,
> The crow a-coming."'

Stella laughed again.

'Why, Ted, you are one of the dumb poets? What in the world put
that into your head?'

'Oh, don't suppose I made up the adventure. I took it from life. I
saw a little lunatic of a lamb caught by his hind end before he was
tailed, and if I hadn't taken him to his mother, the old crow would
have scooped his optics out in no time. You all objected to
"humming." I didn't want the darned sheep to hum; it was you that
would have rhyme, and how could you make "bleating" into poetry
there? I very nearly got into a scot with Stein, he kept on laughing
so much. But then you walked with me up to the Spanish reeds, and
showed me the nest of a superb warbler there—domed, I think you
called it—and told me how you watched the old mater teaching the
young 'uns to fly. And then I made up my mind to ask you if I might
write to you. My heart beat so hard I thought it would crack,
and you said quite carelessly: "Oh yes, Ted, why shouldn't you?" I
couldn't have told why it gave me a lump in the throat the way you
spoke. Then I thought, That little wretch Billy will want to write,
too, and spin away about nightingales, and the Lord knows what!
I never feel such a duffer as I do when I take a pen. I say, Stella,
did you ever keep any of my letters?'

'Oh yes, I think so.'

'I expect you've got a nice pile of love-letters by this time? Now,
tell me true—are there any of them you like better than mine?'

'No; not one.'

The thought welled up bitterly of the letter she had opened with
such insane joy three short days ago. And with this came recollections of the long faithful wooing of her companion—of the devotion

she had taken as carelessly as an unset pebble; and yet, was there anything in the world more rare, more precious? These reminiscences of her untroubled girlhood touched a tender chord. She realized that a love which had its roots so far back in the past had a claim on her loyalty. At the worst, it was less humiliating to marry a man without loving him than to love one already married. Ted, watching her face closely, noted its wistful, softening expression.

'Lookee here, Stella,' he burst out suddenly. 'I am going to run away with you. You will be cross at first, but you will get over it. You know you looked as if you could not speak with passion when I held you that night and asked that I might kiss you. But when we met, you never once thought of bringing it up against me; now did you?'

'No.'

'Oh, good Lord! Stella, why do you keep me on and on hoping, and nothing come of it? Put an end to it. You want to get away; you need a complete change; anyone can see that. You said in July you sometimes thought of marrying me. Yes—no—yes. There it is in the horses' hoofs. Summer, autumn, winter, spring—spring. It is spring now. We won't have the smallest morsel of fuss. If we were married to-morrow, everyone would say: "Well, goodness knows, they've been long enough thinking over it." Let's put an end to it, Stella. Hear the horses' hoofs, every one of them saying "Yes, yes—yes!" Stella, will you marry me?'

There was a long pause. The sound of a railway whistle in the distance, of snowy-breasted sea-gulls calling as they skimmed the waves, the deep, solemn crescendo of the wide sea as it broke on the shining sand, the merry cries of children on the shore—these came borne to them on the balmy spring air. Memories that had a pang beyond the bitterness of death surged up in Stella's mind. To the smallest detail, the hour in which she had listened in speechless happiness to Anselm Langdale's avowal of love rose up before her. An hour so near in time—but in the sensations that turn hours into years remote as the first dawn of consciousness.

'Answer me, Stella,' said Ritchie, his voice now low and husky with contending emotion. 'Don't you know what to say? It's very simple—say "Yes."'

Again there was a long pause.

'Yes,' she answered at last, and Ritchie turned quite pale through the ruddy bronze of his cheeks. For a moment he almost reeled in his saddle and doubted his senses.

'Stella, do you mean it? You will be my wife?'

'Yes,' she said, again looking into his face. He was agitated almost to tears, while she was perfectly calm.

They rode on for a little time in silence. Something like rest stole over Stella. She felt that her course was now fixed, her decision unalterable—and there was relief in the thought. As for Ritchie, he almost feared to give complete credence to the belief that after all these years of unavailing hope—of waiting and rejection—he was in truth an accepted lover. And even he, 'elementary human being' though he might be in one of Stella's old phrases, yet experienced that quick revulsion which so often sets in, of dread because of other possibilities, now that this ardently longed-for happiness seemed within reach. But as the first tumult of thought subsided, his joy rose high.

'Stella, you have said "No" so long; you must keep on telling me it's all right now,' he said in unusually timid tones; 'I can hardly believe in such luck for myself.'

'Don't be too glad, Ted; if you are, you're sure to be disappointed.'

'But if you were me, Stella, you couldn't help being too glad,' returned Ted, with unconscious pathos.

Something in the words struck a chord in Stella's heart. She felt softened and remorseful. She determined that, as far as in her lay, she would quench the rising tide of hard, cold indifference, of scorn for her own life and action, which was the first result of her momentous decision. But when people feel one way and make resolutions in another direction, it is a toss-up with circumstance which will be victor in the first or subsequent encounters.

CHAPTER XLI

WHEN they reached Monico Lodge there was Cuthbert at the door, going away after having waited for some little time. He helped Stella to dismount, and the three went in together.

'Congratulate me, my dear fellow,' said Ted, the moment they went into the drawing-room. 'Stella has promised this very afternoon to be my wife—and this time there is to be no drawing back.'

The brother stared at Ritchie in an incredulous way, and then at his sister.

She suddenly coloured deeply and said:

'Yes, Cuthbert, you may congratulate us; but we are going away almost directly, so as to escape all that—and the wedding-gifts——' She felt compelled to talk in a half-mocking tone, so as to save herself from the imbecility of tears. 'Oh yes, the day after to-morrow, if you please. By the way, I must go and tell Larry—I believe she's in.'

'Stella, darling, may God grant you every happiness!' said her brother, kissing her first on one cheek and then on the other. He felt a pang of misgiving which he could not conquer, and his face and voice were exceedingly grave.

'Now, Cuthbert, don't be so solemn—at any rate, until the ultimate disaster.'

'But you do—you are attached to Ted—or you would never have given your consent?'

'Oh, my dear, it is unsafe to generalize about our delightful sex. Don't you remember what St Teresa said in one of her letters to a Carmelite Father: "Your Reverence made me smile by saying that you could tell her character so well. But we women are not so easily known."'*

'But there *are* some things, Stella, it would be safe to prognosticate of all good women.'

'Oh yes; as, for example, they all have ten fingers, and have learned the Catechism and the Creed. But if it comes to asserting that they believe the one and remember all the rest——'

'But what motive could or would be strong enough with you, darling, except love in some degree?'

'Ah, of course—love. But a woman must not give her love till it is asked. Isn't that one of the demure, unwritten statutes? Well, I am so very proper that I am not going to give it even when asked—not until I am married. It is the process of evolution. In the meantime, Ted vows he has enough for two.'

'Oh, Stella, you pain me! I cannot believe you would look and speak like this if your heart were really touched.'

'Now, Cuth, you know very well if my heart were touched I would be dead. You see, it is a very hard-worked organ as it is. If it went through all the impossible gymnastics ascribed to it by lovers, the human race would have come to an end long ago. When one comes to think of it, perhaps that is the best thing that could happen.'

'You are not well, dear. You flush up feverishly, and then you are pale, with dark rings about the eyes. You looked very different when you came from Lull. Dora and I both noticed it—and you were so dear and tender. We were so delighted. I came to tell you, Stella, that our wedding-day is fixed.'

'Oh! is it to-morrow? Because, if so, Ted and I will be married to-day. Yes, I'm determined not to be like Cinderella, left with the cinders, when you go straight to heaven like Elijah in a fiery chariot.* But then Elijah, poor man! had no Dora.'

'Well, Stella, I should be very unhappy if the girl who promised to marry me could talk like you the day she was engaged. That reckless, mocking tone—no girl who was happy could use it.'

'Unless it were an artifice to conceal her joy,' said Stella, laughing. Then, in a graver tone: 'You see, dear, it does not do to generalize too largely. On looking round among our married friends, does it not strike you that the majority never committed the indiscretion of falling in love at all, or if they did, that they have all they asked for, and nothing of what they hoped, poor wretches? I, for my part—'

Here Laurette entered, followed by Ted. She threw her arms round Stella with a little cry.

'Don't, Laurette; this is what I am determined to avoid,' said Stella, holding her at arms' length. But Laurette was half intoxicated with joy. Not till that moment had she really believed that her schemes would be crowned with such complete success. She pecked once or twice at Stella's cheeks with her hard little lips, and then turned to Courtland, her face wreathed with smiles.

'Isn't it too delightful, after all these years of waiting?' she said to him, pressing his hand with a congratulatory fervour. Courtland, pale and erect, bowed, and murmured something in reply. Then he turned to Ritchie, and took his hand.

'I congratulate you, Ted; you are a very lucky man! I pray God——' There was a sharp break in his voice, and at the sound a cord seemed to tighten round Stella's heart. The old bond between them had been a very strong and tender one. Now that the half-petulant irritation of finding herself, as she thought, displaced in his affection, was lost in the storm that had swept away so many of the old landmarks, her heart went out to him more fully. Only she had to guard against any treacherous yearning for full sympathy and intimate communion. She must be inexorable against her weakness on every side. She was struggling against her whole nature as a strong athlete struggles for victory. That was what made Ritchie's society safer for her in this crisis than that of the old home circle. He was imperturbably good-natured; he had a strong fund of animal spirits, and his hand could never touch any of those inner cords which, if they vibrated at all, brought her in one swift moment face to face with black despair and gnawing jealousy. She conquered the climbing sorrow which her brother's emotion awakened; then going up to him, and putting her hands in his, she said softly:

'Ah, you dear old boy, you have always been so good to me; Ted and I will pull all straight, do not fear. As for you, never forget, though, that you threw me over first.'

She raised the tips of her brother's fingers to her lips as she spoke, and he was instantly melted by her caressing tenderness. She was always confident of winning entire forgiveness for any outbreak of caprice or wilfulness the moment she made up her mind to be quite good. This confidence, modified by an air of imploring entreaty, had always been one of her irresistible moods.

'Pull all straight?—I should think we would!' said Ted proudly, possessing himself of Stella's left hand, while her brother held the right.

'How long do you mean to keep up that wicked little story about my throwing you over?' said Cuthbert, smiling fondly at her as he stroked her hair. 'There never lived the human being who could make me do that. And, Stella, whatever comes or goes, if ever you are in trouble or perplexity, never forget that if need were I would lay down my life for you.' He did not mean to say so much, but there was some undercurrent of feeling at work which he could hardly analyze. He only knew that from the first a strong misgiving beset him as to this marriage.

At Courtland's words a vague alarm rose in Laurette's breast. 'How very absurd!' she thought to herself angrily. 'Women don't want their brothers after they are married—not in that way.'

She herself had only wanted her brother's money, and the means by which she had obtained some of it, and hoped for still more, rose before her, for the first time, in an almost lurid light. A sudden panic fastened on her lest there should be some loophole by which her machinations should be detected. But she had gone too thoroughly to work to be caught in the toils which wreck the half-hearted dissembler. It is not cunning, but simplicity, that must patch and tell a

tale which often carries no conviction in a world where it is a common
trade to make the thing which is seem as though it were not. Simplicity, poor unthrift, who makes no use of all the kingdoms of the
world, and the glory thereof, but to tell the truth, is all too often
shamed into hiding her pensive, virginal, unaffected brow before the
bold, rouged, menacing front of her successful rival—Mendacity.

But Laurette betrayed none of the uneasiness which shot athwart
her mind. Indeed, her anxieties at this time were so multiform that
they might be said to swallow each other, so that, on the whole, she
kept up as gay an appearance as though no cares oppressed her. Chief
among them was her husband's intrigue with this 'wretched little
divorced actress.' This had blossomed apace into a well-concocted
scheme of indefinite migration on his part with her theatrical
company. Laurette knew this definitely by means of examining the
Honourable Talbot's pocket-book, when he slept not wisely but too
well. And yet she felt that her only course was to make no sign; to
feign complete ignorance, and take such action at the last moment,
that is, the eleventh of October, as might be of vital service to her.
Then that letter which she had got Mrs Anson to write. It was only
after fully convincing herself that Langdale's half-erased, mutilated
narrative might not of itself serve her purpose, that Laurette had hit
on the scheme of boldly supplementing it by a communication which
would at once throw light on his supposed story, and his action in
hastening away without seeing Stella. She judged unerringly, too,
that the thought of his hastening back to a loving wife anxious for
reconciliation would stab the girl's pride into more active resistance
against grief than any other theory.

'Stella has it in her to be jealous—one can see that by the way she
took her brother's engagement,' reasoned Laurette. 'And if there is
any occasion on which jealousy may grow into a monster, surely it is
when the man who called you "sweet St Charity," and the innermost
leaf of his heart, is supposed to be steaming away at the rate of
seventeen knots an hour to the beautiful woman he married before
he left school, so to speak. Not that I believe she is really dead—at
any rate, if so, her conduct is very unlike that of other people, who
could do nothing to oblige one in life so much as to leave it. . . .'

Yes, all her calculations had been singularly favoured by Providence; but this speedy engagement was of that order of good
luck which all but frightens one. It was almost sinister—like the

appearance of a sociable vulture in the desert when drawing near a well that may prove empty. All that evening at Mrs Joran's private theatricals the thought rose at intervals, What if Stella and Langdale met abroad? And yet, once the marriage had taken place, what would it avail? There was a dance after the acting was over. Everyone was enraptured with Talbot's masterly performance, and she replied to congratulations on this abominable accomplishment as cheerfully as though it were not drawing a husband and a father, as she styled him, even to herself, in her more melodramatic moments, into the Bohemian depths of a strolling-player's career. But she would save him despite himself—which was usually the way people were saved when once they gave themselves up to the enjoyment of being lost. And to secure that end what means were not legitimate? Yet she could not resist the inclination to reassure herself, by laughing inquiry of a distinguished judge, as to whether deception practised to bring marriage about could in any way invalidate it.

'My dear Mrs Tareling, what could have put such an uncanny idea into your head? What marriage would be safe if once the plea of deception were allowed to batter against the foundations of the holy institution of matrimony?' said the judge, laughing. 'Take the deceptions which Nature puts upon us, to begin with——'

'Now, Sir Henry, you are laughing at me! No one ever knows where Nature begins or ends. I do not mean only with the complexions of my own dear sex.' The judge laughed with real amusement at this sally: Laurette fully knew the value of talking in an amusing way when she had an aim to serve. 'I mean real deception: abstracting letters, and having others written, and things like that, for which I have no doubt you could find awful names in some of your awful books.'

The judge fixed his gray, penetrating eyes on the softly pretty, exquisitely dressed young woman before him, vaguely wondering whose interest she had at heart in this inquiry. 'These bright, pretty young women have often a wonderfully altruistic vein in their natures,' he reflected. Then, in a very lucid unpedantic way, he pointed out that if people did things that had awful names in law-books, they might be brought to account; but people were not supposed to marry because other people abstracted letters or wrote sham ones. Marriage was a contract between this man and this woman for certain ends, clearly set forth in the Prayer-book and elsewhere and under certain conditions. If these conditions were observed, no alleged deception on the part of anyone else could, in the slightest, affect the contract.

'Well, after all, how beautifully simple and reasonable that is!' said Laurette, with a glow of enthusiasm.

Even the term 'alleged deception' carried with it a kind of balm. It made her reflect that not one scratch of her pen had been contained in the letters that had suddenly changed the whole complexion of Stella's life. She had erased, but she had not formed a single letter; and the little note Mrs Anson had written at her dictation was like eternity, without beginning or end, without date or local habitation. After all, what a bulwark to society the law was! Her spirits rose, and she felt like an Eastern hero, as if she were destined to destroy Afrits.

A little afterwards, when in conversation with the Honourable Miss Brendover, this lady said something of having spent the last winter in Berlin, where the musical season had been very brilliant, it flashed through Laurette's mind like an inspiration that Berlin was the very city to which it would be safest for Ted and Stella to go in the first instance. England would not be safe for awhile. Langdale would most likely go on to Brussels before going there. Then he would get the newspaper announcing the marriage, which she would send him the very day after the event came off. Laurette had taken down the address he had inclosed for Stella, which was that of his lawyer in London. Well, after getting that newspaper, he would at once perceive there was nothing to be done but bear his fate. He would not be likely to return to Australia. He would, perhaps, drift about, travelling for awhile. Now, France and Italy were the happy hunting-grounds of all travellers; but Berlin—'My dear Milly, I wish you would tell my sister-in-law-elect about the music in Berlin,' said Laurette. 'I fancy she thought of going to Germany.'

'Oh, and then they will meet Talbot's cousins there—the Avenells! So it will be quite nice and friendly for Mr Ritchie in a foreign land. He does not know German, I think?'

Before the evening was over, Stella had a long chat with Miss Brendover, chiefly about the charms of winter in Berlin. At the same time Laurette duly impressed Ted with the wisdom of going there direct if Stella expressed any wish of the kind.

'I don't care a copper where Stella wants to go,' returned Ted. 'Whatever she wants to do, she shall.'

The subject somehow came up again as they drove home.

'I lost a waltz with you, Stella!' said Ted ruefully. 'What a lot you and that old cousin of Talbot's had to say to each other!'

'Old?—she is charmingly young!' returned Stella. 'I know, because that waltz of Strauss's—by the way, never ask me to dance to it—is one I heard two hundred and fifty years ago. Oh, it was a strange, enchanted sort of country—full of fairy stories, and I believed them all.'

Her cheeks were deeply flushed, and her eyes were shining with a feverish light. Ted was always pleased when Stella was inspired with something of her old gaiety, and yet there was something in the sound of her voice that disturbed him.

'Did you tell Miss Brendover about this country, then? and was that what kept you chatting so long?'

'Oh no—bits of it came trilling back in the music; but between I listened to glowing accounts of wonderful Berlin concerts—eighty trained musicians playing an accompaniment like one man, etc.'

'Shall we go to Berlin, Stella, and take Egypt and the other places on the way back?'

'Happy thought!' cried Stella lightly. 'Charter a vessel direct, before ten to-morrow morning.'

'No, but I am serious, Stella. The *Hindoo Fawn* sails on the sixteenth October.'

'Cannot we get away before then?' said Stella.

Ted's heart thumped wildly at the question.

'There is a French vessel——' he began slowly. But she held up her hands.

'A French vessel—not for your life! There is some very good reason somewhere—in the Book of Proverbs.'*

'There is an Orient steamer on the ninth of October; but—but will your mother consent to such haste?'

'Ah, that is your concern, Ted. You must explain everything when you write. Mind, I take no responsibility beyond the usual fibs of the marriage ceremony.'

Laurette was leaning back in a corner of the carriage, with closed eyes, as if she heard nothing. No one could be more discreet and wary, and less observant, where observation would have been an element of danger. She roused up when they got home, and she sat rattling away to Stella and Ted about all sorts of indifferent things.

'Did you see Mrs Anstey-Hobbs' new poet, Stella—the young man with the sombre expression and the long hair?'

'Is that one of the signs of a poet—not to go to the barber?' asked Ted.

'Oh, besides that, you must write things—

'"What is life but a spectre of bale?
What is joy but a curse that is stale?"'

That is one of the couplets Mrs Anstey-Hobbs quotes in dusky corners with a tremolo in her voice. I wonder why that little Mrs Lee-Towers makes a point of fastening on me on every available occasion of late?'

'Don't you approve of her, Laurette?' asked Stella, with a lurking smile.

'Well, no. I think the way she flirts in public, using the last pattern of young man she approves of like a fan, to keep her husband out of sight, is a little too bare-faced. And then she seems to have them to suit her style of dress. When she is in pale heliotrope velvet, it is that large young idiot with a lisp and flaxen hair. But he seems to be playing truant lately. It must really be a trying moment, when the young man who seemed to have been sent by Heaven into the world to hold your bouquet sympathetically begins to get out of your way.'

'What the deuce does her husband allow it for?—what is he like?' said Ted, who was picking up leaves that had fallen from Stella's nosegay of blush roses, and wondering why Larry did not find it necessary to go to the nursery or somewhere. He had not been a moment alone with Stella since their engagement.

'Oh, don't you know him by sight? He is rather a cadaverous-looking man, with six or seven mouse-coloured hairs on his chin. He looks as if he could ride in the air if he had the proper sort of broomstick. He never opens his lips, unless you make a mistake about figures. No, he isn't amusing; but nothing of that kind excuses a woman in such conduct. You may congratulate yourself, my dear Ted——'

Stella rose with a bored expression. 'Good-night, *mes amis*,'* she said, kissing the tips of her gloved hand to both, and gliding out of the room before Ted could reach the door—a proceeding which need hardly be characterized as unsatisfactory to Ritchie.

'By Jove! I shall never be sure of Stella till we're safely and substantially married,' he said, looking after her with knitted brows.

'True; therefore let it be on the sixth of October, and sail on the sixteenth,' said Laurette decisively. 'You will reach Berlin before the end of November. To be done in that time? Certainly—after a courtship of five years.'

'It's more like ten,' broke in Ted; 'and we were engaged once before.'

'Yes, allude to that. No one can be surprised at your determination to make sure of the young lady now.'

'Allude to it? I don't know how to allude to things. I shall simply put it down in black and white. By the way, Larry, where is Tareling?'

Laurette murmured something in reply which was not audible; but as she offered no explanation, this did not much signify.

'He did his part very well,' said Ted, taking out his cigarcase preparatory to retiring. 'But do you suppose anyone would ever carry on in that way in real life—hocussing* people and stealing letters?'

'Oh, people must put something into plays,' said Laurette contemptuously. As a matter of fact, her own little performance in that line had been infinitely superior, and she may have felt something of the scorn of a finished artist for a pretentious amateur. What did not occur to her was the irony which underlay her discussion of such a theme.

She was preoccupied with thoughts of checkmating Talbot's secret plans, and withal profoundly grateful that she was freed from the haunting fear of being forced to retire to the wilds of the Australian Bush, instead of shining in her proper orbit. She remembered the learned judge's words with a fresh glow of gratitude, and recalled with solemn approval a maxim she had somewhere heard or read, that we can benefit others in no surer way than by making the best of our own lives. How true this was as applied to herself! The best use she could make of her life was certainly to maintain her position in Melbourne society until she might perhaps be called on to take her place among the titled aristocracy of England. And in her efforts to keep this position she was securing Ted's happiness, protecting Stella from the danger of entanglement with a married man, and, most important of all, in a way to thwart the wild folly of her husband and the father of her children. Being in a very wakeful,

active-minded mood, she wrote several letters to members of the
Courtland family. She begged pardon in a pretty, winning way for
siding wholly with Stella and Ted in the arrangement of being
married in time to leave by the sixteenth of October. This was partly
because of business arrangements which compelled Ted to leave by
that date, partly because, after all that had passed, prompt action was
best. She was taking the liberty of seeing to Stella's trousseau so as
to save time: not that it would be a very extensive affair; why should
it? She had so many pretty dresses, and she was going to the great
centres of fashion, etc., etc.

CHAPTER XLII

BREAKFAST was late next morning at Monico Lodge, and the master
of the house did not make his appearance. There were times when
he simply haunted the place—being quite the closest approximation
to a ghost the neighbourhood could produce. It might, however, be
urged by the charitably inclined that his notions of day and night
had been seriously upset by having spent most of his life at the
antipodes—being thirty-one years of age when he left England six
years previously.

'I wrote my letter to your mother this morning, Stella—I want you
just to look over it,' said Ted, as they rose from the table.

Laurette was deep in arrangements for her ball, and left the young
people to themselves in a little morning apartment off the breakfast-
room.

'And mind, Stella, directly after lunch we must go to see about
your dresses,' she said—an announcement which Stella received with
incredulous amazement.

'Stella, have you got a conscience?' asked Ted, as she ensconced
herself in an armchair behind a davenport by the window.

'Yes, occasionally; but it's good to let sleeping dogs lie,'* said
Stella; and then, seeing Ted's aggrieved face, she held out her hand
to him. 'You may kiss the little finger, Ted, who was a traitor on your
side when there wasn't a cloud in the sky.'

'But sooner or later, you know, Stella——'

'Ah, later then! Now, what have you written?'

'"My DEAR MRS COURTLAND,

'"You will be glad to hear that Stella and I are fast engaged once more, and with your kind consent we must be married on the fifth of next month, so as to set sail for Europe on the sixteenth."'

'You see, Stella, I cannot make it any sooner,' said Ted, with a twinkle in his eyes—his line being to keep Stella literally to her mood of last night—'that is, as you object to the French line. There is an extra boat to sail on the eighth.'

She sat staring at him as if she did not hear him. She was following in the wake of a ship that went on its remorseless way day and night, speeding every hour nearer to its goal. Did it bear hearts that beat joyfully at the thought?

'I do not believe you hear what I say, Stella?'

'Oh yes, I do. What makes you think my mother will be glad for me to leave her?'

'I don't; a fellow must say something. But about the French boat?'

'Do not speak of that line. There was only one little Christian boat among them all, and it went down in a frightful storm in mid-ocean—a long way off. But still at times I hear the cries of the drowning; and there is a woman's face. She does not sink, but she has lost everything!'

'Stella, if you want to spin a yarn as you used to, do tell a jollier one than that thing. Anyone would think you saw it, and your eyes are getting larger than ever.'

She got up and looked at herself in a little plush-framed mirror near her.

He followed her, and put his arms round her.

'For God's sake, don't!' she cried, starting back as if she were stabbed. And then the next moment she turned on herself with fierce disdain.

She, whose whole frame had thrilled with rapture at the touch of lips whose kisses were forsworn, what right had she to repulse the honest love of a man who had been faithful to her from boyhood, to whom she had promised all her future life?

'Forgive me, Ted,' she said humbly; 'but I am nervous lately, and you took me by surprise.' She stroked his hand, and he flushed hotly under the touch.

'All right, Stella. Now let's go on with this letter:

'"This hurry is partly because of business arrangements, and also because, being engaged before, and nothing came of it, it's better to avoid accidents. As for me, I have waited so long, and felt often so frightfully down on my luck, I would much sooner the wedding were to-morrow than any other day. You have always been so kind to me, I'm sure you won't say a word against this plan, for I know Stella couldn't bear to do anything against your wishes. It would be only foolish sort of jawing for me to say how much I love Stella. Long before I should be thinking of such things I made up my mind she should be my wife. Many a day since I thought this would never be. But it has come all right now. So hoping you will concur in the above,

"I am, dear Mrs Courtland,

"Yours most respectfully,

"EDWARD RITCHIE.

"P.S.—As Stella can have everything she wants in Paris or elsewhere, it would be foolish for her to lay in a big stock of clothes. The dress she has on now would be the nicest of all for her to be married in. She will have a thousand a year for frills and things, and as much more as she likes. So it would be foolery for her to have an army of trunks full of things she can get where we are going."

—How will that do, Stella?'

'Oh, very well, Ted; but are you sure that we are both awake? On the fifth of next month?'

'Yes, fourteen long days. It's rather a shame, but I suppose we can't fix it earlier? You won't go back on the date, Stella? After all, you know, your mother has had you far longer than she should, if you hadn't gone back on the first racket. Now you write and back me up. You see, Cuth and Dora will be going back with you, and Tom engaged, and Allie soon to be married: they won't miss you, Stella. It's not as though your mother were a duck with one gosling.'

'Oh, Ted, what names!' and then Stella smiled.

'Go on, Stella; write your letter. I want to post it, and then take you for a ride. Look at that young calf of a Dustiefoot, with his snout against the window looking at you. It floors me how he finds out so soon the room you are in.'

'I need not write a separate letter. There is room on this half-sheet of yours.'

Stella took up a pen and wrote hastily.

'DEAREST MOTHER, AND ALL OF YOU,

'Do not be too much taken by surprise. We had better keep to the time named by Ted, as we must get away on the sixteenth. We shall escape all the Apostle spoons* and things every household should be without. I shall be married in a travelling-dress; and I really don't see what I want with any more things, I have been so extravagant this last year; and Tom has given me so many loans. I suppose he will throw an old shoe for good luck, but will it be necessary, when one has a thousand a year for frills? I kiss you all three times on the mouth.

'Your loving
'STELLA.'

'Don't you ever stop to think what you are going to say, Stella?'

'Not when I write to say that we are to be married in fourteen days.'

Ted read the lines Stella had written, and his face gleamed with joy.

'Oh, that is splendid!' he cried; 'but should you put that in about the thousand a year? Shouldn't it be—"Will it be necessary, when we love each other so much?"'

'It is indifferent. One of the advantages of so much social superstition is that a good many things are taken for granted.'

Ted, notwithstanding, made the correction in his uncial, squarely legible writing. Then he dwelt on the last sentence, and looked reproachfully into the girl's face.

'You kiss everyone at Fairacre three times on the mouth, but you don't kiss me once—and in two weeks you leave every man jack of them for my sake. Stella, do you call it decent, or according to God's holy ordinance, as it says in the Prayer-book?'*

He bent over her, and she turned her cheek to him. But he took her in his arms and covered her face with burning kisses. She turned deadly pale and trembled, but remained as passive as if she had been drugged. Then after a little she fought down the crowding thoughts that made the present give place to what had been. Memory, like a rebel, betrayed her to a surging host of recollections that seemed to stamp this moment with a seal of infamy. But the keen pangs of wounded pride, of hopeless love, and jealousy, came to her aid. She conquered her shrinking shame, her instinctive revolt—reminding herself that it was less humiliating to be kissed by unloved lips than by those that were so dear to her.

'Tell me, Stella, you are not sorry you gave me back your promise again yesterday,' said Ted in a low voice.

'Sorry? Oh no—I am glad,' she replied, feeling for the time her words were true—so fiercely did she seek to trample out that smouldering jealousy which was ever ready to leap into consuming flame. He was more than content with the answer. Yet, after she disengaged herself from his arms, he tested her tardy, passionately longed-for submission a little farther.

'Stella, come and kiss me on the mouth three times,' he said, in a tremulous voice.

Almost to her own astonishment she obeyed. Yes, it was part of the bargain. It made this incredible transaction all the more irrevocable. It made those days she would give her right hand to sink in utter oblivion more remote—more impossible. From that day she did not even in thought go back from her approaching marriage. It was as though she had drunk of some opiate that deadened her moral nature. She seemed to escape all fears, all responsibility, and the envenomed darts of memory. She was so much occupied during the day, she danced so much at night, she was so bent on being amused all the time, that none but the closest observer would have doubted the real source of this abandonment to gaiety.

Once or twice Ted, in a clumsy but honest way, tried to speak seriously of his own felt unworthiness, being misled by the statement Laurette had once made as to Stella's suspicion of his failure in conduct. But Stella treated these attempts like jugglers' plates—things to spin in the air, but not to let them down with a crash.

'Have you any wives hidden away, Ted?' she asked, arching her brows at him.

'Oh, come, Stella, you know very well you shouldn't talk in that way.' It was a fact that at this time her irresponsible levity sometimes wounded Ted's moral sense—chiefly because she was so unlike her former self.

'Shouldn't I? Let me assure you people's wives do turn up when they ought to be dead. But you haven't got one at all, it seems. No doubt there was a time when you should have married some, but you didn't—so it is all right. Isn't it beautifully simple?'

It was unpardonable, and Ted, who felt in a dumb way that she was his higher conscience, began to think that after all he had no need to be so remorseful when he thought over the curious difference presented by the spotless record of Stella's life and his own. He supposed women of sense always understood that things were so, though, of course, a line must be drawn somewhere.

Stella was, in truth, passing through that phase of deterioration in which some men gamble and drink deep so as to escape from themselves. She succeeded by ignoring all her better aspirations, all the higher capacities of her mind, in drowning thought, and numbing her sense of what was right to a strange degree. She had a strong will, and the unusual mental discipline through which she had passed early in life had given her a rare power of controlling her thoughts. She exercised both faculties to the utmost degree in casting from her memory the immediate past. But this was so woven into the deepest fibres of her being that to accomplish this object was to become, to a certain degree, morally callous. It was one of those remedies infinitely more injurious to the soul than the original disease.

Laurette was amazed at the change which had come over Stella. She was, at the same time, a little afraid of the element of inconsequence bound up with this alteration. It was all very well as long as nothing in particular happened, but everyone knows that life is full of accidents. It is not easy for women to deceive one another. This is one reason why their strictures on each other often strike men as being malicious. Laurette had a very definite idea that her future sister-in-law was changed—not because she had grown indifferent to Langdale, but because she cared too much. The last night of Stella's stay in Melbourne they had been at a Government House ball, and on their return they sat chatting for some little time.

'I suppose you will really live very little at Strathhaye, Stella, when you return,' said Laurette, who was an adept at leading up to what she wanted to say by beginning a long way off.

'I have hardly considered the matter,' replied Stella, playing with the brilliant diamond hoop which was her engagement-ring.

'You take so kindly to Melbourne life now; and I must say you are likely to be rather spoiled. You will be very popular. What story of yours sent the old Marchioness Lismore* into such roars of laughter?'

'Oh, a rather hideous anecdote about an old aboriginal, who wanted to be baptized while he carried the remains of an enemy in his hair till he should kill the next-of-kin as well. The old dame was talking quite seriously about the possibility of Christianizing our natives, and I felt bound to support her views.'

'Well, she laughed like a regiment—and what a wig she wears, to be sure! The more one reads the society papers and sees of the English aristocracy, the less one is impressed by them. Considering all it takes to keep them going, they should be a little more different from the common herd. I suppose the Marchioness invited you to visit them when you go to England?'

'Yes; but I remembered the fate of your friends the Jorans, and I did not commit myself. Besides, I don't want to go to England much now.'

'But of course you will go with Ted to see Uncle Matthew—and then there are your own friends and relations.'

'I don't know. Claude's wife declares that family circles there get upon one's nerves dreadfully. That, at any rate, is one striking advantage of an aristocracy. They are not formal, and squeezy, and peering timorously at other people to see how they behave.'

'How long do you think you'll be away?'

'Laurette, don't turn into a catechism without the answers. As long as it is quite amusing.'

'You have decided upon Berlin for the winter?'

'Oh yes; we go direct there from Brindisi.'*

'Well, Stella, you are certainly a very fortunate girl—nearly as fortunate as Ted.'

'Call no man fortunate till he is dead, and no woman till she is buried.'

'Oh, of course, I don't at all mean to say that, like everyone else, you won't have your own trials. Men are pretty much alike in many ways. A girl may marry the greatest milksop alive, but after all she is bound to find herself hopelessly behind the scenes.'

'Don't you think, Larry, you might be a little more entertaining? You remind one a little of a vivisector, who for certain experiments makes a lesion in the neck of a guinea-pig, and then pinches its nose to throw it into convulsions. I don't mind so much about my neck, but I am rather sensitive about my nose.'

'Well, Stella dear, you must forgive something to the weakness of a loving sister. I can't help seeing that lately you are more brilliant and somehow harder. In the midst of my joy on Ted's account,

I sometimes ask myself, "Does Stella really love him enough? Will she be able to overlook his faults, and help him, and lead him?"'

'Oh, Laurette, what *have* you been reading?' cried Stella, and she laughed outright, looking on with an animated face, as though she were witnessing a comedy.

But not a muscle of Laurette's face moved, either in mirth or anger.

'Ah, my dear, when you have my maturity of experience as a wife and mother, you will better understand my anxieties. If I thought that you did not really love Ted, I would say to you, even now, "Pause before it is too late!"'

It was inexpressibly comic. Only the play of daily life is often marred by the fact that we generally see—not the whole gem, but merely one or two facets. Yet, on the other hand, to see comedy in its more intimate bearings, as it affects ourselves, might frequently mean that all sense of fun would be merged in that of tragic irony.

Stella sat with such undisguised amusement on her face, waiting for this to go on, that Laurette instantly took up a fresh cue.

'But of course it is only my fears. And what makes it so very safe for you, is having been friends ever since you were babies, I may say. But it's just one of the things we women have to face—to take the world as we find it. To do that in married life, one must start with a good stock of affection. Where should I have been without it? We soon discover that our fairy tales and imaginations have been raised far enough away from reality. Many people were of opinion that if your sister Esther, for instance, had not been so horrified and scornful when she found Raymond went a little into queer* society—my dear, why do you stare so? I mean among the *pêches à quinze sous;** now that you are to be married, one may mention speckled fruit before you—affairs between them might have turned out differently. I dare say she forgave him at intervals; but if a man must forgive his brother seventy times seven,* how often must a woman forgive her husband? It's not put in the Bible, partly, I think, because there is not enough arithmetic going to make it up. And it's not only forgiving, but making light of it in a way. To do that, one must really enjoy one's self—and that's what you have the power of doing. You have to come down a cropper or two in your ideals, but you will soon find that a young married woman in a good position, with plenty of money and some brains, has more advantages, is more perfectly independent, than any other creature in the world. You will get on with all sorts of people. You can have a *salon* if you try, and succeed better than poor Mrs Anstey-Hobbs. If no one else says smart things, you will yourself. And then, of course, you will be sure to have enemies, and they are often far more useful in amusing one than any friends. . . . What could be more diverting than to watch people come to you, their faces covered with smiles, their hearts on their lips, so to speak, as they stretch out their hands to you? . . . And yet you know all the time they never say a true word of you behind your back, unless you are ugly or stupid. . . . I expect you will bring back heaps of lovely things; and of course you will go to Worth as you are coming home. Of course, too, you will go to visit the Lillimore family. Talbot said the other day his mother would be perfectly charmed to know you. There are three unmarried sisters—unfortunately none of them under thirty-three, and none of them very sweet-tempered; but how can you wonder? They are very poor, and their letters are always like Jeremiah's scroll—tenantless lands and mortgages.*

'If ever Talbot succeeds to the title, I shall be at my wits' ends; for what would be the use of being swallowed up in London society, and passing your time scheming how to make ends meet, etc.? They do not even give me any of those little details one longs for so. They write sometimes about the "sausage people," and the "screw-makers," and the "Jew money-lenders," meaning those who have made their money by these articles. But, after all, what is the good of trying to throw names at people about the way their money has been made? Land is going down and down in England. They can't grow wool much, nor wine, nor cotton, and the farmers are going to places where they can make more money, and become gentry on their own account. And there's no class in all the world that need money so constantly in large sums as an aristocracy. They want to be always well amused, and well fed, and well dressed—the dearest things in all the world—and, on top of it all, to do no work, which is dearer than all the rest put together—to be, in fact, almond tumblers,* whose beaks are so soft they must be fed out of a spoon, which is no doubt very genteel, as long as you can get people to feed you. But the Middle Ages are long over. Why, even here, in a properly democratic country, how soon everyone conspires to make you feel your poverty! I have often thought if one continued hopelessly poor all one's life, one would have to take to the love of God—there would be nothing else left.'

'Surely you are not threatened with such destitution, Larry?' said Stella, smiling. 'Why, Ted has more money than be knows what to do with; he must give you some.'

'My dear, that is very sweet and good of you! but you know how absurdly awkward one feels about taking money; and, of course, our poverty, after all, is comparative. It consists largely in having to fall back on second-rate tradespeople—not but what that is a bitter cross in itself: they are more flattered by your patronage, but they charge nearly as much; indeed, they leave out nothing but the style—like Surah, Muslin, and Company, who descend to the paltriest details if you have a dress made at their establishment—even putting the eyelet-holes down as an extra—and then put in sundries one pound fifteen shillings. And there is hardly anything in life more tiresome than a dressmaker who is not quite *chic*. Her fingers are always cold, and she *will* touch your skin, and stick pins in you, and hold things in her mouth, and say in a gushing way, "Yes, madam, it will be a most be-au-ti-ful fit," and then take a cheerful snip out of your arms with her scissors. Stella, you will never know anything of these small miseries. . . . Well, I wish it were possible for me to come to your wedding; but Talbot cannot leave town, as I said, and I must not go without him. But you are to stay with us the few days you are in Melbourne before leaving. What a charming idea that is of Ted's, to drive you in his new drag four-in-hand from Adelaide to Strathhaye!'

Laurette found everything in Stella's lot all the more charming just then by reason of Ted's action in presenting her only that morning with a cheque for two thousand pounds.

CHAPTER XLIII

IT was the evening before Stella's wedding-day. She had returned, in company with her brother Cuthbert and his *fiancée*, and their presence and the interest of their new relationship shielded her from undivided attention. A few days afterwards came Mrs Wallerton, with her children. Everyone knows how a family reunion serves to minimize the concentration of attention on any one grown-up individual of the circle. It is a small republic, in which, after the manner of limited monarchies,* those who reign do not rule.* Claude Hector, aged eight months, being the youngest member, and till then a complete stranger to his older relatives, was a great centre of attraction.

Then Dora, with her pretty, affectionate little ways, drew great attention. If anyone sang or played, Dora always begged for one more song or a little more music. If one spoke a little hoarsely, she never forgot to inquire next morning, with the deepest concern, after the afflicted throat. She was always gliding about, to put a footstool under someone's feet or to recover a straying newspaper or a dropped needle. Then, when anyone spoke, she always listened with the most reverential attention. When Cuthbert spoke, she would often murmur one of his sentences over to herself, as if better to impress it on her memory. She was, in fact, what is known in England as a very sweet girl. In Australia, unfortunately, the species is so rare that no specific name has had to be invented. Dora was to stay at Fairacre for a month after the wedding, and Felix Harrison could not refrain from saying to Allie that the change from Stella to Dora was rather soothing.

'But, indeed, her approaching marriage seems already to have improved her,' the young man said meditatively. He had many good qualities, and withal a liberal estimate of his own abilities. This had long been a subject of serio-comic treatment with Stella.

'I hope Stella won't alter much,' returned Alice, who was embroidering a chair-back* for her own future home. 'I began to think she never would accept Ted——'

'I think she is a very lucky girl, if you ask me. Ritchie simply worships the ground she treads on. And she must be fond of him, though she so long kept up that indifferent way. Why, these last few days at home she spends most of the time with him on horseback.'

Now the last few days had passed, and to-morrow was the wedding-day. Stella sat in the little library on a footstool at her mother's feet. Both windows were open; through one Banksia roses were drooping in heavy cream-coloured clusters; through the other a microphylla rosebush peeped, with its thick foliage of small green leaves, long-spiked buds unclosing, and roses fully blown with deep-pink hearts, and outer petals deadly pale. The sun was setting in golden splendour, and all the atmosphere was warm and rosy; the lovely Adelaide Hills had caught the glow all along their crests with magical effect. The pigeons were flying to their cotes in scores, and the soft beating of their wings in the garden clove the air like silken banners.

'There is one thing that troubles me a little, darling,' the mother said, in her tender voice, with its soft Celtic intonations; 'I thought on your wedding-day you would communicate.* It would be possible to do that with our old friend the Archdeacon, though you have not been confirmed.* I should like you to enter on your new life by drawing near the visible Church.'*

'Mother, I cannot,' answered the girl, with averted face, as she held her mother's hand in both hers.

'Well, my child, you are in God's hands. I do not fear but you will yet find Him who is the soul's most precious possession. In our span of life the rose is ever neighbour with the thorn—the web woven with threads not all of our choosing. And yet God grants us to reap our hundredfold even in this life. In marriage itself, when two hearts and souls cleave together, what deep and sacred happiness has He not granted to us!'

A burning flame of colour rose and spread over the girl's face. How unjustifiable did her marriage appear to her in the white light of her mother's life—one consecrated throughout with fidelity to the higher ideals that sway human conduct.

But she sternly kept the feeling in check. She reflected that for the majority of human beings the best possibilities of life never blossom into fruit. Her marriage had no element of ideal perfection; it belonged merely to the common ruck of such arrangements. And, on the whole, it was the best scheme of existence open to both. 'Ted loves me,' she thought; 'and if I can never love him in the same way, I can at least tolerate him, and be faithful to him even in thought. It was never possible for the women of our race to be otherwise. . . . And then I am safe from the slow canker of disillusionment. Perhaps, in the years to come, I may find it possible to think of—of the spring days at Lullaboolagana as a beautiful dream happily secured from the corrosion of actual life.'

There was a burning flush on her cheeks and a hard brilliancy in her eyes, as she raised her head and put her arms round her mother's neck.

'My darling, wherever you may be, morning and night join your thoughts with mine in prayer,' said her mother. 'And when moments of perplexity come to you, never forget the words, "In your patience ye shall win your souls." '*

'In your patience'—the words haunted her strangely in the silent watches of the night.* Patience, the great keynote of Nature: of God, so far as we can apprehend Him; of man, so far as he can rise to accomplish aught that is to nourish or deliver his kind. That old Gospel of the discipline of sorrow and pain, how fiercely she had come to spurn it, to turn from it as the rock on which human lives were ineffectually offered up! A very Moloch* that demanded all, and gave in return a grave and pale glimmering of a future life so far removed from earth and sense that its possession was a very doubtful gain. And yet—and yet—patience and sorrow, what nobility has man attained without these? what steadfast purpose has he achieved? Would the years here have been in truth so unbearable as she had pictured, surrounded with all the precious charities of serene home-life? At last, in utter impatience, she turned from all these doubts and questions as mere rags of rhetoric that hid from her the true bearings of what her life would become.

'It is because I am going to leave it all that there seems to be healing in the thought of resignation, and leisured quiet, and daily communion with Nature and great thoughts. There would be no end to these eventless days, and the prospect stretching out before me would have frozen me into one of those whimlings* to whom nothing is so real as the wan promises of joy that fade into nothing. It has always made me incredibly dreary when I have seen people stranded in some little inlet of existence; growing gray and faded in trying to persuade themselves that life is not without savour because once on a time they were going to be happy—they were going to hear music, but the harmony never began. With Ted I shall at least keep hold on some of the realities of life.'

She even laughed a little as she recalled the way in which Ted had attempted to reconcile her to the prospect of being so much in his society—reasoning on the subject in his eminently practical, direct way as they rode that morning beyond Coromandel Valley. She had lingered, looking at the views so familiar and well-loved from childhood. Wide fertile valleys irradiated with running water, dotted with prosperous homesteads, folded in by vines, and olives, and fig-trees, surrounded by fertile fields and orchards; sloping hillsides clothed with slender white-stemmed gum-trees; gullies masked with the unbroken shadow of tall, slim stringy bark trees, growing so thick together that one could scarcely walk between them. And then those first glimpses of the silver line of the sea on their return, sparkling in the distance through the quiet shadowy woods like the beginning of a fresh mysterious world. How often had the sight thrilled her with thoughts of the great old classic countries, famous in song and story, which lay far beyond those countless leagues of dividing water—countries whose history and stores of man's highest achievements make so strong a claim on spirits touched to sympathy with the wider issues of human life. All was now within her reach; but as she looked her farewells at these primeval woods, at the calm, beautiful, uncommemorated scenes of her native land, a great pain had fastened upon her heart—a pain, dull, deep, and insatiable, that made her pulses beat slowly, mechanically, as if it were sapping her life-blood.

'Don't look like that, Stella,' Ted had said, after a long silence. 'You will see these places all again as often as you like. We can spend part of each summer among the hills. Did you know my father is going to settle Wattle Cottage on you—that pretty little house on one of the spurs of Mount Lofty?'*

'Oh, mercy, Ted! is there no end to the possessions that are to be heaped on me? And then I must not even take the liberty of looking a little sad, because I am a glorified edition of Curly-locks!'

'Who was Curly-locks? But don't tell me if it's one of those wretched little yarns you make up, with some sort of a ghost in them.'

'No—there is never a ghost, or a banshee, or a lost soul in Curly-locks. It is quite after your own heart:

> '"Curly-locks, Curly-locks, wilt thou be mine?
> Thou shalt not wash dishes, nor yet feed the swine:
> But sit on a cushion and sew a fine seam,
> And feed upon strawberries, sugar and cream." '*

'But the girl after my heart is fonder of a saddle than a cushion. I was reading a novel the other night, Stella, and there was something in it about a strong bond of sympathy between the young man and woman who did most of the spooning.* I'm not sure I know exactly what the fellow meant, but don't you think it's a bond of sympathy between us two that we are both so fond of horses?'

Stella recalled all this, and some more seriously personal talk that followed. After all, she reflected, there could be no one else in the whole world she would marry without being in love with him, except Ted. In the midst of these thoughts she fell fast asleep. Alas! the mysterious phantasies of dreamland were not so reasonable and reassuring as her last waking thoughts. She dreamt one of those life-like, vivid, consecutive dreams with which she had become increasingly familiar of late. She was at Lullaboolagana, out in the Home Field, walking with Anselm Langdale. 'My beloved, there is no one between us—no one,' he was saying. 'To-morrow is our wedding-day. Come and get a wreath of the hymenosperum. That is what I want you to wear instead of orange-blossom.'

They went down beyond the Oolloolloo close to the orchard, and, lo! there was the hymenosperum sheeted with blossoms, and all around the air was rent with songs of birds, and the whole world was glad and surpassingly lovely—even like the holy city, the new Jerusalem, which John saw coming down from God out of heaven, prepared as a bride adorned for her husband.* How wide and full was the tide of joy that welled up in her heart! How starry and fragrant were the flowers they plucked together for her bridal wreath! The sun was warm in their faces, but they could not have too much of these slender, pale cream blossoms. She heard herself laughing happily; and then Anselm held her face to his, and kissed her repeatedly.

'My darling, I am so glad to hear you laugh so on your wedding morning.'

It was her mother who was kissing her softly.

'Oh, it is quite true, then; it is my wedding-day!' said the girl, starting up, her face dyed with happy blushes.

And then her mother kissed her once again, and gently left her, thanking God that her fears had been misplaced. For on the previous evening some curious misgiving had crept into her mind. But now she knew that all was well.

Ritchie had called a little after sunrise with a magnificent bridal bouquet, composed entirely of white fairy rosebuds shaded with maidenhair fern. The mother had taken it softly into her daughter's room. The windows looking eastward were wide open, and the blinds up, according to Stella's invariable custom. The sunrays were falling on her face, which was flushed and radiant like a child's. The mother's heart leaped with grateful joy; and when she heard Stella, still slumbering, break into a ripple of silvery laughter, she could not resist stooping to kiss her awake.

'Thank God my child is so happy!' she murmured gently, as she closed the door behind her.

CHAPTER XLIV

SUMMER threatened to set in early this season. On the fourteenth of October, two days before the Ritchies were to sail, a high easterly hot wind was blowing, and there was something of tropical ardour in the sun. It was exhaustingly unseasonable weather. At Monico Lodge the Venetian blinds of the veranda were closely drawn, and there was that hushed, darkened aspect throughout the house which almost cheats us into believing that without the sky is gray and cool.

'I do envy you, Stella—going straight into the middle of a northern winter,' said Laurette, fanning herself slowly with a wide fan of gray curled ostrich-feathers. She sat opposite to her sister-in-law in the drawing-room, and as she noticed the sharpened outline of her face, and the hectic flush that burned steadily in her cheeks, she was devoutly thankful that the newly-married pair would soon be afloat.

'She is quite capable of having a downright fever,' thought Laurette, 'but the sea-breezes will prevent all that.'

It was indeed curious to notice how the few weeks that had elapsed since Stella left Lullaboolagana had subtly changed the character and expression of her face. The cold look which sometimes marked it before when in repose had hardened into an air of listless hauteur. When she smiled, her eyes, instead of sparkling and gleaming with soft radiance, remained brilliantly hard and unmoved. We are at times almost appalled by the scornful disdain imprinted on women's countenances. Do not let us judge them harshly. Tolerance is not the prerogative of the weaker sex, but often their most savage bigotry of blame is directed against the *rôle* into which they have been cheated by circumstance and their own fatal impatience of suffering. It is not shallow and wilful disesteem of others that makes the hardest lines in their faces, when the tie which is the fount of all human tenderness proves to them an intolerable bond.

'If the summer is to go on from now till March, we certainly must take a little cottage at St Kilda or Brighton,'* Laurette went on, raising her voice a little, doubting whether Stella heard the first remark. Before she could make any response to this the door was hastily opened and Ted came in.

'Isn't Stella here?' he cried—not seeing her at first in the shadowy corner in which she sat with an open book, whose leaves she did not turn. 'Oh, there you are, Curly-locks! Why the deuce do you make the house like a cave, Larry?' he cried, turning to his sister.

'I'll go and amend my ways this instant,' said Laurette, gliding out of the room.

'You mustn't make the room any lighter,' said Stella in a languid voice.

'Why, I thought you were so fond of light and heat. I've often found you in blazing December weather out in the Fairacre garden sitting in the shade without even a hat on. But I'm only too glad, Curly-locks, to hear you wish for anything; besides, I'm going away for the rest of the day, if you can spare me.'

'Oh yes. Where are you going?'

'To Randwick* with two or three other fellows. And do you know, Stella, I'm going to sell Konrad and four or five more colts. I expect John Morton will be here before I get back. Now, before I go would you mind telling me your new name? No larks, Stella. Say your proper go-ashore, newspaper name.'

'Ted, don't be tiresome; and try not to look so complacently, abominably glad. It makes my eyes ache. Most people never look so silly as when they are pleased.'

Ted laughed in an exultant way.

'By George! I hope I'll always look silly in that way. Do you know, Stella, you haven't asked me to do a single thing for you since we were married yesterday.'

'Yesterday! Three hundred and fifty-six years ago! What frightful lies people tell about life being so short.'

'Well, now that I think of it, it is a week and a day. But in sober earnest, Stella, do tell me one little morsel I can do for you. I'm aching all over to do something you would like. Now, didn't I tell you that was for good-luck?' he said, touching the pearl-brooch at her throat.

'Send me back, with Dustiefoot and Maisie, to Strathhaye till you return.'

'And me go to foreign countries without you? I meant something that I could do, Stella. But of course you are joking—you sly little Curly-locks! Do you know what you said in your sleep last night?'

Ted's face was wreathed with smiles; but though the flush on her cheeks did not die away, a certain pallor deepened about Stella's mouth and eyes.

'Did I speak in my sleep? I don't think I used to. What a dangerous accomplishment to evolve!'

'Dangerous? I think it is very jolly, when you are so proud, turning your cheek to me when I want to kiss you. But, you see, I don't mind when you give yourself away in your dreams, calling me by such fond names!'

'You are making that up as you go along, Ted,' she said, with lowered eyes.

'Upon my soul, I am not. You moaned a little. I thought you were having a bad dream, and I stroked your cheek; and then you sighed and said—I heard it quite distinctly—"Dear little leaf of my heart!" Now, you know, you never said anything half as pretty as that to me awake. There, don't go so scarlet! I won't bring it up against you, if you put your two arms around me and say, "I want you not to stay too long away, Ted," and open that little parcel when you are tired of reading.'

Reading! What book has ever been written that can enchain the mind when the heart is throbbing with feverish despair—when the face is blistered with a sense of scorching shame? Yes, she had put up her hands and whispered the words after him in the quiet darkened room; and even in the act it rose up before her like one of the scenes in the 'Inferno' which stamp themselves on the mind of those who are intimate with Dante's 'Divine' poem, like lurid pictures that have been absolutely witnessed. She seemed to see herself among those who smote 'their hands despairingly above their heads, borne along in ceaseless tumult in the atmosphere eternally darkened as with sand driven by the whirlwind.'* A sudden catch came in her breath. She unfastened a slender ribbon that was fastened low on her neck, and drew out the ring that she had daily worn against her heart since the evening she had parted from Langdale. She kissed it as a mother kisses the face of her dead child! 'No, no, no!—I must not wear it,' she moaned; 'I must drive all this away from me. Sleeping and waking I become more enslaved with these memories. I thought to drive them from me by brute strength—to put a barrier between them and my heart; and in place of that they overwhelm me in my sleep—they come back as to a chamber swept and garnished.* And now I learn to juggle and deceive. O God, God!—save me from the leprosy of falsehood to which I have been betrayed!'

Yes, it was true. She had fought down soul and instinct and memory with ruthless violence; but Nature is not to be lightly trifled with. She has strange Nemesis* powers which find their own modes of reprisal. What the girl in her ignorance had dreamt would turn her love and fierce jealousy into a forsworn, perjured and impossible passion had but opened its floodgates. The moment sleep came to her the uncontrolled visions of unconsciousness, the mysterious play of the brain which lies awake and remembers, and keeps time to the beating of the heart, and calls up all the masking simulacrum of life apart from our volition, practised the cruellest treacheries upon her. Forces which had hitherto lain dormant in her nature pulsed into being only to reinforce her forbidden love.

The thought of Ted's untroubled confidence smote on her conscience with intolerable pain. She saw, as with a lightning-flash of insight, all the falsity and degradation of her position. She would tell him all—she must; he was good and generous to her, he would have patience with her, he would give her time to live down the past. . . . This double, treacherous existence was impossible. It would be terrible to speak to him of Langdale—but she would make him understand. He had implored her to let him do something for her, and he would not go back from this wish when he knew all. She would make her confession, and appeal to him. . . . Something of relief came gradually with the thought. The adamant reserve with which she had guarded this terrible crisis of her life had been part of her crushing burden. Yes, Ted would forgive her; and when the keenness of anguish and memory had passed away, she would be a true and loyal wife to him. She might still prove in a faltering, imperfect way, that love and a noble life are one. . . . There was a white gauze scarf looped and interwoven in front of the pale cashmere morning dress she wore. She detached this scarf, and taking the ring with the narrow white ribbon to which it was fastened, she enveloped it, fold upon fold. 'I will not look at it again for long years.' A sudden thought came to her that she would think of Langdale as dead—dead and taken from her for evermore. 'Oh, my love! my love! my love!' she cried, putting down her head, and suddenly her tears fell like summer rain.

She was weeping for the dead. Yes, he was really dead to her—the lover from whom she had parted on that serene night when heaven was flooded as with the twilight of dawn, and the soft mystic glow crept in through the interlaced foliage which hung round the veranda of that quiet house near the borders of the Peeloo Plain. Never again would they stand hand-in-hand looking with radiant faces to the years that were to be all their own. It was a crime to love him; but she might weep for him. She would tame this wild passion which came stealthily back in the visions of the night, when reason was drugged with the poppies of sleep, and conscience had relaxed its vigilance. Day by day she would think of silent graves, and of departed ones who return no more. Her whole frame was convulsed with a storm of sobs. She gave herself up to her long pent-up grief, till its very intensity brought some ray of consolation. She had been so hard, and bitter, and scornful—but she must weep for her dead; she must try and creep back to God, whom she had disbelieved and forgotten. He had wounded her so incurably; it must be that He knew of her poor, maimed, anguish-stricken existence. . . . Let the bells toll, and dust be given back to dust, and let her bow her head and her heart in submissive prayer. Even if God does not care for us, we must still stumble back to Him when the billows of dark despair dash against the frail skiff in which we are launched on the wild, uncertain sea of life. She had joined the sorrow-smitten throng—the great army of earth's bereaved ones. The inextinguishable craving of the heart for communion in prayer overcame her. Crouching low, with folded hands and tear-stained face, the words rose to her lips, joining her petitions with those others, beaten and chastised as she was:

'Our Father who art in heaven, forgive the days of utter rebellion and agony and despair. Forgive the storms of unlighted darkness that toss our souls; those for whom we poor stricken ones mourn are in Thy keeping—safe from the world's slow stain, from the infirmities of old age, from the bitterness of disillusion, from the subtle decay of enthusiasm for all that is good and great. They have reached a continuing city; they are bathed in the light of everlasting life. The currents of time and change, the distraction and vainglory and delusion of the world—these touch them no more forever.

'Our Father, we would that Thy will were ours. . . . We would fain lift up our eyes to Thee, but they are blinded with tears. Yet let us come to Thee, Infinite Source of all good, though our only offering is that of a bruised and broken and sinful heart. The pangs of loneliness and isolation; the rapturous dream of happiness changed into a sword within the bosom; the desolation of days emptied of joy—these are the poor oblations that we bring. Yet may they become to us an inspiration and a stay. When the cruel waves of anguish overcome us; when despair, like an angry sea, threatens to engulf us; when the heavens are dark and starless; when the earth seems empty of all that makes it endurable; when it seems given over to the hopeless mediocrity of natures mildewed with commonness in aim, intention, and achievement; when our days stretch before us blank and purposeless, spent and disconnected, unmeaning and futile as grains of quicksand that a great storm has borne far inland; when hope is dead and faith far off, and fears troop round us like a horde of plotting rebels, saying: There is no God—no soul—no immortality; when the mind is flooded with unbearable recollections of lost joy; when we are listless and indifferent, and overcome with fruitless grief—then, O Kindly Light! let thoughts of Thee and of the great souls whom Thou hast vivified enlarge our natures and illuminate our minds.'

Her sobs died into silence, the bitterness of her grief was spent. The door was opened, but she could only half raise her head, and Tareling, who caught one swift glimpse of her—her face pallid, grief-stricken, and tear-stained—as she crouched in silence like some dumb creature mortally wounded, retreated noiselessly with a startled, almost horrified look. He was in search of Laurette, to make some arrangements for the evening, before he went to his office. He met her in the hall.

'What is the matter with Stella?' he asked quickly, looking at his wife with an indefinable suspicion in his eyes.

'The matter with Stella?' she echoed, with a little, quick throb of terror, which she kept well in hand, however, 'Nothing that I know of—except that she has too many diamond sprays and necklaces and precious stones, and a husband who adores her.'

'Well, I don't know, but I wouldn't mind laying a thousand to one that there was some sort of deception at the root of this marriage. It's not a month since she came here from Lullaboolagana looking like a rose in June.'

'In December you mean, dear. Our roses are very shabby in June; and I am sure Stella will never be in that condition. Oh, about the theatre. You had better book three seats in the dress-circle for us two and John Morton. Stella won't come, and of course Ted will not either. Have you been speaking to her—just now, I mean?'

'No; I should say she is hardly fit to speak to anyone—excess of joy in the possession of Ted and so many diamonds, I suppose.'

Laurette felt anxious, but she avoided the drawing-room for another hour. When she went in she found Stella looking very pale and exhausted, but composed. She had raised one of the blinds, and sat embroidering near the bay-window. There was something in the expression of her face that touched Laurette with a sudden, sharp thrill of compassion. It was no longer hard and listless; all the cold scorn had gone out of it; and in place of these there was an inde-scribable wistful sadness—her eyelids were dark and slightly swollen, and when she looked up one saw that her beautiful radiant eyes had grown heavy and dim. But the only moral and politic course when a bride looks like this is to say nothing.

'Oh, what have we here?' said Laurette, in a half-playful way, holding up the little parcel Ted had left. 'Now, if you are not dying to see this, I am; and may I, therefore, open it for you?' she contin-ued. Stella at once assented. It was a case containing an exquisitely-wrought bracelet, set with extraordinarily large opals—one that Stella happened to notice in a jeweller's window when she accom-panied Ted into Collins Street after reaching Melbourne on the previous afternoon.

'They are really too lovely,' said Laurette, holding them up so that they caught the light and threw it back in a sheaf of quivering rainbow-rays, but with an eerie flame not to be found in a rainbow.

'I shall be afraid to admire anything after this, except the sun and trees,' said Stella, with a tremulous little smile. 'It is so kind of Ted!'—there was a little quiver in her voice, and Laurette suddenly rose and kissed her sister-in-law.

'You are not well, Stella; the weather is so atrocious; do lie down and let me bathe your head.'

But Stella, thanking her, declared there was not much amiss. She would have been glad to lie down, but she felt a stupor of moral and physical exhaustion creeping over her, and feared to give way to it—feared that the purpose she had formed of making a full confession to her husband might slip from her when he returned if she did not resist this benumbing lassitude.

In the afternoon there were callers, and Stella went to her own room to write letters home. The effort seemed to use up all her energies. But she dressed and sat at dinner with the rest, though eating was a mere farce with her. She talked for some little time with Mr Morton—a tall, burly man, with dark curly hair and a sun-bronzed face, but with a voice and manners as gentle as a woman's. She wondered a little that Ted did not come; but when Laurette wished to stay at home with her, and forego the theatre, Stella insisted on being left alone.

'It will not be long before Ted comes,' she said. 'I will rest till then.'

Laurette made her lie down on the sofa in the drawing-room before she went away. But soon after being left alone Stella went into the breakfast-room, which was beyond the dining-room, and communicated with it by folding doors.

Here she was in darkness, except for the light that came in from the dining-room. The gas seemed to beat upon her tired eyes with such wearying brilliance she found the change to the unlighted room very grateful. She opened the window of this little room, and lay opposite to it on the couch, looking out at the starlit sky. At every sound she heard her heart seemed to beat in her ears. The moment Ted came in she must tell him—she must not give herself time to reflect and draw back. She knew it would hurt him, as well as herself, horribly; and yet she had confidence in him that he would not be harsh or ungenerous. He would help her—he would understand. Already, with all her agitation, she felt something of the relief of being freed from the concealment which his own loyalty made all the more intolerable.

Gradually her thoughts became confused—the light of the stars was dimmed with the pale glory of a young moon; the wind, which had been high all day, still rose into fitful gusts, swaying the scanty branches of a Judas-tree that grew near the window hither and thither. She was out in the Fairacre garden—and yet she was looking into Laurette's house, and she saw a form she knew well approaching it. She heard him asking for her, and then gradually all floated from her view. Then there came a troubled dream in which she heard heavy, uncertain footsteps—they sounded near her, and yet they were not mixed up with any story. She was conscious of the thought that these stumbling sounds were real, not part of a dream—and yet she did not wake up.

She had no conception how long she had slept when she became conscious of a low murmur of voices. No, it was not a dream. The moonlight had faded, for the moon was setting. She rose slowly—her temples were throbbing. One leaf of the double folding-doors between the little apartment and the dining-room was half ajar. The murmur of voices resolved itself into words. It was Laurette who spoke.

'Stella is in her own room; she must not know.'

'What has happened?' cried Stella, gliding quickly into the dining-room.

Laurette, in a dark-crimson low-necked silk, as she had returned from the theatre, was standing by the table in the centre of the room. Tareling and Morton were near her, but Ted was not there. The quick look of consternation on all three faces as she entered gave Stella a sickening sensation of fear.

Then, before any could speak, she saw why they looked so strangely. One lay on the couch at the further end of the room breathing heavily, but pale and still. It was Ted; and with a low cry Stella knelt down by him.

'Oh, Ted, Ted, you are hurt!—you do not hear me!' She held his hands—they were cold, and his eyes were not quite closed; but there was no sign of awakening. 'My God, what has happened? He is unconscious!' she cried.

The men looked at her in a strange way, but did not answer.

'No, dear, he is not badly hurt,' said Laurette. She was very white, and her hands trembled as she tried to raise Stella.

'How has he been hurt? You must tell me!' she cried, turning to Tareling and Morton.

Laurette made despairing gestures to them as she stood behind Stella that they should leave the room. But they were so confused that they did not perceive this, or, if they did, failed to understand the drift of Laurette's motions.

'It is not dangerous, Stella,' said Tareling in a low voice, taking her hand in both his.

'Did the doctor say so?' cried Stella. 'Has he gone away? I must see him for myself. Has he been long unconscious?'

'No—not very,' said Laurette.

'But what did the doctor say? What caused this?'

'Stella, it is not dangerous. You may believe Talbot—he knows,' said Laurette desperately. If only these stupid men were out of the way, she felt sure she could invent an illness, or at any rate make up a fictitious account of the doctor's opinion.

'Not dangerous!—to lie like this!' She knelt down again, and held Ted's hands, and whispered his name softly two or three times; but there was not a tremor of consciousness.

The perspiration stood on John Morton's forehead in great drops.

'My dear young lady——' he said, placing his hand kindly on Stella's shoulder. But then utterance failed him.

'Ah, you are deceiving me, you are—I can see it—you look at each other so strangely! Talbot,' she said, going up to her brother-in-law, 'you must tell me the whole truth. It is no use keeping it from me. Tell me what the doctor said?'

'The doctor——' began Tareling. 'The fact is, Stella, we—there is—in an attack like this—well, medical attendance is not usual; we—most men know what ought to be done; it is—er—a form of exhaustion.'

A conviction had seized Stella that Ted must have been dangerously hurt, and that all these blundering equivocations were well-merited efforts to break the news gently to her.

'Do you mean that you have not called in a doctor at all?' she said, looking from Morton to Tareling, and back again at Morton.

He, poor man! could do nothing but wipe his face, and crush his handkerchief into a minute compass.

'Stella dear, you may believe Talbot,' said Laurette once more. 'Everything has been done that is necessary. Ted will be all right when he wakes up a few hours later.'

'Wakes up?' repeated Stella, looking at the group around her with a sharp thrill of ill-defined terror. She saw that Morton was somehow the one most keenly affected. Laurette tried to cajole her. Talbot was infinitely gentle in his manner, yet confused as she had never seen him before; but John Morton's face was a picture of distress and yearning pity.

Going up to him, Stella laid her hand on his arm, and said in a firm voice:

'Mr Morton, I insist upon knowing the truth. There is something you keep back from me. Tell me in one word, is Ted badly hurt? if not, what ails him? You know; I am sure you do.'

'He is not badly hurt; in one way, this is not serious.'

'In one way,' she gasped, with parching lips—'in what way is such protracted unconsciousness not serious?'

Morton had for some years worked a pearling boat off the unknown northern coasts of Western Australia, and had been a spectator and an actor in many wild scenes; but never had he known so acutely miserable a quarter of an hour as the present.

'Well,' he said slowly, thus driven to bay, 'perhaps it is serious in every way, only not as you think. You know the day has been very warm.'

'And the sun,' put in Laurette, 'often affects people without a regular sunstroke.'

But Stella did not even notice her. A glimmering suspicion had dawned on her. Talbot glided out of the room.

'Tell me the truth,' said Stella in a husky voice, still keeping her hand on Morton's arm.

'I thought you knew something of this weakness of Ted's; that he sometimes—not often—forgets himself; takes a little more stimulant than is good for him.'

A low moaning cry escaped from Stella; and she trembled convulsively as if in an ague-fit. They tried to draw her away, but she would not go. She stood as if spell-bound, white and horror-stricken, looking at Ted's insensible form and ghastly unmeaning face.

CHAPTER XLV

STELLA could never recall how the rest of the night passed. She had vague recollections of sitting as if turned to stone, of hearing voices, of speaking herself now and then, of pacing at intervals up and down the room like some creature of the woods that had been suddenly trapped. But look what way she would, Ted's vacant face met her eyes. She could hardly be said to suffer acutely. She was rather in a waking trance, in which the events of the past month rose up before her like a curious panorama, of which she was merely a spectator. Once or twice she found herself planning a secret journey—slipping away into unknown haunts of the desert where she might escape from these endless stratagems that fate was practising upon her. But no coherent plan underlay these vague flights. They belonged rather to those imaginative variations which we sometimes make in a story that is distasteful.

At daybreak Ritchie showed signs of returning consciousness. Not till then could Stella be prevailed on to leave the room. Laurette pleaded with her to lie down and rest, but in vain.

'No one knows of this but ourselves,' she said. 'When we got home from the theatre we found Ted rather confused. He had taken a little raw brandy to steady his nerves, and that, of course, was a fatal mistake. It was an unseasonably hot day, and no doubt he had taken some "long drinks" previously.'

Stella looked at her strangely, but said not a word in reply. She bathed and changed her dress, and went out into the little garden at Monico Lodge and looked at the sun rising with eyes that saw nothing. Her emotion and resolutions of the previous day rose up before her in so mocking and sardonic a light.

After a little time she was joined by John Morton. He, too, had slept but little.

'Stella, will you let me speak to you as if you were a sister?' he said, taking her hand in his. 'You must not think that this is habitual with Ted. It is only a couple of years since he began to forget himself now and then—when he is mixed up with these fast turf people. I asked him a few weeks before he was married whether you knew of this—tendency. He said Laurette told him you had heard something. This is the first time such a thing has happened since he was in the Retreat.'

'The Retreat? What Retreat?'

'You remember, when Ted was at home about Christmas-time, you went to a dinner-party at his father's house?'

'Ah, I remember!' cried Stella, and all the details of that event, and Ted's altered demeanour when he came to bid her farewell, rushed back on her mind.

'Yes; he told me all about it. There is a private Retreat in the western district of Victoria, and Ted, in his disgust at finding that even the prospect of meeting you did not serve to keep him straight, went there for nearly six months. It is only when he is with others—never when he is alone—and a little tells on him. I am certain he will keep straight after this. I know it must vex you terribly; but, Stella, you must not be too angry. Ted sent me to ask you to see him. He is more unhappy than words can tell.'

Stella went slowly into the house. Laurette met her in the hall, and led her into the breakfast-room, where Ted stood pallid and miserable, leaning against the mantelpiece. Laurette would have left them, but Stella called her back. There was something so cold and unmoved in her face and voice that Ted's heart sank, if possible, more than before; but his range of expression was limited.

'I know I have been a thundering jackass, Stella,' he said in a husky voice. 'I don't know how to ask you to forgive me.'

'Do you suppose I do not?' she said in a level voice.

'Don't say you forgive me when you look like that, Stella,' said Ted. 'I know you have a right to be angry.'

'But I am not, any more than if you had small-pox or typhoid—only if it were a merely physical malady you would soon recover. But what hope is there for a vice that wrecks the will so completely—a vice that overcomes a man till he lies sunk below the level of the brutes?'

The words were harsh, yet what added curiously to their force was the quiet, passionless tone in which they were uttered, and the involuntary shudder which shook Stella from head to foot as she spoke.

Ritchie flushed crimson, and for a little he did not speak.

'Do you mean,' he said at last very slowly, 'that I am not to be blamed for this? Because, if you do, you are very much mistaken. I am to blame most damnably, and I have been worse than an idiot; and I say this—if it ever happens again——'

'Why did you say I knew something of this?' said Stella, suddenly turning to Laurette without making any reply to her husband's affirmations.

'Well, I made sure you did by your manner, and that long talk we had before you went to Lull,' said Laurette composedly, meeting her brother's doubting scrutiny without flinching.

Stella put up her hands to her temples, struggling to recollect what the long talk was. And then Laurette, marshalling her forces, went on with calm incisiveness:

'You have seen very little of the world yet, Stella. You have been dreaming over romances, and poetry, and foolish scientific books, and they make you feel as if you knew a great deal. You have several brothers, and are intimate with a good many of their friends. You never saw any of them the worse for drink, so you conclude they never in their lives fell fast asleep with their riding-boots on. That is a little discovery which is generally reserved for the sacred privacy of married life. Take my word for it, there are very few families without one or more in the same boat with Ted. Only, unfortunately, many have no power of pulling themselves up as he has. Now, Stella, let me advise you to rest for some hours. You know this is your last day before sailing——'

Stella, who stood gazing out of the window most of the time while Laurette spoke, upon this turned, and looking at Ted without any trace of emotion in her voice, said slowly:

'It is impossible that I should live with you as your wife. Nothing can alter my determination in that;' and before Ted could say anything in reply she left the room.

He stood for a minute or two as if stunned, and then walked in an aimless way to the window, without saying a word. But after a little he was seized with a fit of dizziness, and sank half fainting on a chair that stood near. Laurette insisted upon his going to bed, and installed herself as his nurse.

This proved to be an eventful day in Laurette's life. The English mail, which arrived that morning by the express train from Adelaide, brought, among other letters, one from his father to Tareling, with the announcement that his eldest brother Cecil had suddenly been stricken down with a stroke of paralysis, and that the physicians held out no hope of his ultimate recovery, though there was no immediate prospect of death. Lord Harewood had been ten years married, and his family consisted of two daughters, the youngest seven years of age. The Earl of Lillimore was seventy-six, and frail for his years, and Talbot was the second son.

In the first moments after receiving this intelligence, Laurette was conscious only of a great and solemn thankfulness. Only for her undaunted efforts, Talbot, who might after this at any moment be called in the kind ordinance of Providence to take his place among the peers of Great Britain, would now be ploughing the main in the society of a disreputable actress! The next moment she was more than ever alive to the necessity of taking instant action, lest Stella should, in her unreasonable caprice, decide not to go abroad. In another fortnight at the most there would be a letter from Langdale, posted at Mauritius. If Stella remained in Australia, Laurette could do nothing to prevent her receiving this or any subsequent letter. Whereas, in her absence, she—Laurette—would speedily write a note to Mrs Courtland, asking that any letters which came from abroad might be forwarded to her—Laurette—in obedience to Stella's wish. She knew the scrupulous way in which the Courtlands would fall in with an arrangement of this kind, without comment or inquiry.

Something would no doubt turn up some day which would make Stella think that there had been some 'extraordinary misunder-standings'—but then at that time Laurette might be safely estab-lished among the hereditary aristocracy of Europe! her husband an earl—her little son a lord! At the thought Laurette could not forbear going into the nursery and clasping the future Lord Harewood fondly to her bosom. . . . Yes, there were occasions in life on which one must act for the present, and not for eternity, or even the remote future. Who was it that advised people to take short views in life?* The counsel was sagacious enough for Solomon himself; for, after all, no people were more egregiously sacrificed at times than those who trusted nothing to the chapter of accidents.

Laurette stole softly into the darkened room in which Ted lay. He looked up eagerly, thinking it might be Stella. At sight of Laurette he closed his eyes in dejected weariness.

'Ted, you must arrange that your voyage is not postponed,' she said, sitting by his bedside.

'I don't see the good of arranging anything, if Stella sticks to what she says, and I believe she will.'

'Fiddlesticks! No doubt she will for a time, but she has a strong sense of humour, and she will soon perceive what a ridiculous atti-tude she takes up. But, at the same time, it becomes you to make con-cessions, and I will be your envoy.'

'What do you mean by concessions?'

'Give in to her whim till you can get her to relent. She cannot cease to be Mrs Edward Ritchie because sometimes you are not as steady as you should be; but if she is wilful, there may be no end of scandal and annoyance and trouble that will only widen the breach. Ask her to start to-morrow with you as arranged, on her own conditions; or I will speak for you, and then bring her in here to clinch the arrangement.'

Laurette found Stella in her own room. She was still curiously unmoved. Laurette told a melting tale of Ted's utter unhappiness and remorse. No, Stella was not angry nor unforgiving; but she could not alter her decision. Did she, then, propose to separate from Ted? She did not know, it was all so dark and horrible. She could not see her way. She must send for Cuthbert; perhaps he would help her to think what was right. She knew there was one crime she must not commit. The story of her friend Cicely's life rose up before her, and she, for the first time since this disastrous revelation burst on her, shed a few scalding, humiliated tears.

'What crime do you mean?' said Laurette in a whisper.

'The crime of adding to the morally-paralyzed lives in the world,' said Stella, in a dry, stern voice.

'What a dreadful idea to take up!' said Laurette indignantly. 'Why, Talbot drinks three times as hard as Ted ever did, and I am sure neither Gwendolen nor Howard is ever likely to be paralyzed. And there's my father—he has drunk pretty heavily at times for the last twenty-six years, and who is more respected than he is—Speaker of the House for so long, and knighted, and all the rest of it?'

Though Laurette was oblivious of that elementary canon of heredity that the further back a quality has been fixed the more likely it is to reappear, her sharp eyes saw that her illustration conveyed no comfort.

'Of course,' she said, going on in an altered tone, 'if you want to send Ted completely to the dogs, you will turn your back on him now. You ought, by rights, to have married him four years ago——'

'I ought to have been told of Ted's vice—and you seem to have prevented his telling me the truth,' said Stella, in a low, hard voice.

'Well, I may have been to blame. You do not know what it is to have an only brother. You may be thankful you were never tempted in the same way. Not many of us fall into temptations that do not beset us. If there were a sort of Greek chorus going on always to warn women off all the possible shoals of matrimony, the world would soon come to a nice pass. You all blame me. It is quite plain that in this matter I am the earthenware pot going down the stream with copper kettles.* But if it was all to come over again I couldn't act differently. Here was Ted hanging after you ever since he was a little shrimp in his first knickerbockers; never thought of any other girl in his life—at least, not to marry her. Uncle was a pig-headed old man, who insisted on Ted leaving college when he was sixteen, because he said a squatter would never want more than to write and see that a book-keeper could add up properly. And then, before he was twenty, Ted is left his own master, with thirteen thousand a year; and since that he has raised the annual income of the station to fifteen thousand. It's ridiculous to speak as if he were a slave to drink, or anything like it. It's only when he goes with that Eversley and Wilmot lot—and now he's got you he'll see precious little of them.'

Laurette spoke in a clear, emphatic voice, and she could see that some of her arguments went home, though Stella made no response. The thought of her sending for Cuthbert had terror in it, if only for the reason that such a course would prevent the pair from leaving by the *Hindoo Fawn*; and if any delay arose, with so many awkward contingencies in the background, no one could tell what might happen.

'Come, Stella, you must forgive Ted. Oh, I know—but what's the good of that sort of forgiveness: "I don't want you to be hanged or quartered—but good-bye"? That won't do, my dear. I am a wife and mother, and my experience of life is much more matured than yours. Take my word for it, forgiveness is the quality that best suits us women—even when we are most sinned against. It does not become us to be too logical, or look too far ahead. It was not for nothing that God made our brains smaller than those of men. Where would I be to-day, and my two little ones, if I had not swallowed a great deal more than ever you will have to overlook?'

'Laurette, I have no doubt you mean very well,' said Stella wearily. 'I do not want to make a public scandal, but——'

'Sail to-morrow as was arranged, Stella, and make your own conditions, till you are satisfied that the episode of yesterday was an accident which won't happen again. Now, be reasonable, and tell me what other plan could Cuthbert, or even an angel from heaven, suggest better than this? What sacredness would the marriage service have if men and women tried to throw the contract over at the first shock? Come on, Stella, and speak to Ted.'

When Stella went into her husband's room, the sight of his haggard face, with its broken, appealing look, smote on her heart.

'Stella, forgive me,' he said, speaking very low, lest he should betray emotion.

'I do,' she said, with bent head. 'I do forgive you, Ted.'

'And, Stella, don't say you don't blame me any more than if I had small-pox. I would sooner, somehow, you thought I was as black as the devil himself, than believe I couldn't help being such an infernal idiot.'

'But, Ted, you know how, less than a year ago, when you were to meet me at your father's, the same thing happened, and now—do I not know that you would not willingly give me pain, that——'

'Thank you for saying that, Stella. May I hold your hand? I know all that—and yet this time it's partly, I know, because I got into my head you knew, and didn't mind so very much. Larry made some mistake, and she thought you knew. And then, you know, I wanted to tell you when I said I wasn't what I ought to be—and you said rather queer things. Of course it was because you didn't really know. I never was so ashamed of myself in my life before, and I'll do whatever you want me to.'

'Oh, Ted, it is all too miserable; it seems as if the things that are worst in life pursued us and hounded us down so that we cannot escape them—so that we cannot help ourselves.'

A scalding tear rolled down Stella's cheek and fell on Ted's hand. Then, so extreme was his misery and remorse, for the first time in his life he moaned aloud.

The thought crossed Stella's mind that she would tell him all she meant to say on the previous night. But the sight of his motionless form and ghastly vacant face, as he lay submerged far below the unconsciousness of brute life, rose before her with cruel vividness. And then she knew that she dared not breathe a word to him of her irremediable bereavement. It would be sacrilege—stealing the oil for common purposes from the lamp that burned in commemoration of her dead.

But a hard unsympathetic antagonism was impossible to her. She was too keenly alive to the tragic element in human affairs—to the multiform aspects in which circumstance, destiny, chance, heredity—call it what we may—so often wove the pattern of our lives with cynical disregard of the designs that make for their salvation and happiness.

As Ted looked at her with dim, appealing eyes, she was sorry for him beyond the reach of words. Yet she was inflexible in the resolve that till the memory of the past had grown more dim, and till the ascendancy of his fatal weakness was disproved, their lives must virtually be lived apart.

'But we can help ourselves—we can yet make it all right, Stella,' he said in answer to her words. 'Only let me be near you—let me be with you—let me look at you day by day—let me do things for you!

. . . It was on the twenty-sixth of last December that I forgot myself before. If on this day twelve months I can tell you honestly that during all that time I have not made such a horrible blunder, will you believe that I can help making a fool of myself, and live with me as my wife? Will you, Stella?'

She made answer that she would, and then he clasped both her hands in a fervent grasp.

'We will travel during that year, Stella,' he went on; and Laurette re-entered the room as he spoke. 'We will sail to-morrow, as we meant to.'

Laurette's face was a little flushed. Her heart rose with a bound.

'You have given your promise, Ted, and I am sure you will keep to it. I will read a verse or two to make you remember it better.'

Laurette, who had the dramatic faculty in some respects to a remarkable degree, caught up a New Testament that lay on the toilet-table, knelt down by the bedside, and, opening the book at random, read the first verses on which her eyes fell:

'"And the lord commended the unjust steward, forasmuch as he had done wisely; for the children of this world are wiser in their generation than the children of light. And I say to you, Make unto you friends of the mammon of iniquity, that when you shall fail they may receive you into everlasting dwellings."'*

Laurette rose from her knees and put away the Testament, feeling for her own part deeply encouraged and reassured. She had heard something of the practice of reading a verse or verses where the Bible happened to open, and her present experience gave her the belief that there was something in it. As far as she had known anything of the sect of the children of light, they were often, in practical matters, conies of the rocks;* and she was well content to be of those who made friends of the mammon of iniquity, which seemed to be a sort of Biblical nickname for worldly prudence.

As for Stella, the feeling overcame her more strongly than ever that she was looking on at dioramic views in a troubled dream, or that she was a supernumerary in a serio-comic opera in which people spoke prose instead of intoning doggerel rhymes. Moral and physical exhaustion was creeping over her, for the time sealing up the sources of emotion. Yet she found herself half smiling as Laurette rose from her knees.

'Stella, promise me that you will rest,' whispered Ted, looking at her worn white face with keen self-reproach. Then he raised her hand to his lips, murmuring his promises anew before Stella left the room. 'What the devil made you read the Scriptures in broad daylight on a Thursday, Larry?' he said when they were alone.

'That's just like you, Ted; you have no imagination,' retorted Laurette. 'You know how they read the Bible at Fairacre night and day; Stella would feel your promise was more solemn—though, of course, in a case of this kind, all is fair in love and war.'

'Don't you believe I am going to funk my promise to Stella,' returned Ted doggedly.

Then Laurette sat by his bedside, and told the wonderful news, which had by this time mounted to her head. A great success is never so intoxicating as when it fairly dawns on the horizon while consummation is yet delayed; for even to the earthliest nature fruition seldom fails to bring its leaden-faced twin-brother satiety.

'Well, Larry, you've kept Tareling in hand better than people expected,' said Ted. 'Those who knew him best said he would never stay in Australia more than a couple of years.'

This little speech opened Laurette's heart.

'My dear boy, no one knows what a struggle I've had to keep Talbot in the narrow path of duty,' she said solemnly. 'Quite recently he was on the point of going off with a wretched little divorced actress who danced and sang, as people used to say, like an angel— as if angels ever made such wicked eyes at the fathers of families!— when she sang,

> ' "Vieni, ben mio, tra queste piante ascose,
> Ti vo' la fronte incoronar di rose,"*

with such brazen archness. I have often thought, and I am sure of it, that in decent theatres, which, after all, owe much of their support to families, effrontery of that kind should be put down with a strong hand. But, however, there Talbot used to sit beside me, gloating on the little Jezebel*—his jewel-gifts shining in her impudent little head—at the very time I shouldn't have known where to turn for a crust, if it hadn't been for the generosity of my good dear old Ted here. You needn't turn rusty, Ted. You have too much of the John Bull* in you in that respect, always trying to hide your generosity under a rough outside. But I must finish about the actress. Yes, I knew everything was arranged; and the precious pair were to be off to

California in a few days. Of course I would not enter upon such particulars to anyone but my own brother; not but what it was one of the stories probably that men grinned over in the Club. Well, what did I do? Flew into a rage, and prepared to run away home on my own account, or melted perpetually into tears? Nothing of the kind. If I had packed up and gone off to Godolphin House, who would have been relieved and delighted? Why, Talbot, of course. And if, on the other hand, I had wept and implored, he wouldn't have come near the place at all. As it was, I never lost his confidence. I was gay and smiling, though my heart might have been in ruins. Suspecting nothing, never dreaming I had an inkling of what was going on, Talbot was so much off his guard that I gleaned all necessary information. I knew the boat, and the hour it was to sail. That morning I had a private interview with our largest creditor, a man to whom we owed five hundred pounds; and I said to him, "If you want to make sure of twenty shillings in the pound of this debt, just see that the Honourable Talbot Tareling doesn't leave by the *Don Carlos* at noon to-day, under the name 'Signor Foscari'"—and he didn't,' said Laurette, nodding triumphantly at her brother, who by this time was listening with a look of interest.

'You are more of a nut* than I ever thought you were, Laurette!' he said with a grim smile.

'Nut or not, I know what I am about. And I would like to know where Talbot would be this day, when there is but a step or two between his being a peer of England and an hereditary legislator of Great Britain, if I didn't possess the necessary tact? Talk of the Prodigal Son! Talbot looked like one that evening, when he came home—only, I suppose, much older. I think a man must have very little idea of fun when he has such an escapade after he has lost all the hair off the top of his head, and his moustache is grizzled. I had got a special friend to get Talbot out of the hands of the creditor at once, and pay the five hundred pounds down. I had the amount by me, you know, out of the money you gave me. Talbot thought I knew nothing of the affair, for he intercepted the letter he had left at the Club to be posted to me the day after he sailed—telling me he would probably be away a couple of years, as he really could not stand Melbourne society any longer. He kindly advised me to economize in his absence at Cannawijera. Oh, I knew what was in it; I saw a draft of the letter in his pocket-book a few days before then. Yes, and he paid this friend three hundred pounds of the debt, which was of course promptly handed to me. I had no scruple in keeping it, for it was part of six hundred pounds I lent him early in October. Yes; all this happened two days before you were married. And there was I, that evening, prattling away about the babies as innocently as Howard boy himself, and the next Government House dinner-party, a specially cosy little affair, for which an invitation had come two or three days before. How a man could give himself up to a Bohemian career with such an invitation staring him in the face I cannot tell. I don't mention myself or the dear children, because it would seem that these are the items which some men part from most easily at times; more especially when they have been importuned for many weeks to hasten away to have their brows coroneted with roses, such as they were. Of course this news will, in a manner, help to steady Talbot. You see his father is seventy-six, and very tottery.'

'But don't reckon upon the old chap giving up the ghost immediately, Laurette,' said her brother, half smiling.

'God forbid!' answered Laurette devoutly.

It was one of the edifying features of her character, in an emergency, that piety of the kind which preachers call 'a bulwark of the State' was always at her command. Then, emboldened by Ted's remorseful mood, and by the thought that at any moment the summons might come which would call Talbot and herself to take their place among the English nobility, Laurette made a full confession to Ted of all their financial difficulties. It would take an additional two thousand pounds to quite clear their liabilities. In any case they would be leaving for England in about nine months. They ought to have a thousand or two in hand for emergencies. The Lillimore estates were in such a state of impoverishment, with so many charges on them, etc. The upshot of these confidences was, that Ted arranged to leave four thousand pounds to Laurette's credit—'for, after all, you've proved yourself a true friend to me, Larry; and though I've put my foot in it so confoundedly, to begin with——'

'Oh, my dear boy, as for that, it will soon blow over. A woman may have principles and theories, but life is so arranged that she soon sees how ridiculous it is to try and act on them. And nothing in this world, nor that which is to come, will, as a rule, enable her to face a ridiculous position for a whole year.'

Thus Laurette, like an artist who knows how and when to strike the desired key-note, went on her way conquering and to conquer. Stella's involved passionate nature, her lack of patience and fidelity to her better self, Ted's fall and remorse, Tareling's chronic servitude to common vice, all under Laurette's cunning fingers were touched into fairy music, which led her to that career of assured triumph she had long felt herself born to achieve. Nor did she fail to acknowledge her obligations to a higher power. An unwavering determination to make the best of life might compass much, but when dealings with such capricious and obstinate material as a girl like Stella are brought to a successful issue, one is bound to recognise the aid of that strain of divinity in mundane matters which 'shapes our ends, rough-hew them as we will.'* This strain of divinity was at times rather obscured in the arrangements of a world in which ready money was an extremely precarious possession with many who might be termed born leaders of society. But who could fail to recognize the finger of an overruling Providence in the series of events that had brought Laurette to her present position?

CHAPTER XLVI

THE *Hindoo Fawn* steamed away at the appointed hour with a large number of passengers, among them rather more than the average mixture of classes who make up the miscellaneous crowds that are constantly to be found going to and fro on the mail-boats between Australia and the old world. They were all there, from the publican who had made a large fortune in a shanty at a new gold-mine, to the Governor whose term of office had expired, and who discussed European politics with an air of lofty reserve, as if sources of information lay in the hollow of his hand denied to such everyday avenues as newspapers. 'Ah, yes, yes; that is the popular rumour,' he would murmur, with an indulgent smile, as though he had a special Asmodeus in his pay in each European Court.* His 'lady,' too, was usually surrounded by a small coterie, who hung on her words with that pathetic docility which oftentimes marks the Australienne who has much money and little culture, and who in provincial simplicity regards a Governor's wife as being necessarily an oracle of fashion and the higher social ethics. But there were many on board the *Hindoo Fawn* who did not join in this form of fetich-worship. Conspicuous among these was Mrs Anstey Hobbs, who formed what might be termed a counter-circle, and numbered among her adherents many of the 'Melbourne people,' and a young man who was supposed to be engaged on a weighty work on Australia. As he had passed four months in the island-continent, had lived only in the cities and among the wealthy grocer order, his qualifications for the task may be imagined. But, then, what he lacked in experience he made up in theories. Even if he had been deficient in these, his friend, Mrs Anstey-Hobbs, would have jogged his imagination.

'The omnipotence of money in our young Republics, that is the bane of our social life, Mr FitzAlan,' she would say sententiously; on which Mr FitzAlan would whip out his note-book and enter the observation with a glow of thankfulness at being able to gather knowledge at so sure and trustworthy a source. 'Look at those exuberant young women sweeping the deck in cream-coloured plush and lace tea-gowns. Their mother laid the foundation of the family's immense wealth by washing in the early days of the Ballarat diggings,* and then the father kept a sly grog-shop. Now their lives are as much divorced from labour as Solomon's lilies.'*

In her desire to be epigrammatic, Mrs Anstey Hobbs occasionally perpetrated a derangement of associations, of which this may be taken as a favourable specimen.

'They keep betting-books, they talk slang, they wear pearls and diamonds at breakfast, and their reading is confined to a few trashy novels and sporting news; their sole idea of conversation is horsy chaff, and their favourite avocation is a pronounced flirtation. Ah, Mr FitzAlan, it is a cruel fate to find one's self bracketed with such people. Yes, people like *you* may discriminate.'

'Well, you have helped me to a much clearer understanding of these young ladies. I fear when my work comes out you will find it enriched with many of your observations, Mrs Anstey-Hobbs. They are so true to the life, so apt, so full of individuality. And that young lady who keeps so much aloof, who has constantly a book in her hands, and seldom speaks except to her husband or dog, or her maid, and has formed no friendship except with a sick ape?'

'Oh, Mrs Ted Ritchie! Well, now, there is a study for you. A few months ago that languid, supercilious, indifferent young person, who preserves such a haughty silence most of the day, was introduced for the first time to what might be termed society. She was delightfully naïve and fresh, interested in everyone and everything—really, one might also say intelligent—her whole face constantly sparkling with enjoyment. She had, too, a very fair idea of talking, perhaps a little too *ingénue** in her delight in entering fashionable society, too ready with a smile when there was no call for it, but on the whole so vivacious and ingenuous that it was quite a pleasure to meet her.'

'You amaze me! What can have wrought so marvellous a change?'

'Money. Fifteen thousand a year is the secret of it all. Mark her cold listlessness, the droop in her mouth, the disengaged air. She is practising the *rôle* of the woman of society to perfection. Oh yes, her sister-in-law may be Countess of Lillimore any day. The two influences combined—wealth and an aristocratic connection—have been too much for her. Just notice, the maid brings her a couple of books, her husband shifts the sunshade, his valet, or groom rather, leads up her dog, and then, for the first time, our fine lady permits herself a feeble smile. One might imagine it was a marriage *à la mode*,* instead of which the young man was the only one she ever cared for, and she had set her heart for years on marrying him. She has accomplished her object—she is wealthy—behold the result! Now, judge whether I over-estimate the exaggerated part that money plays with us.'

Mr FitzAlan was deeply impressed by all this, and more than ever conscious of his great good-fortune in securing so skilful a coadjutor as Mrs Anstey-Hobbs in imparting a lively local colour to his Australian impressions. He made what he would have called a 'study' of Mrs Ritchie. After sketching the exuberant young women whose toilettes on board ship were of so telling a nature, whose fortunes were laid in so dramatic a form, he took up his parable regarding another phase of Australian womanhood—the young lady who belongs socially to a higher grade, but who has lived in straitened circumstances till a lucky marriage has landed her in affluence and wealth. Here the young man warmed to his work, and with those side-lights and cumulative details, which are so much more effective in the tourist's hands than any shred of the truth would be, beset as it is with thorny points which do not adapt themselves harmoniously to neatly packed little theories, he went on to probe and 'accentuate,' as he would term it, the difference of types.

The young persons whose wealth made them so frankly jubilant in its enjoyment had, after all, been born in the lap of luxury. With all their loud, costly, inappropriate costumes, their silken trains dusting the decks of mail-steamers, yet their faith in the almighty dollar as the governing factor of life was not so sublimely immovable as that of the more cultured young lady who had been poor and was suddenly rich—suddenly in touch, through her husband's family, with the proud exclusive aristocracy of England! Then came a fetching picture of the *milieu* of this young lady in her father's house, where she had unwillingly drudged with the maid-of-all-work, and spent a large portion of her leisure in making up cheap dresses that were as faithful a reproduction of the last fashion-plates as circumstances would permit. There was even a light and rapid inventory of the furniture—the varnished side-board, with its plated ware, the imitation Brussels carpet,* the oleographs,* the large supply of the novel of a second-rate order which formed the chief reading of the young lady, whose heart would beat with yearning envy at the facile victories of heiresses—those fortunate beings who command the last triumphs of the milliner's confections, and the man-dressmaker's knowing art—whose coiffure is built up by the cunning fingers of a trained maid. For, under an artless and vivacious appearance, an inflexible purpose lodged itself in this young woman's breast. She would, if possible, be rich! She would cast aside the sordid trappings that bound her, and soar into the empyrean of those whose lives were beautified with wealth! She would become one of the elect who neither toil nor spin.* And all at once this was accomplished. Now mark the outcome. So possessed is this young person with her incredible change of fortune, that her whole nature is transformed. She is penetrated to her finger-tips with a keen appreciation of her good-fortune, and yet she hides her glowing satisfaction under an air of profound indifference, etc., etc.

So enamoured did the young man become of the sketch thus done from life—piping hot, as it were, from the inner reality of things—that he was never weary of adding new touches. Mrs Anstey-Hobbs was delighted. The artist in her, as she would have termed it, expanded in considering this masterly exposition of character. He discovered that his 'study' absented herself from the Sunday services held on deck, sitting apart in the society of her dog and the sick ape. It was then he wrote: 'Nor is this assumption of haughty coldness, of languid scorn, confined to the ordinary intercourse of life. In her determination to be quite above the average herd—to be abreast with the latest development of advanced thought so called—she despises even those outward observances of religion that have consoled humanity through countless aeons of time.' After admiring this phrase hugely for some days, the thought occurred to him that the Church of England Prayer-book was after all dated, and he accordingly made an alteration. This Mrs Anstey-Hobbs called being rigorously critical.

'Each shade, every *nuance* in her nature is subtly touched,' she murmured, adjusting her pince-nez to take a better look at the subject who afforded these masterly discoveries.

'And you tell me that in the weeks immediately preceding her marriage the future Lord Lillimore was struck with the Parisian frivolity she displayed?' said the budding author, cogitating how he might turn the circumstance into a phrase that would swell the general effect. But enough of this young man. He was by no means the funniest example of those Australian tourists whose modes of authorship mark them as chosen morsels for the comic muse.

Needless to say that Stella was throughout entirely oblivious of the speculations to which her altered demeanour gave rise. The change, indeed, was sufficiently startling to attract the attention of one who had known her in the recent past. And we must all have perceived from time to time how a theory protects the average mind from any perception of the truth—the very sun-motes arrange themselves to make the illusion more credible.

It often happens that the sins into which people are betrayed against themselves take long, long years to find out. The seeds have surely been sown, but may it not be that they have died? The sheaves of so many autumns have been garnered, and yet the tares have not destroyed the harvest. May it not be a part of the old superstition of sibyl* and prophet that our deeds still travel with us—their noiseless footfalls ever keeping pace with ours till the moment comes when their shadowy hands hold us faster than adamantine chains? Do not believe it. The root of bitterness is there, and unless we are so forgotten of God that others, rather than ourselves, must suffer for our wrong-doing, the pulse of life beats in the long-buried germ when we least look for its resurrection. But there are retributions which are as the shadow of offences, and follow hard on them like hounds that nothing diverts from their quarry. Of this kind was the bitter humiliation which fell on Stella so swiftly after her unhappy marriage. Yet the depths of listless impassiveness that closed round her at this time were not more the result of that dismal experience than the reaction after those days of strange self-abandonment when the whole forces of her mind had been directed to the effacing all memory of what had been the crowning joy of her life. The inward fever that had preyed on her during the previous weeks now had unrestrained course. One of those dark periods of despair and misanthropical weariness to which the speculative, brooding order of mind is peculiarly liable when fretted and overworn enfolded her for a time like a palpable darkness. That eager unwearied curiosity as to the play and meaning of life which had given her nature so delicately sensitive a texture, so responsive a chord of sympathy, had completely deserted her.

She had been betrayed, and the throes of awakening, of cold, hard disenchantment and disillusion, stifled all spiritual life. At times an intolerable yearning came over her for the sound of a voice, the sight of a face, which could not now be recalled by her without a haunting sense of guilt. And, then, how often it rose up before her: that picture cruelly limned on her brain of Ritchie's face—vacant, senseless, dead!

By the end of the voyage, which lasted nearly five weeks, Stella had recovered something of her old elasticity. Probably the wilful misanthropy which led her to avoid, as far as possible, all intimacy with her fellow-passengers, had co-operated with the health-giving breezes of the sea in restoring her exhausted forces, and expelling the fever that burned in her veins. A recurring weight on her temples, a heavy throbbing that would come back at intervals with no assignable cause, remained. But otherwise her bodily health was restored. The old trick of laughter came back to her with something of the old interest in the endless combinations of the great human comedy. But, unfortunately, the healing process had affected her mind much less than her body. She was harder, less unselfish, less inclined to scan her own action in the misfortune of her marriage with self-accusing justice.

She had been betrayed into marrying a sot. She put it into merciless words with a dull, smouldering resentment, which was directed more against the infinite treachery that life, as a whole, so often practises, than against any individual. Laurette, she knew, had played the traitor. But without any clue to the baseness of her motive, the action, as that of a sister who believed the meanness might work out her brother's redemption, appealed to Stella as one of those vicarious transgressions which, rightly or wrongly, mankind has consented to regard with more leniency than the falseness prompted by purely egoistic aims.

Ted, paradoxical as it may seem, she scarcely blamed at all. He himself had resented her acceptance of his conduct as being beyond his control more keenly than any reproaches. Yet this was the point of view which came back to her with irresistible conviction. Needless to say, it rendered any vivid feeling of indignation impossible. Heredity and circumstance, the two arch-conspirators of necessity—who could resist their action when the moral nature is unfortified by any culture of the soul? And even making allowance for all the complex influences that can be brought to bear on conduct, could any human being's action be shaped by himself apart from external forces?

One disastrous result of the knowledge that had so abruptly broken on Stella in Ritchie's fatal weakness was that she no longer tried to banish Anselm Langdale from her thoughts. He now appeared to her as the mainstay of her better life; she clung to his image as a devotee turns to a relic in the hour of need. As the lassitude of melancholy and fever lessened, the passion which for a time had been kept in abeyance returned, and took possession of her as before. His face and the tones of his voice haunted her night and day; she lived all the hours of their intercourse over again, till at times the longing only to look at him, even from afar, burned in her heart like a slow consuming flame. Alas! this is not the way one thinks of the dead.

It was her dream to sit looking across the sea at dawn, in the starlight and the white moonlight, till the softly-moving waves were transformed into the great inland plain of her native country. The tall kangaroo grass as it bent in soft ripples, the gray-green earth, the distant lines of weeping myall fringing a watercourse, the vague, wide horizons, the moaning sough of the wind as it rose in sighing gusts, sweeping over unpeopled wastes, the muffled beat of the horses' hoofs on the dense herbage, Langdale riding close beside her, his head bent to catch her words—each sight and sound came back to her one by one. In some strange way such visions consoled her. They became the kernel of her inward life. 'I shall never see him again; but he is my friend—my companion. Nothing can take that from me'—so she reasoned.

Outwardly the old footing between herself and Ritchie had been resumed. Stella's whole nature and training made it impossible for her to forego the *bienséances** of life in her intercourse with anyone. Unfailing courtesy and kindliness had been the prevailing notes in her old home. She could repel with signal success attempts at intimacies which did not recommend themselves to her as tolerable. But she could not come in daily contact with one without exercising something of that charm and urbanity of manner which are the birthright of a cultivated, well-descended nature.

As for poor Ted, who, in his dumb way, clung to the pathetic theory that he was responsible for his actions, he endured agonies of contrition when he thought over his unpardonable offence. For some time he did so constantly, cursing himself vehemently the while, to have conquered his deadly enemy for so long, and at the last to fall egregiously when it most behoved him to be a man. Of all the ways that had ever been invented of being a complete idiot—— But it is impossible in these pages to follow the terms that the young man applied to himself. Still, mentally, one gets used to everything, even to having behaved worse than the most pitiable jackass of the most varied adjectival quality; and remorse *per se* was wholly foreign to him. An immovable belief grew on him that never again would he permit himself to be delivered over to the wiles of the devil in such a fashion. He had a small calendar note-book full of racing memoranda, but none of these were of moment to him compared to the little crosses in red pencil with which he marked the flights of the days and weeks. And already Stella belonged to him after a fashion. He watched over her during the weeks of her lethargic prostration with touching devotion. It was only when he found that his constant presence worried her that he absented himself.

There were several other young Australian squatters on board, and though most of them drank a good deal—while the mere sight and smell of stimulants at this time made him shudder—yet he was a good deal in their society. He smoked with them, and lost and won money at various games of chance, and they daily discussed horses and wool and pastoral leases, and all the topics that were of mutual interest. Horses especially never seemed to pall on these young men. The annals of the Melbourne Cup, of the Derby and the Grand Prix, of jockey clubs and the careers of jockeys, were at their finger-ends in an astounding way. The blind devotion of a certain order of minds of the English race to the achievements of young horses is surely, in its way, one of the most curious phenomena of the day. Nowhere, probably, does the craze reach a fuller development than in Australia, where the climate, the universal love for outdoor amusement, the wide-spread tendency to gamble, and the paramount importance of the horse as a mode of locomotion, are all factors that intensify the interest taken in racing.

One of these young men, Aubrey Holland, was a Melbourne acquaintance of Ted's, and he introduced him to Stella. Finding he had travelled a good deal in early youth, she one day endeavoured to glean what aspect of the great centres of art and civilization had most impressed him. Venice? Oh, that was a rum place—a fellow hired a boat to go about instead of a cab. Had he been in Rome? No—o, he didn't think so; but stop—wasn't that the place where they raced a mob of horses bare-backed through one of the streets?* Oh yes, he and his father had been there for three weeks.

Ted's artistic education was a trifle more advanced; for after a pause he asked if that wasn't the old village where they dug up little images with the arms chipped off.

Later, when the two were alone, Ted, seeing Stella smile, asked what the joke was.

'How did you know they dug up little images in Rome?' she said by way of answer.

'Oh, don't you remember that little Cupid you told me about that was in Mrs Anstey-Hobbs' place? You don't seem to cotton much to her now, Stella. I believe you like this little beggar of an ape and Dustiefoot better than anyone on board.'

'Yes; we understand each other.'

'Because none of you talk?'

'That is one reason. Then Dustiefoot has a soul, but does not quite know it. Jacob hasn't got to a soul yet, and I had one, but lost it, so that makes a sort of a bond between us.'

'Then it seems I am the only one of the four of us that has a soul? I can't think how Jacob will live after he parts from you. Shall I try to buy him?'

'Oh, we cannot set up a menagerie.'

'No; as it is, there's you and me——'

Stella began to laugh, but though Ted was delighted at the sound, he had not a notion what amused her, so he went on with his calculation: 'And Dustiefoot, and Maisie, and Ben, and all the luggage.'

The stars were coming out one by one in the ashy-blue sky. The Southern Cross had now disappeared, for they were sailing through the Mediterranean, within a day's journey of Brindisi. But there were new constellations to look for as they began to gleam softly in the depths of the sky. The glow of the electric light suddenly encircled them. Ritchie took out his calendar and counted up his red crosses. Stella was gazing through drooping lashes over the calm gray-blue sea. But instead of the soft swell of the waves against the ship, she heard the muffled hoof-beats of horses falling on the thick sward of the wide Peeloo Plain.

CHAPTER XLVII

THEY reached Berlin early one November morning, three days after they landed in Italy. It was a cold bright day, with a thin insubstantial sort of sunshine and keen gusts of wind laden with the sallow spoils of autumn. Wherever there was a tree with leaves to shed, this wind searched them out, and wrenched them off the stalks, and swirled them away. The rusty red and pale amber of the oak leaves, the delicate wistful green and yellow of the birches, the deep orange of the mountain-ashes, the citron of the common kind, the crimson tufts of the sycamore trees, and the lemon-tinted leaves of the lindens—all were to be seen in the Thiergarten* falling in soft perpetual showers. They fluttered in the air for a moment, and then swelled the banks of autumn foliage piled up against tree-trunks and benches and those quiet nooks in the depths of the wood which even the wind did not readily penetrate.

The pension* of the Baroness von Eisengau, which had been recommended to the Ritchies by Miss Brendover, was close to the Thiergarten; and the large double windows of the suite of rooms which Ted engaged on the second *étage** overlooked the park. The novel sight of a whole wood being shorn of its leaves and left shivering nakedly under a pale cold sky caught Stella's eye at once. Here she took her first long walk since they had left Australian shores. It seemed as though her recovery had been largely dependent on the sea and its invigorating breezes. The day after leaving the *Hindoo Fawn* she felt the old listless languor and mental miasma stealthily creeping over her. Only those who have for a time been victimized by that fell *taedium vitae** which, like a victorious army, beleaguers the very citadel of life, can realize the feeling of helpless subjection that fetters the mind under such assaults. But Stella had so far gained strength that she struggled against the feeling, and simulated an interest she did not feel in the variety and movement of travel.

On returning to the pension, Ritchie, who had been out with his groom to see about hiring horses from the Guldenstern Mews, awaited her with a telegram that had come from his uncle in London. Directly on landing at Brindisi, Ted, instead of writing a letter announcing his arrival and future address, had telegraphed the news—'wiring,'* when practicable, being his favourite mode of correspondence. Now a message had come from the old man, saying he had not long to live, and requesting his nephew's presence as soon as possible.

'I suppose I had better start soon. What do you think, Stella?'

'Oh, go, by all means! The poor old man wants to see you. Has he any children?'

'Two daughters—oldish, I think. I wonder if Hetty and Jemima are like Larry. They say cousins are often more alike than sisters, and, you see, my aunt is my mother's sister. She's a good deal older than my mother, and rather gone in the upper story.* When she writes she always asks the same questions. The last letter I saw of hers, she asked if I was still in college. You see, the governor told her he had sent me there; and it wasn't the habit in the families in England to send the boys to college; so it stuck in the old lady's memory—"Is dear Ted in college still?" says she, with a heavy stroke under "college." Why do some women always put strokes in their letters? I used to get letters once——' Ted suddenly paused, as if struck with the thought that there are some pre-nuptial reminiscences better left in oblivion.

'Well, go on, Ted,' said Stella, with something of the old sense of fun struggling to the surface. 'Was it the adjectives that were always underlined?'

'What are adjectives?'

'Oh, the words that were put before your name, in the letters you used to get once!'

'"My dearly beloved Edward"—are they adjectives? Oh, the "beloved." A serious affair? Well, I don't believe you care a snuff.

Did you never feel a bit jealous of anyone, Stella, except that time when Cuth got engaged? Well, I don't half like going without you. The old aunt will believe I've left college at least, but she'll never believe I'm married when she doesn't see you. "And are you really married, dear?" she'll say every time I see her. And the cousins—I expect they're like Laurette.'

'In what way?'

'Well, like this—always harking back on any point you don't fully explain. "But why didn't Stella come?" That's the way Larry would keep nagging away, till you either made a clean breast of it, or, if that wasn't to be done, cleared out of her way. I'll tell them straight out from the beginning you cried your eyes out to come, but I wouldn't let you because of the fogs. Of course Laurette could well fancy a man and his wife might part soon after the honeymoon without tears—but elderly maiden ladies will find it hard to believe. By the way, Stella, how long is the honeymoon supposed to last? You're not an authority? Lord, I wish *I* were! Well, if they don't suck in the first yarn,* I'll let them believe I wanted to have a bit of a shine all by myself. That'll make the old tabbies sit up—but, of course, being an Australian, they'll take in anything about me. So they may, when all is told. But isn't it rather queer, Stella, how a fellow would sooner any hanged yarn be taken in about him than the truth? It's not only with myself, but I've noticed it over and over again. I had a fellow book-keeping once who had been in quod* for some months. It got to be known, and he pretended it was for putting a knife in a chap— whereas it was for prigging* one.'

'Yes; but the truth is generally even more damaging than the "hanged yarn," you see. I suppose the book-keeper was one of the thirty-three per cent of the educated who go under, and he would be sooner supposed to stab a man than steal from him.'

'Yes, Stella, you're right. As long as people feel they could be different they're ashamed of themselves. But if they got to think they couldn't help it a little bit, and it was all because it was to be, somehow, why—— Look here, Stella, you've been awfully good, I know, over this confounded business; but I wish to God you had given me a rowing, or would speak to me now and then about it—as if you were afraid, don't you know, that I wouldn't keep straight. You are frightfully cut up in one way, and yet in another . . . sometimes it comes over me that you fret because you married me—not because I—I was such an awful idiot.'

Love, even when it has failed to be the saving influence of a man's life, has a curious power of purging the heavy eye. The aspect of the matter, put into such plain terms by Ritchie, was so near the truth that Stella was for a moment conscience-smitten.

'What is the use of talking about it?' she said, lying back in the wide, padded armchair with half-closed eyes.

'I am a twenty-four-carat muff* to bring it up, I know. But, Stella, when I look at you sometimes I feel as if I could not bear it. Always before this you walked as if you were treading on air—your eyes dancing. It didn't matter whether the sun were shining or not, it came in with you. And now you sit by the hour as if you saw nothing. You do not even read. I sometimes think if you would lie up properly till your illness is over it would be better—for you must have some sort of fever hanging about you. You eat next to nothing, and in the morning you look more tired than when you went to bed.'

'Leave it to time, Ted,' she said, gently stroking his brown, strong hand lightly with her slender fingers, which had now a transparent aspect. She wore no rings except her wedding-ring, and it hung so loose that once or twice it had dropped off.

CHAPTER XLVIII

RITCHIE left for England on the following day, and almost to her own surprise Stella found that his absence made a blank. She had not realized till he was gone how his unfailing thoughtfulness led him to anticipate every wish, how his unceasing attentions folded her round on every side. At any time he disliked fuss or demonstration, so much that he would sooner do deeds of kindness or generosity like a thief in the night,* so as to avoid being thanked. But much more was this the case when Stella's large, melancholy eyes and long impassive reveries touched him daily with a fresh apprehension of the heinousness of his past conduct. She had been learning to love him, he thought to himself, when suddenly on that fatal night she saw him 'sunk below the level of the brutes.' The phrase had remained in his mind, and he pondered over it till its full meaning lay revealed.

The dog that sleeps at your door may be stabbed or poisoned, but no form of indulgence will steal his senses from him so that his master may be robbed or murdered without a bark to warn him of his danger. The horse in your stable does not over-drink himself so that he cannot serve you with his docility and speed. He understood what Stella meant when on the journey from Italy she said, in connection with some altercation that had taken place with officials regarding Dustiefoot: 'It is a superstition with me not to say the lower animals. I never hear the phrase without thinking of myriads of human lives compared to which the existence of a toad is a high and holy thing.' He thought over the matter till a curious impetus was given to his imagination. He imagined Stella in some extremity crying aloud to him for help on that night at Monico Lodge—calling him to her aid. No, he could not hear her, he could not be roused . . . he was beyond the reach of all human appeal. . . . Always when he came to that point he indulged in very strong language against himself, but his emotion did not end there. He became skilful in devising ways of serving Stella; and, withal, she knew of old how he hated to be thanked, and that was an added relief. The good people who do so much for us, and then wait hat in hand for a speech of grateful recognition, get hardly used in the end. We learn to avoid them in the day of calamity far more rigorously than those who wilfully throw half-bricks at us.

Ted would even have gone to all Wagner's operas with Stella, though 'Lohengrin,'* to which he accompanied her on the first night they were in Berlin, seemed to him devised to keep people beyond hearing.

'Of course,' he admitted, 'you are glad when the soft parts come, but I would feel so much jollier not to hear any. And then, Stella, to tie a string to the leg of a pigeon and pretend it is the Holy Ghost.* . . . Do you think your mother would like it?'

Stella smiled repeatedly at the inquiry. Ted's direct habit of putting things as they appeared to him into plain phrase never forsook him.

'After all, I think I should enjoy these operas more with you, Ted,' she said, as they were together the half-hour preceding his departure.

Ted flushed deeply, but did not trust himself to reply.

'Whatever you do, Stella,' he said, after a pause, 'don't you go too much into the houses of sick people, to catch fever and things. That Mrs Schulz you went to see to-day—is it anything catching?'

'No, Ted; it is just poverty, and having her husband imprisoned for posting up announcements of a Socialistic meeting. Besides, I am not a favourite of the gods. I am one of the workaday masses who gather up all the arrows on their targets, and still live on. And then, you know, one can die only once.'

'But, Moses, what a jolly difference it makes whether one dies before twenty-four or after eighty! Don't you go and slip me up* with any sell* of that kind, whatever you do. We are going to keep our golden wedding-day one of these years "across the blue Alsatian mountains." Do you remember how Billy Stein used to sing that, making his voice shiver like a jelly?'

Yes, she missed him hourly, and in his absence she made faint efforts to look towards the future without quailing. It was true that even under happier circumstances there could be none of that delicate mental companionship which springs from the mutual insight of affinity, none of that spontaneous interchange of thought, of tender imaginative fancies which are the aerial rootlets of the mind, and make the perennial charm of close intimacy. . . . But life is, on the whole, a rough and ready arrangement, essentially founded on and reinforced by exterior realities, which make a wider claim on our nature than we are always willing to allow.

And after all the young human heart does not doat on being a 'bleeding pageant.'* It is given, rather, to that homely habit known as 'making the best of things,' of finding warmth in the drift-wood fire after the great storms of life have wrecked the gallant barks that set out laden with the fond dreams of youth. With Stella it is certain that her profound capacity of suffering, and her deep tinge of constitutional melancholy, were closely related to that large generosity of nature which is rooted in the love of life. Her wide sympathies, vivid insight, and keen interest in the manifold aspects of the human comedy, could not long lie dormant, when the bitter languor which had for a time overwhelmed her began slowly to be dissipated. She made no rapid strides in recovery. Both sleep and appetite were errant and fitful. In the week that followed Ritchie's departure, it often occurred to her that there was wisdom in his advice that she should for a little time keep to her bed, in the hope of getting rid of that haunting, nameless *malaise*, which at her best seemed never far off.

Yet the worst seemed to be over. Those haunting, life-like visions

of the night, in which she saw Langdale as vividly as in life, in which
the sound of his voice and the touch of his hand thrilled her with
overmastering reality, became gradually less frequent, less absorbing.
And this on the whole reassured her. It enabled her to begin to look
on the past as inevitable and irrevocable—something that had gone
for ever from her—as far as that can be the case with any epoch which
for good or evil has left the deepest imprint on the heart. But
one vision, sleeping and waking, eluded all effort at dislodgment.
Solemn, silent, unpeopled, in the delicate rose twilight—the boundary of earth and sky lost in limitless distance—overhead a few great
white stars swimming into the tender amethyst of the sky. Two riding
side by side, without a single circumscribing line to meet their eyes
in the vast immensity that lay around them. It was a picture that
night and day would rise up before her with incredible intensity of
presence—blotting out for the moment all other sights. Gradually
she came to regard it as one of those consecrated, ideal passages
of life which, like the rapture evoked by high imaginative poetry,
mercifully steeps the mind in forgetfulness of the bald, dreary
stretches of existence that threaten at times to paralyze action and
even thought itself.

That happy girl, with low, fond laughter bubbling to her lips as
lightly as carols float from the throat of a bird, was she not as remote
from Stella's actual self as a scene in an old romance? Let them ride
on in the wistful light that clothes the great Australian plain—those
two whose happiness seemed so inviolable a possession. Let their
hearts beat at the sound of each other's voice as to the cadence of
subtle music. They have passed beyond the inexorable law of change.
They belong to a realm invulnerable to the tooth of Time, where
neither moth nor rust doth corrupt.* Here, in the common life with
which we have to do, love and sorrow alike are blunted by the dead-
ening march of successive days. In place of vivid emotion there falls
a coldness as on the altar of a buried temple. Oh, life, life! is this the
kernel of thy happiness for so many souls—the anguished memories
of hopes that fell like grass before the scythe of the mower?

Thus would the sorrowful girl commune with herself. And yet day
by day the discipline of pain began to direct her thoughts into other
channels. The interest which the first spectacle of life in Berlin had
awakened grew deeper as she saw more of the struggle for existence
around her, more especially among the very poor. She formed new

acquaintances daily. Market-people, poor children, old men dragging burdens beyond their strength, old women sweeping up leaves on the paths of the Thiergarten, the halt and the maimed at street stalls with pitiful little objects of merchandise—they were all ready in their intervals of rest to respond with quick cordiality to her first timid overtures of acquaintanceship. The grief that nestled close at her own heart quickened her observation into an interpretative faculty. Her mind became sensitive to the myriad forms of unhappiness around her, as waters are to the movement of clouds.

She was, during these first days in Berlin, continually on the alert to observe, to sympathize and to help. And with this came something of that renovation of spirit which comes with work and interests that lead the mind away from its own sorrows and ailments.

Ted wrote frequently. His uncle had rallied a little, but the end could not be far off. It seemed he had various reasons for wishing his nephew's presence. 'He is a great deal richer than we any of us knew, and he fancies he owes a good deal to the six thousand pounds I sent when my Uncle Christopher died and left me Strathhaye. You know the two quarrelled so out-and-out when they were young men that they never spoke or wrote to each other for thirty-two years. I did hear something about the reason, that both were in love with Aunt Polly. Lord, how stupid men would feel for quarrelling about a woman if they could see her thirty-two years afterwards!

'The Avenells are here just now. I go a good deal with them to the theatres, etc. . . . I have been twice to see the Lillimores. They came to town lately, and are as kind as they can be. Lady Lillimore is very anxious to know you. Talbot, she says, has told her about you. She is one of the kindest old ladies—something like your mother. I suppose it's the old man Talbot took after. Not that a fellow need take after anyone but himself to turn out pretty crooked. But Tareling seems, at one time or other, to have got into every possible sort of scrape—except work. I suppose he'd think that the biggest misfortune of all. Certainly Larry got a pig in a poke when she married him. But I expect when she's ladyshipped all day long, and has a string of flunkeys to look on when she eats her dinner, she'll be quite pleased with herself. Why don't you write longer letters? I would like to get one every day. You make them just like talking. Hetty and Jemima send their love. They swallowed the yarn about your crying to come with me, and they think if I have to stay much longer you'll come after me. Will you ever want to, Stella? The thought of it makes me go queer all over. It's a week yesterday since I left—but it seems more like a month. The Agent-General* is very kind. I met several Americans at his house the other evening. I tell you what, Stella—I feel quite green with jealousy when I meet Americans. We must have a country of our own, governed by ourselves, and not have the name of being ruled by fellows sent out of the heart of London, to do no good but set people by the ears with their twopenny-ha'penny Government House cliques. In England, unless people know something of racing, they have a notion that Australia is a poky island full of mosquitoes and a few niggers. "*Our* colonies," they say, as if we were bad figs they bought at fourpence a box. I hope that shell-parrot* gave me the straight-tip about living to be seventy-six, if only to live to see Australia a properly independent country. . . . I went to Westminster Abbey the other day, but it's so full of graven images* I couldn't see a mortal thing.'

This letter reached Stella as she was about to set out to pay two visits. The first was to Mrs Schulz, the next to Professor Kellwitz, the Berlin savant she had seen at Dr Stein's early in the year. They met in the Thiergarten two days previously, much to the Professor's delight. He had just received a letter from his Adelaide friends in which mention was made of Stella's marriage. He had to admit a similar indiscretion on his own part. But his wife was just then in Dresden, having been summoned there on account of the dangerous illness of a married daughter. 'Do not wait till she returns before coming in a neighbourly way to look over my books, and carry away any you want to read,' urged the Professor. 'Come on Wednesday, and I shall then be able to show you the last volume published on "Comparative Ethnology," by an old University comrade of Dr Stein's. This is the number of our house. Your pension is within ten minutes' walk of it.'

This was Wednesday, and Stella accordingly made the visit. The Professor had been unexpectedly called out that afternoon, but left a message to say he hoped to be back before Mrs Ritchie left. She was shown into the library and study, where, on the centre of the pedestal table, in its paper binding and uncut leaves, fresh from the printer's, lay the last profound contribution to ethnological science.

The library was a large apartment overlooking the Thiergarten, and lined with books from floor to ceiling on all sides except one, which was covered with engravings and photographs, a large proportion being reproductions of the most ancient and primitive human dwellings of which any record or traces have been discovered. On top of the bookshelves were ranged busts of the immortals. There were tables piled high with books, others with magazines and pamphlets. And even the chairs were not in all cases kept free. But close to the centre pedestal table there was a deep, hospitable-looking couch, to which a long placid career had given a specially alluring aspect. Stella took possession of it, and looked round the room with that quick response to the mere presence of books instinctive to those who love them.

'No doubt there are countless theories and systems reposing in some of these tomes to which time has brought utter ruin,' she thought. 'But all the great brain-nourishers are here—the men whose thoughts "wander through eternity,"* and pierce windows in the souls of successive generations. How even to think of them seems to woo one into a sanctuary where the vehement emotions and storms of life are left behind like a conquered fortress invested with a force which keeps the old rebels in subjection!'

The air of the room, so suggestive of detachment from the ebb and flow of obdurate tides of passionate regret, of revolt and grief, of apathetic indifference, appealed to her, and seemed to carry a message of consolation, of peace. She tried to believe that the vulture-grip of passion had loosened its hold on her. After all, life was not a tale to be cast aside when it does not fulfil its early promises of enchantment—not a harp that is worthless because one string is silenced. The work of the world is carried on mostly by disillusioned men and women. Yes, and by those who throw the whole strength of their lives into action for the common weal. She took up the ethnological work and turned over its pages curiously. But when she tried to read the words swam before her, and her temples throbbed heavily. This was not a new experience, for so much of the invalid still clung to her that any prolonged exertion induced a creeping exhaustion which made thought and action alike difficult. She leant back on the wide yielding couch, saying to herself she would rest a little and then read. In a few moments she was fast asleep.

CHAPTER XLIX

She seemed to have slept but a few moments, when a dream of extra-ordinary vividness took entire possession of her. Langdale was quite near her; he had suddenly entered the room. . . . 'Stella, Stella, my beloved!' he murmured in a hushed voice, looking at her. She would not move, lest she would waken. It was long since she had seen Anselm so clearly; and now, when she saw him, she knew that she had been famishing for a sight of his face. And how close and real his voice sounded with its deep, tender intonations!

He trod gently so as not to waken her. He stood over her, his hand resting on the back of the couch. Her heart began to beat wildly. Ah, would that she might never waken from this vision! It was so palp-able—so much part of herself. It throbbed in every vein of her body. Why had she struggled against this communion as if it were an evil infatuation? It was the saving element left, to steady reason in the wreck that had overtaken her. She knew his face was near hers; she heard herself repeating his name once and again. And then his arms were round her—his breath came in quick pants as he held her to him. She would not open her eyes lest this dream should dissolve.

Dream! Could this be a dream? Could imagination, aided by all the ingenuity of sleep, feign the life-like ecstasy of the kisses softly imprinted on her face?

'Darling, you called me. Are you still asleep?'

In this bewildering dream, which copied life with invincible fidelity, she seemed to open her eyes—and, lo! there he was, close beside her, his face irradiated with joy. 'Oh, Anselm, let me sleep on!' she said faintly. And the dream went on; for he sat beside her, and drew her close to him, so that her weary head lay upon his breast. And so she remained for a little with closed eyes; but at last she began to gather up proofs of being awake. She heard the ticking of a time-piece, the sound of a military band, the muffled roll of carriages. Then timidly she touched the hands that clasped her in so strong and unrelaxing a way.

'Dear little Australian dormouse, does this heavy atmosphere make you so drowsy?' he said with a happy laugh. . . . It was no dream. She gave a low cry of joy, and threw her arms around him. For a few bewildered moments a merciful oblivion overtook her. All the misery and humiliation and endless moral conflict of the past weeks were swept from her. How is one to account for the convictions that suddenly lodge in the heart without a spoken word? The first collected thought which came to Stella was that the dream she dreamt on the morning of her wedding-day was true. No woman stood between her and Langdale—no shadow on his past life divided them; she knew it well, as he drew her close against his heart, murmuring incoherent endearments, and feasting his eyes on her face.

It was much paler than formerly; and surely it was worn, sorrow-stricken, with dark circles round the large eyes, more wistful and *spirituelle** than ever. And those drawn lines round the mouth? She must have suffered much since they parted. The thought sobered the transports of his joy.

'Has my sweet Herzblättchen been ill?'

'Oh, Anselm, Anselm!' was all she could say. And then she screened her face from his sight, hiding it against his breast. All that had happened since they parted in the light of the mystical rose twilight that stole in through the tangled clusters of leaves and purple and scarlet passion-flowers, enclosing the wide veranda of the peaceful home on the borders of the great Australian plain, had for a few tumultuous moments been whirled from her consciousness. And now that the reality, like a hideous nightmare, began once more to reassert itself, she struggled to keep it at bay.

'So you came after all, as you threatened you would; and we have found each other once more—once more!' he said, stroking her hair fondly. She did not look up, but drew a long, low, shuddering sigh, like a child which has been wearied with wandering, but is once more safe in its mother's arms.

'Yes, Stella, we have found each other; this time never to lose one another again—never, till death us do part!'

Oh, merciful Heaven! how the phantom of her wrecked life began to rise and float before her, vivid and pitiful as the wave-washed form of a broken ship that comes with shattered masts and dragging anchors to a wild waste island, in which never a creature of God has lodged and found shelter.

'You got my letter all safe, Liebe. Was it a great shock to you, that enclosure, telling the cause of my visit to England?'

A shudder passed over her, and she moaned a little, but made no reply. Then the reflection dawned on him that, in truth, the news had wounded her cruelly, coming so unexpectedly in the midst of her great happiness. Her face as he had last seen it—the large, radiant eyes, now thrilling him with their steady gaze, then softly veiled with their long dark lashes; the warm, tender damask in her cheeks—her voice, like a hidden bird that sang, had been with him through the weary weeks of separation like a vision of gladness, untroubled by one pang of doubt. Only in the past week or two, when no letters reached him, he had been tormented with fears lest she had fallen ill.

Had this, after all, been the case? She was so wan and silent—so unlike the picture that had been with him day and night. The smiles that rose in her eyes and lingered in them while her face was grave, her low, glad peals of laughter, her quick, imperious gestures, her troops of fancies, blithe and suggestive as the carols of birds in spring, what had become of all these? But he reminded himself that under all the gaiety and quick ardour of her nature there had ever been a strong under-current of almost sombre melancholy. In their separation this had evidently gained the upper hand. Her face would soon resume its old fascinating changefulness—cold, almost hard, one would say, at times, then soft and bright—luminously tender like a wind-flower pearled with dew and softly stirred by the morning air.

In the rush of his sudden joy on seeing her fast asleep in his step-father's house, Langdale had scarcely wondered at Stella's unexpected presence in the Old World. Those who have been in Australia know that people of means there may at any moment embark on a voyage to the Old World—Australia, that vast island-continent, so remote from all the great international centres of activity, is yet in such curiously close touch with all the far ends of the earth. One of the last things Stella had said to him at parting was, 'You know, Anselm, if you are detained in England, just say "Hey presto!" one morning, and there I shall be at your door with a wreath of eucalyptus-blossoms in my hair all ready to go to church. Oh, there are scores of people with whom I could go—Esther to begin with——' Had she perhaps fallen ill and set out with her sister or some friend directly after getting his Mauritius letter, in which he told her of his mother's second marriage, and asked her to address his letters after the beginning of November to No. ——, Thiergarten Strasse? Or was she one of the Adelaide friends of whom the Professor spoke so warmly? But it mattered not how she had come: here she was, and soon she would be her old joyous self again. She had somehow suffered keenly, but the reaction would soon set in. He would not worry her with questions or exclamations over her altered looks. She had looked so much more like her old self when she had been asleep, with a soft flush mantling in her cheeks.

'The moment I got your precious letter I felt I must tell you all before I went away, darling,' he said, in a low, soothing voice. 'Your beloved letter, which I have read till it is almost worn out, and this great lovely lock of your hair—I have kissed it night and morning.'

He had taken the letter out of his pocket-book, and when she caught sight of the closely-written pages and the warm-tinted coiled lock of her hair, the thought of all that lay between them and that happy night, on which she had written with gleeful rapture her first love-letter, made her suddenly turn faint and chill. He saw this, and drawing her nearer to him once more he said:

'Now we need only speak of our joy—of our happiness, without one cloud lingering from the past. It was, as the lawyer said, a false signature. . . . She died a few months after I left England.'

He felt her trembling, and he stroked her face, calling her by all the old fond names.

'Let me take off your bonnet, Blättchen, and your gloves. I want to see and feel your hands in mine.'

She hurriedly removed her gloves, intentionally slipping off the fatal wedding-ring and leaving it in the glove finger. She dared not let the truth come upon him so abruptly. She must somehow tell him—but in what words? After all, Dante showed some inflexibility of imagination in depicting the tortures of the damned. Life furnishes many more terrible situations than those depicted in the circles of the Inferno.*

'I will tell you all there is to tell, Stella, and then we need not return to this. I went from London direct to Brussels, and found the woman who had forged the signature. She admitted the imposition, and I have the needful vouchers in my possession. She was poor, and I knew what *einziges Herz** would wish—I have provided for her. Oh yes, you came and bade me do so. Did you know that you were with me all the time? Your precious little soul came fluttering with me all the way.'

Every word he spoke fell on her now like knotted thongs. But she still clung to him, half hiding her face from his, while the deep, regular beating of his heart seemed to her to measure the moments that lay between her and eternal death.

'Now speak to me a little, my darling. Do you know, I feel as if you would vanish out of my sight! Your presence is so wonderful—so incredible! And I was almost frantic because no letter came.'

'I cannot speak just now, Anselm.'

'My beloved! you have suffered cruelly. Then I will speak till the dear old gaiety and laughter come back. Let me look into your face. Geliebte,* you have been ill. I dreamt you were—over and over again the same dream. Always I wanted to come to you, and always there was some terrible obstacle in the way. I used to set out, and suddenly find myself wandering in unknown places with thick darkness falling, and then there would be great cataracts tumbling over in my path. When I woke up I used to try and laugh at myself. But I was like Macbeth, who couldn't say "Amen!" when he most sorely needed a word of prayer.* I used to think, "After all, that gay, laughing, yet melancholy little witch Blättchen has cunningly infected me with a strain of her Keltic superstition. She is rooted in two nationalities, both a little eerie." Do you remember that tragic dream you had of joining the throng who were in sorrow? Now, confess, beloved, that foolish vision made you a little afraid? But after this you cannot believe in evil dreams. I give you notice that from this day out you must get back all your old mockeries and mischief, and quips and cranks and wreathed smiles. As for me, I foresee that I shall be a dreadful Philistine—as happy as the day is long! "To be happy at home is the ultimate result of all ambition—the end to which every enterprise and labour tends."* Dr Johnson must have known people like me when he said that. Of course, I don't mean only ourselves, Liebe. I have planned every room in the house, and trained creeping laburnum over the front of it, and as for roses, they grow round it like weeds.'

O God! how his words beat upon her heart! Her lips and throat were so parched that she could not speak.

'Ach Himmel,'* he went on, 'what a wretched, downcast creature I was yesterday, when I arrived here and found not a word from you awaiting me!'

'Did you expect me to write?' she asked slowly and with an effort, as she recalled word by word of that abrupt, short letter in which there had been no hint of any future communications.

Surely he forgot how cruelly he had for the time been deceived by that fatal letter, a portion of which he had enclosed to her.

'Expect you to write, Stella?' he echoed, looking at her in amazement. 'You might as well ask if I expected the sun to rise! But then, of course, I did not know you were coming to this side of the world in less than a month after I set sail. How closely, after all, we are enfolded by the tabernacle of clay! Yesterday you were within reach of me, and yet, when I found no letters here, and telegraphed to London and found none had been delayed there nor sent on to Brussels too late to reach me, why, a conviction strong as life fastened on me that something was horribly wrong. I was about to send a cablegram, but found an Australian mail would reach London to-morrow, so I waited to give time to my lawyer to send any on that might have come. But I was as miserable last night as—well, as I am happy now. And my good stepfather would talk of nothing but some funeral scrap that has been unearthed of a hut supposed to date back to the glacial period or some equally impossible time. Yet all the while you were in the city of Berlin! Of course, you did not come alone, Liebe? Is it with Esther you came?'

'No.'

'Tell me, did Hector and Madonna really come? No? Do you want to give me another joyful surprise? Ah, my poor darling! you have been very ill.'

She was indeed paler than ever, and trembling at intervals all over—striving to frame words in which to tell him all, yet shrinking from the task—not as one shrinks from death, but as one shrinks from stabbing the human being who is the dearest loved in all God's wide universe. A species of physical and moral syncope had fallen on her, in which for the time nothing was possible except to half hide her face and hang on every word that Langdale uttered as a miser might gloat over the treasure that is soon to be swept for ever from his possession. A dull wonder had forced itself upon her when he spoke of his disappointment at getting no letter. But she could not think nor reason—she could only, in the feebleness of her great misery, postpone the moment in which the truth must be revealed.

'Did you have a good passage, Liebe? Tell me the very day on which you left. Why, that was just twenty-four days after I did! And our voyage was longer than usual. We had no storms, but shortly after leaving Mauritius our engine got seriously out of gear, and that made us ten days later. Fortunately the sea most of the time was as calm as a great swamp. I used to pace up and down the deck for hours, and fancy we were riding side by side over the Peeloo Plain. Did you not find that a quiet sea under a dim light is wonderfully like a grayish horizonless stretch of Australian scenery? Tell me, Liebe, shall you want to return soon to your beloved native land? But there is a still more important question—one that must be settled this moment—when shall we be married? To-morrow? What! crying, my own? Tell me, Stella, is there some trouble I do not know? Your mother and all—are they well? Did they approve of your coming? Only a brave, intrepid Australian girl could have done such a thing.'

'Oh, Anselm! do not—do not praise me!' she cried in a choked voice.

A wild scheme fashioned itself in her mind to get away before he would learn the truth—to bid him farewell, and then write and tell all and never look upon his face again. But all nerve-power seemed to have deserted her. There was a dull, deep noise in her head, which rose at times and drowned all sound, like waves moaning against a rocky shore.

'Tell me about the Fairacre people,' he said, haunted with the thought that some family trouble weighed on her.

'They were all well. Maisie I brought with me,' she forced herself to say.

'And the friends with whom you came—do I know anything of them? By the way, Liebe, do you know that I hurried here at my step-father's request? I met him going to his beloved museum—one full of miniature specimens of man's primitive dwellings—with some young Royal Highness athirst for knowledge. You must come with me to see them. If you go with the Professor, you will never get away before the dawn of the next century—and that wouldn't suit my plans in the least. You only belovedest—do you remember the butterfly kisses you used to give Lionel? Give me just two of them, in memory of our first delightful squabble over the orphaned little angel.' He held his cheek against hers to feel the flutter of her eyelashes.

But, instead, his face was wet with her tears. Then, for the first time, a sudden pang of fear shot into his heart.

'Your stepfather may soon be here,' she said, raising her pallid, tear-stained face.

'Yes, that reminds me of what I was about to tell you, Stella,' he said, watching her face with a growing apprehension of some unknown disaster dully creeping over him. 'He asked me to hurry here to do the honours of the house for him to an Australian friend—you know he visited South Australia in the beginning of this year—a Mrs Ritchie, he said; do you know her? I fancy I have some association with the name. Perhaps you came with her—and I suppose also you know the Professor?'

'Yes, I know him,' she whispered, looking up into his face in miserable helplessness, her lips dry and quivering, unable to articulate another word. Then he knew that there was some trouble she had to tell him—trouble that she found it difficult to speak of. She had several brothers: perhaps the family had been visited by one of those trials which wound people even more bitterly than death itself. He resolved that she must tell it in the way easiest to her.

'I am teasing you about trifles that do not signify, love. There is some trouble that weighs on you. But do not speak of it to-day if you would rather not. Only remember that any grief which comes to us now must be lighter, because shared between us. Ah, beloved, it seems incredible almost that our great happiness is now assured—within our grasp. . . . Tell me, was there time for you to get the diary-letter I sent from Mauritius?'

'I got only the one terrible letter,' she said faintly.

'Terrible, Stella? Did you, then, blame me so hardly for not telling you all from the first? Perhaps that would have been best; yet it was to save you unnecessary anxiety. But did you not like the long letter, Blättchen?'

'The long letter, Anselm? There was only the one short, dreadful, blotted one, and the part of that letter—the one some woman sent you—saying the rumour of death was untrue.'

She spoke slowly, hesitatingly, as if not certain that the words she used would convey her meaning.

'Stella—my sweet St Charity—tell me what you mean! I have not the least clue. I wrote briefly in a separate note the cause of my visit to England. I knew that virtually I was free to ask you to be my wife, but I wanted the legal vouchers. And, as I said, the moment I got your letter I felt that to keep silence was impossible—might appear to you as a lack of confidence. And I knew—I knew, my darling, I could trust you through life and death. Then, with that brief state-ment, there was a much longer letter—my second love-letter to you, Blättchen—in which I tried to say a little of the thousand things that were in my heart. I enclosed them together, and gave the letter safely into your friend's possession when I found that you had gone out of town, and that there was no possibility of my seeing you. But what other letter do you speak of? My dear one, have you had a fever? Are you mixing this up with some grief?'

'Betrayed! betrayed! betrayed!' she moaned with ashy lips. She had drawn away from him, and leant against the back of the couch, white as death, slowly grasping the treachery that had been put on them.

'Stella, dearest, speak to me; tell me all that causes your anguish. Do you repent coming? Do you love me less than you did?'

'Oh no, no—my only love! God help us!' At the sound of the agony in her voice, something of panic seized him.

'Is it that you did not get my letter—that a false one was given to you?'

'I got a letter addressed in your hand, posted in Melbourne.'

'Posted? But I delivered it by hand when I found that you were away on the twenty-second of September—the day I called.'

'I was not away. I did not go out of Melbourne for half a day during the whole of my visit.'

'Great heavens! what made that woman lie so infamously? Tell me, my darling, what was in the letter you got? You spoke of an unfinished one from some woman. Do you remember the words?'

Stella, roused by the shock of discovering this undreamt-of treachery, repeated, word for word, first, the unfinished letter in some woman's handwriting—then Anselm's, telling of its abrupt beginning and close, with its many erasures, one of them—that at the close—blotted, but not illegible.

'Oh, Stella, could you believe that I would write like that, and enclose such a letter, even if it had come? I would at least have seen you—but, then, you could not imagine that such a diabolical impo-sition was possible. But why did this woman, whom you visited as an equal, behave worse than a common thief?' he asked with gath-ering wrath as he thought of the misery Stella must have endured.

'She had her reasons, and she succeeded—she succeeded,' murmured Stella; and then she slowly rose up. The moment had come when he must know all.

Her gloves fell to the ground, and as he lifted them up a ring fell out of one and rolled under the table.

'Ah, careless little Liebchen, is this the way you let our ring slip off, with its tender old Italian motto? . . . But this is not the ring I gave you, darling child?'

He smiled, but there was a growing fear in his face.

'No, Anselm—I wear that ring next my heart.'

The biting tragedy of their story—fooled and betrayed as they had been on every side—made her marriage appear to her each successive moment more and more in the light of a mocking farce.

'Why, Stella—this is a wedding-ring!'

He looked at her, but she neither spoke nor met his gaze.

'Whose wedding-ring is it?'

He waited for her answer in sickening suspense. To their dying hour they must both remember the awful stillness—broken only by the sullen ticking of a clock, and then the strains of a military band that suddenly broke out into 'Die Wacht am Rhein.'*

'For God's sake, Stella, tell me how this ring came to be in your glove? Whose is it?'

The agony in his voice made the words beat upon her heart with unendurable pain.

'It is mine,' came the answer at last, with a low, wailing sound.

When he heard that, he stood looking at her, his lips parted in breathless, incredulous horror.

Again there was a deep silence. This time it was broken by the miserable sobbing of a woman whose head was bent in bitter shame.

And yet so strong and deep was the man's faith, he had not yet grasped the worst. The wedding-ring was hers. She was, then, on the eve of marrying some man in whose interest, or through whom, all these foul treacheries had been practised. She had carried the ring with her. She was on the eve of marrying, misled by the unscrupulous plotting of this abandoned woman. It must have been with her she had come. Ah, now matters grew clearer. He recalled Miss Morton's story of Stella's supposed engagement—her own admission of having been engaged for a week. It was to the brother of this woman with whom Stella stayed. It was to renew that engagement, then, that this incredible fraud had been practised. And it had almost succeeded. Thank God it was not too late to defeat this wicked, cruel scheme!

These thoughts flashed through his brain like wild-fire. No wonder she was wan with misery. What had she not endured during the nine weeks that had passed since they parted! Oh, to think that through their devilish stratagem she should be made to believe he could have written such words after giving him her entire love and confidence!

'Stella—Stella darling, do not be so broken-hearted. It kills me to see you like this. All will yet be well. We have found each other once more. That makes up for all.'

She struggled for composure, seeking to frame words that would extinguish the last spark of his hope. But she could not—she could not utter them. The exhausting struggle, the determination not to be overborne by grief, the constantly recurring effort to treat the part that Langdale had played in her life as obliterated, had been but a feeble subterfuge. Like a torrent long pent up, the passion of her love rose and took possession of her. What law of God or man could justify the semblance of a marriage compassed by the vilest imposition? She saw that in some way Langdale had not yet comprehended the full extent of the intolerable falsehood. Yes, that was the history of her marriage from beginning to end—an impossible lie.

'Anselm, take me away,' she said, going up to him and placing her hands in his.

'My dear one, do not be afraid. No contract entered upon through such gross imposition can bind you.'

'No—but let us go away.'

'Where would you like to go, beloved?'

'Oh, away to the East—far away from everyone. I do not want anyone in the whole world but you. You do not love me any less? You are my own only love, are you not? Oh, Anselm, do not leave me, whatever happens.'

'Never again, Stella. We shall be married this very day. I shall see these people and return this ring.'

She tried to smile, but broke instead into wild, hysterical laughter. The blood had surged to her head. Her lips and cheeks were crimson—glowing like coals; and there was a glittering light in her eyes.

'Take me away, Anselm. Do not believe them if they say I do not belong to you. It was all a horrible fraud, Anselm. Do you understand me?'

'Yes, my beloved, I understand. I understand how this misery has worked on your mind,' he answered in a low, soothing voice, his lips quivering as he looked at her. His practised eyes read too well the symptoms of the fever that possessed her. It had lain latent in her blood for many days, and had been fanned by this hour of strange, wild misery into fierce life.

'Ah, but I must tell before we go. There must be perfect truth between us. They wove such a frightful mesh of deceit round me. The air is full of it—it chokes me. You and I, Anselm, must be free people under an open sky. No concealment, no duplicity, no seeming. Do you not see how that little rift at the beginning has wrecked us? You wished me to tell Hector and Madonna—but I would not. Ah, dear Madonna, she would not have let their poison fasten on me.— Anselm, for God's sake do not look away! There are tears in your eyes. I may cry, because I am a weak, foolish, faulty woman. But you must not; you must be strong for us both.'

'Yes, my darling, I will be strong,' he replied, in a broken voice. 'And you, my dear one—will you not make me happy by sitting beside me and resting?'

'No, oh no, I must not rest. I must tell you. You must understand how it is. Do you know, Anselm, that treachery is the worst poison of all? I will confess to you that since we have stood face to face to-day I have formed two plans of deceiving you. The first was I would kiss you good-bye as though I would see you again to-morrow, and then write you a letter, and never look into your face again. Was not that a wild infidelity to enter into my heart? Oh, what a wicked, wicked thought—not to see you again, belovedest! And all that has grown out of their duping me. And the other plan—I forget the other plan——'

'Your head pains you terribly, my darling—I know it does.'

'Yes, it beats all over it; and sometimes when your lips move I can hardly hear what you are saying. But I must tell you before you take me away. Do you know, beloved, how I now loathe the smallest speck of concealment? It grows and grows till it makes a horrible stifling atmosphere all round, heavy and thick with poison. It must be like clear, fine crystal all round us. Oh, how they smothered my whole life with lies . . .

'They destroyed your long letter—your beautiful letter, that I would have kissed and put close against my heart, and thanked God

for on my knees day and night—that I would have stolen away to
read over and over to myself till I knew every word of it by heart. It
would have flooded my life with fresh love and hope. But instead of
it they gave me one that was turned into a tissue of awful lies—short,
and hard and cruel, but with your name at the end, clear as the sun
at noon-day. . . . And with your letter they put a woman's lying
message. . . . I saw you day and night—night and day sailing away to
another woman—to your *wife*, to the one who had been misrepre-
sented, who still loved you. I followed you on and on, till you reached
her—till I saw you in her arms, and my blood was on fire. I dared
not go back to the old, quiet, harmonious days, to my mother's peaceful home, where fierce jealousy and the stain of unlawful love were
only things hidden away within the covers of old tragedies. . . . Don't
you understand, Anselm, how I loathed myself—madly, furiously
jealous, because a husband was hastening back to the wife he had
unwittingly wronged! I tried to take comfort in the belief she would
win you back to happiness; but there was insanity in the thought, and
I flung it from me. I seemed to look into black depths yawning in my
soul. I could not deceive myself. I told myself if you had come trampling on the bond that held you, I would have left all and followed
you to the ends of the earth. You were my highest good—my conscience. What you asked me to do I would have done, glorying in the
thought of making some real sacrifice for your sake——'

'Oh, my darling, I know all the depth of your great love. Your eyes
are dim with pain. Let me soothe you into calmness!'

He came to her where she stood, leaning against the back of the
pedestal-table; but when he put his arms round her she drew back.

'No, Anselm; let me tell you all; then I will be calm, and you shall
decide. All these things have been feeding on me, shrivelling all that
was good in me till I began to reconcile myself—to look forward to
a mere blunted, soulless existence as something to live for.'

'Ah, my dear one, you wrong yourself; that you never could do!'

'Anselm, you do not know all. For twenty-three years I have been
slumbering through existence, looking on amused at the play,
untouched by passion, till I knew you. And when the forces that had
thrilled me through and through were turned aside—when all the
better purpose of life was defeated—I consciously made choice of
the lower part, because I knew myself too well to fancy that anything
of the old magic could return. It was so in religion. When the old

vivid faith left me, it never returned; and now do I not *know* what fond delusions we put upon ourselves when we speak of the goodness and fatherhood of God?'

'Hush, my darling; do not speak like that! You know what beautiful holy thoughts came to you.'

'Yes, when you once more woke the deeper, more spiritual, side of my nature. But what became of me when I lost you? The only purpose that made bare existence tolerable was to get away from all that reminded me of the past. No family affection, no love of books, no thought of God, could give me the smallest consolation; all—all was submerged in the fever of passion. Only to forget; and do you not understand, Anselm, that marriage without love was no more forbidding than the whole of existence without love? And then I had known him from childhood——'

'But all that is changed now, Stella. Do not dwell on it, I implore you,' he said. But the fear that had lodged so icily in his breast had deepened, though not an inkling of the dreadful truth had yet come to him.

'And he was rich. Yes, that counts, if you are thrown back on the lees of life. And yet at the last, when it was too late, as I listened to my mother that evening, a conviction came over me, if I had only waited—if I had not been so insanely impatient, bent on drowning my sorrow and humiliation. "In your patience ye shall win your souls." That was one of the things my mother said to me the day before my unhappy marriage.'

'Your "unhappy marriage," Stella! What are you saying?' he cried, drawing close to her, his lips parted in stony horror.

'Yes; is not that what it is called when lifelong vows are made in blind ignorance, though they are found to be impossible lies? though——'

She stopped abruptly. No, not even in that hour, when she was borne by the flood of misery which burst upon her far from the calm reserves of ordinary life, could she reveal the double duplicity of her miserable marriage. Langdale at once interpreted her words and sudden silence to mean that the man to whom she was married was accessory to the criminal imposition practised on her.

'Great God, Stella!—what are you saying?' he cried in a faint voice, his face deadly white.

Strong man though he was, with a training which inures the mind to sudden catastrophes in life, he was forced to lean heavily against an armchair, by which he stood, as the full force of the ruin that had overtaken her life dawned on him.

'Yes, Anselm. Now you know why, after the first joy of seeing you, I was silent and afraid. . . . You know how that ring is part of the mockery. . . . Ah, Anselm, how strangely you look at me! . . . You despise me! Oh, I cannot bear that!'

She gave a low cry, and covered her face with her hands. It was an old, half-childish habit. Often had he seen her indulge in it when telling tales to the Lullaboolagana children in the twilight, or expressing mock contrition for letting fly some shaft of raillery that had too keen an edge. The action, with its old mirthful associations, stung him in that hour of almost unreal misery with intolerable pain. And yet there was a shadow of anger on his face. The revulsion of bitter disappointment, the cruel thought that a little patience, a little waiting would have saved their lives from this dark shipwreck, rendered him for the moment almost blind to her anguish.

'How could you dare to marry any man when you loved another?' he said, looking at her sternly.

'Ah, you are going to leave me,' she said, in a low, broken voice. 'Forgive me before we part, Anselm—forgive me, beloved, for old love's sake! It is getting dark—tell me what to do. I have been piecing my life together, somehow believing those letters; but now—where shall I go? What is to become of me?' She looked into his face in helpless misery, and a sudden desperate resolve formed itself in his mind.

'Stella, we have been criminally, treacherously duped and deceived. But you are mine, and I am yours; and this miserable mockery of a marriage—are our whole lives to be sacrificed to this duplicity?'

'What do you want me to do, Anselm?' she said, drawing nearer to him. 'You must decide quickly. I cannot think, my head swims so strangely. Do not take me away to-day; I must wait.'

He took her hands in his, and they almost scorched him. The delirium of fever was in her face and voice. He fought with the whirl of feelings that threatened to reduce him to the weakness of a woman, and then answered in a low, emotionless voice:

'No, Stella, I will not take you away till you have calmly faced the question in all its bearings. You have been ill for some time. You are in a high fever now. You must rest, Stella; you must regain composure for my sake and your own.'

Even as he looked at her, he saw that a certain vacancy had come into her face.

'You must give me those letters, Stella, that you thought I sent you. They furnish proof of the wicked imposition that misled you. Ah, my darling, my darling, how you have suffered night and day! You must get well and strong. Do not despair; all is not lost.'

His quiet, deep voice penetrated her with an involuntary sense of confidence—of being directed and absolved from the necessity of action. At this time the burning sensation in her temples had increased to an overpowering vehemence.

'I am not as ill as you imagine,' she said, her voice sinking to a whisper. But even as she spoke a dimness fell on her eyes, and she swayed as though she would have fallen. He led her to the chair by which he stood, and knelt at her feet, raising her hands reverently to his lips.

'Stella, you know that there is nothing in the whole world I care for but to help you—to protect you from all evil, do you not?'

'Yes—yes, I do; yes, I do,' she whispered, repeating the words over and over as if they were the refrain of a song. Her face had blanched somewhat, and a great exhaustion was creeping over her.

He released her hands, and she raised them tremblingly, kissing them one by one where his lips had touched them. He saw the action, and he turned away quickly, gazing for a few moments out through the window, but seeing naught.

She leant back with closed eyes as if asleep, but opened them presently, looking round with a perplexed expression.

'I do not know this place, do I? How quiet it is, with the busts of people dead and all the grief hidden away in books. How very, very far away everything seems! But you are here, Anselm? . . . You have not left me?'

'Yes, Stella, I am here.'

Then there was silence again. Presently there was a ring, and the hall-door was opened. Langdale went out and met his stepfather in the hall.

'Well, Anselm, have you seen my Australian friend, Mrs Ritchie?' he asked in a cheery voice, as he put down one or two books and a bundle of proofs damp from the printer's, and drew off his fur-lined gloves. 'Does she not speak German with wonderful verve? She is still here? Ah, that is good—that is good. I thought she would find Kleinsauber's "Comparative Ethnology" a fascinating work. You see, with all her vivacity, she has an unusual love of knowledge. In that she is like your sister Amalie—a combination which is, above all others, calculated to make a woman happy.'

'Very true,' answered Langdale gravely. And then he told the Professor that the Australian lady seemed suddenly indisposed—that he feared she was far from well.

'Ah, now that you speak of it, I have thought each time I saw her that she was greatly paler and thinner. Oh, she is staying only a few houses away. Her husband is in London. She must come and stay with us as soon as your mother returns.'

The good Professor hurried into the study. 'My dear young lady, you are not well. Perhaps you have been reading Kleinsauber's book too closely. You saw it the moment you came in, of course—here on the table? It is wonderful! wonderful!' etc.

The kind, benevolent old face, bending over her with anxious solicitude, helped Stella a little to recall her straying faculties.

When she spoke of going, the Professor proposed to get a hackney carriage, but Stella said the little walk through the fresh air would revive her. The Professor and Langdale walked with her to the pension, and she bade them good-bye at the door, saying that she would be better on the morrow. Early next day Langdale received the two fatal letters, which Stella enclosed with the words: 'To-day I cannot see very well, nor think. Things are going away from me. I only know I will do whatever you wish.'

That night she was prostrated with acute fever. She lay for weeks hovering between life and death. Time after time the crisis seemed to have passed; but a disastrous wave of recollection would sweep over her; and then the fever re-asserted itself once more. But in the end her youth and hitherto unbroken physique triumphed. She struggled back to life shaken and wasted. Day by day she gained a little strength. But mentally a strange change had been wrought. She remembered all that had passed, but the sources of emotion seemed atrophied. It was like a moral aphasia. She had forgotten how to feel; and she shrank from the possibility of mental suffering with a certain morbid horror. All the passion and ardour and power of vivid emotion had left her. If she could be glad for anything, she would have been glad that now at last she knew what it was to have a slug-gish nature—a heart equally steeled against hope and memory.

CHAPTER L

IT was mid-day in Berlin on the last day of February. After a suc-cession of stormy days of unusual severity a hard frost set in, which had lasted now nearly a week. The Thiergarten, all save the foot-paths, was deep in snow, crisp, glittering, and frozen over. The trees, to the tips of the slenderest twigs, were thickly frosted, and gleam-ing in their coating of unspotted purity. But the keen, clear sky, which had lent such brilliancy to the frost for some days, was now completely overcast. Another storm was evidently gathering. The heavens wondrously low down were unbroken in their heavy sombreness—a sullen background piled up with heavy banks of pur-plish-black clouds and vapoury masses of dun-coloured smoke. There was not a break nor a rift—not even a tone of paler gray or lead colour—to show where behind all the sun must somewhere be shining.

The contrast between the lowering sky and the trees in their gleaming delicate white splendour made up a wonderful scene for eyes that had never before seen any of the moods of a northern winter. Stella, who had by this time passed the first stage of conva-lescence, sat by one of the large double windows of their sitting-room in the Eisengau pension looking at the scene with an impassive gaze. A book lay open on a table near her—some needlework had fallen to her feet, where Dustiefoot lay, alternately dozing off into a light slumber, and looking up at his mistress as if longing for some sign of recognition.

Ritchie sat near the open fireplace, the only one in the house, and constructed for an English invalid who had stayed there for a couple of years some time previously. There was a glowing coal fire whose lambent flames were joyously thrown back by blue-and-white tiles that lined the fireplace, each with figures more or less classic or symbolical. Ritchie looked up from the sporting newspaper he was reading and stared into the fire for some time with knitted brows. Then his eyes rested on some of these figures with a look of marked disapproval.

'I say, Stella.'

She turned round with a start.

'I wish you would come and tell me what some of these old hags are doing, or what they mean. Just look at this one with a stick something like a stock-whip handle, and a shock of wool on it.'

He placed a chair for Stella, and she looked at the figure he pointed out with a slow smile breaking on her face.

'Why, that is Clotho, one of the Parcae—the inexorable sisters, the daughters of night and darkness——'

'Well, that is all Greek to me. Why do people put three sulky-looking females round a fireplace—one with a rum sort of stick, the other with a ball of twine, and this savage-looking old party with a pair of shears, as if she were going to cut a fellow's jugular vein?'

'That is her *métier*—her trade. You must know the old Greeks had many tales and symbols of man's life. These are the three Fates—mysterious women who preside over our destinies. Clotho with her spindle spins the thread of life, Lachesis measures its length, and Atropos with the abhorred shears cuts it short.'

'Then, according to that, this is the old vixen who nearly did for you, Stella. Look at the squint of the old banshee. . . . Thank God she didn't have a snip at you with her shears this time, Stella.'

'But it would have been so much easier to die than come back bit by bit so weak and shaken. I remember I had an old doll once I was very fond of. Its hair fell off, and the blue came out of its eyes, and its complexion disappeared altogether. Last of all, a kangaroo pup* of Tom's ran away with it, and took its head off, and I never found it again. But I got the head of another defunct doll, and I got Tom to fasten it on to Sheba somehow. I feel just as she must have felt. Ted, are you sure that Dr Seemann did not screw someone else's head on me?'

'When you talk to me a little I am quite sure he didn't. But, by Jove! Stella, it was an awful close shave. I had just got back from the old man's funeral, and was going into the dining-room to hear the will read when I got the telegram Maisie sent, and for a bit I thought to myself, "It's all U P, old man." For though I didn't say much, I could see you were awfully ill all the time. Once on board ship a fellow who was very ill—he hadn't come out of his cabin the first two weeks—was with me on the deck the first day he came up. We had got pretty chummy, for his cabin was next to mine, and I often did little things for him—roused up the doctor once when poor old Lakemann seemed to be choking. Well, we were walking up and down, and he spied you sitting back and looking away over the sea— one of the Miss O'Briens near you. "Who is that lady?" says he, and I saw he was looking at you. "That is my wife," said I. "No," said he, "I don't mean that lively-looking young lady. I could almost tell without being told she is your wife. I mean that one leaning back, looking exactly like a sleep-walker. She must have seen a ghost some time." He would hardly believe I wasn't putting a hoax on him when I said you were my wife, and not Miss Harry O'Brien. Many a time after that I thought you did just look as if you were awake in your sleep—no, sleeping awake. Oh bother, you know what I mean.'

'Yes; but you must think of something more lively to tell me. I am very tired of myself, Ted.'

'Oh, but I want to talk a little about yourself, Stella. Always when I want to talk to you, since you got well enough to speak, someone is in the way, or you are not up, or you have gone to bed, or there is a silent fit on you—and old Seemann said to me: "Don't make her talk when she doesn't want to till she is built up"—as if you were a wall or a chimney.'

'Has it been very dull for you in Berlin all these weeks, Ted?'

'Well, it didn't matter to me a straw where I was while you were so ill, Stella. But since you've been out of danger I've been toddling round. You see, I know several fellows now. The Avenells came across in the same boat with me. Dick, the eldest of them, is in the British embassy—an attaché they call it. He speaks of his duties, but as far as I can make out, his work is to always wear a neat suit and a flower in his buttonhole, and play scat* and billiards. Of course he has to go to dinner-parties and balls, and the worst of it is he often has to dance attendance on a fat old frump half the night, instead of looking after some pretty girl. That's the very worst aspect of diplomacy, he says. And then Farningham here is very good company—at any rate, he's the sort I get on with. And you like Mrs Farningham?'

'Yes, very much,' returned Stella, but her voice all the time was perfectly level and emotionless.

'Is it Farningham or his wife that is related to the old Professor you met at Dr Stein's?'

'It is Mrs Farningham. Her mother is married to the Professor.'

'And there was a Dr Langdale—who came from the Professor's

every day, sometimes twice, to ask for you, till you were out of danger—isn't he another relation of Mrs Farningham's?'

'Her brother.' She shivered a little as if she were cold, and Ted heaped more coal on the fire.

'Ah, now I begin to get things a little straight. I've sometimes been most awfully mixed up. "My wife's father-in-law," Farningham says, "my stepchildren," "my wife's stepfather," "my mother-in-law," "my wife's mother-in-law," "my brother-in-law," "my wife's brother-in-law," just like one of those affairs like a little telescope you turn round, and see different snaps of things spluttering at you every blessed shake. You see Mrs Farningham's first husband's people are here from America in shoals. It's a jolly good thing there wasn't room for many of them in this pension.'

'Why—don't you like them?'

'Oh, I'd like them well enough, if there weren't so many women among them, with not a blessed turn to do but ask a fellow questions—clatter-clatter all the time, like a bell on a runaway steer. There's one of them a tall, thin woman, with eyes like knitting-pins. She's got about twenty hairs on her scalp, and twenty skewers to keep them in a tiny bob on top of her head, leaving her long, lean neck perfectly bare. I'm not what you'd call a prude, you know, but, by George, the nakedness of that neck gives me a sort of a turn! She writes for two newspapers, and she has a red morocco sort of book, with an indelible pencil, and sometimes she stops in the middle of eating her soup to put something down in this. "I dare not trust my memory, it's so treacherous," she says. "By the Lord," thinks I to myself, "I wish it were so treacherous you'd forget to ask me questions!" Yes, I sit next to her at the table-d'hôte, and there she goes at me hammer and tongs. And the less I know about the things she's interested in, the more I catch her using the indelible pencil on the sly. "Now, Mr Ritchie, you are laughing at me, when you say you *never* heard of Raphael or Michael Angelo,"* she'll say, screwing her long neck round above my head, like a native companion in a fit. Ah, she's yards taller than I am. Wait till you see her. And there Farningham sits on the opposite side of the table, grinning at me like a negro minstrel. Let me see, she's his wife's first husband's first cousin's aunt once removed. Now what relation would you say she is to Farningham?'

'I really haven't the faintest conception,' returned Stella, with a little smile.

'No more has he. But she calls him Charles, and speaks to him solemnly about the privileged classes in England. You know he is to be Sir Charles F. when his governor dies. And then she reminds him of things that happened to his wife's first husband, as if he were the one, you know. Now, I call that deuced awkward; at any rate, it might be in many cases. I dare say it would be more damaging to the other fellow though, if Farningham had been the first husband. They say Mrs Farningham's eldest boy by her first husband will be a millionaire when he is twenty-one; but he is a delicate little chap. Am I talking too much, Stella?'

'Oh no; it's rather amusing. I thought by something Mrs Farningham let fall that some of her American connections were a little trying. But she did not say much; she's very loyal to them.'

'She's a regular trump. She says the right thing to everybody; and she's like you, Stella, she never gets the least ruffled—never sticks her back up, but takes everything as if it were rather fun. She had a bad illness in Dresden, but she has got over it so well—she's better than she was before. I wish you were like that. What does old Seemann mean by some mischief before the fever came on? Was it— was it that shock, Stella? You know what I mean.'

She put up her hands to her head wearily. 'I know what you mean, Ted. But there was something besides that: and the day I was taken ill it came all over again, but worse; only nothing seems very bad now. I do not think I should talk about things that used to hurt me. It cannot be helped any more; nothing can that has gone really wrong.' She gave a long, low sigh, and lay back with closed eyes.

'Don't say that, Stella, please,' said Ted gently. 'It was awfully steep to think I was the cause of all when your life hung on a thread. I used to go to the opera and places; but often I didn't know whether I was standing on my head or my heels.'

'You are not to blame for my illness, Ted. If anyone is to blame, it is Laurette; but I myself most of all. Oh, I don't mean what she concealed about you.'

Ted looked perplexed, but he would ask no questions; and, indeed, he attributed Stella's words to some confusion left by the fever. It may be noted in passing, that Stella did not once suspect him of any complicity in the imposition that had wrecked her life. Only at this period she would have rejected the word 'wrecked' as being too strong. Everything had shrunk so inconceivably. It was as though nothing mattered very much, if only one were left in perfect quiet.

'Dr Seemann is to come only every second day now, he told me,' said Ted, in a cheerful voice. 'What a stunning old chap he is! The best fever doctor in Berlin, they say; and you can't easily beat that. It was the Professor who saw to his attending you.'

There was silence for a few moments, and then Stella said very slowly:

'Do you know when Dr Langdale came to Berlin?' She named him without the least tremor.

'No; but I remember the first time I noticed him particularly. It was two weeks after I came back. I was at the opera-house, with Dick Avenell. We went out into the wide passage behind the boxes, and there Dick met a couple of very lively little French ladies. I don't think they were any better than they ought to be, you know—nothing but a couple of roses and a dagger with diamonds in the handle by way of a bodice. Dick swore I had just come from New Caledonia, and had brought a message from some of their friends there. After a little time, he dodged round a pillar all at once, and left me talking to them alone; at least, they were jabbering away, half in French; and I put in a word edgeways, now and then, in English, but I'm blessed if I could tell what any of us were saying. In the middle of it, who should come round but this Dr Langdale, with his mother! I had seen him once or twice when he came to inquire after you for the Kell-witzes, and he stared hard at me, I can tell you. I didn't know his name till Farningham told me. It seems he's been in Australia for a little time; and he has been a good deal off colour, too, in Berlin. He went to Vienna last week, to see a chum of his who is making a great noise with some operations on eyes, so Farningham told me. It was lucky the Farninghams came here, a few days after I got back from London. I've gone about with him a good deal, and with Dick and his brother Minimus—comical name, isn't it? Comes of three brothers being at a public school together. Now, why do you suppose Dick left me in the lurch like that? He told me plump it was because he saw an old dowager-aunt of a girl he's sweet on, coming our way, and he couldn't afford to be seen with the little Frenchies. A married man, said he, with no end of tin, can stand any racket; but a penni-less attaché has to be deuced proper when on parade. Wasn't that a friendly trick to play a fellow? But he and Minimus are awful fun sometimes. Minimus is supposed to be studying Oriental languages for a "diplomatic career" in India. "People teach languages so much better in Germany," he says; and he goes once a month, perhaps, to an old chap, who swears at him because he is an idle young dog, and makes an appointment with him to come next week to learn some alphabet; but Min. doesn't, as a rule, turn up. He says I'd better give him a billet on my run; he thinks it would be much jollier than spoiling his eyes over rubbishy Eastern pot-hooks. I've often been more miserable than a tuckerless dingo; but still I went to theatres and things. I couldn't nurse you, Stella, you see!'

'Of course not. It was much better you should go about.'

'But now I can look after you a bit, Stella; and that little Maisie— by George, she's worth her weight in gold!'

There was a knock at the door; and in response to Ritchie's robust invitation to come in, a fair, youthful-looking man entered, slight, and rather under the middle height.

'Are you allowed to see people so early in the day, Mrs Ritchie? Why, this is quite the Darby-and-Joan* business—and an open fireplace, I declare!'

'Yes; and the three inexorable sisters—daughters of Night and Darkness—with the spindle-and-shears business, Farningham!' said Ted, with a dignified wave of his hand towards the tiles.

'Why, Ritchie, old fellow, you're coming it strong with the classics. Do tell that to Miss Caroline Sendler. You must know, Mrs Ritchie, that your husband is carrying on a barefaced flirtation with an elderly lady from America—one related to me in some mystical way!'

'I remember. She's your wife's first——'

'Don't—don't, my dear fellow. Let it remain with the dark riddles of a world not realized.* You are really making progress now, Mrs Ritchie?'

'Oh yes, thank you. To-day, I quite know the people from the trees.'

'And do you eat anything? Because I have heard dreadful tales on that score.'

'Now, Stella, tell the truth. Yesterday, you looked at the thigh of a pigeon, and said, "Oh, take it away—it looks so dreadfully pathetic!" And that was your dinner. Yes, upon my honour, Farningham, I had to take it away; and a little while afterwards, when Fräulein—what's her name, the nurse you know?—came in with a little soup, Signora here said, without blinking, "But I've had dinner, you know!"'

'Ah, but that sort of thing will never do. My wife declares she ate all day when she was getting well. And that reminds me why I came!'

'Now you really wound me. I thought it was to find out whether I ate anything,' said Stella, with a little of her old sprightliness.

'So it was; but merely to knock at the door and inquire, and then ask if my wife might come. But this young man was too lazy to open the door, as Fräulein Hennig does. And you look so jolly and cosy, one can't tear one's self away. Now I know why Amalie and I have given up being domesticated. It's the absence of an open fireplace!'

At this juncture another knock was heard at the door, which was speedily opened.

'May I come in?' said a flute-like woman's voice.

It was Mrs Farningham: a tall, graceful woman, with dark eyes and hair, a clear pale skin, a delicately aquiline nose, and an exquisitely chiselled mouth. In feature there was a strong resemblance between her and Langdale, and also at times in expression.

'Ah, you are really better this morning!' she said, taking Stella's hand, and giving Ted a friendly nod.

'I was on the eve of coming to tell you,' said her husband. 'But I suppose I'd better stay a little longer, and then our family circle will be completed by the babies and—collateral branches! You'd better send me away, Mrs Ritchie; for I assure you there is absolutely no end to us! And will you forgive me if I carry your husband off? I am always hiring or buying or exchanging horses; and I always get "choused," he says, if I am alone!'

'Hadn't I better take Dustiefoot for a run, Stella? . . . Lose him? That's more than my place is worth. You may be sure I won't come back without him. Out, boy, out!'

But though Dustiefoot rose up with alacrity at the sound, he got no farther than the door, till he ran back, and put his head on his mistress's lap, looking up fondly into her face.

'Out, Dustiefoot—out!' said Stella; and on this the dog trotted away.

When the two men were gone, Mrs Farningham drew her chair nearer Stella's, saying;

'How did you sleep last night, dear?'

'Tolerably well, thank you, for two or three hours.'

'And after that?'

'Oh, then it was the old stupid story. Endless processions of people filing by, as if I were a mummy holding a levée.'

'And that chamber into which you dare not peep—does it still remain?'

'Yes; and myriads of voices high and low telling me to pass in— but they get fainter night by night. Now, when I waken up in the soft light and see Fräulein Hennig's quiet face, I do not any longer feel like a terrified child that covers its head and trembles because of ghost stories it has heard.'

'Ah, that is a great stage. This is your first serious illness. For the first time you know something of the terror of demoralized nerves. But now that you begin to regain tranquillity the worst is over.'

'Do you think so? I am glad to feel so unmoved; but sometimes— I hardly know why—it frightens me a little that all which used to be so much to me seems so incredibly remote.'

'Oh, that is merely brain exhaustion. As you get stronger—as you are "built up," to use Dr Seemann's words—the old interests will revive.'

CHAPTER LI

MRS FARNINGHAM's prediction was, unfortunately, not verified. Stella's strength slowly returned, but her mental condition remained much the same. As the weeks went on she became, if anything, more silent, more apathetic. The first event that roused her had also the effect of bringing on a feverish attack. It was a great concert given in the Philharmonic Hall in Bernburger Strasse. The conductor and violin soloist were the first of Germany, supported by the full strength of the Philharmonic orchestra. But what made this concert especially interesting was that a 'Sinfonische Dichtung,'* the composition of an Italian musician, was to be rendered for the first time—the music being, in fact, still unpublished.

The theme is taken from the 'Divine Comedy.' It is the love-tragedy of Francesca Polenta, named da Rimini, and of Paolo Malatesta.* It begins in the second circle of hell, guarded by Minos,* who, at the entrance, weighs each transgression, and fixes the grade to which the ill-fated spirit shall be thrust. Deep, slow, mysterious waves of music thrilled the mind with a sudden apprehension of the gloom unpenetrated by the faintest ray of light. Then very slowly there rose, as if in the far distance, the howling of that terrible storm of hell—growing fierce and wild and discordant, as if the sea were riven into mountains and abysmal depths by two opposing tempests, and high above all the cries of lost souls.

After the storm of the elements and of tortured souls falls shudderingly into silence, the compassionate voice of the poet arises as he asks the two who clung together even in hell itself, 'O anime affannate, venite a noi parlar, s'altri nol niega'*—'O ye tired souls, come speak to us, if no one doth forbid it.' Then came the low, anguished, wailing sound of a woman's voice telling her sinful love-story in eternal torment. No sound in life or Nature can surely ever reproduce the piercing pathos of a human voice in hopeless misery like the violin under the touch of a great master.

'There is no deeper sorrow than to recall in misery a happy time.'* There were many eyes dimmed among the audience when the heart-broken confession was translated into passionate, shuddering music. The symphony from beginning to end made a strange impression upon Stella. And as in the leading theme the musician had cunningly woven the story of Lancelot, whose love, too skilfully told by the old romancer, had been such dangerous reading,* so, through all the storm of darkness and despair, through the inexorable remembrance of an hour when overmastering passion trampled duty under foot, Stella was conscious of piercing recollections rising in her brain, which since her illness had no more power to move her than if they were idle spiders' strings. But now they were aflame with vivid terrible life. That woman's voice, pleading, broken, despairing, arose in fitful tones, making the blood start vehemently in her veins—making her shrink and tremble like a creature upon whom suddenly a great burden has been laid.

'It has been too much for you,' whispered Mrs Farningham. 'Let me take you home now. . . .'

'Yes, I really want to leave before anything else drives away the memory of this.'

That night Stella woke, weeping bitterly. In her dreams by night she had been listening over again to the hopeless wailing story told by Francesca to Dante. For days afterwards the fever burned in her veins; and when this passed away she began to avoid people—to shrink from meeting them. She began to walk out a little; but she preferred to go alone to the Thiergarten, with only Dustiefoot as a companion. Even Maisie's presence seemed a trouble to her. When she was with others she had the air of one trying unsuccessfully to understand what was going on around her. She sometimes fell asleep in the daytime, and seemed to wander for years in a strange dark land beset with vague shapes of dread, and then woke up with a start to find her momentary slumbers had not been noticed. She began to confound events with visions of the night. Things that had been said or done in the morning would seem at night-fall to be separated from her by vast tracts of time. She began to have a dread that she could not grasp what people said to her.

One forenoon, as she was alone in the Thiergarten, near the great monument of the nation's victory over France, she suddenly met Professor and Mrs Kellwitz. She looked so timid and startled—almost so confused—on seeing them, that Mrs Kellwitz's motherly heart was wrung with a sudden dread. She knew that Farningham, her son-in-law, and Ritchie had gone to Homburg* together for a week. Yet no one who knew the position of affairs could charge Ted with neglect. He was simply like one who looked on helpless and perplexed. He was always ready at Stella's command; but she had none to give. He was anxious to take her anywhere and everywhere; but she had no wishes except to be left alone. Even a man more gifted with insight and with resources in himself than Ted had ever been, might be excused for taking refuge in the companionship and recreations that were open to him. He was in a foreign land with no occupation beyond amusing himself. And though this is a position that tests the calibre of minds more strongly fortified against the baser temptations of life, yet to one who observed Ritchie closely at this time it would become apparent that the excesses into which he had earlier fallen were due less to inherent weakness than to that Nemesis power which nature often puts forth when but a small part of man's faculties are touched by his daily life.

At this time, also, Mrs Farningham was much engaged among the poor. She had endeavoured, but unsuccessfully, to lead Stella to resume her interest in those she had befriended. But though she gave money lavishly, herself she would not give. She had become conscious of some imminent danger that threatened to engulf her. She avoided contact with all that might arouse her. The chief aim that swayed her at this time was to spare herself morally—to shirk those stormy depths in her nature which threatened ever and anon to surge up and bear her she knew not whither. But on this day Mrs Kellwitz, struck with a sudden fear, would listen to no excuses. 'You must come home with me,' she said decisively. And then, when they reached the house, she sent a messenger for Maisie, and to tell the Baroness that Mrs Ritchie was to be her guest for a few days to come.

During the day she talked to Stella of many things—of books and pictures and music. Once only the girl showed a dawning interest, a little tremor of emotion, and that was when the Italian composer's 'Sinfonische Dichtung' was named. Towards evening Mrs Kellwitz made her lie down to rest in her own cosy sitting-room. After a little she fell fast asleep, and the wide dark circles round the eyes, the noble sweep of the brow, the thin outlines of the cheeks, and the lines round the mouth, all bore the stamp of mental languor, of pain temporarily at bay, but not vanquished. Mrs Kellwitz softly closed the door behind her, and a few minutes afterwards her son Anselm came home.

He, also, was much changed. His face had, in the last few months, grown grave and sad—almost stern in repose. Through his stepfather's intimacy with Dr Seemann, Anselm knew the various phases of Stella's dangerous illness. He knew that latterly the physician was puzzled at the mental rigidity which had fallen on her. He had often seen her at a little distance when she walked in the Thiergarten, and had kept aloof for fear of causing her pain while she was still weak, and also because of the cruel perplexity which entangled their further meeting. Once, indeed, Dustiefoot nearly betrayed him as he sat at a little distance from the bench on which Stella rested—a book in her hand, but not reading. The dog recognised Anselm, and rushed up to him with signs of delight which he would never have bestowed on a stranger. He even rushed backwards and forwards between the two in a joyous way, as if anxious to tell his mistress that an old Lullaboolagana friend was near. But she did not heed Dustiefoot's movements. She sat pale and motionless, with downcast eyes, oblivious to all around her. The sight was more than Langdale could bear. He would have laid down his life to serve her, and yet he dared not speak to her, being in fear lest his face and the sound of his voice would do her harm, and not good. He suffered horribly. Yet he knew that hers was the more intolerable burden. For through all he had work to do, and he was in constant intercourse with people whose knowledge in some one direction exceeded his own—circumstances which serve to make life coherent to the lover of knowledge, even when it has lost its best savour.

To-day, when he came in, his mother observed with concern that the fagged, strained look with which she had been struck on first seeing him when she returned with her daughter from Dresden had deepened rather than become less.

'You are working too hard, Anselm,' she said, looking at him keenly. 'You are as greedy as ever after knowledge. Those lectures of Virchow at the University,* and the honorary work at the hospital, and your writing, and all the rest of it, do not make much of a holiday.'

'You forget, mother, that I had a long one——'

'Oh, in Australia! I hope you don't think of going back there. I think there must be something insidious in the climate—something that undermines the constitution. There is that young lady the Professor met there and found so charming. You met her here, did you not?—Mrs Ritchie, you know——'

'Yes—what of her?'

'Well, I should very much like to have your opinion of her. I have made her come here for a few days. She is sleeping just now. I am exceedingly afraid that there is something very much amiss.'

Langdale felt a terror of what fresh catastrophe might be in store. The fixed look in Stella's face the last time he saw her at a little distance had haunted him night and day.

There is always a shock in hearing our worst fears put into bald, uncompromising words. This Langdale experienced when his mother went on:

'It is not her body now, it is her mind. I am sure of that. Perhaps she would have more confidence in an English doctor. If you would see her here in an informal way—she and your stepfather were so friendly, and Amalie, too, is very fond of her. I hardly know what to think of her husband. Amalie says he is devoted to her—but, if that is the case, she cannot be devoted to him. There must be something very much amiss when two young people drift so far apart at a time like this.'

Poor Langdale! Few situations could have been more ironical in a quiet, unaggressive way than to sit listening to his mother while she calmly discussed the situation which was the very core of the keenest sorrows and interests in his life. So far nothing could have been gained by taking his mother or sister into his confidence as to the relations which had at one time existed between himself and Stella, and the treachery that had come between them. But he was prepared at any moment to tell them all, and to seek their help in somehow averting that darkest of all misfortunes which seemed stealthily creeping nearer. In the meantime he kept silence. He absented himself from home that evening. Next morning he saw Stella alone in the library which had witnessed their first strange meeting in the Old World.

CHAPTER LII

SHE knew he had returned from Vienna some weeks previously, and she was in a manner prepared to see him in his mother's house. Yet, when they stood face to face, something akin to fear was visible in her manner. Otherwise, he was more agitated than she was. They touched each other's hands, and then they sat facing each other in a silence full of ghost-like memories. Stella was the first to speak.

'You have been away, I think,' she said, without looking at him.

He told her something of his journey, of his old friend Max, and his rising renown as an oculist. He noticed that her attention wandered, and that she kept nervously playing with her wedding-ring, which hung looser than ever on her finger. There was a pause.

'Yes, it must have been very interesting,' she said, looking up—a remark that had no direct relation to what he had last said.

Something clutched at his throat and gave him a horrible, choking sensation.

She looked into his face fixedly.

'Don't, Anselm—don't say anything. I cannot bear it. You do not know. I can bear to speak to you now, because everything is all over and done with. But there are times: you do not know——'

She spoke in a low, imploring voice, and then suddenly broke off.

'What do I not know, Stella?' he said, mastering himself with a violent effort, and speaking in a calm, unmoved tone.

'Oh, it would be stupid to tell you. Let us talk of something else—
the weather, for instance.'

This little attempt at recovering something of her old gaiety smote
him to the heart.

'No, I cannot talk of anything else, Stella. I want you to speak to
me of yourself. You know, in the old days, we agreed to be friends.
We can at least be friends.'

'Yes, yes; we can be friends,' she said, and then she suddenly began
to sob.

He kept perfectly silent. When she had recovered composure, he
went on in the same calm voice as before.

'You know, Stella, friends should help one another. I think there
is something you dread. Tell me what it is. I may be able to help
you.'

'Are you afraid, too?' she said quickly. He did not reply immediately. He felt like one groping in the dark, afraid to move too quickly
lest harm should be done. Then she added hesitatingly: 'I have been
afraid for some time. The voices and the faces have gone away. But
there is a silence coming round me, and every day I am more alone—
an abyss between me and everyone that none can cross.'

'No, no, Stella; not so. How many care for you!'

'But I cannot care for them—not in the old way. There is a strange
vacancy, an apathy; it comes creeping, creeping. It is like the
tide rising round a ship that has been stranded. O my God, it is
horrible—it is horrible!' She covered her face with her hands, and as
he looked at her in tearless agony, he trembled as if in an ague fit.
'Do you know what I keep thinking of sometimes?' she said, suddenly looking up. 'Of some old story in Ovid, where one says: "Give
me your hand before I am a serpent all over."* Those old stories
where people were turned into birds, and trees, and reptiles, they are
not so terrible as—as some other things.'

'No, they are not. Only when we see a great danger, the very fact
that we see it shows we may try to avoid it.' His voice almost failed
him once or twice, for there was something in her tone and manner,
even more than in her words, which confirmed his worst fears.

'You still keep up your old habit of taking a book with you when
you go out,' he said presently, in a lighter tone.

'Yes, but I cannot read; is it not strange?' she said, looking at him
with wide-opened eyes.

'Ah, these times come to one,' he answered. 'Now I am going to tell you something about myself—may I?'

'Oh, of course,' she said, with more animation than she had yet shown.

'Well, I have finished that treatise I was writing at Minjah—about the conditions of factory labour. There is some other work I want to do; and, besides, I have gone quite blunt over the thing. The facts, and I believe their inferences, are correct; but the style I am sure is odious. Now, will you go over the MS for me?'

It was some little time before she spoke, and then it was in a hesitating, broken way, which was quite foreign to her old, quick, spontaneous manner.

'I would be so glad to do it, but I lose things so dreadfully—things I have been thinking of. It is as though—I hardly know how to explain it—as if I came on blank spaces in my mind. Words and thoughts drop away out of reach quite suddenly. I am almost afraid to speak to people, lest I might not know what they say. I was afraid even of you. And yet how kind you have always been—except that one letter. But it was because it was wickedly—hurt—and the other one I never got. No, I never got it—never.'

'But about this work I want you to do for me, Stella?' he answered. The clear, harmonious intonations of his voice were lost in a constrained huskiness; but though his heart was throbbing wildly with fierce and contending emotions, his self-possession was outwardly unbroken. 'It is very important I should get the help of some friend; and there is no one whose aid I care to ask but yours. It does not in the least matter about your taking a long while over it. Do only a page or two at a time.'

'I will try to do it; but I will not let anyone see it, for fear it may be wrong. I will try not to make mistakes; but I do not know. It is what you were writing at Lullaboolagana?'

'Yes; and there is one thing more I am going to ask you. There is a convalescent home for little children on the northern outskirts of the town. My mother knows it. Will you let her take you there?'

'Oh, Anselm—no! They will be pale and miserable. They will hurt me; and when things hurt me. . . . Ah, you do not know how dreadful it is!' and a look of helpless fear came into her face, which pierced him like a sword.

Before he could trust himself to answer this objection, she went on, sometimes speaking in a low, hurried voice, at others very slowly, with a curious hesitation, as if the words she sought eluded her, while often she used terms that but approximately expressed what she meant.

'Sometimes at night I keep thinking of a poor half-crazy Welsh-woman who used to wander about, some years ago. She had a great dislike to staying in houses. She always said there were adders in them. She was not so—so badly hurt in her mind, you know, that she ought to be locked up. You know, Anselm, it is true, when people lose everything—when they forget the meaning of all around them—they are locked away like the dead; only they are not quite like the dead. Johanna, that was her name. . . . Sometimes she came to Fairacre, and mother and Kirsty were very kind to her.'

She broke off abruptly, and gave a long shuddering sigh.

'Ah, after all, you have never been at Fairacre!' she said, fixing her great mournful eyes on his face, after a pause. 'It was near the vine-arcade the scarlet fairy roses grew I was to wear the day you came, when the *Pâquerette* reached port. You always liked me to wear roses; and when I flew up to meet you, a bird began to sing as if it were wild with joy. . . . Have I hurt you?' she said falteringly, as he rose and turned away abruptly, his lips trembling and ashy pale. He could not speak.

She stole up to him with a frightened air, and, looking into his face, she saw that his eyes were wet. She gave a little low moan, and put her hand on his arm.

'Anselm, what can I say to make you glad? You were always so serene and hopeful. . . . Do you remember what I said when I sent you those dreadful letters that have been burnt into my brain?— or did I dream it? I shall do what you think is right. . . . I am not dreaming now!'

He turned quickly, raising his hands to draw her to him; but with a strong effort he resisted the impulse. He noticed that, since she began to speak to him, something of the tension in her face had relaxed.

'Tell me about this poor woman, Stella, who used to come to Fairacre,' he said, in as calm a voice as was possible to him.

'About Johanna? The last time she came, she was very strange. She said that when she stayed inside speckled adders crawled round her at night, saying, "'Drown yourself—drown yourself!' There are

three under the table now!" That was what she said, and then mother
tried to soothe her. She said if they were there, we would see them.
But Johanna laughed: it was such a sharp—no, a shrill laugh. I
laughed like her the other night, and it sounded horrible in the
silence. Poor Dustiefoot was frightened; he began to growl at my
door. He lies on the mat outside. . . . You are not angry with me, are
you?' She looked in his face with confused timidity.

'Ah, no, Stella; why should I be?' he said in a choked voice.

She passed her hand wearily over her eyes.

'Well, I have not finished. There is some reason why I began to
tell you. Ah, it was about poor Johanna. Yes, she laughed and said
the adders wouldn't let anyone like mother see them. They were no
fools. "Does it not say in the Word of God, 'Be ye wise as serpents'?"*
That was what she said. "The way they all came staring at me!" she
said. "You see, adders have a great advantage over us in that way,
ma'am, having no eyelashes. If I prayed at all, I think I would pray
that these beasties might be kept from me." Then mother held her
hand, and said, "But you do still pray, I hope?" "Well, no, ma'am,"
she said, "not lately. You see, there's some that the Lord lets off His
hands altogether. If they pray, He turns a deaf ear to them; if they
are in want or sickness, He gives them no wine or mead out of a
crystal cup." . . . She did drown herself at last,' she ended, in an awe-
stricken tone, looking into Anselm's face with startled, wide-opened
eyes.

'Yes, but about the convalescent children?' he said gently.

'Oh, I know now why I told you about this poor woman,' she
answered quickly. 'I am terrified of being hurt, because when I am,
as I was so badly with the music at the Philharmonic Hall, I—I
think it would be better—oh, so much better—to be quite at rest.
Some days ago I walked by the canal——' She suddenly stopped, a
half-guilty look in her face.

'You have been awake very much of late, Stella,' he said, betraying no sign of anguish, save in the constrained accents of his voice.

'Yes; but that is better than to be made to sleep. Often when I am
asleep, everything I touch falls in atoms—everything crumbles away.
Then I dream something dreadful has happened, and I am glad to
wake. But when I am wide awake, it is worse—oh, much worse—
than any dream!'

'But, Stella, these children are not miserable and wretched. It is not a great hospital; there are never more than fourteen. It is a private place, founded by seven ladies—my mother is one of them—for children who have all but recovered from illness. The greatest joy you could give them would be to tell them a little Australian story, or take them out for a drive in the country two or three at a time. My mother and I took four of them up to Treptow the other day. It is on the river, and there is a large coffee-room quite close to the Spree. They sat by the window eating cakes and seeing the boats and barges sail by, and then we went out into the wood behind Treptow, and every little weed they saw gave them joy. You have plenty of time.'

'Plenty of time,' she repeated vacantly, and then a little afterwards, as if the meaning of the words had gradually dawned on her, 'There is endless time—and it is all empty and terrible, and full of crumbling things. I like to go outside because I feel as if I were then away from the corridor—the dreadful corridor. You do not know what I mean by that.'

'No; but you can explain it to me, Stella.'

His calm, even voice seemed to allay her rising agitation. She passed her hand slowly over her brow before answering.

'You know, for weeks back when I try to read, or write, or even sew—whatever it is I try to do slips away from me; even when people talk round me their voices go a long way off. And then I am in a wide, great, empty corridor, where my footsteps make a strange sound. But I do not mind that. It is the long, dark passages that wind out of it. I feel as if I were dragged along them against my will, and at the end there are great cages with iron bars in front, strong iron bars, for there are wild creatures behind them.'

She looked up into his face with a terror in her eyes that made the perspiration stand out in cold drops on his forehead.

'Dear Stella, do not think of them,' he said in a low, imploring voice.

'Ah, but you do not know—they are not savage creatures out of the woods. They are human beings—they are women, some of them; but they beat at the bars and shriek to get out. When I hear them I feel as if I must shriek too. They are mad—they must be kept there because they are more dangerous than wild beasts. Ah, my God! how they terrify me! I keep silent. I say nothing of all this, because people would be afraid of me as I am of these cages, and—and those that are in them.'

'No, no, Stella. That is only how people feel after they have had a terrible illness like yours. To-morrow you must come to see these children——'

'Ah, the children. They have been ill. You are nursing them back to life again—how cruel that is often! They might have died while the world seemed still beautiful, and they could pray to God, "Our Father, who art in heaven, hallowed be Thy name." Think what it is, Anselm, to outlive all that—to know that there is no Father in heaven—that there are people who must be put into iron cages—that you see it coming nearer every day—a terror you cannot name!'

'Stella, Stella, think how wrong it would be to let ourselves sink under one idea—one aspect of life in that way! It is only because your illness still hangs about you that you can have such strange thoughts. If these children were neglected now, when their parents are unable to care for them properly, their constitutions might be injured—impaired for life. It is not that they would die—for most creatures, having once gained a footing in the world, make up their minds to stay if possible. It is that the seeds would be laid for lingering maladies—perhaps for madness itself. That is what you can do, Stella—help to save some people from the wretchedness of lives hopelessly mutilated by disease. I know there are some forms of misery we can do nothing to lessen. It is all the more shame to us if we do not help in things within our reach.'

There was a little touch of sternness in his voice. It hurt him to assume it, but the tone seemed to bring his words home to her more directly.

'You wish me to go to see them? Ah, you think I can speak to them—that they will love me as the children used to——'

'I do not think it—I know it. Once you told me that you were wilful. I did not quite believe it then, but now you are, a little—only you will not persist. Now let me tell you about some of these little ones.'

He made her sit in a large armchair, and placed a cushion under her head, and then sat on a low chair facing her, and told her one or two of those commonplace, everyday incidents in the annals of the poor which come within the ken of all who visit or work among them.

Only he did not let his narrations drop into monologues. He put them in a way that made her ask questions, that roused and interested her. The last child he spoke of was a little one named Gretchen. She had been run over in the streets, taken into one of the hospitals, and discharged while still very weak. At home she was inadequately fed, and when his mother found out about her a tumour had formed under one knee, which threatened to cripple her for life. This had been removed, and she was now in the Home—a plump, merry little thing, who gave names of her own to everyone.

'What do you suppose she calls me, Stella?' he asked.

She smiled. 'One who knows how to scold sometimes?'

'No; something with more unconscious irony than that. "The doctor who has no medicine." Of course a doctor of that sort is all the more welcome to Greta; but, still, the title has its own little stroke of malice when one knows how applicable it often is. And then my mother has a distinctive name, too. One of the other little ones said one day enthusiastically: "Oh, she is an angel!" "Yes, she is," answered Greta; "an angel with a basket." The matron overheard them and told my mother, who is very proud of the definition, for, after all, as she says, how much better it is to have a basket in this world, if you are an angel, than a pair of wings! Yes, she is a child, take her all in all, out of a thousand. So tender, and bright, and unselfish. She has the gift of a sunny nature, and yet she has so much imagination, and she can do so many things—and, by this time, if no one had helped her, she would be either dead or a cripple for life.'

'How old is the dear little thing?'

'Nine last month. My mother has insisted on her staying a few more weeks, so that she may be quite strong. She is knitting a pair of long stockings for Karl, a younger brother. "He is so good and strong, and already he can do many more things than a girl," she told me quite lately. I asked her if she would like to be a boy, and after meditating a little, she said: "No." "Why?" I said. "Because the dear God made me a girl," she answered; and then she added: "And I would wear out my boots so much faster."'

'I must go to see Greta,' said Stella, smiling. 'Yes, it would have been dreadful if her health had been spoiled,' she said reflectively, after a little pause.

Presently Mrs Kellwitz came in, knitting; and when Stella found that some of the convalescent children were badly in need of clothing, she began to make some garments which Mrs Kellwitz cut out for her. That evening, when she bade Langdale good-night, she said softly:

'I am not going to be wilful. I will do what you wish.'

He stood for some moments motionless, while the quick flush that had risen in his face died away. And then he recalled her face and tones during their early interview that day. It was one of those terrible hours which all through a lifetime remain in the memory as if stamped on it by a process apart from ordinary recollection.

He took a letter out of his pocket-book that he had received on the preceding day from Mrs Tareling. He had written to her through a lawyer, stating that he had possession of one of the letters he had left in her hands for Miss Stella Courtland—naming the day and even the hour. One had been mutilated, the other stolen, and a fraudulent document had been put with the falsified one she had delivered. He awaited any explanation she might have to offer before putting the matter into the hands of an eminent firm of Melbourne lawyers for prosecution. The reply was an abject confession. Of course, it was quite false—as abject confessions extorted by fear are apt to be. It was her overwhelming love for her only brother—the adjective 'only' twice underlined. He had loved Stella Courtland passionately from boyhood. She had at one time favoured his suit. (N.B.—It is curious to notice how naturally people slip into this kind of English when they are telling lies.) Then she had at a moment's caprice rejected him. The effect on the only brother was terrible. But still he had ample grounds for hope. Then came Miss Courtland's visit to Lullaboolagana, her return to Monico Lodge. In picturesque English came a graphic description of the terrible temptation to remove a rival from her brother's path. Laurette rose to the occasion. She spoke in such exaggerated accents of remorse, one might imagine she had used a poisoned bowl. Yes, she had been weak—desperately weak and erring, as only a poor foolish woman can be when blinded by affection, etc., etc. But, after all, the past was irrevocable. What but harm could come of stirring up strife?

Langdale asked himself the same question with a sinking heart. Here were full and clear proofs of the treachery by which they had been betrayed. But what could any exposure of this base crime avail? It meant vengeance—nothing more. Publicity could not save them a single pang, nor make the future more hopeful, nor help to divert the doom, worse than death, with which he saw Stella threatened. He paced up and down the room, his sight dimmed, a dull throbbing in his temples, as he recalled her looks and tones in the earlier part of their interview. 'I will do what you wish.' His heart gave a leap as he recalled the words. What action should he take to save her from the wild, dark morass into which her life had been turned?

He had written, sending his letter through an eminent English lawyer, on the morning that Stella forwarded him those fatal documents—one unsigned, cunningly devised to support the lies that were conveyed by the fragments, diabolically falsified, of his own letter, with the purpose of extorting an admission of guilt. But since then all other thoughts had been lost in agonizing anxiety as to the issue of Stella's illness. That had passed, but a worse calamity threatened her. Could he not save her? Could he not stem the bitter waters that had swept away all the joy and pleasantness of her life, and now menaced reason itself? He had resolved to urge no claim—to make no appeal to the love which he knew was still the strongest emotion that swayed her—while any weakness of shattered health clouded or warped her judgment. But now it seemed as if every day, in which she was left at the mercy of the grief and dark fear that had lodged in her mind, rendered ultimate recovery more doubtful. And what prospect did the future hold for her? Was not the slow, dull contagion of this union, so fraudulently compassed, a greater evil than any alternative that lay open to her? And yet, to a proud, sensitive man whose own experience of life had been early dashed with a woman's infidelity, how unendurable was the thought of any stigma cast on the girl whose honour was more sacred to him than aught else in the world! But, then, there are passages in life of so vital a nature that they must be judged wholly apart from the common ineffectual criticism of common minds. It was one of those subtle and cruel complications in human lives in which no action seems possible that is not charged with evil. At last, in despair, he told himself that he would do what he could, and live from hand to mouth; for the present make no plans beyond the passing day—only, as far as lay in his power, he would watch over and shield Stella from harm—seek to guard her from the stealthy foe that had already sapped some of the outworks of the citadel of reason.

Next morning when he went into his mother's sitting-room he found the two in cheerful converse.

'Stella is coming with me to our convalescent children this afternoon,' his mother said briskly. She was one of those generous-minded, whole-hearted, actively kind women whose mere presence throws discredit on the darker evils of the world. 'See how rapidly the child sews!' she said, holding up a small garment which Stella had already completed. 'My dear, it is fatal when I find that people can work like this. I am always turning up with a little bundle of second-hand flannel or calico to be made into small petticoats and knickerbockers.'

'An angel with a basket, in fact, mother,' said her son. And at this they all laughed a little. Langdale noted, with a thrill of gladness, that something of the old look of vivid life had come back into Stella's face.

To do some work, and for his sake, because he wished it——this was the chord that had been struck, and gave a quick response. The mere fact of giving expression to the dread that had so long passed 'in smother,'* and begun habitually to haunt her, served to lessen her fears. After this, Stella went almost daily to the convalescent children. And daily she went over some of Langdale's MS, altering a word here and there, now and then putting in a different phrase. She feared at first to trust her own judgment, when she felt inclined to make changes, but she gained confidence as she went on. And then something of the fascination of brainwork, of that preoccupation with ideas which takes the mind out of itself, laid hold of her.

To think too exclusively of ourselves or our own concerns, even under our best aspects, is, as a rule, to become sad, weary, and discouraged. But to be immured in such thoughts, when the thrill and joy of life are gone, when its best promises are mildewed with disillusion and disappointment, is to poison the very source of sane existence and healthy endeavour. It had been so with Stella, and in the lowest deep of her unhappiness there yet opened the lower deep, that the misery which had overtaken her like a flood was so largely her own doing.

Yes; gradually she crept back from the gulf that had threatened to close over her. The little ones that gathered round her, their faces lighting up with pleasure, drew her to them from day to day, and then they would shyly ask for stories of Australia——that strange, far-away land with strange birds and beasts, and unknown trees that never lost their leaves. Sometimes she would write out beforehand one of the little twilight stories she had told at Lullaboolagana, so that she might not hesitate and be at a loss for words when her little audience clustered breathlessly around her. 'The dear lady'——that was the name by which they learned to call her.

And then it began to be spring once more—the spring of a northern climate, when Nature gradually wakens from her rigid sleep, when the first early blossoms and the first returning birds—those timid evangels of quickening life—thrill the air with messages, which the heart understands but does not put into words.

It was one day early in April. The air had lost its barbarous keenness. The sun shone as if it was getting warm. There were dun-coloured clouds over part of the sky, but between them a wistful azure showed itself, and on the tall, slender birch in the Thiergarten that was opposite Stella's sitting-room a swallow and some linnets were carolling as if they were bent on being marked as the first choristers of the season. Stella had returned from a visit to one of the museums with Professor Kellwitz, and sat by the window as she had entered, in her sealskin coat and toque.* As they returned they met Langdale, and he accompanied them as far as the Pension Eisengau. The incident had brought back the first day they met in Berlin with startling distinctness. They had exchanged few words beyond the ordinary salutations. Mrs Kellwitz and Stella were often together, but she and Langdale met seldomer, and but for a few minutes. Yet these accidental brief meetings surrounded the day on which they took place with an aureole. Stella now sat with lips slightly parted, her hands folded in her lap, looking fixedly before her with a half-startled, dawning sort of expression. Ritchie entered at that moment, and was struck with the air of vividness in her face.

'Why, Stella, you will soon be quite yourself again,' he said, leaning against the mantelpiece near where she sat.

The colour slowly deepened in her cheeks, and she took off her toque.

He suddenly stooped over her, and touched her forehead with his lips. She started as if she were stung. 'You must not do that,' she said, in a peremptory tone.

He was deeply wounded, and drew back, looking at her with a startled expression. 'Perhaps I had better not come into the same sitting-room you are in,' he said, in a rougher voice than he had ever used to her before. A look of cold displeasure settled on her face, but she said nothing.

'While you were so ill,' he went on in a gentler tone, 'and seemed more miserable if I were about, I kept out of the way. Then, as you got better you were kinder to me; you sometimes drove out with me, and let me do things for you. But now again you hardly speak to me once in two days; and as for laughing or joking——' He noticed a look almost akin to terror creeping into her face, and stopped abruptly. 'Forgive me, Stella, if I have been rough,' he said after a little.

Stella had rung the bell, and when Maisie came in she gave her her toque and coat to put away, and asked for her writing-desk. Before she returned an answer to Ted's apology there was a tap at the door, and Mrs Farningham came in.

'Now this is fortunate! I wanted to find you both in,' she said. 'You know, Stella, that my mother and stepfather are going to the East about the beginning of May. Anselm tells me that Johnny's lungs need special care. Well, I mean only to stay in England till the beginning of June; I will then join my mother in Egypt. Now, had you not better come with me? You know how these two men will haunt the racecourses from Dan to Beersheba*—from May to October.'

It had been for some time arranged that the Farninghams and Ritchies would leave Berlin together. The two men were anxious to be in England through the racing season; and their wives, who were neither of them supremely interested in the turf, would thus bear each other company.

Stella became very pale and grave.

'Well, I think that would be far the best arrangement,' said Ritchie. But Stella did not at once reply.

'You see, they could join us in Palestine or Egypt as soon as the St Leger* or whatever the last races they wanted to see were over,' went on Mrs Farningham. She watched Stella a little curiously, and seeing the anxious, perplexed look in her face, she added, lightly turning to Ted, 'You see, Mr Ritchie, your wife is not disposed to lose sight of you for so long—but you think the matter over.'

And with that she left the two alone once more.

'You had better go, Stella,' said Ritchie after a pause.

'I do not know,' she answered slowly. She was like one roughly aroused out of a gentle morning dream. A flood of conjectures, of questions, poured in on her; and the old tormenting habit of finding the train of thought suddenly swamped reasserted itself. But one conviction was clear and steady: if she and Ritchie parted, she would never come back to him again.

He, poor fellow! was touched, thinking her hesitation was due to concern at the prospect of leaving him to his own devices for so long a period.

'Don't be afraid about me, Stella,' he said. 'I made a promise that I would never forget myself in drink again; and I don't mean to put a knife in the contract. I don't take much credit to myself for that; for the more you see of the world, the more there is to open your eyes. We get into a beastly habit of drinking spirits in Australia; but a bottle of good Château Lafite* beats such stuff hollow. You sip glass after glass, and, instead of getting stupider, you are more alive. . . . And then, Stella, while matters are as they are between us, it's easier for me to be out of your sight. You see, if Farningham and I are in England till the end of September, why the year would be up by the time I came to—Palestine, is it? Isn't that the place where the Jews used to play up so before they discovered the Christians? By Jove, you should hear Minimus Avenell talk about the Hebrews!' and Ted laughed at sundry reminiscences.

Somehow the sight of Stella so perplexed and silent at the prospect of parting from him for four or five months raised his spirits.

CHAPTER LIII

DURING the time that intervened between this and the week before they left Berlin for London, Stella remained undecided as to her future movements. Letters came from Adelaide and Lullaboolagana full of tender anxiety regarding her health. Ted had written faithfully, week by week, while she was unable to do so. He had always put the best face on the matter; and when finally out of danger, he had cabled the news. Now letters came in answer to the first short notes she had written, about the middle of February. There was so much rejoicing over her recovery—such loving, thankful congratulations. They were so secure in their confidence that return to health meant love and happiness and safety from all evil. The entire ignorance as to her real life of all who were dear to her in her home and native land separated Stella from them far more than the long weeks of sailing which lay between. Is there anything in human experience more strange, more piercing, than the isolation that surrounds most of us during the darker storms that rend the soul?

'How unaccountable, how incredible, how strange beyond all reckoning!' we say, when some event wholly unanticipated happens in the history of others. We so often forget that the inner lives of even those who are most closely linked to ours are implacably veiled from our gaze. It is with individual as with national life. Outwardly, things may be going on in the old smooth, apparently prosperous fashion. We do not see the inner cone, in which a little speck has appeared that slowly spreads and spreads. We do not hear the tread on the loom where the shuttle at every throw is weaving the inscrutable web of circumstance. At last the catastrophe falls heavily, brutally, without comment or warning; and then, being powerless to do any good, we draw a moral. Its ineptitude, as a rule, is equalled only by our ignorance of the real forces that have been at work.

But lost, undecided, and unhappy as Stella had again become, the old vacant apathy did not return. She worked daily; and those daily hours in which so much of her own personality was lost in thoughts for others, and in matters apart from the groove of her own life, saved her. The day on which she had corrected the last of Langdale's manuscript she met him in Mrs Farningham's sitting-room in the pension. They talked chiefly of Socialism, which was then a prominent topic among those who were inimical or favourable to the movement. Mrs Farningham was gradually becoming a zealous convert.

'After all,' she said, at the close of a spirited, half-jesting controversy between herself and Langdale, 'justice is never done to the poor until those who are in power begin to be terrified. These bungling attempts at State Socialism are valuable as a tribute to the power that lies behind our kinsman Schiedlich* and men like him.'

'Dear old Gottfried, I wish he had not joined the extreme party,' returned Langdale. 'It seems to me he was doing such good work when he was writing calmly and dispassionately.'

'Anselm, you are too provokingly amenable to reason,' said his sister, interrupting him. 'Still, you can persuade Gottfried when no one else can move him. I wish you would take him with you to the East when he is released. You know mother is never so happy as when there is an invalid to care for. And he must be rather broken down, by what you say of him.'

'That is a happy thought,' returned Langdale. 'I shall see if I cannot get him away. He will be at large in a few days hence.'

This was the first time Stella heard of Langdale's intention to go to the East; and as she listened, her face was suddenly suffused with colour.

The rest of the afternoon passed as if enveloped in a mist. Mrs Farningham made Stella lie down, and placed a screen round the couch, trusting she might fall asleep. But she could not rest. She went into her bedroom. Dustiefoot followed her and tried to win her attention. But she did not notice him. She stood before a wide, full-length mirror that was in the room, and looked at her own face in it steadily, till she caught a frightened, cowering look in the eyes which made her shrink and draw back. The unsteady, fiery light in them made her turn deathly pale. . . . She threw herself into an arm-chair and covered her face with her hands. Then the silence became intolerable to her, and she said something aloud—she hardly knew what. The tone must have been strange, for the dog shrank away, looking at her timidly.

'Oh, Dustiefoot, Dustiefoot!—do not be afraid! . . . O my God! why is he afraid of me? . . . I must go to Anselm—I must see him . . . he will know what I should do—he will speak to me. . . .'

Then she broke into bitter weeping—leaning her head on a table near her—with low long sobs like a child who is too spent to weep aloud.

On this Dustiefoot came up and put his head on her lap; then he licked her hands; and this somehow comforted her a little.

'Good dog, good dog!' she said, patting him on the head.

The tears relieved her. After a little she returned to her friends.

'Have you two decided how long you are to be in England?' asked Farningham, after some desultory chit-chat.

'I fear Mrs Ritchie has not yet made up her mind to come with me,' answered Mrs Farningham.

'You had better go, Stella,' said Ted.

'Yes; I shall go,' she answered, her face suddenly flushing.

This decision was greeted by the rest with warm approval.

CHAPTER LIV

TWO weeks after the friends went to London, Mrs Farningham's delicate boy had an attack of hemorrhage. This kept her indoors very much, and altered their plans. It was arranged that she and Stella should leave for Alexandria as soon as the boy was well enough to travel. They were staying in the Westham Hotel, close to Grosvenor Square. One morning, a week before they purposed leaving, Stella went to make some purchases for herself and Mrs Farningham. Not once after the evening on which she announced her intention of going to the East had Stella wavered in her decision. She had improved rapidly in health and spirits. The dark shadow that had for a time hovered over her had disappeared. At times something of feverish restlessness took possession of her. But there was no relapse into moody melancholy or apathy. The steady, unimpaired health, which naturally belonged to her, was once more re-established.

Though it was past the middle of May, the morning was dark and lowering. But Stella was oblivious of all external influences. Ritchie had been anxious to hire a brougham for her daily use; but she prevented his doing so. She said she saw so much more when she was on foot, and all her old love of walking had returned. She had an abounding sense of vigorous life that made physical exertion a necessity. A few paces away from the hotel she met Langdale on his way there.

'Will you please take Dustiefoot back?' she said, her face glowing, her eyes softly lustrous as in the old days. 'When I am looking at things he puts his paws on the counter, and insists on looking too.'

'May I walk a little way with you?' he asked as she gave him her hand. 'I am going into the country for a few days this afternoon.'

'I think Amalie is waiting for you,' she answered. 'Her boy has had rather a restless night again.'

Then he took Dustiefoot back as she wished. No plans nor designs had been formed between them. They met casually now and then, and talked a little of merely impersonal matters; nothing more. But each was conscious that the one step which was to shape their future was taken when Stella decided to go to the East.

In those days she struggled no longer against the rising joy that used to well up in her heart at the prospect of cutting herself finally adrift from the future that had been woven for her by treachery and deceit. The sweet fascination of life had come back to her with redoubled force. On this morning, as she went on her way, she recalled the existence she had led for the past few months with horror—with something of wondering contempt. She had been terrified at the past, oblivious of the present, quailing at the days to come, till she had been on the very brink of madness. And all the time the world was full of interest and movement and joy.

Was there no lurking consciousness of the possibility of remorse swallowing up this intoxicating recaptured happiness? If so, she spurned the thought—cast it aside like one of those malformed little insects that sometimes crawl on the petals of blood-red roses. She was glad that a kind of pagan recklessness, of indifference to far-off consequences, mingled with the tide of her courage and reviving happiness. Once for all she had decided that the problem of her life must be looked at as it was in itself—must be solved apart from authority and tradition. She had been too long cowering like a slave, afraid of others—afraid of herself—afraid most of all of Nature, which in its subtle way had all the time cherished and nursed back into being the one love of her life, compared to which all other bonds were but as flax touched with flame.* The chalice of life's most precious benediction was once more at her lips.

She recalled something that Langdale had once said of the stimulating aura of London—the indefinable demand on one's best powers to polish the rude rocks of capacity into blocks fit for building. But apart from any subtle appeal to the mind, there was a kind of implied union, in the silent fellowship of being successfully alive, which she shared with the crowd around. To be young and well clad, and walk upright with well-moulded limbs, with eyes undimmed with fears, with a capacity for happiness, was a form of responsive loyalty to the life that surged around. Everything appeared to her so unworn and fresh, she was alive in every faculty, and stirred as with the tender novelty in which objects present themselves to us in early childhood. Fancy, imagination, and memory, all were buoyant as young birds that had newly learned to cleave the air.

The feeling now and then was uppermost that she had in some way gone back to an earlier stage of experience—that some indefinable weight had slipped off her. It was as though Nature had taken her by the hand and led her back smilingly from the sophistry of long-accumulated tradition—led her back to the primal instincts of life, blotting out the officious 'thou shalt' and 'shalt not' of defunct generations as impertinent intermeddling with a joy all her own. Perhaps there are forces slumbering in the mind which waken into activity but for one brief hour of the years which are given to us here. It may be that on this morning, if never again, Stella was subtly influenced by the bare, untrammelled aspects of her native land—by the vast unpeopled spaces which hold no claim from the past, and lay no ghostly charges on human beings to postpone their lives for the sake of those who have been and those who are to come. And yet it was vagrant recollections of one of the wildernesses of her country that first quelled the glad ardour of her mood. In the midst of her content at being among crowds of unknown men and women, she recalled how often people spoke of the solitude of a strange city being more absolute than that of a desert. Instantaneously she saw before her an austere stretch of Mallee Scrub. What moody melancholy the reality would evoke—what troops of questions! . . . Questions of what? A quick, inexplicable pang shot through her mind—a dread like that which comes in a dream of the night, when one who has long ago passed beyond reach and recall stands in the masking appearance of life, and the sleeper shrinks from the blank of awakening. But it was a momentary feeling.

She made her purchases, and then passed out of Oxford Street by way of Audley Street, purposely taking a circuitous route to the Westham Hotel. She wanted to walk alone—to give herself up to the full sway of this swift, strong return of mental and physical well-being. But like the refrain of a song which once heard long ago comes back to haunt us one day, we know not why, the thought of the great Mallee desert kept rising up before her: the days she had wandered there—the books she had read—the thoughts that had come to her of the people who had fled from the world and lived in desolate places for the salvation of their soul. What strange delusions men had put upon themselves from age to age, sacrificing the only life they were sure of to vague chimeras of unknown modes of existence!* Then her mother's grave, sweet voice came to her, and she suddenly found the tears rising in her eyes. She wiped them half angrily.

'I must write and tell mother all—all!' she thought.

But the resolve did not quiet the throng of thoughts which began to rise. 'My beloved child, how I long to see you once more! Give me fuller details of your daily life. Why do you say so little of Edward? He wrote with such faithful regularity when you were ill; but since your recovery he writes no longer.' These and other extracts from the home letters, from her mother's especially, rose before her. Nay, it seemed as though one strode beside her to read them to her whether she would or no. She went over the past few months again in self-vindication, as if she were pleading her case before an unseen tribunal.

'See,' she seemed to say, as if addressing a judge, 'how hopelessly all my future would have been wrecked if Anselm had not saved me from myself. It was not one misfortune that overwhelmed me. Had it been only that vile plot of an unscrupulous woman—cheating me out of the one great happiness of life—I would have somehow borne the misery, perhaps overcome it. At least the union would be binding. That I am sure of. But there was a worse betrayal—the moral failure of the man who married me, concealing his subjection to drink. Yes, one may overcome this for a time, but there is always the possibility of a relapse. A year of probation—of what value is that when in one hour all the forces of habit may resume full sway?'

It seemed as though her invisible audience looked at her with stern, searching eyes. The very air became heavy with doubt and suspicion.

'We have made no plans,' she went on, unconsciously entering on the defence that implies accusation. 'We have in common the power of sympathy with wide aims—with impersonal endeavours. We are capable of a great disinterested friendship that time and intimacy can only render more perfect. . . .'

What a strange power of the mind this is—in the hour of keenest elation to become conscious of a cloud of unseen witnesses* who are satisfied with no version of our motives short of absolute veracity. After all that she could urge, Stella was in the end shaken, dissatisfied, restless. 'It is part of the morbid phase through which I have been passing,' she thought. And she mechanically hurried on, as if to escape her self-appointed tribunal, her explanations, the doubts that were incipient fears.

She had followed Audley Street much further than she intended, and now struck out of it eastward, going into a narrow street where, in the distance, she saw one or two cabs. She had got tired, and wished to drive back to the Westham. Before she reached them she was startled by a sudden downpour of rain. At the same moment she found herself opposite the open porch of a church,* into which she went for shelter. There were some women who had evidently come out. Two of them were talking together.

'Which cardinal?' said one.

'Why, Cardinal Newman,'* answered the other.

The name reached Stella, awakening many slumbering

memories—awakening, too, that deep chord of reverent affection which the soul never loses for those who have at one time illuminated and guided it, even though we may have lost the light, though we may have strayed far from the pastures in which still waters flow.*

'Is the Cardinal here?' she asked eagerly.

'Yes—the service is almost over,' answered the woman she addressed; 'but if you go in, and go up near the altar, you can see him very well,' she added kindly.

Acting on the impulse of the moment, Stella went in. But even as she entered some curious intuition crossed her mind—a misgiving, rather, that this simple action might break the purpose round which her happiness, her late triumphant sense of restored well-being, had centred. She passed noiselessly up the left aisle and took a seat not far from the high altar, where she was partly concealed by a pillar.

Yes, the service was almost over; but she saw him clearly—the man whose words so many years ago, in her careless, untroubled girlhood, had so deeply stirred the depths of her inner life; whose voice had been as a voice from heaven to guide her into close communion with God. But the voice had died into silence, and all the glow of dawning intercourse with a kingdom not of this world—all the glad fervour of faith—had left her. And often it had seemed good to her that she had been so early emancipated from the dogmatic finalities, the uncertain certainties, full of contradictions, that men are asked to receive as revelations of the Divine Will. But now that the first spring of youth was barely over, how hard and cruel life had become! and what was the bourne to which she had turned?

Alas! had she so soon again fallen into the clutches of Care and Fear—those haggard visitants, never far off when the conscience is not at peace, but soothed with anodynes? From the moment that she knelt within the church, all that had blinded her was swept ruthlessly away. It was like the letting in of waters, whose rising tide obliterates the paltry landmarks hastily thrown up by invading scouts who had no legal claim to the country. She heard nothing—saw nothing but that pale, spiritual presence; the high, noble brow—the austere, ascetic countenance, furrowed with years and sorrows—a face keenly symbolical of a life consecrated to the service of God and man.

She saw his hands joined and held up in benediction—saw him

turn to the people and make the sign of the cross on them; and she
bent her head in bitter weeping, like a reed shaken by a great storm.*
As smoke vanisheth away* and is seen no more, so was she forsaken
of the happiness—the passionate elation—that had so lately thrilled
her through and through with an exalted sense of vitality.

Low and lower yet her head was bent, while she was rent with
piercing sorrow, and the tears drenched her face like rain. The last
note of the organ died away, the last footfalls of the congregation
retreated, and she was alone in the house of prayer—alone with the
still, small voice* at whose sound our dearest travesties of righteousness shrivel into filthy rags. She had wandered so long and so
far, and near her was the image of the crucified One—whom she had
betrayed like Peter of old. 'And the Lord turned and looked upon
Peter. . . . And Peter went out and wept bitterly.'*

All the unsatisfied yearning for belief, which had so long been
stilled and left a waste place in her heart, rose into new life. And with
this the anguish of a penitent convicted of innumerable treasons
pierced her like a sword.*

There are experiences of the soul that cannot be fathomed. They
are beyond the reach of any plummet that is within our grasp—being
part of the inscrutable mystery of the union of matter and spirit.
There are moments in which the bruised, shaken, sorrowful human
creature sees as by lightning-flashes the wild devious ways by which
the spirit is lured away from the only possession that is everlasting!
In the revulsion of feeling that overwhelmed her, Stella could for a
time frame neither words nor purpose. But from the first she knew
that she dared not follow the path which so short a time before had
been to her as the only one that led into the citadel of life and hope.
Gradually the first bitterness and tumult ebbed away. Some lines that
she had once read to her father came back to her:

> 'But as I raved, and grew more fierce and wild,
>   At every word,
> Methought I heard one calling, Child!
>   And I replied, My Lord!'*

Yes, out of the abysses of exceeding darkness which first fell on her
when she knew that the only purpose which seemed to make life possible must be abandoned, there gradually emerged a faint dawn of
hope. After all her weary wanderings—after her blindness and hard-

ness of heart—after her long conviction that God could only be darkly groped after, never securely hoped in—she knew once more that the chastisement of our peace was upon Him.

'And I replied, My Lord!'

She whispered the words through her blinding tears, and even her great unhappiness was an earnest to her that, notwithstanding her desertion and denial, and callous forgetfulness and unbelief, she had not been cast off utterly.

More and more piercingly she realized how her own pride and vanity and impatience of suffering had been at the root of the evil that had overtaken her. A scorching sense of shame at her infidelity to the higher loyalties of justice, self-sacrifice, and generosity overcame her. Waves of cutting remorse swept over her as she reviewed her conduct in her relationship with her husband. How indifferent and hard she had been all these months—shirking all companionship with him, never seeking to win him to any interest or pursuit beyond the narrow groove in which his life had always run! She was, perhaps, a little unfair to herself as she reviewed her conduct in this respect, as we are apt to be in our self-condemnations as well as in our self-enthusiasms—both in reality being often grounded on ignorance. There are periods in people's lives when everything is against them—when the currents that might have floated them into a quiet haven conspire only to dash them against the rocks. But yet the truth was clear—that on the first evidence of the power of evil habit over her husband she had stood coldly aloof, as if wrong-doing on his part absolved her from all lot or concern in his fate. She recalled how, in speaking of him she had even inferred that he could not help himself—assuming that the spirit of man, no more than his body, can have any source of impulse or action apart from the inexorable links of material causes. Could the spirit of evil itself help to wreck men with a darker atheism than this? . . . 'He had so keen an appreciation of what was good in people—quick to perceive how men's failings and vices are often a forced rather than a wilful product. Always he expected them to live down the evil—to hold to and cultivate the better side of their nature.'*

Where had she read or heard the words? Was not this, indeed, the very core of moral influence? And then came back to her the words of one of the Fathers to one who had tried to take his life: 'Thy crime has made thee mine. See that henceforth thou walkest worthily of me and of God, to whom thou belongest.'* The belief that evil may be overcome—this spring of moral hopefulness—how basely she had denied it by word and action! What had become of the early Church when so much of its endeavours lay among those enslaved, and the descendants of those enslaved by the darkest forms of sensuality, if the half-understood dicta of pseudo-science regarding heredity, and the insignificance of man's will, had prevailed rather than the Divine rule, 'Believe, and thou shalt be saved'?* Oh, how cruelly she had failed in that care for the better nature of the man to whom she had promised her whole life! how completely she had fallen away from that lofty devotion to duty which is the truest, clearest note of womanhood!

And looking steadily into the depths of her unacknowledged thoughts, into the dark recesses of her mind, she convicted herself of having relied on Ritchie's inability to overcome his besetting sin— of having rested on this as a justification of her own future actions.

When the soul is penetrated with a deep sense of guilt, and is prostrated in utter humiliation, no thought overcomes it with such bleeding penitence as this—that it has failed another in the day of need. . . . She was consumed with shame and sorrow, and yet she was quickened by the thought that here her downward course had been arrested by the presence of that priest of the Most High whose words had so early fastened on her heart. Once more she had been drawn as with irresistible cords to the foot of the Cross.

CHAPTER LV

AFTER Stella had fought down the first amazed opposition to her changed plans, a sort of wonder came over her that she should thus throw aside all that seemed like the substance of living for an impalpable shadow—nay, for dark possibilities that began to lower more darkly at her the more she strove to face the future with deliberate calmness. But she did not falter in her purpose, and gradually the powers which man in all ages has found in work and prayer came to her aid. After she had seen Langdale and bidden him farewell, the worst was over. He returned to London three days before Mrs Farningham sailed. When Stella saw him in his sister's sitting-room, he had already learned of the change of plans.

'You must come with me, Anselm, now that Mrs Ritchie has decided to remain. She seems to lose her interest in things mysteriously. She does nothing now but visit rookeries at the East-End. I mean, you must sail in the same boat with me.'

Presently Stella came in.

'You are not so well again,' he said quickly, noticing at once the entire change in her aspect since he had last seen her.

'Oh, I am only a little tired,' she answered, but her face had grown still paler. An old friend of her mother's called, and Mrs Farningham went with her into the nursery.

'Amalie tells me you are not going with her to the East,' Langdale said when they were alone.

'No—and I wanted to tell you personally, and to say farewell.'

'Farewell?' he repeated. He walked hastily to one of the windows; then he came back, and stood by the mantelpiece a little way from where she sat. 'Stella, do not be afraid,' he said, in an agitated voice. 'I shall never say a word, nor urge a claim to your attention, beyond what you judge would be right. You have been so much better; but even in this short time you have lost ground.'

'In my weakness, my selfishness, my forgetfulness of duty, you have been so good to me. You must let me say this before we part,' she said hurriedly, and as if she had not heard what he said.

'So good to you?' he echoed, as if the words hurt him, and then he checked himself. 'Stella, do not try your nature beyond what it can bear. Go with my sister as you purposed doing. I will not see you, nor even write to you. Gain complete strength of mind and body, and then decide what you ought to do. Stella, you may trust me. And if you do not go to the East, let me write to Madonna. It is not fit that you should be left so much alone; you are not as strong as you think. I have written a long letter to Hector, which I delayed sending till you were well enough to read it.'

'We must not send it. We have so far overlived our sorrow without paining others. . . . And now the worst is over.'

There was a little break in her voice as she said the last words. She was outwardly calm, but the anguish at her heart made the words seem unreal even to herself. Langdale looked at her fixedly, and was about to speak, but he checked himself, and again leant against the mantelpiece, shading his eyes with one hand. There was a long pause, and then Stella spoke again:

'Do not fear for me, Anselm. Hitherto I have been thinking chiefly of myself—blaming others for the unhappiness that has overtaken us; brooding over mistakes instead of seeking to set them right. I will no longer think of myself—it is a melancholy subject.'

Her smile was sad, but her face had in it more of the old alertness, the being alive to the curiously unadjusted qualities and defects of life, than she had shown since their first painful meeting in the Old World.

Then she told him what had led to her sudden change of plans. As she did so, something of her old vigour and ardour of expression came back. But in all mental conflicts there are so many forces at work which we but dimly apprehend. We can but say that we have been defeated, or gained a victory, which leaves us more humiliated, more mistrustful of our hearts than ever before. The process we cannot fully explain to ourselves, much less to others.

'You feel just now,' he said slowly, when she had ceased speaking, 'that you should sacrifice all your individuality, all your life, in reparation for a fancied wrong. But can you endure the punishment? Do you realize the peril——'

'No; not punishment!' she said, eagerly interrupting him. 'It is punishment when we are allowed to follow our own devices; when we are dead to endeavour, to patience, to hope—hope, the beautiful spirit that leads us on, white and serene and gentle as the angel of the dew, and bids us never despair of overcoming our own follies, of helping others to better effort and aspiration. I have been so long the unresisting victim of despair; but once more God has called me. Do not pity me, Anselm! Be sorry for me only in the time when I was insensible to duty—deafened with the noise of the chain of mortality so that I could hear none of the voices by which God calls us. Oh! it is true; He does call us, and when we hear Him the poison is drawn out of our darkest sorrows. Dear friend, how can I explain myself? To-day all the sharpest pangs that I have suffered, all that I must endure, seem to me a proof of the love of God. I see that if I had been happy in the way I had chosen, it would mean that He had utterly forgotten me—left me to myself; and when that happens, it is not only ourselves we hurt; we spoil the lives of others.'

'Do not let us deceive ourselves,' he answered, in a voice which, despite his self-control, vibrated with keen anguish. 'We have been robbed and cheated! In our final separation we lose the best possibilities that life can offer. I can only submit. But I cannot pretend to see in this chaos of duplicity any glimmering of Divine guidance. At last it is brought home to me that life may become so poor and maimed a thing that it is not greatly worth having.'

'Oh, do not say that,' she cried, looking into his face imploringly. 'I know that in all the years to come there will be moments of anguished recollection. Twilight or the rose of dawn, a strain of music, a chance picture, the glow of sunset, a bud opening in spring, the song of a bird, any sight or sound that searches the depths of our nature—we know not why—all the things that touch us most may be charged with a burden of sadness—a sense of loss, a pain whose edge can never be entirely blunted. But the pain, and the loss, and the unconquerable yearning, let us take them by the hand, and make them the companions of our wiser hours. In seeking after the best that we can reach, each cup of suffering, every pang of sorrow, may breathe into our lives that finer spirit of all knowledge.'

'Ah, Stella, Stella! must I lose you? hear your voice no more? What can comfort me for this?' he said, looking at her with dimmed eyes. He turned away abruptly, and paced up and down the room. Then he came back to where she stood and resumed in a calmer voice: 'And to make the loss more intolerable there is the fact that our happiness was wrecked by the miserable intrigue of that wretched woman. . . . There are creatures so low down in the scale of nature that the whole nervous system consists of a slender cord, that has a little bulge by way of a brain near the mouth. That is about the type, morally, of a being who could act as she did. And yet she is to go unpunished—screened even from any sense of shame! But no; I shall yet in some way expose her!' said Langdale, with flashing eyes. It was not only the irreparable mischief to both their lives that made Mrs Tareling's immunity from all penalty so intolerable to him, but also the recoil against injustice which, as a rule, moves a man more keenly than a woman. 'Let us admit,' he said in a lower tone, 'that we have been betrayed—but as for consolation——'

'Yes; betrayed by me!' answered Stella in a low voice. Langdale made a gesture of denial; but Stella put her hand on his arm, and, standing close beside him, repeated: 'Yes; it is true. In the end no one can betray us but ourselves. If, instead of being governed by wounded pride and fierce jealousy, I had resigned myself——'

'That is, if you had been some other human being instead of yourself. Stella, this is unreasonable!'

'And then,' she went on, speaking with some difficulty, 'it would be wrong for me not to tell you that in the first bitterness of our meeting I now feel I spoke in a way that reflected unduly on my husband.'

It was the first time she had spoken the word in his hearing, and as he heard it, Langdale coloured deeply.

'You will, I think, believe,' he returned, after a pause, 'that I could not try to urge you to any line of action merely in my own interests. I have been content to drift in this. I have formed plans and given them up. The chief thing was that you should first recover. You had in a measure done so when this ardour for nullifying your life seized you. But beware of doing your own inner nature and instincts a great violence. . . . You were imposed upon and feloniously betrayed. Granted that you should not under any circumstances have been cheated into such a marriage, still, there are certain forms of temptation to which every nature will succumb under given circumstances. But is it right to attempt fidelity to a bond that may eventually wreck your life? Anyone may be hurried into wrong-doing—betrayed into an unmoral course of life—but the fatal thing is the not repenting, or foisting ecclesiastical perversions upon the conscience. Morals have been evolved to save, not to crush us—not to make it impossible for us to work out the salvation of our better natures. Of course, I do not use the word in its priestly sense.'

'You are afraid for me,' she answered in a faltering voice; 'but believe me, weak and unstable as I have before been, I know now that I am no longer blinded. I am not afraid of you, Anselm. I am afraid of myself. If I went now with your sister. . . . Ah, you have understood what it meant. . . . We both know the tyrannical limitations of life. And then, do what we would—nothing could give us back the past—nothing.'

Her voice failed her, and there was silence for a little time.

'I must abide by your decision,' he said in a low voice.

Many thoughts had crowded into her mind that threatened to sweep away her composure. But the necessity of saying something of all she owed to him nerved her.

'Will it comfort you at all to know that you have been in truth my best friend? In the days of my utmost weakness and despair you led me back from the brink of insanity. . . . You were entirely forgetful of self, kind with the delicate kindness of a chivalrous nature—you must hear me. You helped me day by day, and yet kept out of my way. You *knew* you had only to speak in those dark days, and I would have gone with you gladly to the ends of the earth. No tie, no consideration, would have held me; you saved me from worse than death. . . . After all that had happened, you might well have considered that my life was yours. . . . It is so much the creed of the world that a man's strength does not consist in forbearance—in tender consideration of a woman's weakness. . . . Oh my friend, my friend, can you ever know from what an abyss you saved me? A man's life is so much more twofold than a woman's. He has his work and his place to fill in the world. She has the large leisure of home; and if at her side the phantom comes of broken vows and duties trampled under foot, the spring of her life is poisoned at the source. If our lives were given only for such happiness as we could clutch——'

He was deeply touched by the pathetic intensity of her voice—touched, too, by the truth of what she said. He knew how the world is strewn with the wrecks of anarchy in conduct. He was too close an observer of human affairs not to know that the wider and deeper a woman's nature is, the more surely does it suffer under the consciousness of having, in any crisis of life, chosen what was pleasant rather than what was right. And though he held that it would be as irrational to place all who repudiate the bond of marriage on the same level as it would be to condemn the legal tie because of its many and bitter failures, yet, in his calmer, more detached thoughts, all his experience of things as they are led him to shrink from the shadow of blame on the one woman who had exalted and widened his ideal of her sex. And yet, how well he knew that an open rupture, not only with the conventional decorums of society, but with a great law, is infinitely more healthful for a finely-tempered, sensitive nature than the slow moral corrosion of enforced companionship with a hopelessly inferior mind! It was, under the circumstances, inevitable that he should think much worse of Ritchie than he deserved. But he began to perceive that in the awakening of the strong religious instinct of her nature Stella might find an antidote against the more subtle evils of her lot. Only, all his training, as well as his inherited instincts on the question, led him to mistrust the variability of the devotional temperament. Could this impetus last?—or would it turn into a broken reed to wound her more incurably than ever before? Even in the midst of the dull, deep pain, the sense of an all-embracing catastrophe, the utter vacuity that for the time swallowed all which before had been of deep interest to him, this question rose up—forced itself on him.

'This strong influence that has suddenly taken hold of you, Stella—are you sure it is something more than a phantasm that—'

'I am glad you have asked this,' she answered quickly. 'There are some things we cannot well speak of unless we are sure of sympathy. The day after I had been in the church I went again, early in the morning. I felt smitten to the very soul—robbed of all the joy and pride of life. But the moment I looked upon that pale figure nailed on the cross, and knelt, not to pray, but simply to cry like a broken-hearted child who has wandered far, far from its father's house, and comes back too tired and frightened to do more than creep into a corner—then I knew that though I may never be an orthodox Catholic, yet the old faith had so far revived as to be an inspiring rule of life, to give a vivifying motive to every exertion. You know, there *are* some things, after all, that we can be quite sure of. We know, Anselm, you and I, that though our lives are to be widely sundered——'

Langdale gave a great sigh, which was almost a groan. At the sound Stella's face flushed faintly, and with an evident effort at composure she went on:

'Yet the day can never come in which we shall be indifferent to each other. And in the same way we may know, with a conviction beyond dispute, that behind all the confusion and mystery of life there runs a great sane purpose with which we may join our wills and lives. In the end the most we can hope to do must be limited to a small patch of the world, and as far as our personal influence can reach. To spoil that for the sake of any happiness—— You know the rough and ready classifications of the world——'

'I apprehend your meaning, Stella. . . . Certainly, if our lives were given us chiefly for happiness, our parting to-day would be a crime. Perhaps it is not so.'

'In very truth it is not so,' returned Stella, a glow lighting up her whole face as she looked steadfastly at her friend.

'And then, when you come out of the church—when you are in actual contact with the depths of human misery in this vast city— do you find any clue that satisfies your conscience and reason why a world, supposed to be under the loving rule of an omnipotent Creator, should present so strange a spectacle?'

'In the last three days,' she answered slowly, 'I have been a good deal with some people who are working among the poorest and some of the most depraved in the East-End. Ah, my God, what pictures have burnt themselves into my memory!—what ineffaceable ones of the faces of young girls that still keep something of the dewy inno- cence of childhood, and yet are engulfed in living death! Women unsexed, men without manhood, youth without purity, childhood that has never known the sanctity of home—yes, always where there are alleys reeking with bad air, are courts full of filth, where there are men sodden with drink and women in shameless rags, there, everywhere, are children in swarms. Two nights ago I could not sleep. They passed before me in endless processions, those maimed, ruined existences, fit only to be huddled out of sight—to be imprisoned like lepers, so as to stamp out the contagion. At last I could bear it no longer. I rose up in the darkness, and fell on my knees. But I could not pray. "O God, dost Thou not care at all?"—that was all I could say over and over, with a stupid, blank amazement. And then, all at once—how can I tell you? . . .'

The tears forced themselves into her eyes. She was very pale, and her lips were quivering. Yet all the time her face was lit with that grave spiritual light which irradiates the countenance when the heart is quickened with impersonal zeal and thought.

'Try and tell me—I want to know,' said Langdale in a low voice. His eyes were dim with feelings too poignant to be borne with clear sight—too deep to be relieved by words.

'I *knew* that this, even this wild, cruel anarchy, was not born of chaos. It was the shadow side of the highest possibilities of our nature. Because we have power to aspire to communion with God, so human beings have the power to fall and be submerged in the black eddies of shame and pollution. This was the embodiment of that principle of evil which everyone who turns away from the pitiful egoism of self-seeking must strive against—must fight to subdue.

'Then I saw that other great army of which you have often spoken to me—the men and women sown broadcast over the whole land, who, amid all the moral deformity of life, neither flee from the world nor are sick of it, nor despair of the capacity of our common nature for those things which are good and true and of lovely report.* I saw them: women of lonely lives—often undistinguished, unknown—yet firm in the constancy of principle, touched with the gentleness of unweariable love; men of all grades, enfranchised from the corrupt propensities that make our race the willing slaves of evil, steadily, constantly working for the moral renovation of their country—each doing a little, each helping to stem the tide of human misery. Here, a pure-hearted, delicate girl, giving time and thought to hours of intercourse with rough factory lads and girls—wakening in a heart here and there the better impulses that lie dormant, often only because no care nor gentleness has breathed on the timid seeds and wooed them into life. . . . Yes, even the little I have seen helped me to estimate how true was what you once said, that almost all who have any by-play of time and means take thought for some of those less fortunately placed. To touch one or two minds to finer issues— to rescue one or two lives from the appalling depths ready to swamp them—this is not a very bold or ambitious object; and yet to set it before ourselves, we must be sure that no siren voice has deluded us into making the life of any fellow-creature more open to the temptations which beset him, more callous to belief in the goodness of others. Anselm, when these thoughts swept over me, my heart throbbed with gratitude to you—with pride in your unselfish goodness. It was to you I owed it that the Nessus robe of passion* had not scorched and laid waste my life.'

He was too much moved to trust himself to speak for a little time. At last he said slowly:

'I do not think that I will now go to the East. . . . May we not return to the old footing of friends? . . . Let me see you from time to time as long as you are in London. . . .'

There was a pleading tone in his voice to which every fibre of her nature responded. But her victory over herself was too hardly won, too insecure, too bitterly steeped in the struggles that seem to exhaust the very founts of action and resolve. She felt too keenly how impossible the tranquillity of friendship would be for them both for some time to come.

'I think you should go with Amalie—she is very anxious about the boy. I want you to go. . . . And then,' she added, not meeting his eyes while she said it, 'perhaps in the time to come we may both find that a new plan of life opened to us after this parting.'

'If you wish it very much, I will go for your sake,' he answered.

Then she stood up to bid him farewell.

'There is one question, Stella; will you let me ask it? You are satisfied that Ritchie knew nothing of the perfidy practised by his sister?'

'Quite—quite! He is incapable of so mean an action—least of all against me.'

She raised her head proudly, and the look on her face cut him to the soul, and yet consoled him. Let those who have solved the contradictions of our inscrutably involved nature explain the enigma.

There was silence between them for a few moments. Then he took both her hands in his. Each looked for a little into the other's face, and they parted. A few moments after Langdale left the hotel he was hailed by an old friend—a physician—who insisted on carrying him off to St James's Hospital, to see a man who mysteriously kept on living, while every principle known to medical science clearly proved that he should have died three days previously. Stella, in the meantime, was lying prone in a darkened room, lost to all thought or sensation, except the consciousness that her life had in very truth passed from her. But after a time she remembered that she had promised Ted to accompany him that evening to see Irving's 'Macbeth,'* and she knew how infinitely disappointed he would be if she failed to keep the appointment. She therefore rose and summoned Maisie to dress her.

We are aided by the limitations of life, as well as by its rarer hours of illuminating insight. Habit, Routine, Custom—these three gray sisters, who in the liquid dew of youth fill us with languor, with impatient scorn and rebellion—how softly and securely they lead us by the hand when the wine-red roses of passion are overblown and trampled under foot!

CHAPTER LVI

THREE days later Langdale sailed for the East, in company with his sister.

'It beats me hollow, Stella, to imagine why you didn't go with them,' said Ritchie that evening, in a tone of wondering expostulation. Like all solidly practical people, he disliked treating fixed arrangements as airy outlines of things not to be done. And the thought weighed on him still more, that Stella would now be so much alone, while he and Farningham were 'gallivanting about,' as he phrased it, from one racecourse to another. The thought of those endless, horsey, excited crowds, began to weary him in advance. And then Stella's new plan of going so often to church, and so much among the poor, gave Ted a melancholy conviction that she must be 'feeling very low.' He had of late noticed that look again on Stella's face that his acquaintance on board the *Hindoo Fawn* had, in ignorance of their relationship, described as being that of a sleep-walker, or a person who had seen a ghost. Only along with this there was not that shrinking avoidance of his society which had so deeply wounded him for some time before her change of plans. She did not reply to his observation, but took up a letter that lay on a table near her, glanced over it, and then looked up at him, as if about to speak.

Stella had fully decided that Ritchie must ultimately know all. The past would be too full of ghostly memories, too deeply riddled with secret depths, to make their joint lives tolerable, if he were kept in ignorance of the events that had brought her to death's door, and had so much widened the distance between them during the past dark months. In the last heart-searching, self-reproachful days, she had seen how culpable she had been in the old days, in the careless, irresponsible way in which she had accepted Ted's homage for so many years. She realized that if her own happiness had been secured, as Langdale's wife, Ted's life would have been wrecked.

'Even as it is——' she thought, with a sinking heart. And yet the more she strove to see things clearly and dispassionately, the more convinced she was that his weakness in the past had nothing of that moral cretinism which makes the hope of a permanently restored power of will a fond delusion.

'Who shall find a valiant woman? . . . The heart of her husband trusteth in her. . . . She will render him good, and not evil, all the days of her life.'* . . . Yes, this must be her aim; and as the days went on, and the passionate sorrow that had consumed her lost its poignancy, she would learn to acknowledge—nay, to feel—that even if she could, she would not have their marriage undone, at the cost of Ted's misery and probable degradation.

'You married because Laurette behaved worse than a thief and a liar; and now, Stella, you are broken-hearted.'

She knew so well the direct, uncompromising terms into which Ted would put the situation.

'No, Ted, I am not broken-hearted, and I would not if I could go back on our marriage.' On the day that she could say this with truth she would tell him all. Such had been her resolve. But on the evening of this day, when life seemed to be merged into a listless mechanical round, when all the better possibilities of aspiration, and close sympathy, and personal joy seemed to have swept by like a vessel in mid-ocean, while she crouched like a forlorn castaway on a desolate island, watching the last sunrays fall on the gallant barque that would soon be lost to sight, she told herself that such a purpose was idle.

'I can't flatter myself,' went on Ted after a pause, 'that it is on my account you gave Mrs Farningham the slip almost at the last moment.'

He did not speak in an aggrieved tone, but rather with an accent of wistful inquiry, curiously at variance with his words. Stella had almost finished the letter she had taken up when Ted made this second observation. It was one that had reached her on the previous day, from Laurette, in which she implored Stella that the 'mishap' about Dr Langdale's letter might be kept from her brother's knowledge.

'I can see,' she went on, 'by the way Ted writes, that as yet he knows nothing. Dear, dear Stella, this is very noble and generous of you. I dare say your dangerous illness made you see things differently. I have little doubt that you will prevent Dr Langdale, with your usual clear discrimination, from covering himself with ridicule by any appeal to law. . . . After all, people do not marry because others write or suppress letters. Still, I candidly admit that my zeal on Ted's behalf—my fear, too, lest you should find yourself involved in one of those unhappy entanglements which wreck all a girl's future prospects—warped my judgment. It seems as if there were a *vice de construction** in our lives which makes affection, and not honour, the great motive of our actions.

'We are soon to leave for England, and hope to meet you there. Dear Stella, let our reunion be that of those who are not only closely linked by a tender relationship, but also those who have been dear friends from childhood. . . . Might it not be possible for us to take a house together for the rest of the London season? We shall probably be there by the middle of June. Possibly the great mower Death may render it unnecessary for us to *hire* a house. The near prospect of rank and station in Britain—so crammed with cold decorum for the weaker sex, with unbounded opportunities of ruin for men, and with fog for all, if Australian travellers speak truly—makes my heart yearn more than ever for those I love.

'Your little nephew and niece are clamouring round me. When I tell them I am writing to Aunt Stella, they clap their little hands, thinking you are coming; but I tell them you are far, far away, and that we must come to you and Uncle Ted. Dear Talbot is not very well of late—nothing to be at all anxious about. In fact, I think it is connected with his dining so frequently at the Club, with men who, now that he is on the eve of leaving Australia, are anxious to show their cordiality. However, his small ailments make him only more domesticated, and, I may say, affectionate. Perhaps that is why we women are accused of being so fond of nursing. "When pain and anguish wring the brow,"* etc. No wonder we love dear Sir Walter. He understood us well, with all our foibles, which, in the end, seem only to endear us all the more to the best sort of men. By the way, Ted left his "Lady of the Lake" you gave him at Monico Lodge. Shall I bring it to you? But I forget, there will not be time for a reply. When I was at Cannawijera a month ago I thought of your enthusiasm for the Mallee Scrub. Seeing it for the last time seemed to help me to understand your feeling.'

'I had better give Ted this letter to read, and then tell him all. What better opportunity can come? And as for waiting for an indefinite period——' thought Stella wearily. She could speak now without tears or faltering. That strange feeling of unreality which often follows close on prolonged emotion had seized her. It seemed as though she could speak of herself as calmly as if she were a Japanese top-spinner, with whose performances she had nothing to do beyond an amazed looking on.

She glanced up, and found Ted's gaze fixed searchingly on her face. When their eyes met he flushed, and said hurriedly:

'Forgive me, Stella. You look more dead than alive—and here am I slanging* you like a great muff as I am.'

His quick penitence, when betrayed into any natural show of impatience at what must appear to him unreasonable caprice, touched her. And then that saving recognition of what was generous and manly in his nature, of what was faulty in her own, came to her aid. She would not tell him in this cold, abrupt fashion the story of a sister's sordid fraud—of a wife's meditated irretrievable alienation. The day must yet come when in the telling she could rob the tale of its keenest sting.

'You are not slanging me at all, Ted,' she said gently. 'I dare say my conduct appears very silly——'

'Not a bit of it,' answered Ted stoutly. 'And it isn't Mrs Farningham I am thinking of so much as you. She has her brother. By Jove! that man has eyes like a hawk. Did you know that Dustiefoot—you needn't begin to wave your tail, you young Tory! I'm not speaking to you—has a scar on his left paw? When I went on board with the Farninghams the doctor came up to me much friendlier than ever before. I can't help thinking he had some sort of a scunner* against me. I expect it was seeing me talking with those little French rips* when you were lying at death's door, I may say, and his people so much interested in you they used to send him to inquire some-times twice a day. I wonder, though, he didn't send a servant. He must have taken some interest on his own account. But he always seemed as if he would sooner keep out of my way. I expect he thought I was a regular up-and-down fast colonial. Shows how careful a family man ought to be. I'll give Dick a good jawing* about it yet. The moment Langdale came up this young sea-calf* made a tremen-dous fuss over him, and the doctor patted him and talked to him, and then asked him for his scarred paw. "He hasn't got a scar," said I. "My wife is awfully fond of that scallawag. I believe he's always been more looked after than most babies." "Yes, but you know acci-dents will happen to the best-beloved dogs," said the doctor. "I believe Dustiefoot had an accident once;" and he held up his paw, and sure enough there is the mark of some hurt. And then he said——'

'Oh, Ted, please talk of something else,' said Stella, in a low voice, touched to the quick with this careless reminiscence which called up Langdale before her 'with portraiture and colour so distinct'* that his presence seemed to haunt the room.

'All right,' answered Ted placidly. 'I wonder, though, you didn't take a little more to Langdale. He's a good deal like some of those fellows in front of your poetry-books. I don't believe he's well. And

I'm sure, Stella, you're not well. You make me think of a story about a girl you told me long ago out of the "Arabian Nights." I don't remember her name—but as far as being jolly went, she hadn't a leg to stand on.'

'Perhaps it was the orphan who was quite broken-hearted, having no one to befriend her but God,'* said Stella, with a faint smile.

'Oh! but you've got far more to befriend you than that,' returned Ted, with unconscious irreverence. 'But I'll tell you what, Stella: I cannot allow you to be poking about so much among these East-End paupers. If you want to give them money and things, why don't you engage some competent person to do it? There must be no end of people in London who would be thankful to go up those filthy stairs for ten shillings a day or so.'

'Do you think one can do everything by paying money, Ted?'

'Well, if you ask me point-blank, I never thought so little of what money can do for you as at the present moment. Look here!' As he spoke Ted drew a pocket-book out of his breast coat-pocket, and extracted from it a sheet of pale pink note-paper. 'There's your I O U for five shillings you lost to me at euchre last December twelve-months. That night, after I got home, I said to Larry I would keep this bit of paper till everything I had was yours. And now it is; and yet what can I do for you? Instead of flying round with me on a drag with proper thoroughbred horses when you go to places, you pick out a hansom with the screwiest brute you can see, so that you may go slow and give the animal a spell. And as for jewels or dresses, why, you don't spend nearly your own money, and you've never touched any of your settlements.'

'Well, now I am going to ask you for something, Ted. Is all you have really mine?'

'Well, you just try!'

'Give me two hundred acres of Strathhaye.'

'But the whole eighty thousand is yours.'

'Oh, that is too much. Give me two hundred acres to cut up into little farms——'

'Good Lord!' cried Ted, starting up with such a look of horror that Stella fairly smiled. 'But you're only making game of me, Stella! You are not serious! and is it some of the paupers you want to put there?' he cried, a new light breaking in on him.

'Yes; some of the people who come up from the country hoping to get work.'

'But to put them on Strathhaye, Stella? You'd hate the look of them in no time. Oh, I know the sort of farmers they make, with awful whales of horses it would turn a fellow sick to look at, and machinery lying about without even a shed to cover it! No, no, Stella! While you're feeling rather low and going to church so much, you fancy you would like to do this; but to fix them on your own estate instead of well-bred merinoes! You'd be disgusted with them in no time.'

'Well, Ted, you are only judging me by my past character, I know.'

'Now, Stella, don't begin to talk of yourself in such a fashion. Your character indeed!'

'Why, haven't I got any?' said Stella, smiling once again.

'Not in that way. You hear precious little about people's characters till they want to make themselves out better or worse than they are. When you want to speak against yourself you must find someone that knows a little less about you.'

'Well, I did think that with such a large freehold estate——' said Stella slowly.

'Now, I'll tell you what I'll do,' said Ted suddenly. 'There's two hundred and fifty acres of good agricultural land to be in the market next January, at Caradoc, about fifteen miles away from Strathhaye. I'll buy it for you, every acre, and you can put the paupers there.'

'Don't call them paupers, Ted. The Schulz family in Berlin, and others like them in London, self-respecting, thrifty people, but with such heavy odds against them that they must go to the wall in the Old World—these are the kind of families we should help.'

It was a long time since Ritchie had heard Stella speak with so much animation.

'Well, you know you have a lot of money of your own to do what you like with,' he began.

'It will be an investment,' answered Stella.

'At first you'd better make up your mind to *lose* four per cent,' put in Ted.

'No, I won't lose,' she answered confidently. 'You see, you don't know the people, Ted.'

'That just reminds me of what you said once when you were telling me a yarn up in the Moreton Bay fig-tree at Fairacre. It's ages ago, when you were about thirteen—'

'Oh, Ted!—so long ago as that?'

'Well, it's eleven years ago. You used to sit in the fork of the tree with your back against the trunk, with a book; and I would tease you till you told me a story; and sometimes you would make it so creepy I was sorry I asked for it. This time—I remember it well, because it was a week before your father died,' said Ted, lowering his voice—'you looked down towards the sea, and you said there was a ship sailing, sailing away, and at last it came to the strangest country. The people had such small souls that at the Day of Judgment they couldn't be found. The Lord sent squads of angels to look for them, but not one could they fossick out. And there the skeletons had to sit each on its own grave, and the moonlight playing through their bones. That was the only light, and not a blade of grass or a drop of water!'

'Oh, Ted!—are you sure I told you all that?' said Stella incredulously.

'Why, who else could ever think of such things?' returned Ted with assured confidence. 'There was never a sound to be heard but when a big willy-willy* went rushing over the valleys—it was all valleys, full of graves, with skeletons sitting on them, waiting for the souls that couldn't be found. When the storms blew, the air was thick with bones, driven here and there, and at last left in heaps, to get together as well as they could. They used to be so tired and bruised for a long time, they could not move. But at last they began to put themselves together. And that was the only time they could speak. "You have taken part of my backbone," one would say to the other; "This rib doesn't belong to me;" "I am all here but my left leg;" "Who has got my skull?" That last was too much for me. I said, if the skull was missing, the skeleton couldn't speak. But you said I knew nothing about the country. I had never been there. And not only so, but the bone of the little toe could speak far better than a skull. That put the "kybosh" on me completely.'*

'You have got a curious memory, Ted,' said Stella, who had listened with languid wonder to this recital. 'You never seem to remember much of books you read.'

'No; but you tell me things out of them, and I'll remember fast enough. You'll have to come back to that, Stella—keep a school with only me. . . . Is that a letter from Larry?'

'Yes; but I do not think I can let you read it,' answered Stella, taking it up. She was thankful that she had resisted the impulse which had come over her in connection with it. 'They will be in London next month—and, Ted, it may seem selfish to take you away from England when the racing season is at its height, but I want to get away before Larry comes.'

'I'll take you to-morrow wherever you wish to go, Stella,' answered Ted. 'All these months I've been perfectly sick of being able to do nothing for you. As for racing, I told you more than a year ago I was getting full up of it.'

A fortnight later they left for Switzerland, and sailed for Australia early in November.

EXPLANATORY NOTES

These notes identify literary allusions, explain obsolete or colloquial terms, and identify geographical places in cases where some particular significance attaches to their mention or where they have since changed their names. Catherine Martin's reading was extensive and her range of literary reference in *An Australian Girl* is very wide. In cases where I have been unable to identify quotations this has been indicated in the note. Unless otherwise indicated, the date given for literary works is the date of publication and the Bible is quoted from the Authorized (or King James) Version. References to *The Arabian Nights* are by name of tale and use the names given to the tales in Richard Burton's translation (*The Book of the Thousand Nights and a Night*, originally published by the Burton Club). The spelling of Aboriginal words and names varies enormously; I have used Martin's own spelling or the spelling found in some of the works which appear to be Martin's sources. Where possible I have located quotations by reference to book and chapter (or, in the case of letters, to dates) rather than to page numbers in specific editions.

4 *Torrens Lake . . . Park Lands*: the Torrens Lake, an artificial lake formed behind a weir on the River Torrens, lies between the central square mile of Adelaide and the smaller area of North Adelaide, while the Park Lands both surround and separate Adelaide and North Adelaide.

   slips: narrow strips of ground.

5 *gadding tendrils*: see note to p. 201.

   Melbourne Cup: the most famous Australian horse race; it takes place on the first Tuesday in November and was first run in 1861.

6 *dark horse*: a horse which is unknown to the general public and wins contrary to their expectations.

   drag: a horse-drawn private carriage, usually like a stagecoach with seats inside and out.

   a little palm-basket sewn up . . . with a red worsted thread: see 'The Tale of the Three Apples' in *The Arabian Nights*.

   crammer: lie.

7 *parable . . . wet his lips*: a reference to the parable of the rich man and the beggar Lazarus (Luke 16: 19–31), but typically garbled in Ted's retelling.

   tabby: an older woman.

8 *poke borax at me*: make fun of me.

   like chaff that the storm carrieth away: Job 21: 18.

   tucker: food.

13 *spoony*: in love.

14 *a cockatoo . . . a free selector*: under a scheme known as free selection a prospective farmer could select and lay claim to sufficient unalienated Crown land for a small farm and buy it on favourable terms. He was known as a selector or free selector. The term *cockatoo* means generally a small farmer but was often applied specifically to free selectors.

15 *Croesus*: evidently a nickname; Croesus was an extremely rich king of ancient Lydia (560–546 BC).

give ninety Affghanistan camels for an exploring expedition: this reference to Afghan camels suggests that Ted's father, later named as Sir Edward Ritchie, was perhaps based in part on Sir Thomas Elder (1818–97), an extremely rich pastoralist who bred camels at Beltana in northern South Australia, bringing in Afghans to look after them. He lent camels for various geographical expeditions. Like Ted in the novel, he owned many racehorses.

split soda: a bottle of soda divided between two people.

16 *Mile End*: a suburb 1 mile west of Adelaide.

Shorter Catechism: the shorter of the two catechisms approved by the Church of Scotland in 1648 and used for long afterwards as a basic text of Christian education.

collars the tin: takes the money.

17 *seltzer*: soda water; originally a natural mineral water obtained from near Nieder-Selters in Germany.

Noah . . . drank too much wine: for the story of Noah's ark see Gen. 6–8 and for that of his getting drunk, Gen. 9: 21.

going to put a knife . . . 'Here am I': a version of a story related of Abraham and Isaac in Gen. 22.

Abraham was one of those fellows . . . didn't leave his wife at home: this seems to be Ted's gloss on the events related in Gen. 20.

Isaac . . . mess of porridge: a very distorted version of the actions of Jacob and Esau in Gen. 25: 29–34 and 27: 6–29. In the Geneva Bible the heading to Gen. 25 reads 'Esau selleth his birthright for a mess of potage.'

he got put . . . it was a pit: it was Shadrach, Meshach, and Abednego who were placed in a fiery furnace (Dan. 3: 21) and Joseph who is best known as having been cast into a pit (Gen. 37: 24).

18 *Jacob . . . the ten tribes . . . Joseph . . . went down into Egypt*: Ted is confusing Isaac's sons with those of Jacob, who had twelve (Gen. 35: 22–6). From them descended the twelve tribes of Israel, but ten of the tribes were lost after they were carried off into Assyria in the eighth century BC. One of the sons was Joseph, who had a coat of many colours (Gen. 37: 3) and was taken into Egypt (Gen. 37: 28).

Lullaboolagana: this apparently fictional place-name bears some similarity to Mundabullangana, the name of a station in Western Australia belonging to two of Martin's brothers.

18 *Shark's Bay*: or Shark Bay (see p. 58); a large shallow bay in Western Australia, formerly a pearling area.

plunging: recklessly betting.

copper: a penny or halfpenny.

renouncing the devil and all his work: in the Order of Baptism in the Book of Common Prayer godparents, on behalf of the child to be baptized, promise to 'renounce the devil and all his works' as well as 'the vain pomp and glory of this world'.

19 *Hawthorne*: the Melbourne suburb, now spelt *Hawthorn*.

K.G.: Knight of the Garter, the highest-ranking knighthood in the United Kingdom.

20 *the inter-colonial*: the train between Melbourne and Adelaide began running in 1887.

a man shall . . . cleave to his wife: Gen. 2: 24.

fossicked: rummaged

21 *Kooditcha shoe*: the spelling and details identify Martin's source of information as Edward M. Curr's *The Australian Race* (4 vols., Melbourne, 1886–7, i. 148). Curr attributes the practice to the Aborigines west of Lake Eyre in South Australia and explains that *Kooditcha* is the name of an 'invisible spirit'.

23 *blowing me up*: telling me off.

When he has asked . . . bread: compare Christ's question 'what man is there of you, whom if his son ask bread, will he give him a stone?' (Matt. 7: 9).

25 *mariage de convenance*: marriage of convenience.

To save the soul . . . as little intercourse with people as possible: compare the words of the Spanish saint John of the Cross in a letter of February 1598: 'With regard to sins . . . it is well that, in order to duly mourn for them and not fall into them, you have as few dealings as you can with other people' (*The Complete Works of Saint John of the Cross, Doctor of the Church*, trans. and ed. E. Allison Peers, London, 1964, iii. 254).

28 *College Town*: an Adelaide suburb so named from its closeness to St Peter's College (see note to p. 53). It has now been subsumed within College Park.

32 *the Russian and German men-of-war*: in 1882 a Russian fleet anchored off Glenelg near Adelaide; the Russians were entertained at a grand ball. However, visits by Russian naval ships were rare by the late 1880s. Ships of the German imperial navy were likely to call at Australian ports on their way to New Guinea after its annexation by Germany in 1885.

the Grande Chartreuse: a famous monastery in the French Alps; it was the first house of the Carthusians, an order of monks who took a vow of silence.

Brussels pile: a kind of carpet with a woollen pile on a linen backing.

33 *tandem*: a two-wheeled carriage drawn by two horses harnessed one behind the other.

Cremona violin: amongst famous violin-makers from seventeenth- and eighteenth-century Cremona are Niccolo Amati, Giuseppe Guarneri, and Antonio Stradivari.

distingué: distinguished.

Kannawijera: see note to *Cannawijera* on p. 100.

en suite: in a series of rooms opening from one into another.

34 *frugal days of interlinear hash*: compare Crabbe's 'The Patron' from his *Tales* (1812): 'He sometimes saved his cash | By interlinear days of frugal hash' (ll. 355–6).

35 *not wisely, but too well*: compare Othello, who wished to be remembered as 'one that loved not wisely but too well' (*Othello*, v. ii. 343).

Talleyrand . . . what was on the surface: Charles Maurice de Talleyrand-Périgord (1754–1838), a prominent French bishop and politician; quotation not traced.

36 *to show you . . . the glory thereof*: just as Christ was shown this by the Devil during his temptation in the wilderness; see Matt. 4: 7.

37 *the Princess of China*: a princess of China figures in the story of Aladdin and other stories from *The Arabian Nights*.

the central fact . . . marriage: not traced.

38 *Parcae*: the Fates who, in Greek and Roman mythology, determine the fate of individuals by spinning and cutting the thread of life; see p. 391.

classics in Russia backs: 'Russia leather' was strengthened with birch-bark oil and used in bookbinding.

39 *mourir à rire*: the normal French phrase is *mourir de rire*, 'to die of laughing'.

men who married . . . even Molière did: the French comic dramatist Molière (1622–73) married Armande Béjart in 1662. There is good evidence to suggest that she was unfaithful to him.

the babes in the wood: this refers to a well-known story of two children whose uncle hired men to kill them so that he would inherit their property. However, rather than killing them, one of the men left them in a wood, where they died together overnight.

Philemon and Baucis: in the story told by Ovid in his *Metamorphoses* (viii. 618–719), the Phrygian couple Philemon and Baucis asked that they might both die at the same time and when they were very old they were changed at the same moment into intertwining trees.

Goethe's birthday: the birthday of the enormously influential German writer Johann Wolfgang von Goethe (1749–1832).

40 *the shadow of the valley of life . . . than that of death*: compare 'the shadow of the valley of death' (Psalm 23: 4).

He was . . . for ever planting cabbages: the implication is that Ted was always getting on with the practical business of day-to-day life rather than speculating about the future. Compare Michel de Montaigne's comment in his *Essays* (first pub: 1580): 'I would always have a man to be doing, and, as much as in him lies, to spin out the offices of life; and then let death take me planting my cabbages, indifferent to him, and still less of my garden's not being finished' (from 'That to Study Philosophy is to Learn to Die', trans. Charles Cotton).

41 *dickey*: shaky, insecure.

there was a bad 'nick' in him: presumably a reference to Old Nick, the Devil; hence 'there was a devil in him'.

the Athanasian Creed: the Creed of Saint Athanasius. The Book of Common Prayer requires that it should replace the much shorter Apostles' Creed at Morning Prayer on Christmas Day.

Where lies the land to which yon ship must go?: the first line of Sonnet 31 in Wordworth's *Miscellaneous Sonnets* (1807).

42 *en famille*: as a family, without guests.

euchre: a card game of American origin which can be played by two players.

near the foot . . . south-west of Adelaide: the sea, rather than the hills, is a few miles to the south-west of Adelaide, but Sir Thomas Elder's (see note to p. 15) large house, Birksgate, was near the hills to the south-*east* of Adelaide.

43 *portières*: curtains hung over doorways.

'knocked down' a large nugget: spent the proceeds of a gold nugget on heavy drinking.

hook it out of this: leave here quickly.

44 *lick the place into a cocked hat*: Ted's phrase combines the phrase *lick into shape* with *knock into a cocked hat*, meaning 'thoroughly defeat'.

dados: wood or other linings of the lower part of the interior walls of a house.

en rapport with: in sympathy with.

Horace Walpole . . . a lame telescope: in a letter to Henry Conway of 8 June 1747, Walpole writes of a library 'furnished with three maps, one shelf, a bust of Sir Isaac Newton, and a lame telescope without any glasses'.

So many and so many and such woe: compare 'So many and so many and such glee' from Keats's *Emdymion* (1817; iv. 236).

45 *'books' clothing . . . biblia a-biblia*: Charles Lamb uses the phrase 'things in books' clothing' in his essay 'Detached Thoughts on Books and Reading' in *The Last Essays of Elia* (1833) to describe what he calls 'biblia a-biblia', literally 'books un-books', or, as Lamb puts it, *'books which are no books—biblia a-biblia'*.

shady: disreputable.

sprung: tipsy.

46 *a Crimea shirt*: a shirt of coloured flannel commonly worn at the time by working men in the Australian bush.

blowed: euphemistic equivalent to *damned*.

47 *would be regular nuts for her*: would give her a lot of pleasure (in this case, as something to write about).

kotooing: kowtowing.

chouse: swindle.

48 *tenner*: a ten-pound note.

right bower: in euchre, the name for the knave of trumps; it and the other knave of the same colour, the 'left bower', are the two highest cards.

49 *the pride that apes humility*: Coleridge, 'The Devil's Thoughts' (written 1799), l. 24.

all U P with me: all up with me, all finished with me.

50 *Worth*: the Parisian fashion house founded by Charles Frederick Worth (1825–95).

have their numbers taken down: a reference to the practice of putting up the numbers of the winning horses in order to announce the results of a race.

52 *the good old Bishop . . . cost of the cathedral*: if Martin has an actual Anglican bishop of Adelaide in mind it would be Augustus Short (1802–83) rather than his successor, G. W. Kennion, who was aged only 45 when appointed. Surpliced choirs were a mark of the influence of the Tractarian movement in England with its greater emphasis on ritual. They were initially unpopular in some circles in Adelaide but were favoured by Bishop Short (see David Swale, 'Liturgical and Choral Traditions in South Australia', in Andrew D. McCredie (ed.), *From Colonel Light into the Footlights*, Norwood, 1988, 193–207). Only the first stage of the building of St Peter's Cathedral, costing £18,000, was completed before Bishop Short's retirement in 1881; building was resumed in 1890.

53 *St Peter's*: a prestigious Anglican school for boys in Adelaide.

The Lady of the Lake: Sir Walter Scott's long narrative poem, published in 1810.

knock-about hand: an unskilled worker on a farm or station.

54 *the horrors*: a fit of delirium tremens.

nobbler: drink of spirits.

55 *the Zulu War*: the British invaded Zululand in January 1879. After losing several battles they defeated the Zulu army in July of the same year.

60 *Someone has said . . . dull people*: not traced.

buttoned up . . . organ-grinder's monkey: an organ-grinder was an itinerant musician who operated a barrel-organ, a portable mechanical organ; he was often accompanied by a monkey dressed in human clothes.

61 *bise*: a German term for a cold northeasterly wind, especially in Switzerland.

corbie: raven.

sinsyne: since then.

thae: those.

62 *Widdy*: widow.

Brown Street: a road in the central part of Adelaide, later renamed to form the southern half of Morphett Street.

spell: break from work.

Loight Square: Light Square, one of the five squares within the central square mile of Adelaide.

Sisthers av Saint Joseph: the Congregation of the Sisters of Saint Joseph of the Sacred Heart was founded by Mary McKillop and Julian Tenison-Woods in 1866. It was primarily a teaching order but also undertook other kinds of charitable work.

63 *waddies*: wooden clubs.

64 *point de ralliement*: rallying point.

worms of the earth: the phrase comes from Mic. 7: 17, where it is used literally.

take so much . . . clothed: see Matt. 6: 31.

'Tis to no purpose . . . says Plato: this expresses in general terms some of the ideas in Plato's *Ion*, but the actual quotation is from 'Of Drunkenness' in Montaigne's *Essays* in the wording of the 1685–6 translation by Charles Cotton. Moreover, the whole passage in Montaigne is itself taken from Seneca's *De Tranquillitate Animi* (ch. 15).

a brand plucked from the burning: compare 'a brand plucked out of the burning' (Amos 4: 11, as translated in the Revised Version).

65 *Hector . . . the classical hero*: the Trojan hero in Homer's *Iliad*.

unshrived: without having confessed one's sins and received absolution.

cockerel: a young cock; a dialect term.

66 *Once upon a time . . . partly black*: a story of the Narrinyeri people found, amongst other places, in George Taplin's 'The Narrinyeri' (in J. D. Woods (ed.), *The Native Tribes of South Australia*, Adelaide, 1879, 62).

the venomous snake . . . its bite harmless: told in Curr, *Australian Race* (iii. 29–30) as a story of Aboriginal people around the Belyando river in Queensland.

Faust: Goethe's play *Faust*, published in two parts (1808 and 1832).

68 *a house divided against itself*: Matt. 12: 25.

Ligurian bees: in the 1880s this breed of bees, praised for its docility, was introduced from Italy into South Australia and Kangaroo Island was declared a reserve for its cultivation.

Windsor: now a suburb of Adelaide known as Windsor Gardens.

send this to Mr Punch: that is, send it to the magazine *Punch*.

69 *Rosenthal*: a small town about 50 km. to the north of Adelaide; the name was anglicized to Rosedale during World War I, along with other names of German origin.

the pre-Deuteronomic Pentateuch: the first, second, third, and fifth books of the Bible before the addition of the fourth, Deuteronomy. The five together constitute the Pentateuch. The origins and date of Deuteronomy were the subject of much discussion in the nineteenth century.

Die assyrisch–babylonisch Keilinschriften: the Assyrian–Babylonian cuneiform inscriptions. Cuneiform script was developed by the Sumerians, adopted by their successors in Babylonia, and used by later peoples in the Middle East, including the Assyrians, until about the beginning of the Christian era. There was much interest in cuneiform texts in the nineteenth century and in 1850–4 a vast number of clay tablets in cuneiform script were unearthed in the excavation of the Assyrian capital, Nineveh.

when our world . . . had not a name: see Gen. 1: 2–10.

a conscience seared as with a hot iron: 1 Titus 4: 2.

Attila: king of the Huns (d. 453) who invaded and ravaged parts of the Roman empire.

71 *olivets*: olive-groves; an archaism.

72 *Macaroni . . . sticking feathers in it*: from the nursery rhyme 'Yankee Doodle came to town, | Riding on a pony; | He stuck a feather in his cap | And called it macaroni.'

the Grange or Henley Beach: two Adelaide seaside suburbs; the Grange, now known simply as Grange, was so named after the house of that name belonging to the explorer Charles Sturt.

73 *About thee gathered . . . perfumed with ambrosia*: Martin quotes Agamemnon speaking to Achilles in the underworld and describing to him Achilles' own funeral rites (Homer, *Odyssey*, xxiv. 58–9).

amis de la maison: friends of the family.

Montaigne says . . . capable of being so: see 'Of Presumption' in Montaigne's *Essays*, Cotton's translation.

the woman of Samaria . . . the husbands: Christ told the woman of Samaria, 'thou hast had five husbands; and he whom thou now hast is not thy husband' (John 4: 18).

74 *Don Quixote*: the hero, remarkable for his idealistic attachment to the lost world of chivalry, of Miguel de Cervantes' novel of the same name, published in two parts (1605 and 1615).

75 *Blumenthal*: during World War I a place of this name near Gawler was gazetted for a change of name to *Lakkari*.

Dankfest: a harvest thanksgiving festival.

77 *bull*: a statement which contradicts itself.

the spies and Eshcol: Moses sent spies into the land of Canaan and 'they came unto the brook of Eshcol, and cut down from thence a branch with one cluster of grapes, and they bare it between two upon a staff' (Num. 13: 23).

pastorin: pastor's wife.

78 *Kritik of Pure Reason*: the philosophical work by Immanuel Kant (1781). Stella's reading of Kant figures prominently at the end of the story of her spiritual development related by her to Cuthbert in two chapters omitted from the 1891 edition (see Note on the Text).

an old ballad . . . called 'Two King's Children': the widely known German ballad 'Zwei Königskindern' (see Ludwig Erk, *Deutscher Liederhort*, rev. Franz M. Böhme, repr. Hildesheim, 1963, No. 84).

79 *conte à rire*: a funny story.

80 *The old Adam*: Adam as representing human beings in an unredeemed state.

81 *whether the root of the matter is in him*: see Job 19: 28.

as a prey snatched from the snarer: compare 'Surely he shall deliver thee from the snare of the fowler' (Psalm 91: 3).

chosen vessel: Acts 9: 15.

83 *The sun is a woman . . . shoulders*: this story is related in H. E. A. Meyer's 'Manners and Customs of the Aborigines of the Encounter Bay Tribe, South Australia' (in Woods (ed.), *Native Tribes of South Australia*, 200).

Kyirrie . . . Kockadooroo . . . Amathooroocooroo . . . claw of eagle-hawk: Martin's source appears to be Samuel Gason's account of the Dieyerie people of the Cooper Creek area. However, Gason gives *Kyirrie* as the name of the Milky Way and *Amathooroocooroo* as that of the Evening Star and does not mention *Kockadooroo*. He also lists *Kurawurathidna* as the name for 'A cluster of stars representing the claw of an eagle-hawk, seen in the western hemisphere during the winter months' (in Woods (ed.), *Native Tribes of South Australia*, 295).

the ark of Neppelle . . . unfaithful wives: these are both stories of the Narrinyeri people. The version in Taplin's 'The Narrinyeri' (in Woods (ed.), *Native Tribes of South Australia*, 57–8) is closest in its details to Martin's account. It was Nurundere, the most prominent figure in Narrinyeri stories, who caused a flood to drown his wives.

three of the stars . . . deserted husband: this story is told of Nepelle's two wives and Wyungare; see, for example, Taplin's 'The Narrinyeri' (in Woods (ed.), *Native Tribes of South Australia*, 56–7).

84 *one of those hydra-animals . . . respire*: Martin has taken this detail, in Darwin's exact words, from Charles Darwin's *The Origin of Species* (1859; ch. 6). A hydra is a freshwater creature whose body takes the form of a long, thin cylinder.

85 *the horrors of death . . . lying in wait for my soul*: a collection of phrases from the Psalms; see Psalms 55: 4; 124: 5; 31: 9; 22: 6; 38: 2; 9: 15; 63: 1; 74: 1; 102: 4, 6, 7; 20: 4; 141: 7; 59: 3.

86 *who has spiled . . . a good spoon*: spoons were made of horn and a common proverbial phrase was that someone would 'either make a spoon or spoil a horn'.

Ein feste Burg ist unser Gott: 'Our God is a secure stronghold', a hymn by Martin Luther in the *Klug'sche Gesangbuch* (1529).

87 *auld langsyne*: old long-ago; the words are now best known from Burns's song, but he set it to an already existing tune of that name.

88 *Bezer in the wilderness*: a town to the east of the Dead Sea, set aside by Moses as a place of refuge; see Deut. 4: 43.

'delicate as honey born in air': not traced.

pour la guérison de douleur: for the curing of pain.

89 *nervine aliment*: nourishment which is soothing to the nerves.

M. Jourdain's dancing-master . . . applaudissements me touchent: in Molière's *Le Bourgeois Gentilhomme* (I. i), his dancing master explains to M. Jourdain that he yearns for 'a little bit of glory' and that 'applause moves me'.

90 *great fertile young Hercules*: not traced.

92 *ulster*: a long, loose-fitting coat.

cloud: a light woollen scarf.

93 *a very Haroun al Raschid anecdote*: a fantastic story such as those told to Haroun al Raschid, caliph of Baghdad, in *The Arabian Nights*.

bower-bird: a bird which builds itself a bower which it decorates with brightly coloured objects.

swinging: hanging.

94 *Then he brought me . . . weeping for Tammuz*: Ezek. 8: 14.

96 *mia-mia*: a temporary shelter constructed by Aboriginal people.

'possum: the name of this small Australian marsupial derives from a shortening of *opossum*.

Scot: temper.

97 *mise-en-scène*: setting.

98 *in the sure and certain hope . . . the just*: from the Order for the Burial of the Dead in the Book of Common Prayer.

99 *Every body . . . the custody of the elements*: this is very close to passages in St Augustine's *Enchiridion* (ch. 88) and *De civitate* (Bk xxii, ch. 20).

Tatiara district: the area around Bordertown in South Australia, towards the border with Victoria.

100 *in the year of grace 188–*: as Kevin Gilding has shown ('Space Exploration: Catherine Martin, Australia, The World, The Universe and

Whatever', in Caroline Guerin, Philip Butterss, and Amanda Nettelbeck (eds), *Crossing Lines: Formations of Australian Culture* (Adelaide, 1996)), the dates attached to Stella's letters to Cuthbert (including one omitted from the 1891 edition) identify the year as one in which Easter Sunday fell on 1 April; the only possible year for this in the 1880s is 1888. The total action of the novel takes place between December 1887 and November 1889.

100 *Cannawijera*: apparently based on Cannawigara, the name of a real station 11 km. north-west of Bordertown.

Mallee Scrub: an area of bush where the predominant tree is the mallee, a smallish gum-tree which grows in a number of stems; in this case specifically the scrub extending from an eastern section of South Australia into the adjacent area of north-western Victoria.

102 *Dead Sea wilderness . . . great enemy of souls*: see Matt. 4: 1–11 and Luke 4: 1–13.

Dig, and ye shall find; water and ye shall reap: cf. Matt. 7: 7: 'Seek, and ye shall find.'

103 *immortelles*: everlasting flowers.

104 *nearer one still, and a dearer*: 'Or was there a dearer one | Still, and a nearer one | Yet, than all other', Thomas Hood's 'The Bridge of Sighs' (1844), ll. 40–2.

107 *à cœur ouvert et à langue déliée*: with an open heart and an unrestricted tongue.

"sparkle of the glancing stars": Milton, *Comus* (1634), l. 80.

Das Glück ist eine leichte Dirne | Und bleibt nicht lang am selber Ort: 'Happiness is a fickle girl and does not stay long in the same place'; this is the motto to 'Lamentationen', the second book of *Romanzero* (1851) by the German poet Heinrich Heine.

109 *There is . . . more of the fool than of the wise*: from 'Of Boldness' in *Essays, or Counsells, Civill and Morall* (1597, 1612, 1625) by Francis Bacon.

110 *No receipt . . . civil shrift or confession . . . The best preservative . . . admonition of a friend*: both quotations are from 'Of Friendship' in Bacon's *Essays*.

111 *smiles to itself . . . a sin to light the lamps as yet*: not traced.

Some old writers . . . Babylonian naphtha . . . without touching it: this information is given by Plutarch (*c.*46–*c.*120) in his life of Alexander (ch. 35).

113 *put in a box . . . beneath the roaring waves*: see 'The Story of King Shahryar and his Brother' in *The Arabian Nights*.

baskets sewn up with red thread: see note to p. 6.

faces like the moon in the fourteenth night: see 'The Story of King Shahryar and his Brother' in *The Arabian Nights*.

The better to see you with . . . thrown away on Ted: Stella makes an easily recognizable allusion to the story of Little Red Riding Hood.

119 *through a glass darkly*: 1 Cor. 13: 12.

120 *It's better to be born lucky than rich*: this proverb is known in various forms from the early seventeenth century.

121 *The mine had been salted*: an unproductive mine could be dishonestly 'salted' by placing nuggets in it to lure potential investors.

intimes: close friends.

rump and stump: completely.

like Pilate, he washed his hands in public: after the crowd insisted that Jesus be crucified, Pilate washed his hands before the multitude, claiming that he was innocent of Jesus' blood; see Matt. 27: 24.

122 *Nebuchadnezzar, King of the Jews*: the first (historically misleading) line of a children's clapping rhyme. Stella's comment alludes to the fact that the rhyme describes a series of actions. Nebuchadnezzar was ruler of the Babylonian empire and incorporated the kingdom of Judah within his domains.

123 *diablerie*: devilry.

Satan letter: a reference to a letter to Cuthbert, omitted from the 1891 edition, in which Stella imagines what problems would arise if Satan were reformed and returned to Heaven. According to a later letter from Stella, Cuthbert was 'almost shocked' by Stella's speculation.

124 *sacredness of the number seven . . . pre-Semitic civilization of Babylon*: after Semites conquered Babylon in the twenty-fourth century BC they absorbed many beliefs from the earlier Sumerian civilization. The Bible provides us with evidence that the Hebrews, a Semitic people, regarded seven as a sacred number from early times (see e.g. Gen. 2: 2).

125 *trifles light as air*: *Othello*, III. iii. 323.

Mount Tabors and Gehennas: in the Bible both Mount Tabor and Gehenna (later known as the Valley of Hinmon) are sites associated with practices of great evil.

126 *pothooks and hangers*: in handwriting, hooked strokes and strokes with a double curve; children practised these basic strokes when first learning to write.

127 *Moreton fig-tree*: more commonly called Moreton Bay fig; *Ficus macro-phylla*, a very large tree, originally native to parts of northern New South Wales and southern Queensland but widely planted elsewhere as an ornamental tree or to provide shade.

128 *Where is the ship to which yon land must go?*: see note to p. 41.

the cat with one trick: this refers to the fable of the fox and the cat. The fox, who had many tricks, scorned the cat, who had only one trick; but when a hunter and his dogs came the fox was killed while the cat used his one trick, climbing a tree to escape danger, and was saved. The story is well known from its occurrence in collections of Aesop's *Fables* and in the *Tales* of the Brothers Grimm.

128 *cow-lymph*: the liquid taken from the blisters caused by cowpox and used in vaccinating humans against smallpox.

Jack Horner: a reference to the nursery rhyme: 'Little Jack Horner | Sat in the corner, | Eating a Christmas pie; | He put in his thumb, | And pulled out a plum, | And said, What a good boy am I!'

129 *all is vanity and vexation of spirit*: see Eccles. 1: 14, 2: 11, etc.

Mammon: riches; an Aramaic term preserved in English in Christ's words 'Ye cannot serve God and Mammon' (Matt. 6: 24).

esprit: wit.

Parnassus: a mountain in Greece, in ancient times dedicated in part to the Muses and hence traditionally associated with the writing of poetry.

Melbourne Argus: a Melbourne daily newspaper published between 1846 and 1957.

130 *sweetness and light*: a phrase used by Swift in the preface to *The Battle of the Books* (1697–8) and made famous by Matthew Arnold by its frequent use in *Culture and Anarchy* (1869).

borné: limited in outlook, narrow-minded.

132 *en parenthèse*: in parentheses, incidentally. The normal French phrase is *entre parenthèses*.

ruralize: spend time in the country.

a native companion: a large bird, an Australian crane, standing about 1 m. high, otherwise known as a brolga.

135 *mignonne*: dainty.

140 *Is this a dagger that I see before me?*: *Macbeth*, II. i. 33.

I want the share that falleth to my lot now: an allusion to the parable of the Prodigal Son; see Luke 15: 12.

142 *alms to oblivion*: *Troilus and Cressida*, III. iii. 145.

143 *Court Circular*: daily record of activities of royalty published in the newspapers.

144 *chiffonnier*: rag-and-bone man.

146 *artistement*: artistically.

bons mots: witticisms.

147 *salon d'esprit*: literary salon.

150 *Prodigal Son*: see Christ's parable in Luke 15: 11–32.

simulacrum: outward show.

sinews of war: cf. Bacon's comment, 'Neither is money the sinews of war (as it is trivially said)' in 'Of the True Greatness of Kingdoms' in his *Essays*.

154 *the story of the shepherd-boy and the wolf*: an allusion to the ancient fable of the boy who called 'Wolf!' so often for fun when no wolf was actually near the sheep that he was not believed when there really was a wolf.

'We never know,' says Goethe somewhere, 'how anthropomorphic we are.': 'Der Mensch begreift niemals, wie anthropomorphisch er ist', from

Goethe's *Maximen und Reflectionen* (Max Hecker (ed.), Weimar, 1907, No. 203); the maxims are variously numbered in different editions—this one was written in 1823.

en fête: full of festivity.

158 *the Age*: the Melbourne newspaper published since 1854.

162 *the Chins*: one of the ethnic groups within Burma.

164 *home-station*: the main house on a station, a large property for raising cattle or sheep.

165 *Shenstone . . . entangled his shrubberies*: Dr Johnson, in his life of Shenstone in *The Lives of the Poets* (1779–81), writes that on his estate Shenstone 'began . . . to point his prospects, to diversity his surface, to entangle his walks, and to wind his waters'.

166 *a hazel with its 'artless bower'*: compare 'the hazle's artless bower' in William Shenstone's 'Nancy of the Vale, A Ballad' (l. 5). Shenstone's poem is preceded by two lines from Virgil's Eclogue VII; Langdale later compares this same garden to that described in Eclogue I (see notes to pp. 198–200).

place his bark-enclosed dead among the boughs: Curr, *Australian Race,* records this custom for a number of Aboriginal peoples (e.g., i. 88, 164–5, 272).

168 *wore a face of joy . . . glad of yore*: see Wordsworth's 'The Fountain' (1800), ll. 47–8.

171 *'Arabian Nights'*: *The Arabian Nights' Entertainment,* otherwise known as *The Thousand and One Nights,* a collection of Arabic stories widely read in Europe after they were translated into French by Antoine Galland in the eighteenth century; a number of the stories are referred to in the novel. Selections from *The Arabian Nights* were often used as children's reading.

semi-Carthusian: Carthusian monks live a life characterized by austerity, solitude, and silence.

174 *his mattress-grave*: this is the term which Heine himself applied, in the postscript to *Romanzero* (1851), to the sick-bed on which he spent the last nearly eight years of his life after his legs failed him.

175 *Circe . . . with a brazen sickle by moonlight*: in classical mythology Circe turned men into animals with drugs and spells. Circe collecting simples with a brazen sickle derives perhaps from the rather free translation of Ovid's *Metamorphoses* by John Dryden and others where Circe's maidens collect flowers and plants 'With brazen sickles reap'd at planetary hours' (xiv. 223; this detail is not found in Ovid's original text) but is verbally closer to the description in Dryden's *Aeneid* of how the priestess 'Culls hoary simples, found by Phoebe's light, | With brazen sickles reap'd at noon of night' (iv. 744–5) for Dido's pyre.

Beelzebub: Satan.

Mathilde: the name given by Heine to Crescence Eugénie Mirat, a young woman with whom he had a relationship and who later became his wife.

cachet: distinctive mark, stamp.

175 *no life-enjoying . . . an unhappy man*: these words occur in a letter published on 25 April 1849 in the *Allgemeine Zeitung* under the title 'Berichtigung' ('Correction').

176 *certainty of waking bliss*: Milton, *Comus* (1634), l. 263.

The Philistines . . . grind corn at Gaza: the Philistines so treated Samson (Judg. 16: 21).

passionate expression: Wordsworth in the preface to the second edition of *Lyrical Ballads* (1800) describes poetry as 'impassioned expression'.

I could lie down . . . and still must bear: Shelley, 'Stanzas Written in Dejection—December 1818, Near Naples', ll. 30–2.

178 *to dumb forgetfulness a prey*: Gray, 'Elegy Written in a Country Church-yard' (1750), l. 85.

Molière . . . Harpagon . . . 'L'Avare': see Molière's *L'Avare* (1699; III. i), where Harpagon suggests that, while serving his guests, one servant should hold his hat in front of him to conceal an oil stain and another should keep his back to the wall to hide a hole in his breeches.

180 *the waters of Siloe that go with silence*: Isa. 8: 6 in the Douai version. The pool of Siloe or Siloam was a reservoir within the walls of Jerusalem.

presences, unknown as well as unseen: compare Shelley's use of the phrase 'unseen presence' in his 'Ode to the West Wind' (1820), l. 2.

181 *even 'The Babes in the Wood' . . . in the end*: see note to p. 39.

182 *Arcadia*: the idealized pastoral setting of Virgil's *Eclogues* and of later works such as Sir Philip Sidney's romance, *Arcadia* (1590).

183 *laughing-jackass*: kookaburra.

184 *bourne*: ultimate destination, in this case death; modern uses in this sense rather than the original sense of 'boundary' derive from a misunder-standing of *Hamlet*, III. i. 78–80: 'the dread of something after death, | The undiscover'd country from whose bourn | No traveller returns'.

What is the subtlety . . . someone has said: not traced.

opéra bouffe: light comic opera, often of a farcical nature.

186 *Girton*: Girton was established in 1869 as the first women's college at Cambridge University.

le cant Anglais: a French phrase meaning 'English cant'; the French saw cant (hypocritical language) as a particularly English quality.

agaçant: irritating.

187 *anti-Unionists*: those who in the nineteenth century opposed advocates of the reunion of the Roman Catholic and Anglican churches.

189 *of the female 'sect'*: sect in the sense of 'sex' is found in Chaucer and later writers but by the nineteenth century was considered an illiterate or dialectal usage.

190 *the story of the old woman . . . that legend of the nursery*: the old woman cannot get her pigs to jump over the stile so she appeals successively to

various agents (cow, cat, rat, rope, butcher, ox, water, fire, stick, dog) to help her until finally a chain of reactions amongst the agents leads to the dog biting the pigs, which then jump over the stile.

191 *her Adonis of fifty*: in Greek mythology Adonis was a youth beloved by Aphrodite. In 1813 Leigh Hunt was sent to prison for calling the prince regent a 'corpulent Adonis of fifty'.

192 *enough is as good as a feast*: proverbial since at least the fifteenth century.

193 *reaping as we sow*: compare 'whatsover a man soweth, that shall he also reap' (Gal. 6: 7) which has become proverbial in the form, 'As you sow, so you reap.'

you sow tares . . . who spoils the harvest: see Matt. 13: 24–5. *Tares* is used in English Bible translations to denote a poisonous weed growing in wheatfields.

far-off things: see Wordsworth, 'The Solitary Reaper' (1807), l. 19.

196 *plump*: directly and plainly.

197 *Gentle Jesus, meek and mild*: the first line of a hymn by Charles Wesley, first published in 1742.

198 *Virgil's 'Eclogues'*: the references are to the first of Virgil's pastoral poems, the *Eclogues* (written 42–37 BC), which takes the form of a dialogue between Meliboeus and Tityrus.

199 *Amaryllis*: the beloved of Tityrus in Eclogue I, also appearing in other roles in Eclogues II, VIII, and IX.

the lay that Tityrus pipes on his flute: see Eclogue I, l. 10. All editions agree in reading 'lute' but the reference to 'piping' and the allusion to Virgil require the reading 'flute'.

the beech-tree under which Tityrus reclines: in the opening line of Eclogue I, Meliboeus describes Tityrus as lying under a spreading beech-tree.

Afreets: evil demons of gigantic size in Islamic stories.

Hic inter densas corylos: 'here amongst the dense hazel-trees' (l. 14).

Tityrus . . . as high as cypress among bending osiers: see ll. 24–5.

200 *Meliboeus speaks further . . . vineyards*: see ll. 38–9.

willow-bloom on which the bees feast: see l. 54.

the hoarse note . . . the towering elm: see ll. 56–7.

making a bull: see note to p. 77.

201 *vine-buds and gadding tendrils*: compare the 'gadding vine' (l. 40) in Milton's 'Lycidas' (1637).

locust . . . as "though he never should be old": I have not traced the quotation but this is apparently a reference to the story of the ant and the grasshopper in Aesop's *Fables*, in which the grasshopper spent the summer singing without thinking about the coming winter.

all clothed . . . as with a garment: compare Psalm 104: 1–2, 'thou art clothed with honour and majesty. Who coverest thyself with light as with a garment'.

202 *when those that look out . . . daughters of music are laid low*: Eccles. 12: 3, 4.

rail at life in good set terms: compare *As You Like It* (II. vii. 14–17), 'I met a fool | . . . who . . . railed on Lady Fortune in set terms, | In good set terms'.

Seneca: the Roman Seneca (c. 4 BC–AD 65) was the author of numerous treatises on ethics and other subjects.

203 *what Frenchman said that women . . . more truly savage*: perhaps a recollection of Balzac's comment in *Pierrette* (1840): 'Men are supposed to be very savage, and so are tigers; but neither tigers, nor vipers, nor diplomatists, nor officers of the law, nor executioners, nor kings, in their most atrocious acts, can approach the suave cruelty, the poisoned sweetness, the savage scorn of young women toward their sex' (anonymous translator in Honoré de Balzac, *La Comédie humaine*, Caxton edn., London, 1895–1900, xxiv. 160).

the anthropoidal era: the period belonging to the earliest origins of the human race.

On the whole stick close . . . the temple of certainty: see Part I of Goethe's *Faust* (1808), vi. 1990–2.

206 *Confound your eyes*: a milder form of the oath 'damn your eyes'.

211 *Providence . . . those who have no teeth*: compare the proverb 'the gods send nuts to those who have no teeth'.

figmentum malum: evil figment or fiction.

215 *sot*: sat.

spelled: rested.

217 *Werthester Freund*: dearest friend.

219 *what Pliny says . . . beginning of June*: see Bk. XVI, ch. 9 of the *Natural History* of Pliny the Elder (AD 23/4–79).

Pliny the Elder . . . mendaciorum patrem: the Latin means 'father of lies', a phrase usually applied to the Devil after John 8: 44. While it contains much interesting incidental information, Pliny's work contains many scientifically inaccurate details.

writing deep morals upon Nature's pages: Hartley Coleridge, 'The Forget-me-not', l. 8.

220 *Marcus Aurelius . . . it is well to die*: summary of the views of Marcus Aurelius Antoninus (121–80) in Bk. II, ch. 11 of his *Meditations*.

ere sin could blight or sorrow fade: Coleridge, 'Epitaph on an Infant' (1796), l. 1.

223 *Japanese chrysanthemums . . . in honour of this flower*: the annual Feast of the Chrysanthenum is one of the most important of the Japanese flower festivals, the chrysanthemum being the emblem of the Japanese emperor.

224 *Glenelg*: beginning in 1874, incoming mail boats stopped at the seaside town of Glenelg, 11 km. south-west of Adelaide.

King George's Sound: at this time Albany on King George Sound on the southern coast of Western Australia was often the first port of call in Australia for ships coming from England.

Cape Borda: on the north-west tip of Kangaroo Island; it is passed by ships sailing from the west into St Vincent's Gulf, on which Adelaide stands.

Can you keep a secret? . . . best you can: a nursery rhyme said while tickling someone's hand.

La blanche . . . point du tout: 'The white and simple daisy, | Which your heart consults especially | Says: "Your lover, sweet maid, | loves you, a little, a lot, not at all." ' For the custom referred to see p. 254.

225 *Candide*: the philosophical tale published in 1759 by the French writer Voltaire.

her heart . . . the nether millstone: compare 'His heart is as firm as a stone; yea, as hard as a piece of the nether millstone' (Job 41: 24).

227 *the salt-dividing sea*: compare 'The unplumbed, salt, estranging sea' in Matthew Arnold's 'To Marguerite—Continued' (1852; l. 24).

'dolce color d'oriental zaffiro' . . . the murky atmosphere of hell: 'the delicate colour of oriental sapphire'; see the 'Purgatorio', Canto i, l. 13. In the 'Inferno', the 'Purgatorio', and the 'Paradiso', the three books of *La divina commedia* by Dante Alighieri (1265–1321), Dante is led successively through Hell and Purgatory before having a vision of Paradise.

228 *Te Deum*: the common way of referring to the Latin hymn *Te Deum Laudamus* ('We praise you God'), which was often sung as an expression of thanksgiving.

229 *Sir Thomas More's wife . . . practised to her husband*: this information about More's second wife, Alice, is recorded by Erasmus in a letter of 23 July 1519 to Ulrich von Hutten.

merlodeon: the melodeon, a kind of accordion. In a passage omitted from the 1891 edition Dunstan had told a story of how he bought a 'merlodeon' to cheer up his sick wife.

a strayed reveller: from the title of Matthew Arnold's poem 'The Strayed Reveller' (1849).

230 *Mariolatry*: the worship of the Virgin Mary in a fashion viewed by some Protestants as an example of Roman Catholic idolatry.

Breviary: the book setting out the daily requirements of the Divine Office of worship in the Roman Catholic church.

232 *improve the shining hour*: Isaac Watts, 'Against Idleness and Mischief', l. 2, from his collection *Divine Songs for Children* (1720).

bursters: a 'burster' is a heavy fall from a horse.

233 *a local habitation and a name*: *A Midsummer Night's Dream*, v. i. 17.

235 *sundowners*: tramps who arrive at sundown in the hope of receiving shelter and food without working in return.

Cyclopean: in Greek mythology the Cyclops were one-eyed giants who made thunderbolts for Zeus.

236 *flittings*: removals from one place to another (a Scots term).

238 *play the Good Samaritan*: see Luke 10: 25–37.

sup: sip.

239 *Bishop of Noyon . . . out of the head of your bishop*: quotation not traced. All the original editions read 'Noyou' but this is evidently a mistake for Noyon, which was the seat of a bishop.

Dr Johnson's beverage for heroes: according to Samuel Johnson claret is the drink for boys, port for men, and brandy for heroes; see Boswell's *Life of Johnson*, 30 March 1781.

240 *I could not love thee, dear, so much,* | *Loved I not honour more*: Richard Lovelace, 'Going to the Wars', ll. 11–12, from *Lucasta* (1649).

the three ladies of Bagdad: there is a story in *The Arabian Nights* called 'The Porter and the Three Ladies of Baghdad'.

241 *Aladdin, the son of Shamseddin*: the hero of 'Aladdin; or, The Wonderful Lamp' in *The Arabian Nights*. In English versions of the story Aladdin's father is usually either unnamed or called Mustapha.

Nineveh: the ancient city, first excavated in 1843–5.

I have come . . . until you repent or die: see 'The Tale of the Bull and the Ass' in *The Arabian Nights*.

243 *leves well foure paire*: see *The Romaunt of the Rose* (doubtfully ascribed to Chaucer), l. 1698.

the Stella rose . . . starry: *Stella* means 'star'.

246 *ora pro nobis*: pray for us; a request addressed successively to a large number of saints in the Roman Catholic Litanies of the Saints.

247 *Liebe*: dear.

Herzblättchen: a term of endearment, elsewhere translated literally as 'little-heart-leaflet' (see p. 258).

A pard-like spirit, beautiful and swift: Shelley, 'Adonais' (1821), l. 280.

Amore e 'l core gentil sono una cosa . . . Vita Nuova: the first line of a sonnet in Section 20 of Dante's *La vita nuova* (c.1293).

Blättchen: a term of endearment, literally leaflet.

249 *like Hassan's gold covered over by common wood*: in the tale of 'Hasan of Bassorah' in *The Arabian Nights* Hasan's gold is laid in a chest.

250 *'degenerated into a lover'*: the phrase is picked up from Stella's earlier thoughts; see p. 180.

254 *Nothing is better . . . being one in heart*: see Homer, *Odyssey*, vi. 182–5.

Hassan the camel-driver . . . a plume of curled feathers: not traced.

Liebstes Herz: dearest heart.

255 *young leaves . . . the household of King Alcinous*: see Homer, *Odyssey*, vii. 105–6.

O gentle wind . . . how he fareth: from the anonymous ballad, 'Willy Drowned in Yarrow'. There are various versions of the poem; these form ll. 9–16 in the text printed by Palgrave in *The Golden Treasury* (1861).

256 *Whom the gods love . . . in the evening*: a variation on the saying 'whom the gods love die young', which can ultimately be traced to the classical Greek dramatist Menander.

258 *virtuous melodies teach virtue*: this could be seen as a summary of some of Aristotle's comments in his *Politics* (Bk. VIII, ch. 5).

Little-heart-leaflet: a translation of *Herzblättchen*.

259 *Only my love's away, | I'd as lief the blue were gray*: Browning, 'A Lover's Quarrel' (1855), ll. 5–6.

the Foolish Virgins . . . my lamp extinguished: see Christ's parable of the wise and foolish virgins, Matt. 25: 1–13.

niaiseries: childlike babblings; in this context more or less equivalent to the English phrase 'sweet nothings'.

splitter: someone who splits logs into rails, shingles, etc.

263 *There is nothing . . . one of our best-loved novelists once wrote*: not traced.

strait and narrow path: compare 'strait is the way, and narrow is the path, which leadeth unto life' (Matt. 7: 14). *Strait* means 'narrow and difficult to pass through'.

265 *neither life nor death . . . our love*: cf. Rom. 3: 38–9.

266 *Learn by a mortal yearning to ascend, | Seeking a higher object*: Wordsworth, 'Laodamia' (1815), ll. 145–6.

takes the victory from Death and robs the grave of its terror: compare 1 Cor. 15: 55, 'O death, where is thy sting? O grave, where is thy victory?'

the outer court of the Gentiles: non-Jews were allowed to enter this part of the Temple in Jerusalem but the inner court was forbidden to them.

268 *Perfect love casteth out fear*: 1 John 4: 18.

stayed with flagons . . . wine: compare S. of S. 2: 5.

273 *there's many a slip 'twixt the cup and the lip*: proverbial in English in this form since at least the eighteenth century.

276 *She gave me eyes, she gave me ears . . . And love and thought and joy*: Wordsworth, 'The Sparrow's Nest' (1807), ll. 17–20.

277 *Wilhelm Meister . . . Remember to live*: not traced; the reference is to Goethe's *Wilhelm Meisters Lehrjahre* (1795–6) and *Wilhelm Meisters Wanderjahre* (1821).

277 *keep all these things and ponder them in her heart*: as did the Virgin Mary; see Luke 2: 19.

278 *Auf baldige Wiedersehen*: see you again soon.

280 *Chance—chance . . . any philosophy of history*: Charles Augustin Sainte-Beuve (1804–69) wrote numerous critical essays; quotation not traced.

284 *Providence . . . always on the side of the strongest battalions*: a variation on Voltaire's statement 'Dieu n'est pas pour les gros bataillons, mais pour ceux qui tirent le mieux' ('God is not on the side of the big battalions but on that of the best shots') (see his *Notebooks*, ed. T. Besterman, 2nd edn., Geneva, 1968, ii. 54).

286 *Aurora*: the Roman goddess of the dawn.

293 *a dog . . . the death of Procris*: in Greek mythology Cephalus accidentally killed his wife Procris with an unerring javelin she had given him; she had also given him a hunting dog which figures in the painting by Piero di Cosimo (*c*.1462–1515) of her death.

296 *the wisdom of the serpent*: a reference to Christ's words 'be ye therefore wise as serpents' (Matt. 10: 16).

jours insipides: insipid days.

dans ses moindres mouvements: in her slightest movements.

297 *Golconda*: an ancient city in India traditionally seen as a place of immense wealth.

chloral: a drug used as a sedative; addictive if used habitually and toxic if taken in a sufficiently large dose.

hard pan: a layer of hard subsoil, such as clay, lying under soft soil; figuratively, the underlying truth.

a plumb idiot: a complete idiot.

crème demi-double: not full cream (the *crème de la crème*) but cream of half strength.

298 *like a lad of mettle*: see *1 Henry IV*, II. iv. 13.

303 *an old morality*: a medieval morality play in which the characters are personifications of human qualities or abstract notions such as Time.

304 *Where is the land . . . one of Wordsworth's sonnets*: see note to p. 41.

the Australasian: a weekend Melbourne paper associated with the *Argus* and published from 1864.

308 *Your Reverence . . . we women are not so easily known*: from a letter to Father Ambrosio Mariano of 21 October 1576.

309 *when you go . . . Elijah in a fiery chariot*: see 2 Kgs. 2: 11.

314 *in the Book of Proverbs*: the reference to Proverbs is a joking invention.

315 *mes amis*: my friends.

316 *hocussing*: drugging someone for criminal purposes by adding laudanum or another drug to liquor.

317 *it's good to let sleeping dogs lie*: a long-standing proverb found in this form from at least the nineteenth century.

320 *the Apostle spoons*: spoons featuring an image of one of the apostles on the handle; generally given at a christening rather than at a wedding.

according to God's holy ordinance, as it says in the Prayer-book: the words are from the marriage service in the Book of Common Prayer.

322 *the old Marchioness Lismore*: a fictitious person.

323 *Brindisi*: often the first port of call in Europe for ships sailing from Adelaide.

324 *queer*: shady.

pêches à quinze sous: peaches costing five sous, that is, cheap fruit; used metaphorically.

a man must forgive his brother seventy times seven: see Matt. 18: 22.

325 *Jeremiah's scroll—tenantless lands and mortgages*: apparently a reference to the Lamentations of Jeremiah in the Old Testament which records the desolation of the city of Jerusalem after its destruction by the Babylonians.

almond tumblers: a kind of pigeon.

327 *limited monarchies*: constitutional monarchies.

those who reign do not rule: when Louis Philippe became king of the French as a constitutional monarch in 1830, Adophe Thiers wrote of the king's position in words which are usually slightly misquoted as 'Le roi règne mais il ne gouverne pas' ('the king reigns but he does not govern').

chair-back: an anti-macassar, an ornamental covering for the back of a chair to protect it from hair oil.

328 *communicate*: take Holy Communion.

though you have not been confirmed: a rubric in the Book of Common Prayer at the conclusion of the Order of Confirmation stipulates that 'there shall none be admitted to the holy Communion, until such time as he be confirmed, or be ready and desirous to be confirmed'.

the visible Church: the church seen as a visible organization of human beings on earth rather than as a spiritual entity.

329 *'In your patience ye shall win your souls'*: Luke 21: 19 in the Revised Version.

the silent watches of the night: the phrase is a familiar one; compare 'In the sad, silent watches of my night' from Edgar Allan Poe's 'To Helen' (1848, l. 60).

Moloch: a Canaanite god of the Old Testament to whom children were sacrificed; figuratively, something requiring inordinate sacrifices.

whimlings: insignificant people.

330 *Mount Lofty*: the highest point of the Adelaide Hills, overlooking the city of Adelaide.

330 *Curly-locks . . . strawberries, sugar and cream*: a children's rhyme recorded in various forms since the late eighteenth century.

    spooning: love-making.

331 *the holy city . . . adorned for her husband*: see Rev. 21: 2.

332 *St Kilda or Brighton*: seaside places near Melbourne.

333 *Randwick*: a racecourse in Sydney, not in Melbourne.

334 *their hands despairingly . . . sand driven by the whirlwind*: see Dante, *Inferno*, iii. 27–30.

    swept and garnished: Matt. 12: 44.

335 *Nemesis*: the classical Greek goddess who requites human beings for their actions.

346 *Who was it . . . to take short views of life*: the advice was given by Sydney Smith and is recorded in the *Memoir of the Rev. Sydney Smith* by his daughter, Lady Holland (London, 1855), vol. i, ch. 6.

347 *I am the earthenware pot . . . copper kettles*: see Aesop's fable 'The Two Pots', where the bronze pot offers his protection to the earthenware one as they are swept downstream by a river in flood but the latter points out that he will be the one to suffer if they collide. Aesop's moral is to avoid strong neighbours, but Laurette uses the image for her own purposes.

350 *And the lord commended . . . into everlasting dwellings*: Luke 16: 8–9 in the Douai version.

    conies of the rocks: conies are rabbits; compare Prov. 30: 26. 'The conies are but a feeble folk, yet they make their houses in the rocks.'

351 *Vieni, ben mio . . . incoronar di rose*: Come, my love, among these secluded bushes; I wish to crown your brow with roses. The words, written by Lorenzo Da Ponte, are from Susanna's aria in Act IV of Mozart's *The Marriage of Figaro* (1786).

    Jezebel: in the Old Testament the evil wife of Ahab, King of Israel (see 1 Kgs. 16, 18, 21 and 2 Kgs. 9); figuratively, a woman of loose sexual morals.

    John Bull: the archetypal figure of an Englishman.

352 *nut*: apparently Ted means that she is 'a hard nut to crack'.

354 *shapes our ends, rough-hew them as we will*: Hamlet, v. ii. 10–11.

    as though he had . . . in each European Court: in Lesage's novel *Le Diable Boiteux* (1707) Asmodeus the demon opens the houses of a city to view so that his companion Don Cleofas, placed on a steeple, can see the private goings-on in each house.

355 *the early days of the Ballarat diggings*: gold was discovered at Ballarat in 1851.

    their lives . . . Solomon's lilies: a slightly distorted reference to Christ's words, 'Consider the lilies of the fields, how they grow; they toil not, neither do they spin: And yet I say unto you, That even Solomon in all his glory was not arrayed like one of these' (Matt. 6: 28–9).

356 *ingénue*: naïve, artless.

a marriage à la mode: a fashionable marriage without love between the partners.

357 *the imitation Brussels carpet*: see note to p. 32.

oleographs: pictures printed in oil colours in imitation of oil paintings.

one of the elect who neither toil nor spin: see note to p. 355.

358 *sibyl*: a prophetess; originally various particular prophetesses of the ancient classical world.

361 *bienséances*: courtesies.

362 *the place . . . bare-backed through one of the streets*: perhaps Holland has in mind the horse race called the Palio held each year in the Piazza del Campo of Siena.

363 *Thiergarten*: a large park in Berlin.

pension: guest house.

étage: storey.

364 *taedium vitae*: weariness with life.

'wiring': sending a telegram.

gone in the upper story: suffering from loss of memory.

365 *yarn*: a story, often, as here, untrue.

in quod: in prison.

prigging: stealing.

366 *muff*: a fool, a stupid person.

like a thief in the night: biblical uses of the phrase refer, rather differently, to the coming of Judgment Day, the 'day of the Lord' (1 Thess 5: 2; 2 Pet. 3: 10).

367 *Lohengrin*: Richard Wagner's opera of 1850.

to tie . . . the Holy Ghost: the white dove of the Holy Spirit appears from above in Act III, Scene ii of *Lohengrin*.

368 *slip me up*: deceive or disappoint.

sell: a deception or disappointment.

bleeding pageant: presumably a misquotation of Matthew Arnold's 'the pageant of his bleeding heart' from 'Stanzas from the Grande Chartreuse' (1855), l. 136.

369 *where neither moth nor rust doth corrupt*: Matt. 6: 20.

371 *The Agent-General*: the official London representative of an Australian colony.

shell-parrot: literally a budgerigar but used figuratively by Ted.

graven images: the worship of graven images is forbidden in the Second Commandment (Exod. 20: 4).

372 *wander through eternity*: Milton, *Paradise Lost* (1667), ii. 148.

374 *spirituelle*: apparently used with some such sense as 'soulful'; not a normal meaning of the French word.

376 *Inferno*: see note to p. 227.

einziges Herz: my one and only love.

377 *Geliebte*: beloved.

like Macbeth . . . a word of prayer: see *Macbeth*, II. ii. 30.

To be happy at home . . . labour tends: see Johnson's essay, 'Man's Happiness or Misery at Home', *The Rambler* (1750–2), No. 68.

Ach Himmel: Heavens!

382 *Die Wacht am Rhein*: a national song of Germany written by Max Schneckenburger in 1840.

391 *kangaroo pup*: a kangaroo-dog was used in hunting kangaroos.

392 *scat*: or skat; a three-handed card game, originating in Germany and extremely popular there.

393 *Raphael or Michael Angelo*: Raphael (1483–1520) and Michelangelo Buonarroti (1475–1564) are both extremely well-known painters.

396 *Darby-and-Joan*: a loving old couple.

a world not realized: compare Wordsworth's 'Ode: Intimations of Immortality from Recollections of Early Childhood' (1807): 'Blank misgivings of a Creature | Moving about in worlds not realised' (ll. 150–1).

398 *Sinfonische Dichtung*: symphonic poem.

'Divine Comedy' . . . Francesca Polenta . . . Paolo Malatesta: Francesca fell in love with Paolo, her husband's brother, and when their love was discovered they were put to death. The story, related by Francesca to Dante in Book V of Dante's *Inferno*, was a popular one in the nineteenth century and was the subject of Leigh Hunt's poem *The Story of Rimini* (1816) and Tchaikovsky's symphonic fantasy *Francesca da Rimini* (1876).

the second circle of hell, guarded by Minos: in Dante's *Inferno* (v. 4–6) Minos (a legendary king of Crete who in classical mythology became, after his death, the chief judge of the Underworld) sits as judge at the entrance to the second circle of Hell, the place of punishment for those guilty of lust.

399 *O anime affannate, venite a noi parlar, s'altri nol niega*: Dante, visiting Hell, addresses these words to Paolo and Francesca (*Inferno*, v. 80–1).

There is no deeper sorrow . . . a happy time: these are the words of Francesca to Dante (*Inferno*, v. 121–3).

the story of Lancelot, . . . such dangerous reading: it was while reading the story of Lancelot and Guinevere that Paolo and Francesca first kissed (*Inferno*, v. 127–36).

400 *Homburg*: a small and popular spa town near Frankfurt-am-Main.

402 *Virchow at the University*: Rudolf Virchow (1821–1902), pathologist and politician, appointed professor of pathological anatomy at the University of Berlin in 1856.

404 *Give me your hand before I am a serpent all over*: these are the words of Cadmus to his wife Harmonia; see Ovid's *Metamorphoses*, iv. 584–5. They were both changed into serpents by Zeus.

407 *Be ye wise as serpents*: see note to p. 296.

413 *in smother*: in a smouldering fire; the phrase is used figuratively, as it is here, in Bacon's *Essays* in 'Of Suspicion'.

414 *toque*: a woman's small hat with no brim or a very narrow one.

415 *from Dan to Beersheba*: from one end of the country to the other; a biblical phrase, e.g. 1 Sam. 3: 20. Dan and Beersheba were at the northern and southern extremities of the undivided kingdom of Israel in Old Testament times.

St Leger: a horse race in Doncaster in early September; first run in 1776.

416 *Château Lafite*: a red wine from the Bordeaux region.

417 *our kinsman Schiedlich*: Gottfried Schiedlich, in the 1890 edition a prominent Socialist who dies just before he is due to be released from prison. His death provokes a meeting which Stella attends.

420 *flax touched with flame*: that is, something very brief, which flares up briefly but does not last.

421 *unknown modes of existence*: compare Wordsworth's 'unknown modes of being' in *The Prelude* (1850), l. 393.

422 *a cloud of unseen witnesses*: compare 'a cloud of witnesses' (Heb. 12: 1).

a church: the Jesuit Church of the Immaculate Conception in Farm Street built in the 1840s.

Cardinal Newman: John Henry Newman (1801–90), a prominent Anglican theologian who converted to Roman Catholicism in 1845 and was created a cardinal in 1879. Amongst other books he wrote *Apologia pro vita sua* (1864), a work which in the longer version of the novel Stella reports herself as reading (i. 92).

423 *though we may have strayed . . . still waters flow*: see Psalm 23: 2.

424 *a reed shaken by a great storm*: compare 'A reed shaken with the wind' (Matt. 11: 7).

As smoke vanisheth away: compare 'As the cloud is consumed and vanisheth away' (Job 7: 9) and 'a vapour, that appeareth for a little time, and then vanisheth away' (Jas. 4: 14).

the still, small voice: the voice of the Lord (see 1 Kgs. 19: 12).

And the Lord turned . . . Peter went out and wept bitterly: see Luke 22: 61–2.

pierced her like a sword: compare Simeon's words to Mary, 'Yea, a sword shall pierce through thy own soul also' (Luke 2: 35).

424 *But as I raved . . . And I replied, My Lord!*: George Herbert, 'The Collar', ll. 33–6, from *The Temple* (1633).

425 *He had so keen an appreciation . . . the better side of their nature*: not traced.

426 *Thy crime . . . God, to whom thou belongest*: the words of St Gregory of Nazianzus (329–89) to a young Arian zealot who had intended to kill Gregory but instead threw himself at his feet and admitted his purpose. (The wording of the translation follows that given in Frederic W. Farrar, *Lives of the Fathers*, Edinburgh, 1889, i. 751.)

Believe, and thou shalt be saved: compare Acts 16: 31.

434 *those things which are good and true and of lovely report*: based on Phil. 4: 8.

the Nessus robe of passion: to win back his love, Hercules' wife Deianira sent him a robe smeared with the blood of Nessus, the Centaur, whom Hercules had killed. However, the blood was poisoned and the robe clung to Hercules' flesh, causing him intense pain when he tore it off.

435 *Irving's 'Macbeth,'*: Sir Henry Irving (1838–1905), famous as an actor, particularly of Shakespeare. He played Macbeth in 1875 and revived the role in 1888–9.

436 *Who shall find a valiant woman? . . . all the days of her life*: Prov. 31: 10–12 in the Douai version.

437 *vice de construction*: a defect in the making of something.

438 *When pain and anguish wring the brow*: the line is from Sir Walter Scott's *Marmion* (1808; VI. xxx).

439 *slanging*: abusing, scolding.

scunner: a feeling of dislike or repugnance (a Scots term).

rips: disreputable women.

jawing: telling off, reprimand.

this young sea-calf: a sea-calf is a seal; for the figurative use compare Long John Silver's 'what a precious old sea-calf I am!' (*Treasure Island*, ch. 8).

with portraiture and colour so distinct: from Wordsworth's fragmentary poem, 'The Pedlar' (written in 1798), ll. 31–2.

440 *the orphan . . . no one to befriend her but God*: see 'The Tale of the Portress' in *The Arabian Nights*.

442 *willy-willy*: whirlwind.

put the 'kybosh' on me completely: overturned me completely.

American Literature

British and Irish Literature

Children's Literature

Classics and Ancient Literature

Colonial Literature

Eastern Literature

European Literature

History

Medieval Literature

Oxford English Drama

Poetry

Philosophy

Politics

Religion

The Oxford Shakespeare

A complete list of Oxford Paperbacks, including Oxford World's Classics, OPUS, Past Masters, Oxford Authors, Oxford Shakespeare, Oxford Drama, and Oxford Paperback Reference, is available in the UK from the Academic Division Publicity Department, Oxford University Press, Great Clarendon Street, Oxford OX2 6DP.

In the USA, complete lists are available from the Paperbacks Marketing Manager, Oxford University Press, 198 Madison Avenue, New York, NY 10016.

Oxford Paperbacks are available from all good bookshops. In case of difficulty, customers in the UK can order direct from Oxford University Press Bookshop, Freepost, 116 High Street, Oxford OX1 4BR, enclosing full payment. Please add 10 per cent of published price for postage and packing.